Terry Hayes is a former journalist and screen-writer. Born in Sussex, he migrated to Australia as a child and trained as a journalist at the country's leading broadsheet. At twenty-one he was appointed North American correspondent, based in New York, and after two years returned to Sydney to become an investigative reporter, political correspondent and columnist.

He resigned to produce a prominent current-affairs radio programme and a short time later, with George Miller, wrote the screenplay for *Road Warrior/Mad Max 2*. He also co-produced and wrote *Dead Calm*, the film which launched Nicole Kidman's international movie career, *Mad Max Beyond Thunderdome* and a large number of TV movies and mini-series – including *Bodyline* and *Bangkok Hilton* – two of which received international Emmy nominations. In all, he has won over twenty film or television awards.

After moving to Los Angeles, he worked as a screenwriter on major studio productions. His credits include *Payback* with Mel Gibson, *From Hell*, starring Johnny Depp, and *Vertical Limit* with Chris O'Donnell. He has also done uncredited writing on a host of other movies, including *Reign of Fire* with Christian Bale and Matthew McConaughey, *Cliffhanger*, starring Sylvester Stallone, and *Flightplan* with Jodie Foster.

I Am Pilgrim is his first novel. He and his American wife, Kristen, have four children and live in Switzerland.

www.**transworldbooks**.co.uk

I AM PILGRIM

Terry Hayes

BANTAM PRESS

LONDON · TORONTO · SYDNEY · AUCKLAND · JOHANNESBURG

TRANSWORLD PUBLISHERS
61–63 Uxbridge Road, London W5 5SA
A Random House Group Company
www.transworldbooks.co.uk

First published in Great Britain
in 2013 by Bantam Press
an imprint of Transworld Publishers

A CIP catalogue record for this book
is available from the British Library.

ISBNs 9780593064948 (hb)
9780593064955 (tpb)

Addresses for Random House Group Ltd companies outside the UK
can be found at: www.randomhouse.co.uk
The Random House Group Ltd Reg. No. 954009

Typeset in 11/14pt Sabon by Falcon Oast Graphic Art Ltd
Printed and bound in Great Britain by
Clays Limited, Bungay, Suffolk

2 4 6 8 10 9 7 5 3 1

There is no terror so consistent, so elusive to describe,
as that which haunts a spy in a strange country.
John le Carré, *The Looking Glass War*

Down these mean streets a man must go who is not
himself mean, who is neither tarnished nor afraid.
Raymond Chandler, *The Simple Art of Murder*

Part One

Chapter One

THERE ARE PLACES I'LL REMEMBER ALL MY LIFE — RED SQUARE WITH A hot wind howling across it, my mother's bedroom on the wrong side of 8-Mile, the endless gardens of a fancy foster home, a man waiting to kill me in a group of ruins known as the Theatre of Death.

But nothing is burnt deeper in my memory than a walk-up in New York — threadbare curtains, cheap furniture, a table loaded with tina and other party drugs. Lying next to the bed are a handbag, black panties the size of dental floss and a pair of six-inch Jimmy Choo's. Like their owner, they don't belong here. She is naked in the bathroom — her throat cut, floating face down in a bathtub full of sulphuric acid, the active ingredient in a drain cleaner available at any supermarket.

Dozens of empty bottles of the cleaner — DrainBomb, it's called — lie scattered on the floor. Unnoticed, I start picking through them. They've all got their price tags still attached and I see that, in order to avoid suspicion, whoever killed her bought them at twenty different stores. I've always said it's hard not to admire good planning.

The place is in chaos, the noise deafening — police radios blaring, coroner's assistants yelling for support, a Hispanic woman sobbing. Even if a victim doesn't know anyone in the world, it seems like there's always someone sobbing at a scene like this.

The young woman in the bath is unrecognizable — the three days she has spent in the acid have destroyed all her features. That was the plan, I guess — whoever killed her had also weighed down her hands with telephone books. The acid has dissolved not only her fingerprints but almost the entire metacarpal structure underneath.

Unless the forensic guys at the NYPD get lucky with a dental match, they'll have a helluva time putting a name to this one.

In places like this, where you get a feeling evil still clings to the walls, your mind can veer into strange territory. The idea of a young woman without a face made me think of a Lennon/McCartney groove from long ago – it's about Eleanor Rigby, a woman who wore a face that she kept in a jar by the door. In my head I start calling the victim Eleanor. The crime scene team still has work to do, but there isn't a person in the place who doesn't think Eleanor was killed during sex: the mattress half off the base, the tangled sheets, a brown spray of decaying arterial blood on a bedside table. The really sick ones figure he cut her throat while he was still inside her. The bad thing is – they may be right. However she died, those who look for blessings may find one here: she wouldn't have realized what was happening – not until the last moment, anyway.

Tina – crystal meth – would have taken care of that. It makes you so damn horny, so euphoric as it hits your brain that any sense of foreboding would have been impossible. Under its influence, the only coherent thought most people can marshal is to find a partner and bang their back out.

Next to the two empty foils of tina is what looks like one of those tiny shampoo bottles you get in hotel bathrooms. Unmarked, it contains a clear liquid – GHB, I figure. It's getting a lot of play now in the dark corners of the Web: in large doses it is replacing rohypnol as the date-rape drug of choice. Most music venues are flooded with it: clubbers slug a tiny cap to cut tina, taking the edge off its paranoia. But GHB also comes with its own side effects – a loss of inhibitions and a more intense sexual experience. On the street one of its names is Easy Lay. Kicking off her Jimmy's, stepping out of her tiny black skirt, Eleanor must have been a rocket on the Fourth of July.

As I move through the crush of people – unknown to any of them, a stranger with an expensive jacket slung over his shoulder and a lot of freight in his past – I stop at the bed. I close out the noise and in my mind I see her on top, naked, riding him cowgirl. She is in her early twenties with a good body, and I figure she is right into it – the cocktail of drugs whirling her towards a shattering orgasm, her body temperature soaring thanks to the meth, her swollen breasts pushing down, her heart and respiratory rate rocketing under the onslaught of passion and chemicals, her breath coming in gulping bursts, her wet tongue finding a mind of its own and searching hard for the mouth below. Sex today sure isn't for sissies.

Neon signs from a row of bars outside the window would have hit the blonde highlights in this season's haircut and sparkled off a Panerai diver's watch. Yeah, it's fake, but it's a good one. I know this woman. We all do – the type, anyway. You see them in the huge new Prada store in Milan, queuing outside the clubs in Soho, sipping skinny lattes in the hot cafés on the avenue Montaigne – young women who mistake *People* magazine for news and a Japanese symbol on their backs for a sign of rebellion.

I imagine the killer's hand on her breast, touching a jewelled nipple ring. The guy takes it between his fingers and yanks it, pulling her closer. She cries out, revved – everything is hypersensitive now, especially her nipples. But she doesn't mind – if somebody wants it rough, it just means they must really like her. Perched on top of him, the headboard banging hard against the wall, she would have been looking at the front door – locked and chained, for sure. In this neighbourhood, that's the least you could do.

A diagram on the back shows an evacuation route – she is in a hotel, but any resemblance to the Ritz-Carlton pretty much ends there. It is called the Eastside Inn – home to itinerants, backpackers, the mentally lost and anybody else with twenty bucks a night. Stay as long as you like – a day, a month, the rest of your life – all you need is two IDs, one with a photo.

The guy who had moved into Room 89 had been here for a while – a six-pack sits on a bureau, along with four half-empty bottles of hard liquor and a couple of boxes of breakfast cereal. A stereo and a few CDs are on a night stand, and I glance through them. He had good taste in music, at least you could say that. The closet, however, is empty – it seems like his clothes were about the only things he took with him when he walked out, leaving the body to liquefy in the bath. Lying at the back of the closet is a pile of trash: discarded newspapers, an empty can of roach killer, a coffee-stained wall calendar. I pick it up – every page features a black and white photo of an ancient ruin – the Colosseum, a Greek temple, the Library of Celsus at night. Very arty. But the pages are blank, not an appointment on any of them – except as a coffee mat, it seems like it's never been used, and I throw it back.

11

I turn away and – without thinking, out of habit really – I run my hand across the night-stand. That's strange: no dust. I do the same to the bureau, bedhead and stereo and get the identical result – the killer has wiped everything down to eliminate his prints. He gets no prizes for that, but as I catch the scent of something and raise my fingers to my nose, everything changes. The residue I can smell is from an antiseptic spray they use in intensive-care wards to combat infection. Not only does it kill bacteria but as a side effect it also destroys DNA material – sweat, skin, hair. By spraying everything in the room and then dousing the carpet and walls, the killer was making sure that the NYPD needn't bother with their forensic vacuum cleaners.

With sudden clarity, I realize that this is anything but a by-the-book homicide for money or drugs or sexual gratification. As a murder, this is something remarkable.

Chapter Two

NOT EVERYBODY KNOWS THIS — OR CARES PROBABLY — BUT THE FIRST LAW of forensic science is Locard's Exchange Principle, and it says 'Every contact between a perpetrator and a crime scene leaves a trace.' As I stand in this room, surrounded by dozens of voices, I'm wondering if Professor Locard had ever encountered anything quite like Room 89 – everything touched by the killer is now in a bath full of acid, wiped clean or drenched in industrial antiseptic. I'm certain there's not a cell or follicle of him left behind.

A year ago, I wrote an obscure book on modern investigative technique. In a chapter called 'New Frontiers', I said I had come across the use of an antibacterial spray only once in my life – and that was a high-level hit on an intelligence agent in the Czech Republic. That case doesn't augur well – to this day, it remains unsolved. Whoever had been living in Room 89 clearly knew their business, and I start examining the room with the respect it deserves.

He wasn't a tidy person and, among the other trash, I see an empty pizza box lying next to the bed. I'm about to pass over it when I realize that's where he would have had the knife: lying on top of the pizza box within easy reach, so *natural* Eleanor probably wouldn't even have registered it.

I imagine her on the bed, reaching under the tangle of sheets for his crotch. She kisses his shoulder, his chest, going down. Maybe the guy knows what he's in for, maybe not: one of the side effects of GHB is that it suppresses the gag reflex. There's no reason a person can't swallow a seven-, eight-, ten-inch gun – that's why one of the easiest places to buy it is in gay saunas. Or on porn shoots.

I think of his hands grabbing her – he flips her on to her back and puts his knees either side of her chest. She's thinking he's positioning himself for her mouth but, casually, his right hand would have dropped to the side of the bed. Unseen, the guy's fingers find the top of the pizza box then touch what he's looking for – cold and cheap but, because it's new, more than sharp enough to do the job.

Anybody watching from behind would have seen her back arch, a sort of moan escape her lips – they'd think he must have entered her mouth. He hasn't. Her eyes, bright with drugs, are flooding with fear. His left hand has clamped tight over her mouth, forcing her head back, exposing her throat. She bucks and writhes, tries to use her arms, but he's anticipated that. Straddling her breasts, his knees slam down, pinning her by the biceps. How do I know this? You can just make out the two bruises on the body lying in the bath. She's helpless. His right hand rises up into view – Eleanor sees it and tries to scream, convulsing wildly, fighting to get free. The serrated steel of the pizza knife flashes past her breast, towards her pale throat. It slashes hard—

Blood sprays across the bedside table. With one of the arteries which feed the brain completely cut, it would have been over in a moment. Eleanor crumples, gurgling, bleeding out. The last vestiges of consciousness tell her she has just witnessed her own murder; all she ever was and hoped to be is gone. That's how he did it – he wasn't inside her at all. Once again, thank God for small mercies, I suppose.

The killer goes to prepare the acid bath and along the way pulls off the bloody white shirt he must have been wearing – they just found pieces of it under Eleanor's body in the bath, along with the knife: four inches long, black plastic handle, made by the millions in some sweatshop in China.

I'm still reeling from the vivid imagining of it all, so I barely register a rough hand taking my shoulder. As soon as I do, I throw it off, about to break his arm instantly – an echo from an earlier life, I'm afraid. It is some guy who mumbles a terse apology, looking at me strangely, trying to move me aside. He's the leader of a forensic team – three guys and a woman – setting up the UV lamps and dishes of the Fast Blue B dye they'll use to test the mattress for semen stains. They haven't found out about the antiseptic yet and I don't tell them – for all I know the killer missed a part of the bed. If he did, given the nature of the Eastside Inn, I figure they'll get several thousand positive hits dating back to when hookers wore stockings.

I get out of their way, but I'm deeply distracted: I'm trying to close everything out because there is something about the room, the whole situation – I'm not exactly sure what – that is troubling me. A part of the scenario is wrong, and I can't tell why. I look around, taking another inventory of what I see, but I can't find it – I have a sense it's from earlier in the night. I go back, mentally rewinding the tape to when I first walked in.

What was it? I reach down into my subconscious, trying to recover my first impression – it was something detached from the violence, minor but with overriding significance. If only I could touch it . . . a feeling . . . it's like . . . it's some *word* that is lying now on the other side of memory. I start thinking about how I wrote in my book that it is the assumptions, the unquestioned assumptions, that trip you up every time – and then it comes to me.

When I walked in, I saw the six-pack on the bureau, a carton of milk in the fridge, registered the names of a few DVDs lying next to the TV, noted the liner in a trash can. And the impression – the word – that first entered my head but didn't touch my conscious mind was 'female'. I got everything right about what had happened in Room 89 – except for the biggest thing of all. It wasn't a young guy who was staying here; it wasn't a naked man who was having sex with Eleanor and cut her throat. It wasn't a clever prick who destroyed her features with acid and drenched the room with antiseptic spray.

It was a woman.

15

Chapter Three

I'VE KNOWN A LOT OF POWERFUL PEOPLE IN MY CAREER, BUT I'VE ONLY met one person with genuine natural authority – the sort of guy who could shout you down with just a whisper. He is in the corridor now, coming towards me, telling the forensic team they'll have to wait: the Fire Department wants to secure the acid before somebody gets burnt.

'Keep your plastic gloves on, though,' he advises. 'You can give each other a free prostate exam out in the hall.' Everybody except the forensic guys laughs.

The man with the voice is Ben Bradley, the homicide lieutenant in charge of the crime scene. He's been down in the manager's office, trying to locate the scumbag who runs the joint. He's a tall black man – Bradley, not the scumbag – in his early fifties with big hands and Industry jeans turned up at the cuff. His wife talked him into buying them recently in a forlorn attempt to update his image, instead of which – he says – they make him look like a character from a Steinbeck novel, a modern refugee from the dustbowl.

Like all the other regulars at these murder circuses, he has little affection for the forensic specialists. First, the work was outsourced a few years back and overpaid people like these started turning up in crisp white boiler suits with names like 'Forensic Biological Services, Inc.' on the back. Second – and what really tipped it over the edge for him – were the two shows featuring forensic work that hit it big on TV and led to an insufferable outbreak of celebrityhood in the minds of its practitioners.

'Jesus,' he complained recently, 'is there anybody in this country who isn't dreaming of being on a reality show?'

16

As he watches the would-be celebrities repack their labs-in-a-briefcase, he catches sight of me – standing silently against the wall, just watching, like I seem to have spent half my life doing. He ignores the people demanding his attention and makes his way over. We don't shake hands – I don't know why, it's just never been our way. I'm not even sure if we're friends – I've always been pretty much on the outside of any side you can find, so I'm probably not the one to judge. We respect each other, though, if that helps.

'Thanks for coming,' he says.

I nod, looking at his turned-up Industries and black work boots, ideal for paddling through the blood and shit of a crime scene.

'What did you come by – tractor?' I ask.

He doesn't laugh; Ben hardly ever laughs, he's about the most deadpan guy you'll ever meet. Which doesn't mean he isn't funny. 'Had a chance to look around, Ramón?' he says quietly.

My name is not Ramón, and he knows it. But he also knows that, until recently, I was a member of one of our nation's most secret intelligence agencies, so I figure he's referring to Ramón García. Ramón was an FBI agent who went to almost infinite trouble to conceal his identity as he sold our nation's secrets to the Russians – then left his fingerprints all over the Hefty garbage bags he used to deliver the stolen documents. Ramón was almost certainly the most incompetent covert operator in history. Like I say, Ben is very funny.

'Yeah, I've seen a bit,' I tell him. 'What you got on the person living in this dump? She's the prime suspect, huh?'

Ben can hide many things, but his eyes can't mask the look of surprise – a woman?!

Excellent, I think – Ramón strikes back.

Still, Bradley's a cool cop. 'That's interesting, Ramón,' he says, trying to find out if I'm really on to something or whether I've just jumped the shark. 'How'd you figure that?'

I point at the six-pack on the bureau, the milk in the fridge. 'What guy does that? A guy keeps the beer cold, lets the milk go bad. Look at the DVDs – romantic comedies, and not an action film among them. Wanna take a walk?' I continue. 'Find out how many other guys in this dump use liners in their trash cans? That's what a woman does – one who doesn't belong here, no matter what part she's acting.'

He weighs what I've said, holding my gaze, but it's impossible to

17

tell whether he's buying what I'm selling. Before I can ask, two young detectives – a woman and her partner – appear from behind the Fire Department's hazchem barrels. They scramble to a stop in front of Bradley.

'We got something, Ben!' the female cop says. 'It's about the occupant—'

Bradley nods calmly. 'Yeah, it's a woman – tell me something I don't know. What about her?'

I guess he *was* buying it. The two cops stare, wondering how the hell he knew. By morning, the legend of their boss will have grown even greater. Me? I'm thinking the guy is shameless – he's going to take the credit without even blinking? I start laughing.

Bradley glances at me and, momentarily, I think he's going to laugh back, but it's a forlorn hope. His sleepy eyes seem to twinkle, though, as his attention reverts to the two cops. 'How'd you know it was a woman?' he asks them.

'We got hold of the hotel register and all the room files,' the male detective – name of Connor Norris – replies.

Bradley is suddenly alert. 'From the manager? You found the scumbag – got him to unlock the office?'

Norris shakes his head. 'There are four drug warrants out for his arrest; he's probably halfway to Mexico. No, Alvarez here' – he indicates his female partner – 'she recognized a guy wanted for burglary living upstairs.' He looks at his partner, not sure how much more to say.

Alvarez shrugs, hopes for the best and comes clean. 'I offered the burglar a get-out-of-jail-free card if he'd pick the locks on the manager's office and safe for us.'

She looks at Bradley, nervous, wondering how much trouble this is gonna cause.

Her boss's face gives away nothing; his voice just drops a notch, even softer. 'And then?'

'Eight locks in total and he was through 'em in under a minute,' she says. 'No wonder nothing's safe in this town.'

'What was in the woman's file?' Bradley asks.

'Receipts. She'd been living here just over a year,' Norris says. 'Paid in cash, didn't have the phone connected – TV, cable, nothing. She sure didn't want to be traced.'

Bradley nods – exactly what he was thinking. 'When was the last time any of the neighbours saw her?'

'Three or four days ago. Nobody's sure,' Norris recounts.

Bradley murmurs, 'Disappeared straight after she killed her date, I guess. What about ID – there must have been something in her file?'

Alvarez checks her notes. 'Photocopies of a Florida driver's licence and a student card or something – no picture on it,' she says. 'I bet they're genuine.'

'Check 'em anyway,' Bradley tells them.

'We gave 'em to Petersen,' says Norris, referring to another young detective. 'He's on to it.'

Bradley acknowledges it. 'Does the burglar – any of the others – know the suspect, anything about her?'

They shake their heads. 'Nobody. They'd just see her come and go,' Norris says. 'Early twenties, about five eight, a great body, according to the burglar—'

Bradley raises his eyes to heaven. 'By his standards, that probably means she's got two legs.'

Norris smiles, but not Alvarez – she just wishes Bradley would say something about her deal with the burglar. If he's going to ream her out, get it over with. Instead she has to continue to participate, professional: 'According to a so-called actress in one-fourteen, the chick changed her appearance all the time. One day Marilyn Monroe, the next Marilyn Manson, sometimes both Marilyns on the same day. Then there was Drew and Britney, Dame Edna, k. d. lang—'

'You're serious?' Bradley asks. The young cops nod, reeling off more names as if to prove it. 'I'm really looking forward to seeing this photofit,' he says, realizing that all the common avenues of a murder investigation are being closed down. 'Anything else?' They shake their heads, done.

'Better start getting statements from the freaks – or at least those without warrants, which will probably amount to about three of 'em.'

Bradley dismisses them, turning to me in the shadows, starting to broach something which has been causing him a lot of anxiety.

'Ever seen one of these?' he asks, pulling on plastic gloves and taking a metal box off a shelf in the closet. It's khaki in colour, so thin I hadn't even noticed it. He's about to open it but turns to look at Alvarez and Norris for a moment. They are heading out, weaving through the firefighters, now packing up their hazchem pumps.

'Hey, guys!' he calls. They turn and look. 'About the burglar – that was good work.'

We see the relief on Alvarez's face and they both raise their hands in silent acknowledgement, smiling. No wonder his crew worships him.

I'm looking at the metal box – on closer examination, more like an attaché case with a serial number stencilled on the side in white letters. It's obviously military, but I only have a vague memory of seeing anything like it. 'A battlefield surgical kit?' I say, without much conviction.

'Close,' Bradley says. 'Dentistry.' He opens the box, revealing – nestled in foam – a full set of army dental instruments: spreader pliers, probes, extraction forceps.

I stare at him. 'She pulled the victim's teeth?' I ask.

'All of 'em. We haven't found any, so I figure she dumped 'em. Maybe she flushed them down the john and we'll get lucky – that's why we're tearing the plumbing apart.'

'Were the teeth pulled before or after the victim was killed?'

Ben realizes where I'm going. 'No, it wasn't torture. The coroner's team have taken a look inside her mouth. They're pretty sure it was after death, to prevent identification. It was the reason I asked you to drop by – I remembered something in your book about home dentistry and a murder. If it was in the US, I was hoping there might be a—'

'No connection – Sweden,' I say. 'A guy used a surgical hammer on the victim's bridgework and jaw – same objective, I guess – but forceps? I've never seen anything like that.'

'Well, we have now,' Ben replies.

'Inspiring,' I say. 'The onward rush of civilization, I mean.'

Putting aside my despair about humanity, I have to say I'm even more impressed by the killer – it couldn't have been easy pulling thirty-two teeth from a dead person. The killer had obviously grasped one important concept, a thing which eludes most people who decide on her line of work: nobody's ever been arrested for a murder; they have only ever been arrested for not planning it properly.

I indicate the metal case. 'Where's a civilian get one of these?' I ask.

20

Ben shrugs. 'Anywhere they like. I called a buddy in the Pentagon and he went into the archives: forty thousand were surplus – the army unloaded the lot through survival stores over the last few years. We'll chase 'em, but we won't nail it that way, I'm not sure anybody could—'

His voice trails away – he's lost in a labyrinth, running his gaze around the room, trying to find a way out. 'I've got no face,' he says softly. 'No dental records, no witnesses – worst of all, no motive. You know this business better than anyone – if I asked you about solving it, what odds would you lay?'

'Right now? Powerball, or whatever that lottery's called,' I tell him. 'You walk in, the first thing you think is: amateur, just another drug or sex play. Then you look closer – I've only seen a couple anywhere near as good as this.' Then I tell him about the antiseptic spray, and of course that's not something he wants to hear.

'Thanks for the encouragement,' he says. Unthinking, he rubs his index finger and thumb together, and I know from close observation over a long period that it means he'd like a cigarette. He told me once he'd given up in the nineties and there must have been a million times since then that he'd thought a smoke might help. This is obviously one of them. To get over the craving, he talks. 'You know my problem? Marcie told me this once' – Marcie is his wife – 'I get too close to the victims, ends up I sort of imagine I'm the only friend they've got left.'

'Their champion?' I suggest.

'That's exactly the word she used. And there's one thing I've never been able to do – Marcie says it could be the only thing she really likes about me – I've never been able to let a friend down.'

Champion of the dead, I think. There could be worse things. I wish there was something I could do to help him, but there isn't – it's not my investigation and, although I'm only in my thirties, I'm retired.

A technician enters the room fast, yelling in an Asian accent: 'Ben?' Bradley turns. 'In the basement!'

Chapter Four

THREE TECHNICIANS IN COVERALLS HAVE TORN APART AN OLD BRICK wall. Despite their face masks, they're almost gagging from the smell inside the cavity. It's not a body they've found – rotting flesh has its own particular odour – this is leaking sewage, mould and a hundred generations of rat shit.

Bradley makes his way through a sequence of foul cellars and stops in the harsh light of a bank of work lights illuminating the wrecked wall. I follow in his wake, tagging along with the other investigators, arriving just in time to see the Asian guy – a Chinese-American who everyone calls Bruce, for obvious reasons – shine a portable light deep into the newly opened space.

Inside is a maze of cowboy plumbing. Bruce explains that, having torn up the bathroom in Room 89 without finding anything trapped in the U-bends, they went one step further. They got a capsule of Fast Blue B dye from the forensic guys, mixed it into a pint of water and poured it down the waste pipe.

It took five minutes for all of it to arrive, and they knew if it was running that slow there had to be a blockage somewhere between the basement and Room 89. Now they've found it – in the matrix of pipes and illegal connections behind the wall.

'Please tell me it's the teeth,' Bradley says. 'She flush 'em down the toilet?'

Bruce shakes his head and shines the portable light on a mush of charred paper trapped in a right-angle turn. 'The pipe comes straight from Room 89 – we tested it,' he says, pointing at the mush. 'Whatever this is, she probably burnt it then sent it down the crapper. That was the right thing to do – except she didn't know about the code violations.'

With the help of tweezers, Bradley starts to pick the congealed mess apart. 'Bits of receipts, corner of a subway MetroCard, movie ticket,' he recounts to everyone watching. 'Looks like she took a final sweep through the place, got rid of anything she missed.' He carefully separates more burnt fragments. 'A shopping list – could be useful to match the handwriting if we ever find—'

He stops, staring at a piece of paper slightly less charred than the rest. 'Seven numbers. Written by hand: 9. 0. 2. 5. 2. 3. 4. It's not complete; the rest has been burnt off.'

He holds the scrap of paper up to the group, but I know it's me he's really speaking to, as if my job at an intelligence agency qualifies me as a cryptographer. Seven handwritten numbers, half destroyed: they could mean anything – but I have one advantage. People in my former business are always dealing in fragments, so I don't just dismiss it.

Among everybody else, of course, the speculation starts immediately – bank account, credit card, zip code, an IP address, a phone number. Alvarez says there's no such thing as a 902 area code, and she's right. Sort of.

'Yeah, but we connect to the Canadian system,' Petersen, the young detective – built like a linebacker – tells her. '902 is Nova Scotia. My grandfather had a farm up there.'

Bradley doesn't respond; he keeps looking at me for my opinion. I've learned from bitter experience not to say anything unless you're certain, so I just shrug – which means Bradley and everyone else moves on.

What I'm really thinking about is the wall calendar, which has been worrying me since I first saw it. According to the price on the back, it cost forty bucks at Rizzoli, the upmarket book store, and that's a lot of money to tell the date and never use. The killer was obviously a smart woman, and the thought occurred to me it wasn't a calendar at all to her: maybe she had an interest in ancient ruins.

I had spent most of my career working in Europe and, though it's a long time since I travelled that far east, I'm pretty sure 90 is the international code for Turkey. Spend even a day travelling in that country and you realize it has more Greco-Roman ruins than just about any place on earth. If 90 is the country prefix, it's possible the subsequent digits are an area code and part of a phone number. Without anyone noticing, I walk out and head for the quietest part of the basement and make a call to Verizon on my cellphone – I want to find out about Turkish area codes.

As I wait for the phone company to pick up, I glance at my watch and I'm shocked to realize that dawn must be breaking outside – it is now ten hours since a janitor, checking a power failure in the next room, unlocked the door to Room 89 to access some wiring. No wonder everybody looks tired.

At last I reach someone on a Verizon help desk, a heavily accented woman at what I guess is a call centre in Mumbai, and find my memory is holding up – 90 is indeed the dialling code for Turkey. 'What about 252? Is that an area code?'

'Yes, a province . . . it's called Muğla or something,' she says, trying her best to pronounce it. Turkey is a large country – bigger than Texas, with a population of over seventy million – and the name means nothing to me. I start to thank her, ready to ring off, when she says: 'I don't know if it helps, but it says here that one of the main towns is a place on the Aegean coast. It's called Bodrum.'

The word sends a jolt through my body, a frisson of fear that has been barely dissipated by the passage of so many years. 'Bodrum,' she says – and the name washes ashore like the debris from some distant shipwreck. 'Really?' I say calmly, fighting a tumult of thoughts. Then the part of my brain dealing with the present reminds me I'm only a guest on this investigation, and relief floods in. I don't want anything to do with that part of the world again.

I make my way back to Room 89. Bradley sees me, and I tell him I figure that the piece of paper is the first part of a phone number all right, but I'd forget about Canada. I explain about the calendar and he says he'd seen it earlier in the evening and it had worried him too.

'Bodrum? Where's Bodrum?' he asks.

'You need to get out more. In Turkey – one of the most fashionable summer destinations in the world.'

'What about Coney Island?' he asks, straight-faced.

'A close call,' I tell him, picturing the harbour packed with extravagant yachts, the elegant villas, a tiny mosque nestled in the hills, cafés with names like Mezzaluna and Oxygen, awash with hormones and ten-dollar cappuccinos.

'You've been there?' Bradley asks.

I shake my head – there are some things the government won't let me talk about. 'No,' I lie. 'Why would she be calling someone in Bodrum?' I wonder aloud, changing the subject.

Bradley shrugs, unwilling to speculate, preoccupied. 'The big guy's done some good work too,' he reports, pointing at Petersen on the other side of the room. 'It wasn't a student ID Alvarez found in the manager's file – fake name, of course – it was a New York library card.'

'Oh good,' I say, without much interest. 'An intellectual.'

'Not really,' he replies. 'According to their database, she only borrowed one book in a year.' He pauses, looks at me hard. 'Yours.'

I stare back at him, robbed of words. No wonder he was pre-occupied. 'She read my book?' I manage to say finally.

'Not just read it – studied it, I'd say,' he answers. 'Like you said – you hadn't seen many as professional as this. Now we know why: the missing teeth, the antiseptic spray – it's all in your book, isn't it?'

My head tilts back as the full weight of it hits me. 'She took stuff from different cases, used it as a manual – how to kill someone, how to cover it up.'

'Exactly,' Ben Bradley says, and, for one of the few times ever, he smiles. 'I just want to say thanks – now I've got to chase you-by-proxy, the best in the world.'

Chapter Five

IF YOU WANT TO KNOW THE TRUTH, MY BOOK ABOUT INVESTIGATIVE technique was pretty obscure – the sort of thing, as far as I could tell, that defied all publishing theory: once most people put it down, they couldn't pick it up again.

Yet, among the small cadre of professionals at whom it was aimed, it caused a seismic shock. The material went out on the edge of technology, of science, of *credibility* even. But on closer examination, not even the most hardened sceptics could maintain their doubts – every case I cited included those tiny details, that strange patina of circumstance and motivation that allows good investigators to separate the genuine from the fake.

A day after the book's release a flurry of questions began ricocheting around the closed world of top-flight investigators. How the hell was it that nobody had heard of any of these cases? They were like communiqués from another planet, only the names changed to protect the guilty. And, even more importantly, who the hell had written it?

I had no intention of ever letting anyone find out. Due to my former work, I had more enemies than I cared to think about and I didn't want to start my car engine one morning and end up as a handful of cosmic dust running rings around the moon. If any reader of the book was to inquire about the background of the so-called author, all they would find was a man who had died recently in Chicago. One thing was certain, I didn't write it for fame or money.

I told myself I did it because I had solved crimes committed by people working at the outer limits of human ingenuity and I thought other investigators might find some of the techniques I had pioneered useful. And that was true – up to a point. On a deeper level, I'm still young – hopefully, with another, real, life in front of me – and I think the book was a summing-up, a way of bidding a final farewell to my former existence.

For almost a decade I was a member of our country's most secret intelligence organization, which worked so deep in shadow that only a handful of people even knew of our existence. The agency's task was to police our country's intelligence community, to act as the covert world's internal affairs department. To that extent, you might say, we were a throwback to the Middle Ages. We were the rat-catchers.

Although the number of people employed by the twenty-six publicly acknowledged – and eight unnamed – US intelligence organizations is classified, it is reasonable to say that over one hundred thousand people came within our orbit. A population of that size meant the crimes we investigated ran the gamut – from treason to corruption, murder to rape, drug dealing to theft. The only difference was that some of the perpetrators were the best and brightest in the world.

The group entrusted with this elite and highly classified mission was established by Jack Kennedy in the early months of his administration. After a particularly lurid scandal at the CIA – the details of which still remain secret – he apparently decided members of the intelligence community were as subject to human frailty as the population in general. More so, probably.

In normal circumstances, the FBI would have acted as the shadow world's investigator-at-large. Under the perfumed fist of J. Edgar Hoover, however, that agency was anything but normal. Giving him the power to investigate the spooks would have been – well, you might as well have let Saddam loose in the arms factory. For this reason, Kennedy and his brother created an agency that was given, by virtue of its responsibilities, unprecedented power. Established by an executive order, it also became one of only three agencies to report directly to the president without congressional oversight. Don't bother asking about the other two – both of them are also forbidden by law from being named.

In the rarefied atmosphere where those with the highest security clearances reside, people at first disparaged the new agency and its hard-charging mission. Delighted by their cleverness, they started calling it the '11th Airborne Division' – the cavalry, in other words. Few of them expected it to be successful but, as the agency's impressive reputation grew, they didn't find it quite so funny.

As if by common agreement, one part of the name gradually faded, until the entire intelligence community referred to it – in a tone of reverence – simply as 'The Division'. It's not vanity when I say that many of those who worked for it were brilliant. They had to be – some of The Division's targets were the most highly skilled covert operators the shadow world has ever seen. Years of training had taught these men and women how to lie and deflect, to say goodbye and leave not a trace behind, to have their hand in anything and their fingerprints on nothing. The result was that those who hunted them had to have even greater skills. The pressure for the catchers to keep one step ahead of the prey was enormous, almost unbearable at times, and it was no wonder that The Division had the highest suicide rate of any government agency outside of the Post Office.

It was during my last year at Harvard that I was recruited into its elite ranks without even realizing it. One of the agency's outriders – a pleasant woman with nice legs and a surprisingly short skirt who said she was a vice-president with the Rand Corporation – came to Harvard and talked to promising young graduates.

I had studied medicine for three years, majoring in the pharmacology of drugs – and I mean majoring. By day I learned about them in theory; on weekends I took a far more hands-on approach. It was while visiting a doctor in Boston, having read up on the symptoms of fibromyalgia and convincing him to write me a prescription for Vicodin, that I had an epiphany.

Say it was real, say right now it was me behind that desk dealing with the ailments – real and imagined – of the patients I had been quietly observing in the waiting room.

I realized it wasn't what afflicted people that interested me, it was what motivated them. I dropped out of medicine, enrolled in psychology, graduated *magna cum laude* and was close to completing my doctorate.

As soon as it was finished, the lady in the short skirt was offering twice the starting salary of any other employer and what appeared to be almost limitless opportunities for research and advancement. As a result, I spent six months writing reports that would never be

28

read, designing questionnaires never to be answered, before I discovered I wasn't really working for Rand at all. I was being observed, auditioned, assessed and checked. Suddenly, Short Skirt wasn't anywhere to be found.

Instead, two men – hard men – I had never seen before, or since, took me to a secure room in a nondescript building on an industrial estate just north of CIA headquarters in Langley, Virginia. They made me sign a series of forms forbidding any kind of disclosure before telling me that I was being considered for a position in a clandestine intelligence service which they refused to name.

I stared at them, asking myself why they would have thought of me. But if I was honest, I knew the answer. I was a perfect candidate for the secret world. I was smart, I had always been a loner and I was damaged deep in my soul.

My father walked out before I was born and was never seen again. Several years later, my mother was murdered in her bedroom in our apartment just off 8-Mile Road in Detroit. Like I said, there are some places I will remember all my life.

An only child, I finally washed up with adoptive parents in Greenwich, Connecticut – twenty acres of manicured lawns, the best schools money could buy, the quietest house you've ever known. Their family seemingly complete, I guess Bill and Grace Murdoch tried their best, but I could never be the son they wanted.

A child without parents learns to survive; they work out early to mask what they feel and, if the pain proves beyond bearing, to dig a cave in their head and hide inside. To the world at large I tried to be what I thought Bill and Grace wanted, and ended up being a stranger to them both.

Sitting in that room outside Langley, I realized that taking on another identity, masking so much of who you are and what you feel, was ideal training for the secret world.

In the years that followed – the ones I spent secretly travelling the world under a score of different names – I have to say the best spooks I ever met had learned to live a double life long before they joined any agency.

They included closeted men in a homophobic world, secret adulterers with wives in the suburbs, gamblers and addicts, alcoholics and perverts. Whatever their burden, they were all long-practised at making the world believe in an illusion of themselves. It was only a small step to put on another disguise and serve their government.

I guess the two hard men sensed something of that in me. Finally they got to the part of their questioning that dealt with illegality. 'Tell us about drugs,' they said.

I remembered what somebody once said about Bill Clinton – he never met a woman he didn't like. I figured it wouldn't be helpful to tell them I felt the same way about drugs. I denied even a passing knowledge, thankful I had never adopted the reckless lifestyle that usually accompanies their use. I'd made it a secret life and kept it hidden by following my own rules – I only ever got fucked up alone, I didn't try and score at bars or clubs, I figured party drugs were for amateurs, and the idea of driving around an open-air drug market sounded like a recipe to get shot.

It worked – I had never been arrested or questioned about it – and so, having already successfully lived one secret life, it now gave me the confidence to embrace another. When they stood up and wanted to know how long I would need to consider their offer, I simply asked for a pen.

So that was the way of it – I signed their Memorandum of Engagement in a windowless room on a bleak industrial estate and joined the secret world. If I gave any thought to the cost it would exact, the ordinary things I would never experience or share, I certainly don't recall it.

Chapter Six

AFTER FOUR YEARS OF TRAINING – OF LEARNING TO READ TINY SIGNS others might miss, to live in situations where others would die – I rose quickly through the ranks. My initial overseas posting was to Berlin and, within six months of my arrival, I had killed a man for the first time.

Ever since The Division was established, its operations in Europe had been under the command of one of its most senior agents, based in London. The first person to hold the post had been a high-ranking navy officer, a man steeped in the history of naval warfare. As a result, he took to calling himself the Admiral of the Blue, the person who had once been third in command of the fleet: his exact position within The Division. The name stuck but over the decades it got changed and corrupted, until finally he became known as the Rider of the Blue.

By the time I arrived in Europe, the then-occupant of the office was running a highly regarded operation and there seemed little doubt he would one day return to Washington and assume The Division's top post. Those who did well in his eyes would inevitably be swept higher in the slipstream, and there was intense competition to win his approval.

It was against this background that the Berlin office sent me to Moscow early one August – the worst of months in that hot and desperate city – to investigate claims of financial fraud in a US clandestine service operating there. Sure the money was missing, but as I dug deeper what I uncovered was far worse – a senior US intelligence officer had travelled especially to Moscow and was about to sell the names of our most valuable Russian informers back to the FSB, the successor both in function and brutality to the KGB.

As I'd come very late to this particular party, I had to make an instant decision – no time to seek advice, no second guessing. I caught up with our officer when he was on his way to meet his Russian contact. And yes, that was the first man I ever killed.

I shot him – I shot the Rider of the Blue dead in Red Square, a vicious wind howling out of the steppes, hot, carrying with it the smell of Asia and the stench of betrayal. I don't know if this is anything to be proud of but, even though I was young and inexperienced, I killed my boss like a professional.

I shadowed him to the southern edge of the square, where a children's carousel was turning. I figured the blaring sound of its recorded music would help mask the flat retort of a pistol shot. I came in at him from an angle – this man I knew well, and he saw me only at the last moment.

A look of puzzlement crossed his face, almost instantly giving way to fear. 'Eddy—' he said.

My real name wasn't Eddy but, like everybody else in the agency, I had changed my identity when I first went out into the field. I think it made it easier, as if it weren't really me who was doing it.

'Something wrong – what are you doing here?' He was from the south, and I'd always liked his accent.

I just shook my head. '*Vyshaya mera*,' I said. It was an old KGB expression we both knew that literally meant 'the highest level of punishment' – a euphemism for putting a large-calibre bullet through the back of someone's head.

I already had my hand on the gun in my hip pocket – a slimline PSM 5.45; ironically, a Soviet design, especially made to be little thicker than a cigarette lighter. It meant you could carry it with barely a wrinkle in the jacket of a well-cut suit. I saw his panicky eyes slide to the kids riding the carousel, probably thinking about his own two little ones, wondering how it ever got this crazy.

Without taking the gun out of my pocket, I pulled the trigger – firing a steel-core bullet able to penetrate the thirty layers of Kevlar and half an inch of titanium plate in the bulletproof vest I assumed he was wearing.

Nobody heard a sound above the racket of the carousel.

The bullet plunged into his chest, the muzzle velocity so high it immediately sent his heart into shock, killing him instantly – just like it was designed to do. I put my arm out, catching him as he fell, using my hand to wipe the sweat from his forehead, acting as if my companion had just passed out from the heat.

I half carried him to a plastic seat under a flapping, unused sunshade, speaking in halting Russian to the clutch of mothers waiting ten yards away for their children, pointing at the sky, complaining about the weather.

They smiled, secretly pleased to have it confirmed once again that the Slavs were strong and the Americans weak: 'Ah, the heat – terrible, yes,' they said sympathetically.

I took off the Rider's jacket and put it on his lap to hide the reddening hole. I called to the mothers again, telling them I was leaving him momentarily while I went for a cab.

They nodded, more interested in their kids on the carousel than in what I was doing. I doubt any of them even realized I was carrying his briefcase – let alone his wallet – as I hurried towards the taxis on Kremlevskiy Prospekt.

I was already entering my hotel room several miles away before anyone noticed the blood trickling from the corner of his mouth and called the cops. I hadn't had the chance to empty all his pockets, so I knew it wouldn't be long before they identified him.

On visits to London I'd had dinner at his home and played with his kids – two girls who were in their early years at school – many times, and I counted down the minutes to when I guessed the phone would ring at his house in Hampstead and they'd get the news their father was dead. Thanks to my own childhood, I had a better idea than most how that event would unfold for a child – the wave of disbelief, the struggle to understand the finality of death, the flood of panic, the yawning chasm of abandonment. No matter how hard I tried, I couldn't stop the scene from playing out in my head – the visuals were of them, but I'm afraid the emotion was mine.

At last I sat on the bed and broke the lock on his briefcase. The only thing of interest I found was a music DVD with Shania Twain on the cover. I put it in the drive of my laptop and ran it through an algorithm program. Hidden in the digitized music were the names and classified files of nineteen Russians who were passing secrets to us. *Vyshaya mera* to them if the Rider had made the drop.

As I worked through the files, looking at the personal data in the nineteen files, I started to keep a tally of the names of all the Russian kids I encountered. I hadn't meant to, but I realized I was drawing up a sort of profit-and-loss account. By the end there were fourteen Russian children in one column, the Rider's two daughters in the other. You could say it had been a good exchange by any reckoning. But it wasn't enough: the names of the Russians were too abstract and the Rider's children far too real.

I picked up my coat, swung my overnight bag on to my shoulder, pocketed the PSM 5.45 and headed to a playground near Gorky Park. I knew from the files that some of the wives of our Russian assets often took their kids there in the afternoon. I sat on a bench and, from the descriptions I had read, I identified nine of the women for sure, their children building sandcastles on a make-believe beach.

I walked forward and stared at them – I doubt they even noticed the stranger with a burn hole in his jacket looking through the railing – these smiling kids whose summers I hoped would now last longer than mine ever did. And while I had managed to make them real, I couldn't help thinking that, in the measure of what I had given to them, by equal measure I had lost part of myself. Call it my innocence.

Feeling older but somehow calmer, I walked towards a row of taxis. Several hours earlier – as I had hurried towards my hotel room after killing the Rider – I had made an encrypted call to Washington, and I knew that a CIA plane, flying undercover as a General Motors executive jet, was en route to the city's Sheremetyevo airport to extract me.

Worried that the Russian cops had already identified me as the killer, the ride to the airport was one of the longest journeys of my life, and it was with overwhelming relief that I stepped on board the jet. My elation lasted about twelve seconds. Inside were four armed men who declined to reveal who they were but had the look of some Special Forces unit.

They handed me a legal document and I learned I was now the subject of the intelligence community's highest inquiry – a Critical Incident Investigation – into the killing. The leader of the group told me we were flying to America.

He then read me my rights and placed me under arrest.

Chapter Seven

MY BEST GUESS WAS MONTANA. AS I LOOKED OUT THE WINDOW OF THE jet there was something in the cut of the hills that made me almost certain we were in the north-west. There was nothing else to distinguish the place – just an airstrip so secret it consisted of a huddle of unmarked bunkers, a dozen underground hangars and miles of electrified fence.

We had flown through the night, and by the time we landed – just after dawn – I was in a bad frame of mind. I'd had plenty of opportunity to turn things over in my head and the doubts had grown with each passing mile. What if the Shania Twain DVD was a fake, or somebody had planted it on the Rider? Maybe he was running a sting operation I didn't know about – or another agency was using him to give the enemy a raft of disinformation. And what about this? Perhaps the investigators would claim it was my DVD and the Rider had unmasked *me* as the traitor. That explained why I had to shoot him dead with no consultation.

I was slipping even further into the labyrinth of doubt as the Special Ops guys bustled me off the plane and into an SUV with blackened windows. The doors locked automatically and I saw the handles inside had been removed. It had been five years since I had first joined the secret world and now, after three frantic days in Moscow, everything was on the line.

For two hours we drove without leaving the confines of the electrified fence, coming to a stop at last at a lonely ranch house surrounded by a parched lawn.

Restricted to two small rooms and forbidden any contact except with my interrogators, I knew that in another wing of the house a dozen forensic teams would be going through my life with a fine-toothed comb – the Rider's too – trying to find the footprints of the truth. I also knew how they'd interview me – but no amount of practice sessions during training can prepare you for the reality of being worked over by hostile interrogators.

Four teams worked in shifts, and I say it without editorial comment, purely as a matter of record: the women were the worst – or the best – depending on your point of view. The shapeliest of them appeared to think that by leaving the top of her shirt undone and leaning forward she would somehow get closer to the truth. Wonderbra, I called her. It would be the same sort of method used, years later, with great effect on the Muslim detainees at Guantanamo Bay.

I understood the theory – it was a reminder of the world you hungered for, the world of pleasure, far removed from the place of constant anxiety. All you had to do was cooperate. And let me just say, it works. Hammered about details night and day as they search for any discrepancy, you're tired – weary to the bone. Two weeks of it and you're longing for another world – any world.

Late one night, after twelve hours without pause, I asked Wonderbra: 'You figure I planned it all – and I shot him on the edge of Red Square? *Red Square*? Why would I do that?'

'Stupid, I guess,' she said evenly.

'Where did they recruit you – Hooters?!' I yelled. For the first time, I'd raised my voice: it was a mistake; now the team of analysts and psychologists watching via the hidden cameras would know they were getting to me.

Instantly I hoped she would return service, but she was a professional – she kept her voice calm, just leaned even further forward, the few buttons on her shirt straining: 'They're natural and it's no credit to the bra in case you're wondering. What song was the carousel playing?'

I forced the anger to walk away. 'I've already told you.'

'Tell us again.'

'"Smells Like Teen Spirit". I'm serious, this is modern Russia; nothing makes sense.'

'You'd heard it before?' she said.

'Of course I'd heard it before, it's Nirvana.'

'In the square, I mean, when you scouted locations—?'

'There was no scouting, because there was no plan,' I told her quietly, a headache starting in my left temple.

When they finally let me go to bed, I felt she was winning. No matter how innocent you are, that's a bad thing to think when you're in an isolated house, clinging to your freedom, as good as lost to the world.

Early the next morning – Wednesday by my figuring, but in fact a Saturday, that's how disoriented I'd become – the door to my sleeping area was unlocked and the handler hung a clean set of clothes on the back of it. He spoke for the first time and offered me a shower instead of the normal body wash in a basin in the corner. I knew this technique too – make me think they were starting to believe me, encourage me to trust them – but by this stage I was pretty well past caring about the psychology of it all. Like Freud might have said: sometimes a shower's still a shower.

The handler unlocked a door into an adjoining bathroom and left. It was a white room, clinical, ring bolts in the ceiling and walls that hinted at a far darker purpose, but I didn't care. I shaved, undressed and let the water flood down. As I was getting dry, I caught sight of myself naked in a full-length mirror and stopped – it was strange, I hadn't really looked at myself for a long time.

I'd lost about twenty pounds in the three weeks or whatever it was I had been at the ranch and I couldn't remember ever seeing my face look more haggard. It made me appear a lot older, and I stared at it for a time, as if it were a window into the future. I wasn't ugly: I was tall and my hair was salted with blond thanks to the European summer.

With the extra pounds stripped off my waist and butt thanks to the investigation, I was in good shape – not with the six-pack-ab vanity of a movie star but with the fitness that came from practising forty minutes of Krav Maga every day. An Israeli system of self-defence it is, according to people who know, the most highly regarded form of unarmed combat among New York drug dealers north of 140th Street. I always figured if it was good enough for the professionals, it was good enough for me. One day, several years in the future – alone and desperate – it would save my life.

As I stood close to the mirror, taking inventory of the man I saw before me, wondering if I really liked him that much, it occurred to me I might not be the only one watching. Wonderbra and her friends were probably on the other side of the glass, conducting their own appraisal. I may not be on top of anyone's list for male lead in *Deep Throat II*, but I didn't have anything to be ashamed of. No, it wasn't that which made me angry – it was the intrusion into every part of my life, the endless search for evidence that did not exist, the soul-destroying conviction that nobody could do something simply because they thought it was right.

Krav Maga instructors will tell you that the mistake most people make when they fight is to punch someone's head really hard. The first thing you break is your knuckles. For that reason, a real professional clenches his or her fist and uses the side of it like a hammer hitting an anvil.

A blow like that from a reasonably fit person will deliver – according to the instructors – over four newtons of force at the point of impact. You can imagine what that does to someone's face. Or to a mirror. It split into pieces and shattered on the floor. The most surprising thing was the wall behind – it was bare. No two-way glass, nothing. I stared at it, wondering if I was the one that was cracking.

Showered and shaved, I returned to the bedroom and, dressed in the clean clothes, I sat on the bed and waited. Nobody came. I went to bang on the door and found that it was unlocked. Oh, this was cute, I thought – the trust quotient was going suborbital now. Either that or, in this particular episode of *The Twilight Zone*, I would find the house was empty and hadn't been lived in for years.

I made my way to the living room. I had never been in it before but that's where I found the whole team, about forty of them, smiling at me. For an awful moment I thought they were going to clap. The team leader, a guy with a face made out of spare parts, said something I barely understood. Then Wonderbra was putting out her hand, saying it was just work, hoping there were no hard feelings.

I was about to suggest she come upstairs, where I'd visit on her acts of violence, some of them increasingly sexual in nature, but what the team leader said now made me stop – I decided such thoughts were unworthy of someone who had received a handwritten letter from the President of the United States. It was lying on a table and I sat down to read it. Under the impressive blue-and-gold seal, it said that a complete and thorough investigation had cleared me of all wrongdoing. The president thanked me for what he called great courage 'above and beyond the call of duty'.

'In hostile territory, far removed from help or safety, and facing the need for immediate action, you did not hesitate or give any thought to your personal welfare,' he wrote.

He said that while it was impossible for the public ever to know of my actions, both he personally and the country at large were deeply grateful for the service I had performed. Somewhere in it he also used the word 'hero'.

I walked to the door. I felt the assembled eyes on me, but I hardly noticed. I went out and stood on the lawn, looking across the bleak landscape. 'Cleared of all wrongdoing,' the letter had said, and as I thought on that and the other word he had used, it unchained a host of emotions in me. I wondered what Bill and Grace would have thought: would they have found the pride in me I had so long denied them?

I heard a car's tyres crunch up the long gravel drive and stop at the front of the house, but I ignored it. And what of the dead woman in Detroit, the one with the same startling blue eyes as mine? She had loved me, I was sure of that, but it was strange given that I hardly knew her. What would my mother feel if I could have told her?

I kept standing there, shoulders hunched against the wind and the emotional debris swirling around me, until I heard a door open. I turned – the team leader and Wonderbra were standing on the porch. With them was an elderly man, just arrived in the car, whom I had known for a long time. It doesn't matter what his name was – by design, nobody has ever heard of him. He was the director of The Division.

Slowly he came down the steps and stood with me. 'You read the letter?' he asked. I nodded. He put his hand on my arm and exerted a tiny pressure – his way of saying thank you. I guess he knew that any words of his would have little hope of competing with that blue-and-gold seal.

He followed my gaze across the bleak landscape and spoke of the man I had killed. 'If you take the final betrayal out of it,' he said, 'he was a fine agent – one of the best.'

I stared at him. 'That's one way of putting it,' I replied. 'If you take the bomb out of it, 6 August was probably a nice day in Hiroshima.'

'Jesus, Eddy! I'm doing my best here, I'm trying to find something positive – he was a friend of mine.'

'Mine too, Director,' I said flatly.

'I know, I know, Eddy,' he replied, restraining himself – amazing what a letter from the president can do. 'I've said a dozen times I'm glad it was you, not me. Even when I was younger, I don't know if I could have done it.'

I didn't say anything: from what I had heard he would have taken a machine gun to Disneyland if he had thought it would have advanced his career.

He turned his collar up against the wind and told me he wanted me to return to London. 'I've checked with everyone who has to sign off. The decision was unanimous – I'm appointing you the new Rider of the Blue.'

I said nothing, just stared across the blighted fields for a long time, saddened beyond telling by the circumstances and those two little girls. I was twenty-nine years old and the youngest Rider of the Blue there had ever been.

Chapter Eight

LONDON HAD NEVER LOOKED MORE BEAUTIFUL THAN THE NIGHT I FLEW in – St Paul's Cathedral, the Houses of Parliament and all the other old citadels of power and grandeur standing like sculptures against a red and darkening sky.

It was less than twenty hours since my promotion, and I had travelled without rest. I was wrong about the location of the ranch house – it was in the Black Hills of South Dakota, even more remote than I had imagined. From there it was a two-hour drive to the nearest public airport, where a private jet had flown me to New York to connect with a British Airways transatlantic flight.

A Ford SUV, three years old and splashed with dirt to make it look unremarkable, picked me up at Heathrow and took me into Mayfair. It was a Sunday night and there was little traffic, but even so progress was slow – the vehicle was armour-plated and the extra weight made it a bitch to drive.

The guy wrestling the wheel finally turned into a cul-de-sac near South Audley Street and the garage door of an elegant town house swung up. We drove into the underground garage of a building which, according to the brass plaque on the front door, was the European headquarters of the Balearic Islands Investment Trust.

A sign underneath told the public that appointments could be made only by telephone. No number was given and, if anyone ever checked, London directory assistance had no listing for it. Needless to say, nobody ever called.

I took the elevator from the basement to the top floor and entered what had always been the Rider of the Blue's office – a large expanse of polished wood floors and white sofas, but no windows or natural light.

The building itself had a concrete core, and it was from this cell within a cell that I began trying to unravel my predecessor's web of deceit. Late into that first night, I called secret phone numbers which telephone companies didn't even know they hosted, assembling a special team of cryptographers, analysts, archivists and field agents.

Despite what governments might claim, not all wars are fought with embedded reporters or in the glare of 24-hour news cameras. The following day, the new Rider and his small group of *partizans* launched their own campaign across Europe, doing battle with what turned out to be the most serious penetration of the US intelligence community since the Cold War.

We had some major successes but, even though, as time passed, enemy bodies started piling up like cord wood, I still couldn't sleep. One night, chasing down a stale lead in Prague, I walked for hours through the old city and forced myself to take stock of where we were. By my own standards, shorn of all complications, I had failed – after twenty months' unremitting work I still hadn't discovered the method by which the Russians were paying the agents of ours – the traitors, in other words – they had corrupted.

The money trail remained as mysterious as ever and, unless we could track it successfully, we would never know how far the plumes of infection had spread. As a result, I resolved to throw everything we had at the problem but, in the end, none of that mattered: it was a shy forensic accountant and a dose of serendipity that came to our rescue.

Ploughing one last time through the mountain of material seized from my predecessor's London home before it vanished into The Division's archives, the accountant found a handwritten grocery list stuck in the back of a chequebook. About to throw it away, he turned it over and saw it was written on the back of a blank FedEx consignment docket – strange because none of our investigations had shown any evidence of a FedEx account. Intrigued, he called the company and discovered a list of pick-ups from the address, all of which had been paid for in cash.

Only one turned out to be of interest – a box of expensive Cuban cigars sent to the luxurious Burj Al Arab hotel in Dubai. It quickly transpired that the name of the recipient on the FedEx docket was fake, and that would have been an end to the matter – except for the moment of serendipity. A woman working with the accountant had once been a travel agent and she knew that all hotels in the United Arab Emirates are required to take a copy of every guest's passport.

I called the hotel under the guise of an FBI special agent attached to Interpol and convinced the manager to examine their files and give me the passport details of the guest who had been staying in suite 1608 on the relevant date.

It turned out to be a person called Christos Nikolaides. It was an elegant name. Shame about the man.

Chapter Nine

EVERYONE AGREED ON ONE THING – CHRISTOS WOULD HAVE BEEN handsome if it weren't for his height. The olive skin, wave of unruly dark hair and good teeth couldn't overcome legs that were far too short for his body. But money probably helped, especially with the women he liked to run with, and Christos Nikolaides certainly had plenty of that.

A flurry of police database searches showed that he was the real deal: a genuine low-life with no convictions but a significant involvement in three murders and a host of other crimes of violence. Thirty-one years old and a Greek national, he was the eldest son of uneducated parents who lived outside Thessaloniki, in the north of the country. It's important to stress 'uneducated' here, as opposed to stupid – which they most certainly were not.

In the following weeks, as we delved deeper into his life, the family became increasingly interesting. A close-knit clan of brothers, uncles and cousins, the family was headed by Christos's sixty-year-old father, Patros – the family's ruthless enforcer. As they say in Athens, he had a thick jacket – a long criminal record – but this had been accompanied by great material success. An adjustment to the orbit of a US satellite monitoring the Balkans provided photos showing the family's compound in stunning detail.

Set amid rolling acres of lavender, the complex of seven luxurious homes, swimming pools and lavish stables was surrounded by a twelve-foot wall patrolled by what we believed to be Albanians armed with Skorpion machine pistols. This was strange, given that the family was in the wholesale floristry business. Maybe flower theft was a bigger problem in northern Greece than most people realized.

We theorized that, like Colombia's Medellín cartel before them, they had adapted the complex high-speed air and road network needed to transport a perishable product like flowers to include a far more profitable commodity.

But what did a family of Greek drug dealers have to do with my predecessor, and why would he be sending the eldest son a box of cigars at a seven-star hotel in the Middle East? It was possible the former Rider had had a drug habit and Christos was his dealer, but it didn't make much sense: the Greeks were definitely on the whole-sale side of the business.

I was about to dismiss the whole investigation as another dead end – maybe Christos and my predecessor were nothing more than friendly scumbags – when, by good luck, I could not get to sleep on a grim London night. I looked across the rooftops from my apart-ment in Belgravia, thinking of how the two men probably ate together at one of the area's Michelin-starred restaurants, when I realized that the answer to our most difficult problem might be staring me in the face.

What if the Russians weren't responsible for paying our rogue agents at all? Say Christos Nikolaides and his family were responsible for making the payments. Why? Because they were running drugs into Moscow and that was the contribution they had to make to the cash-strapped Russians for the licence to do so. Call it a business tax.

It meant the Greeks would be using their black cash and money-laundering skills to transfer funds from their own accounts into ones in the names of our traitors – and the Russian intelligence agencies wouldn't show up anywhere near the process. Under such a scenario, somebody who had received a large payment – the Rider of the Blue – might send an expensive box of cigars to the man who had just paid him: Christos Nikolaides, on vacation in Dubai.

I put all thoughts of sleep aside, went back into the office and launched an intense investigation – with the help of the Greek government – into the Nikolaides family's deeply subterranean financial arrangements.

It was information discovered during this process that led me to Switzerland and the quiet streets of Geneva. Despite the city's reputation for cleanliness, that's a dirty little town if ever I've seen one.

Chapter Ten

THE OFFICES OF THE WORLD'S MOST SECRETIVE PRIVATE BANK LIE BEHIND an anonymous limestone facade in the centre of Geneva's Quartier des Banques. There is no name displayed, but Clément Richeloud & Cie has occupied the same building for two hundred years, counting among its clients countless African despots, numerous corporate criminals and the rich descendants of a few prominent members of the Third Reich.

Richeloud's was also the Greek family's bankers and, as far as I could see, offered our only way forward. They would have to be persuaded to give us a list of the Nikolaides family's transactions over the last five years – documents which would show if Christos was acting as the Russians' paymaster and, if so, which Americans were on the payroll.

Of course, we could make an application in court, but Richeloud's would claim, correctly, that it was illegal to divulge any information because of the Swiss government's banking secrecy laws – legislation which has made the nation a favourite with tyrants and criminals.

It was for this reason that I contacted the bank as the Monaco-based lawyer for interests associated with the Paraguayan military and arrived on their marble doorstep prepared to discuss a range of highly confidential financial matters. Carrying an attaché case full of forged documents and the prospect of what seemed to be deposits worth hundreds of millions of dollars, I sat in a conference room full of faux antiques and waited for the bank's managing partner.

The meeting turned out to be one of the most memorable events of my professional life – not because of Christos Nikolaides, but thanks to a lesson I learned. My education started with the opening of the oak-panelled door.

It is fair to say a lot of my work has been a row through a sewer in a glass-bottomed boat, but even by those low standards Markus Bucher was memorable. Despite being a lay preacher at Geneva's austere Calvinist cathedral, he was, like most of his profession, up to his armpits in blood and shit. Now in his fifties, you could say he'd hit a home run – a big estate in Cologny overlooking the lake, a Bentley in the garage – but given that he had started on second base, it wasn't really much of an achievement: his family were the largest shareholders in the privately held bank.

He made a big deal of the fact that the room we were in was soundproofed to 'American intelligence agency standards' but failed to mention the hidden camera I had registered in the frame of a portrait on the wall. It was positioned to look over a client's shoulder and record any documents they might be holding. Just to be bloody-minded, I casually rearranged the chairs so that all the lens could see was the back of my briefcase. Amateurs, I thought.

As Bucher worked his way through the forgeries, probably mentally tallying the management fees they could earn on such huge sums, I looked at my watch – three minutes to one, almost lunchtime.

Unfortunately for the Nikolaides family, they had overlooked one salient point as they funnelled more and more money into Richeloud's – Bucher's only child had also entered the banking trade. Twenty-three and without much experience of men or the world, she was working in the more respectable end of the business – for Credit Suisse in Hong Kong.

I glanced at my watch again – two minutes to one. I leaned forward and quietly told Bucher: 'I wouldn't know anybody in the Paraguayan military from a fucking hole in the ground.'

He looked at me, confused – then he laughed, thinking this was an American version of humour. I assured him it wasn't.

I gave him Christos's full name, what I believed to be his account number and said I wanted a copy of the banking records concerning him, his family and their associated companies for the last five years. In a dark corner of my mind I was hoping I was right about this, or there would be hell to pay – but there was no going back now.

Bucher got to his feet, righteous indignation swelling in his breast, blustering about people gaining entry by false pretences, that he had immediately recognized the documents as forgeries, how only an American would think that a Swiss banker would divulge such information, even if he had it. He came towards me and I realized I was being given the singular honour denied to so many dictators and mass murderers: I was going to be thrown out of a Swiss bank.

It was one o'clock. He paused, and I saw his eyes flick to his desk: his private cellphone, lying with his papers – the number he believed known only to his close family – was vibrating. I watched in silence as he stole a glance at the caller's number. Deciding to deal with it later, he turned and bore down on me, wearing his outrage like body armour.

'It's eight o'clock at night in Hong Kong,' I said, without shifting in my chair, ready to break his arm if he tried to touch me.

'What?!' he snapped back, not really comprehending.

'In Hong Kong,' I said more slowly, 'it's already late.'

I saw a flash of fear in his eyes as he grasped what I had said. He looked at me, questions flooding in he couldn't answer: how the hell did I know it was Hong Kong calling? He turned and grabbed the phone.

I kept my eyes fixed on him as he heard that not only was I right about it being Hong Kong but that his daughter – fighting to keep the panic out of her voice – told him she was confronting a major problem. It may have been only lunchtime in Geneva, but for Markus Bucher the day was growing darker by the second.

It seemed that, two hours earlier, all communications within his daughter's luxury high-rise had suffered a major failure – phone, cable TV, Wi-Fi, high-speed DSL had all gone down. A dozen crews from Hong Kong Telecom had started trying to find the fault. One of these maintenance crews – three men, all wearing regulation white boiler suits and necklace ID cards – had found their way into Clare Bucher's apartment.

By the time she called her father she was of the view that they were not, perhaps, what they claimed to be. Her first piece of evidence was that two of them didn't seem to speak any Chinese at all – in fact, they sounded like Americans. The second clue concerned communications equipment. Although she didn't know much about such things, she was pretty sure you didn't need a NATO-style 9mm Beretta pistol fitted with a silencer to fix a line fault.

48

I watched her father's face turn an unhealthy shade of grey as she explained her situation. He looked up at me with a mixture of pure hatred and desperation. 'Who are you?' he said, so quiet as to be almost inaudible.

'From what I've overheard,' I said, 'I'm the only person in the world who can help you. By good fortune, the head of Hong Kong Telecom owes me a favour – let's just say I helped him bid for a successful phone contract in Paraguay.'

I thought at that moment he was going to hurl himself at me, so I got ready to hurt him badly if necessary, and kept talking. 'I'm certain, in the right circumstances, I could call and ask him to have the technicians look elsewhere.'

Somehow Bucher managed to master himself. He looked at me, deeper now in the forest than he had ever thought possible, at a crossroads that would determine the rest of his life.

I watched the battle rage on his face: he could no more abandon his daughter than he could violate everything he thought he stood for. He was paralysed, and I had to help him make the right decision. Like I mentioned, it was a terrible morning. 'If I could just say this – if you decide not to cooperate and the technicians have to eliminate your daughter, I can't influence what they might do to her beforehand, if you understand. It's out of my power.'

I didn't like to use the word 'rape', not to a father. He said nothing then turned aside and vomited on the floor. He wiped his mouth on his sleeve and got shakily to his feet. 'I'll get the records,' he said, lurching forward.

People say love is weak, but they're wrong: love is *strong*. In nearly everyone it trumps all other things – patriotism and ambition, religion and upbringing. And of every kind of love – the epic and the small, the noble and the base – the one that a parent has for their child is the greatest of them all. That was the lesson I learned that day, and I'll be forever grateful I did. Some years later, deep in the ruins called the Theatre of Death, it salvaged everything.

By the time I grabbed his arm, Bucher was already halfway to the door, willing to surrender anything, desperate to save his daughter. 'Stop!' I told him.

He turned to me, close to tears. 'You think I'll call the police,' he shouted, 'with your "technicians" still in her apartment?!'

'Of course not,' I said. 'You're not a fool.'

49

'So let me get the records, for Chrissake!'

'What's to stop you giving me phoney ones or another client's? No, we'll go and look at the computer together.'

He shook his head, panicking. 'Impossible. Nobody's allowed in the back office – the staff will realize.'

It was true except for one thing. 'Why do you think I chose one o'clock, the Friday of a holiday weekend,' I said. 'Everybody's at lunch.' I picked up my bag, followed him out of the conference room and watched as he used an encrypted ID card to unlock a door into the inner offices.

We sat at a terminal; he used a fingerprint scanner to open the system and keyed in the digits of an account number. There they were – pages of Christos Nikolaides' supposedly secret bank records, linked to a matrix of other family accounts. Within minutes, we were printing them all out.

I stared at the pages for a long time – the ledgers of so much corruption and death. The family were billionaires – or close enough not to matter – but the records also proved beyond doubt that Christos was the Russians' paymaster. More than that, just as I'd hoped, the documents also prised open the rest of the enterprise. Regular transfers into other accounts at the bank revealed the names of six of our people whom I would never have imagined were traitors.

Two of them were FBI agents involved in counter-espionage and the other four were career diplomats at US embassies in Europe – including a woman I had once slept with – and for what they had done there was usually only one tariff. In a corner of my heart I hoped they would get good lawyers and manage to plea-bargain it down to life imprisonment. Don't believe what they tell you – it's a terrible thing to hold another person's life in the palm of your hand.

So it was with less satisfaction than I had anticipated that I put the material in my briefcase and turned to Bucher. I told him that in two hours I would call the head of Hong Kong Telecom and have the technicians reassigned. I stood up and, under the circumstances, decided against offering him my hand. Without a word I walked out, leaving him alone – vomit smearing his suit, one hand trembling, trying to decide if the palpitations he could feel in his chest were just nerves or something far more serious.

I didn't know if the man would ever recover, and maybe I would have felt some sympathy for him except for a strange event which occurred in my childhood.

Accompanied by Bill Murdoch, I had made a trip to a small French village called Rothau on the German border. Twenty years and countless adventures have passed but, in a way, part of me has never left that place – or maybe I should say part of it has never left me.

Chapter Eleven

IF YOU EVER FIND YOURSELF IN THE PART OF THE WORLD WHERE FRANCE and Germany meet and want your heart broken, drive up the twisting road from the village, through the pine forests and into the foothills of the Vosges mountains.

Sooner or later you will come to an isolated place called Natzweiler-Struthof. It was a Nazi concentration camp, almost forgotten now, never making it on to the misery-with-a-guidebook tours like Auschwitz and Dachau. You come out of the pine trees and at an intersection there is a simple country road sign: one way points to a local bar and the other to the gas chamber. No, I'm not kidding.

Tens of thousands of prisoners passed through the camp's gates, but that's not the worst thing. The worst thing is hardly anybody has heard of it – that amount of grief just isn't big enough to register on the Richter scale of the twentieth century. Another way of measuring progress, I suppose.

I was twelve when I went there. It was summer vacation and, as usual, Bill and Grace had taken a suite at the Georges V hotel in Paris for most of August. They were both interested in art. She liked Old Masters that told people entering the house that this was a woman of wealth and taste. Bill, thank God, was out on the edge – *dancing* on the edge half the time. He was never happier than when he was finding some new gallery or wandering around a young kid's studio.

Grace, completely disinterested, had long ago forbidden him to hang any of his purchases, and Bill would wink at me and say, 'She's right – whatever it is, you can't call it art. I call it charity – some people give to the United Way, I support starving artists.'

But beneath all the jokes, he knew what he was doing. Years later, I realized what an expert eye he had, which was strange, given that he was completely untrained and his family's only interest had been chemicals. His mother's name before she married had been DuPont.

The second week we were in Paris, Bill got a call from a guy in Strasbourg who said he had a sheaf of drawings by Robert Rauschenberg dating from when the great Pop artist was an unknown marine. The next day, Bill and I got on a plane with a bag packed for the weekend, leaving Grace to indulge her second great passion – shopping at Hermès.

And so it was, once Bill had bought the drawings, that we found ourselves in Strasbourg on a Sunday with nothing to do. 'I thought we might go out to the Vosges mountains,' he said. 'Grace'd probably say you're too young, but there's a place you should see – sometimes life can seem difficult, and it's important to keep things in perspective.'

Bill knew about Natzweiler-Struthof because of his father – he'd been a lieutenant colonel in the US Sixth Army that had campaigned across Europe. The colonel had arrived at the camp just after the SS abandoned it, and he was given the job of writing a report that found its way to the War Crimes Tribunal in Nuremburg.

I don't know if Bill had ever read his father's document, but he found the twisting road without any trouble and we pulled into the car park just before noon, a brilliant summer's day. Slowly we walked into death's house.

The camp had been preserved as a French historic site because so many members of the Resistance had died there. Bill pointed out the old hotel outbuilding the Germans had converted into a gas chamber, and a crematorium packed with body-elevators and ovens.

For one of the few times in my life, I held his hand.

We passed the gallows used for public executions, the building where they had conducted medical experiments, and came to Prisoner Barracks Number One, which housed a museum. Inside – among the prisoners' old uniforms and diagrams of the concentration-camp system – we got separated.

In a quiet corner at the back, near a row of bunk beds where the surrounding ghosts seemed even more tangible, I found a photo displayed on a wall. Actually, there were a lot of photos of the Holocaust, but this was the one that has never left me. It was in black and white and it showed a short, stocky woman walking down a wide path between towering electrified fences. By the look of the light it was late in the afternoon, and in the language of those times she was dressed like a peasant.

By chance there were no guards, no dogs, no watchtowers in the photo, though I'm sure they were there – just a lonely woman with a baby in her arms and her other two children holding tight to her skirt. Stoic, unwavering, supporting their tiny lives – helping them as best as any mother could – she walked them towards the gas chamber. You could almost hear the silence, smell the terror.

I stared at it, both uplifted and devastated by the stark image of a family and a mother's endless love. A small voice inside, a child's voice, kept telling me something I've never forgotten: I would have such as to have known her. Then a hand fell on my shoulder. It was Bill, come to find me. I could see from his eyes he'd been crying.

Overwhelmed, he indicated the piles of shoes and small items such as hairbrushes that the inmates had left behind. 'I didn't realize how powerful ordinary things can be,' he said.

Finally, we walked up a path inside the old electrified fence towards the exit gates. As we wound our way up, he asked me, 'Did you see the part about the gypsies?'

I shook my head: no.

'They lost even more in percentage terms than the Jews.'

'I didn't know that,' I said, trying to be grown up.

'Nor did I,' he replied. 'They don't call it the Holocaust, the gypsies. In their language they have another name for it. They call it the Devouring.'

We walked the rest of the way to the car in silence and flew back to Paris that night. By some unspoken agreement, we never mentioned to Grace where we had been. I think we both knew she would never have understood.

Months later, a couple of nights before Christmas, I walked down the stairs at the quiet house in Greenwich and was stopped by voices raised in anger. 'Five million dollars?' Grace was saying incredulously. 'Still, you do what you like, I suppose – it's your money.'

'Damn right it is,' he agreed.

'The accountant says it's going to an orphanage in Hungary,' she said. 'That's another thing I don't understand – what do you know about Hungary?'

'Not much. Apparently, it's where a lot of gypsies came from; it's a gypsy orphanage,' he said, more or less evenly.

She looked at him like he was crazy. 'Gypsies? *Gypsies*?!'

Then they turned and saw me watching from the doorway. Bill's eyes met mine and he knew that I understood. *Porrajmos*, as the gypsies say in Romani – the Devouring.

After that Christmas, I enrolled at Caulfield Academy, a really phoney high school that took pride in 'providing every student with the means to lead a fulfilling life'. Given the staggering fees, that aspect was probably already taken care of – you had to have about six generations of blue chips behind you even to get in the gate.

The second week I was there we were doing a course to improve our skills at public speaking – only Caulfield Academy could dream up classes like that. The topic someone picked out of a hat was motherhood, and we spent thirty minutes listening to guys talk about what their moms had done for them, which was probably nothing, and funny stuff that happened at the villa in the South of France.

Then I got called on, so I stood up, pretty nervous, and started telling them about pine trees in summer and the long road up into the mountains, and I tried to explain this photo I'd seen and how I knew the mother loved her kids more than anything in the world, and there was this book I'd read by somebody whose name I couldn't remember and he had this expression 'sorrow floats' and that's what I felt about the photo, and I was trying to tie all this together when people started laughing and asking what I was smoking, and even the teacher, who was a young chick who thought she was sensitive but wasn't, told me to sit down and stop rambling on and maybe I should think twice before I ran for high elective office, and that made everybody laugh even louder.

I never got up to speak in class after that, not in the five years I was at Caulfield, no matter what amount of trouble it caused. It made people say I was a loner, there was something dark about me, and I guess they were right. How many of them adopted the secret life or ended up killing half as many people as I did?

Here's the strange thing, though – through all that difficulty and the passage of twenty years, time hasn't dimmed my memory of that photo. It has only made it sharper – it lies in wait for me just before I go to sleep and, try as I might, I've never been able to get it out of my head.

Chapter Twelve

I WAS THINKING OF IT ONCE AGAIN AS I WALKED OUT OF THE FRONT doors of Clément Richeloud & Cie and into the Geneva sunshine. Sure, I could have felt some sympathy for Markus Bucher and his daughter, but I couldn't help remembering that it was Swiss bankers like Bucher and his family who had helped fund and support the Third Reich.

I have no doubt the mother in the photo and millions of other families in cattle cars would have gladly traded the Buchers' couple of hours of discomfort for what they eventually got. It was just like Bill had said all those years ago: it's important to keep things in perspective.

Thinking about the dark history that clung to so much of Geneva's hidden wealth, I walked to the rue du Rhône, turned right, stopped near the entrance to the Old Town and made an encrypted call on my cellphone to a Greek island.

The bank ledgers in the briefcase which was now handcuffed to my wrist were Christos Nikolaides' death warrant, and in the world in which I dwelt there were no appeals and no last-minute stays of execution. As it turned out, killing him wasn't a mistake – but the way I did it certainly was.

There were five assassins – three men and two women – waiting for my call on Santorini. With its azure harbour, achingly white houses rimming the cliffs and donkeys shuttling visitors up to jewel-box boutiques, it is the most beautiful of all the Greek islands.

Dressed in chinos and capri pants, the team was invisible among the thousands of tourists who visit the island every day. The weapons were in their camera cases.

Months before, as the mysterious Nikolaides family had moved ever more clearly into our sights, we had taken an interest in a former ice-breaker called the *Arctic N*. Registered in Liberia, the 300-foot boat, capable of withstanding just about any kind of attack, had been converted at huge expense into a luxury cruiser complete with a helicopter pad and an on-board garage for a Ferrari. Supposedly fitted out for the super-elite Mediterranean charter business, the weird thing was that it only ever had one client – Christos Nikolaides and his entourage of babes, hangers-on, business associates and bodyguards.

All through summer we kept tabs on the boat by satellite, and while we were in Grozny and Bucharest chasing traitors and drug dealers, we watched the endless party glide from St Tropez down to Capri until finally it pulled in to the hollowed-out volcano that forms the harbour at Santorini.

And there the vessel stayed – Nikolaides and his guests relocating every day from the boat's huge sun deck up to the town's restaurants and nightclubs and back down again.

Meanwhile, half a continent away, I waited on a street corner in Geneva for a phone to be answered. When it did, I said three words to a man sitting in a clifftop café. 'That you, Reno?' I asked.

'Wrong number,' he said, and hung up. Jean Reno was the name of the actor who played the assassin in the movie *Léon*, and the team leader sitting in the café knew it meant death.

He nodded to his colleague, who immediately called the other three agents, who were sitting among milling tourists at other cafés. The five of them rendezvoused just near the beautiful Rastoni bar and restaurant, looking for all the world like a group of affluent European holidaymakers meeting up for lunch. The two women in the squad were the primary shooters, and that, I'm afraid, was my mistake.

It was just before two, the restaurant still crowded, when my so-called holidaymakers walked in. The three men spoke to the harried manager about a table while the women moved to the bar, ostensibly to check their make-up in its mirror but in fact noting in the reflection the position of every person in the vaulted space.

Christos and his posse – three Albanian bodyguards and a clutch of chicks his mother had probably warned him about – were sitting at a table looking straight out at the harbour.

'All set?' one of our women asked her male colleagues in passable Italian, framing it as a question but meaning it as a statement. The men nodded.

The women had their tote bags open, putting away their lipstick, reaching for their camera cases. They both pulled out stainless-steel SIG P232s and turned in a tight arc.

Christos's bodyguards, with their True Religion jeans, muscle-man T-shirts and Czech machine pistols, didn't have a chance against real professionals. Two of them didn't even see it coming – the first they heard was the sound of bone breaking as bullets slammed into their heads and chests.

The third bodyguard made it to his feet, a strategy which succeeded only in presenting himself as a bigger target for the team leader. Shows how much he knew. The agent hit him with three bullets, which was unnecessary, as the first one pretty much blasted his heart out the back of his chest.

As is usual in these situations, a lot of people started yelling, to absolutely no effect. One of them was Christos, trying to take command, I guess, scrambling to his feet, reaching under his flapping linen shirt for the Beretta he kept in the waistband of his pants.

Like a lot of tough guys who don't do any real training, he thought he was well prepared by keeping the safety catch off. In the panic of a genuine firefight, he pulled the weapon out, put his finger on the trigger and shot himself through the leg. Fighting the pain and humiliation, he kept turning to face his attackers. What he saw were two middle-aged women, feet planted wide, who – had there been a band – looked like they were about to start a strange dance.

Instead, they both opened up at seven yards, two rounds each. Most of Christos's vital organs – including his brain – were finished before he dropped.

Immediately, the five agents sprayed their weapons across the mirrors, creating a lot of impressive noise and maximum panic. Terrified diners sprinted for the doors, a Japanese tourist tried to film it on his phone and a ricocheting bullet hit a female member of Christos's party in the butt. As one of our women agents told me later – given the way the chick was dressed, the last time she had that much pain up her ass she was probably getting paid for it.

The flesh wound was the only collateral damage – no small

achievement given the number of people in the restaurant and the unpredictable nature of any assassination.

The agents pocketed their weapons, burst out of the front door amid the exploding panic and yelled for someone to call the cops. At a prearranged location – a tiny cobblestone square – they regrouped and boarded four Vespa scooters, permitted for residents only but secured earlier in the day by a large payment to a local repair shop. The team sped into the town's narrow alleys and the leader used his cellphone to call in two fast boats waiting in the next bay.

In three minutes, the assassins reached a scenic cable car that offers an alternative – and far quicker – descent than the donkeys. It takes less than two minutes to take the 1,200-foot drop, and already the boats were pulling into the wharf. The team was halfway to the next island, hurtling across the sparkling blue water in a plume of white spray, by the time the first cops arrived at Rastoni.

To the Greek cops' ribald amusement, they quickly learned that Christos, the first-born and best-loved son of Patros Nikolaides, had been gunned down by two ladies in capri pants and Chanel sunglasses. And that was my mistake – not the killing of him, the women. I genuinely hadn't given it a thought, I just sent the best people for the job, but, as I have to keep relearning, it's the unquestioned assumptions that get you every time.

In the villages of northern Greece, where decisions are taken only in the councils of men, that somebody had assigned women to do the killing was worse in a way than the death itself. It was an *insult*. For the old man, it was as if the killers were telling him that Christos was such a no-account castrato he wasn't even worth a matador.

Maybe Patros, the ruthless enforcer and father, would have ridden out of his compound for vengeance anyway, but when he learned the circumstances, for his dignity as a man, for his *honour* – forget that, given his past, he had none of these things – he believed he had no choice.

The woman agent was wrong about the other casualty too: despite the spandex, she wasn't rented ass at all. She was Christos's younger sister. As I would learn later, for one of the few times in her adult life she was relatively clean and sober in Rastoni. While the other patrons raced for the exits, she scrambled across the shattered glass, bending over her brother, trying to talk him into not dying.

Realizing it was failing, she grabbed her cellphone and made a call. Despite all her years of relentless sex, it was to the only real man in her life – her father. As a result, Patros and his phalanx of Albanians heard before I did exactly what my people had wrought that afternoon.

I hadn't moved from my corner near the Old Town when I got a call ten minutes after he did. It was a text message giving me the price of a *Léon* DVD on Amazon – it meant Christos was dead, the team was safe on board the boats, there was no sign of pursuit. I put the phone away and looked at my watch. Eighteen minutes had passed since I had made the call initiating the whole event.

In the interim, I'd phoned through orders deploying smaller teams to arrest the other six named collaborators, and now the events that started several years ago in Red Square were finally drawing to a close. I suppose I could have taken a moment for quiet congratulation, allowed myself some small feeling of triumph, but I'm prone to self-doubt – always doubting, I'm afraid.

As I adjusted my briefcase – an anonymous young businessman stepping out of the shadows and into the faceless foreign crowd – it was a dead British orator and writer who was on my mind. Edmund Burke said the problem with war is that it usually consumes the very things that you're fighting for – justice, decency, humanity – and I couldn't help but think of how many times I had violated our nation's deepest values in order to protect them.

Lost in thought, I headed for the small bridge that crossed the river. It is eight hundred paces from the edge of the Old Town to the hotel in which I was staying. Eight hundred paces, about four minutes – in terms of history, not even the blink of an eye, really – and yet in that moment all our souls were turning in a few madmen's hands.

Chapter Thirteen

THE HOTEL DU RHÔNE WAS DESERTED WHEN I WALKED IN. THE DOORMEN had gone, the concierge wasn't at his post and the front desk was unattended. More disturbing was the silence. I called out, and when nobody answered I made my way to the bar at one side of the lobby.

The staff were all there, standing with the patrons, watching a TV screen. It was a few minutes before 3 p.m. in Geneva, 9 a.m. in New York. The date was September the eleventh.

The first plane had just hit the north tower of the World Trade Center, and already the footage was being replayed over and over again. A couple of news anchors started speculating that it might be anti-US terrorists, and this theory was met with cheering from several Swiss idiots at the bar. They were speaking French, but my summers in Paris meant I was fluent enough to understand they were praising the courage and ingenuity of whoever was responsible.

I thought of the people at home in New York watching the same footage as us, knowing that their loved ones were somewhere in the burning building and desperately praying that, somehow, they would make it out. Maybe there are worse things than watching your family die on live television, but if there were I couldn't think of any at that moment.

I had a gun in my pocket – all ceramic and plastic, designed to beat metal detectors like the ones at Bucher's office – and I was angry enough to consider using it.

As I fought back my emotions, United Airlines flight 175 out of Boston hit the south tower. It sent everyone in the room, even the idiots, reeling. My memory is that after an initial scream the bar was silent, but that may not be true – all I know is I had a terrible sense of worlds colliding, of the Great Republic shifting on its axis.

Alone, far from home, I feared nothing would ever be the same again: for the first time in history, some unidentified enemy had taken lives on the continental United States. Not only that, they had destroyed an icon which in a way represented the nation itself – ambitious, modern, always reaching higher.

Nobody could say how deep the damage would run, but in the bar life was fractured into disjointed moments – a phone ringing un-answered, a cigar burning to ash, the TV jumping between the immediate past and the terrifying present.

And still people weren't talking. Maybe even the idiots were wondering, like me, if there was more to come. Where would it end – the White House, Three Mile Island?

I left the gun in my pocket, pushed through the crowd that had gathered unnoticed behind me and went up in an empty elevator to my room. I put a call through to Washington, first on a conventional landline connected out of London and then via the Pine Gap satellite, but all communications on the East Coast of the United States were collapsing under the weight of traffic.

Finally, I called an NSA relay station in Peru, gave them the Rider of the Blue's priority code and got through to The Division on an emergency satellite network. I spoke to the Director on a connection so hollow it sounded like we were having a conversation in a toilet bowl and asked him to send a plane so I could get back, wanting to know how I could help.

He said there was nothing I could do and, anyway, he'd just heard from the National Security Council: all flights in and out of the country were about to be halted. I should sit tight; nobody knew where this damn thing was going. It wasn't so much what he said that scared me, it was the edge of panic in his voice. He said he had to go – his building was being evacuated, and so was the White House.

I put the phone down and turned on the TV. Anybody who was alive that terrible day knows what happened: people leaping hand in hand from God knows what height, the collapse of the two towers, the dust and apocalyptic scenes in Lower Manhattan. In houses, offices and war rooms across the world, people were seeing things they would never forget. Sorrow floats.

And though I wouldn't discover it for a long time, watching the cops and firefighters rushing into what would become their concrete tomb, there was one person who saw – in that whirlwind of chaos – the opportunity of a lifetime. She was one of the smartest people I have ever encountered and, despite my many affairs with other substances, intelligence has always been my real drug. For that reason alone, I will never forget her. Whatever people may think of the morality, there was no doubt it took a kind of genius to start planning the perfect murder in the maelstrom of September the eleventh and then carry it out a long time later in a scummy little hotel called the Eastside Inn.

While she was laying her dark plans, I spent the evening watching people jump until, by 10 p.m. in Geneva, the crisis itself was winding down. The president was flying back to Washington from a bunker at Offutt Air Force Base in Nebraska, the fire at the Pentagon was under control and the first bridges into Manhattan were being reopened.

At about the same time I got a call from an aide at the National Security Council who told me the government had intelligence pointing to a Saudi national, Osama bin Laden, and that attacks against his bases in Afghanistan, carried out under the guise of a group of rebels called the Northern Alliance, were already under way. Twenty minutes later I saw news reports of explosions in the Afghan capital of Kabul and I knew that the so-called 'war on terror' had begun.

Claustrophobic, depressed, I went for a walk. The war on terror sounded about as generic as the war on drugs, and I knew from personal experience how successful that had been. The streets of Geneva were deserted, the bars silent, the electric trams empty. I heard later it was the same in cities from Sydney to London, as if for a time the lights had dimmed in the Western world in sympathy with America.

I made my way through what are called the English Gardens, skirted the clutch of Moroccan drug dealers lamenting among themselves the lack of business, thought for a moment of putting a bullet through them just for the hell of it, and walked along the lakeside promenade. Straight ahead lay the exclusive village of Cologny, where Fahd, the ruler of Saudi Arabia, the Aga Khan and half the crooks of the world had their homes. I sat on a bench at the edge of the lake and looked across the water at the United Nations on the other side – brilliantly floodlit, totally useless.

Below it, almost on the lake's edge, rose the grey bulk of the President Wilson hotel, commanding a perfect view of Lake Geneva's most popular beach. Every summer, Saudis and other rich Arabs would pay a huge premium for rooms at the front so that they could watch women sunbathing topless on the grass. With well-stocked mini-bars, it was like an Arab version of an upmarket strip club – without the inconvenience of tipping.

Although it was late, the lights were on in most of the rooms now. I guessed they had realized what sort of shit was about to come down and were packing their binoculars and bags, getting ready for the first flight home.

But no matter what Western revenge would be exacted on Osama bin Laden and Arabs in general, one thing was certain – the events of the last twelve hours were an intelligence failure of historic proportions. The overriding mission of the hugely expensive United States intelligence community was to protect the homeland, and not since Pearl Harbor had these all-powerful organizations screwed up with such spectacular and public results.

As I sat in the cool Geneva night I wasn't pointing the finger at others – none of us was without blame. We all carried the blue badges, we all bore the responsibility. But so did the president and congressmen whom we served, those who established our budgets and priorities. Unlike us, at least they could speak out publicly, but I figured it would be a long wait before the American people got an apology from any of them – the next millennium maybe.

The wind was rising, sweeping out of the Alps and bringing with it the smell of rain. It was a long walk back to my hotel and I should have started then, but I didn't move.

I was certain, even if nobody else was thinking it yet, that pretty soon Lower Manhattan wouldn't be the only thing in ruins – the nation's entire intelligence structure would be torn apart. It had to be if it was going to be rebuilt. Nothing in the secret world would ever be the same again, not least for The Division: people in government would no longer have any interest in secretly policing the covert world; they would only be interested in secretly policing the Islamic world.

I had got up in the morning and, by the time I was ready for bed, it was a different planet: the world doesn't change in front of your eyes, it changes behind your back.

I knew I had none of the language or operational skills necessary for the brave new intelligence world which was about to be born, so I found myself – like Markus Bucher – suddenly at a fork in the road. Unsure what future lay ahead of me, not necessarily seeking happiness, but fulfilment wouldn't be bad, I was lost. I had to ask myself what life I really wanted.

Sitting alone with the storm rolling towards me, I looked back over the years and found, if not an answer, at least a way forward. Rising out of the past to meet me was a remote village called Khun Yuam, just on the Thai side of the Burma border. Looking back, I think the memory of it had waited for years in darkness, knowing its time would come.

It is wild, lawless country up there – not far from the Golden Triangle – and when I was first starting out in this business – I had only been in Berlin for a month – I found myself washed up on its shore. Nothing distinguished Khun Yuam from the other hill-tribe villages, except that five clicks out in the jungle stood a series of grim cinder-block buildings surrounded by guard towers and an electric fence.

Officially a relay post for the Global Positioning System, it was in fact a CIA black prison, part of a vehemently denied but real American gulag: remote facilities used to house prisoners who couldn't be legally tortured back home.

One of the guards had died in-house and, while the Tokyo office normally would have handled it, they were so overwhelmed by yet another Chinese spy scandal that I found myself leaving Europe and flying into a place called Mae Hong Son – the City of Three Mists – on an old turbo-prop.

Most of the time it was a short chopper ride out to the GPS station, but this was the monsoon season and they didn't call it the City of Three Mists for nothing. I rented a Toyota four-wheel drive from a guy who I guessed was a local opium baron and headed for Khun Yuam and its CIA prison.

Passing through spectacular mountains, I came to an ancient cable ferry. It was the only way to cross a roaring river – swollen by the monsoon – a tributary of the mighty Mekong, the scene of so many secret operations and so much US misery during the Vietnam War.

I got out of the car, gaunt and hollow-eyed; I had been travelling non-stop for thirty-two hours, fuelled by nothing more than ambition and anxiety about the mission. As I waited among a clutch of food vendors and villagers, watching a rusty cable drag the flat-bottomed ferry towards us in plumes of spray, a Buddhist monk in saffron robes asked if I wanted a cup of Masala-chai, the local tea. He spoke good English and, with nothing else on offer except the deadly Thai elephant beer, I gratefully accepted.

The monk was heading upcountry too and – given I was supposed to be a WHO expert surveying endemic diseases – it was pretty hard to refuse his request for a ride. We crossed the river in the Toyota, the barge plunging and barely afloat, water blasting over the gunwales and two inches of rusted cable the only thing between us and one of the country's highest waterfalls, half a click downstream. The worst white-knuckle ride of my life.

As we drove out of the gorge, the jungle forming a canopy over our heads, the monk looked at me a little too long and asked about my work. Thanks to my medical training, I gave an excellent account of breakbone fever, but it soon became clear he didn't believe a word of what I was saying. Maybe he knew about the cinder-block camp at Khun Yuam.

He had lived at an ashram not far from New York, so he had more knowledge than you would expect about American life and he spoke intelligently about recreational drugs and the pressures of modern life. I started to get the feeling it wasn't a casual conversation. 'You look hunted,' he said finally, in that Buddhist way, more in sorrow than in judgement.

Hunted? I laughed and told him it was the first time I had ever heard that: people usually put me on the other side of the food chain.

'There is no other side of the food chain,' he said quietly. 'Only the West believes that. Without grace, everyone is running from something.'

Our eyes met. Smiling, I asked if he'd ever considered pursuing a religious life. He laughed right back and wanted to know if I had heard how villagers caught monkeys.

I told him I knew a few things about life, but that wasn't one of them. 'We didn't eat much monkey at Harvard – generally only at Thanksgiving and Christmas,' I said.

So he told me how the villagers chain a ewer – a vase with a narrow neck and a bulbous bottom – to the base of a tree.

'They fill the bottom with nuts and whatever else monkeys like to eat. In the night, a monkey climbs out of the trees and slips his hand down the long neck. He grabs the sweets and his hand makes a fist. That means it's too big to get back up the narrow neck, and he's trapped. In the morning the villagers come round and hit him on the head.'

He looked at me for a moment. 'It's a Zen story of course,' he said, smiling again. 'The point is: if you want to be free, all you have to do is let go.'

Yes, I understood that much, I told him. It was a good story, but it didn't mean anything to me, not now, anyway.

'I suppose not,' he replied, 'but perhaps I was put on the road to tell it to you. You're young, Doctor – maybe the time will come when it will mean something.'

And he was right, of course, the time did come, and in a different way from anything I could have imagined: it was sitting in the Geneva night waiting for a storm, thinking about mass murder in New York and women in short skirts recruiting even brighter young graduates for a new era.

I was thirty-one years old and I realized, through no fault of my own, I had been trained for tank warfare in Europe, only to find the battle was with guerillas in Afghanistan. Like it or not, history had passed me by.

On another level, far deeper, I knew that sooner or later I wanted to find something – something it's hard for me to put a name to . . . a thing most people call love, I suppose. I wanted to walk along a beach with someone and not think about how far a sniper rifle can fire. I wanted to forget that you feel the bullet long before you hear the shot. I wanted to find somebody who could tell me what safe harbour really meant.

I knew with all my heart that, if I didn't leave the secret world now, I never would. To turn your back on everything you know is hard, among the most difficult things you'll ever do, but I kept telling myself one thing.

If you want to be free, all you have to do is let go.

Chapter Fourteen

I WROTE OUT MY RESIGNATION LATE THAT NIGHT IN THE HOTEL DU Rhône, dispatched it by diplomatic courier the next morning and immediately flew to London.

I spent the next three weeks wrapping up my outstanding cases and giving the files to the FBI: in the first of many huge changes to the US intelligence community, The Division had been closed down and its responsibilities assumed – after four decades of trying – by the Feds.

Ironically, my last day on the job was in Berlin, the city where everything had really started for me. I locked the office for the final time and accompanied the staff out to Tempelhof for the flight home. I shook hands with them and, an agent to the end, said I was booked on a later plane.

Instead I walked out of the front doors and, carrying a totally new identity, got a taxi to a car dealership, where I took delivery of a Cayenne turbo. With five hundred horsepower, I figured I was more or less ready for the autobahn.

I threw my bags in the back, was past Frankfurt by evening and crossed the border in the early hours of the morning. Fall had come late that year and even by moonlight I don't think I had ever seen the French countryside looking more beautiful. I flew past villages with romantic names and found the *péage* – a tollway – I was looking for.

If you come into Paris from the south, there's a remarkable point – between the towering high-rises in which the French warehouse their immigrants – where the first sight of the city is almost completely hidden from you. The only thing you see is the Eiffel Tower standing on the horizon.

It was early in the morning, a chill in the air lending a sparkling clarity to everything. I had seen the view many times before but, even so, it took my breath away. The sense of release that had been growing in me through the night finally broke its banks, and I pulled to the side of the road: to be in Paris when you're young and free – well, there's not much on earth better than that.

I rented an apartment in the part of the 8th arrondissement Parisians call the golden triangle, just off the beautiful rue François 1er. Day after day, and late into the night, I wrote the book that few people would read – except for one young woman in New York I would desperately wish hadn't.

After six months, it was done – hundreds of thousands of words, all annotated and checked. I felt the washing out of my earlier life was complete – I had written the final chapter on that era and sent it downstream like a funeral barge into the past. I was proud of the book: call it a public service, call it naive if you want, but I thought if my expertise could help defeat just one man like Christos Nikolaides, then it was a candle worth the burning.

After careful vetting by a team of analysts working for the Director of Intelligence, the book was published by a small house that specialized in harrowing memoirs about escapes from Castro's Cuba and female honour killings among Arabs. In other words, it was a secret subsidiary of the CIA.

Such a publisher was obviously accustomed to authors whose identities had to be concealed but, even so, my case was complicated: when I gave up my badge it was decided I knew enough about national security that nobody could ever know who I was or what job I had done. Without meaning to, the secret world took my identity and my history from me.

When the book finally appeared, not only was Jude Garrett given as the author's name, but an entire identity had been created for him. Anybody who made inquiries received the following biography:

Jude Garrett, a graduate of the University of Michigan, spent over fourteen years in law enforcement, first with the Sheriff's department in Miami and then as a special investigator with the FBI. He died while on assignment in Chicago. The manuscript of this book, which he had researched extensively, was found in his study shortly after his death and represents the last testament of one of the world's finest investigators.

And it was true – some of it, anyway. There had been an FBI agent called Jude Garrett, and he was dead – a car wreck on his way home from work. Unmarried, a loner with few interests outside work, the publishers simply appropriated his identity and gave him a literary accomplishment in death he had never found in life.

I have to admit I liked his biography and I liked the fact he was dead. I mean, who would go looking for a dead man?

Well, somebody did.

With the book finally published, the funeral barge almost lost to view, I had started for the first time in my adult life to live in a world without secrets. I looked at all the laughing women, hips swinging, sashaying down the wide boulevards of Paris, and as spring became summer I started to believe anything was possible.

The problem with the spy business, though, is that while you can resign you can never leave. I suppose I didn't want to acknowledge it then, but too much wreckage floats in the wake of a life like mine – people you've hurt don't forget. And at the back of your mind is the one lesson they drummed into you when you were young and your whole career was ahead of you: in this business, you can't learn by your mistakes. You don't get a chance. Make one, and you're dead.

The only thing that will save you is your intuition and your trade-craft. Burn them into your soul. I suppose I must have listened because, still only nine months into my retirement, I noted a cab with a passenger circling the block. Nobody does that in Paris. Given the chaotic traffic, it could take hours.

It was just after eight, a busy Friday night, and I was at a sidewalk café on the place de la Madeleine waiting for an ageing doctor. He was a gourmand whose young Russian dates usually cost more for the night than the dinners he lavished on them, so he was always short of cash. To my mind, genteel poverty was a great advantage in a medical practitioner. It meant that when he was giving a diagnosis and writing a prescription he was prepared to listen to a patient's own suggestions, if you catch my drift.

I didn't mark the white taxi the first time it passed – not consciously anyway – but somewhere in all my tradecraft the ever-changing tangle of traffic must have been registering. The second time it went by I knew it had been there before.

Heart spiking hard, I didn't react – that was the training kicking in. I just let my eyes follow it as casually as I could, cursing that a combination of headlights and traffic prevented me from seeing clearly who was in the back. It didn't matter, I suppose – I just think it's nice to know the identity of the people who've come to kill you.

The tide of vehicles carried the taxi away, and I knew I didn't have long: the first pass they locate you, the second they plan the angles, the third they fire. I dropped ten euro on the table and moved fast on to the sidewalk.

I heard a voice behind, yelling – it was the doctor, but I didn't have time to tell him we couldn't help feed each other's habits tonight. I jagged left into Hédiard, the city's best food store, and moved quickly past pyramids of perfect fruit and into the crowded wine section.

Everything was unfolding in a rush – like it always does in such situations – and while I didn't have any evidence, my instinct was screaming that it was the Greeks. The old man not only had the financial clout but also the deep emotional motive to search for revenge – the sort of incentive every missed Christmas and birthday would only have made stronger. He also had easy access to the personnel: crime intelligence reports from any police force in Europe would tell you that half of Albania was involved in the murder-for-hire business.

From Hédiard's wine department, a door accessed a side street and I went through it without pause, turning left. It was a one-way street and I walked fast towards the oncoming traffic, the only strategy in the circumstances. At least you can see the shooter coming.

Scanning the road ahead, I realized I was acting to a well-organized plan. I didn't know it until then but, wherever I went, part of me was always thinking about the best way out, an unseen escape programme constantly running in the background of my mind. My biggest regret was about my gun.

A cup of coffee, a quick meeting with the doctor and a cab home – half an hour maximum, I had figured. That meant the gun was in a safe back at the apartment. I had grown sloppy, I guess. Even if I saw them coming, there was little I could do now.

Home was exactly where I was heading – first thing, to open the damn safe and get myself weaponed up. I turned right, walked fast for a block, turned left and met the rue du Faubourg Saint-Honoré exactly where I wanted – just down the road from the Élysée Palace. Whichever Greek or Albanian was in the taxi would know it was the safest street in Paris – snipers on the rooftops, the whole length under constant anti-terrorist surveillance. Only now did I feel comfortable enough to grab a cab.

I got the driver to stop hard against my building's service entrance. By cracking open the door of the cab and staying low I could unlock the steel door and get inside without anybody seeing me. The driver thought I was crazy – but then his religion thinks stoning a woman to death for adultery is reasonable, so I figured we were about even.

Slamming the door behind me, I ran through the underground garages. The limestone building had once been a magnificent town house, built in the 1840s by the Comte du Crissier, but had fallen into ruin. The previous year it had been restored and turned into apartments, and I had rented one on the first floor. Even though it was small, normally someone in my situation would never have been able to afford it, but my material circumstances had changed – Bill Murdoch had died three years ago while I was on a brief assignment in Italy.

I wasn't invited to the funeral, and that hurt – I just got a note from Grace telling me he had died suddenly and had already been buried. That was my adoptive mother for you – jealous to the end. A few months later I got a letter from a lawyer saying Bill's matrix of companies – controlled by an offshore trust – had been left to Grace. It wasn't unexpected – they had been married for forty years. The letter said that, while there was no provision for me, Grace had decided to set aside enough money to provide me with an income of eighty thousand dollars a year for life. It didn't spell it out but the tone was clear: she believed it discharged all her responsibilities towards me.

Two years after the arrangement – almost to the day – Grace herself died. I felt her earlier behaviour relieved me of any obligation and I didn't go back for the huge society funeral at Greenwich's old Episcopalian church.

Again, and not for the first time, I was alone in the world, but I couldn't help smiling at what a difference two years can make: had the order of their deaths been reversed, I knew Bill would have made a substantial bequest to me. As it was, Grace left everything to the Metropolitan Museum of Art to rebuild the Old Masters gallery in her name.

This information was conveyed in a letter from the same lawyer who also mentioned that there was a small matter concerning Bill's estate that needed to be finalized. I told him I'd see him at his office in New York when I was home next – and then let it pretty much slip from my mind. The cheques from Grace's bequest arrived regularly and it meant I could live a life far more comfortable than anything the government had ever envisaged with their pension.

The most tangible benefit was the apartment in Paris, and I found myself racing through what had once been the mansion's kitchen – converted to a plant room – and flying up a set of fire stairs towards my home. I opened a concealed door next to the elevator and burst into the small foyer.

A woman was standing there. It was Mme Danuta Furer, my seventy-year-old neighbour, who lived in the mansion's grandest apartment. The perfectly groomed widow of some aristocratic industrialist, she had the uncanny ability to make everyone else feel like a member of the Third World.

She saw my tongue moistening my dry lips, shirt hanging out. 'Something wrong, Mr Campbell?' she asked in her inscrutable upper-class French.

She knew me as Peter Campbell, on sabbatical from my job as a hedge-fund manager – the only job I knew of which would enable somebody my age to afford to live in the apartment and not work.

'Fine, Madame – just worried I left the oven on,' I lied.

The elevator arrived, she got in and I unlocked the steel-core door into my apartment. Bolting it, not turning on any lights, I sprinted through the living room with its beautiful bay windows and small but growing collection of contemporary art. Bill would have liked that.

In the gloom I ripped open a closet in the dressing room and keyed a code into a small floor safe. Inside was a large amount of cash, a pile of papers, eight passports in different names and three hand-guns. I pulled out a 9mm Glock fitted with an extended barrel – the most accurate of them all – checked the action and grabbed a spare clip.

As I slipped it into my waistband, I dwelt on something that had been ricocheting round my head all the way home: if it was the Greeks, how the hell had they found me?

One theory I could come up with was that the Russians had stumbled across something and passed it on to their former partners, just for old times' sake, you know – and a bucketload of untraceable cash.

Or had I made some tiny mistake at Richeloud's that Markus Bucher had passed on to his clients and which had allowed them eventually to discover who I was? But, in either case, what had led the Greeks to Paris? For God's sake, I was living under a completely different identity.

The knock on the door was firm and definite.

I didn't react. I had always known that a hostile would have little difficulty getting into the building – François, the middle-aged, snivelling concierge, was always leaving the front doors open as he plumbed new depths of servitude. No sooner would he have heard Mme Furer coming down in the elevator than he was probably out in the street alerting the limo driver and fussing around to make sure he was registering ever more clearly on her Christmas gift list.

Without hesitation I did exactly what the training says – I moved fast, silently, into the back of the apartment. One strategy experienced assassins use is to attach a couple of ounces of Semtex – a plastic explosive with the consistency of clay – to the frame of a door before ringing the bell.

The perpetrator takes cover – in this case it would be in the elevator car – and detonates it with a call from a cellphone. Eight ounces of Semtex brought down Pan Am flight 103 over Lockerbie, so you can imagine what half that would do to a steel door and anybody looking through a peephole.

I backed through the dining room, grabbed a jacket to cover the Glock and headed for the spare bedroom. When the building had been the Comte du Crissier's mansion his staff had used a hand-cranked elevator to send meals up from the kitchen to the dining room. This dumb waiter had terminated in a butler's pantry – which was now my spare bedroom.

During the renovation the shaft had been converted to carry electrical wiring and, under the guise of installing high-speed computer cable to monitor the activities of my non-existent hedge fund, I got permission for a contractor who had installed surveillance equipment on The Division's behalf to access the shaft. Having him fit a ladder inside, giving a route to the basement, I figured made the place almost worth the sky-high rent. Right now it was priceless.

I opened a closet door, pulled off an access panel and in less than a minute was heading into a narrow lane at the back of the building. Any moment I expected to hear the nineteenth-century facade and the heritage-listed bay windows heading towards a messy landing on the Champs-Élysées.

Nothing. What was stopping them? I guessed that, having lost me down at the place de la Madeleine, they had returned immediately to my apartment. Uncertain if I had arrived back yet, the knock on the door was an attempt to find out.

Just as well I hadn't answered. I was almost certain there were two of them – that's how many I would have used – and they were hiding right now near the elevator, waiting for me to return. That gave me a chance – if I entered by the front doors and took the stairs, I was pretty sure I could surprise them. I was never the best shot in my graduating class, but I was good enough to take them both out.

I slowed to a walk as I emerged from the lane, and ran a professional eye over the pedestrians, just to be certain that the guys inside didn't have help on the street. I saw women on their way home from shopping at the luxury stores on avenue Montaigne, couples walking their dogs, a guy in a Mets cap with his back to me – a tourist by the look of it – window-shopping at the patisserie next to my building, but I didn't see anyone who fitted the profile I had in mind. I turned to the vehicles and, equally, there was no white cab or shooters sitting in parked cars that I could see.

I moved up close behind a fifty-year-old woman in high heels and her boyfriend, twenty years her junior. They wouldn't completely shield me from a sniper on a roof but they would certainly make the job more difficult. Under cover of them, I steadily closed down the distance to my building: eighty yards, forty, twenty . . .

As I passed the patisserie, the guy in the Mets cap spoke to my back: 'Wouldn't it have been easier just to open the fucking door, Mr Campbell?'

My heart stopped, every fear I had collapsing into the void that was once my stomach. In the next moment two distinct and contradictory thoughts fought for primacy. The first was: so this is how it ends? The retired agent outsmarted on a street in Paris, shot through the head, probably by somebody standing inside the patisserie. *Vyshaya mera* to me, I guess, bleeding out on the sidewalk, a man I don't even know pocketing the gun as he and the guy in the Mets cap walk away to be picked up by – what else? – a white taxi.

The other thought was – there's no way they're killing me. Even if there was a shooter on a building or in a room at the Plaza Athenée hotel, the guy in the cap would have signalled silently and the marksman would have done his job. They don't talk to you in the real world: only in movies do the bad guys have this pathological need to tell you their life story before they pull the trigger. Out here, there's too much danger and your mind's way too revved not to just get it over with. Look at Santorini.

Nevertheless, there was always a first time – so I still wasn't sure whether to piss myself from fear or from relief. I looked at the man: he was a black guy in his fifties with a lean body and a handsome face, worn around the edges. More Reject China than fine Limoges, I told myself. This assessment was confirmed as he stepped a little closer and I realized he was limping badly on his right leg.

'I think you called me Mr Campbell. You're mistaken,' I said in French, filling every syllable with my best imitation of Parisian disdain. 'My name isn't Campbell.' I was buying time, trying to work out what was going on.

'I guess that's one thing we agree on,' he said in English, 'given that no Peter Campbell holds a Wall Street trading licence, and the hedge fund he manages doesn't exist.'

How the hell did he know that? I shifted casually, putting him more squarely between me and the patisserie window.

'So if you're not Campbell, who are you?' he went on. 'Jude Garrett, FBI agent and author? Well, that's difficult too – him being dead. Here's another weird thing about Garrett,' he said calmly. 'I spoke to his cousin down in New Orleans. She was pretty amazed about his literary achievement – she doubted he ever read a book, let alone wrote one.'

He knew all this stuff about me, but I was still alive! That was the important point and he seemed to be missing it. I scanned the rooftops, trying to see if there was a sniper.

He watched my eyes, knowing what I was doing, but it didn't affect his swing: 'This is what I figure, Mr Campbell-or-whoever-you-are, you live under a fake identity but you wrote the book using a dead man's name, just to be safe.

'I think you worked for the government and only a handful of people know your real name. Maybe not even that many.

'To me, that says it's probably not wise to ask what kind of work you did but, the truth is, I don't care. Your book is the best work on investigative technique I have ever read. I just want to talk about it.'

I stared at him. Finally, I got it out, speaking in English: 'You wanna talk about a book?! I was gonna *kill* you!'

'Not exactly,' he said before lowering his voice. 'Do I call you Mr Garrett?'

'Campbell,' I shot back through clenched teeth. 'Campbell.'

'Not exactly, Mr Campbell. I think if anyone was gonna do the killing, it was actually me.'

He was right of course, and – as you'd expect – that made me even more pissed. He put out his hand, unsmiling. I'd learn in time he was a man who hardly ever smiled.

'Ben Bradley,' he said calmly. 'Homicide Lieutenant, NYPD.'

Unsure what else to do, I gripped his hand and we shook – a cop who was learning to walk again and a pensioned-off covert agent.

I know that, on that night, encountering each other for the first time, we both thought that our race was run, our professional lives had ended, but here's the strange thing: that meeting was of huge significance.

It mattered – my God, did it matter. All of it turned out to be important, all of it turned out to be connected in some strange way: the murder at the Eastside Inn, Christos Nikolaides gunned down in a bar in Santorini, the failed covert operation in Bodrum, my friendship with Ben Bradley, and even a Buddhist monk travelling down a road in Thailand. If I believed in fate, I would have to say there was some hand guiding it all.

Very soon I would learn that one great task still lay ahead of me, one thing which – more than any other – would define my life. Late one afternoon, a short time hence, I would be dragged back into the secret world, and any hope I had of reaching for normal would be gone, probably for ever. Like people say – if you want to make God laugh, tell Him you've got plans.

With precious little information and even less time, I was given the task of finding the one thing which every intelligence agency fears most: a man with no radical affiliations, no entry in any database and no criminal history. A *cleanskin*, a ghost.

I'm afraid that what follows isn't pleasant. If you want to sleep easy in your bed, if you want to look at your kids and think there is a chance they will live in a world better than the one we leave behind, it might be better not to meet him.

Part Two

Chapter One

NO MATTER HOW MANY YEARS MAY PASS, EVEN IF I SHOULD BE LUCKY and grow old in the sun, he will always be the Saracen to me. That was the code name I gave him in the beginning and I spent so long trying to discover his real identity it is hard to think of him as anything else.

Saracen means Arab or – in a much older use of the word – a Muslim who fought against the Christians. Go back even further and you find that it once meant a nomad. All of those things fitted him perfectly.

Even today, much of what we know about him is fragmentary. That's not surprising – he spent most of his life running between shadows, deliberately covering his tracks, like a Bedouin in the desert.

But every life leaves a trace, every ship a wake, and even though it was often just a glimmer of phosphorescence in the dark, we chased them all. It took me through half the souks and mosques of the world, into the secret archives of Arab states and across the desk from dozens of people who might have known him. Later – even after the events of that terrible summer were over – teams of analysts interrogated his mother and sisters for weeks on end and, while I might be accused of putting words into his mouth or thoughts into his head, I make no apology. I ended up knowing more about the Saracen and his family than any man on earth.

One thing beyond dispute is that when he was very young he was swept up in a public beheading. That was in Jeddah, Saudi Arabia's second-largest city and, by popular agreement, its most sophisticated. Believe me, that's not saying much.

Jeddah lies on the shore of the Red Sea and, by the time the Saracen was fourteen, he was living with his parents and two younger sisters in a modest villa on its outskirts, close enough to the water to smell the salt. We know this because many years later I stood outside the old house and photographed it.

Like most Saudis, the boy's father, a zoologist, despised the United States and what the Arab newspaper called its 'paid-up whore': Israel. His hatred, however, wasn't based on propaganda, the plight of the Palestinians or even religious bigotry – no, it ran much deeper than that.

Over the years, he had listened to both Washington and Tel Aviv and, unlike most Westerners, he believed what our political leaders told him – their objective was to bring democracy to the Middle East. As a deeply devout Muslim, such a prospect filled him with anger. Being well educated, at least by local standards, he knew that one of the foundations of democracy was the separation between religion and the state. Yet, to many Muslims, the religion *is* the state. The last thing they want is to separate it.

In his opinion, the only reason that infidels would advocate such a thing would be in order to divide and conquer, to hollow out the Arab world and destroy it, pursuing a campaign the Christians had begun with the First Crusade a thousand years ago and had continued ever since.

It would be easy to dismiss the zoologist as an extremist, but in the twilight world of Middle East politics he was in the *moderate* wing of Saudi public opinion. There was one thing, however, which did set him apart from the mainstream: his views on the royal family.

There are many things you can't do in the kingdom of Saudi Arabia – preach about Christianity, attend a movie, drive a car if you're a woman, renounce your faith. But towering above them all is a prohibition on criticizing the House of Saud, the ruling dynasty, made up of the king, two hundred powerful princes and twenty thousand family members.

All through that year, Jeddah was awash with whispers that the king had allowed American troops, the soldiers of an ungodly country, into the Prophet's sacred land. Equally disturbing was information filtering back from Saudi dissidents in Europe about prominent princes losing fortunes in the casinos of Monte Carlo and showering gold watches on young women from 'modelling' agencies in Paris. Like all Saudis, the zoologist had always known about the gilded palaces and profligate lifestyle of the king, but bad taste and extravagance are not *haram* – forbidden – in Islam. Prostitution, gambling and alcohol certainly are.

Of course, if you live in Saudi Arabia you can express your disgust about the policies of the king and the behaviour of his family, you can call it an offence against God if you want and even advocate their forced removal. Just make sure you do it in the safety of your head. To speak to anyone who isn't your wife or father about it, even in the most abstract fashion, is reckless. The Mabahith, the Saudi secret police – a law unto itself – and its network of informers hear everything, know everything.

It was late on a spring day when four of its agents, all wearing the white tunics called *thobes* and the usual red-and-white-check head-dress, visited the zoologist at work. They showed their identity cards and led him out of his office, through an area of laboratories and work stations and into the car park.

The twenty other people working in that section of the Red Sea Marine Biology department watched the door slam behind him, nobody saying a word, not even his three closest friends – one of whom was almost certainly the informer.

We will never know exactly what the zoologist was accused of, or what defence he offered, because Saudi judicial proceedings, conducted in secret, aren't concerned with time-consuming niceties like witnesses, lawyers, juries or even evidence.

The system relies entirely on signed confessions obtained by the police. It's strange how methods of torture are one of the few things which cross all racial, religious and cultural boundaries – poor militia in Rwanda who worship ghosts use pretty much the same methods as rich Catholics supervising state security in Colombia. As a result, the Muslim cops who took the zoologist into a cell in a Jeddah prison had nothing new to offer – just a heavy-duty truck battery with special clips for the genitals and nipples.

The first the zoologist's family knew of the catastrophe engulfing them was when he failed to arrive home from work. After evening prayers they made a series of phone calls to his colleagues, which either went unanswered or were met by contrived ignorance – from grim experience, people knew that those listening in would target anyone trying to help a criminal's family. Increasingly desperate, the zoologist's wife finally agreed to her fourteen-year-old son heading out to try to find him. She couldn't do it herself because Saudi law forbids a woman to be in public unless she is accompanied by her brother, father or husband.

The teenager left his mother and two sisters and set off on his dirt bike, a gift for his last birthday from his dad. Keeping to the backstreets, he drove fast to a group of seaside office blocks, where he found his father's car alone in the parking lot. Only in a police state does a child pray for nothing more serious than a crippling accident to have befallen their parent. Beseeching Allah that the zoologist was lying injured in the darkened building that housed his office, the boy approached the entrance.

A Pakistani security guard stationed in an alcove in the gloomy interior was startled when he saw a boy's face peering through the glass doors. Yelling in bad Arabic, he motioned the kid away, grabbing a billy club, ready to unlock the doors and use it if he had to.

But the boy didn't flinch – calling back desperately in Arabic, imploring the help of the Prophet, saying something about a missing father. It was only then that the guard realized the visit was connected to the event that had caused a tidal wave of whispered gossip all afternoon. He stared at the child's drowning face – he was far too young to be clinging to such tiny hopes – and lowered the club. Maybe it was because he had kids of his own, but the tectonic plates of the guard's universe shifted, and he did something totally out of character – he took a chance.

With his back turned to the security cameras monitoring the doors, gesticulating as if shooing him away, he told the boy what little he knew: four members of the state police, led by a colonel, had taken his father away in handcuffs. According to their driver – a fellow Pakistani to whom he'd taken a cup of tea – they had been secretly investigating the man for months. But listen close, he said, this was the important part: they were talking about charging him with 'corruption on earth', a term so broad as to be meaningless except for one thing. It carried the death sentence.

'Tell your family,' the Pakistani continued, 'they'll have to act fast if they're going to save him.'

With that he threw the doors open as if he'd lost patience and, for the benefit of the cameras, started swinging the billy club with a wild vengeance. The boy ran for the dirt bike and kicked it to life. Caring nothing for himself, he sped across the parking lot, nearly lost it in a drift of sand and flew through the gates.

Though no one will ever know for sure, I imagine that – mentally – he was being torn in two: as a child, he desperately wanted the comfort of his mother but, as a man, the head of the household in his father's absence, he needed the counsel of other men. There was only one way this conflict could be resolved; he was an Arab, and that meant two thousand years of baggage about male pride. So it was inevitable that he would turn north, into the darkest part of the city, towards the house of his grandfather.

Even as he drove, a sense of informed doom started to grow upon him. He knew his father was as good as locked in a cattle car being driven by state security and he realized it would take a huge amount of *wasta* to alter the course of that journey. In the absence of democracy and efficient bureaucracies, *wasta* is the way the Arab world works; it means connections, influence, a web of old favours and tribal history. With *wasta*, doors – even to palaces – open. Without it, they remain forever closed.

The boy had never thought about it before, but he saw now that his family, including his grandfather, whom he loved so dearly, were modest people: modest in ambition, modest in their connections. For them to influence state security and have what was considered an attack on the House of Saud dismissed would be . . . well, it would be like taking a knife to a nuclear war.

By the end of the night – after the long and closed counsels of his uncles, grandfather and cousins had failed to initiate one significant phone call – he knew he was right about their chances. But that didn't mean that any of them gave up: for five months, the family, close to collapse under the stress, tried to penetrate the Saudi gulag and find one tiny life hidden in its labyrinth.

And what did they get for their trouble? No information, no assistance from their government and certainly no contact with the zoologist. Like the victims of 9/11, he had just gone to work one morning and never returned.

The man was lost in a surreal maze, trapped among the living dead in hundreds of crowded cells. It was here he quickly learned that everybody ends up signing a confession – a testament to the twelve-volt lead-acid battery – but that among the inmates there were two distinct groups.

The first surrendered themselves to their fate, or Allah, and just scrawled their name on the damn thing. The second group figured their only hope was to sign the document in order finally to get before a judge. They could then recant their confession and proclaim their innocence.

This was the strategy the zoologist adopted. The Saudi judicial system, however, has developed a way of dealing with this: the prisoner is simply returned to the police to explain his change of mind. It's far too depressing to go into the 'enhanced' methods used against these men and women – suffice to say, nobody has ever gone before a judge and recanted their confession a second time. Never.

Having at last admitted and been convicted of seditious statements and corruption on earth, the zoologist's journey through the system ground to a sudden halt.

The cause was traffic problems in downtown Jeddah: at least ten days' notice was needed to close the huge car park outside the main mosque. Only then could the white marble platform be erected in its centre.

Chapter Two

SPECTATORS STARTED GATHERING EARLY IN THE MORNING, AS SOON AS they saw the barricades going up and the special team of carpenters erecting the platform. Public announcements about impending executions are rare in the kingdom but, by cellphone and text message, the word always spreads.

Within hours, large crowds were streaming into the car park and, by the time a twelve-year-old boy – the Saracen's best friend – drove past with his father, he knew exactly what it meant. It was a Friday – the Muslim day of rest – and the traffic was terrible so it took the kid over an hour to get home. He immediately grabbed his bicycle and rode eight miles to tell his friend what he had seen.

Fearing the worst, mentioning nothing to his mother or sisters, the Saracen got on his dirt bike, piled his friend on board and headed for the Corniche, the road that runs beside the Red Sea into downtown Jeddah.

Just as the two boys caught sight of the sea, noon prayers had finished at the main mosque and hundreds of men were spilling out to join masses of spectators waiting in the parking lot. In the harsh summer light the men in their stark white *thobes* made a stunning contrast to the knots of women in their black *abayas* and face veils. Only little kids in jeans and shirts added a splash of colour.

Executions are about the only form of public entertainment permitted in Saudi Arabia – movies, concerts, dancing, plays and even mixed-sex coffee shops are banned. But everybody's welcome, women and kids too, to see someone lose their life. Eschewing such modern innovations as medical injections or even the firing squad, the Saudi method seems to be a real crowd-pleaser: public beheading.

It was close to 110 degrees on the Corniche that day, the heat bouncing off the asphalt in shimmering waves, as the dirt bike threaded rapidly through the weekend traffic. Up ahead, chaos was unfolding: the road was being torn up for a new overpass, construction machinery blocked all but one lane and cars were tailed back for blocks.

Inside his sweltering helmet, the zoologist's son was also in chaos – frightened almost to vomiting, desperately hoping it was an African drug dealer being taken to the platform. He couldn't afford to think that, if he was wrong, the last he would see of his father would be him kneeling on the marble, the flies already buzzing, the silver sword disappearing in a fountain of red.

He looked at the impenetrable traffic ahead and swung the dirt bike off the shoulder and, in a whirl of dust and debris, blasted into the badly cratered construction site.

Despite the size of the crowd gathering for the display, there was little noise in the parking lot – just the murmur of voices and the sound of a mullah reading from the Qur'an over the mosque's public address system. Gradually even the quiet voices fell silent as an official car made its way through the cordon and stopped at the platform.

A powerfully built man in an immaculate white *thobe* got out of the vehicle and mounted the five steps to the platform. A polished leather strap ran diagonally across his chest and terminated on his left hip, supporting a scabbard which held a long, curved sword. This was the executioner. His name was Sa'id bin Abdullah bin Mabrouk al-Bishi and he was acknowledged as the best craftsman in the kingdom, his reputation built primarily on a procedure called a cross amputation. Far more difficult than a simple beheading and meted out as punishment for highway robbery, it requires the rapid use of custom-made knives to cut off a prisoner's right hand and left foot. By applying himself diligently to this process, Sa'id al-Bishi had over many years steadily raised the overall standard of Saudi Arabia's public punishments. Only occasionally now did the public see an executioner having to keep hacking at a prisoner's head or limbs to detach them from his body.

Returning greetings from several onlookers, al-Bishi had barely had time to familiarize himself with his workspace when he saw a white van push through the crowd. A policeman lifted a barrier and the air-conditioned vehicle stopped next to the steps. The crowd craned forward to catch sight of the occupant as the rear doors opened.

The zoologist stepped out of the van into the cauldron barefoot, blindfolded by a thick white bandage, his wrists handcuffed behind his back.

Among those watching were people who knew him, or thought they did, and it took a moment for them to recognize his features. God knows what the secret police had done to him in the previous five months, but he seemed to have shrunk – he was a shell of a man, broken and diminished at least in his body, like those translucent old people you sometimes see in retirement homes. He was thirty-eight years old.

He knew exactly where he was and what was happening; an official of the so-called Ministry of Justice had arrived at his cell forty minutes earlier and had read him a formal decree. It was the first he knew that he had been sentenced to death. As two uniformed cops led him slowly to the steps of the platform, witnesses said he raised his face to the sun and tried to straighten his shoulders. I'm sure he didn't want his son and daughters to hear that their father didn't have courage.

On the Corniche, gridlocked drivers watched with a mixture of disgust and envy as the dirt bike blasted past, using the construction site as a private freeway. Damn kids.

The young boy slid the bike past coiled fire hoses used to spray the overworked Bangladeshi construction workers and prevent them passing out from heat exhaustion, then weaved through a forest of concrete pylons. He had about seven minutes to reach the square.

I don't think, even later in life, he could have explained why he undertook that wild ride. What was he going to do there? My own belief is that, in his fear and anguish, all he could think of was that he was of his father's soul as much as his body and such a bond would accept nothing less than his presence. He swung the bike hard left, through a wasteland of piled debris, and flew even faster towards a road that fed into the square. It was blocked by a chain-link fence but, on the other side of bundles of steel reinforcing rods, he saw an opening just wide enough to squeeze through. Allah was with him!

He slid the bike even tighter left, slaloming through the bundles of rods, sending up clouds of fine dust, closing fast on the narrow gap. He was going to make it!

The zoologist, blindfolded on the platform, felt a hand fall on his neck and press him down. It belonged to the executioner and he was being told to kneel. As he lowered himself, the feeling of the sun on his face indicated that he was facing Mecca, forty miles away. Directly in its path was his house, and the thought of his wife and children sitting in its loving confines sent a shudder of loss through his body.

The executioner gripped the man's shoulder – the swordsman had been here many times before and he knew the exact moment when a man might need steadying. A voice called out a command on the mosque's public address system.

All across the square, stretching from the austere Ministry of Foreign Affairs building to the grass in front of the mosque, thousands of people knelt to face Mecca in prayer. As with all devout Muslims, the zoologist knew the words by heart, and he spoke them in unison with the crowd. He also knew their exact length: by any reasonable estimate, he had four minutes left on earth.

The boy, half blinded by the dust kicked up by his swerving bike, didn't see one bundle of the steel reinforcing rods until a second too late. Protruding at least a foot from the others, one of the rods was already sliding between the spokes of his front wheel when he first registered it.

His reaction time was incredible – he hurled the bike to the side, but not quite fast enough. With the front wheel spinning, the rod tore the spokes apart in a fury of ripping metal. Chunks of thin alloy ripped through the bike's gas tank and cylinder head, the wheel collapsed, the front forks dug into the dirt and the bike stopped instantly. The zoologist's son and his friend kept going – straight over the handlebars, and landing in a tangle of flying limbs and spraying dirt. Badly stunned, the dirt bike fit only for the scrap heap, they were barely conscious.

By the time the first of the shocked motorists watching from the Corniche had reached them, the prayers in the parking lot had finished and the crowd was rising. The executioner stepped close to the kneeling prisoner and the whole square fell silent. The swordsman made a slight adjustment to the angle of the zoologist's neck and those spectators near enough saw a few words pass between them.

Many years later, I talked to a number of people who were in the square that day. Among those I spoke to was Sa'id al-Bishi, the executioner. I had tea with him in the *majlis* – the formal reception room – of his home, and asked him what the zoologist had said.

'It's rare a man can say anything in that situation,' Sa'id al-Bishi told me, 'so of course it stays in your mind.' He took a long breath. 'It was brief but he said it with conviction. He told me: "The only thing that matters is that Allah and the Saudi people forgive me my sins."'

Al-Bishi fell silent and glanced towards Mecca – apparently, that was it. I nodded reverently. '*Allahu Akbar,*' I said in reply. God is great.

He took another sip of tea, gazing into the middle distance, lost in thoughts about the wisdom a man finds in his last moments. I kept looking at him, moving my head sagely. The one thing you don't do in any Arab country is accuse a man of lying, no matter how indirectly.

As a consequence, I just kept looking at him, and he kept staring off at wisdom. Outside, I could hear the water tinkling from a fountain in his beautiful courtyard, the sound of servants bustling in the women's quarters. Being state executioner must have paid pretty well.

Finally he began to move uncomfortably in his seat and then he shot a glance at me to see if I was just the quiet type or if I was really calling him on it.

I didn't take my eyes off him, and he laughed. 'You are an intelligent man for a Westerner,' he said, 'so now let us discuss what he really said, shall we?

'When I bent down to the prisoner I told him to expose as much of his neck as possible and not to move – this would make it easier on both of us. He didn't seem to care, he just motioned me closer. Someone must have injured the inside of his mouth – an electrode, maybe – because he had trouble talking. "You know the king?" he whispered.

'It took me by surprise, but I said I'd had the honour of meeting His Majesty several times.

'He nodded as if he expected it. "Next time you meet him, tell him this is what an American once said – you can kill a thinker but you can't kill the thought," he said.' The executioner looked at me and shrugged.

'And did you ever tell him?' I asked. 'The king, I mean.'

The executioner laughed. 'No,' he replied. 'Having seen the alternative, I enjoy having my head on my shoulders.'

I didn't need to ask what happened next – other people in the car park that day had told me. As al-Bishi finished his brief words with the prisoner, a strong breeze sprang up off the Red Sea – nearly everyone mentioned it because it was so hot on the asphalt. The executioner stood up and drew his sword in one fluid movement. He took a single step back from the prisoner and measured the distance expertly with his eye before securely planting his feet.

The only sound was static from the mosque's public address system. Al-Bishi held the long sword out horizontally, straightened his back and lifted his jaw to accentuate his profile – when I met him I couldn't help but notice his vanity. One-handed, he swung the sword up high and, as it reached the apex of its arc, every eye in the square followed, almost blinded by the white sun directly above.

He paused, the sword dazzling, as if to milk the drama from the situation – then he locked his second hand around the handle and brought the blade down with breathtaking speed. The razor's edge hit the zoologist square on the nape of the neck. Just as he had been asked, the prisoner didn't move.

The thing everybody tells you about is the sound – loud and wet, like someone whacking open a watermelon. The blade sliced through the zoologist's spinal cord, the carotid arteries and the larynx until the head was separated.

It rolled across the marble, eyelids flickering, followed by an arc of blood from the cut arteries. The zoologist's headless torso seemed to float for a moment, as if in shock, and then it pitched forward into its own fluids.

The executioner stood in his unmarked *thobe* and looked down at his handiwork, the static on the public address was replaced by a Muslim prayer, a swarm of flies started to gather and the crowd in the square broke into applause.

The dead man's young son – breathing hard from trying to run, badly grazed all down his left side, a handkerchief wrapped around one bloody hand – limped into the car park just after his father's body had been loaded into the startling coolness of the white van. That was the reason the vehicle was air-conditioned – not for the comfort of the living but to inhibit the stench of the dead.

Most of the spectators had gone, leaving just the cops to take down the barricades and a couple of Bangladeshi labourers to wash down the marble.

The boy looked around, trying to see somebody he recognized to ask them the identity of the executed prisoner, but the men were moving fast to escape the wind, pulling their chequered headscarves down like Bedouin to protect their faces. On the far side of the patch of grass, the *muezzin* – the assistant to the mosque's leader – was closing wooden shutters, sealing the building against what was looking more and more like a major sandstorm.

Whipped by the wind, the boy ran and called to him through the iron railing, asking him for a name, a profession. The *muezzin* turned, shielding his face from the sand, shouting back. The wind snatched away his voice so there was only one word the boy heard. 'Zoologist'.

Footage from Saudi surveillance cameras monitoring the square – dug out a long time later – showed that the *muezzin* went back to his work and didn't even see the kid turn away and stare at the marble platform, his body battered by the burning wind, his heart obviously consumed by utter desolation. He didn't move for minutes and, determined to act like a man and not to cry, he looked like a windswept statue.

In truth, I think he was probably travelling fast: like most people who suffer great horror, he had come unstuck in space and time. He probably would have remained standing there for hours, but one of the cops approached, yelling at him to move, and he stumbled away to escape the cop's vicious bamboo cane.

As he headed through the whirling sand the tears finally burst through his iron resolve and, alone in a city he hated now, he let out a single awful scream. People told me later it was a howl of grief, but I knew it wasn't. It was the primal scream of birth.

In a process as bloody and painful as its physical counterpart, the Saracen had been born into terrorism in a windswept car park in central Jeddah. In time, out of abiding love for his father, he would grow into a passionate believer in conservative Islam, an enemy of all Western values, an avowed destroyer of the Fahd monarchy and a supporter of violent jihad.

Thank you, Saudi Arabia, thank you.

Chapter Three

DESPITE ITS HUGE WEALTH, VAST OIL RESERVES AND LOVE OF HIGH-TECH American armaments, nothing really works in Saudi Arabia. The Jeddah bus system, for example.

With his dirt bike wrecked, the zoologist's son had no alternative means of transport, which meant that – due to the system's erratic timetable and the worsening dust storm – news of the execution beat him home by twenty minutes.

His extended family had already gathered in the villa's modest *majlis* and his mother was filling her relatives with growing terror. Between waves of pain and disbelief, she was railing against her country, the Saudi judicial system and the royal family itself. Although no Saudi man – let alone society itself – had ever been able to admit it, she was almost always the smartest person in the room.

Her bitter assault came to an end only when someone looked out of a window and saw her son approaching. Barely breathing through her tears, she met him in the hallway, desperately worried that – tragedy piled upon tragedy – he had witnessed his father's execution.

When he shook his head, recounting fragments about the bike wreck in the construction site, she slumped to her knees for the first and only time, thanking Allah for every wound on his body. The boy bent down, raised his mother up and, over her shoulder, saw his two young sisters standing alone, as if marooned on their own private island of despair.

He gathered them all into his arms and recounted the final grief that had weighed on him all the way home but hadn't yet occurred to any of them – as an executed prisoner, there would be no funeral or burial, no closing of his father's eyelids, no washing and shrouding of his body under Islamic ritual as their final kindness to him. His remains would be thrown into common ground and buried in an unmarked grave. If they were lucky, one of the workers would lay him on his right side and face him towards Mecca. If they were lucky.

In the months which followed, according to the mother in her long-delayed interrogation, the oppressive cloud of loss that settled over the house had little to disturb it. Apart from close relatives, there were no visitors or phone calls – the nature of the crime meant the family was ostracized by friends and the community at large. In a way, the family too had been cast into an unmarked grave and buried. Even so, the steady passage of the days finally dulled the keen edge of their grief, and the boy – an outstanding student – at last picked up his books and started to continue his studies at home. More than any other thing, it steadied the family. After all, education is a grab for a better future, no matter how impossible the prospect may seem at the time.

Then, eight months after the execution, the eastern sky broke with an unheralded dawn – unknown to the family, the grandfather had been working relentlessly on their behalf. Through what little *wasta* he commanded and the payment of bribes he could ill afford, he had succeeded in obtaining passports, exit permits and visas for his daughter-in-law and the three kids. Certainly it was a testament to how much he loved them, but the truth was the family was an embarrassment to the authorities and they were probably pleased to see them go. Whatever the subtext, he arrived late, gave the family the startling news and told them they would leave early in the morning, before the people whose help he'd purchased had a chance to change their minds.

All through the night they packed what little possessions they cared about, took one last turn through their memories and, with nobody to bid farewell, were on the road by dawn. The convoy of four overburdened family vehicles drove for twelve hours, across the breadth of the country, through timeless desert, past never-ending oil fields, until at dusk they saw the turquoise waters of the Arabian Gulf.

Looping across the sea like a necklace was the glittering causeway that connected Saudi Arabia to the independent island nation of Bahrain. It ran for sixteen miles over bridges and viaducts, a triumph of Dutch engineering known as the King Fahd Causeway. Every mile, giant billboards of the Saudi monarch smiled down on the family as they crossed the ocean, an irony not lost on the boy: he was the man who had signed the decree executing his father. Fahd's hated face was the last thing he saw of his homeland.

After paying another bribe at the border, the grandfather and three cousins were allowed briefly to enter Bahrain without papers to ferry the family's goods to a house the old man had rented through a friend of a neighbour. Nobody said anything, but all their hearts sank when they saw it.

The dilapidated home stood in a small square of dirt in a semi-industrial section of Manama, the country's capital. The front door was hanging open, the plumbing barely worked and electricity served only two rooms – but there was no going back now and anything was better than life in Jeddah.

With the family's meagre goods finally unloaded, the boy's mother stood with the old man in the decaying kitchen, quietly trying to thank him for everything he had done. He shook his head, pressed a small roll of banknotes into her hand and told her he would send more – not much, but enough – every month. As she bit her lip, trying not to cry at his generosity, he walked slowly to his grand-daughters, who were watching from the dirt yard, and put his arms around them.

Then he turned and hesitated – he had left the hardest part to last. His grandson, aware of what was coming, was trying to look busy opening boxes on the back porch. His grandfather approached and waited for him to look up. Neither of them was quite sure, as men, how much emotion to show – until the grandfather reached out and held the boy tight. This was no time for pride; he was an old man, and only God knew if he would ever see his grandson again.

He stepped back and looked at the youngster – every day he thought of how much he resembled his own boy, the one they had executed. Still, life lives on in our children and their children, and not even a king can take that away. Abruptly he turned and walked towards the vehicles, calling to the cousins to start the engines. He didn't look back lest the family see the tears rolling down his cheeks.

The boy, surrounded by his mother and two sisters, stood in the gathering darkness for a long time and watched the tail lights of their former lives disappear into the night.

Chapter Four

TWO DAYS LATER, FOR THE FIRST TIME IN HER ADULT LIFE, THE children's mother went out in public unaccompanied by an adult male. Despite her fear and embarrassment, she had no choice – if she didn't keep the children occupied their loneliness and new-found poverty might overwhelm them.

Adrift in a foreign land without relatives or friends, she found the local bus stop, bundled the kids on board and walked for hours with them through the city's shopping malls. It was a revelation. None of them had any experience of a liberal interpretation of Islam, and they looked wide-eyed at posters for American movies and Bollywood musicals, stared at Western women in tank tops and shorts and couldn't believe Muslim women in elaborate *abayas* who had surrendered their veils for Chanel sunglasses.

For the boy, one thing above everything else swept his feet from under him. The only female faces he had ever seen were those of his mother and close relatives – he hadn't even seen women in photographs: magazines and billboards showing unveiled women were banned in Saudi Arabia. So, in the shops of Bahrain, suddenly afforded a basis of comparison, he learned something which otherwise he would never have known – his mother was beautiful.

Of course, all sons think that about their mothers, but the boy knew it wasn't prejudice. She was still only thirty-three, with high cheekbones, flawless skin and wide almond eyes that sparkled with intelligence. Her nose was fine and straight, leading the eye directly to the perfect curve of her mouth. More than that, her recent suffering gave her a grace and hauteur far above her modest position in life.

One night not long afterwards, with his sisters in bed, he sat beneath a bare light strung across the kitchen and haltingly told his mother how lovely she was. Laughing, she kissed the top of his head, but in bed that night she cried quietly – when a boy started to notice a woman's beauty it meant he was growing up, and she knew she was losing him.

In the weeks that followed she succeeded in enrolling the three kids in good schools and the boy, after six attempts, found a mosque that was rigid and anti-Western enough to have met with his father's approval. A fifteen-year-old who walked in off the street, un-accompanied by any male member of his family, was an unusual addition to any group of worshippers, so, on the first Friday after prayers, the imam, blind since birth, and several other men invited him for tea in a beautiful garden at the back of the building.

Under a purple jacaranda tree the boy volunteered almost nothing about the events that had brought him to Bahrain, but the men weren't easily diverted and, unable to lie to the imam, he finally told them in fractured vignettes the story of his father's death. At the end the men bowed their heads and praised his father. 'What son – what devout Muslim – could not be proud of a man who had spoken out in defence of his faith and its values?' they asked angrily.

For a boy who had been shamed and rejected by his community, who had been lonely for so long, it was a salutary experience. Already the mosque was starting to fill the emotional void at the centre of his life.

The blind imam told him that God sends only as much suffering as a man can handle. Therefore the horrific events in Jeddah were a testament to his father's deep devotion and courage. With that he reached out and ran his fingers over the teenager's face, committing him to memory. It was a sign of respect, a special welcome into their fellowship.

The boy – saying only that the worshippers were highly educated – told his mother nothing of the lectures he attended most nights at the mosque. It was men's business, the imam said, and a man could speak freely only if he knew it would not be repeated.

And while the boy took those first steps into violent politics with what turned out to be a cell of the Muslim Brotherhood, the rest of the fleet was sailing in the opposite direction. Unlike most people in Bahrain, the family didn't have a TV, but the girls' exposure to pop culture increased every day – at school, in malls, on billboards – and as with every other country in the region, popular culture didn't mean Arabic.

The growing Americanization of his sisters caused escalating arguments between the boy and his mother until one night she spoke to him hard and straight. She told him Bahrain was their only future and she wanted the girls to fit in, to find the love of friends – she wanted that for all her kids – and if it meant rejecting everything about the way they had lived in Saudi then she would not cry one tear for something that had brought them so much misery.

She said loneliness was a razor that cut a heart to shreds, that a child had a right to dream and that if the girls didn't strive to be happy now they never would. She told it to him with insight and honesty, and why shouldn't she? She might as well have been talking about herself. He had never heard his mother so on fire and he realized that while to the outside world she was still a Muslim, at the heart of her – feeling abandoned by God – she really worshipped only life and her children now. Deeply troubled, he reminded her that Allah was watching them and made his way to bed.

After he fell asleep, his mother went to the girls' room, woke them quietly and put her arms around their shoulders. She told them she knew they were growing towards a different light but they could no longer offend their brother in his own house. The music had to stop and, when they left the house for school, they would wear the veil.

The girls were like their mother, in looks and temperament, and they both started objecting. She silenced them and told them it was because their brother loved them and he was only trying to discharge the huge responsibility he felt towards their father. She looked at their faces, pleading with her to change her mind, and she almost smiled – she was about to share a secret with her girls, and she had never done that with anyone except her own mother.

'I need your help,' she said. 'There's something I have to raise with him that's very important – he'll never agree if he thinks you are being corrupted.'

The two girls forgot their protests, wondering what on earth their mother was planning to broach.

'We can't go on like this,' she said. 'It's not just the house, your grandfather isn't young – what happens if he dies and the money stops?' She let the grim ramifications sink in before she told them: 'I have applied for a job.'

Of all the lessons the girls would learn as young Muslim women, the one their mother demonstrated that night was the most important: to take command, to realize that the only stairway to heaven is the one you build yourself on earth. They stared at her in wonder. A job?!

She told them she'd heard about the opening from one of the mothers at their school and had phoned the company weeks ago. She had been on the point of giving up, but a letter had arrived that day asking her to come for an interview. She explained she had said nothing to their brother in case she wasn't hired – let's be honest, she said, it was almost certain she wouldn't get it, not on her first try – as there was no point in having an argument without anything to gain. Beyond those simple facts she would tell them nothing, insisting that it was late and they get to sleep.

By morning the girls had thrown their support behind their mother in the only way they knew how – the posters were down, the stacks of magazines were stuffed in garbage bags and all their music and make-up was hidden away.

On the day of the interview, with the kids at school, their mother gathered what little savings she had and, following a carefully thought-out plan, went to a small boutique in one of the best malls and bought a good knock-off of a Louis Vuitton handbag and a pair of Gucci sunglasses.

In the public washroom she swapped out her handbag, dropped the old one in the trash and removed her veil. She was determined to give herself every advantage, including the one commented on by her son a few months earlier. Overcoming a lifetime of modesty wasn't easy, though, and even with the sunglasses in place she still couldn't work up the courage to look at herself in the mirror.

Appearing modern and very beautiful, she finally slipped out of the door and walked to the office tower next door: the head office of Batelco, the local telephone monopoly. Tingling with fear and excitement, she sat on a couch and waited to be called for the interview. It occurred to her that her feelings weren't far removed from those on her wedding night – and right now she felt about as naked.

No wonder women enjoy going out like this, she thought.

A secretary approached and showed her into a conference room, where two men and a female executive explained that the company was expanding its number of 'customer relations' officers. What did she think of that? She told them it was a good idea – the company's reputation for service was so bad it was difficult to believe they even had any to start with.

The senior guy stared at her and then laughed. All day they had heard prospective employees tell them what an outstanding company it was. Finally they were interviewing someone who at least understood the job was necessary. Still smiling, he said most of the work was dealing with customer complaints about overcharging, explaining billing cycles, unlocking the mysteries of pricing plans.

She told them she didn't have any experience but she was still an expert; as a widow on a small income she had to understand and analyse all the household bills, including Batelco's. Out of anxiety she kept rattling on, not realizing that even though they were nodding their heads, the panel members were barely listening.

They knew the job was more about handling irate subscribers than technical qualifications. The woman in front of them seemed to have a rare combination of intelligence and style – enough to give pause to even the most rabid customer.

The committee looked at one another, communicating in a shorthand of raised eyebrows and tiny shrugs, and without a word between them came to a decision. The senior guy interrupted and asked if she could start on Monday. She was so excited she couldn't answer, and it was only after he repeated the question that she managed to say yes.

She walked out of the conference room with a maelstrom of thoughts crowding her head but, even in the midst of it, she knew she couldn't share the news with her daughters. Everything could still fall at the last hurdle: her son.

After dinner, casually, she asked him to go with her to the nearby grocery market. She had been planning it all afternoon and, as they set out, she saw that her timing was perfect. It was the start of the weekend and groups of youths had gathered outside a car customizing shop, squads of Pakistani men who lived on site at local factories squatted on street corners and carloads of rowdy boys headed into movie houses in the city. As they walked, she pointed out every unsavoury aspect and told him that soon, veiled or not, the girls would be of an age where they would no longer be able to leave the house.

He nodded; he'd thought about it too. As a male, he was the head of the family and responsible for the women's virtue.

'We have to move to a better area,' she said.

'Sure,' he replied. 'And how do we pay for it?'

'I get a job,' she said quietly, conveniently omitting to mention she already had one.

He stopped and stared at her. 'That's ridiculous!' he said.

She lowered her veiled face in obedience, wisely letting the first blast of anger and surprise blow by. He turned to walk on towards the grocery store but she didn't move.

'Ridiculous maybe, but give me an alternative,' she said steadily. 'How else do we keep the girls safe?'

He continued towards the store. And still she didn't move, determined to fight her son for a chance at a better life.

'We can't live on charity for ever!' she called after him. 'What man would want it? No mother would allow it. With a job we could afford a new life—'

She didn't finish. He turned and stalked back to her, furious. 'The answer is no – it's wrong!'

He started dragging her by the sleeve, but she had seen the opening she had been so desperately hoping for. 'A woman working may not suit some idea of manhood, it may offend a few wild-eyed imams, but it isn't *wrong*,' she said coldly.

Her son glimpsed the chasm opening in front of him, but he couldn't take back what he had said. Instead, he tried closing the whole subject down, indicating the groups of men watching the unfolding domestic dispute. 'Come on!' he said. 'You're making a spectacle of us!'

But she wouldn't move. 'It's years since I did my religious studies,' she said, 'so tell me – where in Islam does it say it's wrong for a woman to take honest work?'

'It's wrong because I say—' but she didn't even let him finish that nonsense.

'Your opinion is greater than the Prophet's, peace be upon him?' she wanted to know.

To even think such a thing was a sacrilege, and for a moment he couldn't reply.

His mother hammered the advantage: 'It was God's will you took your father's place – now start acting like him. You think he would want his daughters living like this? You think he'd want his *wife*?!'

The boy knew the answers. He looked across the vast expanse of gender that separated them, and into a tiny window. It was the narrow slit in her veil – for over a thousand years the only way by which men and women in the Arab world have observed each other.

She held his gaze with her beautiful, shadowed eyes. 'I asked if you thought your father would want us living in these circumstances – now answer me,' she demanded.

He tried to stare her down, but she wouldn't have it and his eyes slid away. She was still his mother and he loved her dearly. 'How much would a job pay?' he asked at last.

Chapter Five

THE FAMILY'S INDIAN SUMMER MIGHT HAVE CONTINUED FOR EVER except for a group of Bangladeshi construction workers.

Within a month of her son agreeing that she could work, they had moved to a house in a good neighbourhood and, five days a week, she got on the bus with her daughters and went to her job. Never before had she felt so much purpose in her life, or such quiet enjoyment of her two girls. It came to an end two days after the construction workers started building a small office block next to the boy's school.

Unfamiliar with the finer points of site preparation, the Bangladeshis drove a mechanical backhoe through the underground water and power lines, killing off the air-conditioning in the school. While the hapless driver looked at his barbecued machine, the kids cheered him from their windows, fully aware they would be given the rest of the day off.

The Saracen decided to surprise his mother and take her for lunch, but the Manama bus service was about as reliable as Jeddah's and he arrived a few minutes after the Batelco building had closed for the break. Assuming she was inside in the staff cafeteria, he went to the mall to get a drink and to consider how he might spend his free afternoon.

He stepped off an escalator, saw her from thirty yards away and, in that moment, whatever small life he had constructed for himself in Bahrain fell to pieces. Unveiled and wearing lipstick, her Gucci sunglasses pushed up on to her head, she was having lunch at a café with a group of co-workers.

He stared at her unveiled face and make-up, shattered. She might as well have been naked in his eyes. Even worse than her immodesty, though, were the four men who were sitting at the large table. One look at them, and he knew they were not the fathers or brothers of any of the other women.

A wave of sudden retching, of betrayal, almost choked him and, just as he beat that back, he was swamped by the rolling desolation of failure: he realized that he had let his father down in the worst imaginable way.

He considered confronting his mother in front of them, covering her face and dragging her home – but somehow he managed to force his legs to walk away. Angry, wounded virtually beyond repair, he went to the only refuge he knew – the mosque – desperate for comfort and advice from the imam and the other soldiers of the Muslim Brotherhood.

He returned home so late that night and was deliberately so tardy in getting up the next morning that he didn't see his mother and sisters until dinner time. Strangely, he made no reference to what he'd seen at the mall but, all through the meal, his mother was aware something was wrong.

When the girls had gone to bed she asked him what it was but, withdrawn and surly, he wouldn't be corralled into talking about it. The only thing she could think of was that it had something to do with a girl, so she decided not to pressure him; she'd had brothers herself and she knew how hard the teenage years were for boys.

It took several days, but he finally sat down and spoke with her. With downcast eyes, he said that, after months of introspection, he had decided to follow a religious life and would one day – God willing – become an imam.

She looked at him, taken aback, but made no attempt to interrupt. Whatever dreams she'd had for her son, they had never included that.

He told her quietly that he knew a spiritual life was a hard road but, since the death of his father, religion had brought him greater consolation than anything else and, as the imam had told him on several occasions, it was a decision of which his father would have been immensely proud.

His mother knew that was true and, while it explained his recent silence, she couldn't help but think there was something else about the decision she didn't understand.

She stared at her only boy – every month looking more like his father and making her love him all the more deeply for it – trying to will him to tell her everything, but he just looked up and met her gaze, unwavering.

'I'm sixteen in two weeks,' he said, 'but I still need your permission to get a passport. I want to go to Pakistan for a month.'

She said nothing, too shocked – Pakistan? Where did that come from?

'It's during the long summer vacation, so it won't affect my studies,' he continued coolly. 'Outside Quetta there's a famous *madrassah* – a religious school – that has a perfect course for young men starting out. The imam tells me it will set the high standard for the rest of my career.'

His mother nodded; she could almost hear the blind man saying it. What would he know about her son? The boy was tall and strong, surprisingly athletic, and she doubted that a life of religious study would ever satisfy him. 'Even if I agreed – how could we afford it?' she asked, opting for the most reasonable-sounding objection first.

'The course is free,' he said, 'and the imam has offered to pay the air fare. Other members of the mosque have said they'll write to friends to arrange accommodation.'

She bit her lip – she should have anticipated something like that. 'When would you leave?' she asked.

'Ten days,' he replied, daring her to say it was too soon.

'*When*?!'

'Ten days,' he repeated, knowing she had heard well enough.

It took her a moment to stop her heart's wild tattoo. Only then could she try to address her fear that if she didn't help him it might open a gulf which might never be healed.

'What do you say?' he asked, the tone aggressive enough for her to understand the answer he expected.

'I'd never stand in the way of such an honourable ambition,' she said at last. 'But of course I have concerns of my own, so it depends on meeting with the imam and making sure I'm satisfied with the arrangements.'

He smiled pleasantly as he got to his feet. 'No problem. He's expecting your call.'

Two days later, reassured by her meeting, she signed the

application for an expedited passport, and that afternoon he went to the office of Pakistan Air and bought his ticket.

By then his mother had realized he would be away for his birthday and, in the flurry of packing and shopping, she and the girls took on one extra burden – organizing a surprise birthday celebration for the day of his departure. It was a poorly kept secret, but he seemed to play along, feigning not to notice the extra food being brought in and the invitations going out to his school and the mosque.

By 4 a.m. on the day of the party, however, he was already awake and fully dressed. Silently he slid into his sisters' room and stood at the end of their beds. They were exhausted, having stayed up until midnight completing the preparations, and neither of them stirred.

He looked at their lovely faces sailing quietly across the dark oceans of sleep, and perhaps it was only then he realized how much he loved them. But this was no time for weakness, and he tucked a copy of a Qur'an inscribed with his name under their pillows and kissed them one last time.

With a heart heavier than he could have imagined, he made his way down the hall and opened the door into his mother's room. She was asleep on her side, facing him, lit by a soft glow spilling from a night-light in her bathroom.

Unknown to any of them, he had returned to the airline office three days earlier and changed his ticket to a 6 a.m. flight. Ever since seeing his mother in the mall, he had masked his feelings, but he wasn't sure he could continue to suppress them during the emotional turmoil of what only he knew would be a farewell party. He had told them he would be home in a month, but that wasn't true. In reality, he had no idea if they would ever see each other again.

Looking at his mother now, he knew there was no easy way. Growing up in the desert, he had only ever seen fog once in his life. Early one morning, his father had woken him and they had watched a wall of white vapour, otherworldly, roll towards them across the Red Sea. Now the memories came towards him like that: her belly growing large with one of his sisters, his father hitting her hard across the mouth for disobedience, her lovely face dancing with laughter at one of his jokes. The rolling mass of human emotion – hope to despair, childish love to bitter disappointment – wrapped its strange tendrils around him until he was lost in its white, shifting universe.

He would have remained adrift in tearful remembrance except for a distant *muezzin* calling the faithful to prayer. It meant dawn was breaking and he was already running late. He moved to the bed and bent close to the woman's face, feeling her sleeping breath gentle on his cheek. They say that when men are dying in battle their fingers nearly always twist into the soil, trying to hold on to the earth and all the pain and love it holds.

The boy didn't realize it but, had he looked down, he would have seen his fingers wrapping tight into the coverlet of his mother's bed. As he kissed her forehead he murmured a single word, something he had never said to her before: he spoke her name, as if she were his child.

He pulled himself to his feet and backed out of the door, keeping his eyes on her for as long as possible. Quickly he grabbed his backpack, emerged into the new day and ran fast down the path lest the tears overwhelm him and make his feet follow his heart and turn him back.

At the far end of the street, as arranged, a car was waiting. Inside were the imam and two leading members of the Muslim Brotherhood. They greeted him as he scrambled into the back seat, the driver slipped the vehicle into gear and it sped off to drop him at the airport.

His mother woke two hours later, rising early to finish the arrangements for the party. In the kitchen she found a letter addressed to her. As she started reading it she felt as if cold water was rising up from the floor and crushing her lower body. She felt her legs go from under her, and she only just managed to find a chair before she fell.

He told her in simple prose about seeing her in the mall with her shame in full flower, of how he was certain his sisters were complicit in her behaviour and that his only ambition had been to protect the women, exactly as his father would have wanted.

As she read on, two pages in his best handwriting, she was taught a lesson many other parents have learned – it's usually your children who wound you the most ferociously.

Finally she came to the last paragraph and realized she had been completely deceived by the imam. What she read destroyed the last strands of her tenuous control and she fell into a chasm of loss and guilt and terrible fear.

Her son wrote that he was going to Quetta but there was no famous *madrassah* there, just a different type of camp hidden in the high mountains. There he would undergo six weeks' basic training before being taken along an old smugglers' route and over the border into the battlefield.

He said he had never had any intention of following a religious life. Like any truly devout Muslim, he was going to Afghanistan – to wage *jihad* against the Soviet invaders who were killing the children of Islam.

Chapter Six

DURING THE NINE YEARS OF THE AFGHAN WAR, OVER A MILLION PEOPLE died. The Saracen wasn't one of them – a fact which, given what he did later, would make most people question if not God's existence then at least His common sense.

After crossing the border, the Saracen fought the Soviets for two years until, one cold February night – eighteen years old and grown tall and hard – he stood on a ridge and looked down on a road that stretched all the way to Europe.

Behind him a crescent moon cast its light across serried ranks of peaks and crags where another ten thousand battle-hardened *mujahideen* were also standing like sentinels.

All of them had seen remarkable things – how fast a Russian prisoner can dance when doused with gasoline and set on fire, what their own dead looked like with their genitals hacked off and stuffed in their mouths – but on this, a night of a million stars, they might as well have been standing on the fifth ring of Saturn watching the Imperial Starfleet fly past. Nobody had seen anything like it.

For forty miles along the wide valley below – and according to reports on the Afghan military radio, for a hundred miles beyond that – the two-lane blacktop was packed with low-loaders, trucks, and tank transporters. Every few miles fires were burning, lighting up the night like some Christo version of funeral pyres. As vehicles drew alongside the fires, the soldiers riding shotgun would toss out surplus material: snow suits, ration boxes, tents, first-aid kits.

Now and again ammunition or flares would go in by mistake, sending the men on the vehicles diving, lighting up the sky like dismal fireworks, throwing one of the largest convoys ever seen on earth into blinding moments of sharp relief. The vehicles were heading towards the Amu Darya river and the border with Uzbekistan: the huge Soviet 40th Army – the army of the Afghan occupation – was pulling out, defeated.

The Saracen, along with the other *mujahideen*, knew exactly why the Soviets had lost. It wasn't because of the rebels' courage or Moscow's determination to fight the wrong war. No, it was because the Soviets were without God: it was the *mujahideens' faith* that had brought them victory.

'*Allahu Akbar!*' a voice called from the top of one of the highest pinnacles. 'God is great.' Ten thousand other voices took it up, shouting in reverence, listening to it echo. '*Allahu Akbar!*' – on and on it went, raining down on the Soviets as they ran for home. Afghanistan, the graveyard of so many empires, had claimed another victim.

Two weeks afterwards, twenty heavily armed men rode on horseback into the snow-swept village where the Saracen was camped with other battle-scarred foreign fighters.

The leader of the visitors was called Abdul Mohammad Khan and, even in a time of giants, he was a legend. In his forties when the Soviets invaded, he took his clan to war, was led into a trap by two 'military advisers' from another tribe, captured in a wild firefight and tortured in a Kabul prison to the point where even the Russian guards were sickened. He escaped during a bloody prison uprising and, holding his body together more by willpower than with bandages, made his way back to his mountain stronghold.

Six months later, his health partly restored, he fulfilled the ambition which had sustained him throughout the hours of pummelling and electrodes in Kabul – his fighters captured alive the two men who had betrayed him. He didn't torture them. Blocks of heavy steel were strapped to their backs, and they were laid naked – face up – in large moulds. Unable to stand, they thrashed with their arms and legs as they watched liquid concrete being poured into the moulds.

Once it had covered their bodies and faces just enough to drown them, the concrete was stopped and allowed to set. The outline of their thrashing limbs and screaming faces were now captured for ever in the stone – a grotesque bas-relief.

The blocks containing the entombed men and their eternal attempt to escape were set in the wall of the fortress's luxurious meeting room, available for the enlightenment of anyone who came to visit Lord Abdul Mohammad Khan. Nobody ever betrayed him again.

When he arrived at the freezing village with his military escort, he had already – as a warlord without peer and a deeply devout man of faith – appointed himself governor of the province. It was in that capacity he was travelling through his huge domain in order to thank the foreign fighters for their help and to arrange their repatriation.

Throughout that long journey there was one man more than any other he wanted to meet. For two years he had heard stories of the Saracen, who had campaigned throughout the mountains with a forty-pound Blowpipe missile system on his back and an AK-47 over his shoulder.

In the years of war which had followed the first Soviet tanks across the Afghan border, the Russians had lost over three hundred and twenty helicopters. Three of them, all fearsome Hind gunships, were taken out by the young Arab and his Blowpipe – two in the very worst months of the war and one in the last week of the conflict. By any standard it was a remarkable achievement.

Abdul Khan – limping for ever thanks to his stay in what the Soviets affectionately called the Kabul Sports Club, his haggard and handsome face never far from a smile even when he was turning men into concrete sculptures – held court before the assembled men and listened to their requests for everything from medical treatment to travel expenses. Only the Saracen – standing at the back – said nothing, wanted nothing, and the warlord admired him even more.

After everyone had eaten dinner together in the village's communal kitchen, the governor motioned for the Saracen to join him alone in an alcove near the roaring fire. With the wind whipping up the valleys and howling all the way to China, the flurries of snow piling in drifts against the huddled houses, Abdul Khan served the tea himself and said he had heard that the young man was a deeply devout Muslim.

The teenager nodded, and Khan told him that there was a religious scholar, a former *mujahideen* commander who had lost an eye in battle, who was setting up his own elite *madrassah* in the city of Kandahar. His students were all former fighters and, if the Saracen wished to study Islam in all its glory, then Governor Abdul Khan would be happy to meet the cost.

The Saracen, sipping from his steel cup and dragging on one of the governor's American cigarettes, had heard of Mullah Omar and his group of Taliban – the Arabic word for a person seeking religious knowledge – and, though he was flattered by the governor's offer, he shook his head. 'I'm going home, to the country where I was born,' he said.

'To Jeddah?' the governor asked, unable to mask his sharp surprise. On other nights, around other fires, he had heard men tell the story of the execution that had started the youth on his long road to *jihad*.

'No, Riyadh,' he said, and the governor guessed now what he was talking about. Riyadh was the Saudi Arabian capital, the ruling seat of the king and the House of Saud. 'You've heard what they did to my father?' the young man asked, watching the older man's deep-set eyes.

'Men have spoken of it,' the warlord replied quietly.

'So you understand – I go to start the work of revenge.'

It was said without rancour or emotion, purely as a matter of fact. Even so, if most young men had said such a thing the governor would have laughed and offered them another one of his fine cigarettes. But most youths had never faced a Soviet Hind helicopter gunship in full rampage, not once, not even in their worst night-mares. Watching the Saracen, the governor wondered, not for the first time, if he himself could have found the courage – armed with nothing more than a Blowpipe – to have done it. Like everybody else in Afghanistan, he knew the missile was one of the worst pieces of shit ever invented, almost guaranteed to result in the death of anyone unfortunate enough to use it.

Shoulder-fired, the four-foot missile used a manual-guidance system: in other words, you fired the missile and then used a joystick on a small radio box to steer it to the target. As if that wasn't dangerous enough, the missile made such a bright flash at launch that the intended victim, usually a helicopter, invariably saw it coming.

Immediately, the crew on board would turn the craft, bringing their multi-barrelled machine guns and fifty-calibre cannons to bear. Firing a hailstorm of metal, the pilot would try to annihilate the operator and his joystick before he could steer the missile home.

To be seventeen years old, alone, with no parent to bury you let alone protect you, to stand at sunset on a mountain scree in Afghanistan with only the long shadows to hide you, with shards of rock and bullets blasting past as hardened airmen unleash the dogs of hell, to stand in the eye of a twister with the world whirling and disintegrating all around, to hear the deafening roar of rotors and engines, the scream of machine gun and cannon as it approaches fast, to hold your ground, never to run or flinch and to work a joystick in the face of onrushing death, to count the endless seconds for a horse of the apocalypse to turn away in fear, to twist the stick and guide the warhead into the soft underbelly of its engine and feel the heat of the explosion then smell the death and burning flesh and realize suddenly it wasn't your own, not this time anyway – well, there are not many men who can do that.

Three times the Saracen played one of the deadliest games of chicken ever known, and three times he won. Lord Abdul Khan would never laugh at anything such a young man said.

'Stay,' the warlord told him quietly. 'The Saudis will arrest you the moment you arrive. With your name and a history of *jihad* you won't get past the border.'

'I know,' the Saracen replied, pouring them both more tea. 'When I leave I go to Quetta – a thousand dollars in the arms bazaar there buys a passport in any name you want.'

'Maybe – but be careful, most Pakistani forgers are shit. What nationality will you take?'

'I don't care, anything that'll get me into Lebanon. There's a medical school in Beirut that's one of the best.'

Abdul Khan paused. 'You're going to study to be a doctor?'

He nodded. 'If I'm no longer a Saudi, how else can I return to my country and live there?' he said. 'It's closed to foreigners but not to doctors – a foreign Muslim with a good medical degree is guaranteed a visa. It has one other advantage. The Mabahith won't spend time monitoring a doctor. They're supposed to save lives, aren't they?'

Abdul Khan smiled but just kept looking at him. 'It'll take years,' he said finally.

'A lifetime maybe.' The Saracen smiled back. 'But I have no choice, I owe it to my father. I think that's why God kept me safe on the mountain – to destroy the House of Saud.'

The governor sat in silence for a long while – he had never thought the young fighter could do anything that would impress him more than facing down the Hinds. He had been wrong.

He swirled the tea in his cup and finally raised it in salute – he knew more about revenge than most men. 'To Saudi Arabia and vengeance then,' he said. *'Insha'Allah.'*

'Insha'Allah,' the Saracen replied. God willing. And for close to fifteen years that was the last word that passed between them; the governor and his escort left at dawn the next morning. Three weeks later, though, after the foreign fighters had struck their camp and were waiting for the last snowstorm of the year to pass, two of the governor's young nephews dragged themselves into the village.

They had been forced to turn their mounts loose in the blizzard and, while the horses made their way down to safer ground, the two youths climbed on through the storm. Unannounced, completely unexpected, they brought a small oilskin package with them for the Saracen, the legendary *mujahideen* who was only a little older than they were.

Alone in the kitchen with him, they waited while he signed for its contents. Inside was a Lebanese passport in a false name – not some bad fake bought in the bazaar in Quetta but a genuine book with every detail properly registered, traded by a corrupt Lebanese Embassy employee in Islamabad, the Pakistani capital, for ten thousand US, cash.

Equally importantly, it contained visas and permits that showed that the bearer had entered from India three years earlier in order to gain his high-school diploma from a respected international school. Tucked in the back was four thousand US dollars in well-used bills. There was no letter or explanation, there didn't need to be: it was like a properly maintained AK-47, a gift from one warrior whose war had finished to another whose campaign had just begun.

With the spring melt starting, the Saracen started his long trek out of Afghanistan. As he walked the back roads, the signs of the war's destruction were everywhere: towns laid to waste, devastated fields, bodies in ditches. But already families were planting the most lucrative of all cash crops – opium poppies. As he neared the Pakistani border he met the first of five million refugees returning to their homes, and from then on he swam against a rising tide of humanity.

At the border all semblance of control had collapsed and, un-noticed, he crossed out of Afghanistan late on a cloudless afternoon – a young man with a fake past, a false identity and a real passport.

No wonder, when the time came, it took me so long to find him. As I said – he was a ghost.

Chapter Seven

THE SARACEN MADE IT DOWN TO KARACHI BY THE FIRST BLAST OF THE monsoon. The huge city sprawls along the Arabian Sea, and he used a few of his dollars to buy sleeping space on the deck of an old freighter heading out to Dubai. From there, a dozen airlines fly directly to Beirut and, a week later, the passport fulfilled all its expensive promise when he passed unchallenged through Lebanese immigration.

Beirut was a disaster story in itself, half of it in ruins and most of its population wounded or exhausted. But that suited the Saracen – the country was recovering from fifteen years of civil war, and a rootless man had no trouble passing for a native in a city full of shattered lives.

He had always been a good student and, with six months' hard work, helped by tutors he met at the city's most radical and intellectual mosque, he easily passed the next sitting of the college entrance exam. Like most students, the high cost of tuition was a problem, but fortunately he found a State Department scholarship programme which was aimed at rebuilding the nation and fostering democracy. The staff at the US Embassy even helped him fill in the forms.

Flush with US aid money, the Saracen devoted the long days – interrupted only by prayer and simple meals – to the study of medicine; the nights to terror and revolution. He read all the big ones – Mao, Che, Lenin – and attended discussions and lectures by wild pan-Arab nationalists, Palestinian warmongers and several men who could best be described as Islamic cave dwellers. One of them, on a fund-raising visit, was forming an organization which translated as 'the law' or 'the base' – al-Qaeda in Arabic. The Saracen had heard

116

of this tall sheikh, a fellow Saudi, while he was fighting in Afghanistan but, unlike everybody else in the mosque that day, he made no attempt to impress Osama bin Laden with fiery rhetoric – proof yet again that the quietest man in the room is usually the most dangerous.

It was at another of these discussion groups, this one so small it was held in a dingy room normally used by the university's stamp club, that he encountered an idea that would change his life. Ours, too, I'm sad to say. Ironically – because the guest speaker was a woman – he almost didn't attend. She gave her name as Amina Ebadi – although that was probably an alias – and she was a political organizer in the huge Jabalia refugee camp in Gaza, home to over a hundred and forty thousand Palestinian refugees, one of the most deprived and radical square miles on earth.

The subject of her talk was the humanitarian crisis in the camp, and a grand total of ten people showed up. But she was so accustomed to swimming against the tide of international in-difference it didn't worry her – one day, somebody would hear her, and that person would change everything.

It was a brutally hot night and, in the midst of her address, she paused and took off her half-veil. 'There are so few of us, I feel like I'm among family,' she said, smiling. None of the tiny audience objected and, even if the Saracen had been inclined to do so, it took him long enough to recover from the sight of her face that the oppor-tunity was lost.

With only her serious voice to go by, he had drawn up a mental picture of her that was completely at variance with her large eyes, expressive mouth and flawless skin. Her tightly pulled-back hair lent her a boyish quality and while, individually, her features were far too irregular to be considered attractive, when she smiled everything seemed to coalesce and nobody could have ever convinced the Saracen that she wasn't beautiful.

Although she was about five years his senior, there was something – the shape of her eyes, her hunger for life – that reminded him of the elder of his sisters. He hadn't had any contact with his family since the day he had left Bahrain, and a sharp wave of homesickness suddenly hit him.

By the time he had ridden it out, the woman was saying something about 'the near enemies'.

'I'm sorry,' he said. 'Could you repeat that?'

She turned her large eyes on the self-possessed young man, the one somebody had told her was a deeply devout medical student but who she guessed from the weather-beaten face was almost certainly a returned *jihad* warrior. She knew the type – the Jabalia camp was full of *muj* veterans.

Addressing him with the great respect he deserved, she said that nearly all the Arab world's problems were caused by what could be called their near enemies: Israel, of course; the ruthless dictatorships scattered throughout the region; the corrupt feudal monarchies like Saudi Arabia who were in the pocket of the West.

'I hear all the time that if our near enemies are destroyed then most of the problems would be solved. I don't think it's possible – the near enemies are too ruthless, too happy to oppress and kill us.

'But they only survive and prosper because they are supported by the "far enemy". A few forward thinkers – wise people – say that if you can defeat the far enemy, all the near enemies will collapse.'

'That's what I like about theories,' the medical student replied, 'they always work. It's different if you have to try to implement them. Is it even possible to destroy a country as powerful as America?'

She smiled. 'As I'm sure you know, the *jihadists* broke the back of an equally powerful nation in Afghanistan.'

The Saracen walked the five miles home in turmoil. He had never had a clear idea of how to bring down the House of Saud, and he had to admit there was a reason why all Saudi dissidents were based overseas: those who lived or travelled inside its borders were invariably informed upon and eliminated. Look at what had happened to his father. But never to enter the country and yet force the collapse of the Saudi monarchy by inflicting a grievous wound on the far enemy – well, that was a different proposition!

By the time he turned into the doorway of his tiny apartment he knew the way forward: while he might still become a doctor, he wasn't going back to Saudi Arabia. Again, he didn't know how to do it yet – Allah would show him when the time was right – but he was going to take the battle to the one place which loomed larger than any other in the collective Arab imagination.

It would take years, on occasions the hurdles would seem insurmountable, but his long journey to mass murder had begun. He was going to strike at the heart of America.

Chapter Eight

TEN YEARS AFTER THE SARACEN'S REVELATION AND HALF A WORLD AWAY, I was on a sidewalk in Paris arguing with a stranger, a black guy with a limp.

Lieutenant Bradley would end up holding my life in his hands but, in the short term, I was silently cursing him to hell. In telling me that he wanted to discuss my book, he had comprehensively destroyed all the layers of false identities I had so carefully constructed around myself.

Seemingly unaware of the detonation he had caused, he was now explaining that an hour earlier he had arrived outside my apartment just in time to see a person who he thought was me get into a cab. He had grabbed his own taxi, followed me to the place de la Madeleine, circled the block trying to find me and, when that failed, had returned to the apartment to pick up the trail. It was he who had knocked on the door and, not sure whether I was inside or not, had decided to wait in the street to see if I turned up.

I got the sense he thought this was all pretty amusing and I started to dislike him even more. As much as I wanted to blow him off, I couldn't – I was scared. He'd found me and, if he could do it, so might someone else. The Greeks, for instance. Everything, my feelings included, had to be set aside until I found out how he had done it.

'Fancy a coffee?' I said pleasantly.

Yeah, he'd like that, he said, volunteering to pay. That was a mistake. Given the part of Paris we were standing in, he'd probably have to cash in his pension plan for an espresso and an eclair, but I wasn't in the mood to show any mercy.

We started walking down rue François 1er a few paces apart, in silence, but we hadn't gone more than five yards before I had to stop: Bradley was gamely trying to keep up, but the limp on his right leg was worse than I had realized.

'Birth defect?' I asked. I can be fairly unpleasant when I'm angry.

'That's the other leg,' he shot back. 'I got this one last year.'

'Work or sport?' I was having to walk with him, so it seemed unreasonable not to continue the conversation.

'Work.' He paused fractionally. 'Lower Manhattan, ran into a building without thinking. Wasn't the first time I'd done it, but this one was different – lucky it didn't kill me.' It was clear from his tone he didn't want to elaborate on the circumstances.

'Looks like your hip,' I said, as we continued even more slowly, pretty sure I was right from the way he was rolling and what I remembered of my medical training.

'They replaced it with titanium and plastic. Said I'd need a lot of physio but, shit, not eight months.'

A homicide cop, a destroyed hip, titanium pins to hold the bone together – sounded like a large-calibre gunshot wound to me. He didn't volunteer anything else, and I have to say that, despite myself, I was warming to him – there's nothing worse than cops with war stories. Except maybe spooks.

We stopped at the lights, and I pointed at a limestone hotel with three new Rolls-Royce Phantoms parked in front of it. 'The Plaza Athénée,' I said. 'We can get a coffee there.'

'Looks expensive,' he replied, unaware that very soon he would understand the true meaning of that word.

We went through the revolving door, across a marble foyer and into the hotel's grand gallery. From there, tall doors opened on to one of the most beautiful courtyards in Paris.

Totally enclosed, overlooked on all sides by bedrooms, its walls were covered in ivy. The balconies set among the greenery were shaded by red awnings, and guests could look down on a concert grand, elaborate topiaries, numerous Russian oligarchs and a variety of other Euro-trash. We took a table at the back, almost hidden from view, and the battered cop started to explain how he had deconstructed the legend of one of the world's most secret agents.

Though he didn't say it in so many words, it quickly became apparent that the injuries he had sustained when he ran into the building were far more serious than a smashed hip. One lung had collapsed – another bullet, I guessed – his spine had been injured and he had sustained a bad blow to his head, all of which added up to three weeks in intensive care.

For the first week it was a near-run thing if he'd survive, and Marcie wouldn't leave his side. Somehow, she and the physicians rolled the stone back from the cave and, eventually, he was released to the high-dependency unit. There it became clear that his ailments were more than physical. Whatever abyss he had looked into meant he barely talked and appeared to feel even less. Maybe it was fear, maybe it was cowardice, maybe there was someone he couldn't save – he never explained – but whatever it was he'd encountered in that building meant he'd left a lot of himself behind.

'I was alive, but I was a shadow of the person who'd gone to work that day,' he said quietly. 'The numbing, the emotional disconnection, was worse than any physical injury – not just for me, for Marcie.'

Not even the love of his wife could turn his face towards the light, and I was certain, though he never used the term, that he was suffering from what was once called shell shock and was now termed post-traumatic stress disorder. After weeks of anti-anxiety drugs but little improvement, the doctors suggested that taking him home might offer the best chance of reconnecting him. They probably needed the bed.

Marcie spent two days rearranging the apartment – turning a corner of their bedroom into an area for his physiotherapy sessions and filling it with his favourite books, music and anything else she thought might engage him.

'It didn't work,' he added. 'I had too much anger and a bad case of what the psychologists called "survivor guilt".'

For the first time, I realized that others must have died during the incident – a partner, I wondered, a couple of members of his team? In retrospect, I was pretty dumb about the whole situation but, in my defence, I had no time to consider any of it in detail – he was hurrying on.

He said that whatever hopes Marcie had of nursing him back to health with love were soon overwhelmed by the terrible toll mental illness can take on even a good relationship.

Because he had been injured in the line of duty, she didn't have to worry about his medical bills and, after three soul-destroying weeks, she finally got the number of a highly regarded residential-care facility in upstate New York. In the bleakest hours, she wondered whether, once her husband had been admitted, he would ever come home again.

I've been to enough Narcotics Anonymous meetings to know it only takes about twenty minutes before somebody gets up and says they had to hit bottom before they could start the long climb out. So it was with Marcie. Sitting up late one evening, she'd begun filling in the forms she had received that morning from the Wellness Foundation in Hudson Falls.

With Ben asleep in the next room – watching people die over and over in his dreams – and a questionnaire taking her back through so many shared experiences, she found herself deeper in the canyons of despair than she had ever been. She didn't know it, of course, but she had finally found 'bottom'. One question asked what personal items the patient would enjoy having with them. Nothing really, she answered – what was the point, she had tried providing all of that. As she was about to continue, she stared at the word and a strange thought took hold. 'Nothing,' she said quietly.

Marcie was a smart woman – a teacher at a charter high school in New York – and, like most women, she had thought a lot about love. She knew, even in marriage, if you advanced too far to please the other person it let them edge away, and you ended up always laughing and fighting and screwing on their territory. Sometimes you had to stand your ground and make them come to you – just to keep the equilibrium.

She turned and looked at the bedroom door. She knew she had done so much to try to restore her husband's mental health that the equilibrium was way out of line. Maybe the trick was to make him emerge from the deep cell he'd built and edge back towards her.

When Ben woke seven hours later from his drug-assisted sleep, he thought he was in the wrong life. This wasn't the bedroom he and Marcie shared, this wasn't the room he had closed his eyes on. Yes, the doors and windows were in the same place, but all the things that individuated it, that made it his and Marcie's space, were gone.

There were no photographs, no paintings and no mess on the floor. The TV had gone and even the kilim they both loved had silently disappeared. Apart from the bed and some physio equipment there was, well – *nothing*. As far as he could see, it was the white room at the end of the universe.

Confused about where he really was, he swung off the bed and, hobbling from his smashed thigh, crossed the room. He opened the door and looked into a parallel universe.

His wife was in the kitchen, trying to hurry up her coffee. Bradley watched her in silence. In the twenty years they had been together, she had grown ever more beautiful in his eyes. She was tall and slim with simply cut hair that accentuated the fine shape of her face but which, more importantly, seemed to say she didn't care much about her own good looks. That, of course, was the only way to handle such a gift, and it made her appear even more attractive.

Looking at her in the midst of the home they loved gave him a terrible catch in his throat. He wondered if he was being shown what he had left behind; maybe he had never got out of the building and was already dead.

Then Marcie realized he was there and smiled at him. Bradley was relieved – he was pretty certain people who saw a dead guy in their bedroom doorway didn't act like that. Not Marcie, anyway, who didn't care much for Hallowe'en and had a deep aversion to graveyards.

For the first time in months Marcie's spirits ticked higher: the new strategy had at least made him come to the cell door and look out. 'Another minute and I'm leaving for work – I'll be back in time to get dinner,' she said.

'Work?' he queried, trying to get his mind around the idea. She hadn't been to work since he was injured.

She said nothing – if he wanted answers, he was going to have to work for them. He watched her jam a piece of toast in her mouth, grab her travel cup of coffee and head out the door with a small wave.

It left Bradley marooned in the doorway, so, after a moment of silence and unable to keep the weight on his strapped leg, he did the only thing he thought sensible – he left the parallel world and went back into the white room.

He lay down but, try as he might, he couldn't think clearly about what was happening with so many psychoactive drugs in his body. In silence, alone in the decaying morning, he decided the only practical thing to do was to wean himself off them. It was a dangerous but crucial decision – at last he was taking responsibility for his own recovery.

Despite her promise, Marcie didn't fix him dinner that night; he was in a fitful sleep so she decided to leave him be. Instead of a meal tray, she placed a new hardcover book on his bedside table, hoping that, with nothing else to occupy him, he would eventually pick it up. The idea for the book had come to her that morning, and immediately after school she had hurried down to a store near Christopher Street. It was called Zodiac Books, but it had nothing to do with astrology – it was named after a serial killer in Northern California whose exploits had spawned a one-maniac publishing industry.

Marcie had never been inside Zodiac – she only knew of it from Ben – so when she climbed the set of steep stairs she was amazed to enter a space as big as a warehouse, stacked with the greatest repository of books about crime, forensic science and investigation in the world. She explained to the ageing owner behind his desk what she was looking for – technical, factual, something to engage a professional.

The owner was six foot seven and looked more like he belonged in the backwoods than in a bookshop. A former FBI profiler, he slowly unfurled himself and led her past shelves coated with dust and into a row of books and periodicals marked 'New Releases'. Some of them must have been forty years old. From a small carton on the floor, newly arrived from the publisher, he lifted out a buff-coloured doorstop of a book.

'You told me he's sick,' the Sequoia said, opening the highly technical material to show her. 'Fifty pages of this should finish him off.'

'Seriously,' she said, 'is it any good?'

He smiled, swept his hand around the room. 'Might as well throw the rest away.'

As a result, the book which I had spent so many months writing ended up sitting on Bradley's bedside table. He saw it when he woke early the next morning but made no move towards it. It was a Saturday, and when Marcie brought his breakfast in he asked her about it. 'What's it for?'

'I thought you might find it interesting – look at it if you want,' she said, trying not to put any pressure on him.

He didn't glance at it, turning instead towards his food.

Throughout the day, every time she came in to check on him, her disappointment grew. The book hadn't been touched.

She didn't know, but Bradley had been in a turmoil of his own since the moment he woke, coming down off the drugs, a jackhammer of a headache splitting his skull as his body adjusted, a kaleidoscope of thoughts all let loose, making him remember when he didn't even want to think.

By the time she was fixing dinner, Marcie had given up hope. With no sign of interest in the book from her husband she found the forms from the Wellness Foundation and started rehearsing how she was going to tell him it would be best if he went back to hospital. She couldn't come up with any way of spinning it so that it didn't sound like a defeat, and she knew it might shatter him. But she had run out of mental highway and, close to tears, she opened the door into the bedroom and braced herself for the imminent wreck.

He was sitting up in bed, thirty pages into my book, sweating hard, face etched with pain. God knows what effort it had taken for him to get that far, but he knew it was important to Marcie. Every time she came in, she couldn't stop her eyes sliding to the book.

Marcie stared, frightened she was going to drop the tray, but decided that by even acknowledging the event she might scare him back into the cell, so she just continued normally.

'It's bullshit,' he said. Oh God. Her soaring spirits nosedived, ready for another one of his episodes of wild anger.

'I'm sorry, the man in the shop told me—' she replied.

'No, not the book – the book's fantastic,' he said irritably. 'I mean the author. Call it intuition, call it what you like, he's not FBI. I know those guys – they don't work the frontier. This guy is something special.'

He motioned her closer, indicating where he'd marked things he had found arresting. And she never remembered seeing any of it, stealing glances at her husband, wondering if his spark of engagement would light a fire or whether – as with people she had read about who emerged from comas – it would die quickly and he would sink back into the void.

He took the dinner napkin off the tray and used it to wipe the sweat from his face. It gave Marcie a chance to leaf back to the beginning of the book. She stopped at the few lines of biography, but a picture of the author was conspicuous by its absence. 'Who is he, then?' she asked. 'Who do you think Jude Garrett really is?'

'No idea. I'm hoping he'll make a mistake and tell us by accident,' he said.

All through the weekend, to Marcie's relief, the fire kept blazing. She sat on the bed as he ploughed through the pages – reading out slabs to her, arguing ideas back and forth. And as he went deeper, continually thinking about the science of investigation, he was forced to consider the one crime he had tried so hard to forget. Fragments of what had happened in the building kept floating to the surface of his mind, dragging the breath and the sweat out of him.

On Sunday night, seemingly out of nowhere, the words over-topped the dam and he told her that at one point he was trapped in what felt like a concrete tomb and that it had been so dark he hadn't been able to see the face of the dying man he was with. He started to cry as he said that all he had been able to do was to try to catch his last words – a message for his wife and two young kids – and for the first time, as her husband cried in her arms, Marcie thought everything might be okay.

Slowly, he went back to reading, and Marcie stayed with him every word of the way. Hours later, Bradley said he thought the author was too smart – he wasn't accidentally going to reveal his identity. Jokingly, he told her the test of any great investigator would be to discover who the guy really was. They turned and looked at one another.

Without a word, Marcie went into the next room and got her laptop. From that moment on, discovering my identity became their project, their rehabilitation, the renewal of their love story.

And for me? It was a disaster.

Chapter Nine

NINETEEN WORDS. SITTING IN THE PLAZA ATHÉNÉE, NOT ADMITTING TO anything, I'd asked Bradley what had made him think the author was in Paris, and that's what he told me. Out of a total of three hundred and twenty thousand words in the book, nineteen fucking words had given my secret away.

Seven of them, he said, were an attempt by the author to describe the different colours of decaying blood. I remembered the passage exactly: I had compared the shades to a particular type of tree I had seen change from bright red to brown every fall of my childhood. So what? Checking every detail, Bradley said he called a professor of botany and asked him about the tree. Apparently, they were unique to the Eastern Seaboard and I had unwittingly identified at least the general area where I grew up.

The other twelve words, two hundred pages later, concerned a murder weapon: the stick used to play lacrosse, something which I said I recognized because I had seen students at my high school with them. Bradley told me that if you call the US Lacrosse Association you will learn there are one hundred and twenty-four high schools on the Eastern Seaboard which offer it as a sport. They were getting closer.

By then Marcie had located Garrett's cousin living in New Orleans and learned that the guy's reading extended to four letters: ESPN. The cousin said that Garrett had graduated high school in 1986, and Bradley guessed, from two references in the book, that the real author was from the same era.

He called the one hundred and twenty-four high schools which played lacrosse and, as an NYPD detective, requested the names of

127

all male students who had graduated between 1982 and 1990 – expanding the search, just to be on the safe side. Very soon, he had a long list of names – but one which he felt sure included the identity of the real author.

Working through it would have been overwhelming – except they were mostly private schools and they were always looking for donations to increase their endowment. The best source of money was former students, and there were not many databases better than an alumni association with its hand out. They had extensive records of all their former pupils, and Bradley combed through pages of lawyers and Wall Street bankers, looking for anything out of the ordinary.

He had nothing to show for his trouble until, one night, in the names from a school called Caulfield Academy, he and Marcie came across a person called Scott Murdoch.

'He had graduated high school in '87,' Bradley told me, biting into the world's most expensive eclair. 'He was accepted to Harvard, studied medicine and got a doctorate in psychology. A great career lay ahead of him, but then – nothing. The alumni association had no address, no work history, no news. From the minute he graduated they knew less about him than anyone else. He had simply disappeared. Of everyone we looked at, he was the only one like that.'

He glanced up to see what I was thinking. I didn't speak, I was too preoccupied – it was strange hearing the name Scott Murdoch after so many years. Sometimes – in the worst moments of the secret life, when I was both judge and executioner – I wondered what had happened to that person.

After a long silence, Bradley soldiered on. 'Following weeks of research, Harvard told me that Dr Murdoch took a job at Rand – they knew because he was recruited on campus and they found a record of it. But here was the strange part: Rand was certain it had never heard of him.

'So were the professional associations, licensing boards and all the other organizations we contacted.

'As far as we could tell, when Dr Scott Murdoch left Harvard, he walked off the face of the earth. Where did he go? we asked ourselves.'

A chill which had started at the base of my spine was spreading fast. They had unearthed Scott Murdoch and they knew that he had vanished. That was a fine piece of work, but not half as good, I suspected, as what was coming.

'We had an address for Scott Murdoch from his years at high school,' Bradley continued. 'So we headed out to Greenwich, Connecticut. I spoke to somebody through an intercom, told 'em it was the NYPD, and the gates swung open.'

I looked up at him – wondering what he and Marcie, a couple struggling to get by in Manhattan, must have felt when they drove up the endless drive of my childhood home, past the ornamental lake and the stables, and stopped at what has been described as one of the ten most beautiful houses in the country. Coincidentally, Bradley answered my question. 'We never knew houses like that existed in America,' he said quietly.

The current owner, a well-known corporate raider, told them that both the elderly Murdochs were dead. '"I heard they only had one kid," he said. "No, I have no idea what became of him. Must be loaded, that's all I can say."'

The next day, the two investigators searched the registry of deaths and found the entries for Bill and Grace. 'We even spoke to a few people who'd been at both funerals,' Bradley said. 'They all told us Scott wasn't at either one of 'em.'

It was obvious from his tone he thought that was the strangest part of all, but I had no intention of telling him that I would have done everything possible to attend Bill's funeral – if only I had known about it.

I think Bradley knew he had hit a nerve, but I figured he was a decent man because he didn't pursue it. Instead he told me that, by then, they were confident Scott Murdoch was their man. 'Two days later, we knew for sure.'

Apparently, he and Marcie had sent my social security number – or at least the one I had at Caulfield Academy and Harvard – to Washington for extensive checking. They wanted to know where it was issued, had it ever been replaced and a list of other details which might give a clue to Dr Murdoch's whereabouts. When the answer came back it was alarmingly brief: no such number had ever been issued.

I sat in silence. Some back-office idiot in The Division had screwed up monumentally. I knew instantly what had happened. Years ago when I took on a new identity, ready to go into the field for the first time, a special team had eliminated my old name and history. They closed bank accounts, cancelled credit cards and expunged passports – sanitizing anything that would tie a covert agent back into his former identity. The agent was supposed to have drifted off overseas, like many young people do, and disappeared.

One of the clean-up team – either overzealous or poorly supervised – must have decided it would be even more effective to eliminate my former social security number. They could have told social security I had died, they could have let the number lie fallow, they could have done a hundred different things, but the one thing they should never have done was ask for it to be *eliminated*.

That mistake led to the situation I was now facing – a kid in Connecticut had an identifying number that, according to the government now, had never been issued. You didn't have to be Bradley to work out something strange was going on.

'I figured to have a social security number vanish into a black hole, it had to be done by the CIA or something like that,' the cop said. It confirmed what he had started to suspect: although many details were altered in the book, the cases it dealt with were from the secret world.

An evening which had started out as a pleasant rendezvous with a pliant doctor had turned into a disaster and was rapidly getting worse – the book had led Bradley to Scott Murdoch and convinced him that he was the same person as Jude Garrett. Now he knew what sort of work I did.

But how bad was it really? I asked myself. Very bad, the agent in me replied. I figured this might be my last night in Paris.

With no time to waste, I spoke to him with a quiet ruthlessness. 'Time's short, Lieutenant. Answer me this. So you think Garrett is a spy – but the man could have been anywhere in the world. What made you look in Europe?'

'The school,' he said.

The school? How the hell would Caulfield Academy know I had been stationed in Europe?

'When we visited the campus, some of the faculty remembered him. Weird kid, they said, refused to speak in class but brilliant with languages – especially French and German. If he was working for some black government agency, I figured they wouldn't send him to South America, would they?'

130

'Maybe not,' I answered, 'but there are 740 million people in Europe and you end up in Paris? Come on – someone told you where to find him, didn't they?'

That was every agent's real nightmare. Betrayal, either accidental or deliberate, was what killed most of us. The cop stared, disgusted anyone would think that his abilities were so limited. 'It was a damn lot harder than a tip-off.'

He said that after months of searching for Scott Murdoch, and convinced that the guy was working for an intelligence agency, he realized he had to look for him under a different name. If Murdoch was a US covert agent, how would somebody like that enter a foreign country? He guessed that the best and safest method would be to assume the identity and job of a minor government employee – a junior trade analyst, a commercial attaché or something similar.

Because Bradley's father had worked in Washington, he knew all such appointments were recorded in a variety of obscure government publications. The announcements usually included information like education, age, professional history, zip codes, birth dates and other seemingly unimportant details.

Lying awake one night, he tried to imagine what it would be like to keep assuming new identities, under stress at every border, struggling to keep an endless list of lies straight in your head with never time to think, just to answer.

He knew if it was him, even to have a chance, he would have to populate the fake identities with easily remembered facts – a phone number from childhood, a genuine birth date with the year changed, the real first names of parents.

'You get the drift,' he said as we sipped our coffee, a universe away from the razor-wire at a checkpoint on the Bulgarian border, being questioned by some thug in a uniform, his breath reeking of cigarettes and last night's dinner, turning your documents over in his hand, throwing questions at you out of left field, alert for any hesitation, only too happy to make a hero of himself and call out to the unshaven Vopos that he didn't believe this American or Briton or Canadian or whatever you happened to be masquerading as at that time in that place on that day.

Yeah, I got his drift, but I was too shaken to reply. Armed only with his intelligence, Bradley had divined exactly how covert agents entered a country and how they controlled the endless detail on which their lives might depend. In all honesty, I was finding it hard to remain angry with someone I was coming to admire so much.

Bradley said he discussed his theory with Marcie and they decided to experiment. From all the information they had compiled on Scott Murdoch's early life, they assembled a list of twenty minor facts. While she went to work, he spent the day at his computer downloading the last ten years' editions of one of the publications which recorded government appointments – the weekly Federal Register.

One evening, he and Marcie entered the facts into a search robot and, hoping to find a match for any of them, turned it loose on the register's huge number of announcements.

Thirty-six hours later they had three hits. One was the zip code of Greenwich, Connecticut – used by a man appointed as a US delegate to the International Arts Council in Florence – and which may or may not have meant something. Another concerned a trade attaché who had played squash at Harvard, just like Scott Murdoch, and looked very promising – until they realized they were reading his obituary. The third was someone called Richard Gibson, a US observer at a meeting of the World Meteorological Organization in Geneva. His mini-biography included a birth date the same as Scott Murdoch's and a summary of his education. His high school was given as Caulfield Academy.

'We searched the alumni records, but nobody called Richard Gibson had ever been at Caulfield,' Bradley said quietly.

It was a remarkable achievement. He and Marcie, starting with nothing more than the name of a tree in Connecticut, had found Richard Gibson, the cover I had used to enter Geneva for my chat with Markus Bucher at Richeloud & Cie.

The name Gibson was the proof of principle – now they were certain that the method worked, they went at it full tilt. Three weeks later the system identified a minor official working at the US Treasury who had gone to Romania for a conference. The name the man was using was Peter Campbell.

'I called the Romanian Finance Department and found a guy who had helped organize the event. He had a copy of Peter Campbell's entry visa, including his passport details. A buddy at Homeland Security ran a check and found the same passport had been used to enter France.

'The French government said Campbell hadn't just entered the country, he had applied for residency in Paris. On his application, he said he was the manager of a hedge fund, so Marcie called the Securities and Exchange Commission. Nobody named Peter Campbell had ever held a securities trading licence and the hedge fund didn't exist.'

I watched in silence as Bradley reached into his jacket, took out two pieces of paper and laid them on the table.

The first was a page from an old high-school yearbook showing a photo of the four members of the Caulfield Academy squash team. One teenager stood apart – as if he played with the team but wasn't part of it. His face and name were circled: Scott Murdoch.

The second piece of paper was a passport photograph attached to the French residency application in the name of Peter Campbell. There was no doubt that the two photos were of the same person. Me. I didn't say anything.

'So this is how I figure it,' Bradley said. 'Scott Murdoch went to Caulfield Academy, studied at Harvard and joined a government black programme. He became a covert agent, used a hundred different names, and one of them was Campbell—'

I kept staring down at the yearbook photo, trying to recall the members of the squash team. One guy was called Dexter Corcoran – a big creep; everybody hated him, I remembered that. The others – even bigger assholes – I couldn't even remember who they were. Deliberate suppression, a psychologist would have called it.

'Maybe Dr Murdoch was thrown out of the secret world or his soul just got tired of it – I don't know,' Bradley was saying. 'But he entered France on Campbell's passport, wrote a book to pass on what he knew and published it under the name of Jude Garrett, a dead FBI agent.'

When I still didn't respond, he shrugged. 'And so the two of us end up here.'

Yes, and there was no doubt about it: it was a brilliant piece of work by Bradley and his wife but – like I said – it was their discovery today, somebody else's tomorrow.

There was only one thing left for me to do, so I stood up. It was time to start running.

Chapter Ten

BRADLEY CAUGHT UP WITH ME AT THE DOORS LEADING FROM THE hotel's beautiful courtyard into the grand gallery, moving surprisingly fast, given his limp.

I had said a curt goodbye and headed out, but he managed to grab my arm before I knew he was following. 'I have a favour to ask,' he said. 'That's why Marcie and I came to Paris.'

I shook my head. 'I've got to go,' I said.

'Listen – please . . .' He took a breath, struggling with what he was about to say. But I didn't give him a chance. I pushed his hand away and started to leave.

'No,' he said, in that authoritative voice. I looked around and saw that people at the nearby tables were watching us. I didn't want to create a scene and it gave him a moment.

'Go down deep enough into darkness and nothing's ever the same,' he said quietly. 'Being injured made me think differently – about life, my relationship with Marcie and my work. Especially my work. If there was one positive—'

I'd had enough. 'I'm sorry,' I said, 'the injury must have been terrible and I'm glad you came through okay, but there are things I've got to arrange.' I didn't have time for a sob story or to hear reflections on life from a man I would never see again. I was getting out of Paris, running for cover and maybe my life, and I didn't have time to waste.

'Just one minute – one more,' he said.

After a beat I sighed and nodded – I suppose I owed him some small courtesy for telling me how my former life could be laid bare so effectively. But I didn't bother moving, and everything about my

134

body language told him the Wailing Wall was in Jerusalem and to just get it over with.

'You never asked about how I got my injuries – and I want to thank you. Professionals usually don't, of course. Most of us have been in bad situations so there's not much point in talking about it.'

Yeah, yeah – enough about correct professional conduct. What do you want to ask me? I thought.

'I told you I was trapped in a building. It was a little more than that – I was in the North Tower of the World Trade Center when it went down.'

Chapter Eleven

BRADLEY KEPT TALKING BUT, TO THIS DAY, I HAVE NO IDEA WHAT HE SAID. Somehow we returned to our table, but I was too preoccupied with cursing my stupidity to listen. No wonder he had post-traumatic stress disorder, no wonder he had weeks in intensive care, no wonder he was suffering from survivor guilt, no wonder he needed an impossible investigative project to bring him back from the dead.

Bradley had said he was holding some guy in the dark, listening to him die. Meanwhile, outside their concrete tomb, Lower Manhattan was on fire. And yet I was so smart I had worked out it was a gunshot wound to the hip and another one that took out his lung. If that was the best I could do, it was probably a good thing that I had retired.

I was shaken from my harsh self-appraisal by his voice – he'd taken his cellphone out and was asking me something. 'Mind if I make a call? I want to check in with Marcie.'

I nodded. He waited for her to answer, turned away, and said a few brief words I couldn't hear. As he hung up, he motioned for more coffee and pastries. I hoped he had a credit card with no limit.

'I only mentioned September eleventh,' he said, 'because it's the basis for what I want to ask you.'

'Go on,' I said softly, trying to make up for even thinking the poor mother should have gone to the Wailing Wall.

'As part of my recovery, I finally went back to Ground Zero, to the spot where the North Tower had stood,' he said. 'I looked at it for a long time – God, it was cold – and I finally realized that I was so damned angry I had no hope of ever making a full recovery.

'But I wasn't angry at the hijackers – they were already dead. And it wasn't because of the injuries I had received – c'mon, I was *alive*.

'I was angry about injustice – about the uncaring way the world works. I knew a lot of ordinary people had died that day not because of fire or falling masonry but because of their *compassion*. It was their desperate attempts to save other human beings – often total strangers – that had ended up costing them their own lives.'

He took a sip of coffee, but I knew he didn't want it. He was buying time, trying to work out how best to go on. I just waited. To my mind, he'd earned the right to take as long as he needed.

'Ever think about how many disabled people were working in the Twin Towers that day?' he asked finally.

'No, it never crossed my mind either,' he continued, 'not until just after the planes hit. Of course, if you were in a wheelchair your problems were far worse than anyone's – it wasn't as if you could try to get out by elevator. That's one thing we all know, isn't it? Those signs are always warning us to use the stairs. But say you can't walk? If I ever get trapped in a burning building, Mr Campbell, all I ask is that I can use my legs. Just an even chance to run or die. That's not asking much, is it? An even chance.

'There was a guy – he was working for a financial-services company – who had listened to all the fire drills and knew where his evacuation chair was. Ever seen one of those? It's like an aluminium dining chair with long handles that stick out front and back so people can lift and carry you.

'He was a paraplegic, and I suppose he was proud he'd overcome his disability and had a job. Might have had a wife and kids too, you never know.

'September eleventh was the first day of school, and a lot of people were late. It meant he was alone in his corner of the North Tower when the American Airlines plane hit.

'The impact jumped his wheelchair halfway across the room. Through the window, he saw a blast of flame arcing into the sky and he knew he had to move fast or he was dead.

'He found his evacuation chair, balanced it on his lap and headed for the emergency stairs. On the way he got drenched – the sprinklers came on and with it the lights gave out.

'He got out into the elevator lobby, but there were no windows so it was dark. It was the building-maintenance guys who gave him a chance. A few years back, they had used glow-in-the-dark paint on the emergency doors so that in a disaster people could still find them. God knows how many lives the decision saved that day.

'He propped open the door into Stairway A with his wheelchair and positioned his evacuation chair inside. He wasn't a strong guy, but he transferred himself across.

'Immobilized now, he sits in an emergency stairway inside a burning building and does the only thing he can. He waits.

'There are three emergency staircases in the North Tower. Two are forty-four inches wide, the other is fifty-six inches. It's a big difference – in the wide one two people can pass each other and it's not as tight on the turns. Those turns would be critical for anyone trying to carry what is really a stretcher with a seat. As you can imagine, fate being a bitch, the paraplegic guy is on one of the narrow staircases.

'All through the building people are deciding which way to run – towards the ground or up to the roof for a helicopter rescue. Those that go up die – the door on to the roof is locked to prevent suicides.

'Stairway A is full of dust, smoke, people and water. Like a fast-running stream, it pours down the steps from overworked sprinklers and busted pipes. But the guy in the evacuation chair doesn't call out, doesn't ask for help. He just waits. For a miracle, I guess.'

Bradley paused, thinking about miracles, I suppose. For a moment, as he started speaking again, there was a tremor in his voice, but he managed to control it. 'A long way below, some middle-aged, not very fit, guy hears about the man in the chair and starts yelling. He wants volunteers to go back up with him and help carry him down.

'Three men step forward. Ordinary guys. They follow the middle-aged man up the stairs, pick up an end of the chair each and choose the right way – they don't go up, they carry him down. Through the crush of people, the smoke, the water and those corners that were too fucking tight.'

He paused again. 'They carried him down *for sixty-seven floors*! And you know what they found when they got to the bottom? No way out.

'It had taken them so long that the collapse of the South Tower next door had destabilized its neighbour. Ahead of them was just fallen concrete. Behind them was the fire.'

Bradley shrugged. I remained silent. What was there to say, even if

I could trust my voice not to falter? *Sorrow floats* was all I could think of.

'They turned back, reached a door on to a mezzanine and got in to the lobby. A short time later, everything went to hell when the building crashed down. The wheelchair guy and two of the rescuers somehow made it to safety, but two of those who saved him didn't.' He paused for a moment. 'You know what took their lives, Mr Campbell?'

'Compassion?' I said.

'That's right, like I told you – it wasn't the falling masonry or the fire that killed them. It was their goddamned attempt to help some-body else. That was where my anger came from. Where was the justice in *that*?'

He caught his breath for a moment before saying softly, 'I wasn't sure I wanted to live in a world like that.'

I knew then that Bradley had visited Ground Zero in more ways than one. I pictured him in the snow at dusk, a tiny figure in the acres of emptiness where the Twin Towers had once stood, doing his best to find a reason for living.

Thankfully, Marcie was with him, and he said they held hands as he told her about his despair. 'So what are you going to do about it?' she wanted to know, totally matter-of-fact.

He told me he looked at her in confusion, no idea what she meant. 'Yes, I got it, Ben, you don't want to live in a world like that,' she said. 'Okay. But as people say – are you gonna curse the darkness or light a candle? So let me ask you again: what are you going to do about it?'

That was Marcie – she had become so tough, she wasn't surrendering an inch any more.

'She was right, of course,' Ben continued. 'And we talked about what to do all the way home.

'Because of my injuries, I didn't know much about the 9/11 invest-igation, and as we walked uptown I listened as she told me fifteen of the nineteen hijackers were Saudis, how bin Laden's family were spirited out of the country in the aftermath, that most of the perpet-rators were in America on expired visas and several of 'em had learned to fly planes but hadn't shown any interest in landing them.

'It became clear that, even though the hijackers had made scores of mistakes, they were still better than us – and if anyone doubted it,

139

there were three thousand homicides on my turf that proved it. By the time we reached the Village I realized that an idea was taking shape.

'I worked on it through the night, and the following day – a Monday – I went to New York University and lit my candle.'

He said that, in a large office facing Washington Square, he explained to the college executives that he wanted to start an event that would become as famous in its way as the World Economic Forum in Davos – an annual series of lectures, seminars and master classes for the world's leading investigators. A place where new ideas would be exposed and cutting-edge science displayed. He said it would be moderated by the top experts in their field, crossing all disciplines and agency boundaries.

'I pointed through the window,' Bradley told me, 'to where the Twin Towers had stood. 'Men like that'll come again,' I said, 'and next time they'll be better, smarter, stronger. We have to be too – all of us who are investigators have got one clear objective: we've got to beat them next time.'

'There were eleven people in the room and I figured I'd won over three of 'em, so I told the story of the guy in the wheelchair and I reminded them that they were the closest college to Ground Zero – they had a special responsibility. If they weren't going to stage it, who would?

'By the end, half of 'em were ashamed, a few were in tears and the vote in support was unanimous. Maybe next year I'll run for mayor.' He tried to laugh, but he couldn't find it in his heart.

He said the arrangements for the World Investigative Forum were going better than he had expected, and he rattled off a list of names of those who had agreed to teach or attend.

I nodded, genuinely impressed. He said, 'Yeah, it's all the big ones,' and then looked at me. 'Except one.'

He didn't give me a chance to reply. 'Your book has had a huge effect,' he continued. 'Being over here, you probably don't realize, but there's hardly an A-list profess—'

'That's why you came to Paris,' I said, 'to recruit me?'

'Partly. Of course, I came to finally solve the mystery of Jude Garrett but, now that I have, here's a chance for you to make a contribution. I know we can't say who you really are, so I thought you could be Garrett's long-time researcher. Dr Watson to his Holmes. Someone who helped—'

'Shut up,' I said – something he probably wasn't used to hearing. I was staring at the table and, when I looked up, I spoke low enough to ensure it was for his ears only.

'Right now,' I said, 'I'm gonna break all the rules of my former profession – I'm going to tell you the truth about something. This is probably the only time you'll ever hear it from someone in my line of work, so listen carefully.

'You did a remarkable job in finding me. If I ever did another edition of the book, I would include your work for sure. It was brilliant.'

He sort of shrugged – flattered, I think, really proud, but too modest to express it.

'You found a lot of names, unravelled a lot of cover stories, but you didn't find out anything about what I actually did for my country, did you?'

'That's true,' Bradley replied. 'I'm not sure I wanted to. I figured anything that secret was best left alone.'

'You're right about that. So let me tell you. I arrested people, and those I couldn't arrest I killed. At least three times I arrested them first and then I killed them.'

'Jesus,' he whispered. 'Our country does that?'

'I think homicide detectives and judges have a name for it, don't they? I can tell you, though, those sort of actions can weigh heavily on a man's spirit – especially as he gets older. One thing I can promise you: nobody could ever accuse me of discrimination. I was ecumenical in my work – I took down Catholics and Arabs, Protestants, atheists and at least a few Jews. The only ones who seemed to miss out were the Zoroastrians. Believe me, I would have included them too if I knew exactly who they were. Trouble is, a lot of the people I hurt – their friends and family, mostly – aren't active practitioners of what you and I might call Christian principles, Mr Bradley. Specifically, they don't care too much for the bit about turning the other cheek. You know the Serbs? They're still angry about a battle they lost in 1389. Some people say the Croats and Albanians are worse. To people like that a few decades hunting me wouldn't even count as a weekend. I'm telling you this so that you can understand – I came to Paris to live in anonymity. I've been trying to reach for normal. Tonight hasn't exactly been good news, so I won't be running any workshop, I'm running for my life.'

I got up and held out my hand. 'Goodbye, Mr Bradley.'

He shook hands, and this time made no attempt to stop me. The courtyard had emptied and Bradley cut a forlorn figure sitting alone among the candles as I made my way out.

'Good luck,' I called back. 'The seminar's a great idea, the country needs it.' I turned to continue on my way – and came face to face with a woman.

She smiled: 'I take it from the look on my husband's face the answer was no.' It was Marcie. Bradley must have told her where we were when he phoned her.

'You're right,' I said. 'I can't take part – he knows why.'

'Thank you for giving him the time, though,' she responded quietly. 'For spending so long listening to him.'

There was no resentment or anger – her only concern seemed to be her husband's welfare. I liked her instantly.

Bradley turned away from watching us and tried to attract the waiter's attention, calling for the bill.

'You know, Ben admires you tremendously,' Marcie said. 'I don't suppose he told you, but he read the book three times just for pleasure. He always says he wishes he could have done half the things you wrote about.'

For a moment I glimpsed a different Bradley – a top-flight investigator who believed he had never played in a league big enough to match his talent. More than most people, I knew that professional regret was a terrible thing to live with and, as often happened, I started thinking about two little girls and what I did in Moscow a long time ago.

Marcie had to touch my arm to break me out of the alley of my memories, and I saw she was handing me a business card. 'It's our number in New York. If you ever get a chance, call him – I don't mean now, some time in the future.' She saw my reluctance and smiled. 'A few years would be fine.'

But still I didn't take it. 'He's a good man,' she said seriously. 'The best I've known; better than most people could ever imagine. It would mean a lot to him.'

Of course I knew I would never call but it seemed so unnecessarily hurtful not to take it that I nodded. As I was putting it in my pocket, Bradley turned back, and he and Marcie's eyes met for a moment across the silent courtyard.

In that unguarded second, neither of them aware that I was watching, I saw them stripped of their social armour. They were no longer in Paris, nowhere near a five-star hotel; I saw in their faces they were exactly where they had been before and after the North Tower fell – in love. They weren't kids, it certainly wasn't infatuation, and it was good to know that in a world full of trickery and deceit something like that still existed. Maybe the evening hadn't been a complete bust after all.

The moment passed, Marcie looked back at me and I said goodbye. I went through the tall doors and paused at the lectern where the courtyard's maître d' stood in judgement. He knew me well enough and after I thanked him for his hospitality I asked him to send the trolley over one more time and gave him two hundred euro to cover the bill.

I have no idea why I paid. Just stupid, I guess.

Chapter Twelve

THE AMERICAN AIRLINES FLIGHT ARRIVED IN NEW YORK EARLY IN THE morning – towers of dark clouds hiding the city, rain and wild winds buffeting us all the way down. Two hours outward bound from Paris, the FASTEN SEATBELT sign had come on and, after that, conditions had deteriorated so rapidly that all in-flight service had been suspended. No food, no booze, no sleep. Things could only get better, I reasoned.

I was travelling on a perfect copy of a Canadian diplomatic book which not only explained my seat in First Class but allowed me to avoid any questions from US Immigration. They processed me without delay, I retrieved my luggage and stepped out into the pouring rain. I was home, but I found less comfort in it than I had anticipated. I'd been away so long, it was a country I barely knew.

Eighteen hours had passed since I had left the Bradleys at the Plaza Athénée. Once I realized my cover had been blown I knew what I had to do: the training was unambiguous – run, take shelter wherever you can, try to regroup and then write your will. Maybe not the last part, but that was the tone in which a blown cover was always discussed.

I figured America was my best chance. Not only would it be harder for an enemy to find me among millions of my own, but I knew if I was ever going to be safe I had to erase the fingerprints I had left behind, making it impossible for others to follow the path Ben and Marcie had pioneered.

I had covered the distance between the Plaza Athénée and my apartment in six minutes and, as soon as I walked in, I started to call the airlines. By luck, there was one seat left in First Class on the earliest flight out.

It is strange how the unconscious mind works, though. In the ensuing chaos of grabbing clothes, settling bills and packing my bags, the two letters from Bill and Grace Murdoch's lawyer suddenly floated into my thoughts for no apparent reason. I rummaged through a file of old correspondence, threw them into my carry-on and turned to the only issue which remained: the contents of the safe.

It was impossible to take the three handguns, a hundred thousand dollars in different currencies and eight passports with me, not even in my checked luggage. If the metal detectors or X-rays picked it up – even as an alleged diplomat – I would come under intense scrutiny. Once they discovered it was a fake book, as they surely would, I would have weeks of explaining to do – first about my real identity and then about the other items. All guns, false passports and contact books were supposed to have been surrendered when I left The Division.

Instead I slit open a seam of my mattress, removed some of the filling and taped the tools of my trade inside. Once I was in America, I would call François, the snivelling concierge, and have him arrange for a moving company to transport all my furniture back home. With everything secure, I glued the seam closed, refitted the mattress cover and called a cab to take me to Charles de Gaulle.

Ten hours later I was standing in the rain at Kennedy, telling another cab to head for midtown. On the way I called the Four Seasons, one of those hotels where sheer size guarantees anonymity, and booked a room.

After three days of traipsing between realtors I rented a small loft in NoHo. It wasn't much but it caught the morning light and, on my first day living there, I found the letters from the lawyer and called to make an appointment.

We sat in his expansive office in the late afternoon, looking all the way up Central Park, and what he had described as a small matter concerning Bill's estate managed to change my life for ever.

For several days afterwards I walked the city late into the night, turning the matter over and over in my head, trying – as a psychologist would say – to internalize it. I let my feet carry me wherever they chose, passing crowded bars and restaurants, skirting the long lines outside the hippest clubs and latest movies. Finally, footsore and painfully aware of how little experience I had of what people call a normal life, I began to accept what the lawyer had told me. Only then did I turn to the problem of fingerprints.

My first call was to an FBI supervisor – the woman to whom I had handed over The Division's European files when the agency was closed down. She contacted one of her deputy directors, whispered that I had once been the Rider of the Blue, and I sat down with him a day later in a shabby conference room in a bland downtown tower.

After I had asked to speak to him alone and his two aides had closed the door behind them, I explained that Scott Murdoch's social security number had been eliminated and the danger that presented to me. It took him a moment to master his incredulity but, once he had finished cursing whoever was responsible, he made a phone call and set about having the number restored.

'I'll flag it – I'll make sure if anybody ever inquires about the number, you'll be warned,' he said. 'What else?'

'Someone to go in and alter computer databases. There's a lot of information about me – or the aliases I have used – which has to be lost.'

'Government or private computers?' he asked.

'Both,' I said. 'Everything from the records of an alumni association at a school called Caulfield Academy through to scores of announcements in the Federal Register.'

'No hope,' the deputy director said. 'Databases are *stripper rules* – the Supreme Court says we can look but we can't touch. It'd be illegal for me even to point you towards somebody who could help.'

I pressured him, telling him about the years I'd served my country, explaining why I needed him to break the rules.

He nodded thoughtfully, then something seemed to tip him over the edge and he started ranting. 'Break the rules? You're asking me to get involved in computer hacking – any idea how much that costs the community? This isn't geeks, that was years ago – cyberspace is ram-raiders now. Smash into a site, ignore the damage, steal anything of value—'

I was stunned – I didn't care about the Supreme Court or modern developments in cybercrime, I just wanted to clean up my past. I figured I must have touched a nerve, but that wasn't going to help me get to safety.

He was on a roll, though, and he wasn't stopping. 'There's a level even higher than the rammers,' he continued. 'Call 'em cat burglars – they get in, copy everything and nobody knows they've been there. They're the brilliant ones. Had one guy, stole fifteen million mortgage files. *Fifteen million*! Each one included someone's credit-card details, social security number, bank account, home address. Know what he was gonna do with 'em?'

'Identity theft?' I said, no idea why we were still talking about this.

'Of course. But he wasn't going to use it himself – oh no, that was too much like hard work. He was going to sell 'em to the Russian mafia. A buck each for the first million, he told us, just to get 'em in. Then he was gonna ride the up-elevator until he got ten bucks a file. Figured he'd make a hundred million. For sitting in front of a screen.

'You know how much the average bank robber gets?' he asked, leaning over the table. 'Nine thousand bucks and maybe a bullet. Who do you think found the right business plan?'

I shrugged. I really didn't care.

'The guy is twenty-three, probably the best in the world.'

'How long did he go down for?' I asked, trying to show some interest.

'Not decided. Maybe zip; depends if he keeps cooperating and helps nail the samurai crackers that are doing equally bad stuff. Battleboi was his online handle, so that's what we call him.'

'Battleboy?' I said, not certain I'd heard right.

'Yeah, with an "i". Hispanic fucker. Grew up in Miami but lives nearby now, just off Canal Street, above Walgreens.'

He looked at me and our eyes met. The scales fell away and I realized why he had been telling the story.

'Anyway, enough about my problems – I have to stop before I say something illegal,' he said. 'Anything else I can do?'

'Nothing – you've done more than enough. Thank you,' I said warmly.

He got up and started to lead the way out. Pausing at the door, he turned to face me: 'I'm glad I could help with the social security problem. I know your reputation – a lot of us do – and it's been an honour, a real honour, to meet the Rider of the Blue.'

He said it with such admiration, his handshake strong enough to turn coal to diamonds, it took me aback. He and his aides watched in silence, with respect I suppose you could call it, as I walked towards the elevator. Flattered as I was, I couldn't help thinking of how a man gets burnt out long before his reputation.

Once outside, I got a cab and rode across town, looking out at the passing faces. With the shadows lengthening into night, I once again had a strange feeling of detachment, of being a stranger in my own land. I knew if a person kept travelling down that road they ended up dying to the world – you see them sitting on park benches, in reading rooms at public libraries, alone at railroad stations. Some future, I thought. But there was nothing I could do: the caravan rolls on, the dogs keep barking and it was imperative that I buried my past.

The cab stopped in front of Walgreens; I walked the length of the building and found a doorway tucked into the wall. There was only one intercom and the few words next to it were in Japanese. Great.

Wondering if somehow I had misunderstood the FBI guy, I pressed it anyway.

Chapter Thirteen

A MAN'S GRUFF VOICE ANSWERED IN ENGLISH. I TOLD HIM A MUTUAL friend who worked on the twenty-third floor of a nearby building had suggested I call around. He buzzed me in and I climbed a flight of stairs, noting that someone had worked hard to conceal four closed-circuit cameras monitoring the stairway. Worried about the Russian mafia, I guessed.

I turned into a corridor, and it was only after my eyes had adjusted to the gloom that I saw him: Battleboi was standing straight ahead, just inside the type of steel door which would have made a crack house proud. The most surprising thing about him wasn't his size – though he weighed in at around four hundred pounds – the shocking thing was that he was dressed like a medieval Japanese *daimyo*. A samurai cracker of the first order, I realized.

He was wearing a shockingly expensive silk kimono and traditional Japanese white socks notched for the big toe, his black hair oiled and swept back tight into a topknot. If anybody ever needs a Hispanic sumo wrestler, I know just the guy. He bowed slightly, the minimum of good manners – I guessed he didn't like our friend from the twenty-third floor very much – and stood aside to let me enter.

Admittedly, his feudal lands only extended to four rooms on a side street, but beautiful tatami mats covered the floors, *shoji* screens separated the spaces and on one wall was an antique painted screen of Mount Fuji which I bet would have cost at least twenty thousand of his most expensive files.

Once across the threshold, I only just avoided a social disaster – at the last moment I realized I was supposed to swap my shoes for a pair of guest sandals. While I undid my barbarian boots I asked what I should call him.

He looked blank. 'What do you mean – they didn't tell you?'

'Well, yeah, they told me,' I replied. 'It just doesn't seem right calling somebody Battleboi to their face.'

He shrugged. 'Doesn't worry me, dickhead,' he said, and led the way to a pair of cushions on the floor.

'The deputy director says you're cooperating with him,' I said, as if I were there with The Man's complete authority.

He looked at me with disgust but didn't deny it. 'What do you want?'

As we sat cross-legged I explained about deleting every reference to Scott Murdoch from the databases held by the alumni associations of my former schools. I figured that was as good a place as any to start.

He asked who Murdoch was and I told him I didn't know. 'It's been decided to deep-six his past – that's all we've got to worry about.'

He asked for Murdoch's date of birth, details of the alumni associations and a host of other questions to make sure that he got the right person. After I answered, he adjusted his kimono and said we'd start in a few minutes.

'*Cha, neh?*' he said casually, but I got the subtext: I was supposed to look blank and feel inferior but, honestly, I wasn't in the mood.

I reached into memory, to a summer long ago. I was on a blood-soaked beach, surrounded by a rash of beheadings and scores of samurai committing ritual suicide. In other words, I had spent my vacation reading Shōgun. Out of all those epic pages I remembered a few key phrases – *cha* was tea.

'*Hai, domo,*' I said, hoping my memory hadn't failed me and I was saying 'Yes, thank you' and not 'Go fuck yourself.'

I must have got it right. 'You speak Japanese?' he said, with a mixture of astonishment and respect.

'Oh, just a little,' I said modestly.

He clapped his hands, and one of the screens slid open. A slim Hispanic chick dressed in a red silk kimono entered and bowed, prompting in me a question which has occupied the minds of great philosophers since time immemorial. How come unattractive guys nearly always get the hot women?

She was a couple of years younger than him, with large eyes and a sensuous mouth. On closer inspection, it was clear she had freely adapted the traditional kimono – it was much tighter across her hips and boobs than you would ever see in Tokyo. To facilitate movement, she had slashed it at the back from the hem up to her thigh and as she moved across the room it was obvious from the way the silk rippled and clung to her she didn't have to worry about panty-lines and bra-straps. She wasn't wearing either. The overall effect was both alluring and crazy.

'Tea?' she asked.

I nodded, and Battleboi turned to me. 'This is Rachel-san.' She glanced my way and gave the thinnest of smiles.

Battleboi? *Rachel-san*? *Old Japan above Walgreens*? No matter what the FBI said about his abilities, I didn't hold out much hope. It looked to me like I was dealing with a pair of care-in-the-community cases.

Three hours later, I was forced to revise my opinion drastically. Not only had Lorenzo – at least that's what Rachel had called him once – deleted all references to me from the alumni-association records, he said he could do the same to the far more complex files held by Caulfield Academy and Harvard themselves.

'You can get rid of an entire academic and attendance record?' I asked. 'Make it look like Scott Murdoch never even went to Caulfield or Harvard?'

'Why not?' He laughed. 'There are so many people on the fucking planet now, that's all we are – lines of code on a hard drive. Take the lines away and we don't exist; add to it and we're really somebody. Want a full professorship – tell me the faculty. Need a hundred million large? Wait while I manipulate some binary code. By the way, you can call me God if you like.'

'Thanks, but I've kinda come to like Battleboi.' I smiled.

Late that night, I watched as he consigned the last of Dr Murdoch's academic achievements to the electronic void. 'It's a shame – all that study, and now it's gone,' he said.

There was little I could say, too awash with memories, especially of Bill – he'd driven up in his old Ferrari to Boston, the only person who had come to see me graduate.

Once Lorenzo was satisfied that he hadn't left behind any sign that he had accessed the data, I told him about the next item on my list:

the information that had to be excised from government computers and job announcements.

'How many entries?' he asked.

'A couple of hundred, probably more.'

From the look on his face you would think I had invited him to commit *seppuku*.

'Let me guess – this is urgent, *neh*?' But he didn't wait for a reply; he knew the answer. 'You got copies of these announcements, or do we have to dig 'em out ourselves?'

I hesitated. Ben Bradley and his wife had all the information, but they were the last people I wanted to ask. 'I'd have to think about that,' I replied.

'If we've gotta start from scratch, it could take months. Let me know what you decide,' he said, and started closing down his racks of hard drives.

As he walked me to the door, he'd become relaxed enough for a little small talk. 'I've been studying Japanese for three years – bitch of a language, huh? Where'd you learn it?'

'*Shōgun*,' I said simply and, after he had overcome his shock, I have to say he took it with enormous good grace. The mountain of flesh shook as he laughed at his gullibility and, with his eyes dancing and that great generosity of spirit, I glimpsed what Rachel must have first seen in him.

'Shit,' he said, wiping the tears from his eyes, 'and I've spent the last six hours feeling inadequate – just like being in high school again.'

As I put my boots back on, emboldened by our laughter, he asked: 'What exactly do you do at the FBI?'

'I don't . . . It's complicated. I suppose you could say I used to be a fellow traveller with them, that's all.'

'Are you Scott Murdoch?'

I laughed again. 'You think if I had those qualifications I'd be sitting on my ass talking to you?' I hit just the right tone of bitterness and humour – I'm a helluva good liar when I need to be.

'Whoever you are, you must be tight with the twenty-third floor.'

'Not really. Why?'

'I was hoping you could put a word in with the deputy director, ask him to go easy on the charges.'

'My understanding is, if you keep cooperating, there may not be any charges.'

'Sure,' he laughed bitterly. 'That's why they've set up a special division for cybercrime. It's their brave new world – I figure they'll bleed me for everything I've got then double-cross me. You know, just to make an example.'

I shook my head, telling him he was paranoid, they didn't operate like that. But of course he was right. Some months later they hit him with every charge they could find, then offered him a plea deal that was no deal at all. In the end, unable to afford any more lawyers – he had even sold his treasured Mount Fuji screen – he was forced to sign it. Fifteen years in Leavenworth was what he got.

And he would have languished there, virtually forgotten, except that – in a frightening avalanche of developments – the search for the Saracen hit a desperate pass.

Chapter Fourteen

THE SARACEN ARRIVED AT THE SYRIAN BORDER JUST BEFORE LUNCHTIME, getting off the bus from Beirut with a leather medical bag in one hand, a nondescript suitcase in the other and a remarkable plan in mind.

It was five years since he had graduated, with honours, as a doctor, and those were the missing years, the hungry years. It took me a long time to piece together his movements during that period, but one thing was beyond doubt – by the time he fronted the Syrian immigration officer he had solved the riddle which had occupied all his waking moments. He knew how to attack America.

As a doctor who claimed to be on his way to work in the sprawling refugee camps, he had his Lebanese passport stamped without any difficulty. Skirting the taxi drivers and assorted hustlers, he turned left in the trash-strewn parking lot and found a public bus that would take him into Damascus.

At the city's main bus depot he checked his two bags at the stored-luggage counter, exited a side entrance and started to walk. He was determined to leave as little evidence as possible of his movements and, for that reason, he wouldn't even take a cab.

For over an hour he made his way down dusty roads and through increasingly grim neighbourhoods – Damascus is home to almost two million people, five hundred thousand of whom are impoverished Palestinian refugees.

At last, at the intersection of two freeways, he found what he was looking for. Beneath the elevated roads was a no man's land, a petrified forest of concrete pylons blackened by diesel fumes. The area was decorated by coloured lights, limp flags and quotes from

154

the Qur'an which attested to the proprietors' love of honesty. They were used-car lots.

Here, at the bottom of the automotive food chain, the Saracen chose an ancient Nissan Sunny. While the salesman praised the skill of a man who could see past the rust and find the diamond on the lot, the Saracen paid in cash. He added an extra five Syrian pounds in order to dispense with the transfer papers, and headed off into the dusk. The car burnt more oil than gas but the Saracen didn't care – transport was only the vehicle's secondary purpose. The primary one was accommodation. He knew that even in cheap hotels people remembered too much, and he spent three hours driving the city before he found a secluded area at the back of a supermarket parking lot and took up residence.

Over the weeks that followed he assembled the material he needed for the task ahead and let his personal hygiene go to hell. He started wearing clothes that were increasingly grimy and, while this might have offended his own standards, he had little choice – his plan depended on him being a perfect version of a homeless man. Finally, after one long surveillance trip to the battlefield, he was ready.

On the outskirts of Damascus, a four-storey glass and concrete building stood almost alone. The sign out front said THE SYRIAN INSTITUTE FOR ADVANCED MEDICINE, but its exact purpose was unclear – nobody could remember the last time the country's leaders sought medical treatment anywhere except in the private clinics of London or Paris.

Because Western intelligence was worried that the building was being used for nuclear or biological research, one of eight US satellites which patrolled the Middle East kept the institute under constant surveillance. It photographed faces through windows, recorded all deliveries and monitored the chemical signature of emissions but, unfortunately, didn't take any photos of the immediate surroundings. As a result, there have never been any images of the homeless man who, according to a later report by the Syrian secret police, arrived in bits and pieces.

Early one Friday evening a security guard, passing through a garden at the end of the building, saw that an old tarp had been strung between two palms, colonizing under its shade a stand-pipe used to water the plants. A few days later a tiny cooking ring, a salvaged gas bottle and a battered cool-box also took up residence.

But still the scores of people who walked by on their way from the parking lot to the front of the institute hadn't actually seen the homesteader – not even after a well-worn copy of the Qur'an in an antique binding and two threadbare blankets appeared.

By then it was too late to do anything about it – Ramadan, the ninth month in the Islamic calendar and by far its most sacred, had started. The holy book on the blanket acted as a mute reminder to everyone that beggars, travellers and the poor have to be provided for under Islam. What True Believer would have a homeless man removed during Ramadan?

It was only then, protected by his religion, that the Saracen appeared, abandoning the Nissan in the supermarket parking lot, emerging on foot out of the dry scrub, settling in under the tarp as if he already belonged, which I'm sure was his plan. Bearded and ragged, wearing the anonymous long tunic and headdress of the countless thousands of Palestinian refugees, he cracked open the stand-pipe for some drinking water and started reading the Qur'an.

At the ordained times he filled his saucepan, performed the washing that precedes the five daily prayers and pointed his mat at what was either Mecca or the security guards' toilet, depending, I suppose, on your view of the world.

Nobody complained about his presence, and he was over the first hurdle. The next morning he started work – washing the windows of parked cars, sweeping up trash and generally acting as guardian of al-Abah Parking Lot Number Three. Like most refugees, he never asked for money but he did place a saucer on the walkway – just in case someone felt a sudden urge to fulfil their charitable obligations.

By any measure, it was brilliant. Several weeks later, after the mutilated body of one of the institute's most senior officers was found, the police and Syrian spooks flooded the surrounding buildings, finally targeting the homeless man and trying to build a photofit. Everybody they spoke to was in agreement: five foot eleven, say, about one-eighty, heavily bearded and then – well, pretty much nothing.

In the secret world, a disguise and life story that have been invented to hide someone's real identity is called a legend. The ragged guardian of al-Abah Parking Lot Number Three – a Saudi Arabian, a graduate in medicine from Beirut University, a hero of the

Afghan War – had created a legend as a Palestinian refugee so effective it had rendered him virtually invisible. For a professional to have done it would have been a great achievement; for an amateur without resources or training, it was remarkable.

A week after his arrival, the Saracen established the habit during the hottest part of the day of crouching with his Qur'an in a grove of palms near the building's front door, taking advantage of a cool breeze from a faulty air-conditioning conduit. While people smiled at his ingenuity, the truth was he didn't give a damn about the heat – he had lived in the outer ring of hell during blazing summers in Afghanistan, so fall in Damascus didn't worry him. No, the area under the conduit allowed him to see, through a plate-glass wall, the exact security procedures which applied to everyone entering the building. Once he was convinced he understood them, he set about weighing – both figuratively and literally – the people who worked at the place.

The deputy director of the institute was always among the last to leave. In his fifties, his name was Bashar Tlass, a relative of one of Syria's ruling elite, a former prominent member of the country's secret police and – I'm sorry to say – an unmitigated piece of scum.

But neither his high position, his qualifications as a chemical engineer nor his love of the slow garrotte during his career with the secret police had any bearing on why he was chosen. It would have been a great surprise to everybody, Tlass included, that the reason he was killed was because he weighed one-hundred-and-eighty pounds – or at least as near as the doctor, sitting among the palm trees, could tell.

Having identified his target, all the Saracen had to do now was wait. Throughout the Muslim world, Ramadan's thirty days of fasting, prayer and sexual abstinence end with an explosion of feasting, gifts and hospitality called Eid al-Fitr. The evening before the festival of Eid, almost everyone leaves work early to get ready for the ritual of dawn prayer, followed by a day of huge banquets.

Damascus was no different and, by 4 p.m., banks and offices were locked, shops were closed and the roads increasingly deserted. Tlass walked out the front door of the institute and heard the security guards at their console behind him activate the electronic locks. It meant the building was completely empty, and he knew – as did everyone else – that as soon as he was out of sight the guards would

157

arm the rest of the system and quietly head home to make their own preparations for the festivities.

Years ago, the director had tried to get the guards to work over Eid but had run into so much opposition, including from the employees' mosques, that everybody had immediately reverted to the prior practice of contrived ignorance. And anyway, nobody knew better than Tlass that the country was a police state – who would be foolish enough to try to break into a government building?

He got the answer to that question a few minutes later as he walked down a path between the gardens, heading for his car. The few surrounding buildings and parking lots were deserted, so he was mildly alarmed when he turned a corner and, momentarily enclosed by hedges and palms, heard a rustle of movement behind him. He swung round, then almost smiled as he realized it was just the stupid Palestinian, the man who kept insisting on washing the windshield of his SUV even though he had never dropped so much as a piastre into the tin saucer for his trouble.

Now the beggar thought he had him cornered, bowing all the time as he came closer, holding out his saucer for money, murmuring the traditional greeting '*Eid Mubarak*'. Tlass gave the greeting back, as tradition demanded, but that was all he was giving – he brushed the saucer aside and turned to continue down the path.

The Saracen's arm exploded across the tiny distance between them and, in one blurred moment, it locked tight around Tlass's neck, startling and choking him in equal measure.

The deputy director's first thought, born out of fury, was that there was no way he was letting him have any money, the refugee would have to kill him to get it. The second was how could a beggar, living on nothing more than garbage, be so fucking strong?

Already Tlass was gasping for breath and, as he dredged up from memory the unarmed combat move to counteract a choke hold, desperately trying to implement it, he felt a searing pain rip into the base of his neck. Blinded by the swelling heat of it, he would have screamed if he could have found the air. He knew immediately it wasn't a knife – that would have slashed his throat and sent the warmth of his own blood streaming down his chest. The thought had barely formulated itself when a ball of fire burst into the muscle of his neck and started bullying into his bloodstream.

The pain staggered him, but he knew now what it was. A syringe, with the plunger being driven down hard. Given the circumstances, it was an impressive piece of reasoning – entirely accurate too. Confused and terrified, Tlass knew he had to yell for help quickly, but whatever chemical was flooding his body suddenly meant the muscles of his mouth wouldn't say the words that were screaming in his head.

The chemical flood hit his limbs – he realized with a wild rage that nothing could stop it now – and he saw his car keys fall from the jelly that used to be his hand. His attacker's fingers flashed out and caught them in mid-air and it seemed to tell Tlass, more than any other thing, that he was in the hands of a master.

Chapter Fifteen

TLASS BUCKLED AT THE KNEES. THE SARACEN CAUGHT HIM BEFORE HE fell and half carried him towards his vehicle – a black American SUV, the same one whose windshield he had washed so many times. Halfway there, he stopped.

He smacked Tlass hard across the face and saw the prisoner's eyes spark with pain and fury.

During the planning, one of his major concerns had been that intravenous sedatives recovered from a body might contain a chemical marker that would allow them to be traced to a batch number. Such a number would lead to the regional hospital he had been working at in Lebanon, and it wouldn't take diligent investigators – a team from the Syrian secret police, for example – very long to start working through the list of employees and find that he was supposedly on vacation during the relevant period.

There were, however, enough donkeys hauling carts in Beirut for the city to have developed a large and unregulated market in veterinary products. As a result, it was an ampoule of an untraceable horse tranquilliser that was ripping through Tlass's body now, and the Saracen only hoped he had calculated the dose correctly – enough to inhibit any muscle control but not so much that it caused the victim to pass out. If Tlass's eyes glazed over, the man would be useless – whatever else happened, the prisoner had to stay alert.

Whack! The Saracen hit him across the face again for good measure, then resumed hauling him towards the SUV. Just as he had learned by observing Tlass while he washed the windshield, he used the button on the key to unlock the doors, opened the rear one and bundled the prisoner inside.

The interior of the vehicle was like a cave. All through the searingly hot countries that extend from the Mediterranean down past the Arabian Gulf, there is one unfailing way to work out who has *wasta* and who doesn't. The slang word for it is *makhfee*, and it means tint – as in the coating you put on car windows to keep the sun out. Restricted by law to 15 per cent, the more *wasta* you have, the more *makhfee* you can get away with.

Tlass had a great deal of *wasta* indeed, and the windows of his Cadillac were tinted to an intimidating 80 per cent – making the cabin almost completely private, ideal for what was about to take place within. The Saracen swung in behind his prisoner, slammed the door, climbed into the driver's seat, put the key in the ignition and turned the engine on. He wasn't going anywhere, but he needed the air-conditioning blowing as cold as possible. He flicked the switch that operated the rear seats and watched the bench lie down until Tlass was flopping about on a flat platform like a tuna on the deck.

Working to the choreography he had planned for weeks, he pulled rolls of thick electrical tape out of his pocket and scrambled on to the platform. Tlass watched in mute terror as the master grabbed his wrists, taping them to grab handles on the doors, spreading him out face up, just as Tlass had once done to a naked woman he had taken great pleasure in 'interrogating' until she became too exhausted to scream and he had grown bored and garrotted her.

The master then taped Tlass's feet, thighs and chest to the platform, making sure he couldn't move. What happened next, however, was the strangest thing of all – the master taped Tlass's forehead and chin tight to the headrest, holding his head as rigid as if it were in a workshop clamp. Tlass tried to speak, wanting to know what the hell he was doing – after all, it wasn't as if you could use your head to escape. But no words would come from his drooling mouth.

With quiet satisfaction, the Saracen saw him trying to speak, watched his terrified eyes dart about: he knew for certain that he had got the dose of sedative right. Certain that Tlass, spreadeagled, was incapable of movement, the Saracen opened the rear door, checked the surrounding area was clear, slid out and ran to his encampment.

In one crashing move he pulled the tarpaulin down from its anchors and piled his gas ring and other possessions on to it, leaving nothing behind to help the forensic analysts. He tied the tarp into a bundle, flung it over his shoulder and picked up his old cool-box, carefully packed by him earlier in the day, as if he were preparing for some bizarre picnic.

The last thing that he had stowed in it was what had caused him the most anxiety – a large bag of ice. For weeks he had mulled over the problem of how to acquire it but when the answer came it was disarmingly simple – he asked the friendliest of the security guards, the same one who had told him about the practice of the guards disappearing for Eid, to help him keep some drinks cool for his own simple celebration of the festival.

'Would it be possible to have some ice from the refrigerator in the staff kitchen?' he had asked the guard, and the good Muslim had duly delivered it a few hours ago.

'*Eid Mubarak*,' they had said to each other as the Saracen stashed it in the cool-box – on top of two small plastic containers, some food scraps and several bottles of cordial, which were really just a blind. The real contents of the cool-box – the rest of the specialist equipment he needed – were hidden in a concealed compartment at the bottom.

With the cool-box under his arm and the bundle on his back, he ran to the SUV. Tlass heard a rear door open, and his wild eyes swivelled to see the Palestinian load his possessions on board, swing himself in behind and slam the door shut. Ominously, the master reached forward and hit a switch, operating the central-locking system, sealing them inside.

The Saracen reached down and emptied the deputy director's pockets, setting aside his cellphone, opening up his wallet, ignoring the money and credit cards and finding exactly what he needed – Tlass's security key card.

Feeling more confident by the minute, he knelt down, carefully positioned himself close to Tlass's head and took the lid off the cool-box. He unloaded the food and released the catch that allowed him to remove the false bottom. From out of the hidden compartment he took a heavy plastic pouch rolled and tied with a cord and laid it down beside him. Next he began to fill the two plastic containers with ice – and there was something in the calm and orderly way he did all these things that Tlass recognized.

The fucker's a doctor! he said in his head, it being the only place he could speak right then. His eyes darted around frantically: the startling insight had made him more frightened than he would have ever thought possible.

What sort of sick fuck with all that study behind him – and a good career ahead as long as he kept his nose clean – would sweep up a parking lot? he wanted to know.

Somebody with a plan was the answer he immediately gave himself. And, in his experience, men with plans were usually fanatics, not the sort of people you could reason with – even if you could get your muscles to say the words you so desperately needed to.

The doctor took a pair of clear plastic gloves out of the secret compartment. They terrified Tlass in some even deeper place. *What are they for?!* he tried to scream.

As if in answer, the doctor spoke to him. In different circumstances, people had complimented him on his bedside manner. 'I'm going to take your eyes,' he said.

Chapter Sixteen

WHAT DID HE SAY?! TLASS SCREAMED TO HIMSELF. WHAT DID THE *fucktard say about my eyes?!*

The Saracen watched as panic spiked in the two dark orbs – in truth, he had no interest in explaining to Tlass what he was doing, but he needed the rush of fear and adrenaline to dilate the pupils and engorge the organs with blood. The more blood in them, the longer the eyes would retain the appearance of life after they had been removed.

'I don't know you,' the Saracen told him, 'so it's nothing personal.' But of course the Saracen did know him – he knew him in the way that he was always imagining the men who had led his father into a cell in Jeddah so many years ago.

Nothing personal?! Tlass yelled inside his head. He was right, the guy was a fanatic – that's what the fanatics always said. He tried to muster every hidden reserve, every ounce of energy, willing his muscles to act, trying to buck himself free. The Saracen watched a tiny ripple of movement shimmy down the man's body. It was sad, really.

Tlass's eyes filled with tears – of fear, of frustration, of hate. The Saracen reached down, picked up the plastic pouch and untied the cord, allowing it to unroll. It was a surgical kit, and he was happy for Tlass to see it. Another spike of adrenaline and fear, he hoped. Out of one of the pockets he drew an instrument – a four-inch steel scalpel.

Tlass stared at it – a fucking scalpel? He had to do something! Anything! There was the spike, the Saracen noted with satisfaction. 'I think the right eye first,' he said.

By marshalling every sinew in his diminished body, Tlass managed to speak. 'No,' he gasped in a strangled whisper.

If the Saracen heard him, he made no sign. 'Removing the eyes is a relatively easy procedure,' he said calmly, wrapping his fingers around the handle of the instrument

Tlass started climbing a black wall of terror and despair as he watched the scalpel slide towards what many people regard as the most vulnerable part of their body. The blade loomed huge in his right eye as the doctor's thumb and forefinger kept his eyelids apart.

With one deft movement, the Saracen started cutting the lids away. 'Technically speaking, it's called an enucleation,' he said helpfully.

Tlass thought he was going to vomit – he wanted to vomit; anything that might stop the madman.

Blood ran down, half obscuring the sight in his right eye. He could feel the lunatic's thumb working between the bridge of his nose and the side of the eyeball. The Saracen was pushing the eyeball aside, finding the orbital muscles that held it in its socket, slicing the sinew.

Tlass was drowning under cresting waves of pain. But still he could see out of the eye that was being operated on. Ha, it wasn't going to work! The Saracen located the last anchor: the optic nerve and the blood supply which coiled around it. Then he cut it.

Half of Tlass's visible universe instantly disappeared, sucked into a black hole. The eyeball popped out.

The Saracen had to work fast now, tying off the blood supply to the eyeball with a ligature, trying to keep as much fluid as possible trapped within it, plunging the ball into the ice to slow its deterioration. It was the same reason the air-conditioning was blasting. He turned his attention to the left eye – as fast as he had been before, he worked at twice the speed now.

Tlass lost the other half of the universe in a few seconds, the pain so intense he was barely conscious enough to realize that he was totally blind now.

The Saracen opened the locks of the Cadillac, hit the parking lot running and sprinted for the front doors of the institute. In his hand he carried Tlass's two eyes, firmly nestled in their separate containers of ice.

But they were only the first part of the jigsaw – the next problem was the question of weight.

Chapter Seventeen

THE ENCRYPTED KEY CARD WHICH THE SARACEN HAD TAKEN FROM Tlass's wallet did its job instantly, and the front doors of the institute slid open.

Although the security desk was unmanned and the building deserted, the metal detectors were still operating. He stepped through without any difficulty – hours ago, he had taken off his watch and emptied his pockets. He strode six more paces and stopped.

In front of him was a narrow corridor – the only way forward and blocked at the far end by an automatic steel door. Between him and that, the floor consisted of a long metal panel.

Through the plate-glass window, while supposedly enjoying the broken air-conditioning conduit, he had unlocked one of the building's many security secrets: the floor was a hidden scale. Before stepping on to the metal you had to swipe your encrypted card through another reader. A computer then married the name on the card to a database which checked the weight of the individual.

If it hadn't been for that precaution, the Saracen could have grabbed Tlass by the scruff of the neck and walked through behind him. But two men of one-eighty standing on the floor would have shut the building down.

Still wearing the surgical gloves, the Saracen ran Tlass's card through the reader. He stepped on to the scale with no idea what tolerance for error the system operated on, half expecting shutters to fall from the ceiling, trapping him.

Nothing happened – his guess that Tlass had been the same weight as him was right. Now for the last hurdle: a retina scanner. He put the ice containers on a ledge and took an eye in each hand, noting which was left and which was right. Holding a slippery ball in his thumb and forefinger, he jammed them hard against his own eyelids, deep into the bony socket. Unable to see, with only hope and prayer to sustain him, he turned to face the scanner in the wall.

He knew his gloved hands were no problem – the system was designed to ignore plastic or wire-framed glasses, contact lenses, make-up and anything else. It was interested in only one thing – the blood vessels in the membrane at the back of the eye, each pattern unique among the six billion individuals on earth, even those born as identical twins.

The manufacturer claimed the technology could not be beaten and, while it was true that the retinas of dead people decayed very fast, the real question was whether eyes taken from a living person and fewer than three minutes old would have enough blood left in them to convince the software that this was Bashar Tlass standing in front of it. The Saracen had no way of knowing the answer, and probably nobody else did either – it wasn't as if someone had ever volunteered to find out.

As a result of his observations, the Saracen knew that most people faced the scanner for about two seconds, so he forced himself to count to three and turned away. He dropped the eyes in the ice and turned towards the metal door at the far end. Again he started counting – the longest he had seen anybody wait for it to open was to a count of four.

He reached a slow six and knew he would have to run. His abort strategy was to smash through the plate-glass window on the assumption that the key card and doors would have been frozen by the system. Once outside, he would drive the SUV to an area near a garbage dump which he had already reconnoitred, terminate Tlass and walk twenty miles to the bus station. He would then take the first bus to the border and hope he could get across before they closed it.

At the count of eight he was turning away, his planning curdling into self-loathing, fear hammering urgency into every movement, when the steel door slid open. He was in.

The reason for the delay would remain a mystery – perhaps subtle changes to the eyes had confused the system and forced it to use a more complex algorithm, or maybe it had to rouse itself from a stand-by mode – but he didn't care. He strode along the corridor, through the steel door and into a large atrium, all the time anticipating a sense of elation at his achievement. Instead, his hopes plunged.

Because of high walls, razor wire and surveillance cameras, he had never seen anything of the institute except the front facade. Without thinking about it, he had predicated the size of the building on that information. As it turned out, that was a serious error – perhaps a fatal one. Now inside the atrium, he could see that the place was huge.

Only Allah knew how long it would take him to find what he was looking for in a place so large, while out in the world, at some stage, probably very soon, Tlass would be missed. When his friends or family couldn't reach him in the office or on his cellphone, somebody undoubtedly would drive into the parking lot to look for him.

How long that gave him, the Saracen couldn't tell – maybe they were already on their way – but he knew now that time was short and the job was huge. As a Turkish proverb says, it was going to be like digging a well with a needle.

Unarmed, totally at the non-existent mercy of anybody who came, he sprinted down the first of five broad corridors and jagged right when he reached an intersection. He stopped in mid-stride: armoured glass and an unmanned security desk blocked the way.

Two guards, sharing a weekend tea with him just after he had arrived, had mentioned a special security measure somewhere deep in the building which, based on their description of it, told him that it included a backscatter X-ray. Impossible to smuggle anything past because it rendered you as good as naked, the X-ray could also check a huge range of body measurements – the length of the right femur, the distance between the nose and an ear lobe. Unlike with a retina scanner, you had to be who you claimed you were.

No advanced medical facility in the world boasted armoured glass and backscatter X-rays, and the Saracen knew that behind them undoubtedly lay all the most horrific things which were really being researched at the institute. He never thought he would be able to access the inner bastion, and he didn't care. If he was right, he didn't need to.

He turned and returned fast to the intersection – a foreign man in a foreign land, desperately trying to find something rare but, strangely, completely *harmless* – just a box of small bottles used to protect the people who worked there.

As he plunged into the next maze of corridors and offices, through pools of deep shadow, past looming shapes that could have concealed any manner of threat, lights along the baseboards and in the hallways suddenly burst to life. He stopped and wheeled on the spot.

Somebody had entered the building and activated the lights! He listened with every cell of his being for a clue to their position. From far away he heard a phone ring, a tap dripping, an exterior shutter banging in the wind. Its beat was almost identical to the rhythm of his pounding heart. He listened for footsteps, the squeak of clothing, the clink of an unholstered weapon. Nothing.

Then he realized, and fear went back into its cave – the lights were on a timer and night must have fallen outside.

Chapter Eighteen

ALL ACROSS THE INSTITUTE'S DESERTED PARKING LOT, SODIUM STREET lights hissed to life. Tlass couldn't see their yellow glow, he would never see anything again, but he heard them and his heart soared: the arrival of night meant the clock was running out for the filthy Palestinian.

A monstrous red pain had been spearing deeper into his forehead, and he could still feel blood weeping from his eye sockets, but the sedative was wearing off and although the pain increased exponentially so did Tlass's energy.

He was a strong man, a fit man, but what was that worth if the spirit was broken? The thing which was parachuting him down, the secret knowledge sustaining him, was the fact that he had already been running late when he left the building. Now night had come, he knew the alarm would be raised in earnest.

His wife and four adult children, waiting impatiently at his eldest daughter's house for a poolside gathering, would have already tried phoning all the numbers they could think of. One of his two barrel-chested sons – both making a name for themselves in their father's old outfit – would even have slipped inside and made a call to their father's mistress, ready to berate her for keeping him from his family obligations.

Unable to locate him and with darkness falling, the two boys, he was certain, were getting into one of their cars to trace his route, worried he had been involved in a wreck. As members of the secret police, both of them were always armed, and now all Tlass had to do was stay alive and help them find him as fast as possible. Despite his injuries, despite the pain and nausea, he knew how to do it.

Working his face from side to side, loosening the bands of electrical tape binding his head, he gradually ripped his hair, flesh and beard free of it. It was an agonizing task but if he could get his head loose he could use his teeth to rip at the tape around his chest and liberate his arms.

Earlier, he had felt the fanatic pull the cellphone from his pocket and then seen him grab the car handset out of its cradle. Moments later he had heard both phones being smashed to pieces on the asphalt. But the idiot had left the engine running in case he needed a fast exit and, knowing nothing about luxury cars, didn't realize it meant the hands-free phone system was working. If Tlass could get his arms loose and lunge forward to the driver's seat he didn't need his eyes to find the button on the steering wheel which activated the car phone. And he certainly didn't need the handset.

The last call he'd made had been to his eldest son's cellphone that morning, and hitting the steering wheel button would redial it automatically. All Tlass had to do was speak loud enough for the microphone above his head to pick it up. 'Office. Car park,' he whispered, practising.

His son would recognize his voice, and Allah help the Palestinian when the two boys arrived. The woman's cries for mercy just before he first entered her – and then her pleas for a quick death many hours later – would sound like soft poetry compared with the song his sons and their colleagues would make the fucker sing. He was still repeating the two words – louder, stronger – when he finally tore his head and chin free of the tape. He gasped with the pain and would have cried for real if he'd had any tear ducts left.

He sat for a moment to recover from the agony, and anybody cupping their hands against the glass and looking through the Cadillac's smoked windows at that moment would have seen a man with empty eye sockets, clumps of hair missing from his head and strips of flesh ripped from his face.

Had they continued to watch, they would have seen him lean forward to tear at the tape around his chest with his teeth and – given his wild determination – they would have said it would be only a matter of minutes before he was free.

Chapter Nineteen

A TINY SALVAGE DIVER WORKED TIRELESSLY ON THE WRECK OF A Spanish galleon as five beautiful clownfish swam through the bubbles pouring from his helmet.

The wall-sized aquarium's eerie glow lit the waiting room of the institute's lavish executive wing, casting a shimmering shadow of the Saracen across the opposite wall. As he moved through the silent space – close to despair, not sure which corridor or alcove to explore next – he hesitated at the sight of the brilliantly coloured fish.

He hadn't seen them for twenty years or more, but he knew what they were. '*Amphiprion ocellaris*,' he said, surprised he could remember their biological name after so much time. Of all tropical fish, they had been his father's favourites and, often, when he worked at the weekend, he had taken his young son into his sea-front office and planted him among the huge research tanks. The largest was filled with sea anemones, the beautiful but treacherous flowers of the marine world.

'Look at the clownfish,' his father would say. 'They're the only fish in the world which the anemone's tentacles don't poison and kill. Why? That's what I'm trying to find out.'

Now, so many years later, alone in a secret weapons establishment, the irony of it wasn't lost on the Saracen. Just like his father, he too was consumed by the search for something which gave protection against a deadly pathogen.

He would have liked to linger with the fish a moment longer, try to remember more of what innocence was like, but there was no time. He started to turn away – and stared straight down a dark passage that he hadn't even noticed. At the far end was a door, and somehow he knew it was the room he was searching for, even before he saw the Red Crescent fixed to the wall.

The sign, the Islamic version of the Red Cross, indicated it was the building's first-aid and medical centre. He had been told of its existence by a former employee – a nurse he had worked with at the hospital in Lebanon – but it was his father's clownfish which had guided him to it and he took that as a sign from Allah.

The door into the first-aid clinic wasn't locked, and he moved inside fast, heading through the treatment areas until he found the supply rooms at the back. The purpose of the centre was to handle any on-site illness and to conduct physicals for new employees – hence it had ECGs, treadmills, defibrillators, respirators and enough other equipment to make any hospital proud.

In the centre of it all was a drug dispensary, and the Saracen entered it with the easy familiarity of someone with years of experience in hospitals. The wall behind a counter was taken up with boxes of pharmaceuticals and racks of surgical supplies. Another wall housed locked cabinets faced with steel grilles which the Saracen knew contained the Class A drugs: narcotics, hallucinogens, amphetamines and various opiates used as anaesthetics.

He ignored everything – at the back was a smaller room, and in it he saw the row of refrigerated cabinets which had brought him to this godforsaken country and forced him to live like a dog in a parking lot.

In a surge of hope and anxiety, he moved along the glass-fronted refrigerators. His expert eye registered pouches of blood products, vials of temperature-sensitive drugs and, as in hospitals everywhere, the food and drink of the staff. But nothing of what he needed. With each step his desperation grew – maybe every scrap of gossip he had heard, every assumption he had made, had added up to nothing more than a grand delusion. Like a fool, he had believed what he wanted to believe . . .

Then he looked in the last cabinet and bowed his head in a silent prayer. On a rack were eight cardboard containers holding rows of tiny glass bottles, and printed across the front of them was a complex technical description that told the Saracen they were exactly what he was looking for.

He opened the unlocked cabinet and removed six of the vials from a half-empty box. The clear fluid they held was the direct result of an experiment in a small English village two hundred years earlier, and it occurred to the Saracen, wrapping them in a cloth and putting them in his pocket, how much he and the clownfish would soon have in common. He too would be able to move through a beautiful but hostile environment totally protected from the deadly poison it contained. It can't be overstated what it meant to him: in the desperate months during which I tried to find him, and even as my journey escalated into a horrifying race, I only ever discovered two scraps of paper that pointed to his identity. On each of them was written the word 'clownfish'.

With the vials safely in his pocket, he turned to the drug register lying on a counter and accounted for the bottles by carefully altering several entries going back three years to make sure nobody ever found out that any of them were missing. He put the register back, headed to the corridor, closed the door and, thanks to his plastic gloves, left the clinic with no forensic trace of ever having entered it. He ran past the aquarium and into the long, silent corridors which led to the front doors.

He estimated that in two more minutes he would be home free. There was only one problem – the prisoner in the SUV was about to beat him across the line.

Chapter Twenty

SNAP! THE ELECTRICAL TAPE BINDING TLASS'S CHEST BROKE AS HIS TEETH ripped through the final strand. Bleeding from a fractured incisor but barely noticing, he tore his arms loose of the remnants of the tape and sat upright.

With blood returning into his hands, making him gasp with pain, he threw himself forward and started to free his legs and ankles – falling back every time he lost his balance, pitching himself forward to continue, already imagining his hands on the steering wheel pressing the phone button, followed by the sound of his boys hitting their siren and minutes later screeching into the parking lot.

It wasn't salvation he was starting to taste on his lips. It was revenge. He ripped his first leg free and used his booted foot to smash and kick the last of the tape away. Groping in his perpetual darkness, he scrambled to his knees. He was free.

Two hundred yards distant, the glass doors of the institute slid open and the Saracen, having retrieved the plastic containers with the eyes, sprinted out of the building and on to the path leading to the parking lot. In twenty seconds he would be in the Cadillac. With its engine running, he would throw it into gear and be heading out of the parking lot by the time the institute's electronic locks and computers had resealed the building.

Already he could see the alien glow of the sodium lights ahead. He swerved left across garden beds and saved himself a few seconds, bursting on to the asphalt and seeing the black SUV dead in front of him. The vehicle was rocking on its suspension. Somebody inside was moving . . .

Tlass – a man possessed – was scrambling fast over the flattened seats towards the steering wheel, making the suspension shudder. He crashed into the back of the driver's seat with his shoulder, recovered and somehow tumbled between the front seats. He put one hand out to break his fall and, by good fortune, grabbed the wheel.

The Saracen dropped the plastic containers holding the eyes and pounded towards the vehicle. He had no idea what Tlass was trying to do – hit the accelerator and crash the car, smash the gear stick and disable it, lock him out – but he figured all the danger came from the driver's seat.

In those few frantic paces, he made a decision on which both his and Tlass's lives would turn. More importantly, it would determine the fate of his entire plan. A better man – a man with a wife and children and dreams for them, no matter how modest, a man who had seen less of killing and more of love, a decent man in other words – would have wasted time by opening the door. But the Saracen did exactly what I or any other real killer would have done – he decided to punch his fist straight at the tinted glass of the driver's window.

With his arm cocked, he had a moment of panic: what if the glass was armoured? It would have been, too, had Tlass still been in the secret police, but the Cadillac – big and flashy – was his private vehicle. Anyway, the Saracen had no time to reconsider . . .

Tlass had already hauled himself into the driver's seat, found the phone button and pressed it. The system was beeping fast as it dialled the number. Help was a few digits away. Three, two . . .

A white Toyota Land Cruiser – siren blaring, red-and-blue lights flashing behind its radiator grille, no cars on the holiday eve to impede its progress – barrelled down a freeway skirting the edge of the old oasis, heading straight for the institute. Inside, Tlass's two buzz-cut sons scanned the road ahead for fire trucks, ambulances, a broken guard rail or any other sign of a wreck.

The phone on the Toyota's dashboard rang and the brothers looked instantly at the caller ID on the screen. It was their father at last!

The Saracen's fist appeared in a shower of glass, taking Tlass across the bridge of the nose. It was a wild punch, the sort any Afghan *muj* would have been proud of – smashing the man's septum, spraying blood, sending him half sprawling into the passenger seat, drowning him in pain.

The taller of Tlass's boys, riding shotgun in the Toyota, pulled the phone out of its cradle and spoke one urgent word: 'Dad!' There was no response.

His father was crumpled in a whimpering, blinded mess across the centre console of his SUV. But he was still conscious: he could hear his son calling to him with escalating urgency. Like a deathbed convert, all Tlass had to do was find the strength to say the few words which would bring salvation. In this case: 'Office. Parking lot.'

Confused – with no idea how the phone could be working without a handset – the Saracen heard an unknown voice yelling for his father and saw Tlass rise on to his shoulder, his mouth starting to move to reply. For the second time in as many moments, the Saracen made an inspired decision – he ignored Tlass and his own confusion, reached out, turned the ignition key in the lock and yanked it out, switching off the engine, killing the electrical system and disconnecting the phone.

Tlass, unable to see what was happening, tried to beat back the pain flooding out from his splintered nose. All he knew was that he had not had a chance to say the words which would save him, and he started to haul himself up.

In the speeding Toyota the two men heard the connection fail, and the taller one immediately redialled their father's car. They still had no idea where he might be, so his brother continued to charge towards the institute.

Tlass was up on one elbow when he heard the passenger door of the SUV being thrown open. He felt the Saracen's powerful hands grab him by the lapels and haul him across the console into a sitting position in the passenger seat. He tried to resist, but it was to no effect.

The Saracen extended the passenger seatbelt and kept looping it tight around the prisoner's bloodied neck and arms, holding the exhausted man upright in the seat, binding him tight. He snapped the buckle of the seatbelt home, checked that Tlass was completely immobilized and scrambled out of the vehicle. He ran across the parking lot, scooped up the plastic containers with the eyes and sprinted back to the vehicle.

As soon as he turned the engine on the phone began ringing again. The Saracen would have liked to switch it off but, knowing nothing about the system, decided not to touch it. He backed the SUV out hard and made sure the wheels crushed the glass from the broken window. He would have preferred to pick it up, leaving no evidence at all, but he wasn't willing to spend the time. First, the disembodied voice and now the drumbeat of the phone told him the hounds were loose and, while he had no idea how close they were, the delay in searching the building and his shredded nerves were screaming that he needed to change his plan fast.

He swung the wheel and hit the gas, fishtailing out on to the access road. Instead of joining the freeway and heading towards a long-term parking lot at the airport, where he had intended to execute Tlass and abandon the car among thousands of others, he decided to trigger the fall-back plan and ditch the vehicle as fast as possible.

It was for that reason, and that reason alone, that everything went to hell for the rest of us. He kept going around the access road and sped out the back of the complex. Tlass's sons, pistols in their laps, came off the freeway and through the front entrance and missed seeing the black Cadillac by no more than ten seconds.

Ten seconds – nothing really – but it was enough. It meant, not for the first time, that the lives of countless people would turn on a tiny event. If only the bomb hadn't been placed under an oak table in the Führer's conference room. If only the Tsar of Russia hadn't executed Lenin's brother. *If only* – but it has been my unfortunate experience that you can't rely on divine intervention, and that fate favours the bad as often as the good.

The men in the Toyota arrived those few seconds too late and didn't see their father's car, which meant they didn't give chase, they didn't capture the Saracen and nobody ever discovered that six small glass vials were missing.

Chapter Twenty-one

EVEN BEFORE THE SONS HAD FINISHED SEARCHING THE CLUSTER OF parking lots, the Saracen had found the road he wanted. He turned on to it, switched off the Cadillac's headlights and was swallowed up by the long, pot-holed blacktop.

On one side was a municipal dump, and the Saracen made sure that he travelled slowly enough not to raise the flocks of seagulls that attended it or scare the wild dogs constantly roaming its perimeter. On the other side was a wasteland of scrub, its only landmarks the hulks of abandoned vehicles and a canal overgrown with reeds and full of fetid water.

The Saracen slowed at a chain-link fence, nosed the Cadillac through a gate hanging on its hinges and pulled to a stop in a deserted cul-de-sac which serviced what some optimistic realtor had once called an industrial estate. Fronting the road was a shamble of buildings forming an auto-repair yard which was probably a chop-shop, a low-slung warehouse selling reconditioned washing machines and five converted garages used to package lamb delicacies. With food, sometimes it's better not to know.

Thanks to the pain, the seatbelt around his neck that was as tight as any garrotte, the fever and a galloping infection from the un-sterilized scalpel, Tlass had plunged into a twisted and psychedelic unconsciousness. The Saracen opened the door, untied the belt and pulled him out into the rotting silence. The warm air Tlass dragged into his lungs allowed a splinter of reality to enter his fevered world and he managed to hold himself upright, tottering.

'You do good work with the garrotte – one professional to another,' he said through his damaged larynx. With which he collapsed to the broken asphalt and started whispering in weird fragments about God and the heavenly light show.

The Saracen knew where it came from: like people who have had arms amputated and can still feel their fingers, a person who had lost the use of their eyes often saw displays of spectacular lights. The Saracen left Tlass to his private aurora borealis, gathered the things he needed from the back of the SUV then dragged the prisoner by his collar to a garbage skip full of refuse from the meat works.

He saw that, among the reeds and stunted bushes, primeval shapes were moving – little more than pools of greater darkness – and he knew the wild dogs were coming. The meat works was a favourite feeding ground among the stronger ones, and now they could smell sweat and blood they knew that an animal, a large animal, was in trouble.

The Saracen propped Tlass up in the garbage skip. He took the dead eyes out of the icy containers, jammed them back in their sockets and deftly wound a piece of ragged fabric around the man's head. It looked like a dirty blindfold, but it's real function was to hold the eyes tight in place.

As Tlass felt a sudden coldness on his fiery flesh, the kaleidoscope of lights faded and, in his madness, he thought they were ministering to his wounds. Sure he had wanted to kill them, but now, like most people subjected to torture, he felt an outpouring of gratitude for even the smallest kindness. 'Thank you for the bandage,' he whispered.

At the thought of the crisp, white dressing his spirits rose and he turned his attention to the suffocating stench of blood, vomit and defecation. He knew from his experience in the secret police exactly where he was – he had been dragged back down into the cells. Pretty soon somebody would come, strip off his clothes and hose him down. The jailers never touched the shit-covered clients themselves, so it would be a pair of female prisoners.

Usually the guards made the women do it naked and, when they were close enough, Tlass had to remember to try to get a feel – the guards always laughed at that. He heard a sharp click of metal. It made him pause; the sound was familiar, like a . . . like . . . ? Then it came to him through his fever and he laughed – it was just like a pistol being cocked. That was ridiculous – nobody was ever shot in the cells, it was far too messy. And why treat his wounds if they were going to execute him? No, it had to be something else.

'Who's there? Somebody there?' he called out in what he thought was a strong but friendly tone.

The only person present – sighting down the barrel of an Afghan-era pistol he had taken out of the secret compartment in the bottom of the cool-box – heard him croak the question, the words badly slurred and barely audible, and ignored it. The Saracen was standing six feet away, just far enough, he estimated, not to be hit by bone and blood, aiming at the blindfold covering Tlass's left eye.

Trying to hear, certain there was someone else in the cell, Tlass held himself perfectly still. The Saracen knew there would never be a better moment. Truly he was blessed. He squeezed the trigger.

Crack! Tlass felt the pain of . . . and then felt nothing more. A spray of bright blood, bone chips and brain exited the back of his head just as the Saracen sensed a scurry of movement behind and wheeled fast. It was the wild dogs running for cover.

The Saracen turned back, aimed and fired again, this time hitting the dead man on the right side of the blindfold, destroying – with luck – any evidence that the eyes had been surgically removed. His hope was that the investigators would think Tlass himself, having forgotten something, had returned to his office and was robbed and abducted only after he left the institute a second time. That way it wouldn't even occur to them that anything had been stolen from inside the building.

Obviously, the less they knew the better and, to that end, he was pleased when he heard the dogs returning, loping through the darkness, anxious to eat their fill of the evidence. By then he had parked the Cadillac in the darkest corner at the back of the auto-repair yard, confident that any casual observer would think it was just another vehicle waiting to get chopped. From the back of the SUV, still wearing the plastic gloves, he removed everything that might be of any interest to the forensic experts.

Carrying the cool-box and the rest of his possessions, he set off into the wasteland. He moved quickly and kept the pistol cocked in one hand – just in case some of the dogs decided they preferred their human on the hoof.

At the municipal dump he smashed the cool-box to pieces and scattered everything else from his camp among the piles of refuse. He knew that, two hours after dawn, they would have already been retrieved by scavengers and recycled into the lawless refugee camps.

Apart from the syringe, a cardboard ticket and some loose change, all he had left in the world was a pistol, his father's Qur'an and the six glass vials. In his view, those tiny bottles made him the wealthiest person on earth.

Chapter Twenty-two

THE SARACEN WALKED FOR HOURS, GUIDED ONLY BY THE WAN starlight. After leaving the dump, he cut across the scrub and followed the canal until he finally found a rickety wooden structure which passed as a bridge.

He crossed it and trudged for miles along the reeds before seeing what he needed: the rusting chassis of an old four-wheel drive half submerged in the rank and muddy water.

He filled the plastic containers with the syringe, Tlass's wallet and other effects, weighed them down with pebbles and threw them into the middle of the canal.

It was with terrible regret that he raised the pistol and drew his arm back – the weapon had been with him longer than any of his other possessions except his father's Qur'an, but it was the one thing that tied him inextricably to Tlass's murder and he felt he had no other option. He threw the gun well and it landed in the water next to the rusting chassis. If they came down the canal, dragging a metal detector through the water, they would just think it was part of the vehicle.

Quickening his pace now, he turned towards the distant glow of lights that indicated Damascus.

Four hours later, footsore and filthy, he handed over the cardboard ticket at the luggage counter of the bus depot and retrieved his suitcase and medical bag. He undid the coded lock-strap securing the suitcase, took out a slim roll of bills, paid for the storage and gave an attendant one pound for the use of a small wash cubicle.

It was two hours until the first bus left for the Lebanese border and on from there to Beirut, and he used the time to trim his beard and to shower until his flesh was almost scrubbed raw. From out of the suitcase he put on his cheap Western suit, shirt and tie and placed two of the stolen glass vials, their identifying labels pulled off, in his medical bag, hidden in plain sight among other bottles and medicines. By the time he emerged carrying his passport and luggage, he looked exactly like what he would claim to be if anyone questioned him: a devout Lebanese doctor who, having worked in the refugee camps, was now on his way home.

He had put the filthy clothes that had helped create his Palestinian legend into a plastic bag and, as he walked to the rattletrap bus, he threw it in a large charity bin. The only other stop he made was to drop the trash from a meal he had bought of pitta bread, fruit and tea into a garbage bucket and, though it would have seemed entirely innocuous to any onlooker, it was significant.

Shortly after 4 a.m. he took his seat at the back of the bus – almost exactly an hour before Tlass's two sons, long delayed by having to search in ever-widening circles but attracted by the sound of wild dogs fighting, found the body of their father.

Despite the ungodly hour and the fact that it was one of Islam's most important holidays, their membership of the secret police meant they knew exactly who to call. The news was conveyed to the highest circles of government and very soon the airwaves were full of phone conversations and text messages on supposedly secure communications networks.

Echelon sucked them all up.

Echelon never tires, never sleeps. It patrols the vast emptiness of space without needing air or food or comfort, it works as a silent thief at the world's fibre-optic hubs and it commands countless radomes – the clusters of giant golf balls – on military bases across the globe. In total, it listens to every electronic communication on earth, a vast satellite and computer network so secret that its existence has never been acknowledged by the five English-speaking nations which established it during the Cold War.

The billions of bytes of data it collects every nanosecond are downloaded to a collection of super-computers at NSA headquarters at Fort Meade, Maryland, where highly classified software utilizes key words, patterns of phrases and even – by several secret accounts – speech recognition, to pull out any fragment worthy of further investigation.

And there were plenty of fragments in Damascus that night. Echelon listened as one of Tlass's sons, grief-stricken, phoned his sister and told her there would be the mother-of-all crackdowns on the dissidents and enemies-of-the-state likely to have been responsible. 'Allah help them and their families,' he said.

The US intelligence analysts, assessing the intercepts, came to a similar conclusion – Tlass was a man with such a reputation for cruelty there must have been a long line of people only too happy to have fed him to the dogs. A revenge killing in a failed Arab state is of little interest to US security, so the event was quickly dismissed.

That was a terrible mistake – and so was the fact that Syrian state security, contending with the early hour and the holiday weekend, didn't close the border immediately.

Chapter Twenty-three

THE OLD BUS SPUTTERED AND BELCHED THROUGH THE NIGHT, CRAWLING through the extensive roadworks on Syria Route One and – having negotiated them – was forced to stop only for *fajr*, the dawn prayer.

When it finally reached the border, surly immigration and customs officers examined the Saracen's documents, looked him up and down and only treated him with anything approaching respect when they realized he was a doctor. Had they bothered to search him, though, they certainly would not have found four of the glass vials – their contents were hidden in a place far beyond their reach. They were in his bloodstream.

The last thing he had done before leaving the wash cubicle in Damascus was to take a special two-pronged needle from his medical bag, dip it into the contents of the vials and prick and scratch the solution into the skin of his upper arm until it was bleeding freely. He knew the dose was four times greater than normal, but he intended to do everything to give himself as wide a margin of safety as possible. He bandaged his arm, put his shirt on and crushed the empty vials beyond recognition. That was what he had dropped in the garbage bucket along with the rubbish from his meal.

As he was being processed at the border, he was already, as he had anticipated, coming down with a fever, prickling sweats and a searing headache. He just hoped he could make it to a cheap hotel in Beirut before it got too bad. The symptoms he was feeling were almost identical to those experienced by a young boy in the English village two hundred years ago, the first person to undergo a procedure thought up by a local doctor called Edward Jenner. He was the scientist who pioneered vaccination.

For that is exactly what the Saracen had done – he had risked his life, broken into a weapons lab and killed a man he had never met in order to steal a vaccine. And here was the truly strange thing – in the washroom he had vaccinated himself against a disease which no longer existed, that presented a threat to no one, which had been totally eradicated from the planet just over thirty years ago.

Prior to that, however, it was the most catastrophic disease known to man, responsible for more human death than any other cause including war, killing over two million people annually as late as the 1960s – the equivalent of a new Holocaust every three years. The disease was known to science as *Variola vera* and to everyone else as smallpox.

The complete eradication of the virus was one of the reasons why so few places on earth even had the vaccine – apart from research facilities and secret weapons labs, it was no longer needed. Not unless – of course – like the Saracen, you were planning to synthesize the virus and were worried that one tiny mistake in that almost-impossible process would infect and kill you. For that reason he had sought out a state-of-the-art vaccine, one which no doubt had been thoroughly tested and proven effective, and which would now allow him to make as many errors as he needed.

Not all vaccinations 'take', and not all vaccinations work the same way in different people. In order to try to compensate for that and – as I said – offer himself as much protection as humanly possible, he had quadrupled the dose. No wonder he was feeling sick but, for the Saracen, the fever was good news: it meant that his body was being challenged and his immune system was mobilizing to fight the invader. The vaccine had 'taken'.

While an immigration officer was waiting for the computer screen in front of him to assess the Saracen's passport, a phone in the nearby office started ringing. By the time someone had answered it and relayed the order to close the border, the officer had waved the Saracen through and into Lebanon – a man with a false name, a real passport and a growing immunity against the world's most deadly pathogen.

Chapter Twenty-four

I CAN'T DENY THAT THE FEELING HAD BEEN GROWING ON ME FOR DAYS. I am not in the bag for fate or destiny, but not long after I had left Battleboi and was walking home through Manhattan's darkened streets, I had an overwhelming sense that some force of nature was coming to meet me.

I entered my small loft with its chronic undertow of loneliness and began to search through the bags that I had brought from Paris. No sooner had I said goodbye to Battleboi than I decided that the only way to deal with the hundreds of government announcements that were threatening my life was to ask Ben and Marcie to hand over what they had found. Frankly, I didn't think that either the hacker or myself would have the time or the skill to duplicate their work. At last I found what I was looking for: the jacket I had been wearing at the Plaza Athénée the night I met them. Inside the pocket was the business card Marcie had given me and which I had taken with such reluctance.

It was too late to phone them that night but early the following evening I put a call through. It was Marcie who picked up.

'This is Peter Campbell,' I said quietly. 'We met in Paris.'

'It didn't take you long to call,' she said, overcoming her surprise. 'Nice to hear from you. Where are you?'

'In New York for a while,' I told her, cautious as ever. 'I was wondering if you and your husband might be willing to let me have the research material on Scott Murdoch that he told me about.'

'Ben's not at home . . . but sure, I don't see why not.'

'Thank you,' I said, relieved. 'Can I come and get it?'

'Not tonight – I'm meeting him for a movie, and tomorrow

we have dinner with friends. What about Friday, around seven?'

A delay of two days was a lot longer than I wanted, but I wasn't in a position to object. I thanked her, made a note of the address and hung up. Being a highly experienced professional, a man skilled in the tradecraft of the clandestine world, a person who – as I think I mentioned – had been trained to survive in situations where others might die, it would be reasonable to assume that I would see an ambush coming. But not me – the high-school teacher raised in Queens played me off a break and I didn't even suspect it until I stepped into the apartment.

The lights were low, 'Hey Jude' was playing on the stereo, the room was filled with the smell of home cooking and a table was set for three: I had been invited for dinner. I guessed the whole evening would be devoted to pressuring me to change my mind about Bradley's seminar, but there was no way out, not when people have spent months compiling a dossier on your life and you're a beggar for their files.

'You shouldn't have gone to so much trouble,' I said, doing my best imitation of a smile.

'The least we could do,' Marcie replied, 'considering all the trouble we have caused you.'

Bradley appeared, hand extended, asking me what I'd like to drink. As it happened, I was in one of my periodic 'cease and desist' phases: I had decided New York would be a fresh start, a perfect opportunity to try to get clean, and it wouldn't be just lip service this time – I'd even got the schedule of the local Narcotics Anonymous meetings. Being an addictive personality, however, I couldn't do anything in moderation – not even sobriety – so I had also sworn off all alcohol. This was going to be a long evening.

Bradley returned with my Evian. While Marcie went to check on dinner, Bradley took a shot of his liquor and guided me towards the white room at the end of the universe. Except it wasn't that any more – the kilim was on the floor, the drapes rehung and the only evidence of the desperate drama that had played out within its walls was the physiotherapy equipment in the corner.

Dozens of file boxes were standing next to it. Bradley pointed and smiled. 'This is your life, Mr Murdoch.'

As I bent and glanced through them, I was shocked at the extent of their research – the boxes were filled with computer print-outs, data-storage disks and copies of everything from Caulfield Academy yearbooks to the annual reports of UN agencies. I took a folder at random – it was their master list of the aliases I had used – and the names brought a rush of memories.

Bradley watched as I turned the pages. 'Marcie and I have been talking,' he said. 'Do you mind if we call you Scott?'

'What's wrong with Peter Campbell?' I asked.

'I just thought . . . at least between ourselves, it'd be easier to use your real name. That's how we've always thought of you.'

I looked at him. 'Trouble is, Ben, Scott Murdoch's not my real name either.'

Bradley stared, trying to compute it. Was I lying, trying one last gambit to throw them off the track they had followed so assiduously, or was this my poor attempt at humour?

I indicated the list of aliases. 'It's like all the rest. Just another false identity – a different time, a different place, a different name.' I shrugged. 'It's been my life.'

'But . . . you were Scott Murdoch at school . . . just a kid . . . That was years before the secret world,' he said, even more perplexed.

'I know. Nobody would have chosen what happened – but that's the way it turned out.'

I watched the investigator's mind race – the child's name that was no real name at all, my absence from either of the funerals, the fact I didn't seem to have inherited any of the Murdochs' wealth. He looked at me and realized: I was adopted, I wasn't Bill and Grace's natural child at all.

I smiled at him, one of those smiles that has no humour in at all. 'I'm glad you didn't try to go back any further than Scott Murdoch. Everything before Greenwich is mine, Ben – it's not for anyone else to see.'

There was no doubt he understood it was a warning. The three rooms on the wrong side of 8-Mile, the woman's features which had faded in my memory with every year, the real name she gave me – they were the very core of me, the only things I owned that were indisputably mine.

'Who cares about a name?' Bradley said at last, smiling. 'Pete's fine.'

Marcie called out, and the evening headed down a track I would never have expected. For a start, she was a superb cook, and if

190

excellent food doesn't put you in a good mood you've probably been *supersized* one time too many. In addition, they didn't mention the seminar and I had to admit that signing me up didn't appear to be on their minds. I started to relax, and the idea occurred to me that they knew so much about my background that, for them at least, it was like having dinner with an old friend.

Bradley had scores of questions about the book and the cases it dealt with and Marcie took obvious delight in watching her clever husband try to pin me down on details I was forbidden to talk about. During one particularly torrid session she laughed and said she had never seen him so pissed off in her life. I looked at her and couldn't resist joining in.

When someone makes you laugh, when they've invited you into their home and tried their hardest to make you welcome, when they've given you boxes of material that just might save your life, when they've hauled them down into the street and helped you load them into a cab, when you're standing under a street light in Manhattan and all that's waiting for you is an apartment so cold you call it Camp NoHo, when you're lost in your own country and the world's promises haven't amounted to very much, when you have the inescapable sense you are waiting for some future which might not be very pleasant, when they smile and shake your hand and thank you for coming and say they have no way of contacting you, you've got a hard choice to make.

I paused, all my tradecraft and experience telling me to write down a fake phone number and drive away with their research. What did I need them for now? But I thought of the warmth with which they had greeted me, Bradley's joy in the music he had chosen for the evening and, I'm sorry, I couldn't do it. I took out my cellphone, pulled its number up on the screen and watched Marcie write it down.

In the weeks that followed they would call, and we would catch a movie or go to a club and listen to the old blues-men that Bradley loved, jam the night away – always just the three of us. Thank God they never tried to set me up on a date or went off piste and mentioned Bradley's seminar.

During that time Bradley underwent a battery of physical and psychological tests and, much to his relief, was passed fit to return to work. He still limped a little and, because of that, he was on lighter duties than normal but sometimes, usually late at night, he would get hold of me and ask if I wanted to drop by a crime scene where he thought there was some element which might interest me. On one particular evening he left a message while I was attending one of my regular twelve-step meetings. By this stage, I had switched my patronage to AA – as Tolstoy might have said, drug addicts are all alike, whereas every alcoholic is crazy in his own way. This led to far more interesting meetings, and I had decided that, if you were going to spend your life on the wagon, you might as well be entertained.

The meeting – held in a decaying church hall on the Upper West Side – came to an end, and I left my fellow outcasts milling about the foyer. I walked east, enjoying the unseasonably warm evening, and it wasn't until I saw the Gothic towers of the Dakota that I thought to check my phone for messages. I saw Bradley's number and figured he must have turned up another one of his rock 'n' roll ghosts, so I was surprised when I clicked play and heard him, for the first time since we had met, ask for help.

'I've got a murder case that's very strange,' he said on the message. Explaining nothing more than the fact that it concerned a young woman, he then gave me the address of a sleazy hotel where he wanted me to meet him.

It was called the Eastside Inn.

Chapter Twenty-five

THE WOMAN RESPONSIBLE FOR THE KILLING IN ROOM 89 HAD USED MY knowledge, my experience, my *brain* to commit the murder, and that made me – at least by my count – an accessory to the crime.

I wasn't going to let something like that ride, so once the coroner's assistants had zipped up the bag containing Eleanor's body I walked out of the room – angrier than I had been for a long time – and headed down the stairs.

I found what I was looking for – the door to the manager's office – in a small alcove near the reception desk. Alvarez, or one of the other young cops, had locked it when they left, so I stepped back and smashed the sole of my shoe hard into the wood just below the handle.

The sound of splintering wood brought a uniformed cop. 'I'm with Bradley,' I said, with an air of complete authority. He shrugged, I finished kicking and stepped into the scumbag's lair – rank with the smell of body odour and cigarettes.

Amid the squalor, a tall metal filing cabinet had been pivoted aside, revealing a hidden space in the floor. Set into the cavity was a heavy-duty safe. The burglar, being an expert, must have known exactly where to look and had already worked the combination and opened the safe door.

Among the cash and documents were computer print-outs of the hotel's accounts, a couple of cheap handguns and scores of tiny colour-coded sachets. I bent down and held a couple of them up to the light: the green ones contained coke; crack rocks were in black; tina – appropriately, I suppose – was in ice-blue. Other colours meant other product – just like in any good warehouse. The scumbag had missed his calling – he should have been running Wal-Mart.

Staring at the stash, I would be a liar to say I wasn't tempted, especially by the Percodan in the yellow sachets. I reached out to see how many there were – you know, just out of curiosity. Strangely, I found my hand pausing before it touched them and then slowly moving aside. Who says that twelve-step programmes are a waste of time?

I lifted the computer sheets and other documents out of the safe and sat down at the battered desk. That was where Bradley found me thirty minutes later.

'What are you doing?' he asked, leaning against the door frame, so tired his face looked like an unmade bed.

'Helping out.'

Surprise made him perk up. 'I thought you were retired.'

'I am, but call me old-fashioned – somebody uses a book I wrote to murder a young woman and it pisses me off.'

He walked in and lowered himself gingerly into a chair. He'd told me that he figured his leg would probably trouble him for the rest of his life, more so when he was tired.

'You should go home and get some rest,' I said. 'Your team finished yet?'

'Half an hour; they're packing up now. Find anything?' he asked, indicating the documents littering the desk.

'Yeah.' I pushed a folder towards him. 'That's the file for Room 89. Your detectives glanced through and they were right – she moved in over a year ago and paid in advance. But the details are a total mess, not even any specific dates. I figure it's kept deliberately confusing—'

'In case the tax people run an audit?' Bradley interrupted.

'Exactly. So I went to the bottom of the drug safe. Down there I found the computer print-outs of the real accounts. They're perfect, every cent accounted for.

'They have to be – they're kept for the wise guys who own the joint, so you can imagine what they'd do if the scumbag tried to rip 'em off.'

I pointed at one of the items I had marked. 'You can see it here – the killer moved in on September eleventh.'

The unmade bed shifted into furrows of surprise. He leaned forward, looking closely at the entry. 'You sure?'

'Yeah, a time stamp indicates she checked in around five o'clock – about six hours after the Twin Towers fell.

'You were still in surgery, Ben, but I guess – like me – you've read the stories about that day. The whole area was a war zone, ash raining down, people running for their lives, everybody thinking even worse was to come.

'For hours before she checked in there was so much smoke in the air it would have seemed like night, cars stood abandoned in the road, everything was silent except for the sirens.

'I remember reading that a priest was walking through the streets calling for people to make their last confession. It was end-of-days stuff and, according to the computer print-outs, even the pimps and whores at the Eastside Inn knew it. The night before, ninety rooms were occupied. The night of the eleventh there were six. The whole joint – the whole *neighbourhood* – had moved out.

'But our killer makes her way to this place. She must have walked, picking her way through the wreckage. Imagine it, Ben – filthy from falling dust, probably unrecognizable, her shoes almost burnt through from the hot ash and maybe a bandana across her face to try to block the acrid fumes.

'Finally, she pushes through the front door and takes off the bandana – she doesn't start with the disguises until the morning, and that means the scumbag's the only one who knows what she looks like, if he can remember. Not that we'll find him, anyway.

'She tells him she wants a room. Like I said, she doesn't belong here, but already she knows she's gonna stay – the print-outs show she paid for two months in advance.'

I pushed the account details aside. 'Why, Ben?' I asked. 'Why did she do all that? There was nowhere else to stay, this was the only hotel in New York? She virtually walked over hot coals because she liked it so much?'

He pulled a Camel out of a pack left lying on the desk. Sometimes he just liked to hold one. I made a mental note to talk to him about the value of twelve-step programmes.

'You got all that from some columns of numbers?' he asked, impressed. I didn't say anything.

'I don't know why she did it,' he said at last. 'I've got no idea.'

195

'Nor do I,' I replied, 'but something happened. Something happened that day which changed everything for her.'

He shrugged. 'Sure – it did for a lot of people.'

'Yeah, but none of them checked into the Eastside Inn. She was determined to hide her identity and live off the grid. I think she made her mind up that day – she was going to murder someone. Checking into the Eastside Inn was the start of her preparations.'

The cop looked at me, and he knew it was a bad development: a person who had spent so much time planning a crime was far less likely to have made a mistake. His shoulders sagged as he thought of the long investigation ahead, and that, combined with the ache in his leg, was enough to make him look like he was about to crawl into the unmade bed.

I glanced up and saw someone pass the door. 'Petersen!' I yelled. 'You got a cruiser outside?'

'I can get one,' he countered.

'Throw your boss over your shoulder,' I said. 'Take him home.'

Bradley objected, but I cut him off. 'You said yourself they were packing up – nobody's gonna solve it tonight.'

Petersen had never heard Bradley ordered around before, and he couldn't hide his delight. He bent as if to follow my instruction but his boss pushed him away, telling him there was always a vacancy on the sewer patrol.

Petersen smiled at me. 'How about you – you need a ride?'

'I'm fine, I can make my own way home,' I said. It wasn't true, though – I wasn't going home, I was going to where I figured the killer had started her own journey on that terrible day. I was going to Ground Zero.

Chapter Twenty-six

I'VE BEEN TO MANY SACRED PLACES, BUT NONE SO STRANGE AS THE sixteen acres of Ground Zero. It was a construction site.

In the time which had elapsed between the attack on the Twin Towers and Eleanor's murder, the whole area had been turned into a massive pit with almost two million tons of rubble being removed to prepare it for rebuilding.

Eventually new towers would rise from the scar and on them would be plaques carrying the names of the dead until, in less time than most of us would credit, people would hurry past, barely remembering they were on hallowed ground.

But on this quiet Sunday the sight of that raw expanse was one of the most moving things I had ever seen: the very desolation of the place was a more eloquent statement of what had been lost than any grand memorial. Staring out at it from the viewing platform, I realized that the attack was imprinted so deeply on our minds that the building site formed a blank canvas, an empty screen on which we projected our own worst memories.

With breaking heart I saw the brilliant blue sky again and the burning buildings, I watched people wave from jagged windows for help that would never come, I saw the wounded run down dust-filled streets, I heard the crashing thunder of the collapsing buildings and I saw rescue workers write their names on their arms in case they were pulled dead from the rubble. I smelt it and lived it and tried to say some quiet words to the twenty-seven hundred souls that would never leave that place. Twenty-seven hundred people – over a thousand of whose bodies were never found.

It was a wonder that any were recovered. At fifteen hundred

degrees Fahrenheit, human bone turns to ash in three hours. Fires in the World Trade Center reached two thousand degrees and weren't extinguished for a hundred *days*.

It says in the Qur'an that the taking of a single life destroys a universe, and there was the evidence in front of me – twenty-seven hundred universes shattered in a few moments. Universes of family, of children, of friends.

With the rising sun bringing light but little warmth, I left the platform and started to walk. I didn't know what I was looking for – inspiration probably – but I had no doubt that the killer had started her journey to the Eastside Inn from very close to the path I was following.

There was no other way to get to the hotel – just after the first plane hit, the Port Authority closed all bridges and tunnels into Manhattan; buses, subways and roads across the island either stopped running or were gridlocked; a hundred minutes later the mayor ordered the evacuation of the entire area south of Canal Street. To make it to the hotel, she must have already been inside the exclusion zone.

As I walked, I tried to imagine what she was doing in this part of town at what I figured was around 9 a.m. on a Tuesday morning – work perhaps, a tourist heading for the observation deck on top of the South Tower, a delivery-truck driver, a criminal with a meeting at one of the law firms? Why was she here? I kept asking. If I found the answer, I knew I would be halfway home.

And while it was true I had no idea what I was looking for, I certainly wasn't prepared for what I found.

Lost in speculation about her movements on that day, it took me a minute to notice the small shrines which had appeared on either side of the pathway. For the thousands of people who had never had the bodies of their loved ones returned, Ground Zero seemed to stand in lieu of a cemetery. In the weeks following the attack they had come and stood in silence – to think, to remember, to try to understand. But as the months rolled by and they visited on anniversaries and birthdays, Thanksgiving and other holidays, it was only natural that they left flowers, cards and small mementos. Those shrines were now dotted along the fences and pathways.

Almost beside me were several soft toys left by three young kids for their dead father. Pinned on the wire was a photo of them, and I stopped and looked – the eldest must have been about seven. In the picture they were letting go of balloons so that, according to their hand-penned note, their dad could catch them in heaven.

I walked on and saw several shrines created by elderly parents for their lost children, I read poems from men whose hearts were breaking and looked at photo-collages assembled by women who could barely contain their anger.

Strangely, though, in the midst of so much sorrow, I wasn't depressed. Maybe I was wrong, but it seemed to me that something else was shining through – the triumph of the human spirit. All around I saw that shattered families were making a promise to endure, I read about men and women who had risked their lives to save unknown strangers and I saw more photos of dead firefighters than I cared to count.

I stopped at the epicentre, alone among so many home-made memorials, and bowed my head. I wasn't praying – I'm not a religious man, a person of The Book, as they say – nor was I particularly affected by so much death. I've been to Auschwitz and Natzweiler-Struthof and the ossuary at the Battle of Verdun, and death on an industrial scale had long ago ceased to amaze me. But I was humbled by so much raw courage – probably because I am so doubtful of my own.

Pain and suffering were imprinted on me very young – you see, as a kid, I was inside the apartment when my mother was killed. Don't get me wrong, I'm not particularly afraid of dying, but all I have ever asked for was that, when the time came, it was fast and clean. I've always had a great fear of being hurt like my mother, of not being able to stop the pain – that was the secret terror which waited for me where the street lights end.

With the bravery of ordinary people memorialized all around me, and reminded once again that when it comes to courage I'm a flawed man, I turned for home. That was when I saw it – a white board hanging on the wire, half hidden by a curve in the path, easily overlooked except for the accident of the rising sun glinting off its surface. There was a larger than usual pile of bouquets lying at its foot, and that was what drew me towards it.

Written on the board, rendered in a careful hand, were the names of eight men and women, all with photos. A caption said that they had been brought out alive from the collapsing North Tower by one man – a New York cop. A teenage girl whose mother was one of those rescued had created the shrine, and it was a loving tribute to the courage of a single man. The girl's narrative listed the people the cop had saved and they included: a lawyer in her power suit, a bond trader with a picture-perfect family who looked like a real player, a man in a wheelchair . . .

'*A man in a what?*' I said to myself. My eyes flew down the board and found a photo of the cop who had been responsible for getting them all out. Of course I recognized him – Ben Bradley. As I said, it was the last thing I had expected to find.

When Ben had told me in Paris that he was trapped in the North Tower of the World Trade Center, I had assumed he had been inside the building on business, but I was wrong. The teenager had the real story. She said he was on Fulton Street when he saw the plane hit and a huge section of the tower blossom into the sky like a massive exit wound.

With debris raining down and everyone starting to flee, he pinned his shield on his shirt collar, dumped his jacket and sprinted for the tower. Like New York City itself, it was Bradley's darkest moment and his finest hour.

Five times he made his way in and out of the building, each time climbing an emergency stairway against the sea of people coming down – trying to see how he could help, who he could save. At one stage, standing on an elevator landing on the thirtieth floor – with the first of two hundred jumpers hurtling down the façade – Bradley had to wrap his shirt around his mouth so that he could breathe. In the process he lost his shield, his only form of identity.

Expecting the worst for himself, he plunged into a deserted office and found a marker pen to scribble his name and Marcie's phone number on his arm. He looked out the window and couldn't believe it – a hundred and twenty feet away the South Tower was collapsing. Until then, he hadn't even known it had been hit.

He ran for safety to Emergency Stairway A and it was then someone told him that there was a guy in a wheelchair way up above, waiting for help. Thanks to the teenager's account, I learned that Bradley was the middle-aged guy who had called for volunteers, led the other three men up to find the crippled man and carried his evacuation chair down the sixty-seven floors.

The teenager wrote that the team found their way to the

mezzanine and somehow got the evacuation chair and its occupant outside. Terrified that the tower would collapse, they ran for safety. One of the rescuers – a big guy, a young insurance salesman – realized the other members of the team were running on empty, dropped his corner of the chair and threw the crippled guy over his shoulder. He yelled at Bradley and the other two – a security guard and a foreign exchange dealer – to beat it.

Two minutes later the world caved in – the North Tower collapsed from the top down as if it were being peeled. Everything in those minutes was random, including death – the insurance salesman and the crippled guy took cover in a doorway that offered no protection and escaped the falling debris unharmed. Ten feet away the security guard sustained a direct hit from a blast of rubble and died instantly. Bradley and the forex dealer threw themselves under a fire truck that got buried by a mountain of concrete.

Trapped in an air-pocket, it was the forex dealer – thirty-two and a millionaire – who Bradley held tight and whose dying message he memorized to give to the guy's family.

Five hours later a fire crew with a sniffer dog hauled Bradley out, saw the details on his arm, called Marcie and told her to get to Emergency as fast as possible.

I stood for a long time in silence. It was one of the most remarkable stories of courage I had ever encountered, and I knew that the following day I would offer Bradley the only thing of value I could give. I would tell him I would invent one last legend and talk at his damn seminar.

I turned away and started to think about what I would say to a gathering of the world's top investigators. I figured I would claim to be Peter Campbell, a former doctor turned hedge-fund manager. I would tell them that I had first met Jude Garrett back in my medical days when he consulted me on a murder he was investigating. We became friends and there was hardly a case or investigative technique he had pioneered which he didn't discuss with me. I would reveal it had been me who had found the manuscript of the book after he died and that I was the one who had prepared it for publication. I would lead them to believe, as Bradley had suggested, that I was Dr Watson to his Sherlock.

It wasn't perfect, but it would do. Mostly, I was confident because I knew Campbell's academic credentials and a host of other details I would need to invent would survive almost any scrutiny. I could rely on Battleboi for that.

Sure, I could establish Peter Campbell's legitimacy, but what would I actually say when I addressed them? I wondered if it would be possible to take such elite investigators into an unsolved case, to lead them through the strange details of a brilliant crime – in other words, could I throw open for discussion the murder at the Eastside Inn?

It certainly had all the right elements for a good case study: a woman who changed her appearance every day, a hotel room washed down with industrial antiseptic, a body whose teeth had been pulled and the killer's use of Jude Garrett's own book, the one that had caused such a stir among the attendees, as a step-by-step manual.

But they were just facts, and the audience wouldn't be satisfied with that. 'Give us a theory,' they would say. 'Where's the narrative? Why September eleventh? Isn't that the first thing a brilliant man like Jude Garrett would ask?'

And they were right, of course – of all the days, why that one? I thought that if I was Garrett – which, fortunately, I was – I would tell them—

A startling thought swept into my head. Pressured by my imaginary performance, I had an idea of why, when everyone else was running, she was looking for a place to stay.

Say there was somebody she wanted to murder but she had never known how to do it without being caught. Just assume she worked in one of the Twin Towers and was running late that morning. Say she wasn't at her desk but was standing outside and saw the buildings burn and fall. If all her work colleagues were dead, who would know she had survived?

She could just vanish. All she needed was a place to stay, and to make certain that nobody ever recognized her. Then she could commit the murder whenever it suited her.

I mean, there's no better alibi than being dead, is there?

Chapter Twenty-seven

ALTHOUGH I MET BEN AND MARCIE FOR DINNER THE FOLLOWING NIGHT, I said nothing to Ben about my newly minted theory – I wanted to keep turning it over in my mind like some complex architectural model to see if it held together.

In return for Marcie's home-cooked meals I had invited them to Nobu and, somewhere between the shrimp tempura and the yellow-tail, I did, however, mention that I had changed my mind – I would be happy to take part in the seminar.

They both stared at me. It was Marcie who spoke first. 'Let me guess, you've found Jesus too?'

I smiled, but – men being men – there was no way I was going to embarrass either myself or Bradley by talking about the shrine I had seen at Ground Zero and the emotions I had experienced when I read about his bravery.

'Maybe it's being home again,' I said. 'But I think it's time to give something back to the community.'

Bradley almost choked on his sake. He and Marcie exchanged a glance. 'That's wonderful,' Bradley said. 'Why not join Neighbourhood Watch too? Just out of curiosity – any chance of telling us the real reason?'

'Not really,' I replied, smiling back, thinking quietly about the sixty-seven floors and the fact that the man in the wheelchair, to judge by his photo, was a heavy-set guy.

The silence stretched on, and at last Marcie realized I had no intention of explaining any more and she launched into a new subject. 'Have you thought about going back to your childhood home?' she asked.

Surprise changed sides. I stared at her like she was crazy. 'Greenwich, you mean? What – press the intercom and ask the corporate raider if I could take a look around?'

'You can try that if you like, but having met him, I don't think it'll work,' she said. 'I just thought you might have seen the bit in *New York* magazine.'

I lowered my glass of water and looked a question at her.

'A local garden society is showing the grounds to raise money for charity,' she explained. 'If you're interested, Ben and I would be happy to go with you.'

My mind was spinning – go back to Greenwich? – but I didn't pause. 'No, but thanks. It's just a house, Marcie – it doesn't mean anything to me. It was all a long time ago.'

Naturally, as soon as we had separated after dinner, I bought a copy of the magazine and, the next day, I called the Connecticut Horticultural Society and purchased a ticket.

Bill would have loved it. 'Two hundred dollars to see a few trees? What's wrong with Central Park?'

It was a glorious Saturday morning, the sun climbing in a cloudless sky, as I wound through Connecticut's leafy avenues. I could have told the cab to take me up the drive to the front of the house, but I wanted to walk – I figured it would be best to give the memories a chance to breathe. The huge wrought-iron gates were open and I gave my ticket to an old lady with a rosette and stepped into the past.

It was amazing how little had changed in twenty years. The sycamores still formed a canopy over the pea-gravel drive, the European beeches continued to add depth to the hillsides and in their cool glades the rhododendrons were as beautiful as ever. Halfway up the drive there was a break in the foliage, designed to give visitors their first view of the house. If it was meant to shock, it never failed.

I paused and looked again at Avalon. It stood in the distance, its facade reflected in the broad waters of the ornamental lake. Bill's grandfather had gone to England in the 1920s and stayed with the Astors at Cliveden, their stunning Italianate pile on the Thames. He returned with dozens of photos, showed them to his architect, and told him to 'build something like that, only more beautiful'.

The house was finished six months before the Crash. Along with

Marjorie Merriweather Post's Mar-A-Lago in Palm Beach, it was the last of the great American mansions of the twentieth century.

My eye tracked along its walls of Indiana limestone, aglow in the morning light, and found the three tall windows at the northern end. It was my bedroom and maybe you can imagine how a room like that felt to a kid from my part of Detroit. The memory of those frightening days carried my eyes down to the lake where I had spent so much time walking alone.

Under a row of pin oaks I saw the grass promontory from which, years later, Bill taught me to sail. As a child he had spent his summers in Newport and fell in love with the twelve-metre yachts which competed for the America's Cup. One day he came home with scale models of two of the greatest boats ever to have had keels laid down. *Australia II* and *Stars and Stripes* were over five feet long, their sails and rudders remote-controlled, driven only by the wind and the skill of the operator. God knows how much they cost.

I can still see the madman now, sprinting down the lake, trimming his sails, trying to cover my wind and beat me around every buoy. Only when I had defeated him three times in a row did he take me out on Long Island Sound and teach me the real thing in a two-man dinghy.

I don't think I'm a boastful person, so maybe you will trust me when I say that sailing was the one thing for which I had a natural gift. Apart from deceit, of course. So much so that one Saturday, sitting on the upturned hull, Bill told me he thought I had a chance of going to the Olympics.

Knowing I always kept myself apart from others, he had the good sense to suggest one of the solo classes – a Laser – and worked hard with me every weekend. It didn't matter in the end – when I was about sixteen, lost and angry about life, having nothing else to rebel against, I gave it up. I told him I wasn't going to sail again, and I thought in my naivety and cruelty that the look of disappointment on his face was some form of victory. A hundred times I must have thought of ways to take it back, but I wasn't smart enough to understand that an apology is a sign of strength, not weakness, and the opportunity vanished with the summer.

As I stood on the drive after so many years and looked at the lake again, I realized why I had come back. He was dead but I wanted to talk to him.

I made my way up to the old house. Marquees for the silver-service lunch stood on the lawns and the doors into the house were roped off – only committee members and VIP guests with passes were making it past the security guards. Getting inside might have presented a problem for even a highly trained agent, but not to someone who had spent their childhood in the house.

At the back of the service buildings I found the door into a gardeners' change room had been left unlocked, moved through it quickly and entered the cavernous garage.

On the wall on the far side, I reached above a set of workshop shelves and hit a button hidden under a row of power sockets. A section of the shelves creaked open – an underground passage led into the house. Built by Bill's father, ostensibly to access the garage in icy weather, its real purpose was far different.

According to the old housekeeper, the colonel – having conquered Europe with the Sixth Army – came home and launched a similar campaign with the maids. He established his headquarters on the daybed in his study, a room which offered a long view of the drive and gave that week's subject plenty of time to get herself dressed, head down the passage and into the garage before the colonel's wife reached the front door. The housekeeper always said the plan was so good her boss should have made General.

I paused in the passage and listened for any sound from the study. Nothing, so I turned the handle and stepped through the door concealed in the room's antique panelling.

Grace would have had a coronary. Gone were her priceless English antiques and the Versailles parquetry, replaced by plaid couches and a tartan carpet. Over the old fireplace, acquired from some chateau, where her finest Canaletto had once hung, was a portrait of the owner and his family, staring at some far-off point as if they had just discovered the New World. The only possible improvement would have been if it were painted on black velvet.

Ignoring their heroic gaze, I crossed the room and opened the door into the entrance hall. I heard voices – all the good and the great were congregating in the formal living rooms – but the two gorillas at the front door had their backs to the interior, so they didn't see me head up the stairs. At the top, it was one of those moments.

The raider hadn't turned his decorator loose on the first floor, so the years promptly fell away and my childhood was all around me.

I walked down the beautiful corridor – I think I said it was the quietest house I had ever known – and opened the door at the north end.

The layout of the rooms was unchanged, the weight of the past almost palpable – a large sitting room, a bathroom, walk-in closets and a bedroom overlooking the woodland. There were a dozen other similar suites in the house, and it was obvious the raider's family had never used this one.

I stood silently for minutes without end, just remembering, until at last I perched on the bed and looked at a seat built into a bay window. Whenever Bill came to talk, he always sat there, his face framed against the copper-beech trees in the woods behind. Slowly I let the focus of my vision blur, and I swear it was as if I could see him again.

In my heart, I told him all the things I had never been able to say in life. I said he had cared for me when he'd had no obligation of blood or friendship to do so and I told him that, to my mind, if there was a heaven, there would always be a place for someone who did that for a child. I confessed that whatever good was in me came from him but the acres of darkness were all my own, and I told him that he was forever in my thoughts and there wasn't a day went by when I didn't wish I could go sailing again to make him proud. I asked for his forgiveness for not being the son he had so desperately wanted and, after that, I sat in stillness.

If anybody had walked in and seen me with my head bowed they would have thought I was praying, and I must have stayed like that for a long time because the thing that stirred me was the sound of a violin. The two hundred dollars had bought not only the silver-service lunch but an accompaniment by a chamber ensemble, and I guessed everybody was starting to head into the tents. I stood up, took one last look at my past and headed for the door.

Chapter Twenty-eight

I CAME DOWN THE STAIRS AND WAS HALFWAY ACROSS THE FOYER, twenty feet from the front door and freedom, when I heard her. 'Scott . . . ? Scott Murdoch? Is that you?'

The voice was familiar, but I couldn't put a face to it. I kept walking – another few paces and I would be safe, swept up in a crowd approaching the exit. Four paces now. Three—

Her hand caught hold of my elbow and brought me to a stop. 'Scott – didn't you hear me?'

I turned and recognized her. She was wearing the purple rosette of a committee member and I realized I should have known she would be there – she had always loved gardens. It was the one thing she and Grace had in common and it was the primary reason for their friendship.

'Oh, hello, Mrs Corcoran,' I said, smiling as best I could. She happened to be Dexter's mother, the creep who had been on the Caulfield squash team with me, and I had suffered through any number of team-building events at her house.

'I can't believe it's you. What are you doing here?' she said.

'You know – just looking around . . . for old times' sake,' I replied. Her eyes flicked across my jacket and failed to find the identity tag that would have given me entry. I could tell she was desperate to ask how the hell I had got past security, but she decided to let it ride.

'Walk me to lunch,' she said, linking arms with me. 'We'll catch up on everything, then I'll introduce you to the owner. Delightful man.' Her voice dropped conspiratorially. 'Nothing he doesn't know about the markets.'

But I didn't move, an edge to my voice. 'No, I was just leaving, Mrs Corcoran – I've seen everything I wanted to.'

She looked at me, and I think in that instant she realized the visit had meant something important to me.

She smiled. 'You're right. Silly of me. Forget the owner – he's an awful man, to be honest. The wife's even worse – fancies herself as a decorator.' Her laugh had always been brittle, like a glass breaking, and it hadn't altered.

She took a step back and ran her eye up and down. 'You look well, Scott – the years have been good to you.'

'You too,' I said, shaking my head in fake wonder. 'You've barely changed.' I couldn't believe I was saying it, but she nodded happily – flattery and delusion were part of the air she breathed.

We continued to look at each other for an awkward moment, neither of us quite sure what to say next. 'How's Dexter?' I asked, just to get over the hurdle.

A shadow of confusion fell across the tightly drawn skin of her face. 'That's strange. Grace said she wrote to you about it.'

I had no idea what she meant. 'I didn't have any contact with Grace for years. Wrote to me about what?'

'That'd be Grace,' she said, doing her best to smile. 'Not interested unless it was about her. Dexter's dead, Scott.'

For a moment I couldn't get the gears to mesh: he was a strong guy – always sneering at people – but still, dead? That was a bit extreme. Because I was an outsider who never spoke to anyone and he was loathed, the rest of the squash team always made sure we were paired together and, more than anyone, I had to endure his racquet-throwing and taunts.

His mother was watching my face, and I was thankful I didn't have to fake it – I was genuinely shocked. She herself was fighting to blink back the tears – no easy thing given how much skin the plastic surgeons had cut away over the years.

'I asked Grace to tell you, because I knew how tight you two were,' she said. 'He was always saying how often you would go to him for advice, not just on the court either.'

Corcoran said what? I would have rather gone to Bart Simpson for advice. Jesus Christ.

'We can be honest now, Scott – you didn't belong, did you? Dexter said that's why he always stepped forward to partner you – he didn't want you to feel like you were excluded. He was always very thoughtful like that.'

I nodded quietly. 'That was a part of Dexter a lot of people didn't see,' I said. I mean, what else could I do – he was her only child, for God's sake. 'What happened?'

'He drowned – he was at the beach house by himself and went for a swim one night.'

I knew the stretch of beach – it was dangerous even in daylight; nobody in their right mind would go swimming there in the dark. Fragments of things I had heard drifted back – he had flunked out of law school, ugly stories about hard drinking, time spent at a rehab clinic in Utah.

'Of course there were spiteful rumours,' his mother said. 'You know what people are like – but the coroner and the police both agreed it was an accident.'

I remembered his grandfather had been a prominent judge – on the Supreme Court – and I figured somebody had put the fix in. If there was a note in the house I suppose it was handed privately to his parents and they destroyed it.

I've had too much experience of death for someone my age but even that couldn't inoculate me. I always thought it would be me, but Corcoran – the dumb sonofabitch – was the first of my class to pass from this world, and it must have taken the colour from my face.

'You're pale,' Mrs Corcoran said, touching my arm to comfort me. 'I shouldn't have said it so directly but, Scott, I don't know any correct—'

She was swallowing hard and I thought she was going to cry but, thankfully, she didn't. Instead she forced herself to brighten. 'And what about you – still in the art business?'

Grief hadn't unhinged her – that was the legend I had created for friends and family when I first went into the field for The Division. Legally, nobody was allowed to know of the agency's existence, so I had spent months crafting my cover story before the Director finally signed off on it.

Arriving at Avalon unannounced one Sunday, I told Grace and Bill over lunch that I was sick of Rand, sick of research, sick of psychology itself. I said the greatest thing the two of them had given me was an interest in art and, as a result, I was leaving Rand to start a business dealing in early twentieth-century European paintings, basing myself in Berlin.

As legends went, if I do say so myself, it was good – it allowed me to travel anywhere in Europe for my real work and at the same time provided a reason to lose contact with my former acquaintances until I was virtually forgotten. And, obviously, it had been believable – here I was, so many years later, listening to a woman who had been a friend of Bill and Grace asking me about the art racket.

I smiled. 'Yes, still chasing canvases, Mrs Corcoran – still squeezing out a living.'

She looked from my cashmere sweater down to my expensive loafers, and I realized my mistake – out of deference to Bill's memory I had dressed up for the occasion.

'I suspect more than squeezing,' she said, eyes narrowing.

I didn't want her to think my fictitious business was successful, or else people might start asking why they had never heard of it, so I took the almost revolutionary step of telling the truth. 'I was lucky,' I said. 'Maybe you already know – Grace left me some money.'

She paused. 'I would have bet everything I owned against that,' she said softly.

'Yeah, she could be pretty aloof,' I replied, 'but underneath I suppose she must have felt something.'

'Obligation, if you ask me,' she replied tartly. 'They're dead now, so I don't suppose it matters – Grace never wanted you, Scott, not even from the beginning.'

Whatever difficulties I'd had with my stepmother, I had never expected to hear it put so bluntly. I wondered if Mrs Corcoran was exaggerating, and a look of doubt must have crossed my face.

'Don't stare at me. I heard her say it – about a week after you arrived from Detroit. We were having coffee out there.' She pointed towards the lawn that overlooked the lake.

'Bill, Grace and I were watching you – the nanny had you down at the water's edge, looking at the swans, I think.'

As young as I was, I remembered that – I had never seen swans before and I thought they were the most beautiful things in the world.

'Bill wouldn't take his eyes off of you,' Mrs Corcoran continued. 'To be honest, I've never seen a man so taken with a child. Grace noticed it too. She kept looking at him and then, very quietly, she said: "I've changed my mind, Bill – a child doesn't fit in with us."

'He turned to her. "You're wrong," he said. "It's exactly what we need. *More* kids – give this place some damn life."

'There was a finality to it, but Grace wouldn't let it drop, determined to have her way – apparently they only had a few days to tell the agency if they were going to keep you.'

Mrs Corcoran paused to see my reaction. What did she expect – is there anyone who doesn't want to think their parents loved them?

'Yeah, Grace was an experienced shopper,' I said. 'She took everything on a sale-or-return basis.'

The old woman laughed. 'That's why I always liked you, Scott – you never let anything hurt you.'

I just nodded.

'Anyway, the argument between them became increasingly bitter until finally Grace lost her temper. "You know your trouble, Bill?" she said. "You're a porter – you see anyone with baggage and you've always got to help them."

'With that, she told him you'd be leaving in the morning, and headed for the house, claiming she was going to check on lunch. Nobody saw her for the rest of the day. Bill sat in silence for a long time, his eyes still fixed on you, then he said, "Scott will be staying at Avalon until he goes to college, longer if he wants. He'll stay because the porter says so – and Grace will have to accept it."

'I didn't know what to say. I'd never seen that steely side of him – I'm not sure anybody had. Then he turned to me and said the strangest thing.

'You probably know Bill wasn't a spiritual man – I never once heard him talk about God – but he said that every night he sat by your bed while you slept. "I think Scott was sent to us," he told me. "I feel like I've been chosen to care for him. I don't know why I think it, but I believe he's going to do something very important one day."'

Standing in the old house with so many years gone by, Mrs Corcoran smiled at me. 'Did you, Scott? Was Bill right? Did you do something very important?'

I smiled back and shook my head. 'Not unless you think finding a few lost canvases is important. But Bill was a fine man and it was good of him to think like that.'

From out on the lawn, we heard someone calling Mrs Corcoran's name – she probably had to give a speech. She patted my arm, starting to go.

'Well, who knows?' she said. 'You're not old, there's still time, isn't there? Goodbye, Scott.'

But there wasn't – time, I mean. I was still in my thirties, but my race was run. Only a fool would think it could turn out otherwise. So – say hello to the fool, I have often said to myself when I think back on those days.

Chapter Twenty-nine

THE SARACEN, NEWLY ARRIVED IN AFGHANISTAN, WAS TRAVELLING FAST, sticking to the sparsely populated valleys for as long as he could, always heading east. It had been almost fifteen years since he had been in the country as a teenage *muj*, but every day he still saw evidence of the old Soviet war: abandoned gun emplacements, a rusted artillery piece, a goat-herder's hut bombed into oblivion.

Creeks and rivers ran along the valley floors, and they provided safety. The fertile strip on either side of the watercourses was planted with only one thing – marijuana – and the tall, moisture-heavy plants provided good cover from US thermal-imaging equipment.

Finally, however, he had to abandon the valleys and climb into the forbidding Hindu Kush mountains. In the steep forests he followed the tracks made by timber cutters, hoping the surveillance drones would see his packhorses and dismiss him as one more illegal logger. But above the treeline, every breath a labour because of the altitude, there was no cover and he had to quicken his pace even more.

Late one afternoon, in the distance, he thought he saw the mountain scree where he had brought down his first Hind gunship, but it was a long time ago and he couldn't be sure. Toiling higher, he crossed a narrow ridge and passed shell casings and rocket pods of a far more recent vintage.

In the years since he had last seen the country as a *muj*, the Afghans had known little but war: the Russians had been replaced by the warlords; Mullah Omar's Taliban had defeated the warlords; America, hunting Osama bin Laden, had destroyed the Taliban; the warlords had returned; and now the US and a coalition of allies were fighting to prevent the re-emergence of the Taliban.

The used ammunition told him he must be close to Kunar Province – referred to by the Americans as 'enemy central' – and, sure enough, that night he heard Apache helicopters roaring down a valley below, followed by an AC-130 gunship which people said fired bullets as big as Coke bottles.

In the following days he was stopped numerous times – mostly by US or NATO patrols but twice by wild men who described themselves as members of the Anti-Coalition Militia but who he knew were Taliban in a different turban. He told them all the same thing – he was a devout Lebanese doctor who had raised money from mosques and individuals in his homeland for a medical mercy mission. His aim was to bring help to Muslims in remote areas where, because the continuous wars had destroyed the country's infrastructure, there were no longer any clinics and the doctors had fled.

He said he had sent his supplies by boat from Beirut to Karachi, flown to join them, bought a truck, driven through Pakistan into Afghanistan and, at the Shaddle Bazaar – the world's largest opium market – had traded the truck for the ponies. All of it was true, and he even had a cheap digital camera on which he could show photos of himself tending to the sick and inoculating kids at a dozen ruined villages.

That – combined with the fact that every time his caravan was searched they found a wide range of medical supplies – allayed both sides' fears. The only items he carried that led to questions were a pane of thick, reinforced glass and several sacks of quicklime. He told anyone who asked that the glass was used as an easily sterilized platform on which to mix prescriptions. And the quicklime? How else was he to destroy the swabs and dressings he used to treat everything from gangrene to measles?

Nobody even bothered to reach deep into the small saddlebag which held his clothes and spare sandals. At the bottom of it was a collapsible 'helmet' with a clear plastic face plate, a box of R-700D disposable face masks, a black bio-hazard suit, rubber boots, Kevlar-lined gloves and rolls of special tape to seal every join from the helmet to the boots. If the equipment had been found he would have told them that anthrax occurs naturally among hoofed animals – including goats and camels – and that he had no intention of dying for his work. As further proof, he would have shown them vials of antibiotics he was carrying, stolen from the hospital he had been working at in Lebanon, which was the standard drug to treat the disease. But the men he ran into were soldiers – either guerillas or otherwise – and they were looking for weapons and explosives, and nobody asked.

The only time he straight-out lied was if they asked where he was heading next. He would shrug, point at his possessions and say he didn't even have a map.

'I go wherever God takes me.' But he did have a map – it was inside his head and he knew exactly where he was going.

On three separate occasions, NATO troops, having searched him, helped load his supplies back on to the ponies. The hardest part was lifting and securing the pairs of heavy-duty truck batteries on to the four animals at the rear. The batteries were used to power small refrigerated boxes, and the soldiers smiled at the doctor's ingenuity. Inside were racks of tiny glass bottles which would help countless children: vaccines against polio, diphtheria and whooping cough. Hidden among them, indistinguishable except by an extra zero he had added to the batch number, were a pair of bottles which contained something vastly different.

At that time, only two examples of the smallpox virus were supposed to exist on the planet. Kept for research purposes, one was in a virtually impenetrable freezer at the Center for Disease Control in Atlanta and the other was at a secure Russian facility called Vector in Siberia. There was, however, a third example. Unknown to anyone in the world except the Saracen, it was in the two glass vials on the back of his wiry packhorse deep in the Hindu Kush.

He hadn't stolen it, he hadn't bought it from some disaffected Russian scientist, it hadn't been given to him by a failed state like North Korea which had undertaken its own illegal research. No, the remarkable thing was that the Saracen had synthesized it himself.

In his garage.

Chapter Thirty

HE COULD NEVER HAVE DONE IT WITHOUT THE INTERNET. AS THE search for him became increasingly desperate, I finally discovered that, several years after he had graduated in medicine, the Saracen took a job in El-Mina, an ancient town in the north of Lebanon.

He worked the night shift in ER at the local hospital – hard and exhausting work in a facility that was under-equipped and under-staffed. Despite the constant fatigue, he used every spare moment to secretly pursue what he considered his life's work – *jihad* against the far enemy.

While other soldiers-of-Allah were wasting their time at hidden boot camps in Pakistan or fantasizing about getting a US visa, he was reading everything he could find about weapons of mass destruction. And it was only the Internet that had given a doctor at an old hospital in a town nobody had heard of widespread access to the latest research into every major biological killer in the world.

In one of those unforeseen but deadly consequences – what the CIA would call blowback – the World Wide Web had opened up a Pandora's box of terrible possibilities.

The Saracen hadn't been raised like Western kids so he didn't know much about computers, but he knew enough: by using a good proxy connection he managed to undertake his relentless search in complete anonymity.

For months, helped by his knowledge of medicine and biology, he concentrated on what he considered the most achievable bio-warfare candidates – ricin, anthrax, pneumonic plague, sarin, tabun and soman – all of which were capable of causing widespread death and even greater panic. But all of them came with enormous shortcomings – most of them either weren't infectious or were most effective if used as part of an aerial bombing campaign.

Frustrated at his lack of progress, fighting waves of despair, he was in the middle of researching anthrax – at least the raw bacteria was obtainable; it was widespread in the Middle East, including Lebanon, but it would still have to be 'weaponized' – when he read something that changed the very nature of the world in which we live.

Nobody much noticed it.

In the online pages of *The Annals of Virology* – a monthly which doesn't exactly fly off the shelves – was an account of an experiment conducted at a lab in upstate New York. For the first time in history, a life-form had been built entirely from off-the-shelf chemicals – all purchased for a few hundred dollars. It was late in the afternoon and for once the Saracen forgot to kneel for *maghrib*, the sunset prayer. With increasing wonder, he read that the scientists had successfully recreated the polio virus from scratch.

According to the article, the aim of the researchers was to warn the US government that terrorist groups could make biological weapons without ever obtaining the natural virus. Good idea – there was at least one terrorist who had never thought of it until he read their research. Even more alarming – or perhaps not, depending on your degree of cynicism – was the name of the organization which had funded the programme with a three hundred thousand dollar grant. The Pentagon.

The Saracen, however, was certain that the startling development had nothing to do with the Defense Department or scientists in New York – they were merely the instruments. This was Allah's work: somebody had now synthesized a virus and opened the door for him. On the other side was the Holy Grail of all bio-terror weapons, a wildly infectious agent transmitted by the simple act of breathing, the most potent killer in the history of the planet – smallpox.

In the weeks which followed, the Saracen learned that the researchers, using polio's publicly available genome – its genetic map – had purchased what are called 'nucleic acid base pairs' from one of the scores of companies that sell material to the bio-tech industry. Those base pairs cost the princely sum of ten cents a piece and, according to an account on an Internet discussion forum for biology geeks, were ordered by email. Because the sales company's online system was fully automated, the report on the forum said, there was no name verification and nobody asked why the material was being purchased.

Once the New York lab had acquired the microscopic building blocks, the scientists spent a year arranging them in the correct order and then – in a skilful but publicly known process – gluing them together. The Saracen, being a doctor and with a dozen manuals on molecular biology at hand, soon understood enough of the process to suspect that what could be done at a lab in upstate New York could be duplicated in a garage in El-Mina – if he could locate one thing.

He had read about it somewhere, and he started searching. After two hours online he found it – the smallpox genome. Once one of the world's most closely guarded secrets, the virus's complete chemical and genetic map had fallen victim to the explosion of knowledge about biology and the worldwide dissemination of complex scientific papers over the Internet. There were no gatekeepers any more, and potentially lethal information was haemorrhaging all the time – while it had taken the Saracen two hours to locate the genome, had he been more experienced at searching the Web he would have found it on a dozen biology or research sites in less than half the time. I know because I did.

From the article in *The Annals of Virology* the Saracen knew that polio had 7,741 base pairs, or letters, in its genome. Now he saw that smallpox had 185,578 letters, greatly enhancing the difficulty of re-creating it, but he was riding a wave of knowledge and optimism and he wasn't going to let a small thing like an extra 178,000 letters deter him.

He quickly decided his first objective was to protect himself: smallpox is a merciless pathogen and it was almost certain that somewhere in the complicated and unstable process of trying to synthesize it he would make a mistake. Many mistakes, probably, and the first he would know of his exposure would be when the fever hit and, a short time later, a rash of fluid-filled blisters appeared. By then it would be over: no cure for smallpox has ever been found.

He had to locate a vaccine, and it was the pursuit of that goal that made him take a six-week vacation. Instead of heading to Beirut and flying to Cairo to visit friends, as he had told the medical director of the hospital, he had boarded an early-morning bus for Damascus.

There he killed Tlass, stole the vaccine, used the double-pronged needle on himself and crossed the border back into Lebanon.

He spent five days locked in a hotel room fighting the terrible fever which had accompanied the huge dose of vaccine he had taken. Once that had passed and the telltale scab and scar had formed on his arm, he returned to El-Mina. Though, outwardly, nothing had changed, his life had entered an entirely new phase: he was ready to start on his history-making journey.

Chapter Thirty-one

THE FIRST THING HE DID WAS SET ABOUT SEALING THE GARAGE UNDER his small apartment and turning it into a makeshift bio-containment laboratory.

He had one advantage in performing the work – there was a good example close at hand. While everything else at the El-Mina hospital was falling apart, it had a two-bed isolation ward and an attached lab. Because anthrax was endemic to the region, the hospital had been able to take advantage of a World Health Organization programme to help developing nations combat the disease. Forget that the hospital didn't have some of the most rudimentary equipment necessary for saving lives, the Geneva organization had provided a small fortune to build a first-rate facility.

As far as the Saracen knew, it had only been used once in ten years and had become little more than a temporary storage shed. Nevertheless, it was an excellent blueprint for his own lab, and it also ended up providing half the practical equipment he needed – incubators, a microscope, culture dishes, pipettes, sterilizing cabinets and a host of other items. They were never even reported missing.

Over the following week, using a computer and an Internet connection he had set up in the lab, he assembled a list of over sixty bio-tech companies worldwide which would provide DNA material of fewer than seventy letters without asking for name verification or any further information.

A long time later, on first hearing this, I didn't believe it. To my despair, I went online and did it myself.

But before the Saracen could order DNA he had to locate two crucial pieces of equipment: gene synthesizers – machines about the size of a decent computer printer. It took him an hour. The dizzying progress in the bio-tech industry meant the market was awash with equipment at hugely discounted prices which was no longer the fastest or the best.

He found two synthesizers in excellent condition, one on eBay, the other on usedlabequipment.com. Combined, they cost under five thousand dollars and the Saracen was thankful that doctors were well paid and he had always lived such a frugal life. He could well afford them from his savings and what was even more important to him was that the sellers also had no interest in who the purchaser was – all they wanted was a valid credit-card number. An anonymous Western Union money transfer was just as good.

He started work the day the second machine arrived and, that evening, he was surfing the Web, adding to his already vast library about viruses and biology, when he glanced through the latest online edition of the prestigious periodical *Science*. One of its lead stories was about a researcher who had just synthesized an organism with 300,000 letters. In the short time since he had decided on his course of action, 185,000 letters had already faded into history. That was the pace at which genetic engineering was advancing.

After he finished the article he knew that smallpox was within his grasp and his date with destiny confirmed. He prayed late into the night – it was a huge responsibility and he asked Allah to make sure he used it well.

Six months later, having glued and re-glued, backtracked, researched and re-learned – using not only his knowledge but the vast array of cheap equipment that was rapidly becoming available – he completed the task.

To the best of his ability, one molecule at a time, he had re-created smallpox. According to every test he could run, it was identical to its naturally occurring equivalent.

In the thousands of years since the virus had made the jump from some other life form into humans, there have been two different types of smallpox – *Variola minor*, often called cottonpox, which was rarely fatal, and its bigger brother, *Variola major*, the disease which had proved devastating to human populations ever since mankind had started to congregate in large tribes. It was that virus – with a death rate of about 30 per cent – which the Saracen had synthesized. However, within *Variola major* there were a host of different strains, some far more lethal than others.

Knowing that, he began to refine and challenge his virus, a well-established method of forcing it to mutate time after time, attempting, in the slang of some microbiologists, to KFC or deep-fry it, trying to turn it into a red-hot strain of what was already the hottest agent on earth.

Satisfied that it was as lethal as he could make it, he set out to modify its genetic structure. That was the simplest, but also the most dangerous, part of the entire exercise. It was also the most necessary . . .

Once the naturally occurring form of smallpox had been eradicated from the planet, the World Health Organization found itself holding a huge stockpile of vaccine doses. After several years, when everyone was convinced that the virus would not re-emerge, that protective reservoir was destroyed. Similarly, although a vast number of people had been routinely vaccinated against smallpox – primarily children in the Western world – the Saracen also knew that the vaccine started to wear off after five years and, as a result, virtually nobody on earth had any immunity.

That was ideal for his purposes – except for one problem. The United States, the target of his assault, had become increasingly concerned about a bio-terror attack and in the wake of 9/11 had decided to produce and warehouse over three hundred million doses of vaccine, one for every person in the country. When the Saracen had first read about it, the information had cast him into despair. Sitting up for an entire night researching vaccination, he learned that anything up to 20 per cent of a population would remain unprotected: the vaccine didn't take in a significant number of people and it can't be given to pregnant women, newborn babies, elderly citizens or anyone with a damaged immune system.

Even so, the existence of the vaccine stockpile shook him badly and, just before dawn on that long night, he had considered abandoning his plan and looking for a different weapon. But, once again, the ongoing explosion of scientific knowledge – or Allah – came to his rescue.

Delving deeper into the literature, he found a research report from a group of Australian scientists. Working at a facility in Canberra, the nation's capital, the scientists had been trying to find a way to control the breeding cycle of mice. Working with mousepox, a disease closely related to smallpox, they had spliced a gene from the immune system known as IL-4 into the virus. What they found was startling: the virus crashed through any vaccine that had been given to the mice and wiped them out.

The addition of one gene – just one gene – had made the virus into a vaccine-buster.

The Saracen, with hope renewed, started following the obscure research trail. In rarely visited corners of the Web – frequently following nothing more than casual leads mentioned in scientific forums – he found that a number of researchers throughout the world had tried, with varying degrees of success, to duplicate the Australians' result.

With daylight flooding into the world outside his cocoon, he worked on and stumbled across a newly posted report from several Dutch agricultural scientists working with cowpox. They had decided to splice a slightly different gene into the virus and had not only succeeded in evading the vaccine but had managed to repeat the process every time.

The Saracen knew that the gene in question was readily available from the same companies that had supplied him with the nucleic acid base pairs. He ordered it immediately, opened the tiny package two days later and took science into uncharted waters.

He knew that the massive dose of vaccine that he had used on himself would provide no protection if he was successful in constructing a weapons-grade smallpox virus: he would be as good as naked in the hot zone. As a result, he stole a complete bio-hazard suit from the hospital to protect himself against infection and then drove to the coast. He travelled slowly along the road that ran parallel to the sea until he found a diving shop. Inside, he paid cash for four scuba tanks of oxygen and an air regulator, loaded them into the back of his car and returned to his cocoon.

Every time he worked on his vaccine-resistant virus it took him twenty minutes to put on the pilfered bio-hazard suit and attach his specially modified breathing apparatus, but the scientific work was easy. Partly as a result of the expertise he had gained and partly because the new gene contained only three hundred or so letters, he finished splicing it into the virus less than a month later.

It was this potential cataclysm that was contained in the two glass vials with the extra zero, and there was a simple reason why the

Saracen had brought them to Afghanistan: all his remarkable work would have been for nothing if he had made a mistake and the virus didn't work. He was well aware that smallpox occurred only in humans – not even our closest relatives, chimpanzees and monkeys, were capable of catching it. That meant the only way for him to be certain it was as deadly as the original and to discover if it could crash through the vaccine was to conduct a human trial.

It was deep in the mountains of the Hindu Kush that he planned to find the three subjects necessary for his dark experiment.

Leaving Kunar Province and its US patrols far behind, he found a dry riverbed which, due to the decay of the country's infrastructure, now served as a road. For days on end he walked along it, sprayed with dust by passing trucks and the ubiquitous Toyota 4-WDs, but, finally, on a blazingly hot morning, he realized he was getting close to his destination: ahead, silhouetted against the sky, he saw four men on horseback with AK-47s, standing guard.

The Saracen led his small caravan forward, turned a bend in the river and saw, some distance ahead, a town of mud and stone that appeared little changed since the Middle Ages. On the opposite bank, commanding a pass deeper into the mountains, stood a heavily fortified group of buildings built into a cliff face.

Once a nineteenth-century British fort, it had been turned into a home, a stronghold and a seat of regional power. The Saracen passed under the remains of a road bridge, climbed on to a pitted blacktop and headed towards it. Halfway along what had once been a major road, he walked between a jumble of giant boulders and – emerging on the other side – found himself face to face with two of the horsemen.

They commanded the road, their rifles levelled casually at his chest. The Saracen knew they would be more than happy to pull the trigger.

'Who are you?' the one with fine gold inlay along the stock of his weapon – the more senior of the pair – asked.

The Saracen started to answer but stopped, realizing the name he was using – the one on his passport – would mean nothing. Instead, he indicated the entrance to the fort.

'Give him a message, please. Tell him the boy with the Blowpipe has returned.'

Chapter Thirty-two

IN THE YEARS THAT HAD PASSED SINCE THEIR LAST MEETING, LORD Abdul Mohammad Khan had come to look more like a medieval painting than a warlord. His skin was the texture of tooled leather and he wore a *chapin* – the long traditional Afghan robe – of the finest cloth, a gold dagger as a symbol of his authority, and highly polished calfskin boots. Unfortunately, the effect was ruined by a gold Rolex as big as a microwave.

The years hadn't been kind to him – then again, the years are never kind to anyone in Afghanistan – but he could boast of one thing few of his contemporaries could: he was still alive. In his late sixties now, he was the warrior-father of his clan, and both soldiers and visitors stood aside in true deference as he limped through his stone-paved compound. All of them wondered who the muscular man was who had arrived at the gate and who Lord Khan had rushed to meet with such speed.

Some said he was a former comrade, a *muj* hero, while others claimed he was a doctor who had come to treat Khan for some terrible illness. Whatever the stranger's background, he was being afforded an honour denied to any of them: the great Khan had his arm around the man's shoulder, personally escorting him into his ornate audience chamber.

The room had once been the office of the British commander of the North-West Frontier and, as a result, featured high ceilings, a fireplace imported from England and a raised platform on which had stood the commander's desk. This was now covered with antique carpets fit for a museum and silk cushions that had crossed the border from palaces in Iran and China. A gold brazier burned incense in the corner, the fireplace housed all the equipment for making tea, but, of all the exotic and beautiful things in the room, it was the wall opposite the fireplace that monopolized every visitor's attention.

Khan watched from beneath hooded eyes as the Saracen caught sight of the massive concrete blocks set into it. The visitor stopped and stared at the bas-relief of the struggling limbs and screaming faces of the two men who had betrayed Khan, captured for ever – crystallized – in the moment of death. For some reason, he had always imagined the men were not much more than boys, but now he saw they were full-fledged warriors – tall and heavily armed – and that made their terror even more powerful.

The Saracen walked closer. Age and smoke had given the blocks a patina the glow of honey, and he was surprised at how much they resembled something cast in bronze. Lord Khan came to his side. 'You like my sculpture, huh? You know what their names are?'

The Saracen shook his head. Even though he had been told the story many times, he had never heard that part.

'Dumb and Dumber,' the warlord said, and roared with laughter. 'That's what a CIA guy called 'em when he visited years ago – now it's the name everyone uses.'

The Saracen stiffened slightly. 'Does the CIA come here often?'

'Every few years,' Lord Khan said with a shrug. 'Always trying to buy my support for whatever faction they're backing that month.' He walked towards the fireplace. 'I've never taken their money but, I have to admit, I like their sense of humour.'

An old man sitting cross-legged in the gloom, his eyes misted with cataracts, unfurled himself, about to start preparing tea for his master and the guest. Lord Khan stopped him and turned to the Saracen, indicating the staff and a dozen bodyguards spread around the room. 'You want them to leave?'

The Saracen nodded – privacy was exactly what he needed.

Khan smiled. 'I thought so. Nobody comes to Afghanistan on a social visit.'

As the room emptied, he began spooning leaves into a pot. 'You remember the last time I served you tea?'

'The war was over,' the Saracen replied. 'We were striking camp; you and I sat in the kitchen smoking cigarettes.'

Lord Khan's face softened – they had been good times, full of comradeship and courage, and he liked to recall them. 'I was heading home, you were starting on a much longer road.'

The Saracen said nothing, taking two delicate cups out of a rack, placing them next to the fire to warm.

'The last time I looked,' Lord Khan continued quietly, 'the House of Saud still had its palaces and power.'

'For how much longer?' the Saracen asked, equally softly. 'Maybe we'll learn soon enough if they can survive without the help of the far enemy.'

The two men looked at one another. 'When I heard you were a travelling doctor,' Lord Khan said, 'I wondered if you had changed, mellowed as you got older . . .' His voice trailed off. 'So you are still doing God's work, then?'

'Always. I need three people, Abdul Mohammad Khan, three dispensable people. If you can help, I am sure God will be well acquainted with what you do.'

'What do you mean exactly – how dispensable?'

The Saracen made no reply; he just turned and looked at Dumb and Dumber.

'Oh,' said Lord Khan, 'that dispensable.' He needed time to think, so he walked to a balcony overlooking the compound and started yelling orders to the soldiers gathered below. Whatever the risks, he realized, he had little choice: the Saracen had been willing to lay down his life for Khan and his people, and that was a debt which could never be repaid. He returned to finish making the tea. 'Any preference regarding the prisoners?' he asked.

'Jews would be perfect,' the Saracen said.

Lord Khan laughed at the joke. 'Sure,' he replied. 'I'll check the local synagogue.'

The Saracen grinned back. They both knew there hadn't been a Jew in Afghanistan in decades, not since the last of the once-flourishing community had been forced to run for their lives.

'Seriously,' the Saracen continued, 'they have to be young and healthy – and no Muslims.'

'Or Americans,' Lord Khan added. 'Abduct one of them and it brings down a world of grief on everyone.'

The Saracen nodded: 'If Muslims are excluded, it means it has to be foreigners – so I guess there will be trouble enough without asking for more.'

The proposal had one huge chance of success, Lord Khan thought. Afghanistan was awash with potential victims: European aid workers, Christian missionaries, English reconstruction workers, international journalists.

Though he said nothing, he also knew men who had been in the kidnapping-for-ransom business for years. They were a gang of a dozen brothers and cousins who had once fought under his command and now lived across the border in Iran. Just as importantly, they would die for Abdul Mohammad Khan if he asked – he had once saved their mother's life.

'One final criterion,' the Saracen said. 'The prisoners don't have to be men.'

That pleased Lord Khan – women made it a lot easier. They were more difficult to abduct but easier to control and conceal: no foreign soldier would ever dare look beneath a black veil and full-length robe.

'Can you give me three weeks?' Khan asked. The Saracen couldn't believe it – he would have waited three months if he'd had to. Not trusting words to express his gratitude, he reached out and warmly embraced the old warrior.

Their business concluded, Lord Khan pulled a bell rope, summoning his staff back into the room. He didn't say it but the less time he spent with the Saracen alone, the easier it was to disclaim any knowledge of future events.

'And what of you, my friend?' he said as the door opened and his guards entered. 'You are blessed with a wife?'

Lord Khan was making casual conversation for the benefit of his retainers, but he knew from the shadow of grief that passed across his visitor's face it was a question which would have been better left unasked.

'I was blessed,' the Saracen replied softly. 'Immediately after I graduated as a doctor I went to Gaza, to the Jabalia refugee camp. I knew that was where the people's need was the greatest.'

Several guards and retainers exchanged a glance – Gaza was not somewhere to be taken lightly; it was probably the only place in the world that made Afghanistan look safe.

'I had heard a woman lecture about it while I was studying medicine in Beirut; she was the one who introduced me to the idea of the far enemy,' the Saracen continued.

'After I arrived I found her again. Two years later we were married and then—' His fist clenched and he shrugged, the simple action conveying more about loss than any words.

'How did she die?' Lord Khan asked. Nobody in the room took their eyes off the visitor.

'An Israeli rocket – she was a passenger in a car.'

There was a long silence. None of the listeners had anything new to add; everything they felt about the Israelis had been said long ago.

'She was targeted?' Lord Khan asked finally.

'They said she wasn't – collateral damage. But you know how the Zionists lie.'

Khan nodded his head then spoke reverently. 'Peace be upon her. What was her name? I will pray for her.'

'Amina was what most people knew her by. Amina Ebadi,' the Saracen said. 'My wife, the mother of my only child.'

Chapter Thirty-three

THAT NIGHT THE SARACEN SET UP HIS MAKESHIFT CLINIC ON THE verandah of the guest house, and it was while standing there two days later, tending to a child with a shattered leg, that he saw Lord Khan and his bodyguards ride out.

The story in the fortress and town was that the warlord had decided to visit the far-flung graves of his five younger brothers, all killed in various conflicts, but in truth he was riding hard for the Iranian border.

Three weeks later he returned, exhausted and complaining of a sharp pain down his left arm, which was purely an excuse to rouse the visiting doctor from his bed. They sat alone in the guest house, once more drinking tea, the Saracen listening intently as Lord Khan told him to be ready to leave immediately after dawn prayers.

Pulling out a US Army survey map and tracing the route, Khan said the Saracen had four hundred miles of hard travelling ahead of him. Avoiding villages, sticking to old *muj* supply trails, he would travel alone through some of the harshest and most remote territory on earth. At eight thousand feet, halfway up a mountain which had never been named, only numbered, he would find a Soviet forward observation post which had been left in ruins years ago.

There, he would rendezvous with a group of men and, in the solitude of the high peaks, far from any form of civilization, his prayers would be answered.

'Have the prisoners been taken yet?' the Saracen asked, heart soaring.

'Tonight. They have been watched and chosen – two men and a woman. The woman is pregnant.'

231

Chapter Thirty-four

THE SARACEN DIDN'T SEE THE EIGHT TRIBESMEN WHO BROUGHT THE merchandise. It was night and they arrived at the old observation post in silence, the hooves of their horses wrapped in rags to muffle the sound.

It wasn't just the Saracen who never laid eyes on the strange caravan – in the week preceding their arrival, nobody else had either. For seven days the tribesmen had made camp just before dawn, slept during the daylight hours and travelled as fast as their horses would carry them through the night.

I know this because a long time later – after the events of that grim summer were over – a team of Special Forces and CIA agents secretly crossed the border into Iran, stormed the men's fortified village and interrogated them with what used to be called 'extreme prejudice'. I'm sure none of the eight ever fully recovered.

Of course, not even the tribesmen were on Mountain 792 long enough to witness exactly what the Saracen did but, having seen all the secret evidence and, as I mentioned earlier, knowing more about him than anyone on earth, I am probably in the best position to say what happened up in the high mountains – an area which, despite the Saracen's constant prayer rituals, must have given an entirely new meaning to the term 'godforsaken'.

Even though the tribesmen had muffled their ponies well, the Saracen knew that they were there. Four days earlier, he had arrived and set up camp in the observation post's old bunkhouse, blasted deep into the rock, and it was inside the cave that he awoke with a start. It was either his battlefield intuition or the restless movement of his horses that told him that he was no longer alone on the mountain.

Lying motionless, he assumed that by choosing the small hours of a moonless night, their ponies carefully silenced, the kidnappers didn't want to be seen even by him, so he made no move to go and greet them.

After thirty minutes he thought he heard the slap of reins, as if a horse was being urged into a trot down the mountain, but he couldn't be sure. He gave it another twenty minutes then scrambled out on to the broad rock shelf.

The tribesmen – halfway down the mountain and pausing to water their ponies – looked back and saw the tiny glow of a hurricane lantern. That was all they saw of the person who, very soon, would become the most hunted man on earth.

The kidnappers had left the three prisoners chained to ringbolts which had once secured a communication mast, and it was there that the Saracen first saw them – bound hand and foot, gagged, the woman half shrouded in the black robe that had been used to disguise her on the wild journey.

Satisfied that they were properly secured, the Saracen approached them and lifted the woman's robe in order to examine her more closely. Underneath, he saw that her cotton shirt was crumpled and ripped and her jeans had lost the buttons at the fly. He couldn't help but wonder what had happened to her on the trip – the outlaws who abducted her might have been devout Muslims, but they were also men.

Her tattered shirt barely covered her belly and the Saracen, being a doctor, guessed from the sight of it that she was about four months pregnant. A different man – a less religious and a more humane man – might have been affected by it. But not the Saracen: the prisoners weren't people to him, they were a gift from God.

He turned and saw, hanging on the steel mount that had once supported a pair of Soviet field binoculars, that a package containing not only the keys to their manacles but their passports and wallets had been left for him.

As the gagged prisoners watched, he opened the documents and learned that the woman was Italian, twenty-eight years old, unmarried, an aid worker with WorldVision. He guessed that she had been grabbed while on one of her field trips, probably betrayed by the people she was trying to help.

He turned to the back of the woman's passport and looked at the photograph. Though nobody would have known it from her filthy state, it showed she was a pretty woman: long, dark hair, a ready smile, deep-green eyes. Those eyes didn't leave the Saracen's face, trying to communicate, pleading, but he ignored them and turned his attention to the men.

The younger of them was Japanese. In his mid-twenties, he sported spiky hair and a barbed-wire tattoo around one muscular forearm. The Saracen had seen enough of popular culture in Lebanon to know that the man would be considered hip or cool. He disliked him instantly. According to his documents, he was a free-lance sound-recordist. In light of the dangers in Afghanistan and the voracious demand of the 24-hour news channels, he was probably making a fortune, which would explain the four thousand dollars and the two small foils of cocaine tucked in the back of his wallet.

The guy shackled beside him – the oldest and calmest of them all – was a Dutch engineer. His book said he was forty-six, and the photos in his wallet revealed he was the father of three teenage kids. The visas indicated he had made a career out of hardship postings – Nigeria, Iraq, Bosnia, Kuwait – and survived them all. Not this time, *Insha'Allah*, the Saracen thought.

He looked at them all again. Though his face didn't show it, he was delighted: they were physically strong and his medical eye told him they were all in good health. If his home-made virus could kill them, it could kill anyone.

There was one other piece of good news: given their situation, they were relatively calm and he guessed that the tribesmen had told them they were a commodity in a well-worn financial transaction. Apart from opium poppies and hemp plants, kidnappings for ransom had become about the only growth industry in Afghanistan. The outlaws would have told the victims that, as long as they behaved properly and their employers knew how to play the game, no harm would come to them. A couple of weeks of living rough, then they would be back in their air-conditioned compounds, their employers would be a few hundred thousand dollars lighter, and a group of villages with no running water or means of support would have enough to live on for another ten years.

The Saracen took the gags out of their mouths and threw them three water bottles. They had barely finished drinking before they started trying to communicate with him. Because English was the only language the three prisoners had in common, they tried it first. The Saracen shrugged, feigning that he had no idea what they were saying. Having had no success, the woman tried the few bits of Urdu, the national language of Pakistan, she had picked up while working there. After that it was Dari, the most common of the Afghan languages, but the three prisoners' pronunciation was so bad and their vocabulary so limited even they had no idea what they would have said had he replied.

Instead he spoke to them fast in Arabic, and now it was their turn to look confused. With seemingly no hope of communication, the Saracen turned and walked into the bunkhouse. By the time he brought the horses out, the three prisoners were speaking softly to one another in English, their discussion confirming what the Saracen had guessed: they were certain they had been abducted for ransom. The Japanese hipster even suggested they try to drag the chain in order to give the AWAC overflights, or whatever other means were being employed, the best chance of finding them.

The Dutch engineer had been watching the Saracen, and he wasn't convinced he was just a lowly escort. There was something in his economy of movement, the coiled energy, that made the Dutchman think it wouldn't be wise to toy with him. He'd seen the same quality in the battle-hardened guerillas in Kosovo, the toughest men he had ever known.

'I think we should let the negotiators play it out,' he advised. 'We've got a saying in Holland: "If the shit is up to your neck – whatever you do, don't make waves."'

Before they could discuss it further, the Saracen yelled at them. Although they couldn't translate the words, they clearly understood the zipping motion he made across his mouth: he wanted silence and, when he took his prayer mat out of his saddlebag, they understood why. Dawn was breaking and it was time for the first prayer of the day.

As soon as he was finished, the Saracen picked up his AK-47, took the safety off, set it to full automatic and undid their leg manacles. One by one, their hands still cuffed, he bundled them on to the back of the horses, shoving hard on the Japanese guy's injured arm – wounded when the outlaws did the uptake – being particularly brutal to him. Nobody was going to drag the chain on this excursion.

The first day's travel was the easiest, but by nightfall the three prisoners were still exhausted and saddle-sore. The Saracen ordered them off the horses, manacled them by lengths of chain attached to a steel spike he had driven into the ground, and set about building a fire while they shuffled behind boulders to pee and crap.

With his back to them, he prepared a pot of tea black and sweet enough to mask the taste of the strong sedative he had added, then poured it into three mugs. Throughout the terrible day he had refused to pass the water canteens around, despite their mimed pleas, and the prisoners drank long and deep of the tea. The Saracen threw blankets down on the ground next to the fire and, within an hour, his charges, still manacled and cuffed, had all slipped into a deep and strange sleep.

The Saracen approached the woman, who was lying on her face, legs apart, one knee cocked up, and knelt beside her. With the two men passed out, there was no risk of him being disturbed, and he reached out and lowered the jeans with the missing buttons until her brief white panties were exposed.

He stared for a moment, then his hand touched her exposed buttock and slid slowly towards the softness of her inner thigh. Only at the last moment did he recall that he was a man of God and a doctor and stop himself. He turned away, breathing hard, and looked up at the starlit night. He murmured a prayer for forgiveness, took several minutes to compose himself and then opened the small roll of medical supplies which he had taken from a packhorse earlier in the night. Inside was a tube of numbing gel, a bi-pronged needle and the two remaining glass vials of smallpox vaccine that he had stolen from the facility in Syria.

During the day's long ride he had decided that she would be the best candidate to test whether the virus could break through the vaccine and, as a result, he had to immunize her as fast as possible. He had quickly dismissed the idea of vaccinating her in the arm – he didn't want her to be able to see the site and start asking herself what it meant – and had concluded that the point where her buttocks met would be best. She wouldn't be able to see it and she would almost certainly believe it was a saddle-sore.

Apart from his brief encounter with temptation, the vaccination went off without difficulty, and the following morning the woman woke with a fever, a searing headache and a swollen sore on her butt.

236

The Saracen listened as the men speculated that something might have bitten her in the night and then watched them turn and mime to him that the woman would have difficulty riding. The Saracen mimed back that it was a saddle-sore, gave them full canteens of water and placed a blanket over the woman's saddle to cushion it for her. He even helped boost her up into the seat.

For six more days, travelling both by day and night, stopping only when he was too exhausted to carry on, the Saracen rode behind them, using a knotted rope to keep the horses, and sometimes their passengers, awake and moving.

Within twenty-four hours of the inoculation, the woman's fever had started to diminish and, though he had no way of knowing – short of removing her jeans and seeing if there was a scar – he was confident that the vaccine had taken.

Climbing higher every hour, they took a long, looping route to avoid any human settlement and headed deep into the bleakest part of the Hindu Kush. Despite their overwhelming fatigue, the prisoners weren't surprised at the pace the Saracen set: everybody in Afghanistan, on both sides of the kidnapping divide, knew that one of the rules of the business was that, immediately after the uptake, the merchandise had to be kept moving.

Nevertheless, understanding the reasons didn't make the journey any easier, and by the time the Saracen arrived at his final destination, the prisoners were barely conscious from exhaustion. They raised their lolling heads – it was just after midnight – and looked at an abandoned village so remote and hidden that a mountain herdsman would have been hard pressed to find it.

Not the Saracen, though – he knew it as well as any place on earth.

Chapter Thirty-five

LEAVING THE PRISONERS HANDCUFFED, HE HOBBLED THE HORSES AT THE entrance to the village, held his weapon at the ready and returned to the heady days of his youth.

Back in his laboratory in Lebanon, he had come to the conclusion that there was only one place remote enough to conduct his human trial – the ruined village where he had bivouacked for over a year during the Soviet war.

Now, as he walked its broken streets – every building familiar, every blackened fire-pit full of memories – he sang out a greeting in Arabic. *'Allahu Akbar,'* he called.

He had no way of knowing if the Taliban, a group of war refugees or one of the endless caravans of drug couriers had colonized the place, and he had no intention of bringing his prisoners in until he knew that he was alone.

'Allahu Akbar.' God is great. And the only reply he received was the sound of the wind, the constant biting wind he remembered so well, the one that blew all the way to China. Confident he was alone, he turned past the old mosque and stepped into the kitchen where he had first shared a cigarette with Abdul Mohammad Khan.

The ghosts danced all around him – he could almost see the bearded faces of the other *muj* who had been sitting in a semicircle, making their final requests of the great warlord. They were all so young then, so alive. For the Saracen it was before he was married, before he had a child of his own, and for a moment he remembered what it was like to have so much road in front of you and barely any behind.

He pulled himself out of his reverie, lit a fire in the hearth for probably the first time since the *muj* had left and made a makeshift stable in the area where the grain had once been stored. Only then did he bring the prisoners in, chain them to the old sinks, refill their water bottles and give them each two of the hardtack biscuits which had sustained them since their capture and which they had now come to hate.

They ate them mechanically, too exhausted to care, and didn't even bother spreading out their bedrolls, curling up instead on the old straw piled in a corner. For the two men, it was the last unfevered sleep they would ever have.

The three of them woke in the morning to the sound of hammering. The Saracen had been up for hours, rebuilding one of the stone storehouses perched on the edge of a cliff, not far from the mosque. The three prisoners could see, by looking through chinks in the wall, that he had repaired one section which had collapsed and was now using one of the horses to haul in a hardwood door which would replace the flimsy one that had fallen from its hinges. It was clear this was going to be their cell.

Only once did the Saracen enter the kitchen, and that was to retrieve the pane of reinforced glass from boxes containing what, to the prisoners, looked like medical supplies. They watched him return to his building site and set the glass halfway up a wall and seal it into the stone with a mixture of mud and mortar. A window? That was strange, the prisoners thought. But it wasn't a window at all – it was an observation panel.

Just after lunchtime, wordlessly he transferred them to what would become their stone tomb. Once inside, they looked around and saw that he had thrown a pile of saddle blankets into a corner for bedding, dug a toilet pit behind a rough curtain and provided a box of hardtack, four large casks of water and a wood stove with a good supply of fuel. Once again they tried to communicate with him, demanding to know how long they would be kept in the airless room, but he just checked the chains that secured them to ringbolts in the wall and left.

A short time later they heard the sound of the horses' hooves on the stone roadways and, by climbing up on one of the water casks to peer through the observation panel, they saw that he was riding out with his string of ponies. Where in God's name could he be going? The nearest human habitation had to be at least several days' travel away, even on a fast horse, and it was unlikely he would leave them unguarded for that length of time.

Even so, they set about trying to work the ringbolts free of the rock in which they were set. It was an agonizingly slow and thankless task – the only implements were shards of wood from their fuel pile – and after four hours they had made hardly any impression on the granite and mortar, when they heard the horses returning.

Again using the observation window, they saw that the Saracen immediately disappeared into the maze of crumbling streets and houses, digging and hammering, then periodically returned to the packhorses and unloaded several grey metal boxes and at least a dozen wooden barrels. Where he had found them, they had no idea.

That night, for the first time since he had entombed them, the cell door opened. The Saracen entered and wordlessly laid down three plates of what looked like a vegetarian curry accompanied by a pile of the circular flat bread the Afghans call *naan*. It was the first hot food the prisoners had seen in almost two weeks, and they fell upon it ravenously. As plain as the food was, the Dutch engineer said laughingly it was the finest meal he had ever eaten.

Within an hour they were in a strange, dreamless sleep. No wonder – both the naan and the curry were laced with a barbiturate called pentobarbital, a drug so powerful as a sleeping aid that it is recommended by most groups which advocate euthanasia.

Just before 2 a.m., the Saracen, carrying a small surgical kit and an oil-filled hurricane lamp, re-entered the cell. He looked terrifying, dressed in his full black bio-hazard suit, Kevlar-lined gloves and helmet with its clear plastic face plate. On his back was an oxygen tank feeding air through a regulator into his taped and sealed lifeboat.

Working quickly, trying to preserve as much of the oxygen as possible, he knelt beside the woman, removed her jeans, pulled aside her smelly underwear and checked the site of the vaccination. With quiet satisfaction, he saw the flat scar and knew that the vaccine had taken perfectly. She was as well protected as modern science could make her.

He replaced her clothing and started working on the sound-recordist first. He rolled up the sleeve of the man's T-shirt and looked at the barbed-wire tattoo. The Saracen hated tattoos and chose that as his spot.

He took out a syringe and checked its plunger through the clear plastic of his face plate. Satisfied, he reached over to the kit and removed one of the two glass vials with the extra zero added to its batch number. It was sealed with a special rubber top and the Saracen, holding the syringe in his Kevlar-gloved hand, pushed the needle through the rubber and into the bottle.

With the sound of his rapid breathing rattling through the oxygen regulator, he pushed air into the vial then pulled on the plunger and filled the syringe with what could be the most lethal pathogen on the planet. Time would tell.

By the dim light of the hurricane lamp – definitely a scene from the inner circle of hell – the man in the black bio-hazard suit bent over the prisoner and, with a final prayer to Allah, slowly slipped the needle into the barbed wire.

The Saracen was a good doctor, long experienced in administering intravenous medications, and the young Japanese hipster barely stirred in his drugged sleep as the needle went deeper and found the vein. Gradually the Saracen pressed down on the plunger and watched the level of clear fluid drop as it poured into the victim's bloodstream. After ten seconds it was done and the young man sighed quietly and rolled over in his sleep.

The Saracen immediately put the glass vial and syringe into a special red bio-hazard container which he had filled earlier with industrial-strength Lysol disinfectant.

Next, he turned his attention to the Dutch engineer, repeating the procedure on the man's thigh and only stopping when – for a moment – he thought the initial needle prick had woken him. He was mistaken and, gripping the syringe firmly, he pushed down and attempted to separate the man from his wife and three kids, as surely as if he were holding the barrel of the AK-47 to his temple.

With his experiment complete, he picked up his surgical kit, the bio-hazard container and the hurricane lamp.

In silence – even the sound of the air regulator seemed to have stilled – he headed for the door, praying hard that his virus was deep fried and that the extra gene had made it a weapons-grade vaccine buster.

Chapter Thirty-six

I DON'T SUPPOSE THERE ARE MANY GOOD WAYS TO DIE, BUT I KNOW one of the worst: far from home and family, chained like a dog in an abandoned village, your body collapsing under the onslaught of smallpox and only a bearded face at a sealed glass window to hear your screams for help.

All the prisoners had woken late the following morning with a headache hammering at the base of their skull. They wondered if it was a reaction to the food but not for a minute did they think they might have been drugged. Why would anyone do that? It wasn't as if they might escape – they were chained to ringbolts in a stone cell.

When the two men finally dragged themselves up to wash at a small basin, they both found what appeared to be a small bite mark: a reddened area on one man's tattooed bicep, the other guy with one on his thigh. Their immediate thought was scorpions or spiders, and they set about using an oil lamp to search every inch of the cell, to no avail.

As the day wore on, and through the next twelve days, the fevers and night sweats got steadily worse. It fell to the woman to try to tend to them in the stifling cell. She changed their blankets, brought them food, mopped their burning bodies and washed their soiled clothes. All the time she was surrounded by their sweat, their breath and their spittle – she didn't realize it, but she was swimming in an unseen ocean, surrounded by billions of molecules of infection, a place white-hot with the pathogen.

On one occasion, desperate to get fresh air into the cell, she stood on one of the water casks and looked out of the window to try to attract the Saracen's attention. What she saw scared her more than any other thing during their long ordeal, and she couldn't say why. He was standing thirty yards away and was talking animatedly on a satellite phone. Up until then, she had assumed he was just a labourer in their particular enterprise but now she thought he might not be the monkey after all – perhaps he was the organ grinder. Due to the way he was holding the phone, she could see his face clearly and she thought from the movement of his lips and the few words which she could decode that he was speaking in English. He rang off, turned and saw her at the glass. A look of dismay, followed by wild anger, crossed his face and she knew in that instant she had witnessed something she was never meant to see.

It didn't help her, though.

That afternoon, all the men's symptoms, which had been steadily accruing, avalanched – the fever went suborbital, the blisters that had been forming on their limbs swept across their outer extremities and filled with pus, the nights became filled with hallucinatory dreams, their veins and capillaries started to burst, turning their skin black from haemorrhaging blood, forcing the flesh to split from their skeleton, their bodies expelling strange odours, and the pain got so bad that they screamed for two days until they probably died from exhaustion as much as anything else.

Every few hours, the Saracen's face would appear at the window to check on the progress of his creation. What he saw, to his delight, was the results of a very hot virus indeed and, while he couldn't be sure, it appeared to be a type of *Variola major* called haemorrhagic smallpox. Known among researchers as 'Sledgehammer', it causes catastrophic bleeding in the body's largest organ – the skin – and is one hundred per cent fatal. *One hundred per cent.*

By the time the men had died, the woman herself was suffering from a rocketing temperature and horrifying night sweats and she knew that she was now rapidly circling the drain. Late one night the Saracen watched with satisfaction as she staggered to the basin to cool her burning face and found the first blisters on the back of her hand. In that moment, the Saracen knew that not only had he synthesized a red-hot virus which was highly infectious but the addition of the extra gene had also allowed it to crash through the best state-of-science vaccine. It was, without question or salvation, a terror weapon to end all terror weapons.

Because she had seen the future, both for herself and the unborn child with which she had already fallen in love, she took it even harder than the men, and the Saracen resorted to gazing at the spectacular view, stuffing his ears with cotton and reciting the Qur'an to drown out her cries.

When she finally bled out, he didn't move. He wanted to savour the moment: the three bodies proved that he was now within reach of an event which terrorism experts have found so frightening they have given it a special name. They call it the 'soft kill' of America.

Chapter Thirty-seven

THIS IS THE UNALLOYED TRUTH: WITHOUT AN EFFECTIVE VACCINE, NO country on earth could survive an orchestrated smallpox attack, not even a country of 310 million people which is responsible for over 50 per cent of the world's wealth, which had enough nuclear armaments to destroy the planet a hundred times over and had produced more Nobel prizewinners in science and medicine than any other nation on earth. It would be as helpless in the face of *Variola major* as the three prisoners who were lying dead in their own fluids in the stone tomb.

But just one man, one virus – could it really be done? The Saracen knew it could and, surprisingly, so did Washington.

It was called Dark Winter.

That was the name of a bio-terror simulation conducted at Andrews Air Force Base in the spring of 2001. Years later, working in Lebanon, the Saracen had read a report into the exercise's findings on the Internet. Even if he had never thought of weaponizing smallpox, the once-secret report would have certainly pointed him in the right direction.

Dark Winter postulated a smallpox attack on the United States in which one infected person entered a shopping mall in Oklahoma City. It then plotted the spread of the disease and projected the number of casualties. Thirteen days after the sole infectee entered the mall, the virus had spread to twenty-five states, infected hundreds of thousands of people, killed one third of them, overwhelmed the healthcare system, sent the economy into free fall and led to a more or less total collapse in social order. Naturally, the virus was indiscriminate in whom it attacked and cops, firefighters and health workers fell victim as fast as the population in general – probably faster – and looting and fires broke out unchecked. Hospitals were forced to lock and barricade their doors. The exercise was stopped early: nobody needed to learn any more.

All of those who read the report and participated in its production probably had the same thought – that was one infected person in a mall in Oklahoma City carrying a not particularly hot strain of the virus. Imagine the New York subway, Macy's Thanksgiving Day Parade or the Superbowl.

And while the government eventually ordered the production and stockpiling of the vaccine, no real funding was given to finding a cure for the disease – the only certain way to consign smallpox to history and take it off the shelf of potential weapons. As many people have noted: generals are always fighting the last war, not the next one.

And what if there were twenty, a hundred, a thousand infected people? Although the Dark Winter report never made it specific, all the CIA analysts, bio-defence experts, epidemiologists and their endless computer simulations appeared to assume that the person in Oklahoma City was a suicide infectee – someone deliberately dosed with the virus and then let loose in America.

But to the Saracen, the use of suicide infectees – known as vectors to pathologists – was nonsense. While it might be possible in a refugee camp in Gaza to find young martyrs willing to walk into a café wearing bomb belts, killing yourself in one magnificent blast was very different from the slow agony of smallpox. Having worked alongside his wife in the camps, the Saracen knew no would-be warriors would find anything heroic in pus-filled blisters – even if you could get them through US Immigration in the post 9/11 world.

No, he had thought up something far more effective than any scenario imagined by the American experts. By his estimate, his plan would provide at least *ten thousand* vectors spread throughout the length and breadth of the far enemy.

The soft kill of America indeed.

Chapter Thirty-eight

THE SARACEN TOOK THE COTTON OUT OF HIS EARS AND HEADED towards the village. At its edge, he stopped at a small cairn of stones he had placed there and counted every step as he walked forward. After nine paces he moved hard to the left and avoided a buried land-mine.

The whole village was booby-trapped – a task he had undertaken as soon as he had secured the prisoners in their stone tomb. Accompanied by his packhorses, he had set off along a maze of precipitous paths which led even higher into the towering mountains. After several wrong turns when his memory failed him, he found – in a chaos of wind-torn boulders – the entrance to a complex of caves.

The mountains were studded with such places – some natural, others hollowed out with dynamite – all used by the *muj* during their protracted war with the Soviets. This one, an ammunition dump, was built by the Saracen and his comrades then abandoned on the day the war ended.

By the beam of a flashlight he made his way into the deepest cavern. The light swept across the walls, revealing boxes of mines, grenades, mortars and other ordnance, which had sat untouched for so many years. Nearly all of it had been supplied by the CIA, so it was good quality – none of that Soviet or Pakistani crap – and the thin mountain air had preserved it better than any underground bunker.

The Saracen found what he needed, transferred it into grey ammo boxes and a dozen wooden barrels and returned to the village. All that afternoon and late into the night he rigged improvised explosive devices and booby traps along the alleys and throughout the ruined buildings. The reason was simple: unlike his attitude to the Soviets, he had respect for the US forces and many of their allies.

Ever since he had devised the human trial he had known that UN troops would be searching for the prisoners – with growing determination when they received no ransom demand – and though he believed they would never come to a wrecked village as remote as this, he wasn't taking any chances.

Now, with his mission almost at an end, he had to follow his secret signs carefully to avoid tripping an unseen wire or opening the wrong door. One mistake and he would join the Italian woman and her two friends in the choir invisible.

He made it back to the kitchen, fed the horses, cooked his dinner and slept better than he had in months. He woke with the dawn and, after the ritual washing and prayers, set about moving out. He had already dug a large pit behind the village headman's house and now he filled it with bags of the quicklime he had carried with him specifically for the purpose. The chemical would destroy the bodies and so degrade any other material thrown into the pit that no forensic specialist in the world would be able to find a clue about what had happened in that lonely and evil place.

Dressed in his bio-hazard suit, with one of his last tanks of oxygen strapped to his back, he used a hand bit to drill a small hole in the heavy wooden door. He slid a plastic tube with a small nozzle attached to the end of it through the hole, put the other end into a large container of Lysol and used a foot-operated pump to spray gallons of the disinfectant over the bodies and the interior of the cell. When he felt he had covered as much as possible, he swapped out the disinfectant for an old military can full of gasoline. He sprayed the fuel inside, dousing the bodies, the straw, the wooden beams, and the stone itself. He pulled out the plastic tube and filled the hole with a gasoline-soaked rag, put a match to it and moved back fast to safety.

He had been in two minds about torching the cell in order to help sterilize it, afraid that the smoke would attract attention, but the day was clear and bright and he was confident that the timber inside was so old that it would burn fast and clean. He was right about that, but he was astonished by the ferocity of the fire – as if nature itself were offended by what had been done within its walls.

Once the flames were out, he extinguished the embers with more Lysol and, still wearing his bio-hazard equipment, used the horses, coils of rope and several meat hooks to haul the charred bodies into the pit. They were closely followed by everything else that had been touched or used by any of them during their stay – plates, utensils, syringes, the burnt remnants of the saddle blankets. Still in the suit, he showered himself in disinfectant, stripped naked, showered himself again in the Lysol, dressed and tossed the suit into the quicklime.

It was dusk, and he'd almost finished refilling the grave when he went back to the kitchen to get the last two bags of lime to spread around the top of the pit in order to deter any wild animals.

Inside, the horses were waiting, ready to be saddled, and the solitude and silence of the high mountains was almost oppressive. Even the wind had dropped to a whisper.

He didn't hear a thing, and he would never have had any warning of the shit that was coming in at over two hundred miles an hour – except for the horses.

Chapter Thirty-nine

THE SOVIETS HAD STARTED IT, AND THE UN AND US TROOPS HAD followed: all the assault helicopters in Afghanistan were fitted with silenced rotors and engines. It meant you didn't hear them until they were right on top of you.

At least humans didn't. The *muj*, however, had realized the horses were different and, long ago, they had learned to read their ponies' behaviour as if their lives depended on it.

The Saracen, lifting the bags of lime on to his shoulder, heard two of the ponies snicker and turned to look. It had been years since he had seen horses act in that way, but it might as well have been yesterday. Helicopters were coming!

He dropped the bags, grabbed his AK-47 and a backpack containing his passport, money and medical equipment, untied the horses, whacked them on the rump and sent them bolting into the falling night. He knew they would make their way down to the valleys below, where the villagers who found the eight prized mountain ponies – worth the equivalent of one large Hino truck – wouldn't jeopardize their good fortune by reporting it to anyone.

Two minutes later, three UN choppers, with twenty Australian troops aboard, landed – alerted by a report from a satellite that was using thermal imaging to scan remote areas for the abductees. Ironically, it was the virus and not the fire which had sent up a red flag. Because of the high fever which accompanies smallpox, the analysts interpreting the satellite images looked at the thermal footprint captured a day previously and did not even consider that it could have been generated by three people. More like eight, which was about the size of the group they were hunting. It never occurred to anyone – not the analysts, nor the CIA agents at Alec Station handling the recovery operation, nor anyone else at the agency – that a single man could be in control of three prisoners. Kidnappings didn't work like that.

Consequently, when the Australian troops scrambled out of the choppers expecting to find a small group of Taliban or a caravan of drug runners, they had planned for at least five potential hostiles and the possibility of crossfire slowed them down considerably. So did the first improvised explosive device.

When two of the privates, following correct procedure, came to a doorway into a house on the edge of the village, they stepped to either side of it and kicked it open, triggering two large landmines attached to the back of it. That explosion severed a wire disguised to look like an old laundry line stretched across the alleyway, detonating a mortar bomb behind them. The two privates had found their crossfire – they never had a chance.

The officer closest to them – a lieutenant by the name of Pete Keating – didn't bother consulting with his commanding officer, a captain standing several hundred yards away, a man who most of the squad considered if not downright dangerous, at least a fool. Keating ordered everybody back and flung a cordon round the entire village – something they should have done the moment they set down but which the captain hadn't thought necessary.

'What are the towel-heads gonna do – try and walk down the mountain?' he had asked. 'If they're in there, we'll give 'em a chance to surrender. Just yell out, "Hey, fellas – it's washday and we've got the machine,"' he had said, confirming to his men just what a racist fool he was.

Keating had tried again to convince him to surround the village, was refused and sent the men in cautiously. Now he was trying desperately to pick up the pieces. He dispatched four men to check on the two privates – not that he held out any hope – and the rest he deployed in two sweeping arcs to secure the village finally.

Three hundred yards away, the Saracen was running fast, body-swerving, keeping count of every step – heading for the village well and a steep slope which led to a barely discernible path and, beyond it, the freedom of the mountains.

Had Keating been less decisive and delayed by a minute, the Saracen would have escaped the cordon. But the lieutenant, fine soldier that he was, didn't hesitate and almost within sight of the path, the Saracen had to throw himself behind the well to avoid four approaching infantrymen.

Now he was trapped inside the iron circle and he knew that the young soldiers were giving the world its best chance of avoiding the catastrophe that had been so long in the making. He crouched and darted for a low rubble wall. He made it unseen and was back in the streets, where one false step, one misremembered wire, would cost him his life.

The soldiers were moving slowly, checking every building, detonating the IEDs as they found them, advancing in ever-tightening circles. The Saracen sprinted down a curving lane, through an old goat shed, and then had to beat a rapid retreat as he almost stumbled on top of more soldiers. He backtracked past the headman's house and into a rubble-strewn alley.

In his panicked state, it was a bad mistake: the path ahead was blocked by a pile of masonry. There was no way back: the encircling troops were so close behind that he could hear their personal communication devices. He unslung his AK-47 – better to die like a *muj* than forced to kneel like a dog – and looked to heaven for guidance.

He got it: the rooftops. If he could only get on to them, there were none of his booby traps up there so he would be able to move much faster. He gambled everything on it – racing towards the approaching troops, trying to get to a stone water cistern before they rounded a bend and saw him.

He reached the cistern, springing on to the flat top and using it as a stepping stone to scramble on to the roof of the old mosque. Moments later, as he lay flat, trying to control his gasping breath, the soldiers passed below. Then they stopped, trying to pick up the noise of anyone moving among the houses ahead.

There wasn't a sound, the silence so deep on the mountaintop that Lieutenant Keating – on the outskirts of the village and commanding his men by radio – started to wonder if the village was deserted. Maybe the place had been booby-trapped years ago by the departing *muj*. But why would they do that? The only people likely to reoccupy the houses were poor Afghan families or itinerant goat herders. No, the more likely explanation was that they had stumbled on some target of high value and the hostiles were lying low, watching. As a consequence, the silence was about the most dangerous thing Keating had heard and he spoke quietly to his squad on the radio. 'Slowly,' he said. 'Take it slow.'

The Saracen forced himself to stay frozen for a slow count of seven. He took off his soft leather sandals and, in his thick woollen socks, darted silently across the old mud tiles. He jumped one narrow alley, nearly plunged through a hole where the tiles had collapsed and threw himself behind a low parapet. That was when he saw his chance.

Peering through a small gap in the masonry, invisible to the Australians' night-vision goggles, he registered soldiers coming down three separate alleys. That was the tightening noose he had to either bend or break if he was going to escape. He put his sandals back on, dug his chin so hard into the masonry it started to bleed, pressed the assault rifle tight into his shoulder and thanked Allah it was fitted with a flash suppressor and a silencer.

A lesser combatant, a man who had never been a guerilla, would have shot to kill. But the Saracen knew his business well – on average it takes seven men to treat and evacuate a badly wounded soldier. The dead need nobody.

He chose one target in each of the three different alleys. If he hadn't had a silencer, they would hear the first shot and duck for cover; if it hadn't been for the flash suppressor they would see his position and rip him and the parapet to shreds with automatic fire.

He fired. The troops didn't even hear the three tiny pops through their static. One got it in the thigh – he was as good as dead unless they got a tourniquet on him. One took it in the throat, and there was probably nothing anyone could do for him. And the last had his forearm shattered, which was good enough for a lot of pain. All three went down screaming, their comrades diving for defensive positions, everybody trying to take each other's back.

Good troops, disciplined troops – and these were very good troops indeed, despite their captain – will do anything for their wounded. In the chaos of trying to help their downed comrades and locate the enemy, amid the darkness and terror of a firefight, groups of them were forced to scramble from piles of rubble to gaping doorways.

From behind the parapet the Saracen watched the circle bend – and then crack. It wasn't much and it probably wouldn't last long but maybe it would be enough. He didn't crouch – he just rolled down the sloping roof, his backpack and rifle clutched to his chest, and went over the falls. He watched the wall of a building flying by – Allah help him if he broke his leg – twisted in mid-air and crash-landed on his hip. The pain almost swamped him, but he got to his feet and ran. This was no time for an old *muj* to whimper or limp: he was a veteran of the most cruel war in decades and he wasn't going to cry like some Christian now.

He sprinted for the one twisting alley that would lead him through the broken cordon, momentarily out of sight of a clutch of soldiers thanks to the leaning facade of a ruined house. If the soldiers moved ten feet either way . . .

He made it through the noose. He passed a crescent moon he'd scratched on a wooden door, hoped to God he remembered well, and started to count. He ran twenty-five paces forward, took three left, successfully skirted a buried mine and saw the safety of the mountains directly in front.

From behind, he heard a soldier yelling at his comrades to hit the ground. He fully expected to hear the deafening rattle of carbines and lose all control of his legs as the bullets hit his exposed back and severed his spine. Instead, the soldier had found a trip wire leading to two grenades hidden in a pile of old oil drums. As his comrades hunkered down, the soldier jerked the wire.

The grenades exploded and, in their brilliant flash, Lieutenant Keating – running forward to try to reseal the cordon – saw the Saracen outside the noose, sprinting for the safety of a group of tumbled-down walls. Keating fell to one knee, slammed the stock of his carbine into his shoulder and fired. He had been trained by Special Forces, so he knew what he was doing: he bracketed three rounds in each burst and panned left to right and back again fast.

A few inches either way – one lucky shot even – and everything would have been different. But that wasn't in the stars that night – high-velocity rounds blasted stone and dirt all around the Saracen but none put him down. Keating cursed the night-vision goggles and the inevitable disconnect between eye and trigger. The Saracen, of course, thanked the hand of God.

He rounded a corner of three wrecked walls while in full flight, jagged left, swerved hard right and, still clutching his backpack and rifle, slid and tumbled down a steep slope and into the all-embracing darkness of a rock-strewn gully.

A young Australian officer had glimpsed him in the flash of a grenade for a fraction of a second. That was the only time the Saracen was ever seen by either civilian or military authorities. Until I met him, of course.

Chapter Forty

THE AUSTRALIANS DIDN'T PURSUE THE SARACEN, WHICH WAS A MISTAKE, but their mission was to find the three kidnapped civilians, not to chase a lone insurgent. As it turned out, though, in a night dogged by bad luck, there was one piece of overwhelming good fortune: because it was the Australian captain who had taken the round in the thigh, it meant that Lieutenant Keating was in command.

He was only twenty-six years old but he had already done one tour in the 'Ghan, so even at that age his face was full of years. He came from a little town called Cunnamulla – it's mostly wheat country that far out west, on the edge of what Australians call the never-never, so hot that the locals claimed a pervert was a man who preferred women to beer – but some of the neighbours ran a few sheep so Keating knew from an outbreak of foot-and-mouth disease what quicklime was used for.

That was why, when they finally made it into the kitchen and he saw the two discarded bags lying on the floor, he felt as if the ground was shifting under his feet. Quicklime was totally alien to that part of the world, and why would anyone have gone to the trouble of carrying it in? Not kidnappers, surely. He still believed the IEDs indicated that a high-value asset was being protected in the village, but he was no longer certain it was still alive. He immediately told his men to get their flashlights out and start looking for a grave or burial pit.

First they found the charred remains of the stone storage house, and it was while Keating was trying to work out what that meant that an urgent shout rang out.

It was one of the young grunts. Not bothering with his

communication headset or correct procedure, he yelled to his mates: 'I've found it – bring me a shovel.'

Keating heard, and he and several of his men came running – carefully because of the threat of unexploded IEDs – to the area behind the headman's house. One look at the freshly turned soil – deep and wide enough to contain God-knows-what, traces of lime scattered around – and Keating was in no mood for taking any chances.

'Get back now! Everybody deploy to the LZ. Move!'

One of the sergeants – like all the others, no idea what was going on – turned to Keating. 'What about searching the remaining houses, boss? Might be more hostiles.'

Keating shook his head. The elaborate IEDs and the fact that nobody had tried to nail the squad made him certain that the village's only occupant had disappeared into the night. 'No, Sarge – whatever it is, I think we've found it.'

At the landing zone – the wounded being treated, the squad's lone medic trying to get an IV into the captain's arm – Keating immediately used the secure communications network to put a call through to their base.

The Medevac choppers were already on their way to uplift the wounded, and the base operator, two hundred miles away in an air-conditioned blockhouse, assumed the officer was calling to hurry them up and that pretty soon he'd start whining about how they were on the front line *and all they needed was some goddamn support*. Just like they always did.

But Keating cut through the guy's bored update on the choppers and told him they needed a hazchem unit on the mountainside *right now*. Being the army – of course – that started a host of questions, requests for authorization and confusion about the chain of command. Keating knew it could go on for hours, so he yelled at the hapless operator: 'We may have been exposed – are you listening? For all I know it's nuclear. Certainly something serious.'

Like the operator, Keating's men – including the barely conscious captain – were stunned. For a moment even the rising wind seemed to be swallowed by the silence. Then the operator started speaking fast, telling him to hold on while he opened a host of channels so that Keating could go through the chain of command as fast as possible.

Keating hung up – he knew that losing the connection would

galvanize them into even more hurried action: in the army – as in life – sometimes you had to create a crisis in order to get people's attention. He didn't believe it was nuclear, but his intuition told him they had stumbled on to something evil and he didn't know any other way to convey the urgency. He'd already decided he was going to get his ass busted for overreacting, but what else could he do?

While the staff officers back at base spun into a whirlwind of activity, what none of them realized was that, if the captain hadn't been shot, if Keating had grown up somewhere other than in the Australian west, had he not known the look and use of quicklime – if it hadn't been for these things and a whole lot more – the team of men in spacesuits equipped with their inflatable silver dome and towers of Klieg lights would never have arrived in time.

As it was, their fleet of Chinook helicopters landed with less than an hour to spare – any delay would have meant the quicklime would have done its work and they would never have found the corner of one saddle blanket.

Chapter Forty-one

BY THE TIME THE CHINOOKS HAD LANDED, THE SARACEN WAS ALREADY down the first of the precipitous slopes and crossing a narrow, windswept plateau. If the Western world had got lucky by having Keating take command on the mountaintop, the Saracen had also encountered his own share of good fortune. He was on horseback.

His climb down the slope had become increasingly difficult, thanks to his injured hip. His experience as a doctor told him it wasn't broken but, whatever damage he had done, he was finding it increasingly difficult to walk.

Without a crutch or length of wood to take the weight, he knew that, pretty soon, he would have to find a cave or a hole in the ground to lay up in for at least a few hours to try to rest it. That's when, just as he started across the plateau, he saw the horse.

It was one of his pack ponies, looking lost and forlorn in the starlight, which had become separated from its brethren. It recognized his voice and, hoping as much for company as some treat, trotted towards him obediently. He grabbed the lead rope he had slashed earlier in the night, used it as a makeshift halter and scrambled on to its back.

He urged it into a canter and travelled fast across the plateau, found a path that the goat herders used in summer to access the high pasture and gave the pony its head. Mountain-bred and sure-footed, it carried him quickly down the crumbling path, instinctively avoiding the washaways of loose gravel and never losing its head, even when the drop below its hooves was a thousand feet or more.

By the time dawn came, US and UN helicopters were over the narrow plateau and searching hard, but they thought they were looking for a man on foot and they predicated all their arcs and grids on that assumption. Given that the terrain was riddled with ravines and caves, both of the natural and man-made variety, it was a slow and laborious process for the pilots and their spotters.

The perimeter of the search was steadily expanded, but the horse kept the Saracen well beyond its growing reach and, within two days, he had fallen in with a tribe of nomadic herders, riding with them during the day and sleeping between their tents at night.

Early one morning, travelling along a high ridge, he saw the old Trans-Afghan highway bisecting the valley below. He took his leave of the nomads and turned towards it.

Two hours later he had joined a river of broken-down trucks, speeding Toyota pick-ups and overcrowded buses and vanished into the chaos of modern Afghanistan.

Chapter Forty-two

THE MEN IN THE WHITE NBC SUITS – NUCLEAR, BIOLOGICAL AND Chemical – worked methodically inside their translucent silver dome. Mobile generators and sophisticated filters carried away the smell of dank earth and raw quicklime, replacing it with purified air kept at an unwavering sixty-eight degrees Fahrenheit.

Despite their slow progress, it took the technicians and their supervisors only a few hours to decide there was no nuclear material on the mountaintop.

This discovery didn't do much for Keating's reputation – or his career prospects. 'An alarmist' was about the kindest thing anyone in the chain of command had to say, before they pretty much lost interest in the entire exhumation. The general consensus among the hazchem crew was that some drug courier had decided to bury a couple of horses – either his own or, more likely, those belonging to some rival. When it came to feuds, everyone agreed, the Afghans were in a league of their own.

But there was one detail they couldn't sneer away, and that was the quicklime. It was what sustained Keating throughout those hard days – that and his overwhelming belief there was something badly awry, something deeply sinister in the jumble of buildings. Adding that feeling to the village's isolation and its spectacular view, he even gave it a name: the Overlook hotel, he called it.

Then the men inside the dome found the first charred body. Or at least what was left of it. They established that it was a woman and, though they had no evidence, they were certain that deeper down they would find two more dead – one Japanese and one Dutch. What sort of kidnapper dumped the uptake into a lime-filled pit without even making a ransom demand?

Beside the body, deep in a chemical sludge, they found what was left – barely two inches square – of what looked like a saddle blanket. They didn't know it, but on the last night of her life the woman had clutched it to her face and tried to asphyxiate herself to stop the relentless flood of pain. As a result it contained her saliva, blood, strands of tissue and a complete panel of genetic material from the blisters that had formed in her mouth and throat.

The blanket was still locked in her partly burnt hand, protecting it from the worst of the flames when the Saracen used the horses to drag her into the pit. Another hour and the quicklime would have destroyed it completely.

Worried now, and forced to acknowledge it might not be a kidnapping at all – instantly rehabilitating Keating's reputation and career prospects – the NBC team and their supervisors greatly accelerated the workrate. Their first task was to discover exactly what they were dealing with, so they sealed the small square of blanket into an airtight bio-hazard container, secured it within another lead receptacle and sent it, first by helicopter and then on a special overnight jet, to Fort Detrick in Maryland.

Chapter Forty-three

FORT DETRICK, PART OF THE UNITED STATES ARMY MEDICAL COMMAND, is made up of a collection of buildings and campuses set on twelve hundred high-security acres just outside the town of Frederick.

One of the largest of the campuses houses the nation's leading biological-warfare agency – the Research Institute of Infectious Diseases, an organization so steeped in secrecy that a number of conspiracy theorists have claimed that it was the lab where the government created HIV.

If they were right, perhaps the long, low building not far from what used to be known as Anthrax Tower was also where NASA staged the moon landing. Nobody knows, because very few people, not even those with security clearances as high as mine, have ever been allowed on to the site.

It was at one of the facility's bio-safety labs that the sealed box from Afghanistan arrived on a Sunday morning. Because nobody at the Overlook hotel knew what they were dealing with, it hadn't been marked as top priority.

For that reason, it was placed in a queue and wasn't opened until just after 9 p.m. By then, the only microbiologist working was a guy in his forties called Walter Drax – a petty, resentful man who was happy to work the graveyard shift because it meant he didn't have to put up with what he called the assholes and knuckle-draggers. In his mind, the A&Ks were a large cohort, one that included most of his co-workers and certainly everyone in management – the people who, he believed, had blocked every possibility of promotion and the higher pay it provided.

Working alone under what are called Biosafety Level Four

conditions, in a lab kept at negative air pressure, wearing a suit not dissimilar to the Saracen's, his air regulator connected to an overhead supply, he unsealed the box in a special cabinet, removed the small piece of saddle cloth and prepared it for analysis.

Peering at the screen of his electron microscope, he couldn't believe what he was seeing. Heart racing, sweating hard inside the bio-safety suit, he checked it three times – even changing out the microscope and going back to his work station and consulting the relevant literature and the institute's classified manuals – before he was convinced.

He was looking at *Variola major*. Instinctively, he knew that it was a very hot strain, but what really terrified him was what he saw when he looked deep into the knot of DNA at the centre of it: it had been genetically engineered. He had no doubt that it was a weaponized, military strain of the pathogen – a no-holds-barred weapon of mass destruction.

By unpicking the DNA knot and comparing the images in the manuals with what he could see through the microscope, he quickly learned that somebody had inserted a specific gene into it. There was only one reason he could think of why somebody would do that: the virus had been constructed to be vaccine-evasive.

If it worked – and Drax could see no reason why it wouldn't – nobody in the world, not even the Nazis with their cattle cars and canisters of Zyklon-B gas, would ever have been in possession of a more efficient killer.

The normal procedure in such an event – if anything in such circumstances could ever be considered normal – was for Drax to phone his duty supervisor at home and inform him of what he had found. But Drax didn't want to do that. He was damned if he was going to give any of the A&Ks a place in the institute's history – that *celebrityhood* – that he knew the discovery of weaponized smallpox would entail.

I mean, he told himself, the whole place still talks about the guys who found the Ebola virus in a damn monkey.

Instead, he decided to make an end-run around them all and speak to his cousin. He didn't like her much either, but she was married to a special assistant at the National Security Council – a man who Drax privately called Lip Gloss, given how smooth he was at sucking up to his superiors.

When he got him on the line, Drax – without explaining anything about the small square of saddle blanket – said he needed to speak to the highest-ranking member of the US intelligence community he could contact this late on a Sunday night. Lip Gloss laughed and said things didn't work that way and he'd better tell him what it was all about and, anyway, what was wrong with his own superiors, and surely they had a protocol in place—

Drax wasn't in any mood for delay. 'Oh, sorry,' he said. 'Perhaps you need some directions to Shut-Up Village. There's a secure line directly into the lab. Now do it – get somebody to call me, it's a national emergency.'

He hung up before Lip Gloss could reply and then sat down to wait. He hadn't felt so good in years.

It was the phrase 'national emergency' and the fact that Drax worked for the pre-eminent bio-defence laboratory which convinced Lip Gloss to call the Deputy Director of National Intelligence, a man whom he knew well because their teenage sons played baseball on the same team.

As a result, it was the deputy director who called Drax and listened with avalanching dismay as the technician told him about the piece of material that had arrived from Afghanistan and the different types of smallpox.

'Given the panic something like this would cause, I wanted as few people as possible to know – I thought it best to try and go straight to the top,' Drax told him.

The deputy director congratulated him on his foresight, told him to speak to nobody and to sit tight until he called back. The deputy director, however, had one immediate and overwhelming problem: was Drax telling the truth? Hadn't it been a scientist in the same unit at Fort Detrick who had been suspected of manufacturing anthrax and sending it through the post to several US senators? On the other hand, while the guy he had been speaking to on the secure line certainly sounded like a nightmare, that didn't necessarily mean he was a Fort Detrick nut-job.

He called the head of the institute, a high-ranking military officer and a well-respected scientist in his own right, swore him to secrecy, explained what he had been told and asked him – no, ordered him – to get to the lab immediately to confirm the provenance of the sample and examine Drax's findings.

Forty minutes later, sitting in front of Drax's electron microscope, the head of the institute called back and gave the deputy director the news the guy had been dreading. Now the machinery of government, and the sense of panic, started to go into overdrive. All that occurred while only two people at the nation's huge bio-defence facility – the organization that should have been at the epicentre of events – had any idea what was actually happening. As far as end-runs went, it was spectacular.

For the rest of us, it was fortuitous – it meant the government at least had a chance of keeping the situation secret. If the Saracen were to learn he was being hunted, he would either go to ground immediately or accelerate his plans. Maintaining secrecy was paramount and, in that regard, the next few hours would be critical . . .

Chapter Forty-four

THE SECRET HELD. BY MIDNIGHT ON THAT SUNDAY NIGHT ONLY NINE people in the world – apart from the Saracen – knew the truth. A short time later, even though I had long ago surrendered my badge, I became the tenth.

The first two initiates – Drax and his boss – were at the army's Research Institute of Infectious Diseases. The third was the Deputy Director of National Intelligence. Once he had confirmed the truth of what he had been told, he made an urgent phone call and the head of his department – the Director of National Intelligence – became the fourth.

The director, no grey bureaucrat, was steeped in the history and practice of the sprawling intelligence community: he had started his career at the National Security Agency, analysing photos of Soviet military installations taken by U2 overflights, and had then moved into covert operations with the CIA. Thanks to his dark history of targeted killings in that section and the fact that he was the most softly spoken person ever to work in Washington, he was given a nickname, which had followed him throughout his storied career. Whispering Death was what they called him.

He phoned the president, asleep in his bedroom in the family quarters on the second floor of the White House, and waited a moment while the commander-in-chief shook the sleep out of his brain and moved into the study next door. It was past 11 p.m. by then.

The president had been widowed for the past seven years and he didn't move into the adjoining room for fear of waking anyone; he had lived a monastic life since his wife had passed and he slept alone. No, he wanted to buy himself a little time to grab a robe from the back of the door. He could tell from the time of the call and the tone of Whispering Death's voice that something huge had happened, and he didn't want the damned *New York Times* reporting that he was lying in bed in his underpants when he heard.

Sitting at his desk, the president listened as Whisperer told him that a sample of live smallpox had been recovered from an abandoned village in Afghanistan, that it wasn't just ordinary smallpox, it appeared to have been engineered to crash through the vaccine, that the genetic analysis indicated it had been made from individual components that were readily available throughout the world, that the virus appeared to have undergone a dry-gulch clinical trial in the Hindu Kush mountains, that three innocent people were dead, and the only suspect, a person who nobody knew anything about, had escaped and undoubtedly vanished into one of the nearby Arab nations, which had a combined population of about four hundred million people. In short, they were facing a potential catastrophe.

It was in those circumstances that the president – who was very pleased he had put on his robe – became the fifth person to know the secret.

Neither he nor the Director of Intelligence had any doubt – not then or in any of the weeks that followed – that America was the target. With a sinking heart and growing anger, the president asked the director how long he thought they had before an attack was launched.

'I don't know,' Whispering Death replied. 'All I can tell you is that somebody – or some group – appears to have synthesized it and now has good reason to believe that it works. Why would they delay?'

'I understand,' the president said coldly, 'but you're the Director of National Intelligence, I need some sort of time frame – a best guess, anything.'

'How would I know? Damn soon, that's all I can say.' It was a small blessing that the White House recording system extended to the president's private study – it meant that there was now a historical record of the only time Whispering Death had ever been known to raise his voice.

He told the president he was about to call for a car and would be at the White House in twenty minutes. He rang off and sat in contemplation for a moment. In the long silence of his fear, he couldn't help thinking that Fort Detrick had once again lived up to its nickname – Fort Doom.

Chapter Forty-five

AS THE GOVERNMENT CAR SPED THROUGH THE DESERTED STREETS towards the White House, Whispering Death sat in the secure cocoon at the back, the thick glass privacy screen raised – and made a series of phone calls. The first one was to order the immediate arrest of Walter Drax. Even the most cursory glance at the guy's human-resources file showed he was a man with too much anger, a loose cannon who could never be trusted not to talk or boast.

A few minutes later, six men in three black SUVs gained access to the institute's campus, were met by several of the on-site security guards and walked into Drax's lab. With pistols clearly visible under their jackets, they told the institute's director to return to his office, flashed Drax some IDs which may or may not have been genuine FBI shields and told him he was under arrest on suspicion of espionage. Drax, looking completely flustered, told them he had no idea what they were talking about – he was a loyal American, had been all his life. They ignored him, read him his rights and, when he asked to see a lawyer, told him that would be arranged once he had been formally charged. Of course they had no intention of doing that – instead they took him to an airfield just the other side of Frederick where a waiting government jet flew them to a private airstrip in the Black Hills of South Dakota. From there, more government SUVs transported him to a remote ranch house and the bleak rooms it contained.

Ironically, in one of those strange coincidences that life sometimes throws up, it was the same house that I had been taken to after I had killed the Rider of the Blue – appropriated and put to a similar use by other members of the intelligence community after The Division was disbanded. Like myself so many years before, Drax and his secret were now lost to the world.

The second phone call Whisperer made – well, actually it was three phone calls – was to the ambassadors of Italy, Japan and Holland. He told them with deep regret that he had just learned that their nationals were dead, killed by their kidnappers when they realized troops were closing in. 'They made a hurried attempt to bury the bodies and we are exhuming the site now,' he said. 'Obviously, forensic tests and formal identification will take some time.' He told them that, for operational reasons, the information had to be kept secret and, while he didn't say so explicitly, he gave the impression that a hot pursuit was still in progress.

His last call was to the head of the CIA. Offering no explanation, which wasn't uncommon in the shadow world, he told him to organize to have the men in the NBC suits at the Overlook hotel informed that all tests had come back negative. Because they were no longer needed, they were to return to base immediately. Only after they had left were the CIA's own operatives to move in, seal the pit and secure the site completely.

By the time he had finished the phone calls – plugging the most obvious means by which the secret might escape – he had entered the gates of the White House.

Chapter Forty-six

THE SURPRISING THING ABOUT JAMES GROSVENOR WAS THAT HE WAS highly intelligent, personable and modest – in other words, a man far removed from the typical politician. Nobody had intended, least of all himself, that he would ever become the President of the United States.

He had been a businessman for nearly all his working life, the major part of it spent taking over distressed manufacturing companies and turning them around. Call him old-fashioned, but he believed in American industry, the skill of American workers and that hardworking men and women deserved a living wage and decent health care. One thing he didn't believe in was unions – if capital conducted itself properly, there was no need for them. Needless to say, his employees repaid him with their loyalty, and their productivity rates were always among the highest in the country.

The success – and the wealth – that followed his approach allowed him to take over ever larger enterprises and gave him a media profile as a man committed to saving the nation's industrial base. Phoenix Rising was the name given to the segment about him on *60 Minutes*. Shortly after it appeared he was offered the job of Secretary of Commerce and, having enough money and happy to take on a new challenge, he accepted. For a self-made man, government administration and its endless bureaucracy was a revelation, but he was not a man for turning and he made such a success of it that when the Secretary of Health was swept aside in a corruption scandal he moved to that department.

His wife had died from breast cancer and he brought to the

department a fierce commitment that hadn't been seen for years in the musty building on Independence Avenue. He was widely seen as championing the rights of ordinary citizens – much to the anger of the powerful health-care lobby – and that only served to raise his public profile even higher. Two years later he was asked to take the second slot on a presidential ticket. The candidate was a woman – the first ever to stand for the highest office on behalf of a major party – and Grosvenor knew that he had been selected to balance the ticket with a strong male presence.

None of his friends expected him to accept, but he and Anne had never had any kids and he found it harder and harder to fill the hole left by her passing. His answer was to work harder and find even greater challenges. Beneath the energetic exterior, he was a sad man – a decent one too.

After two days' careful thought he accepted but, in the private counsels of his own mind, he didn't give himself or the candidate much chance of prevailing. Nor did the polls. The country had already elected a black president, but accepting a woman as commander-in-chief just seemed a bridge too far at that stage of the country's evolution.

Then, while speaking at a rally in Iowa ten weeks before the election the candidate suffered a brain aneurysm. If the images of her crumpling to the stage and suffering a grand seizure weren't bad enough, the next four days as she lingered on life support while her family kept a bedside vigil were even worse.

Throughout it all, Grosvenor maintained not only his own schedule but undertook the majority of her engagements too, virtually single-handedly keeping the campaign alive. At every opportunity he spoke of how he had handled his own wife's illness and reminded the audience of what was really important in all their lives – good health, long life, the love of others. For once in a political campaign, it sounded genuine.

He had always been witty, a kind of twinkly, handsome man, and the polls tightened. But the real turning point came on the night the family decided to take the candidate off life support. Grosvenor was at the hospital and, after it was all over, he stepped outside a side door to get some air. Moments later, the candidate's husband joined him, both of them thinking they were completely unobserved.

But somebody was watching – a hospital worker, probably – and whoever it was captured the scene on a cellphone camera. Grainy, recorded at a substantial distance, it was an indistinct video but certainly clear enough to see the candidate's husband break down and start to cry. After a pause, when it was clear the man couldn't master his emotions, Grosvenor reached out, put his arms around the man and held him close for several minutes.

Two men, neither of them young, standing outside a hospital, one of them a candidate for vice-president and supporting the other in his time of anguish, was such a human, unscripted moment that, minutes after the anonymous camera-person uploaded it on to the Internet, it went viral. For the duration of the film clip, the electorate saw behind the curtain of image and spin, and what they recognized in the man who stepped to the front of the ticket was, I believe, a person not too different from themselves.

On the first Tuesday in November it wasn't a landslide, but Grosvenor – perhaps the most unlikely candidate in modern American politics – won enough to get him over the line. 'I'm Lyndon Johnson – without the assassination,' he told friends just before the inauguration.

But the one question nobody could answer – the one completely hammered by his opponent during the campaign – was whether James Balthazar Grosvenor had the steel necessary to handle a full-on crisis.

All of us – the nation, the world, the man himself – were about to find out.

Chapter Forty-seven

WHISPERING DEATH ENTERED THE OVAL OFFICE TO FIND THAT THE secretaries of state, defense and homeland security had been summoned and were already seated in front of the Lincoln desk. President Grosvenor's chief-of-staff was taking notes and using a small MP3 player to record what was said – whether it was for posterity, his autobiography or to boost his memory, nobody seemed quite sure.

The bare bones of the situation had already been explained to the three secretaries by the president, and that now made nine people privy to the secret. With the core of the government assembled, Grosvenor told them that there would be no greater act of treason than for any of them to divulge the threat that now confronted the nation – that meant to their wives, their children, their mistresses, page boys or anybody else they damn well cared to name.

They nodded their heads gravely, and Grosvenor just hoped it was genuine. He was about to launch into a hastily handwritten agenda when the Secretary of Defense interrupted. 'In light of what we know, wouldn't it be a good idea if we started with a reading from scripture or a short prayer?'

Grosvenor saw Whispering Death and the Secretary of State raise their eyes to heaven and realized that he had at least two atheists in the kitchen Cabinet.

'It's a fine idea, Hal,' he replied evenly to the Defense Secretary, 'and I'm sure all of us will ask privately for whatever spiritual help we need as the night wears on. For the moment, let's keep going, shall we?'

It was a good, diplomatic answer and it seemed to satisfy both Hal

Enderby, the Secretary of Defense, and the atheists sitting behind him.

The president turned to Whisperer. 'First, are we certain that the virus has been designed to try to crash through the vaccine?'

'Yes,' replied Whisperer. 'There's one gene – apparently associated with the immune system – that has been grafted on to its DNA. There is no way it's a random occurrence.'

'Will it work? Could it defeat the vaccine?' the president asked. 'I mean, this is way out on the frontier – it's never been done before, has it?'

'Unfortunately, sir, that's not true,' replied Whisperer, looking around, letting everyone know with his eyes that what he was about to say was highly classified. 'During the late 1980s the Soviets had at least ten tons of smallpox which they had developed for use in MIRV warheads.

'According to a highly placed asset of ours, that material had been engineered to be vaccine-evasive. I think we have every reason to believe it is possible.'

The revelation by the country's leading spook cast an instant pall over the room, broken only by the sole woman in the meeting – the Secretary of Homeland Security.

'But that doesn't mean this version works. The Russians are one thing, terrorists are completely different. We have no way of knowing, do we?' she said.

'I think we know,' President Grosvenor said. 'The man in the Hindu Kush had three prisoners – it's inconceivable his experiment didn't include vaccinating one of them and testing to see if the virus broke through.'

'That's my reading,' Whisperer agreed. 'Obviously, it worked – all the prisoners are dead.'

'It means we have no line of defence,' said the president. 'Three hundred million doses of vaccine are probably useless.' Silence filled the dimly lit room. 'We should have developed an anti-viral drug – a cure. That was the only real security,' Grosvenor said, almost to himself.

'That door's closed. There's no time now,' the Secretary of State, an older man who already looked exhausted, responded.

Grosvenor nodded and turned to Whisperer. 'And this is what they call a hot virus?'

'Very hot,' Whisperer said. 'I believe that was deliberate too. The hotter the strain, the faster it burns out.

'A virus isn't exactly alive,' he continued, 'but it's certainly not dead. It can't live outside the host – in this case, the human body.

'The faster it destroys the hosts, the faster the epidemic wanes. I don't believe whoever developed this wants to destroy the world – just us.'

'That's comforting,' the president said ironically. 'Okay – the man that got away. How do we find him?' He turned to the chief-of-staff. 'Echelon?'

Within five minutes the chief-of-staff had made the phone calls that would deliver to the Oval Office everything that Echelon had overheard. To keep the amount of material manageable, Whisperer had suggested restricting the initial 'pull' to a wide arc surrounding the mountaintop in the Hindu Kush over the last twelve days. Even so, he knew that the volume of data would be staggering.

There were no landlines in the area, of course, and cellular masts outside Kabul and a few other major cities were non-existent, so that meant satellite phones. While Echelon loved them – it was one of the easier signals in the world to vacuum up – the problem was that the Stone Age nature of all other communications in Afghanistan meant that everyone carried one. Drug traffickers, arms smugglers, warlords, Taliban commanders, aid workers, journalists, village headmen, doctors and travelling government officials were all equipped with them.

Add to that ten different local languages and over forty dialects – to say nothing of codes and encryption which ranged from the rudimentary to the sophisticated – and it made the amount of material overwhelming.

Nevertheless, if the lone man who Lieutenant Keating had glimpsed on the mountaintop had used a satellite phone anywhere near the village, Echelon would have heard and recorded it. Of course, the president knew there was no guarantee that the man even *had* a satellite phone but, in the present circumstances, he had little choice – when you don't have anything else, you go with what you've got.

Responding to a direct order from the president, the water-cooled IBM Roadrunner computers at Fort Meade – among the fastest-processing clusters in the world – immediately started scanning their databases.

If they found nothing on the first pull, their circle of search would extend out mile by mile until it covered not just countries, but sub-continents. Literally, they were looking for a single voice among tens of millions.

Chapter Forty-eight

IN THE MEANTIME, THE FIVE MEN AND ONE WOMAN SEATED AROUND the Lincoln desk tried to develop the outline of a plan. Almost immediately, they were at war among themselves.

The only thing they agreed on was that there should be no change to the nation's threat status: it was at a low level and, in order to avoid panic and unwanted questions, it had to stay there. But in the two hours that followed, the atheists and the God-botherers took to each other's throats on almost every idea, then suddenly teamed up against the president on several others, split among themselves, formed uneasy alliances with their former opponents, returned to their natural alliances and then sallied forth on several occasions as lone gunslingers.

'It's worse than a meeting of the *loya jirga*,' the chief-of-staff said quietly into his MP3 player. The *loya jirga* was the grand assembly of all the Afghan elders. The reason it was called that was because the word 'clusterfuck' had already been taken.

By the time exhaustion was creeping in, everybody had lined up against Whisperer, who, they all thought privately, was the most obstinate man they had ever met. 'Oh, get your hand off your dick!' the Homeland Secretary told him in exasperation at one point. It was so unladylike, such an un-Christian turn of phrase, even she was shocked that she had said it. Then Whisperer laughed, good man that he was, and everybody else joined in.

As a result, they were all in a better mood when Whisperer suddenly came up with the first genuinely good idea. He was the one who thought up Polonium-210.

The reason why they had all found him so obstinate was that he

279

refused to move forward on any suggestion until somebody could explain to him how you could launch a worldwide dragnet for a man without revealing why you wanted him.

'So we go to the Pakistanis and say we desperately need your help but, sorry, we won't tell you the reason,' he said. 'Not only will they be offended, but it will lead to speculation and, in my experience, when enough people speculate, somebody always gets it right.'

Later on, after they had all finished laughing at the homeland secretary's brain-snap, Whisperer was taking them through the problem yet again: 'We're talking about using the resources of the entire US intelligence community and its allies. That's over a hundred thousand people chasing one man. Everybody's going to assume it's a terrorist and what are we going to say . . .'

His voice trailed away as his mind, running ahead of his voice, hit an unseen ramp and launched into clean air.

The president looked at him. 'What's the matter?'

Whisperer smiled at them. 'What we are going to say is that we have highly credible intelligence that the kidnapping of the foreign nationals was part of a much larger plot.

'It was to raise money in order to try to acquire a gram of Polonium-210.'

'A nuclear trigger?' the Secretary of State said.

'That's right,' explained Whisperer. 'We'll say that either the man, or the organization he's part of, are in the final stages of building a suitcase nuclear device.'

As the idea sank in, the others looked like cavemen who had just discovered fire. 'Everybody will help,' the Secretary of Defense said. 'There's not a country in the world – not even the lunatic fringe – who wants someone building a dirty bomb in their backyard.'

'It'll give us a reason to launch the biggest manhunt in history,' Whisperer replied. 'It's so serious, nobody will question it – who'd make up something like that? Of course, we'll act reluctant even to reveal it—'

'But we'll leak it ourselves,' the homeland secretary added. 'Something reputable – the *Times* or the *Post*.'

Whispering Death smiled – now they were getting the idea.

'It'll cause panic,' the chief-of-staff said, making sure that his sensible counsel was loud enough for the recorder.

'Sure it will – but not as much as smallpox,' Whisperer responded.

He had already thought of the public reaction and didn't believe it was a deal-breaker. 'It's one bomb, one city. The president can assure the public we have the resources to stop it.'

Everybody turned to the commander-in-chief to see his reaction and were surprised to find that the sadness on his face was even more pronounced than usual.

'It's a terrible commentary on our times,' he said, 'when a suitcase nuclear bomb is more palatable than the truth.'

They weren't stupid people, none of them, and it gave them all pause to think. Where did it start? they must have wondered. How did the world ever get this crazy?

But Whispering Death was a practical man, the toughest of any of them, and he didn't believe there was any profit in spending too long reflecting on Man's enmity to Man.

'It means we can cover the airports and borders with agents and arm them with scanning devices. It won't matter what we call 'em – Geiger counters or whatever – as long as they read body temperature.

'That's one of the first signs of infection with smallpox. Naturally, we'll pay close attention to Arabs or Muslims – so what if it's profiling? Anyone with an elevated temperature will be directed to secondary screening and quarantine if necessary.'

The Secretary of State interrupted. 'Is that the most likely method of attack, people deliberately—'

'Suicide infectees,' Whisperer said, picking up the thread. 'Several years ago, we ran an exercise called Dark Winter, and that's always been the favoured hypothesis.

'If we can nail one of the vectors, then track it back – reverse-engineer their movements – we'll find the people responsible.'

There was silence, but Whisperer knew it was the silence of success, not disappointment. It had taken hours, but now they had a workable strategy. In the circumstances, it was an excellent plan, and they couldn't be faulted for the fact that their faces were showing a small flush of hope and confidence.

It was just a pity it didn't have a chance of working.

First, no matter how many agents were put on the case, there was only a handful of people who knew of the Saracen's movements, and they certainly weren't disposed to help anybody. When Lord Abdul Mohammad Khan heard that all hell was breaking loose and that the

Pakistanis, the Afghans – and even, for shit's sake, the Iranian government – were searching for a man who had been travelling through the Hindu Kush and was supposedly trying to acquire a nuclear trigger, he couldn't be sure it had anything to do with the doctor who had once been such a fiend with a Blowpipe. But, just to be on the safe side, he sent a courier – one of his grandsons, so he could be trusted completely – with a verbal message to the Iranian kidnappers. The content was simple: it told them, on their mother's life, that he expected them not to say anything about what they had done for him in grabbing the three foreigners. The message back was just as simple. On their mother's life, their lips were sealed.

The second problem was that the people in the White House believed in the weight of numbers, they believed in agents at every airport, they believed in scanners and elevated body temperature. They believed, like an article of faith, in suicide infectees as vectors. The Saracen, however, didn't and, in view of the fact that he was the one with the smallpox, that was a critical distinction.

Dawn was touching the horizon, and the Secretary of State had just asked if they could get some food sent in when they heard from Echelon.

Chapter Forty-nine

TWO PHONE CALLS. THE FIRST PULL FROM ECHELON HAD PRODUCED TWO satellite calls and both of them fitted the search criteria better than anyone could have expected.

Made three days apart, both of them were slam-dunk in the designated time frame and, although there had been a fair amount of atmospheric interference – probably another storm moving through the Hindu Kush or that damned wind blowing all the way to China – the NSA analysts who had handled the high-priority search for the White House were certain they had been made within a few miles of the ruined village.

It was quite possible that they were made from *within* the village, but that level of precision would have to wait for the IBM Roadrunners to try to determine the exact coordinates by filtering out the interference.

In addition, the two people on the line – the man in the Hindu Kush and a woman at a public phone box in southern Turkey – were both speaking English, although it wasn't their native tongue.

The president and Whisperer, listening to the chief-of-staff's report, looked at one another, and their expression said what the three Cabinet secretaries were thinking: *could it get any better than this?*

Then their luck ran out.

The two people on the phone might have been using English, but it didn't help much. On the first call the man said very little; it was as if he was listening to a report. While the woman did nearly all of the talking, she was very smart – she had pre-recorded it, probably on a cellphone. What she had to say was culled from the BBC, CNN,

MSNBC and a host of other English-speaking TV news services. Although she interrupted her recording a couple of times and offered what seemed to be additional information, it was impossible to get an idea of her age, level of education or anything else that FBI profilers might have been able to use.

The actual content of this weird conversation was even more mysterious. Half of it was in coded words which clearly didn't match whatever the other content was. The expert analysts who had reviewed it were of the opinion that she was giving information about a medical problem, but that in itself was probably code for something else.

The second call was even shorter. Again, she had pre-recorded it, and it seemed like some sort of update. The man thanked her and, even across the passage of time and so many miles, you could hear the relief in his voice. He spoke for six uninterrupted seconds then rang off.

The people in the Oval Office were totally perplexed. What started with so much promise a few minutes before had now turned into a labyrinth of problems.

The chief-of-staff glanced again at the report which had been emailed over and told them that Echelon had searched its entire database for the last six years to see if the sat-phone had been used to make or receive any other calls. There was nothing – just the two phone calls, like single atoms drifting in cyberspace; virtually incomprehensible.

And yet, even in the mess of code and voices borrowed from news programmes there were clues. Four words, mistakenly spoken by the woman at one point, were in Arabic, and the man cut her off harshly in the same language – admonishing her for using it. So they were Arabs: or maybe that was a rehearsed, deliberate mistake to make anybody who was listening leap to a certain – and wrong – conclusion.

There was another clue: in the background at the Turkish end of the conversation, the thrum of roaring traffic almost drowned out the sound of muzak or a radio station or *something*. But not quite – there was what sounded like music, and the analysts figured it had been transmitted down the phone line as the woman played her recording into the mouthpiece. What it was, however, they couldn't tell. Their report said they would have to drill down for weeks to try to get an answer from what they had recovered.

Normally, such background noise wouldn't have mattered – Echelon would have been able to identify the location of the phone box within moments. But the Turkish phone system was far from normal. Whoever at Echelon had designed the software that worked as a thief at a country's regional telephone hubs didn't count on shoddy workmanship, illegal connections, undocumented repairs, mysterious rewiring to avoid being charged, epidemic corruption and constant technical failures. All that Echelon could do was narrow the phone box down to the centre of a small city: somewhere inside a five-mile radius a woman had received two phone calls, their report said, as traffic passed by and some sort of music played in the background.

'What about voice recognition?' the president asked, focusing on Echelon's most highly classified capability. His voice sounded even more fatigued than he looked.

'The woman didn't speak long enough in one stretch to get a sample,' the chief-of-staff said, looking further down the report. He turned to the three secretaries, knowing they had never been admitted into Echelon's innermost secrets . . .

'The system needs at least six seconds. It then compares elements of a voice to over two hundred million other voices – terrorists, criminals, guerillas – from information gathered from databases throughout the world,' he said, warming to the subject. He'd always loved technology.

'But that's just the start. The real game-changer is it can break down each vowel and sound into a digital—'

'That's enough,' Whisperer interrupted, his eyes telling the chief-of-staff that one more word and, under the provisions of the National Security Act, he would be allowed to get up and throttle him.

'What about the man?' he asked. 'Did they get six seconds of him talking?'

'Yeah, they got a good enough sample from him,' the chief-of-staff said, still smarting from being slapped down by the Director of National Intelligence. 'But there was no match – there wasn't even a subset of voices he was close to – not in English or Arabic. It says here: "completely unknown to any intelligence or law-enforcement database".'

The development scared Whisperer deeply. He didn't tell the president or the others, but the one thing which no intelligence agency in the world could deal with was a cleanskin. Where did you start with a person who had no history, no form, no record? Whisperer had never met one in his life – not a genuine one – and he had never wanted to.

The others noticed the anxiety in his sombre face and, in the short, awkward silence that followed, they realized that their luck wasn't coming back.

The president was the first to pull himself together and exercise the leadership they needed. He told them that, for all their hours of frustration and cratered hope, one thing remained true: there was a woman in southern Turkey who knew the man's identity and had spoken to him. She had given him information which, it seemed, was very important. Why else would he, in the middle of testing a virus he had synthesized – a remarkable achievement – have gone to the trouble of calling her? Not once, but twice. Anybody smart enough to engineer a deadly virus must have known there was a risk somebody would be listening. Why did he do it? What was so important? More importantly – who was the woman?

'So . . . we go to Turkey,' he said in conclusion. 'How?'

Of course, the secretaries of defense, homeland and state – the Gang of Three was what Whisperer had started calling them in his head – were all for sending in the Fifth Army and the Mediterranean Fleet and storming the beaches. A hundred thousand agents wouldn't be enough for what they had in mind. The president calmed them down.

'We've caught a glimpse of somebody,' he said. 'If we charge in, if we flood the zone, she'll take fright and head for Syria, Saudi, Yemen – you name it – some hole we might never be able to dig her out of.'

He had read about the mistake George Bush had made when they were chasing Osama bin Laden and he had flooded the zone in Tora Bora. The number of people on the ground and the depth of agency infighting ended up undermining the operation completely. Eventually, they got him by good old-fashioned intelligence work. 'What do you say, Whisperer?'

'On the money. The effectiveness of any operation is in inverse proportion to the number of people used,' he said, ready to go to war with the Gang of Three if he had to. 'It's the type of work covert

286

agents do, the best of 'em anyway. We send in a Pathfinder and, if he's good enough, and our luck comes back, he'll find out enough to light the way for the rest of us.'

The Gang of Three said nothing, probably still dreaming of massive bombing runs and the opening scenes of *Saving Private Ryan*. 'Who do we send?' the president asked.

'I don't know,' Whisperer replied, and that was why the president respected him so much: he was one of the few people in Washington willing to admit he didn't know something. 'I'll come back to you.'

The same thought ran through all their heads. One man, that was all, a Pathfinder alone in a strange country. Not a job for a man afraid of cracking, for someone who had never learned to dance.

The six people in the Oval Office decided there was little more they could do while they waited for Whisperer. The man himself stood up and deftly scooped up the copy of the Echelon report the chief-of-staff had put on the coffee table – he didn't want that left lying around.

As the keepers of the great secret headed for the door, one last thought occurred to the president and he called out to Whisperer: 'Where exactly in Turkey are we talking about?'

Whisperer leafed through the pages of Echelon's report. 'A province called Muğla,' he replied. 'The name of the town is Bodrum.'

Chapter Fifty

WHISPERER DIDN'T SHOWER, DIDN'T EAT, DIDN'T REST. HE CALLED AHEAD from his car to have every current government file on southern Turkey downloaded and on his office computer by the time he got there. He wanted to know as much about the area before he even thought about which agency – let alone which operative – he was going to tap as the Pathfinder.

Hence, immediately after arriving from the White House, he spent the morning shut inside his large office with the blinds drawn and the door closed, hunched over his screen.

He had just finished a State Department analysis of Turkey's current political situation – another ten pages of fellatio, he thought to himself – and picked up a thin file which had been sent to the US Embassy in Ankara, the country's capital.

It was from a homicide detective in the NYPD, and it was asking for help in discovering the names of all female US citizens who had applied for Turkish visas in the last six months. Whisperer didn't know it, but Ben Bradley had come up with the idea – a good idea too – that somebody who had a Turkish phone number and an expensive calendar featuring spectacular Roman ruins might be thinking of going there.

Whisperer saw that it concerned some murder at a hotel called the Eastside Inn – not the sort of place he would be staying anytime soon to judge by the grainy photos attached to the police crime report – and was about to lay it aside.

Then he stopped. The eye for detail that he had developed as a young man when analysing spy photos of Soviet military installations had never left him. By habit, he always looked deep into the background of any shot, and now he was looking at a man barely visible in the shadows of a murder scene.

Whisperer knew him. Even in the photo he seemed to be a man apart, just watching – as he had probably spent half his life doing.

Whisperer stared at the image of me for a long time, thinking, then pressed a button on his desk, summoning his special assistant. A man in his late twenties, well tailored and ambitious, entered almost immediately.

'I want you to find a man,' Whisperer told him. 'I don't know what name he uses now, but for a long time he called himself Scott Murdoch.'

The special assistant looked at the photo Whisperer pushed across the desk, the face in the background carefully circled. 'Who is he?' he asked.

'Years back he was known as the Rider of the Blue. He was probably the best intelligence agent there's ever been.'

The special assistant smiled. 'I thought that was you.'

'So did I,' Whisperer replied, 'until I met him.'

Chapter Fifty-one

THE CROWD HAD STARTED TO ARRIVE EARLY, STREAMING INTO THE largest auditorium on the campus of New York University. Frankly, I didn't think the room would be big enough to hold them all. It was the first day of Ben Bradley's long-planned symposium – the Davos Forum for investigators and the technicians who worked in the pit-lane on their behalf.

They came from twenty different countries – even a two-man delegation from the Bosnian police department who didn't speak English but had convinced someone in authority that they should attend. By all accounts, they were having a whale of a time in New York and, over early-morning coffee, they communicated to Bradley their support for making it an annual event. They suggested holding the next one in Vegas.

After Bradley's welcoming address, in which he recounted some of his own experiences on 9/11, including the plight of the guy in the wheelchair – conveniently omitting the part about how he had saved him – he was given a large round of applause. That was the cue for him to introduce a hitherto unknown colleague who had assisted Jude Garrett on so many of his investigations. In other words, I was on.

Thanks to Battleboi and the databases he had manipulated, I was now Peter Campbell again. When I had visited him in Old Japan to ask for help with the new identity, I asked if he could make the new identity convincing, given that we only had limited time.

He nodded. 'We've got one huge advantage – people believe what they see in databases. They've never learned the most important rule of cyberspace – computers don't lie, but liars can compute.'

I laughed. 'Is that why you're so good – you're a gold-plated liar?'

'In a way. I guess I believe in alternative realities. Look around, I live in one. I suppose they're one big lie.

'I've never said this to anyone,' he continued, 'but in a fair fight I'm better than your buddies at the FBI or any of those secret-agency guys.

'You see, to them, alternative realities or cyberspace is just a job. Because I'm big and unattractive, it's different – I don't like the real world much.' He indicated the racks of hard drives. 'This is my life.'

'Funny,' I replied. 'I've never thought of you as big or unattractive. I've always thought of you as Japanese.'

I saw from his face how much it meant to him. 'You're probably right, though,' I continued, 'about being the best. I'll tell you this – if I ever got into a tight corner and needed computer help, you'd be the guy I'd call.'

He laughed and finished his cup of tea. 'You wanna start?'

By the time I left, Peter Campbell was a graduate of the University of Chicago who went on to study medicine at Harvard and then spent years helping Garrett with his research. As I had planned earlier, Campbell was the one who had found the manuscript of Garrett's remarkable book and, because I had access to his meticulously kept files, the publisher had asked me to edit it. As a result, I had an encyclopaedic knowledge of all his cases – I mean, it was almost as if I had investigated them myself.

So when, as Peter Campbell, I stood up in front of the congregation of my peers, I started nervously but quickly found my groove. I talked about Garrett's reclusive nature, how I was one of the few friends he had had and the fact that, essentially, he lived a double life: while everyone knew he was an agent with the FBI, most of his work was for agencies in what I coyly termed the 'intelligence sphere'.

I expanded on a number of those investigations – the ones featured prominently in the book – and when I thought I had caught their interest I opened the cases up to discussion and questions. The place exploded. I have to say I sort of began to enjoy it – it's a weird thing to stand on a stage and hear your peers attack, analyse and praise you. A bit like reading your own obituary.

There was a woman in a turquoise shirt sitting at the front who led the charge – dissecting evidence, analysing motive and asking pointed questions. She had a good mind and an even more attractive face – hair with a natural kick, high cheekbones and eyes that always seemed close to laughter. At one point she said: 'I noticed a few things he wrote in the text – I don't think he liked women very much, did he?'

Where did she get that idea? I was under the impression that I liked women very much. 'To the contrary,' I told her. 'Furthermore, when he did venture out, women seemed to find him extremely charming and – I don't think I'm being indiscreet – very sexually attractive.'

She barely blinked. 'Charming, smart – *and* sexy? God, I would have liked to have met him!' she said, to a huge round of applause and cheering.

As I grinned at her I realized that all the months of reaching for normal might be achieving something, and I was attracted enough to hope that later in the day I might find the chance to talk to her and ask for her number.

In the meantime, I changed gear. I told them about a case which – were Jude alive – he probably would have found the most interesting of all. I told them about the day the Towers fell and the murder at the Eastside Inn.

'Ben Bradley spoke earlier about the man in a wheelchair,' I said. 'What he didn't tell you was this – he was the one who led the group that carried the guy down.'

There was a moment of shocked silence in the auditorium, then a rolling wave of applause for him. Ben and Marcie – she was sitting next to him – stared at me in surprise. Until then, they had no idea that I knew about Ben's bravery, but I think they understood then why I had agreed to speak.

'He didn't find Jesus at all,' Marcie said to her husband, feigning surprise.

'No, we should have realized he'd learn the truth – he's a damn investigator,' Bradley said, berating himself, getting to his feet to acknowledge the crowd.

When the clapping stopped, I continued. 'But that was a day full of remarkable events. Ben's was just one of them. Earlier in the morning, a young woman was running late for work. As she approached the Towers she saw the first plane hit and realized that

– as far as the world was concerned – she was already at her desk, as good as dead.'

For the second time in less than a minute Bradley was taken aback. I had never shared my theory with him, and he raised his hands, as if to say, Where the hell is this going?

So I told him – and the crowd. 'You see, the woman whose tardiness had just saved her life wants to kill somebody, and now she's got the perfect alibi: she's dead.

'So she walks through the chaos and fear until she finds a place where she can live off the grid and nobody will find her. It's called the Eastside Inn.

'Whenever she goes out, she disguises herself and, on one of those trips, she borrows a textbook – probably the definitive work on how to kill somebody and how to get away with it. We all know the book – it was Jude Garrett's.'

That caused a stir, a sharp intake of breath among the delegates. Bradley caught my eye and clapped silently – yeah, he was saying, it was pretty damn good.

'She invites a woman – young, probably attractive – to the Eastside Inn,' I said.

'A little drugs, a little sex. Then she kills her date – exactly by the book, so to speak, and disappears.

'When the NYPD arrive they find a victim with no face, no finger-prints and no teeth. So that is what they've got – a victim nobody can identify and a killer nobody suspects because she's dead. Why the murder? Who are these people? Where's the motive? What does it mean?'

I paused and looked around. People were shaking their heads in quiet admiration for the crime. 'Yes,' I said. 'You're right – impressive. Jude had a name for ones like this. He called 'em the *mind-fuckers*.'

People laughed, and the comments and ideas started slowly but quickly avalanched. By then, however, I was barely listening – I had seen three men enter at the back of the hall and sit silently in the last row.

For that reason, when the attractive woman in the turquoise shirt came up with a brilliant idea, I barely registered it. Although I recalled what she had said weeks later, I still cursed myself for not paying attention to it at the time.

The only thing I could plead in my defence was that I knew the secret world and I knew what the men at the back were doing there. They had come for me.

Part Three

Chapter One

THE FUNNEL WEB, NATIVE TO AUSTRALIA, IS ALMOST CERTAINLY THE most venomous spider in the world – worse even than the Brazilian wandering spider and, God knows, they're bad enough.

A long time ago, I investigated a case where the neurotoxin from a funnel web had been used to kill an American engineer, an asset of one of our covert agencies working in Romania. As part of the inquiry a biologist showed me one of the black, full-bodied creatures – a Sydney male, the most venomous and aggressive of the species.

I promise you, if you had never seen a spider before – if you didn't know an arachnid from a hole in the ground – the moment you saw a funnel web you would know you were looking at something deadly. There are men – and a few women – like that in the secret world. You sense immediately that they haven't been touched by the humanity that inhabits most people. It is one of the reasons I was pleased to leave their environment and chance my hand in the sunlight.

It was three of them who were waiting at the back of the auditorium for the session of the forum to end. As soon as the delegates had filed out for lunch, leaving just myself and Bradley at the front and the two Bosnians sleeping it off near the sound console, they made their way towards us.

Bradley had seen them earlier. 'You know them?'

'In a way,' I replied.

'Who are they?'

'Better not to ask, Ben.'

The cop recognized the danger in them, and he certainly didn't like the way they were rolling, but I put my hand on his arm. 'You'd better go,' I said quietly.

He wasn't convinced. I was his colleague and, if there was going to be trouble, he wanted to be there for me. But I knew why men like that had been given the job – somebody was sending me a message: there won't be any negotiation, just do what they tell you. 'Go, Ben,' I repeated.

Reluctantly, glancing over his shoulder, he headed for the door. The spiders stopped in front of me.

'Scott Murdoch?' the tallest of them, and obviously the team leader, asked.

Scott Murdoch, I thought to myself – so, it was that far in the past. 'Yeah, that's as good as any,' I replied.

'Are you ready, Dr Murdoch?'

I bent and picked up my fine leather briefcase – a gift to myself when I had first arrived in New York and mistakenly thought it was possible to leave my other life behind.

There was no point in asking the men where we were going – I knew they wouldn't tell me the truth and I wasn't ready yet for all the lies. I thought I deserved just a few more moments of sunshine.

Chapter Two

THEY DROVE ME TO THE EAST RIVER FIRST. AT THE HELIPORT A CHOPPER was waiting, and we flew to an airport in Jersey, where a business jet took off the moment we were on board.

An hour before sunset, I saw the monuments of Washington silhouetted against the darkening sky. We landed at Andrews Air Force Base and three SUVs driven by guys in suits were waiting for us. I guessed they were FBI or Secret Service, but I was wrong – it was far above that.

The guy in the lead vehicle hit his bubblegum lights and we made good time through the choking traffic. We turned into 17th Street, reached the Old Executive Office Building, passed through a security checkpoint and headed down a ramp into a parking area.

That was as far as the spiders were going – they handed me off to four guys in suits who took me through a reception area, along a windowless corridor and into an elevator. It only went down. We stepped out into an underground area manned by armed guards. There was no need to empty my pockets – I was put into a back-scatter X-ray and it saw everything, both metal and biological, in intimate detail.

Screened and passed, we got on to a golf cart and drove down a series of broad passages. As disorienting as it was, that wasn't the strangest thing: I got the sense nobody was looking at me, as if they had all been told to glance away.

We reached another elevator – this one ascended for what felt like six floors – and the four guys in suits handed me over to an older man, better dressed, with greying hair. 'Follow me please, Mr Jackson,' he said.

My name wasn't Jackson, I had never heard of Jackson, my many aliases had never included Jackson. I realized then that I was a ghost, a shadow without a presence or name. If I didn't know before how serious it was, I did then.

The silver fox led me through a windowless area of work stations but, again, nobody looked in my direction. We went through a small kitchen and into a much more expansive office. At last there were some windows, but the gloom outside and the distortion caused by what I supposed was bulletproof glass made it impossible to get any sense of where we were.

The silver fox spoke quietly into his lapel mic, waited for an answer, then opened a door. He motioned me forward and I stepped inside.

Chapter Three

THE FIRST THING THAT STRIKES YOU ABOUT THE OVAL OFFICE IS THAT IT'S much smaller than it appears on TV. The president, on the other hand, seemed much bigger.

Six-two, his jacket off, heavy bags under his eyes, he rose from behind his desk, shook hands and indicated we should move to the couches in the corner. As I turned towards them I saw that we weren't alone: a man was sitting in the gloom. I should have guessed of course – he was the person who had dispatched the spiders, the one who wanted to make sure I understood that the summons was non-negotiable.

'Hello, Scott,' he said.

'Hello, Whisperer,' I replied.

Back in the day, we had met a number of times. Twenty years older than me, he was already elbowing his way to the top of the intelligence heap while I was a fast-rising star at The Division. Then the Twin Towers fell and I took a different path. People say that on that afternoon – and late into the evening of September eleventh – he wrote a long and stunning deconstruction of the entire US intelligence community and its comprehensive failings.

Although nobody I knew had ever read it, apparently it was so vicious in its appraisal of individuals – including himself – and so unsparing in its critique of the FBI and CIA that there was no hope for his career once he had given it to the president and the four congressional leaders. Being an intelligent man, he must have known what the result would be: he was committing professional suicide.

Instead, as the full scale of the disaster became apparent, the then-president decided he was the only person who appeared hell-bent on honesty rather than covering their ass. Whatever the Latin is for 'Out of Anger, Victory' should be Whisperer's motto; within a year he had been appointed Director of National Intelligence.

I can't say that during our professional encounters we liked each other much, but there was always a wary admiration, as if a Great White had come face to face with a salt-water croc. 'We've got a small problem,' he said as we sat down. 'It concerns smallpox.'

I was now the tenth person to know.

The president was sitting to my right and I sensed him watching me, trying to gauge my reaction. Whisperer, too. But I had none – no reaction, at least not in the conventional sense. Yes, I felt despair, but not surprise. My only real thought was about a man I had met once in Berlin, but it wasn't exactly the situation in which to mention it, so I just nodded. 'Go on,' I said.

'It appears that an Arab—' Whisperer continued.

'We don't know he's an Arab,' the president interrupted.

'The president's right,' Whisperer acknowledged. 'That could be an attempt at disinformation. Let's say a man in Afghanistan who spoke some Arabic has synthesized the virus. In the last few days he's run a test on humans – his version of a clinical trial.'

Again they looked at me to see my response. I shrugged – I figured if you'd gone to the trouble of creating it, you would probably want to test it. 'Did it work?' I asked.

'Of course it fucking worked! We're not here because it failed,' Whisperer said, irritated by my apparent equanimity. For a minute I thought he was going to raise his voice, but then he didn't.

'Further, it appears that the virus has been engineered to crash through the vaccine,' he added.

The president hadn't taken his eyes off me. After more silence from me, he shook his head and sort of smiled. 'I'll say one thing for you – you don't scare easy.'

I thanked him and met his gaze. It was hard not to like him. As I said, he was far removed from a normal politician.

'What else have you got?' I asked.

Whisperer reached into a document case and gave me a copy of the Echelon report. As I started reading it, I saw that nothing had been blacked out or excised – I had been given raw, unsanitized intelligence, and it made me realize how panicked they were. Looking back, I think as the afternoon wore into night, they truly believed that the whole country was going over the falls together.

'Two phone calls,' Whisperer said as I laid the report down. 'Three days apart.'

'Yeah,' I replied, thinking about them. 'The guy in Afghanistan makes the first call. He phoned a public phone box in Turkey and a woman was waiting for him. She had spent hours coding up a message, so she was well aware he was going to call. How did she know that?'

'Prearranged,' Whisperer responded. 'You know the drill. On a certain day, at a certain time, he would call—'

'From the middle of the Hindu Kush? While he's testing a remarkable bio-terror weapon? I don't think so; he wouldn't risk it. I think it's more likely some event had happened and she needed to speak to him urgently.

'That means,' I continued, 'she has some way of letting him know that he has to call her.'

The president and Whisperer sat quietly, considering it.

'Okay,' the president said. 'She contacted him. Why didn't Echelon hear it?'

'A lot of possibilities,' I said. 'Outside the search area, a message sent days before to an unknown cellphone, a hand-delivered note. It could be anything. My guess would be a bland message on an obscure Internet forum.'

'It'd make sense,' Whisperer said. 'The man would get an automated text alert telling him so-and-so had posted a new profile or whatever.'

'Yeah, and as soon as he saw the alert he would know what it really meant – to call her. So he does it the first chance he gets, from a totally different phone.

'He listens to her coded message and it gives him certain information. It also tells him to call back in three days. He does, and that's the second call.'

'Two phone calls and some sort of alert or message we can't identify,' the president said. 'It's not much, but it's about all we've got.'

He looked straight at me. 'Whisperer says you're the best man to go into Turkey and find the woman.'

'Alone?' I asked, completely non-committal.

'Yes,' said Whisperer.

That figured, I thought. I would have used a Pathfinder too: some-one to go in under deep cover, a person who could feel their way along the walls of a dark alley, a man who would be parachuted in to light the way for the assault troops to follow. I also knew that most Pathfinders didn't enjoy what intelligence experts called 'longevity'.

'What about Turkish intelligence?' I asked. 'Will they be there to help?'

'Help themselves maybe,' Whisperer said. 'Any information they get, I'd give it an hour before they're leaking it – or more likely sell-ing it – to half the world.'

When Whisperer said he wanted somebody to go in 'alone', he meant alone. I sat in silence, thinking about Turkey and a host of other things.

'You don't seem very enthusiastic,' the president said at last, look-ing at the anxiety on my face. 'What do you say?'

The phone rang, and I figured, given the scale of what we were dis-cussing, it had to be important – probably North Korea had just launched a nuclear attack to round out an otherwise perfect day.

As the president answered – and turned his back to give himself some privacy – Whisperer opened his cell to check his messages. I looked out of the window – it wasn't every day you got the chance to admire the view from the Oval Office – but, the truth was, I didn't see a thing.

I was thinking about failed dreams, about reaching for normal and an attractive woman in New York whose phone number I would never know. I was thinking about the fourth of July, days on the beach and all the things that so easily get lost in the fire. But mostly I was thinking about how the secret world never leaves you – it's always waiting in the darkness, ready to gather its children back again.

Then a bad feeling about what lay ahead took hold of me, and I saw something, I saw it as clear as if it was on the other side of the glass. I was sailing an old yacht with patched sails, the wind driving me hard across a foreign sea, only the stars above to guide me in the darkness. There was nothing but silence, a silence so loud it screamed, and I saw the boat and myself grow ever smaller. Watching myself vanish on the black and endless water, I was scared, scared in a pit-of-the-stomach, end-of-days way.

In all my years of terrible danger, it was the first time I had ever imagined or felt such a thing. You don't need a doctorate in psychology from Harvard to know that it was a vision of death.

Badly shaken, I heard the president hang up and I turned to face him. 'You were about to tell us,' he said. 'Are you going to Turkey?'

'When do I leave?' I answered. There was no point in arguing, no point in complaining. Dark omens or not, life has a way of cornering us. A person either stands up or he doesn't.

'In the morning,' Whisperer said. 'You'll go in under deep cover. Only the three of us will know who you are and what your mission is.'

'We'll need a name, something to know you by,' the president added. 'Any preference?'

The yacht and the ocean must have been still raw in my mind because a word rose unbidden to my lips. 'Pilgrim,' I replied quietly.

Whisperer and the president exchanged a glance to see if there was any objection. 'Fine by me,' Whisperer said.

'Yeah, it seems to fit,' the president replied. 'That's it then – Pilgrim.'

Chapter Four

BY THE TIME I LEFT THE WHITE HOUSE IT WAS LATE ENOUGH FOR THE evening traffic to have thinned. Whisperer and I were in the back of his government car, heading across town. The director looked terrible; every hour without rest was taking its toll and, after twenty-two hours of being drowned by the crisis, his face was as grey as a tombstone.

Even worse, the night was nowhere near done yet.

As there were only the three of us who knew the real purpose of my assignment – and nobody had any intention of expanding that number voluntarily – Whisperer had already offered to be my case officer. I would be the agent on the ground and he would have the job of 'running' me. As with any joe and his case guy, there were a million details we had to work through, and I assumed we were heading to his office to get started. The plan was for me to be on a commercial flight to Turkey in less than twelve hours.

Earlier, after the president had shaken hands and offered me a choice of souvenirs, either a framed photograph of himself or a set of White House golf balls – I have to say, in the circumstances, he had a pretty good sense of humour – Whisperer had stayed behind for a private discussion. I was quarantined in an empty office by the silver fox and, after five minutes, the director had reappeared and escorted me down to the White House garage. To minimize the number of people who saw me, we took the stairs and had barely gone a dozen steps before Whisperer started to wheeze. He was carrying too much weight and it was obvious he and exercise were barely on nodding terms.

I had hoped we would be able to spend the time in the car

working on my legend but, once he had murmured instructions to the driver and raised the glass privacy screen, he checked his phone again for messages and pulled a battery-operated blood pressure monitor out of his briefcase.

He rolled up his shirtsleeve, slipped the cuff over his upper arm and pumped it up. As it deflated, he looked at the digital reading on the tiny screen. So did I.

'Jesus,' I said. 'One-six-five over ninety – you're gonna die.'

'No, no – it's not too bad,' he replied. 'Imagine how high it'd be if I talked like a regular person.'

Whisperer wasn't known for his jokes, and I appreciated the effort. He put the monitor away and slumped deeper in his seat. I figured he needed a few moments to roll back the fatigue, so I was surprised when he looked out of the window and started to speak.

'It's my anniversary, you know – thirty years tomorrow since I joined the agency. Thirty years, and not a day of peace. That's the way in our business, isn't it? Always at war with fucking somebody.'

I could see his face reflected in the glass. He looked far older than his years and, despite the bravado, I think he was worried about the blood pressure and how much more abuse his body could take.

'Three marriages, four kids I barely know,' he continued. 'Still, it's been a rewarding life compared to a lot of men's. But you'd be a fool not to think: Has anything I've done really made a difference?

'You won't have that problem, will you?' he said, turning to look at me. 'Pull this off and, fifty years from now, they'll still be talking about Pilgrim.'

Maybe I'm lacking in something, but things like that don't matter much to me. They never have. So I just shrugged.

He turned back to the window. 'It's genuine, isn't it? You really don't give a shit, do you? But I envy you – I wish I were twenty years younger. I would have liked just one chance to make it all count.'

'You can have this one, Dave,' I said softly. 'I'll give it to you for free.' Dave was his name, but hardly anyone remembered it any more. 'It scares the crap out of me.'

He gave a small laugh. 'Then you hide it damn well. I stayed behind with the president to find out what he thought of you.'

'I figured as much.'

'He was impressed, said you were the coolest sonofabitch he'd ever met.'

'Then he needs to get out more,' I said.

'No,' Whisperer replied. 'I was looking at your face when I told you about the smallpox. Maybe this is the apocalypse – the four horsemen are saddled up and on their way – and you showed no emotion, no panic, no *surprise* even.'

'That's true – the bit about surprise, anyway. I wasn't.'

'No, *no*. Anybody would—'

I was getting annoyed, pissed off at having been dragged into a life I really didn't want to have any part of.

'I wasn't surprised,' I said sharply, 'because, unlike all the so-called Washington experts, I've been listening.'

'To what?' he responded.

I glanced ahead and saw we were slowing for a long tailback.

'Ever been to Berlin, Dave?'

'Berlin? What's Berlin got to do with it?'

Chapter Five

WHISPERER DIDN'T KNOW WHERE I WAS GOING BUT HE DECIDED TO roll with it. 'Yeah, I was in Berlin in the eighties, just before the Wall came down,' he said.

I should have remembered, of course – he was with the CIA back then, the station chief in the hottest spot of the Cold War, what was then the capital city of espionage.

'You recall the Bebelplatz – the big public square in front of the cathedral?'

'No, that was over in East Berlin. Guys in my job didn't climb the Wall much.' He smiled, and I got the feeling he liked remembering the old days, when the enemy was the Soviets and everybody knew what the rules were.

'When I was first starting out,' I continued, 'I was posted to The Division's Berlin office. It was from there I went to Moscow and had my meeting with the then Rider of the Blue.'

He looked at me for a long moment, realizing that we had never spoken about it. 'That was a helluva thing,' he said. 'In the middle of Moscow, too. I always thought it took a truckful of courage.'

'Thanks,' I said quietly. I meant it too – that was really something coming from a man with his résumé.

'Before any of that,' I said, 'on a Sunday I would often walk to the Bebelplatz. It wasn't the grand architecture that took me there – it was the evil of the place.'

'What evil?' he said.

'One night in May 1933 the Nazis led a torch-lit mob into the square and looted the library of the adjoining Friedrich-Wilhelm

University. Forty thousand people cheered as they burnt over twenty thousand books by Jewish authors.

'Many years later a panel of glass was set into the ground to mark the spot where the fire had been. It's a window and, by leaning over, you can look into a room below. The room is white, lined from floor to ceiling with plain shelves—'

'An empty library?' Whisperer said.

'That's right,' I replied. 'The sort of world we'd live in if the fanatics had won.'

'A good memorial,' he said, nodding his head. 'Better than some damn statue.'

I looked through the windshield. The tailback was starting to unknot.

'After a couple of visits to the plaza,' I continued, 'I realized the empty library wasn't the only interesting thing. An old city cleaner with watery eyes, a guy who was there every Sunday sweeping up, was a fake.'

'How'd you know?' he asked, professional curiosity piqued.

'His legend wasn't quite right. He was too thorough in his work, the grey overalls were tailored a bit too well.

'Anyway, one day I asked him why he swept the square. He said he was seventy years old, it was hard to find a job, a man had to earn an honest living – and then he saw the look on my face and didn't bother lying any more.

'He sat down, rolled up his sleeve and showed me seven faded numbers tattooed on his wrist. He was Jewish, and he pointed at groups of old men of his generation, dressed in their Sunday suits, taking the sun on nearby seats.

'He told me they were Germans – but like a lot of Germans they hadn't changed, they'd just lost. In their hearts, he said, they still sang the old songs.

'He told me he swept the square so that they would see him and know: a Jew had survived, the race lived on, their people had *endured*. The square was his revenge.

'As a child it had been his playground – he said he was there the night the Nazis came. I didn't believe him – what would a seven-year-old Jewish kid be doing in that place?

'Then he pointed at the old university and said his father was the librarian and the family had lived in an apartment behind his office.

'A few years after the bonfire the mob came for him and his family. Like he said, it's always the same – they start out burning books and end up burning people. Out of his parents and five kids, he was the only survivor.

'He passed through three camps in five years, all of them death camps, including Auschwitz. Because it was such a miracle he had survived, I asked him what he had learned.

'He laughed and said nothing you'd call original. Death's terrible, suffering's worse; as usual the assholes made up the majority – on both sides of the wire.

'Then he thought for a moment. There was one thing the experience had taught him. He said he'd learned that when millions of people, a whole political system, countless numbers of citizens who believed in God, said they were going to kill you – *just listen to them.*'

Whisperer turned and looked at me. 'So that's what you meant, huh? You've been listening to the Muslim fundamentalists?'

'Yes,' I replied. 'I've heard bombs going off in our embassies, mobs screaming for blood, mullahs issuing death decrees, so-called leaders yelling for *jihad*. They've been burning books, Dave – the temperature of hate in parts of the Islamic world has gone out to Pluto. And I've been listening to them.'

'And you don't think we have – the people in Washington?' He said it without anger. I was at one time a leading intelligence agent, and I think he genuinely wanted to know.

'Maybe in your heads. Not in your gut.'

He turned and looked out of the window. It was starting to rain. He was quiet for a long time and I began to wonder if his blood pressure had taken off again.

'I think you're right,' he said at last. 'I think, like the Jews, we believed in the fundamental goodness of men, we never thought it could really happen. But *damn*, they've got our attention now.'

We drove through a set of electric gates and stopped at a small guard booth. We hadn't gone to Whisperer's office at all, we were at his house.

Chapter Six

THE CURTAINS WERE DRAWN IN WHISPERER'S STUDY BUT AFTER SEVERAL hours, through a narrow gap, I saw the rain clear and a blood-red moon rise. It was a bad omen, I thought.

Normally, I was too much of a rationalist to give any weight to such things, but the vision of the old yacht on a foam-flecked sea had shaken me badly. It was as if a corner of the universe had been lifted and I saw the road ahead. Not a road exactly, I corrected myself – a dead end.

Thankfully, there was too much work to let me dwell on it. We had come to Whisperer's house because he knew that in any covert operation your own side was always the greatest danger. More agents were lost to gossip, speculation and inadvertent comments than to any other cause, so Whisperer made an end-run of his own – we never went near the office and its inevitable talk.

He had inherited the home from his father, a merchant banker turned senator, and it was a beautiful, sprawling place that had found its way on to the National Historic Register. As a result, we set up headquarters in the study of a house which had once been owned by a relative of Martha Washington's.

Thanks to Whisperer's position in the government, its communications were almost as safe as the White House: constantly monitored for bugs and other electronic intrusions and equipped with an Internet connection that was part of the government's Highly Secure Network.

As soon as we entered the study Whisperer threw off his jacket, loaded up the coffee machine and started a series of deep-breathing exercises. He said they were to help control his blood pressure, but I didn't believe him: the old campaigner was shrugging off the rust of the past and getting ready to flex muscles which hadn't been used in years. David James McKinley – failed husband, absentee father, Director of United States Intelligence, a man saddened not to have found a place in the pantheon – might as well have been back in Berlin. He had gone operational.

He immediately called in secretaries, special assistants, executive aides and two phone operators – a dozen people – and set them up in various parts of the house. He made it clear his study was off limits to everyone, and the beauty of it was that nobody even knew I was in the building.

With a back office in place, Whisperer and I set about trying to master a million details, the sort of things that might mean life or death when you were hunting terrorists in southern Turkey, a country on the frontier of the badlands, less than a day's drive from Iraq and Syria. Although we didn't discuss it, we both knew what we were really doing: we were sending a spy out into the cold.

Every few minutes Whisperer headed out to the back office to pick up files and assign tasks. Naturally, the staff were aware they were involved in something big, so their boss started to drop clever hints. The result was that when the news broke about the nuclear trigger the people closest to the investigation immediately assumed they were part of the search for the terrorist who was trying to buy it. Dave McKinley trusted nobody, and it was little wonder people said he was the best case officer of his generation.

In the wood-panelled study, I had already decided that the public phone boxes in the centre of Bodrum were the best place to start. Given what we had, they were about the *only* place to start. Of course, Turkish Telco had no reliable map of them, so Whisperer and I decided I would have to cover the five square miles on foot.

He called the head of the NSA and requested that a satellite photo of the town centre be emailed to the house immediately. While we waited for it to arrive he went to the dining room, where the executive assistants were headquartered. He asked one of them to call the CIA and tell them they had six hours to deliver a smartphone fitted with a specially enhanced digital camera. The camera, in turn, had to be married to the phone's internal GPS system.

The idea was that I would take high-quality photographs of every phone box in Bodrum on my cellphone, posing as a visitor snapping street scenes in the Old Town. The photos would then be automatically downloaded on to the map, and I would have a complete record of the look and exact position of every phone box in the target area.

Somewhere on that list would be the one we were looking for. We knew that a woman had entered it on specific dates and, in the early evening on both occasions, had spoken to the man we had to catch. There was traffic noise in the background so that ruled out any in pedestrianized areas. There was also music. What that was we had no idea – we were waiting for the NSA to try to isolate, enhance and identify it.

As an investigative plan, focusing on phone boxes wasn't much, not much at all – if it was a patient, you would have to say it was on life support – but in one way it was enough. My journey had started.

With the first step of the investigation prepped, Whisperer and I began work on my legend. We had come to the conclusion that, with precious little time to organize it, I would go into Turkey as an FBI special agent working on the murder at the Eastside Inn.

There were major problems with it – why was the FBI investigating a New York homicide, and why had they taken so long to get involved? Nor could I go into Turkey uninvited – we would need permission from their government – and we were worried that even on a good day the link between the murder and Bodrum, a few digits of a phone number, would look pretty tenuous.

Then we had a piece of luck – or at least that's what it looked like. We should have known better, of course.

Chapter Seven

IN THE MIDST OF TRYING TO JUICE MY SHAKY LEGEND, WHISPERER GOT A phone call from the family room. That was where his two special assistants – each with a security clearance high enough to have access to most government documents – were stationed.

Whisperer went out to see them and returned a few minutes later with a file that had just arrived from the State Department. It contained a ten-paragraph account – brief, sketchy, frustrating – of the death of an American citizen several days previously in Bodrum.

A young guy had died and, I have to admit, as grim as it was, it sounded like good news to us – such a death might warrant the FBI's legitimate interest.

Whisperer handed me the file and, while the victim's full name was at the top, I didn't take it in. It was one of the later paragraphs that caught my attention: it said he was known to his friends and acquaintances as Dodge.

'Dodge? Why Dodge?' I asked Whisperer.

'Like the car,' he replied. 'The guy was twenty-eight years old and the heir to an automobile fortune – he was a billionaire. I guess his buddies could either call him Dodge or Lucky.'

'Not that lucky,' I said as I read on. According to the account, he and his wife were staying at one of Bodrum's clifftop mansions – known as the French House – when he either slipped, jumped or was pushed on to the rocks a hundred feet below. It took boats and divers over two hours to retrieve the body from the pounding sea.

'I don't think it's going to be an open-casket funeral,' Whisperer said when I had finished looking at the attached photos and laid the file down.

There was no evidence, and maybe I was prone to looking for connections where none existed – I admit I enjoy a good conspiracy theory as much as the next person – but I couldn't help wondering about a link between a scrap of paper found in a drain at the Eastside Inn and the mangled body of a billionaire.

'What's your bet?' I said as I turned. 'Just chance, or are Dodge and the woman's murder in Manhattan connected?'

Whisperer had read the files on the woman's case when we were working on my legend and he was as qualified as anyone to make a judgement.

'Almost certainly – but I don't care,' he replied. 'All that concerns me is that half an hour ago, as far as a legend was concerned, we were polishing brass and calling it gold. Now we've got a billionaire American who has died in questionable circumstances. A *well-connected* American—'

'How do you know he's well-connected?'

'Show me a family with that much money that isn't.'

'There is no family – just the wife; the report says so,' I argued, playing devil's advocate.

'So what? There'll be aunts, godparents, lawyers, a trustee. I'll get the back office to start checking, but with a billion dollars there's gonna be somebody.'

He was right, of course – growing up with Bill and Grace, I knew that. 'Okay, so a trustee or lawyer hears Dodge is dead. What then?'

'I ask the State Department to call him. They say they have concerns about the death but they need someone with authority to request the government's help. The lawyer or trustee agrees—'

'Yeah, I'd buy that part – he's got a duty,' I added.

'The State Department suggests he call the White House and make a formal request,' Whisperer said. 'The chief-of-staff takes the call. He says he understands – the trustee wants a proper investigation. It's a foreign country; anything could have happened. So what does the White House do?'

'They tell the FBI to send a special agent to monitor the inquiry.'

'Exactly,' Whisperer said. 'And here's the best thing – Grosvenor can call the President of Turkey personally to organize it. A billion dollars and the name of a great automobile family – it's believable that he would do that.'

We both knew: as of that moment I was an FBI special agent. 'What name do you want?' Whisperer asked.

'Brodie Wilson,' I answered.

'Who's he?' Whisperer said. He knew the drill – he wanted to make sure that if sometime very soon the questioning got really tough, I wouldn't get confused about my name.

'A dead guy. He was my stepfather's sailing partner. Bill said he was the best spinnaker man he ever saw.' Suddenly – I couldn't explain why – I felt a great wave of sadness roll over me.

Whisperer didn't notice; he was too busy being a case officer. 'Okay, you were born on Long Island, sailed every weekend, birth date is the same as yours, next of kin is your widowed mother – okay?'

I nodded, committing it to memory. The information was for the passport – a dog-eared version with plenty of stamps which would have to be produced by the CIA within the next few hours. Whisperer was already picking up the phone – conferencing in the family room, kitchen and dining room – to start organizing it and a host of other details that would transform a fake name into a real identity.

I took the opportunity to think: on the ground in Turkey I would need a conduit, some way of communicating with Whisperer. I couldn't call him directly – an FBI agent would be of interest to the Turkish version of Echelon, and they would almost certainly be listening to every call. But if I was investigating the link between Dodge's death and the murder at the Eastside Inn, I could legitimately speak to the New York homicide detective in charge of the case.

My idea was that Ben Bradley could act as our mail box – taking cryptic messages and relaying them between the two of us. As soon as Whisperer was finished on the phone, I explained it to him. He wasn't sure.

'What was this guy's name again?' he asked.

'Bradley. Ben Bradley,' I said.

'He's trustworthy?'

Whisperer was somewhere far beyond exhaustion but even his face came alive when I told him about the Twin Towers and what Bradley had done for the guy in the wheelchair. 'He's a patriot,' I said.

'Sixty-seven floors?' Whisperer replied. 'He's not a patriot, he's a fucking athlete.' He picked up the phone and made arrangements for the FBI to go and collect him.

Chapter Eight

BRADLEY WAS ASLEEP WHEN THE PHONE WENT. TWICE HE LET IT GO TO the answering machine, but when the apartment's entry intercom shrilled he felt he had no choice but to answer that. An unknown voice at the front door of the building asked him to pick up his goddamn phone immediately.

With Marcie at his side, Bradley lifted the handset and was told there was a car waiting outside. He was needed downtown at the FBI's headquarters now. He tried to find out what it was about, but the guy on the other end of the line refused to say.

After pulling on his Industries and a sweatshirt – it was 2 a.m. – he was taken to the same nondescript building I had visited some months before and escorted to the eleventh floor. A night-duty agent showed him into a soundproofed room, empty except for a secure phone line and a chair, and then left, locking the door behind him. The phone rang, Bradley picked it up and heard my voice at the other end.

I told him there wasn't much time, so he had to listen hard. 'My name's Brodie Wilson, I'm a special agent with the FBI. Got it?' I'll give Ben his due – he took it in his stride.

I said that in a few hours I was heading to Bodrum and gave him a brief rundown on Dodge's death. He immediately started asking about a connection to the woman at the Eastside Inn, but I cut him off – that investigation wasn't our primary concern. I told him I would be calling him from Turkey and his job was to listen carefully and to relay what I said to a ten-digit number I was about to give him.

'You must never try to record what I say – not under any

319

circumstances. It's memory and notes alone,' I said, more harshly than was necessary, but I was worried. The Turkish version of Echelon would know if he was using a recording device and that would send up a forest of red flags.

'You may be asked to send messages back to me. Same deal, okay? Here's the ten-digit number—'

I was partway through it when he stopped me. 'That's wrong,' he said.

'No it's not,' I replied testily. I was dog-tired too.

'It can't be right, Scott – I mean, Brodie – there's no such area code.'

'Yes there is.'

'No, I'm telling you—' He tried to argue, but I stopped it.

'It's an area code, Ben! People just don't know about it, okay? Nobody does.'

'Oh,' he said, and I finished giving the number to him. I didn't tell him, but he now had the number of the Director of US Intelligence's high-security cellphone – something known to only five other people, one of whom was the president.

Without knowing it, Ben had joined the big time.

Chapter Nine

WHISPERER HAD BEEN ON THE PHONE TOO. BY THE TIME I HAD FINISHED with Ben he had organized a myriad other details – everything from an airline ticket and credit cards to the junk that would be found in Brodie Wilson's pockets.

Foremost among the material that would turn my name into a believable legend was a four-year-old laptop with plenty of miles under the hood. It would include an email program with hundreds of old messages, both business and private, as well as documents and downloaded files about past cases.

'You're going to have to go through it on the plane and try and familiarize yourself with the crap,' said Whisperer.

'Concentrate on the file with your family photos. You're divorced but you've got either two or three kids – I can't remember exactly what I told them. You can fudge stuff about past investigations, but of course you can't do that with your family. I said you were devoted to them.'

'Any of it encrypted?' I asked.

'Password-protected and some low-level code but they could bust it pretty quick. If we armour-plated it, I figure that would raise too many weird questions.

'They'll also be loading in iTunes and you'll get an MP3 player. But I'm warning you – the geeks at the agency have God-awful taste in music.'

'Thanks – I'll probably have to become a rap fan,' I replied. I heard cars crunch along the gravel driveway and I guessed it was the back-office staff heading out, their work done. 'When will everything be ready?' I asked.

'Six a.m. Your clothes, passport and laptop will be dropped at the security post, and the guard will put it in the kitchen for you.'

We had already organized for me to use his guest bedroom, so it meant I'd get two hours' sleep before I had to be on the move again. Thank God for adrenaline, I thought.

'The taxi's due just before 7 a.m.,' he continued. 'I've arranged one meeting for you before you get on the plane. The details will be with your stuff.'

His face looked like death, and we both knew there was no way he would be awake before I left. The only thing remaining was to say goodbye.

He took all our notepads and USB drives, threw them in the fireplace and put a match to it. I'm sure it wasn't in the manual, in the section about the proper destruction of classified material, but at least the fire gave the room a homey feel and took the chill off our feelings about what lay ahead.

'I wish I could be there to have your back,' he said sincerely. 'Especially when your back's against the wall. But I won't be.'

'Nobody will,' I replied.

'You're right about that – you're on your own.'

Our eyes met and I expected him to put out his hand to shake and wish me luck, but he didn't.

'You're not like me; you're not like any agent I've ever known, Scott. Your weight is your heart,' he said.

I thought about that for a moment. My weight was my heart? Nobody had ever said that before, but there seemed a truth to it.

'You feel things maybe more than you should,' he said. 'There are circumstances in which that could make things very difficult for you.'

He turned and poked the fire. It wasn't comfortable to hear, but he had a right to say it – he was my case officer.

'If for some reason it all goes to hell and you're certain they're going to work on you, don't wait too long – hit the eject button.'

'Take myself out, you mean?'

He didn't answer, not directly. 'Ever get to Afghanistan?' he wanted to know.

'No, I didn't,' I said.

'Lucky you. I did a few years in Kabul – twice. The Brits were there a hundred years before us, but things weren't much different. They used to have a song they'd sing:

> '*When you're wounded and left on Afghanistan's plains,*
> *And the women come out to cut up what remains,*
> *Just roll to your rifle and blow out your brains*
> *And go to your god like a soldier.*'

He sort of shrugged, trying not to make too much of it. 'So yeah, like the English soldiers said – "roll to your rifle". There's no point in suffering, Scott – no point in dragging it out.'

I knew it then, I knew without a doubt, that he had gone down into the archives and read my file.

Chapter Ten

YOU COULDN'T REALLY CALL IT SLEEP – AFTER A RESTLESS FEW HOURS
lying on the covers in Whisperer's guest room, I got up with the first
light. I had heard the back door of the house open earlier, so I wasn't
surprised to find the fiction of my new life sitting on the kitchen
bench.

I opened the battered suitcase – the Samsonite I had supposedly
used for years on both family vacations and work assignments – put
the rest of the material inside and went back to the bedroom.

After showering, I looked through the clothes that had been
supplied and was pleased to see that most of them had tags from
stores in New York. Somebody knew what they were doing. I
selected an outfit that an FBI special agent would wear when travelling
to an exotic place. In other words, I dressed like I was going to the
office but left off the tie. I checked the leather wallet with its credit
cards, slipped it into my jacket and looked at the passport.

At some stage during the previous night Whisperer and I
had taken a photograph of myself against a white wall and he had
emailed it to the CIA over in Langley. I looked at the photo now,
pasted into the well-used book, and I had to say the techs had done
a good job with their nuclear-powered version of Photoshop. The
hair was a different style and there were fewer lines around my eyes.
It was me, just five years younger.

I checked my possessions one last time, packed the clothes and
toiletries into the Samsonite and turned to the carry-on they had provided. Inside I put my travel documents, passport, laptop and a
partly read copy of a book they had given me for the plane. I looked
at its cover and smiled.

I guess somebody had thought hard about what an FBI special agent would use to entertain himself on a long-haul flight and decided that a serious work dealing with the science of investigation would be ideal. It was my book. I have to say I was pleased – not out of vanity, but because it meant I wouldn't have to wade through a novel on the off chance that some border guard questioned me about it.

On top of the book I placed the Beretta 9-mil pistol in its holster – standard issue FBI – and the box of ammunition they had provided. It would have to come out first and be shown to airport security, along with the document in my wallet that gave me authority to carry it 'in all and every circumstance'.

I closed the door quietly and, wearing another man's clothes, left the house in the shallow light between dawn and morning. I passed the guard in his security box but he didn't do anything more than glance in my direction then turn away. The taxi was waiting on the other side of the electronic gates, and I threw my suitcase and carry-on into the back seat and climbed in.

Whisperer had organized for it to take me to my meeting, but I had already decided to change the arrangements. I told the driver to head to Union Station and drop me at the car-rental offices. I wanted to try out the passport, driver's licence, credit cards and anything else I could think of in Brodie Wilson's wallet. It was better to find out that somebody had screwed up whilst I was in DC than under surveillance at Istanbul airport.

Everything went through, and after a few minutes I had entered the address of my meeting into the vehicle's navigation system and was heading into the morning rush.

Forty minutes later I pulled through the gates of a Virginia horse farm, drove down a long drive and stopped in front of a beautiful farmhouse. Almost immediately a man came out to meet me. In his early eighties and lonely in his rolling acres – his wife dead for ten years past and the horses long since gone – he was only too happy to spend a couple of hours talking to me about his life's work.

A Nobel prizewinner, he had once been the world's leading virologist, part of the team that had long ago planned the eradication of smallpox. He had been told I was an FBI researcher conducting a threat analysis into biological weapons. The truth was that Whisperer wanted me to have as much knowledge as possible in the hope that some tiny detail, a fragment of information, would prove to be the key at some later date. It was either a very good idea or an index of his desperation – take your pick.

From his library the old guy produced bound volumes of scientific journals and faded notebooks containing his research notes. While I read through the information he fed me I asked him if anyone had ever come close to finding a cure for any version of smallpox.

He laughed – that dry, rasping laugh some old people have when there's not much life left. 'After the virus was eradicated, science lost interest – all the money and research went into AIDS, that's where the glory was.

'There were no prizes awarded because there was no pressing need, and no cure because there was no research,' he said.

'So all we need is half a dozen suicide infectees and we've got a full-on catastrophe,' I replied.

He looked at me like I was crazy. 'What's wrong?' I asked.

'Human vectors?' he said. 'Is that what you're saying? And tell me, how will these suicide infectees get here – in carts with stone wheels?'

'What do you mean?' I asked.

'Four thousand years ago the Hittites sent people infected with plague into the cities of their enemies. As far as I know, that was the last time anyone used human vectors in biological warfare.'

He might have won a Nobel Prize, but his history didn't sound right to me. 'No, all the government studies have been based on people being sent into the country—'

His skull-like head started wagging in anger. 'That's because governments don't know shit,' he said. 'Even British soldiers – who weren't exactly scientific geniuses – came up with the idea of using contaminated goods to wipe out Native Americans.'

'Blankets you mean—?'

'Of course I mean blankets – fresh from their smallpox ward. That was almost three hundred years ago, and things have come a long way since then. You read the news? Every week there's some story about poisonous pet food from China being recalled, adulterated toothpaste turning up on the docks, imported baby food contaminated with melamine. And these are accidents. Imagine how easy it would be to do it deliberately.'

He looked up to see if I was following him. I got the feeling he had been beating the drum for years but nobody had started marching.

'Go on,' I said.

His voice was quieter, but it wasn't due to fatigue or old age: it was resignation. 'You know, we've outsourced everything in this country. Do we actually make anything any more? When you rely on imports for so much, there's no security. Not real security. Who the hell would bother with vectors?

'I'm not an alarmist, I'm a scientist, and I'm saying you can forget them. It's contamination that is the risk. Find something ordinary and send your pathogen in from overseas – the new version of the blanket. That's how a modern, intelligent enemy would do it.'

He ran his hand through where his hair once would have been. 'I'm old and I'm tired, but it will happen, and it'll happen in the way I've explained. A writer called Robert Louis Stevenson once said that "sooner or later we all sit down to a banquet of consequences".

'He was right – so I say pull up a chair and pick up your fork, the time is coming when we'll all be chowing down.'

Chapter Eleven

WHEN I ARRIVED AT THE HORSE FARM, I HAD FAITH. I BELIEVED IN rock 'n' roll, the Western dream and the equality of man. But most of all I believed in a worldwide dragnet for an Arab fugitive and that temperature checks at every border would keep the pin in the grenade.

By the time I left, I still had faith in rock 'n' roll, but little else. The old man with the translucent skin and impatient manner had convinced me that what he termed a 'modern, intelligent enemy' would never be caught by rounding up the usual suspects. Nor would there be any suicide vectors.

As I left his tree-lined drive and headed towards National airport, I realized that we were chasing a new kind of terrorist. I saw the future and I knew that the day of the fundamentalist and fanatic had passed. In their wake, a new generation was emerging and the man with the smallpox – highly educated and adept with technology – was probably the first. The cave-dwellers with their bomb belts and passenger planes converted into missiles looked like dial-up. This man was broadband. And say he was flying solo? If he had done it by himself, then that was an even more astonishing achievement.

Nobody likes to think they might have met their match, especially not an intelligence agent selected and trained to be the best on the battlefield, but that was my deeply held fear as I arrived at the airport. And I have to say, as the Saracen and I circled closer to one another in the weeks which lay ahead, I saw nothing to put that feeling back in its box. He would have been brilliant in any area he had chosen to pursue.

So it was in a sombre frame of mind that I dropped the rent-a-car, headed through security and boarded the plane to La Guardia in New York. From there I took a cab to JFK – I was a live agent now, arriving exactly like any genuine Manhattan-based federal agent – and made the flight to Istanbul with barely twenty minutes to spare.

For the next six hours I buried my head in the emails, photographs and case notes that formed the skeleton of Brodie Wilson's life. Only when I had put flesh on the bone – giving names to my kids, assigning them birth dates which I would remember even under duress, listening to the God-awful music loaded on the MP3 player – did I close the computer and tilt the seat back.

I wasn't going to sleep. I wanted to think about the one other thing which had been on my mind: what was in my file.

Chapter Twelve

I HAVE SEEN MEN SO SCARED THEY DEFECATE THEMSELVES. I HAVE SEEN men who are about to die get an erection. But I have only ever seen one man so terrified that he did both at the same time.

He was a prisoner at Khun Yuam, the CIA black prison hidden in the lawless jungle along the Thai–Burma border. As I mentioned, I went there as a young man because one of the guards had died in questionable circumstances and, given the nature of the dark arts that were practised within its walls and the high value of its prisoners, any unusual death had to be investigated. That was my job, as raw and inexperienced as I was.

The military guard who died – an American of Latvian descent known as Smokey Joe – was an unpleasant piece of work, the sort of guy who would break your arm then knock you down for not saluting. He had been found floating in a back eddy of a roaring river and, while somebody had gone to a lot of trouble to make it appear that he had fallen from a dilapidated rope footbridge, I wasn't convinced.

I chose a CIA interrogator from the prison's staff because he was about the same size as Smokey Joe and, without telling him why, asked him to accompany me to the bridge. A dozen of his colleagues and an even larger number of guards walked with us, everybody expecting me to explain my theory of exactly what might have happened. Instead, I had a long length of elasticized rope. Too worried about losing face in front of his colleagues, the CIA guy barely objected when I tied the rope around his ankle, secured the other end to a thick wooden beam and told him to jump.

Five times he either made the leap or we simulated someone pushing him, and we quickly established two things: it would have

330

been impossible under those conditions for Smokey Joe to have left a smear of blood I had found on a boulder halfway down and – second – the interrogator didn't have much stomach for makeshift bungee jumping.

The splash of blood meant that the guard would have had to be hurled off the footbridge like a javelin and, on account of his size, it would have taken two men. It wasn't hard to narrow down the suspects – the bridge was only used by prison guards going to buy cheap booze at a smugglers' camp on the nearby border or opium couriers avoiding military patrols on the highway. I opted for the opium couriers.

For several days I camped under a rocky overhang near the bridge with six Special Forces soldiers attached to the CIA. It was just before dusk on the fourth day when we heard someone coming – a tough guy with a fair bit of Montagnard tribesman in him by the look of his face. He was barefoot and shirtless, a long scar from what was probably a machete running across his ribs. Over his shoulder he had an old M16 assault rifle and a filthy Mickey Mouse backpack. Inside it, undoubtedly, were bricks of No. 2 opium wrapped in rags, starting their long journey on to the streets of America and Europe.

He was whistling an Elton John number through stained teeth when the Special Forces guys jumped him. 'Crocodile Rock' died in his throat, the M16 fell, he didn't have time to get out his long-bladed machete and he stared at me with a mix of defiance and hatred. Two minutes of listening to his glib story about only rarely using the trail and being in Chiang Mai a week ago and I knew he was lying.

I decided to take him back to the cinder-block prison, where I thought a few days in the crushing heat of one of the solitary-confinement cells might make him more cooperative. The CIA guys, most of whom liked Smokey Joe because of his willingness to hit prisoners without being asked twice, had other ideas. They didn't feel like wasting time by interviewing him or asking a young guy from The Division if they could take over the interrogation.

Deciding to use what their manuals coyly called 'enhanced inter-rogation techniques', they filled a large concrete bathtub in a corner of the prison hospital. Only when the water was almost at the top did a couple of guards drag in the courier – blindfolded, shackled hand and foot.

Almost immediately I wished I had told the agency guys it was my case and to get the hell back to their cages. Sure, you can convince yourself the rules of life are different when you're working in the national interest, but this wasn't even remotely connected to that. When I look back I think I was overawed or I just wanted to be part of the team – the psychology of the small group, as the experts call it. Whatever it was, to my shame, I said nothing.

Stripped to his threadbare underpants, eyes covered, the courier had no idea where he was or what was happening, so he was already close to panic as they lashed him face up to a long length of board and lifted it off the floor.

Four of them – obviously well-practised in the technique – carried it over the bathtub and tilted it backwards so that his head, all except his mouth and nose, were in the water. He tried to fight – to no avail – and it was clear from his gasping breath he thought that, any moment, he was going to be lowered another couple of inches and drowned.

Two more of the interrogators took up a position on either side of his struggling body. One slapped a towel over the prisoner's mouth and nose and, once it was firmly in place, the other swamped it with water from a large bucket.

The water took a moment to soak through the fabric then went straight down the courier's inclined throat. The water in his wind-pipe combined with the sensation of a wave hitting his face convinced him he had been plunged underwater and was drowning. The gag reflex, uncontrollable, kicked in as he fought to stop the water entering his lungs . . .

The water kept coming. The sense of drowning erupted into even greater terror and the gagging became a rolling sequence of spasms. They went on and on until he got an erection, clearly visible through his underpants, and then defecated in the water.

Men laughed, but I stared at him – I felt ashamed and dis-honoured, experiencing every spasm as if it were me that was strapped helpless to the board. Some people say that compassion is the purest form of love because it neither expects nor demands any-thing in return. I don't know if what I felt that day for a Thai drug runner was compassion, but I can say for certain I had never seen terror like it. All I could think of was that he was probably a better man than most – my parched mouth, panicking heartbeat and sweat-drenched body told me I couldn't have stood it for half as long as he had. I felt sick.

The agents stopped. They took the towel off his face, left him blindfolded and asked if he wanted to talk. Too distraught to form any words, fighting for every breath, his spastic hands trying to tear at the restraints, he said nothing. The senior CIA guy told his men to put the towel back on and keep going.

That's when I found my voice.

'Stop now, or you'll all be on a charge,' I said, trying to make it sound as cold and ruthless as possible. They looked at me, eyeing me up. I had no choice then – I either had to win or be emasculated for whatever remained of my career.

'I can make it a Critical Incident Investigation if you like. You wanna try explaining what this guy has got to do with national security? Kramer, you want to go first?'

After a moment that seemed to last a year the senior guy – Kramer – told them to put the towel away and take off the blindfold. The drug courier looked up at me, this tough guy with machete scars who probably thought he had no problem handling pain, and it was pathetic to see how thankful he was. 'You ready to tell us what happened?' I asked him.

He nodded, but he couldn't stop his hands from shaking – they had broken him, that was for sure. Years later, when the CIA water-boarded Khalid Sheikh Mohammed – al-Qaeda's military commander – he set a new world record by withstanding it for two and a half minutes. The courier had lasted twenty-nine seconds, which was about average.

Once he had been released from the board and was slumped on the floor, he told us he had been on the bridge with two brothers. They ran the high-country opium lab where the drugs originated and were the ones who had decided to turn Smokey Joe into a human javelin. The courier said he had never laid a hand on the man, and I had the feeling he was telling the truth.

He explained that the guard had developed a nice little earner shaking down the drug couriers as they crossed the river gorge: he'd turned the dilapidated footbridge into Thailand's first toll road. Initially he had been satisfied to unwrap the raw No. 2 and take a line of shavings off the brick – clipping the ticket, so to speak. He would then trade the shavings with the smugglers for booze, which he would sell at the prison. Of course, he got greedy and the shavings became massive offcuts – so large that the two brothers finally decided that a toll road wasn't in northern Thailand's best economic interest.

We had found our answer and, while there would be no Critical Incident Report, we all had to submit our own version of the case to our superiors. I'm sure the CIA's account said they had only used reasonable force, while mine, of course, said the opposite. That would have been an end to it – who in the intelligence community would have cared about a Thai drug courier? – except there would have been one section of the CIA's report I couldn't dispute.

Kramer would have recounted that he saw fear on my face, that it appeared I had felt so much for the man being interrogated that my body was rigid and drenched in sweat. He might even have questioned my courage and whether I was suitable for front-line service. In his own way, he was probably saying that my weight was my heart.

It was that report which Whisperer would have read when he called up my file from the archives. I have had many years to consider my own weaknesses, and I have to say that what Whisperer told me as I was leaving was probably right – for me, there was no point in suffering. End it quick.

I looked out of the window and saw the broad sweep of the Bosporus and the domes of Istanbul's magnificent mosques. The wheels hit and held on the runway. I was in Turkey.

Chapter Thirteen

OLD PASSENGER JETS THUNDERED DOWN THE ASPHALT AT ANOTHER airport – this one was in Islamabad. The Saracen had followed the Trans-Afghan Highway down to Kabul and found himself in an outer ring of hell – the Afghan city was overwhelmed by US and Coalition forces and haunted by the constant threat of suicide bombers.

After a day of prayer and uneasy rest, he had travelled the well-trodden invasion route down to the Pakistan border, crossed the frontier among a tide of other travellers and made his way through Peshawar and on to Islamabad.

The flight to Beirut was late – every flight out of Pakistan was late – but he didn't care. He was safe. If the Americans or Australians or whoever they were who had almost captured him up at the ruined village had somehow managed to discover his identity he would have been grabbed the moment he handed over his passport at check-in.

Instead, it was just the normal situation – the perfunctory look at the passport, a glance at the ticket and then the obligatory small talk while the counter clerk waited for his 'tip' to make sure that the checked suitcase was sent to Beirut and not to Moscow. He paid the bribe and headed towards the gate. Heavily armed men in uniform were everywhere but there was nothing you could call genuine security: as usual, too many guns, not enough brains.

He boarded the flight, flew to Beirut, returned to his bleak apartment in El-Mina and immediately went to work. He had resigned from the local hospital months earlier, but before he left he had raided its chaotic storeroom and taken with him two white bio-hazard suits and their air regulators, boxes containing ten thousand small glass vials which he had ordered especially for his purposes and a book of the hospital's official dispatch dockets.

All of these things he had stored in his garage. Wearing one of the suits and an oxygen tank, he set about producing as much of his super-virus as possible. Perhaps it was because of the spectacular results he had seen in the Hindu Kush or maybe it was thanks to his growing expertise, but the process went much faster than he had expected.

Day after day, working with large pharmaceutical tanks he had rigged into a sort of makeshift bio-reactor, he transferred the deadly virus into the glass vials, sealed their rubber tops with a special machine he had acquired for the purpose and stored them in industrial refrigerators he had purchased second-hand in Beirut.

As he approached the end of his production run, he took a day off, travelled to Beirut and stood in a queue for two hours to buy a newly released cellphone, the one featured in a Hollywood movie that all the young kids seemed to want. He paid cash for it and then walked several miles and bought a pre-paid SIM card which would give it a year's cellular service. The only thing that remained was to gift-wrap it.

The following Friday after prayers, he gave the present to another member of the congregation – a teenager with whom he had become friendly shortly after arriving in town. The boy reminded the Saracen a lot of himself at the same age – fatherless, deeply religious and full of fiery dreams about the irresistible rise of Islam.

The kid was so poor that when he pulled off the wrapping paper and saw the gift his eyes widened and he was barely able to believe it was his. The Saracen explained he was leaving El-Mina to find work and a new life in one of the fast-growing Muslim communities in Europe. The phone was a gift to remember him by, and all he asked in return was that the young man do a simple favour for him.

'When I have found somewhere to live, I will call on the new phone, make arrangements to send a key and ask you to open my garage for a Beirut courier who will pick up some boxes. Do you understand?'

The boy nodded and repeated the instructions perfectly. Men – even young men – in the Muslim world take the obligations of friendship far more seriously than their counterparts in the West, and the Saracen had no doubt that the teenager would fulfil his request to the letter. With tears in his eyes and no inkling of the plot in which he was now a participant, the teenager reached out and embraced the Saracen, a man he had often wished had been his real father.

The Saracen walked away without looking back. He had already spoken to the Beirut courier – twice weekly, his refrigerated truck arrived at the hospital to pick up or deliver blood and drugs. The Saracen told him there were boxes of medical supplies in his garage which would need to be sent to him and asked him to be on standby for a call.

With his arrangements almost complete, the Saracen arrived back at his apartment and went into the garage. The gene-sequencing machines, bio-safety suits and other equipment were already gone, smashed and burnt into an unrecognizable pulp and taken out to the local garbage dump in the boot of his car. He boxed up the vials of sealed virus, attached the hospital's official dispatch dockets and, in the appropriate field, marked them as 'expired vaccine'. The exact address they were being sent to would have to wait – he didn't know it yet – but he could rely on the boy with the cellphone to fill it in when the time came.

He put the boxes in the refrigerator, locked the garage and went upstairs to his living quarters. Sweating, he packed the only other things that he really cared about – photos, keepsakes and small mementos of his wife and son – into a crate which would go into a storage locker he had rented in Beirut. He was almost finished when three men from a local charity arrived in a pick-up truck to collect his single bed, desk and other household goods. Once the items were loaded, he stood alone in his empty apartment.

He looked around at the two rooms one last time – they had been good years, productive years. Lonely years, too. There were times he missed his wife and boy so much that the pain was almost physical but, looking back, maybe the way things had turned out had been for the best. No, it was *definitely* for the best. It was Allah's will.

Known only to himself, he had set a date for the soft kill of America, a day that would live in history long after he was gone. The date was 12 October, which he knew was Columbus Day, the day when America was discovered by Europeans and all the world's real troubles had begun.

How appropriate, he thought to himself with pleasure, that future generations would mark that same date as the beginning of the far enemy's decline.

He had worked hard but, if he was going to meet his deadline, there was still no time to waste. He walked out of the door, turned the key in the lock and headed for Germany.

Chapter Fourteen

I PASSED THROUGH TURKISH IMMIGRATION WITHOUT DIFFICULTY AND BY the time I reached the baggage claim my Samsonite was on the carousel. As I walked to get it, I saw that no other luggage from my flight had arrived yet and I knew what had happened – mine had been unloaded first and sent to the on-site office of MIT, the Turkish intelligence agency, to be inspected and photographed.

I wasn't offended: I was supposedly a sworn officer of a foreign power and it was understandable that they would take an interest in me, but – for God's sake – couldn't they at least have done it professionally and sent it on to the carousel with the rest of the bags from my flight? I looked around the customs hall but I couldn't see anyone who appeared to have me targeted. They were probably in a room above, checking me out on one of their closed-circuit cameras.

I walked through customs unchallenged, plunged into a sea of taxi touts and found the shuttle to take me to the domestic terminal. It made the international version seem deserted – there were men with large brass urns on their backs selling cups of apple tea, makeshift stalls with sugar-laden pastries and guys roasting nuts over coal braziers. Forget that it was close to a hundred degrees, the heat hit you like a wall, and the Fire Department would have taken a week to get through the traffic.

I joined a queue at a Turkish Airlines check-in desk and finally inched my way forward until I faced a young woman with heavy gold jewellery, far too much make-up and a crisp headscarf covering her hair – according to Islam, a woman's crowning glory. She took my suitcase, swapped my ticket for a boarding pass and pointed me in the direction of my gate.

The line at security stretched for more than a block, but I managed to circumvent it by approaching one of the supervisors and telling him, in English and the few words of Turkish I had at my command, that I was carrying a gun. I was quickly escorted into a windowless office where five men, all in suits and smoking heavily, examined my passport, agency shield and other documents, including a copy of a letter from the White House to the President of Turkey thanking him for assisting the FBI 'in this sad and unfortunate matter'.

That was the document which did the trick, and two of them summoned a golf cart and had me driven down to the Milas–Bodrum gate. I was the first passenger to arrive and, with well over an hour to spare before we were due to depart, my plan had been to open the laptop and continue studying my past cases. It didn't happen.

No sooner had I sat down than I glanced up at a television screen suspended from the ceiling. It was tuned to a Turkish news channel and they were showing stock footage of some mountains in Afghanistan. I thought it was just another story about the endless war and was about to turn away when they cut to a diagram of a suitcase and the elements that were needed to make a dirty bomb.

I knew then that Whisperer had leaked the story about the Saracen trying to buy the Polonium-210 and, while I had no direct evidence, I was certain he had done it to coincide with my arrival in Turkey. No wonder the MIT agents over at international arrivals had been so sloppy with my suitcase – they would have been distracted by the breaking news of the biggest story in international terrorism for years. I smiled in quiet admiration: that was the definition of a good case officer – to orchestrate a perfect diversion to take the heat off his joe.

I stood up and asked a woman at the desk if I could borrow the remote for the TV. For the next hour, as the waiting area filled with my fellow passengers, I surfed the BBC, CNN, MSNBC, Al Jazeera, SkyNews, Bloomberg and half a dozen other English-speaking news channels to follow the story of the nuclear trigger. As usual, it was mostly the same small amount of information endlessly recycled, but every now and again a new morsel was added for the anchors and the experts to chew over: more than two thousand intelligence agents were to be dispatched to Afghanistan and Pakistan; the governments of Saudi Arabia, Iran and Yemen had pledged their cooperation; the White House announced that the president would address the nation.

I was looking forward to hearing what Grosvenor would have to say but, just as the press corps rose to their feet and a camera grabbed a shot of Grosvenor approaching the lectern, they made the final call for my flight.

I returned the remote, walked down the skybridge, found my seat and, fifty minutes later, caught a glimpse of the turquoise waters of the Aegean Sea – probably the most beautiful stretch of water in the world – as we circled wide and came in to land at Milas airport. It was twenty-five miles inland from Bodrum and after I had gone through the ritual of retrieving the Samsonite yet again – there was no MIT to provide unseen assistance this time – I found my way to the car-rental desk.

It took an age. Computers didn't appear to have reached the Turkish frontier – all the paperwork had to be completed by hand and copies distributed to various desks. A Fiat four-door was finally brought round to the front and, after myself and two of the office staff had succeeded in converting the navigation to English, I headed out of the airport and hit the road for Bodrum. Thanks to the traffic, I didn't make much progress and when I finally crested a rise I saw why – up ahead was a convoy of garishly painted eighteen-wheelers and flatbeds. The circus was in town – literally.

This was no cheap sideshow – it was the Turkish State Circus complete with, according to a billboard on the side of one of the semis, 'one hundred tumblers, eighty hi-wire artists and four snake charmers'. Thankfully, on the outskirts of Milas they pulled into an exhibition ground where they were setting up the big top, the bottleneck cleared and I hit the gas.

Five miles on, I rolled down the window and let the hot breeze wash over me, surrounding me with the scent of pine forests and the promise of another deadly mission. Yes, I was long retired and scared; yes, I was alone and living an elaborate lie. But there was part of me that was so alive it was almost intoxicating.

Chapter Fifteen

THE MILES FELL BY THE WAYSIDE QUICKLY. I DROVE PAST OLIVE GROVES and tiny villages of white Cubist houses, on distant hills I saw derelict windmills which peasants had once used to grind flour, but I was damned if I could see the one thing I needed.

I was looking for somewhere to stop that wouldn't arouse suspicion, the sort of place a newly arrived FBI agent might pause to enjoy the sunshine and check his phone messages. Several miles past a larger village with a small mosque and a thriving farmers' market – unchanged in centuries by the look of it – I swept round a curve and saw a café with a panoramic view coming up on my right. I had reached the coast.

I pulled into the café's car park, stopped well away from its open-air terraces and ignored the view. I got out of the car, opened my cellphone and, as I looked at the screen, ostensibly to check my messages, I restlessly wandered around the Fiat. The whole thing was a sham, a performance enacted for the benefit of the occupants of any vehicle who might have been following me. I knew there would be no messages – what I was doing was running a program that the techs at Langley had implanted in the phone's software. Near the back of the vehicle the phone started beeping and, as I moved closer, it got louder. Somewhere inside the right rear wheel arch – and accessed through the trunk, I guessed – was a tracking transmitter which had been installed, no doubt, by my buddies at MIT. They wanted to know where I was – there was no surprise in that – but I was quietly pleased about the way they had done it. As any experienced agent would tell you, it was a lot easier to dump a car than a tail.

Satisfied that I was travelling solo, I turned my phone off, removed its battery, slipped both parts into my pocket and turned to the view. No wonder the café was crowded: the rugged hills tumbled down to the waters of the Aegean and the whole of Bodrum was laid out in front of me. It was late in the afternoon, the sunlight washing across the marinas and the two bays that hugged the town, highlighting the walls of a magnificent fifteenth-century castle built by the Crusaders which stood on the headland between them. The Castle of St Peter was its name, I recalled.

It was over ten years since I had last seen the town and it had grown and changed, but that didn't stop the memories crowding in. For a moment I was a young agent again, watching as the lights from exclusive hotels danced on the water, listening to music from a myriad nightclubs fill the night air. How could a mission which had started with so much promise end in such disaster?

I tried to shrug the memory off and walked to one of several large pairs of binoculars that were fixed to tripods for the benefit of tourists with a few lire to spare. I slipped the coins in and saw in stunning detail expensive villas clinging to the cliffs and a host of remarkable yachts, all of them far too big for any marina in the Mediterranean or Aegean, riding at anchor offshore. I swept past them and tilted up until I found a mansion which stood alone in acres of gardens on a headland.

Built over fifty years ago and with tall colonnades, vine-covered loggias and cascading terraces, it had a faintly Roman air. Its shutters were closed and, with the headland losing the afternoon light, it seemed to sit in brooding shadow. As impressive as it was, I didn't like the house: even at that distance there seemed something sinister about it. I had no particular knowledge of it, but I was certain it was the French House and that it was from the end of its sweeping lawn that Dodge had plunged to his death.

I returned to my car and drove down into Bodrum, heading back into my past.

Chapter Sixteen

THE HOTEL I WAS BOOKED INTO WASN'T WHAT ANYONE WOULD CALL fashionable – I mean, people weren't drilling holes in the walls to get inside. Those sorts of places were down on the waterfront with 24-hour champagne bars, open-air dance clubs, and Ukrainian models doing lingerie shows on private beaches.

Mine was in a backstreet with a car-repair shop at one end and a used-furniture shop at the other. Built out of cement block which had been painted a pale blue, 'tired' was about the kindest word that could be applied to it. When I drew up outside I was forced to admit that the staff in Whisperer's makeshift back office had done an outstanding job – it was exactly the sort of place you would expect an FBI agent travelling on his country's dime to stay.

Even as I walked up the front steps I knew what I would find inside: faded curtains, a limp buffet for breakfast and a pair of potted palms clinging to life. The man standing behind the reception desk, like the hotel itself, had seen better days. Over the years all his features appeared to have been battered every which way but loose. I learned later that he had once been one of Turkey's most successful amateur middleweights. If that was the look of a winner, I certainly didn't want to see the loser. Yet, when he smiled – and he smiled in expansive greeting as I walked through the door – his face was so full of vitality and goodwill it was impossible not to like him. Pumping my hand, he introduced himself as the manager and owner, pulled out an index card on which I was required to write my name, passport details and home address, and took imprints from three credit cards. 'Just to be on the side of the safe,' he confided happily.

Let's just say his English was idiosyncratic.

'It's a great pity of the shame you weren't here on the Saturday night, Mr Brodie David Wilson,' he continued. For some reason he had decided that all English speakers had to be referred to by the full name given in their passports.

'The fireworks were of a nature rarely by anyone to be seen.'

'Fireworks?' I asked.

'Zafer Bayrami,' he replied.

I had no idea what he was talking about. Maybe it was some kind of blessing. 'Zafer Bayrami?' I said.

'The Day of Victory. All peoples of the world know of this date – the nation of great Turkey wrung the heads of enemies that were mainly of the Greeks.'

'Ah,' I replied. 'No wonder there were fireworks.' The Turks and the Greeks had been at it for centuries.

'I went up for the watching on the roof. A huge bomb of the phosphorus exploded over the headland of the south. The Greece peoples probably thought we were attacking again.' He thought this was a fine joke and laughed loudly.

'The southern headland,' I said. 'Isn't that where the French House is?'

A shadow passed over his face. 'Yes.'

'And somebody died there on Saturday night, didn't they?'

'A misfortune of the first rank, a man of very few years. Terrible,' he said, shaking his head in sadness. I think he had such a love of life that he found the death of just about anyone upsetting. Well, maybe not if they were Greek.

'Is that why you have come to us – for the investigate, Mr Brodie David Wilson?'

'Yeah,' I said. 'Who told you that?'

'The police,' he replied, as if it were perfectly normal. 'They were here of this morning, two of them. The woman one left you a message.'

He handed me an envelope and called for the bellhop.

Chapter Seventeen

MY ROOM WAS PRETTY MUCH WHAT I HAD EXPECTED, EVEN DOWN TO the faded curtains and a small pile of magazines with coffee stains on the covers.

No sooner were we inside than the bellhop, an Albanian drifter in his late twenties, started opening and closing closet doors in the age-old belief that the greater the activity, the bigger the tip. I didn't pay much attention: my interest was catching up on the nuclear trigger and seeing what the president had said to calm the nation.

I found the remote and switched on the TV in the corner. I got Al Jazeera, which was leading with the story but had managed to find their own angle – they were telling their mainly Arab audience that the developments over the last twelve hours would mean an explosion of racial profiling at airports and travel terminals throughout the world. For once – even though they didn't realize why – they had got it absolutely right.

I started to channel surf and got two local news stations, a women's talk show, several strange soap operas which were so brightly lit they hurt your eyes, and then I was back at Al Jazeera. That couldn't be right – where was the BBC, CNN and all the others? – and I started hitting buttons. I was okay with guns but remotes weren't my strong point.

I explained to the bellhop – half in mime, half in Turkglish – that I wanted to watch the English cable news channels. I even wrote out the names for him to make sure he understood.

'No, no – not here,' he kept repeating, pointing at Al Jazeera, making it clear that, if you wanted English news, that was your only option. He was so adamant that I was forced to accept it – as far as

346

Bodrum was concerned, none of the English-language channels were available.

After he left I slumped into a chair. The situation was serious for one simple reason: the messages from the woman in Bodrum to the man in the Hindu Kush were entirely composed of fragments from English-speaking news channels.

We knew from the CIA analysis of the recordings that the audio quality of the news programmes was too good to have been taken from a computer: they were recorded up close to a TV's speakers, and I had been harbouring a mental image of the woman carefully recording and editing the material.

But if you couldn't get the stations in that part of Turkey then she must have recorded the material elsewhere and driven to the phone box in Bodrum to send the messages. It meant she could have come from hundreds of miles away – from Iraq or Lebanon or *anywhere*, for God's sake.

I ran my hand through my hair. By that time I had been in Bodrum for ten minutes and already the potential background of the woman had expanded exponentially. Dog-tired, I decided to put the problem aside and stick to my original plan. That had been to shower, grab my cellphone and – using the map of central Bodrum I had committed to memory – start locating and photographing phone boxes. It didn't quite work out that way.

It was 3 a.m. when I woke up, still in the armchair, and I figured somebody walking the streets and taking photos at that time – even if parts of Bodrum were still partying – would draw exactly the sort of attention I wanted to avoid.

With no alternative and deciding to have at least one good night's sleep, I was getting ready for bed when I saw the envelope from the Bodrum cops. That contained even worse news.

In a few brief lines – thankfully, in good English – it said they had tried to contact me before I left America in order to save me the journey. They said that the evidence in Dodge's death was clear and overwhelming: it was a tragic accident and, as a result, the investigation was being terminated.

Chapter Eighteen

WITHOUT AN INVESTIGATION, THERE WAS NO NEED FOR AGENT BRODIE Wilson in Bodrum.

Take it slow, we're not finished yet, I told myself as I arrived at police headquarters right on nine the following morning.

That was the time the cop who had signed the letter had suggested that I should call by and meet her.

'You'll have no problem in making the afternoon flight out of Bodrum,' she had written. 'It shouldn't take more than twenty minutes to bring you up to date.'

Once inside, I was handed over to a young cop in a beautifully pressed uniform and the shiniest boots I've seen outside of a Marine honour guard. He couldn't have been more than sixteen. He led me out the back, up a flight of stairs and into a warren of offices occupied by the detectives. At the end of a corridor we entered a room with two desks and a view into the courtyard of an adjoining house. The whitewashed home was falling down, plaster crumbling from its walls, broken tiles scattered across the roof, but it didn't matter. It was rendered beautiful by virtue of two old frangipani trees in its courtyard.

Only one of the desks was occupied. A young woman with a tumble of dark hair – obviously a secretary – was behind it, with a phone to her ear and typing on a computer which was so old it had probably arrived pre-loaded with *Pong*.

The secretary was one of those women where everything about her was extravagant – her gestures, her boobs straining against a tight blouse, her make-up, her ass in a pencil skirt. The moods, too, one suspected. As I waited for her to finish, it occurred to me that, in

348

many ways, she represented the contradictions of modern Turkey – she was young in a culture wedded to the past, unabashedly female in a society dominated by men, irreligious and Western-looking in a country where one face was always turned east towards Islam.

And, of course – for a deeply conservative nation – there was one last contradiction, the biggest of them all. Drugs. Turkey had become the critical link in the most lucrative trafficking route in the world, a modern Silk Road which transported opium, semi-refined heroin and fine-grade hash from Pakistan and Afghanistan into Western Europe, over the border to Lebanon or across the Caucasus mountains into Russia. If drugs were just another modern commodity – like oil, pumped down transnational pipelines – Turkey had become the biggest interchange in the world.

I knew about it because of Christos Nikolaides, the Greek drug dealer whose death I had ordered in Santorini. In pursuing him I had learned from the DEA that Patros Nikolaides and six other major cartels were wound tight into Turkey – especially this part of Turkey – and despite valiant efforts by some fine Turkish officers, corruption had blossomed and profits had become ever more spectacular.

The secretary showed no sign of finishing the call so I pulled up a chair and fell to thinking about Patros and his Albanian enforcers. Once I had returned to the safety of America, the man had slipped from my mind but I had to admit it was ironic how, under the pressure of the crisis we were facing, I had been drawn back into a corner of the world he knew so well. I wondered where he was – still behind his twelve-foot walls in Thessaloniki, tending to his lavender plants and mourning the loss of his son, I hoped.

I was wrong not to have thought harder about it – spectacularly wrong – but the woman finally hung up, turned her appropriately extravagant smile on me, straightened her blouse in case I hadn't yet noticed what she considered her two best assets and asked if I was Brodie Wilson.

I nodded, and she told me that her boss was running fifteen minutes late. 'She takes the little dude to a corner park every morning. Her car, it just got up and died. It's Italian – the car, I'm talking about – which explains why it's a piece of shit.'

I deduced from this that she must have had a boyfriend who was Italian. It also seemed that most of her English had been gleaned from modern American music, summer blockbusters and chatting on the Internet.

'"The little dude"?' I asked.

'Her son.'

'Is her husband a cop too? That's the way it usually works in this business.' I didn't care much, I was just making conversation – you know, shooting the breeze.

'No, she's divorced.'

'How old's her son?'

'The little dude's six.' She obviously liked the expression; I guess it made her think she was just as hip as any visiting American.

'That's hard, being a single mom with a boy that age.'

She shrugged – I doubt she had ever thought about it. Out of nowhere, disaster arrived and tried to shake hands with me. 'You have children, Mr Wilson?'

'No, no little dudes,' I said, not concentrating and inadvertently telling the truth – at least the truth about myself but in direct contradiction to my legend. I immediately realized the mistake, thought of trying to bite the words back but dispensed with that stupid idea. Somehow I managed to keep my cool.

'Not that live with me,' I continued with a smile. 'I'm divorced, that's why I know how difficult it is – my former wife keeps telling me.'

She laughed, not noticing anything untoward. Good recovery, I thought, but my palms were damp and I gave myself a metaphorical slap across the head to wake me up. 'Is that your boss?' I asked, trying to change the subject, pointing at a photo on the other desk.

It showed a smiling woman dressed in a headscarf and coveralls halfway up a ladder, whitewashing the side wall of a small Bodrum house. It must have been shot down in the old port – a large building next door carried a sign in English and Turkish: GUL & SONS, MARINA AND SHIPWRIGHTS.

'Yeah,' the secretary said, coming to my side. 'That was a couple of years ago, just after she arrived.' I looked more closely at the photo – she was a beautiful woman, in her thirties, sort of exotic too: high cheekbones and large almond eyes.

'She's very attractive,' I said.

'Thank you,' a voice said icily from behind. 'People say I get it from my mother.'

350

I turned, and it was the cop, of course. She put her handbag and cellphone down and turned to the secretary. 'Go to your desk, please, Hayrunnisa.'

Hayrunnisa didn't need to be told twice. The cop was dressed in a headscarf that was tucked into a high-collared jacket that fell to her knees. Underneath it she wore a long-sleeved blouse and wide-legged pants that brushed the top of a pair of high heels. Everything was of good quality – stylish too – but there wasn't an inch of flesh exposed except for her hands and face. This was the other side of Turkey – conservative, Islamic, deeply suspicious of the West and its values.

'My name is Leyla Cumali,' she said. She didn't offer her hand, and you didn't have to be a detective to work out she didn't like me. Maybe it was because I was an investigator trespassing on her patch, maybe because I was an American. Probably both, I decided. Apparently, in Turkey, two strikes and you're out.

'It's a pity you've come so far for so little,' she said, sitting down at her desk. 'As I said in the note, the death of the young man was clearly an accident.'

'When do you intend to finalize it?' I asked.

'Today. The case file will go to my superiors later this morning. Assuming everything is in order, it will then be forwarded to the department head in Ankara, who will close and seal it. That's a formality.'

'I'm afraid it will have to be delayed,' I said. 'I need to review the investigation before any decision is made.' I'm not usually so abrupt, but I couldn't let it get away from me; somehow, I had to buy some time.

She tried to mask it, but she was instantly angry – I could see it in the almond eyes. She fixed them on mine, trying to make me offer some conciliatory gesture, but I had been stared down by better men than her.

'I don't think there'll be any need to delay,' she said finally. 'Like I mentioned, I can take you through this in twenty minutes. Less, probably. That's how clear cut it is.'

She opened a filing cabinet, pulled out a stack of files and found a photo of the lawn at the back of the French House. She slapped it down on the desk.

'This is where he fell,' she said, indicating a hundred-foot drop down the face of a sheer cliff.

The crumbling precipice was rendered safe by a double-bar wooden fence which ran around the entire private headland and terminated at a beautiful gazebo on the tip of the point.

'Four metres north of the gazebo he either climbed on to the fence or stepped over it,' she said. 'We know the exact spot because one of my forensic team found a single thread from the chinos he was wearing snagged on a splinter.'

Her English was damn near perfect, but she hit the term 'forensic team' a little too hard – still seething, she was letting me know she wasn't from the backwoods and they had done their work in a thorough and modern fashion. I started to ask a question, but she rolled over me.

'You asked for a review, let's finish it. The young American died at 9.36 p.m. We know because his cellphone was in his pocket and the clock stopped when he smashed on to the rocks. That was six minutes after a large phosphorous star exploded above the headland. It marked the start of a firework display. I doubt you would know but Saturday night was—'

'Zafer Bayrami,' I said.

She was surprised. 'Congratulations,' she replied. 'Perhaps you're not as ignorant as most of your countrymen.'

I let it ride – what was the point? I had far more difficult problems to deal with than her attitude.

'The victim – Mr Dodge – had been sitting in the library of the house, drinking alcohol and taking drugs – the toxicology report shows it – when the phosphorous star exploded and marked the start of the evening's festivities.

'He picked up a pair of binoculars – we found them just inside the railing – and walked down the lawn to watch the fireworks.'

The binoculars set an alarm ringing – my radar said there was something wrong – but I didn't have time to think about it: I wanted to concentrate on what she was saying, and she was going at warp speed.

'To get a better view of the fireworks, he either stood on the railing or swung himself over it. Disoriented by the cocktail of drugs and alcohol, on unfamiliar territory, perhaps confused by the constant explosions of light, he lost his footing on the crumbling cliff edge and couldn't recover. He fell. Are you with me, Agent Wilson?'

I nodded.

'We re-created the scene with a dummy of exactly his height and weight. One point eight seconds after he fell, he crashed through some bushes clinging to the cliff. You can see the broken branches, and we found several tufts of hair in the foliage. You may find this interesting: his trajectory was totally consistent with a man slipping.

'Here are the records of those tests.' She slid a small pile of technical graphs across the table.

'We think he tried to grab on to a branch – there were lacerations on one hand – but he kept falling until he hit the rocks one hundred and four feet below. That's a ten-storey building. Among many other injuries, he broke his spine in two places and died instantly.'

I nodded – that was what the State Department file had given as the cause of death. I had to admit it – she and her forensic team had done an outstanding job. God help us, I thought. I had no choice except to keep attacking.

'There were security people on the estate,' I said. 'Plenty of people on boats. Some of them must have been close to the headland. Who heard him scream?' I was just probing.

'Nobody. Even if he did scream, the sound of the exploding fireworks would have drowned it out. Was that the question you were going to ask?'

'No, actually, it wasn't,' I replied testily. 'I wanted to know exactly who else was on the estate that night.'

'That's funny,' Cumali replied, her voice freighted with sarcasm. 'Exactly the same question occurred to us. Apart from the security detail, there was nobody. He was alone.'

'How can you be sure?' I asked. 'It's a huge estate.'

She gave me a withering look. 'Six point nine acres in total,' she said, opening another folder and taking out more photos. With them was a wad of blueprints.

'The only people who rent it are hugely wealthy – as a result, there are one hundred and eight cameras which monitor and record the perimeter. The system was installed by one of the world's leading security corporations – American, you'll be pleased to know – and it's impossible to step on to the grounds without being seen and recorded.'

She dealt out photos showing dozens of different cameras – cameras mounted on poles, on the sides of buildings, hidden in foliage. Some were fixed, others pivoted; all were equipped with infrared and night-vision hardware. Looking at them as an expert, I knew it must have cost a fortune.

She followed up with some of the blueprints. 'These are the specifications of the system – you can see there isn't an inch of the perimeter that isn't covered.'

Next came a series of reports which showed that the cameras had been working perfectly. I didn't look at them – I was sure she was right. Things were getting worse by the second. I might be able to delay her by a few days but, beyond that – well, it was looking impossible. 'What about the cliff?' I asked. 'What was to stop somebody climbing up it?'

She sighed. 'There is a small beach at one end – the German Beach, it's called – which has a boat ramp, a salt-water pool and boathouse. It is part of the estate and attached to it is a guardroom.

'Two men were inside and four cameras monitor the steps up to the estate and the entire cliff face. You want to know how good the motion-controlled cameras were? There was a slight blur recorded by one of them that took our interest – then I realized it had captured the victim's body plunging past. One fiftieth of a second and it got it.'

I looked out at the frangipani trees, buying myself a moment, trying to gather my thoughts for another assault. 'So you say Dodge was alone – except of course he wasn't,' I said. 'There was the security detail. What was to stop one of them approaching from behind and tipping him into eternity?'

She barely looked at her notes; she could have shot it down blind-folded. 'There were eighteen men on duty that night.' She laid out mugshots of them all; more than a few gorillas in their ranks.

'Like many people in that business, some of them weren't good men, but that wasn't important: they were not allowed to patrol the grounds. They had to stay in the security posts, monitor their TV screens and only leave in groups of six with a supervisor if the perimeter was breached.

'All the posts were under camera surveillance,' she continued. 'The recordings show nobody left any of them for an hour either side of Mr Dodge's death. I'm sorry to disappoint you, but the security team are clean.'

'You're not disappointing me,' I lied. 'I'm just trying to get to the truth. Yes, the guards may be clean – unless the tapes or disks were doctored.' I was grabbing at anything I could lay a hand to, but I tried to carry it off with a certain panache.

'They're disks,' said Cumali, not buying the panache or much of anything else. 'They've been checked. All of them have embedded code, which means, if you edit them, it shows up immediately. I'm told it's the same system used at the White House.'

She was right about that, and the beauty of the security precautions at the French House was that the wealthy people in residence had total freedom. They weren't under constant surveillance – which probably meant a great deal to rich dilettantes using drugs – but nobody could enter the grounds without being observed and challenged. The occupants were probably as safe as they would be anywhere in the world.

'What about motive?' I said, trying not to show it was just another flip of the card, another roll of the dice.

'The wife, of course. The dead man had no siblings, his parents were dead and she was the only heir. Her name is Cameron.' She slid a photo across the desk.

Cameron – photographed in long shot and looking at the camera – had it all going on. She was in her mid-twenties – tall and elegant, a cool haughtiness that you usually only find in models and those who are truly beautiful. According to the State Department report, she had been working as a 'personal shopper' at the Prada store on Fifth Avenue when she met him. It figured – how else was a chick from nowhere going to meet a young billionaire? At the laundromat?

'How long had they been married?' I asked, still looking at Cameron's face. She was that kind of woman.

'Eight months.'

I stared at Cumali for a beat. 'Eight months and a billion-dollar payout – that sounds like quite a motive to me.'

The cop shook her head. Why wasn't I surprised? 'From 8 p.m. she was in her husband's helicopter with four other partygoers – visiting a series of clubs along the coast. We've seen the CCTV footage from all of them – every minute was accounted for.'

I could imagine it – other revellers arriving at dance clubs in Porsches, BMWs and perhaps a few Ferraris. Then she turns up with her posse in a Bell JetRanger. It's hard to beat a billion dollars.

'Okay – say she's clear,' I theorized. 'She got someone to do it for her.'

'Who? They knew a few people – other rich couples who'd sailed down from Monaco and St Tropez – and they met some foreigners here. Acquaintances, really. We interviewed them all, but there wasn't anybody you could remotely think was acting on her behalf.'

'A hired hand,' I threw back. 'A paid killer.'

She laughed – but not because she found it funny. 'How do you find someone like that?' she demanded. 'Not a bungling lowlife but some top-class assassin? Somebody who won't take the deposit and just walk away? Anyway, you've still got the problem that he was alone on the estate.'

'A billion dollars, though,' I said, more to myself than her, 'that's a helluva lot of money.'

'What is it with Americans?' she asked with contempt. 'Why do you automatically think of killing? If she wanted money – a few million would be enough – why wouldn't she just divorce him?'

I was tired, I was frustrated, I was desperately worried about trying to pump air into an investigation that kept deflating. But mostly I was sick of the woman and her attitude to me and my country. I wanted to round on her, I wanted to pay out on her own failings, I wanted to ask about the drug trade and the new Silk Road and genocide against the Kurds and anything else I could lay a hand to, but I reined it in – I had to, for the greater good, and all that.

'Was there a pre-nup?' I asked wearily.

But she wasn't interested. 'I didn't inquire,' she said. 'What was the point? As I've said, there was nobody else on the estate, the only person with any motive was twenty miles away, Mr Dodge's actions were clear and unambiguous, the forensic evidence is irrefutable. It was an accident.'

She started to gather up the photos and reports, ready to be put back in the filing cabinet. 'That's the review for you, Mr Wilson. I think even the FBI would agree that the Turkish police have done a thorough and professional job.'

'I'll need those files, the raw data and everything else, Detective,' I said, indicating her stack of material. I expected an explosion, and I wasn't disappointed.

'*What?*' she replied.

I caught sight of Hayrunnisa watching our faces, loving it.

'I told you, I need to conduct my own review,' I said evenly.

'No,' Cumali replied. She repeated it in Turkish for added confirmation.

'I've come a long way, Detective Cumali. My visit has been organized at the highest levels of government. Do you want me to call and say I'm not getting the cooperation I need?'

She didn't move. Nor did the secretary – she had probably never heard her boss threatened with a bazooka before. I put my hand out for the files, but Cumali shook her head.

'They're the originals. Anyway, they're mostly in Turkish,' she said.

'I'm sure a lot of them were translated for the widow,' I countered, but she made no move to give them to me. 'Please, Detective – don't let's do this,' I said.

She didn't take her eyes off me – and then appeared to give in. 'How long do you need them for?' she asked.

'Three days, maybe four,' I said. It wasn't much, but I figured it was the best I could do.

She looked at the secretary, still deeply angry – and that should have warned me that she had a plan. She spoke harshly in Turkish, but there was one word I understood because it was so close to the English: *fotokopi*.

'Thank you,' I said politely.

'There's nothing here for you in Bodrum, Agent Wilson,' she said after a moment. 'Nothing at all.'

With that she turned her back and started to examine her schedule and mail. She didn't look up when Hayrunnisa returned with the photocopied files. Not even when I put them in my back-pack and walked out of her office.

357

Chapter Nineteen

OF ALL THE DEATHS OF ALL THE PEOPLE IN ALL THE WORLD – WE HAD TO choose Dodge's. What had seemed like a piece of good fortune had turned out to be a terrible mistake.

With his death so clearly an accident, there was nothing to investigate and, with nothing to investigate, Brodie Wilson might as well have got on a plane and gone home. Detective Leyla Cumali had called that one right.

I had bought myself a few days, but that was nowhere near enough. As I left the stationhouse I thought yet again how it was the assumptions, the unquestioned assumptions, that get you every time. Whisperer and I should have drilled deeper and asked ourselves exactly *what* I was going to investigate. In fairness, we were tired and desperate when we made the decision and, in most circumstances, the death of a twenty-eight-year-old man on sea-swept rocks would have presented *something* worth investigating. But excuses were no good, we had nailed our flag to the mast and – like any number of pirates – we paid the price when the ship went down.

The question was: what was I going to do about it? The short answer was: I had no idea. I have a way of dealing with stress, though – I either walk or I work. Bodrum offered the opportunity to do both and I reminded myself that the major mission – or at least a first step on it – was identifying the phone boxes in the Old Town.

So I pulled the cellphone with its specially modified camera out of my backpack, reinserted the battery and, at the end of the street, I turned right. I was working to the inner map I had in my head and, after five minutes' fast walking, at last feeling the anxiety subside to a manageable level, I reached the edge of the search area.

I had divided it mentally into sectors and I wound back to a much slower pace, determined not to allow any potential target to escape my notice or the camera. It wasn't easy. For most of the year Bodrum is a sleepy town, home to about fifty thousand people, but in summer the number swells to half a million and, even though it was the tag end of the season, the streets were crowded with vacationers, scenesters and the vast universe of people who prey on them.

I passed countless shops selling Turkish leather sandals and rare Persian carpets, nearly all of which had come overland from some factory in China. Every hundred yards there were aromatic bars specializing in what, in Spain, would be called tapas but that far east was known as *meze*, and no matter what time of the day or night they were always full.

Every time I saw a phone box I photographed it, confident that the software in the phone was downloading it on to the map and recording its exact position. Somewhere along the line I grabbed a kebab wrapped in pitta and sat on a bench under a jacaranda tree to eat it. Only after a few minutes did I look in the window of the shop beside me. On display was an outstanding collection of saxophones and classic electric guitars. I stepped to the door and looked into the dark cavern beyond.

It was one of those places – my sort of places – that you hardly see any more. One side of the cave was occupied by piles of sheet music, racks of vinyl records, bins of CDs, and if somebody had told me there were boxes of eight-track cartridges out back I would have believed them. The other side was given over to instruments – enough Gibsons and Fender Stratocasters to make any rock 'n' roll tragic smile – and a host of Turkish folk instruments I couldn't put a name to, let alone a sound.

The guy smoking behind the counter – in his forties, a musician by the look of his weathered jeans and dreamy eyes – motioned me to step inside. At another time, in another life, I would have spent hours inside, but I spread my hands in mute apology and got on with the task at hand.

In the hours that followed I took enough photos of phone boxes outside tourist shops and corner markets to last a lifetime, waited an age to cross a main thoroughfare to shoot one ten yards from a BP gas station and found at least six that looked as if they had been brought in from another country and illegally connected to the overhead lines. No wonder Turkish Telecom had no record of them.

By late afternoon, footsore and thirsty, I found myself in a small public square. I sat down at an open-air café and my first thought was to order an Efes beer but, thankfully, I have some degree of self-awareness and I knew that in a mood of anger and despair I might not have stopped at one. I ordered a coffee instead and began the task I had been avoiding all day: I opened the backpack, took out the files concerning Dodge's death and began to examine the disaster into which Whisperer and I had stumbled.

Twenty minutes later I was certain something was badly wrong with the police investigation. The key wasn't in the interviews, the forensic examination or the analysis of the security footage. It was in the toxicology report.

Along with a lot of the other files it had been translated for Cameron's benefit, and Detective Cumali was right, it showed there were drugs in his body, but I doubt if she had any way of judging what those levels really meant. Indeed, the final page of the medical examiner's report merely stated they were sufficient to have significantly impaired the victim's judgement and balance.

'"Significantly impaired"?' Holy crap, the young billionaire had gone nuclear. From my medical training and own dark experience I knew he couldn't have introduced that level of drugs into his blood-stream in a matter of hours – not without overdosing. Dodge had been on an epic binge: three or four days, by my reckoning.

Unlike Cumali – or any of her forensic team – my chequered past also gave me an expert insight into the actual effects those drugs would have had on him. There was tina, of course – there was always tina these days – its faithful little sidekick GHB, or EasyLay, to cut the mood swings and a good lacing of Ecstasy to soothe the soul. Sleep was always the enemy of somebody on a binge, and that's why there were the heavy traces of coke: to keep him awake. I was certain that nobody on a four-day drug blitz, using a cocktail of those substances, would have had any interest in fireworks. That was Sunday school compared to the light show going on in his own head and genitals.

Then I remembered the alarm that went off over the binoculars. I realized what my problem was: who would take binoculars to look at fireworks exploding almost overhead? Not unless you wanted to blind yourself. And why go to the very end of the property and stand

360

on a cliff edge – wouldn't the lawn or terraces have offered just as good a view? Even the most chronic drug users have *some* instinct for self-preservation. No, something else had induced him, in that state of heavy drug intoxication, to grab the binoculars and head down to the cliff face.

I didn't know what it was – I didn't know the answer to a lot of things – but I did know that the situation wasn't as bleak as it had appeared in Detective Cumali's office, as I drowned in her disdain and the smell of frangipani.

I thought again of that bottle of Efes. Better not, I decided: hope was even more dangerous than despair.

What I really needed was my car.

Chapter Twenty

THE FRENCH HOUSE WAS EASY ENOUGH TO FIND. ONCE YOU HEADED OUT of Bodrum and reached the southern headland, you took the long road that wound up through overhanging cypress trees and drove until you could go no further.

It was almost dark by the time I reached it. The large wrought-iron gates blocking the road, backed by black canvas for privacy, were closed, and the lanterns on top of the stone pillars remained unlit. A police car stood almost unseen in a small grove of trees and, when I drew to a stop, an overweight cop leaned out of the window and started yelling in Turkish and waving me away.

I turned off the engine and got out of the car. He threw his door open, snarling, and I saw his hand reach for his billy club. I'm sorry to report that Turkish cops don't have a reputation for asking twice but, fortunately, I beat him to the draw. I had my gold shield out and pointed at his face before he got within range.

He stared at it for a second, pissed off, then returned to his squad car. I heard him arguing on his radio and, when he was finally told what to do, he hoisted up his pants and took his sweet time approaching a small pedestrian gate opened by an electronic keypad. The device was set into concrete, a twelve-digit version, custom-made and impenetrable: nobody would be removing its face plate and trying to manipulate the circuitry any time soon. Two cameras mounted on the high wall – one fixed, one sweeping and motion-activated – held us in their glass eye. On the second try, the cop, consulting a scrap of paper, got the code right, the gate swung open and he stepped back. As I passed, I could smell the booze on his breath.

The gate clicked shut behind me and, alone in the gloom, I saw that an expanse of grass a hundred feet wide circled the grounds inside the wall. I guessed it was an electronic moat, monitored by cameras and probably loaded with motion detectors. No interloper, even assuming they could have scaled the wall, would have had a chance of crossing it undetected and reaching the treeline on the far side. The house had been built decades ago, back when Bodrum would have been an unknown fishing village, but even then somebody had gone to extraordinary lengths to ensure their security, and I wondered why.

I followed the tree-lined drive, my shoes crunching on the gravel, heading down a tunnel of overarching boughs. It grew steadily darker and quieter and, though I couldn't explain why, I undid my jacket and made sure I could reach the Beretta tucked into my belt at the back. It was that sort of place, that sort of night.

The drive dog-legged round a silent fountain and revealed the house. The sight did nothing to comfort me: it was huge and dark and what had seemed sinister through a telescope from far away looked in close-up as if it wanted to overpower you. Most houses built in spectacular locations, even old houses, are designed for the view, with wide windows and long runs of glass. The French House had broad eaves, an oak front door and windows recessed deep into the cut-limestone facade. It felt like it had been built for privacy – an impression given even more emphasis because all the shutters at the front were closed.

I skirted round the side of the building, avoiding the pools of dark shadow closest to the wall, and passed a helicopter landing pad and a stone-built security centre near the garages. It was empty. Leading away from it was a path, and I followed it through a high hedge and on to a terraced lawn. The view was amazing – a necklace of distant islands, the floodlit Crusader castle, the lights of Bodrum hugging the bays – but I didn't like it. Not at all. Call me paranoid, but I couldn't shake the feeling that there was somebody in the house watching me.

I turned and looked back. It was in darkness, so quiet a coma seemed to have settled over it. The shutters on the ground floor were open here, but all the rest were shut. I took my jacket off, laid it on a teak bench and walked down the sweeping lawn towards the wrought-iron gazebo. Halfway down, I heard something in the acres of silence and swung round fast to look at the house – on a third-floor terrace a shutter was swinging on its hinges. It could have been the wind, and I had no way of knowing if it had been fastened when I first looked at the house.

I reached the gazebo, took four paces to the north and climbed over the railing. This was where Dodge had been standing when he tumbled down, and I suddenly felt nauseous: the drop was so precipitous and the surging water, far below, so disorienting that I felt as if I were being pulled towards it. The ground beneath my feet was crumbling and I knew the railing behind was too far to reach. I thought I felt, or heard, something close behind me – I wasn't sure – but there was no time to yell. I wheeled hard, launched myself at the railing and grabbed it. There was nobody there.

I caught my breath and climbed back on to solid ground. I was stone-cold sober and yet, once I was on the wrong side of the fence, I could have easily fallen. What the hell had Dodge been doing down there?

From the safety of the barrier fence, I looked at the view again. I tried to imagine what it must have been like: the air full of explosions and multicoloured rockets, the sound of music drifting across the water from party boats and dance clubs, the silver moon running ladders of light halfway to Greece. Underneath it, stumbling a little down the lawn, came a man on a four-day drug binge, maybe trying to wrench himself back to sobriety and calm the raging testosterone and whirling paranoia. But why, I asked myself again, why head for the gazebo?

My guess was that he had been looking for something, probably in the water out in the bay. The closer he got to it, the better the chance he had of seeing it. That's why he had brought the binoculars and had either stood up on the railing or stepped over it. But what had he been looking for?

The records of his cellphone, included in the documents Detective Cumali had given to me, showed that he hadn't received any calls for at least an hour either side of his death. The surveillance cameras also showed that, during that same period, nobody had left the guardhouse to speak to him.

Yet something or somebody had induced him to grab a pair of binoculars, leave his lovely friend tina, step out of the library, cross the formal terrace and head down the lawn to try to see something in the dark waters of the bay.

Say it was a person who – literally – had led him down the garden path to the gazebo. The most logical explanation was that they knew either how to beat the surveillance system or how to enter the estate inside the electronic moat. It had to be somebody Dodge knew or trusted, otherwise he would have raised the alarm. They could have then pushed him over the edge and left by the same route they had entered.

Almost immediately another thought followed: if it was murder, I had only seen one in recent memory anywhere near as good. That was half a world away, at the Eastside Inn. Any doubts I had about a connection between the two deaths were vanishing fast.

I turned, walked up the lawn, picked up my jacket and climbed the steps to the formal terrace. It was time to enter the dark and brooding house.

Chapter Twenty-one

I TRIED THE HANDLES ON TWO SETS OF FRENCH DOORS WITHOUT success. The third one was unlocked, which meant that either the absent security people were very sloppy or there was somebody inside.

I took the small flashlight attached to my key ring, turned it on, stepped into the salon and closed the door. By the narrow beam of light I saw a beautiful room. Whoever decorated it had taste: Grace would have felt right at home, I thought. Most of the furniture was English antique – restrained, elegant and fabulously expensive. The mellow parquet floors were covered in large silk rugs and the ivory-coloured walls hung with half a dozen paintings by the biggest of the big-name Impressionists.

The thin beam of light swept past them and fell on a pair of tall doors that led into the library. In many ways it was a more beautiful room than the *salon* – it was smaller and that made the proportions better, and the rows of books gave it a warmer, more informal mood. I wasn't surprised that Dodge had made it his headquarters.

A deep leather armchair had a side table next to it and, though the drugs had been removed, the paraphernalia was still there: the silver foils, a glass pipe, half a dozen bottles of Evian, cigarettes and an overflowing ashtray. Through a wall of French windows the chair commanded a panoramic view of the sea and sky – hell, if he had wanted to see the fireworks he wouldn't have even needed to stand up. The effect in the room would have been even more remarkable thanks to two huge gilt mirrors on either side of the fireplace directly behind the chair.

They struck me as being incongruous in a library – I knew Grace

366

would never have approved – but even the rich have their idiosyncrasies.

I stepped over the crime tape securing that side of the room – it didn't matter, the Turks said the investigation was over – leaned on the back of the chair and looked out at the view. I tried to imagine what somebody could have said to him which would have made him leave the safety of his headquarters.

I reached down into my mind, holding my breath and trying to swim deeper. Once again, just like when I had stood in the room at the Eastside Inn and realized that it was a woman who was living there, I shut everything out . . . The answer was close . . . lying just the other side of knowing . . . if only I could touch it . . . a person he knew had come through the tall doors . . .

I didn't hear it, but the concealed door behind me opened. It was one of those ones you find in a lot of old libraries – decorated with the spines of books to make it blend seamlessly into the rest of the shelves. Whoever stepped through it must have been wearing rubber-soled shoes, because I didn't hear a footfall on the silk carpet. But there is a sound clothing makes when it moves – or maybe it's not even a sound, more like a disturbance of the air – that is almost impossible to conceal. I felt it then.

Heart leaping into my throat, I reached behind me, drew the Beretta in one fluid motion, slipped off the safety, turned fast, crouched low to reduce my size as a target, spread my feet, raised the weapon as a direct extension of my right arm and crooked my finger round the trigger – exactly as they had taught me so many years ago when I was young and didn't know yet what it was like to kill a man and see the faces of his two young girls in my dreams.

A different man, a less troubled man, would have shot. Instead, I hesitated and looked down the barrel and saw a barefoot woman dressed in black – which was appropriate, given that she was newly widowed. It was Cameron.

'Who the hell are you?' she asked, trying to appear calm in the gloom, but the gun had scared her and she couldn't stop her hand from shaking.

I holstered it. 'My name is Brodie Wilson. I'm—'

'The FBI guy? Cumali, the Turkish cop, said they were sending someone.'

'Yes.'

'The FBI always walks into people's houses unannounced?'

'I apologize,' I replied. 'I was under the impression it was empty. I came to look around.'

Her hand had stopped shaking, but she was still rattled and she pulled out a cigarette. But she didn't light it – it was one of those electronic jobs favoured by people trying to kick the habit. She let it dangle from her elegant fingers. 'Does the FBI normally investigate accidents? Who asked you to come to Bodrum?'

'One of your husband's lawyers or trustees, I believe.'

'That figures,' she said. 'Who was it – Fairfax, Resnick, Porter?'

It seemed from her list there were a lot of her husband's circle who didn't approve of a sales assistant – even if it was Prada – hitting the jackpot. 'I don't know,' I said.

She laughed, without any humour. 'You wouldn't tell me even if you did, would you?'

'No,' I replied.

She took a drag from the electronic cigarette. From anybody else, it would have appeared ridiculous.

'The house looked deserted,' I said. 'I'm sorry about the gun, but you surprised me.'

She didn't bother answering. I got the feeling she was sizing me up.

'How did you get on to the estate?' I asked, trying to keep the question as casual as possible.

'What do you mean?' she replied.

'I came through the front gate – there weren't any cars parked there and the cop on duty didn't say anything about you being at home.'

'Our boat is moored in the bay – that's where I've been staying since the accident. One of the dinghies brought me over and I walked up the steps.' She must have seen a shadow of doubt cross my face, because she shrugged. 'The dinghy is in the boathouse. The crewman is still down there – go and ask him if you want.'

'Of course not,' I replied. 'It's your house, you can do whatever you like. That was you up on the terrace, was it?'

She hesitated. 'I didn't realize you were watching.'

'I was down on the lawn – I couldn't be sure, I thought I saw a shadow.'

'A shutter was blowing in the wind,' she replied.

I turned quickly – from somewhere far away, I thought I heard a door close. 'Is there somebody else in the house?'

'No. Why?'

'I thought I heard . . .' I listened harder, but I couldn't catch it. Everything was silent.

'It's an old house,' she explained. 'If the wind hits from the south it comes up through the basement.' She started to turn lamps on. I couldn't tell whether it was to distract me or because she was genuinely tired of the dark.

In the soft light I saw her clearly. Jack Lemmon once said of Marilyn Monroe that she was lightning in a bottle. He could have been describing Cameron. Willowy and athletic, her skin so fine it seemed to reflect light, I realized it then – and saw it several times later: she had a way of tilting her head and sharpening her eyes that made whoever she was talking to think they were the only person in the room, if not the world.

She was smart too – I knew because I had read a transcript of the interview which the Bodrum cops had conducted with her on the night of the so-called accident. Told she wasn't allowed to have a lawyer present, trying to understand a translator's fractured English, exhausted and alone, she remained polite and helpful throughout the hours of questioning. Lose your temper in Turkey and – guilty or not – you could find yourself in a world of trouble. Intelligent *and* self-possessed – remember that, I thought.

Satisfied with the lights, she turned and opened one of the bottles of water.

'The Turkish police told me you are the sole heir to your husband's estate,' I said, with as much neutrality as I could summon.

She took a drink. 'Is this a formal interview, Mr Wilson?' she asked sensibly.

'No, but I can make it one if you want.'

She shrugged. 'There's no secret to it. Yes, I'm the heir.'

'Was there a pre-nuptial agreement?'

She hesitated, and I could tell she wasn't going to answer. 'Our New York office can subpoena the documents if you want. From what you said earlier, I'm sure the lawyer or trustee would be happy to assist us.'

'Yes, there was a pre-nup,' she said, sucking it down.

'What were the terms of that agreement if you got divorced?'

She took another drink. 'For the first five years I got forty thousand dollars a year. After that, it rose by small amounts until I was fifty. Then – to use the lawyer's term – I became "vested" and the pre-nup no longer applied.'

'Forty thousand a year for five years,' I said. 'That must have been about what you were earning at Prada.'

'Pretty much.'

'And what do you get now that you are his widow?'

'It's a trust . . . it's complicated – I'm not sure anyone knows exactly—'

'How much?' I repeated.

'About one point two billion,' she said, and turned away.

The figure hung in the air for a moment – figures like that often do – then she turned and looked at me. To my surprise, she was shaking with emotion, her eyes alive with anger.

'Do you know why I was closing the shutter on the terrace? Do you know why I was up there? That was the bedroom my husband and I shared. I come over here from the boat every night, I walk up the lawn and I go to that room.

'If I lie on the bed, I can smell him, I can believe that if I were to roll over he'd still be there.

'People can say whatever they want about the money – some sheets in a bedroom in a rented house are all that I have left of him. I loved my husband, Mr Wilson.'

Her eyes welled up. She fought back the tears and, in that moment, she had such dignity and courage it was hard not to feel your heart go out to her. If it was an act, she needed to get her acceptance speech ready.

'Now, I want you to leave. Any further questions, you can speak to the Turkish police. They're in charge of the investigation, and they have a full record of the interview I gave. I've got nothing more to add.'

As I crossed the terrace, heading towards the front gate, my inclination was to believe her but, of course, you never know. About to turn the corner of the building, I glanced back. She was standing on the terrace, alone in the shadow of the brooding house, barefoot and achingly beautiful, staring towards the gazebo and the spot where her husband had died. I thought for a moment she was going to turn and look at me, but she didn't.

I entered the long driveway, the night engulfed me and the sinister house receded into darkness. I had arrived with doubts and I left convinced that somebody had induced Dodge to swap his drugs for binoculars and take that last walk.

It was a good theory, but it wouldn't suffice, not if I was going to stay in the game. Leyla Cumali would make sure of that – she had developed her own version of events and burdened it with her professional reputation. She couldn't afford to be wrong, and she would do everything possible to send the American intruder on his way.

What I needed was proof.

Chapter Twenty-two

I WOULD NEVER HAVE FOUND IT IF IT HADN'T BEEN FOR A SET OF TRAFFIC lights.

I had driven down from the southern headland and hit the out-skirts of the town at that time when restaurants transform into bars, women start thinking of ditching their stilettos and normally sober couples begin ordering just one more glass of raki.

The traffic lights – at a busy intersection with a club on one corner and a construction site on the other – changed from green to amber. I was close enough to have been able to run the light but, as there were so many mopeds working to their own rules and crowds of pedestrians with a buzz on, I decided not to risk it.

Waiting for the green, I glanced across at the construction site and among the graffiti supporting various political parties was a tattered poster advertising an all-night rave that had been held on the night of Zafer Bayrami. It showed a stylized graphic of the harbour, the French House on top of the headland and the huge 'bomb of the phosphorus' exploding above it. Shredded magnesium was what it was, I thought idly, remembering my chemistry classes at Caulfield Academy. It was the same material old-time photographers used in their exploding flashguns, I rambled on mentally.

Then an idea struck me that was so far out I had to repeat it to myself. After I had, it seemed even more outrageous.

I knew Dodge had been in the library when the starburst exploded – Cumali had said so, and there was no evidence to disprove it. It meant he would have been sitting in the leather armchair with a pair of large mirrors behind him when the magnesium burst outside the tall glass doors. There was a chance, I figured, that those seemingly unconnected elements – the magnesium and the mirrors – would provide the proof I desperately needed.

I was so engrossed by the idea that it took me a moment to register that the drivers behind were laying on their horns and I had a green. I hit the gas, rummaged one-handed through the files Cumali had given me, found a note to the medical examiner with her mobile number attached to it and pulled out my cellphone. I was halfway through dialling when I realized that a woman with a six-year-old child might not appreciate being woken and, anyway, what was she going to do that late at night?

Instead, I decided to drive to the hotel, get on the Internet, find the home page of the Uffizi Gallery in Florence and hit every one of their email addresses with my phone number and an urgent request for help.

The Uffizi, a former home of the Medicis, was one of Europe's greatest art museums, home to the finest collection of Renaissance paintings in the world. When I was young, Bill and Grace had taken me down its corridors half a dozen times and, on one occasion – the visit I had enjoyed most – Bill had arranged for us to tour what the museum director modestly called their 'workshop': an art-restoration facility unequalled on either side of the Atlantic. It was the workshop's facilities I needed now, and I hoped that, when the museum staff arrived early in the morning, somebody would get my message into the right hands and they would contact me.

I pulled up at the hotel, parked the car and headed to the front desk to get my room key. The manager handed me another envelope.

'I hope this is not news of the type which might cause Mr Brodie David Wilson the great sorrow,' he said. The envelope was unsealed and I figured he had already read the message and it was almost certainly going to cause me the great sorrow.

I was right. It was from Leyla Cumali, telling me she had discussed with her superiors my 'request' for a delay in finalizing the investigation into Dodge's death.

'After examining the file and all supporting documents, my superiors have decided that no delay can be justified on investigative grounds.'

She said the chief of police and his senior officers had concluded it was a clear case of 'death by misadventure' and, as a result, the file would be forwarded to Ankara in the morning, Dodge's body would

373

be released to his wife for burial and the passports of their friends and acquaintances would be returned, allowing them to leave town immediately.

'The Bodrum Police Department thanks you for your interest and have been proud to offer the FBI every possible assistance,' she wrote. 'Please feel free to keep the copy of the material we provided to you for your files.'

No wonder Cumali had seemed to surrender a little too easily. I was sunk if the cops implemented what they had decided – there would be no need for the FBI in Bodrum, and reopening the investigation would be impossible. The body would be gone and any potential witnesses scattered around the world. My inclination was to call Cumali immediately, but my calmer instincts prevailed. I could phone her in the morning; the priority was the Uffizi.

The manager was watching me closely, and I told him that life was full of the sorrow but to this type of problem Brodie David Wilson was no stranger. Hell, I was so tired I was starting to talk like him. I went to my room and, after bombing the Uffizi with emails, all I wanted to do was crawl into bed.

But there was one more call I had to make. I put the battery into my phone and called Ben Bradley. I told him the local cops were convinced Dodge's death was accidental and were closing down the investigation.

'Christ,' Bradley replied.

'Yeah. They're wrong, too. I'm working on something to keep it open, but you'd better let the other interested parties know.'

'Anything I can do?' Bradley asked.

'Appreciate it,' I replied, 'but my mess, my clean-up.'

I hung up but left the battery in the phone just in case there was an urgent response. As tired as I was, I hadn't even got to sleep when it started ringing. 'I forgot to ask,' Bradley said. 'When do you think you'll know if your idea has worked?'

I knew it was from Whisperer, and I could almost hear the panic in his voice.

'This time tomorrow,' I said. 'I may have to go to Italy in the morning.'

Chapter Twenty-three

I WOKE AT SEVEN AND IMMEDIATELY CALLED CUMALI ON MY CELLPHONE but got sent straight to voicemail. I left a message to call me urgently and kept trying the number but, after twenty minutes, I still hadn't managed to talk to her.

I went down to the front desk, took another tour through the English language with the manager and discovered from him the address of Gul & Sons, Marina and Shipwrights. I entered it into the Fiat's navigation system and, seven minutes later, I was in the old port, standing in front of the house Cumali had been painting in the photograph.

It had once been a fisherman's home, two-storey, with terracotta pots and window boxes full of flowers. I was surprised – there was a joy and softness to the house which I certainly hadn't seen in the woman. I walked up the front path and rang the doorbell. There was no answer.

I crossed a small patch of lawn and headed down a driveway wedged hard against the tall wall of Gul's marina and looked in the garage. The piece-of-shit Italian car was in there – black paintwork and its hood up – but there was no sign of life. I moved closer to the back of the house and listened: there wasn't a sound or movement except for a tabby cat scratching its ear inside the kitchen window.

Back in the car, glancing at my watch, I started driving a grid, steadily expanding out from the house, looking for a corner park. I had to find her soon. Ten minutes later, I saw a small piece of grass with half a dozen kids playing on the swings. Their mothers were hovering around them and, to my immense relief, Leyla Cumali was among them.

I parked and scrambled out. She had her back to me, pushing her son on the swing, so I was only a few yards from her when one of the other mothers called out to her in Turkish and pointed in my direction.

The detective turned, saw me and, in that moment, there was so much anger in her face at the unexpected intrusion that I could hardly credit it. But there was something else . . . something furtive . . . in the way she moved to gather up her son. The instant impression I had – the blink moment, so to speak – was that I had walked into a secret.

As she glared, the boy peeped one eye out from behind her skirt and I smiled at him and said, 'This must be your son.'

To my credit, the expression on my face didn't change as – more confident – he stepped further out from behind his mother and I saw that he had Down's syndrome.

Like every one of those kids I have ever encountered, his face was beautiful – smiling and full of innocence. He said something to me in Turkish which I guessed was 'Good morning' and, for some reason, instead of trying to communicate in a language he didn't understand, I took it into my head to bow to him. He thought this was about the funniest thing he had ever seen and did a pretty good bow back. The mothers and the other kids, all of whom were watching, laughed, and that only encouraged him to bow several times more to the crazy American.

The only person who didn't think it was funny was his mother. 'How did you find me? My note made it clear, I'm not willing to argue—'

'I'm not here to argue,' I interrupted. 'I want you to come to the French House with me.'

That took some of the horsepower out of her anger. 'Why?'

'I think Dodge was killed, and we may be able to prove it.'

'Murdered? How did anyone get on to the estate?'

'I don't know. The first step is to prove there was somebody else in the house. I think we can do that.'

She thought for a moment then shook her head. 'No. The evidence clearly shows—'

'Forget the evidence. Evidence is a list of the material you've got. What about the things you haven't found? What do you call that – unimportant?'

It was a quote from my book and I immediately berated myself – again I had stepped outside my legend – then I remembered the book had been packed as part of my on-plane reading and I let the self-admonishment go. Cumali still wasn't convinced.

'We have to do it now – before the investigation is closed,' I pressed.

'No – my superiors have already signed off on it.'

I had to work hard not to lose my temper. 'If I turn out to be right and the Bodrum police have released the body and returned people's passports, there's going to be hell to pay. Not from me – from the highest levels of government.'

She wavered. The other mothers and kids started to head to school, waving goodbye to Cumali and her bowing son.

'I can't go now,' she said. 'I have to drop my son at the nanny's. The car is broken, it takes time—'

'I'll drive you,' I replied, pointing at the Fiat.

She didn't appear to like it, but, equally, she couldn't see any way out, so she nodded in agreement. The little boy, on the other hand, thought it was great and took my hand as I walked them to the car.

Cumali opened the back door, ushered her son inside and climbed in beside him. It was bad enough for a Muslim woman to share a car with a man she barely knew; for her to travel in the front seat would have been unthinkable.

As she gave directions, I spoke over my shoulder. 'I think you should call your office – tell them something has come up and get them to delay sending the file to Ankara.'

She didn't respond, so I glanced in the rear-view mirror and saw her staring at me, cold-faced. It wasn't going to be pretty when she heard my idea, but there was nothing I could do about that. After a moment I saw her take out her cellphone and she started speaking in Turkish.

She hung up and told me that she'd left a message for her chief and had asked several of her colleagues to meet us up on the southern headland. Calling in reinforcements, by the sound of it. I didn't get a chance to say anything about it – the young guy started speaking animatedly in Turkish. I looked in the mirror again and saw Cumali listening hard. It was obvious she wanted him to know that his thoughts were valued and, the more I watched, the more I realized she had endless patience with him.

'My son wants me to tell you that we are going to the circus on Thursday,' she translated. 'He says we'll start with the Grand Parade and then watch acrobats and lions, clowns—'

'And snake charmers,' I added. 'I saw it when I was arriving – please tell him it looked like a great circus.'

Cumali translated, the boy laughed and quickly it turned into what sounded like an argument. Finally, she explained: 'My son said to ask if you would like to come with us but I said you had a meeting that night – you were very busy.'

I caught her eye in the mirror. 'Yeah, a shame about the meeting,' I said. 'I would have liked to come. Please apologize to him.'

She spoke to him in Turkish, then told me to make a left and stop twenty yards up the road. We pulled up outside a modest house with a row of garden gnomes along the front path, a kid's slide on a square of grass and a Coca-Cola distribution warehouse opposite. The engines of two large trucks, manoeuvring in and out of the drive, were so loud I didn't get a chance to say a proper goodbye to the little guy before his mother had him out of the car, through the gate and walking towards the house.

A young woman, probably in her late twenties, dark-haired and badly obese, opened the door and kissed the little boy on his head. As Cumali spoke to the nanny, it gave me a chance to think again about the furtive moment in the park. The easy take-home was that it had been caused by the boy's Down's syndrome, that his mother had instinctively tried to protect him from my intrusion. But I didn't believe it was that – both Cumali and her son were totally comfortable among the other people and kids. No, I had a feeling it was something quite different, but I had no idea what it might be. A mother and her child, playing in a park – so what?

By then Cumali was returning and her son was standing in the doorway, lifting his hand in farewell to me. Even though I was behind the wheel, I managed to perform a fairly good bow, and his face lit up. He gave me two back.

Cumali climbed into the back seat and I remained looking at her son for a moment. He was a great kid and it was a terrible thing – there was no way to spin it, I'm sorry to say – it was a terrible thing that I ended up doing to him.

I put the car in gear and drove towards the French House.

Chapter Twenty-four

CUMALI'S COLLEAGUES HAD ALREADY ARRIVED, AND THE TALL GATES were open. We drove down the long driveway and found three of them waiting near their cars, all in plain clothes, smoking, a couple on their cellphones.

Two of them looked like your average gumshoe. The other one, though, had corruption written all over him. He was in his mid-forties, tall and overweight, a sausage-fingered vulgarian in a slick suit. Cumali introduced him, but I was damned if I could catch his name. To be on the side of the safe – so to speak – I decided to call him 'Officer'.

As the cops rang the doorbell, my cellphone vibrated in my pocket. It was the fourth time since I had found Cumali at the park, but I decided again not to answer it. I guessed – I hoped – that it was somebody from the Uffizi, and I didn't want to have to rush through an explanation. I would need plenty of time to take them through what, I assumed, would be one of the strangest ideas they had ever heard.

There was no answer to the bell and Cumali opened the door with her pass key. Inside, it was as gloomy as ever and, though I hadn't been in this part of the house, I led them through a baronial dining room and into the library. The only thing that had changed since the previous evening was that the curtains had been drawn and I assumed that, after I left, Cameron had spent time in the room with the memory of her dead husband. Unless, of course, I really had heard a door close and whoever else was in the house had come and sat in the library for the evening.

I drew the curtains back, let the light flood in and turned to face the four Turkish cops. 'I told Detective Cumali that I don't believe Dodge was alone on the night he died. I think a visitor came into this room – somebody he knew.'

'How did they get on to the estate?' the guy I was calling Officer asked belligerently. Typical.

Frightened we were going to waste time down that rabbit hole, I went back at him just as hard. 'Go with it for a minute – assume the visitor knew how to beat the system, say he knew a place where the cameras didn't mesh, figure he found a way over the wall, think *anything* right now. It doesn't matter.'

'Okay, hurry up then,' said one of the gumshoes.

I ignored him. 'The lights are off, the curtains are open – it said so in the crime-scene report.' I pointed at the leather armchair. 'The two of them are here – the visitor standing, Dodge sitting next to his stash. He's on a binge and he's not leaving.'

'But the visitor's got a plan – he's going to induce Dodge to go down to the gazebo then tip him over the cliff.'

'What does he say to get him down there?' the officer interrupted.

'I don't know,' I replied.

'Sheesh – what do you know?'

'I know that while the visitor is speaking to him, the fireworks start,' I said. 'It begins with a white star exploding over the head-land. Everybody says it was huge—'

'Yeah, you could have seen it in Istanbul,' the other gumshoe offered.

I smiled politely – Istanbul was five hundred miles away. 'But that was the one thing the killer hadn't thought about,' I continued. 'The nature of fireworks.'

The cops all looked at each other – what was the FBI idiot talking about now? Fireworks were fireworks.

At least I had their undivided attention. 'To be bright enough to be seen in Istanbul, it would have contained shredded magnesium. That's common in big fireworks – for a moment, it turns night into day. That's why old-time photographers used it in their flashguns.'

'Look,' Cumali said. 'Fireworks, magnesium – does this mean any-thing?' It got a chorus of agreement from the others.

'It means we've got a flash and we've got a subject – Dodge and his visitor,' I replied. 'All we need is film.'

I pointed at the two huge mirrors next to the fireplace. 'Mirrors

380

are glass backed with a coating of silver nitrate. What is silver nitrate? It's another name for film stock – it's exactly what they once used in movie cameras.'

Nobody said a word; they just stared, trying to compute it.

'It was all here,' I said. 'A flash. A subject. Film. I believe we've got a photograph of whoever was in this room. I think it's imprinted on the back of the mirrors.'

Still they said nothing, continuing to look at me in disbelief. I can't say I blamed them – even I thought it was pretty wild.

Cumali recovered first. 'Just to be clear – you think you're going to "develop" the mirrors?' she asked.

'Yeah.'

'Where – One-hour Photo?'

I smiled but, before I could respond, the officer launched in. 'This is ridiculous – photographs on the back of mirrors,' he sneered. 'We're wasting our time,' and he motioned to the others to head out. He probably had some criminals he needed to shake down.

I couldn't help it, I turned on him. I've never had much stomach for corruption. 'Why do you say it's ridiculous? Because it's never been done before? The FBI are the guardians of the best crime lab in the world, you hear me? The best. We're accustomed to pioneering things. How would you know what's ridiculous and what isn't?'

The spark in his pudgy eyes and the curl of his lip told me I had made an enemy for life. I didn't care. Before things spiralled down any further, my phone went again and, glancing at the screen, I saw that it was an Italian number.

'That'll be the Uffizi Gallery in Florence,' I told them. 'I'm going to ask for their help in recovering the image.'

One of the gumshoes – apparently, he was the leader of the group – shook his head. 'No,' he said. 'There won't be any help – not from the dagoes or anyone else. The mirrors stay where they are. This is reaching for straws, or however you people say it.'

'Okay,' I said. 'Okay. I am now making a formal request, on behalf of the FBI, to take possession of the mirrors for forensic examination. If you refuse I will need your reasons in writing so that I can forward them to the White House and the relevant officials in Ankara.'

Silence. My phone rang again, but I made no attempt to answer it. We all stood there without a word. Just before the phone stopped, the leader shrugged. 'Take the damn mirrors then,' he said angrily. 'Waste your time if you want to.'

'Thank you,' I replied. 'Who do I call to make arrangements to get them down?'

The officer laughed. 'No idea. Try the FBI lab – they know everything, I'm sure they can help.'

The two gumshoes smiled broadly. Cumali looked embarrassed by her colleagues but, when the leader motioned them out on to the terrace, she followed obediently.

As they lit cigarettes and walked down the lawn – enjoying the view, bitching about me I'm sure – I called the Uffizi back. Someone had alerted the director of the workshop, and it was to him – probably the leading art-restoration expert in the world – that I explained what I needed.

Once he had stopped laughing, he got me to take him through it again. After a dozen or so questions he finally agreed – I guessed more for the challenge of it than any other reason – but made me understand that he had virtually no expectation it would work.

'I suppose it's urgent?' he asked.

'Of course,' I said. 'Isn't everything? I'll get them to you as fast as possible.'

The moment he had rung off I made one more call and – from a far different quarter – also received a promise of help.

Chapter Twenty-five

THE MANAGER OF MY HOTEL ARRIVED AT THE FRENCH HOUSE WITH TWO beaten-up trucks and eight companions who looked like they were on day release. Shame on me for judging them by appearance – they turned out to be some of the finest, most hardworking men I had ever encountered.

They were friends of the manager, he had rustled them up at a moment's notice, and when I met them at the front of the house and told them I would pay them, they all refused.

'These men peoples say that of the money today they have no kissing-love,' the manager translated, sort of. The more I heard him, the more he sounded like one of those online translation programs. 'Is enough for them of the great estate they have the chance to see,' he said.

It appeared that none of the men, like almost everybody else in Bodrum, had ever been through the tall gates, and they were only too willing to heed the manager's call for help. As I led them around the house, heading towards the rear terrace, we encountered Cumali and her colleagues on their way out. There was a moment of embarrassment when the two parties confronted each other, but the manager stepped off the path and his workers followed suit to allow the cops to pass.

It so happened that I was in a position where I could see the manager's face clearly and the look of disdain as the officer walked by was almost palpable. The manager turned, saw me looking at him and smiled. Once the cops were out of earshot, he walked to my side: 'He is the name of a man we call SpongeBob.'

All the workers nodded. 'SpongeBob?' I said. 'Like the cartoon?' The manager nodded and mimed a sucking motion.

'Ah,' I said, 'the big sponge,' and rubbed my thumb and

forefinger together in the universal symbol of bribery. The manager and his friends laughed, and one of the men spat on the ground. For a moment we had transcended all language, and we turned the corner of the house.

After allowing them a minute to stare at the view, I led them through the French doors into the library. Two of the men were carpenters and, while they discussed the logistics of building crates to protect the mirrors, several others returned to their trucks for ladders and tools.

I wandered out on to the lawn and started trying to call somebody at FedEx who could organize, at short notice, to pick up the mirrors and fly them to Florence. I was waiting for yet another customer-service rep to call back when the manager hurried to my side, obviously upset and wanting me to follow him into the house. For a moment I thought they must have dropped one of the mirrors, but I realized I would have heard it smash and I put that possibility aside.

I temporarily gave up on FedEx, followed the manager up to the terrace, went through the doors and into the library. I stopped. The men – silent and standing to one side – were watching me. They had removed both mirrors, and I looked at the dressed-stone walls where they had been hanging.

When I first saw the mirrors, I had thought they were incongruous but I had put it down to someone's eccentricity. It wasn't – the mirrors had been used to cover two large swastikas that had been carved into the stone. They were the real deal too, beautifully chiselled, both surmounted by the imperial eagle of the Third Reich. I stared at them. As a child, I had seen swastikas in the Kommandant's office at Natzweiler-Struthof and, for a terrible moment, I saw the woman again with the baby in her arms and the two children holding tight to her skirt.

I walked towards the foul things, watched by the manager and his friends, all of them seemingly shamefaced. Turkey had been neutral in the Second World War, but they all knew what the symbols represented and I think they were deeply offended at what had been found in their town.

I reached up – I really didn't want to touch it – and ran my finger along the chisel marks. It came away thick with dust: the mirrors had been put in place years ago.

I turned to the men. 'Why do they call it the French House?' I asked.

Chapter Twenty-six

IT WASN'T THE NAME OF THE HOUSE, NOT ORIGINALLY. WHEN IT WAS built, just after the end of the war, it had been called *La Salle d'Attente*. The Waiting Room. Waiting for what? I wondered.

I was sitting with the manager and his team on the steps leading from the terrace down to the lawn, the Aegean Sea laid out in front of us and a warm breeze rustling through the palm trees above. The men had brought out their lunch and insisted I share their meal of olives, cheese and wood-fired bread. It was only by showing them my FBI shield and telling them it was forbidden that I managed to avoid the wine and raki that seemed to accompany every mouthful. I was grateful they had got the mirrors down before lunch.

We were engaged in what was, to put it mildly, a chaotic conversation – and not because of the booze. All the men, the manager included, had their own version of the history of the house. None of them were old enough to remember its construction, so they relied on stories that had been passed from mouth to ear by their grandparents.

The one thing everybody agreed on was that the house had been built by a German woman. As far as I could tell, that had been in 1946, barely a year after the war had finished when Germany – with seven million dead – was in ruins. The story was that her family had moved their assets to Switzerland before the outbreak of hostilities and that her fortune had survived intact. Maybe it was true: there were Germans who had done exactly that – ask the guys at Richeloud's.

The consensus among the storytellers was that the woman had flown into the old grass runway at Milas, was met by a car, inspected the site at lunchtime and flew out two hours later. After a few months, a construction team arrived.

Back then, there were hardly any roads, so all the tradesmen and engineers, as well as the building materials, had to be brought in by barge. The gaunt men – all Germans – built bunkhouses and a field kitchen and, for reasons only they knew, had nothing to do with the villagers.

After two years, with the house complete, the last of them demolished their simple barracks, landscaped the gardens and pulled out. All that was left to mark their stay was the name of the small cove at the base of the cliff, inaccessible except by boat, where they had landed the barges and swum every evening. 'This sand of the water,' the manager said, 'is what the Bodrum peoples call—'

'The German Beach,' I said.

The men told me that, despite all the effort and expense, nobody had lived in the villa – at least not permanently. At first, lights would come on every few months, stay lit for a week or so, then go dark again. Everybody assumed it was a vacation home, but the carefully planted foliage and the privacy of the land made it impossible even to glimpse the people who called the Waiting Room their temporary home.

The Waiting Room, I thought again – such a strange name. 'Why was it changed?' I asked them.

The manager laughed and didn't need to consult his colleagues. 'It was of the nature very simple,' he said. '*La Salle d'Attente* made a complication far too much for the fisherfolk to pronunciate. They knew of the language in which it was spoken, so they did the shrug and called it the French House. Over the years, it did a catch-on and all peoples named it the same.'

The seasons passed, the men said, the foliage grew thicker and the villa seemed to fall into a long sleep, eventually becoming unvisited for years at a time.

Slowly at first, then more rapidly, tourism changed the coast – marinas sprouted in the harbour and other beautiful villas were built on the headland. Then, about eight years ago, a man came – nobody knew who he was – and opened up the house. A few weeks later, teams of renovators arrived from overseas and set about updating the mansion, even installing a state-of-the art security system. Finally, the twenty-first century had caught up with the French House.

A few months before that particular summer season started, a local realtor received a call from someone who said it was time the mansion earned its keep: it was available for vacation rentals at two hundred thousand US dollars a week.

The men smiled at the amazing figure and did the shrug.

'Who was she, the woman who built it?' I asked in the silence, thinking about the swastikas.

They shook their heads: it was a mystery. The manager looked at his watch and told the men they had better finish loading up if the mirrors were going to make it to the airport on time. The team re-corked their bottles, got to their feet and headed back to the terrace.

I turned and walked down the garden. Halfway, I stopped and looked back at the house. It was certainly sinister, and my impression had been right when I had first seen it from the driveway: it had been built for privacy. But the Waiting Room – why call it that? And what of the people who came and stayed briefly all those years ago? Who were they?

I don't know why I thought of it – maybe it was the sweep of the sea, perhaps it was the sight of a freighter on the horizon – but I have learned to trust my intuition. A ship, I thought. That was what they were waiting for: a ship.

The manager was on the terrace, waving to get my attention. 'The loadings of the mirror are all system go and finished,' he called. 'We only need now the person of you.'

I smiled and headed up to join the convoy to Milas airport.

Chapter Twenty-seven

I FLEW INTO FLORENCE AT DUSK, NOT A CLOUD IN THE SKY, THE GREAT Renaissance city laid out below in all its haunting beauty. I was in the cockpit of a FedEx plane that had been diverted from Istanbul to pick up two large crates as a special favour to the FBI.

The pilots, a pair of cowboys – one English and the other Australian – invited me to sit in the spare seat up front. Had I known they would spend the entire flight arguing about cricket, I would have stayed in the back.

A truck from the Uffizi headed on to the apron to meet us and, between the gallery's three storemen and the two cricket-lovers, the large crates were craned out of the belly of the plane and into the back of the truck in a matter of minutes. As much as any city on earth, Florence itself is a work of art, but seeing it again brought me little joy. The last time I had walked its streets had been with Bill and, once again, I found myself overcome with regret about the way I had treated him.

We entered the city in the twilight, travelled down narrow side streets little changed in five hundred years and stopped outside a pair of huge oak doors I dimly remembered. The workshop was located in a separate complex to the museum – a group of old cellars and warehouses, their stone walls six feet thick – which had once housed the Medicis' vast stores of grain and wine.

Cameras checked every inch of the street before the oak doors swung back and the truck entered a huge security area. I climbed out of the cab and looked at the hi-tech consoles, squads of armed guards, racks of CCTV monitors and massive steel doors that barred further entry into the facility. The place bore little resemblance to the one I had visited so many years ago, and I wasn't surprised – the Uffizi had been bombed by terrorists in the early nineties, and the museum obviously wasn't taking any chances.

Two guards approached and fingerprinted the storemen and driver with handheld scanners. Even though the men had known each other for years, the guards had to wait for the central database to validate the men's identities before the steel doors could be opened. As the truck and its cargo disappeared inside, I was left behind. A guy in a suit appeared, arranged to have me photographed for a security pass and told me the director and his team were waiting.

With the pass pinned to my coat, a guard strapped a copper wire trailing to the floor around my ankle: any static electricity generated by my clothes or shoes would be carried away by the wire and sent to ground, avoiding any risk of a spark. After robbery and terrorism, a tiny flash igniting the volatile chemicals used in art restoration was what facilities like the workshop feared most.

The Uffizi specialized in repairing large canvases and frescoes and, though there had been many changes since my previous visit, the director had told me on the phone that they still had the huge photographic plates and chemical baths necessary for that work. It was those that would very soon determine the future of my mission.

The man in the suit led me to an elevator, we went down six floors and I stepped into what looked like a conference room: four opaque glass walls, a long table and, on one side, two technicians sitting at computer screens connected to a huge array of hard drives.

Three women and half a dozen men stood up to greet me. One of them extended his hand and introduced himself as the director. He was surprisingly young, but his long hair was completely grey and I guessed that the risk of ruining priceless works of art must have taken its toll. He said that, in the few hours since we had first spoken, the people gathered in the room had put together a strategy to try to recover an image from the mirrors. None of them, he said, held out much hope.

'Then again,' he added with a smile, 'sometimes even art restorers can work miracles. Ready?'

I nodded, and he flicked a switch on the wall. The four opaque walls turned completely clear. They were made from a type of glass called liquid crystal – an electrical current had rearranged the molecules and turned it transparent.

We were standing in a glass cube, suspended in mid-air, looking down on a remarkable space.

As big as a football field and at least sixty feet high – arched, vaulted and pure white – it was probably even older than the reign of the Medicis. Standing in it, dwarfed by the vast expanse, were hydraulic hoists for lifting monumental statues, gantries to raise and lower oil paintings, stainless-steel cleaning baths big enough for an obelisk and a steam-room to remove centuries of grime from marble and stone. Moving between them were silent, battery-operated fork-lifts, small mobile cranes and dozens of supervisors and specialists in white scrubs. Some workshop – it looked as if NASA had taken over the catacombs.

Almost directly beneath me a Titian was being cleaned and, not far away, men and women were working on a set of bronze doors by Bernini which I had once seen at the Vatican. But most spectacular of all was a group of panels which had been joined seamlessly together and fixed to one wall. Produced from the huge photographic plates used in its restoration, it had been put there either as an inspiration or a memento of the facility's outstanding work.

It showed da Vinci's *The Last Supper*.

It was life-size and as vivid as if it had been painted yesterday, and I had a fleeting sense of what it must have been like five hundred years ago to have entered the convent of Santa Maria delle Grazie and seen it for the first time.

The director, putting on a wireless headset, pointed out two gilt frames standing against the wall. The mirrors had been removed and both of them were hanging from an overhead crane. As we watched, it lowered them into a tank of blue liquid – a solvent which they were hoping would separate the film from the glass without damaging it. If it failed, or the silver nitrate fell apart, we could all go home.

Almost immediately, a large tent was lowered over the tank, blacking it out. 'If they can get the silver nitrate off, it has to be treated like a film negative – it can't be exposed to light,' the director said.

I was consumed by doubt. What hope was there really? Sure, the Uffizi had restored Michelangelo's marble *Pietà* after a deranged Australian had taken a hammer to it, but even they didn't believe you could tease an image out of old mirrors.

The director clamped the headset to his ear, listened for a moment then turned to the rest of us: 'It worked – they've got the film off intact.'

As the others smiled and clapped, he turned to me: 'They'll encase the film in a frozen slab of gelatin to stabilize it, then move it into the darkroom for processing.'

Two minutes later, men in white scrubs wheeled a large trolley out of the tent and pushed it into a glass-sided freight elevator. I watched the two mirrors, wrapped in foil blankets, rise up.

The elevator stopped at a block-like room, cantilevered over the vaulted space, which I guessed was the darkroom.

'It could take a while,' the director said, 'but once they've "developed it" the technicians will be able to tell if the film has captured anything.'

Chapter Twenty-eight

I WAS SITTING IN THE UFFIZI'S STAFF CANTEEN WITH THE REST OF THE team, picking at a meal of espresso and more espresso, when the call came.

The director took it on his cellphone then turned to me, but spoke loud enough for everyone to hear: 'There's something on the film.'

We ran down white, silent corridors, past a startled group of wealthy donors being given a behind-the-scenes tour, into a freight elevator and towards the conference room.

Through its glass wall we saw the technicians huddled round one of their two large computer screens, one of them at the keyboard while the water-cooled hard drives spun fast.

The director had kept up with me all the way. 'Whatever they found on the silver nitrate will have been digitized and put on to disk. That's what they're looking at.'

We sprinted through the doors. The image of two people – just two people standing in the room – was all I needed. Anything to identify the visitor would be a bonus.

There was nothing on the screen. Well, that wasn't exactly true – there was a darkness of varying shades, like looking at a pond on a moonless night. The director must have seen the distress on my face.

'Don't panic – not yet,' he said. 'They'll use the software to force the image, then try to fill in the missing microscopic dots from the surrounding fragments. It's the same method we use on damaged frescoes.'

But I *was* panicking – he would have been too if he had known how much was really at stake. The young tech at the keyboard, his skin as white as the walls, was entering command after command. I looked at the intense, almost religious concentration on his face: he certainly hadn't given up, and that was comforting.

Slowly, almost imperceptibly at first but gathering pace as the hard drives spun even faster, a shape emerged from the dark ocean. I could tell from the warning lights blinking amber on a series of controllers that they were pushing the system close to its limits, but those guys weren't for turning either. I saw part of a room surface from the pond: fragments of a chandelier, the outline of windows looking out on to a view, the side of a fireplace. It was definitely the library in the French House, or *La Salle d'Attente* or whatever other damned name anybody wanted to call it. I could barely believe it.

'I think we've got a person,' the pale technician said over the clapping. He pointed at a section of the pond water – darker than the rest but containing a shadowy outline – cordoned it within an electronic grid and poured in a constant barrage of light and pixels and there was the leather armchair – I could see it!

Hands sweating despite the constant and relentless air-conditioning, I could make out a blurred head, the crook of an arm, a part of the neck of a man in the chair. It was almost certainly Dodge. The techs kept going, the warning lights drummed out an even faster beat and the dark water surrounding the armchair sprang into sharper relief.

Dodge was alone.

Even so, the director and his team turned to me – elated, calling out in celebration. The plan which they had designed and implemented had been successful: they had recovered an image from an almost unheard-of medium. There was no doubt it was an outstanding achievement. Equally, there was no doubt it didn't help me at all.

'What's wrong?' they asked as they saw my face.

'I knew there was a man sitting in the chair. I'm looking for another person. I need two people. What about the second mirror? It'll show the room from a different angle.'

We turned: the pale guy and his colleague already had the second image on the screen. You didn't need to be an expert in computer graphics to see it was far more degraded – the ocean of blackness was deeper and the available light thin and full of shadow. We might as well have been underwater.

The technicians moved faster. The darkness disappeared and the guy at the keyboard once again dragged fragments of the library out

393

of the depths. Parts of the chair and table emerged, but their shapes were far less distinct and already the warning lights had hit the amber and a few of them were starting to blink red. My hopes nosedived.

The techs themselves looked disheartened, frequently glancing up to see more of the warning lights crossing over and yet achieving no real improvement in the image.

That was the trouble with luck, I figured – it runs out. I felt the director and other members of the team shoot glances at me, knowing how disappointed I must be, wondering how I was going to take it.

All the lights were red and I realized the techs had stopped trying to enhance the image – they had reached the limits of the technology. The half-formed image of the library hung on the screen like a quiet reminder of failure. The pale tech leaned closer to it, pointed at one section of the darkness and said something in Italian I didn't understand. The director and the rest of the team peered at the spot he was indicating, but it was clear nobody could see anything.

The tech – not very confident because he was doubting his own eyesight – dropped a grid over the section. Ignoring the red lights, he zoomed in on it, manipulated the pixels and tried to coax the truth out of them.

Nothing.

His colleague stepped in and hit a command. The area under the grid inverted – the black becoming white, as if it were now a negative image. Suddenly we could all see something – a vertical shape almost out of frame. The two techs worked together fast, pushing the software and the hard drives beyond their operating limits. Warning boxes popped up, but the guys cancelled them out as soon as they appeared. The red lights weren't flashing – they were a solid bar.

Still the guys kept going, but there didn't appear to be any discernible improvement – a solid shape teasing us, that was all. Then they turned the image back from the negative and removed the grid and the zoom.

It was there! Indistinct, spectral-like, but the shape had become a person standing in front of the fireplace. It was impossible to distinguish anything specific – even if it was a man or a woman – but that didn't matter. There were definitely two people in that room.

The director and his team stared at it for a moment then cheered, while the two technicians got to their feet and hugged their colleagues.

I pulled my eyes away from the screen, smiled, put my hands together and applauded them all: they didn't know it, they would never know, but the Pathfinder was back in business.

Chapter Twenty-nine

I STEPPED THROUGH THE OAK DOORS AND INTO A NIGHT SO CRISP AND clear that the old cobblestones and Renaissance facades seemed almost too vivid, like the landscape of some strange video game. Only the crowds on the streets and the complete lack of taxis convinced me it was real.

I had two calls to make and was waiting for the first to pick up as I headed past the workshop's exterior cameras and into a wide thoroughfare.

Leyla Cumali answered and, without any preamble, I told her I had a photo showing that Dodge and another person were in the library six minutes before he was killed. There was a stunned silence at the other end.

I filled the empty space by telling her that the director of the Uffizi workshop was preparing a full report which he would send to her with a copy of the photograph.

'I'll let my colleagues know,' she said finally, unable to keep the defeat out of her voice. I was sure SpongeBob and his buddies were going to be overjoyed.

'It doesn't look like we have any choice,' she continued. 'We'll open a homicide investigation tonight.'

'Good,' I replied. 'Good.'

'How did you know Dodge wasn't alone?' she asked, a little of the old disdain creeping back.

'It was the drugs – and the binoculars. Nobody needs binoculars to look at fireworks.'

'Then why did he have them?'

'You have to take it step by step. Somebody obviously knew how to get on to the estate in secret,' I told her, still trying to find a damn cab.

'They entered the house and found Dodge in the library. It was a friend of his, or at least an acquaintance – if it was a stranger he would have raised the alarm.

'I'm almost certain the visitor was feigning distress. They told Dodge something that alarmed him enough to cut through his wild libido and the swirling craziness of the drugs.'

'What did they tell him?' she wanted to know, impatient.

'If you reread the interviews you carried out with his acquaintances, at least six of them volunteered that he loved his wife very much.'

'That's right,' Cumali added.

'Cameron was out bar-hopping in the JetRanger that night. I think the visitor told him that the helicopter had just crashed in the bay.'

Silence. Cumali didn't respond – there was just a sharp intake of breath.

'Dodge would have believed the visitor without question,' I continued. 'There's a landing pad on the estate and he would have thought she was on her way home.

'Trying to sober up, he grabbed the binoculars to search the bay and he and the visitor ran on to the lawn. He wasn't looking up at fireworks, he was looking out at the water – and the further he went on to the headland, the better chance he had of seeing something. That's why he chose the spot four yards from the gazebo: there wasn't any foliage, the only tree was the one he hit halfway down – and he had a much better view of the bay.

'When he couldn't see anything – why would he? there was nothing out there – he either stood on the railing or climbed over it.

'He would have had the binoculars to his eyes when he felt a push on his back. To the killer it probably didn't even feel like murder – just a gentle helping hand.

'So gentle, in fact, that when you did the tests with the dummy it was totally consistent with a man falling.'

I let my voice trail away: there was no point in recounting his plunge down the cliff face and the hit on the rocks – there was no dispute about any of that.

Cumali didn't respond and finally I had to ask: 'Are you still there?'

'I'm here,' she said. 'I'll make sure nobody's passport is returned. We'll start now. I'll draw up an expanded list of everyone he had contact with. Like you said – the visitor had to be somebody he knew.'

'You can discount Cameron or the others in the helicopter – they couldn't have visited him in the house, they were supposed to be fighting for their lives in the water. And you were right – I don't think anybody was paid to do it. The answer lies in the circle of friends.'

There was another element to the murder she didn't know about, one she could never know. Call it a tiny signature, but it had made me really angry. I was certain that the thread from Dodge's chinos had been planted on the railing to make sure the cops would come to the right conclusion.

A case in which the killer had followed exactly the same procedure was featured in my book.

Chapter Thirty

I HAD FINALLY LOCATED A CAB, WHEN I HEARD THE BAD NEWS.

Having finished the phone call with Cumali, I had seen a vacant cab and dashed into the traffic to grab it. It was a miracle that any pedestrian could survive a horde of Italian drivers but somehow I scrambled inside, and asked the driver to take me to the airport.

I was returning to Bodrum as fast as possible and as soon as I had tightened my seatbelt – wishing it was a full racing harness given the way the guy was driving – I made the second phone call. It was to Ben Bradley.

When he picked up, I told him I was in Florence. 'We're back in business,' I said, elated. 'It's a murder – let the other parties know.'

'I've been trying to call you for two hours,' he said.

'Sorry,' I replied. 'I had the battery out of my phone.' There was only one reason he would have been calling – a message from Whisperer – and I knew that couldn't be good.

He rattled on about the murder at the Eastside Inn – but that was just camouflage – then mentioned that some colleagues of ours had run a series of tests, computer modelling, in fact, that I needed to know about.

Ben didn't understand what he was saying – he was relaying a message – so there was no point in asking him questions. All I could do was listen with a sinking heart.

He said that the guys had come up with an interesting date – they were saying 30 September.

'But you know what computer geeks are like,' he continued, and I got the feeling he was reading from a script. 'It's hard to tie 'em down; they say you have to allow a two-week contingency for any unforeseen problems – so they're saying the second week of October.'

I hung up and sat very still, lost in thought for a long time. I knew from Ben's message that Whisperer had ordered a team to model – probably under the auspices of some war-game – how long it would take a civilian to churn out a significant amount of smallpox virus using publicly available equipment. Working from that, they had calculated that it could be done by the end of September and then added a couple of weeks leeway.

We had a date now – all time, all events, all hope, was running to one point in time. Call it 12 October, I told myself – Columbus Day. The anniversary of my mother's death.

Chapter Thirty-one

WHEN THE CUSTOMS OFFICERS OPENED THE SARACEN'S WELL-WORN luggage they found neatly folded slacks, two dress shirts, a doctor's kit of a stethoscope and thermometer, a copy of the Holy Qur'an and an English magazine. It wasn't the *Economist* or the *British Medical Journal*. It was called *Bra-Busters* and offered at least a D-cup on every page.

The two customs officers didn't say anything but exchanged a look that spoke volumes. 'Typical Muslim,' they appeared to say, 'devout on the outside and, like everybody else, a dog on the inside.'

Had the men been a little more observant, they would have noticed that the holy book was zipped into a completely separate pocket of the carry-on, as if it had been quarantined from the filth with which it had been forced to travel. The Saracen had bought the magazine at the airport in Beirut in case German immigration had directed him to one of their interview rooms and put him through the hoops. The last thing he wanted was to look like a devout Muslim – the way the world had developed, if you had to cross a border, it was safer to be a hypocrite than a man of God.

In the event, though, the magazine wasn't necessary. He had arrived at Frankfurt airport – Europe's largest and busiest – at the height of the morning rush, just as he had planned. He knew from experience that a visitor was far less likely to be scrutinized when the lines were long and the immigration officers tired and overworked.

After an hour in a queue he presented himself to a young officer in a drab brown uniform. The man glanced at the photo in the Lebanese passport then at the person smiling in front of him: nice suit, beard trimmed to little more than a stubble, handsome face. A doctor, according to the arrival card he had filled in.

'The purpose of your visit?' the young officer asked, first in German and, when that received a blank stare, in English.

'A medical conference,' the Saracen replied. Apart from banking, Frankfurt's major commercial activity was hosting huge conventions and trade fairs – all at a specially constructed showground called the Messe. The Saracen produced the tickets and pass that he had purchased online and laid them on the desk. The officer barely looked at them, but the Saracen knew that it was the details – things like the girlie magazine and, in Damascus, the dirt under the fingernails – which turned a legend into reality.

The officer glanced at the return ticket, ran the passport through his scanner and looked at the computer screen. Of course it came back clear: the book was genuine and that name had never been on any kind of watch-list.

'How long will you be staying?' he asked.

'Two weeks,' the Saracen replied. 'Maybe a little more, depends on how long the money lasts.' He smiled.

The officer grunted and stamped the passport for three months. Everyone got three months. Even if the passport of a card-carrying member of al-Qaeda had come back clear, he would have been given three months. Germany wanted its Messe visitors to stay – it liked the money they spent.

Of course, the Saracen planned to stay longer than two weeks but, even if the immigration officer had just granted him the fortnight, it wouldn't have mattered. The Saracen knew what every illegal immigrant in the world was well aware of – immigration enforcement in Europe was even more slack than border control. Keep your nose clean and your shoulder to the wheel and you could stay as long as you wanted. The long-term future was fine too – every few years, they offered an amnesty. Where was the incentive ever to leave?

The Saracen picked up his bag from the carousel, suffered the indignity of seeing the snide glance between the customs officers, was sent on his way and walked into the kerbside chaos of the huge airport. Squeezing along the sidewalk, he dumped the girlie magazine and its temptations into a trash can, found a bus to take him into the city and vanished into the alternate universe of Islamic Europe.

It was a strange world, one which I had experienced when I was stationed in Europe. Chasing down leads and contacts on a dozen different cases, I had walked through scores of grim industrial cities and visited the countless Stalinist-style housing estates on their outskirts. But for anyone who hadn't seen such places, it would have been hard to credit the gradual transformation that had taken place. The most common name for a baby boy in Belgium was now Mohammad. Three million Turkish Muslims lived in Germany alone. Almost 10 per cent of the population of France were followers of Islam.

As a Swiss writer once said, 'We wanted a labour force, but human beings came,' and what nobody had foreseen was that those workers would bring their mosques, their holy book and huge swathes of their culture with them.

Because of Islam's commitment to charity and the explosion in the size of the Muslim population, every city quickly came to host an austere, male-only hostel – supported by donations – where devout Muslim men could eat halal food and bed down for the night. It was to the Frankfurt branch of such a 'safe house' that the Saracen travelled on his first day in Europe, still amazed at the ease with which he had crossed its border.

The following day, poorly dressed in jeans and scuffed workboots, he put his luggage into a long-term locker at Frankfurt's main railway station and bought a ticket from a vending machine. Already letting his beard grow out – just another face among the mass of blue-collar Muslims – he caught a train to Karlsruhe. Situated on the edge of the Black Forest, the city had been bombed back into the Stone Age during the Second World War and the decades which followed had seen it rebuilt as a sprawling industrial centre. Among its factories was one which was crucial to the Saracen's plan.

While he was still living in his apartment in El-Mina he had spent hours trawling the Web until he located a mosque with the exact geographical attributes he needed. As a result, when he got off the train from Frankfurt, he knew exactly where he was going. He found his way to Wilhelmstrasse and, halfway along it, saw a former corner shop – ironically, once owned by a Jewish family killed in the Holocaust – that sported a tiny minaret. The only feature that distinguished it from the twelve hundred other Islamic prayer centres in Germany was that it was almost within sight of the chosen factory, the European subsidiary of a major US corporation.

It was Friday and, right on schedule, the Saracen entered the mosque moments before evening prayers. Once they were finished, as tradition demanded, the imam approached the stranger and welcomed him on behalf of the congregation. Invited to take tea with them, the Saracen – reluctantly, it seemed to the men who had gathered around – explained that he was a refugee from the latest war in Lebanon.

Giving a credible performance as just one more displaced person looking for a new life in Europe, he said he had paid a group of people smugglers almost everything he had to take him by boat to Spain and from there across a borderless Europe by truck. He looked up at his fellow worshippers and his voice faltered, making it impossible for him to go into detail about the terrible journey.

I have to say it was a nice touch, and most of the listeners – blue-collar workers too – nodded in understanding: the details may have been different, but they too had entered Europe in a similar fashion.

The so-called illegal immigrant said he had been staying with a cousin in nearby Frankfurt but, desperate for work and down to his last few euro, he had made his way to Karlsruhe in the hope of finding a job. With the hook baited, he claimed he used to work in the shipping department of a big corporation in Beirut.

'*Insha'Allah*, maybe there is something like that available in the large factory at the end of the road?' he asked.

Nearly all the worshippers worked at Chyron Chemicals and, exactly as he had anticipated, they promptly took the bait and offered to make inquiries among their workmates and colleagues. He thanked them by offering an obscure but appropriate quote from the Qur'an, which confirmed to them that their first impression of him had been correct: most assuredly, he was an honourable and devout man.

Telling them that he was embarrassed, he said in a quiet voice that he didn't have money for food or another rail fare and he was wondering if there might be one of the 'safe houses' he could stay at until he found work. Of course the congregation took him in, arranging meals and shelter – after all, one of the Five Pillars of Islam was to provide for the poor.

And so, without even realizing it, in little more than an hour, the Saracen had become their responsibility. They were the type of men who took such things seriously and, three days later, their inquiries and advocacy paid off: a Turkish supervisor in Chyron's dispatch department reported that there was a place for the refugee as a storeman on the graveyard shift.

After prayers that night the men, so happy for him they took him to a café for dinner, told the Saracen about the remarkable working conditions he would enjoy: the on-site health care, the subsidized cafeteria and the beautiful prayer room. What none of them mentioned, however, was that all the jobs had once been held by Americans.

The old Nobel laureate in Virginia had been right when he had asked if the greatest industrial nation in history actually produced goods and machinery any more. Millions of jobs, along with most of the country's manufacturing base, had been exported over the decades, and a great deal of the nation's safety had disappeared with them. As for Chyron Chemicals, the danger was particularly acute – it was a drug manufacturer and exporter, one of the most respected in the world. Though few people realized it, the heartland of America was really only as safe as an anonymous factory in a city hardly anybody had ever heard of.

In a better world, the Saracen – seated in the café with its laminated tables and strange Turko-German music – would have had a final hurdle to overcome. Indeed, for a time, he believed it was the single thing most likely to cause his plan to fail. Surely, he had asked himself back in El-Mina, wouldn't the American Food and Drug Administration inspect drug shipments for possible contamination?

He found the answer on the Web – a transcript of a congressional hearing into the FDA which told him that one country alone had over five hundred factories exporting drugs and their ingredients to the USA.

'How many of those facilities did the FDA inspect during the previous year?' a congressman asked.

'Thirteen,' came the reply.

The Saracen had to read it through again to make sure he had understood it correctly: only thirteen out of five hundred factories had been inspected. And that country was China, the nation with the worst history of product safety in the world. He knew then that nothing from Chyron – a subsidiary of a US corporation based in a First World country – would ever be inspected.

At 10 p.m. on the night following the celebratory meal he walked along a deserted Wilhelmstrasse, presented himself at Chyron's security gates, was issued an employee pass and given directions to the distribution warehouse. There he met the Turkish supervisor, who, escorting him past endless pallets of drugs awaiting shipment to cities across the United States, explained his duties to him. None of the pallets were guarded, nothing was locked and sealed – they never had been; nobody had ever thought it necessary. Then again, nobody had ever thought it necessary to lock the cockpit doors on passenger jets either.

After the supervisor had left for home and the Saracen was alone in the cavernous warehouse, he took out his prayer mat, pointed it towards Mecca and said a prayer. A child who had been introduced to misery in Saudi Arabia, a teenager who went to wage *jihad* against the Soviets in Afghanistan, a deeply devout Muslim who had graduated with honours in medicine, a man who had fed a stranger to wild dogs in Damascus, a zealot who had dosed three foreigners with smallpox and watched them die in agony, gave thanks to Allah for the blessings which had been bestowed upon him.

Before he finished, he rendered one final thanks to God – for the woman in Turkey who had done so much for him.

Chapter Thirty-two

I LANDED BACK IN BODRUM JUST AT DAWN. I HAD NO LUGGAGE AND, with a freshly issued visa in my passport, combined with my FBI shield, I passed through Turkish immigration without delay. I walked out of the terminal, located my car in the parking area, and headed on to what is known as the D330 to Bodrum.

Everything was fine for fifteen minutes but, despite the early hour, I then ran into a long tailback of eighteen-wheelers, tourist coaches and countless Turks blasting their horns in frustration. I pulled off at the first opportunity and headed south-west, in the general direction of the sea, figuring that sooner or later I would either hit Bodrum or hook back on to the highway.

It didn't work out that way: I ended up in a lonely area scarred by landslips and jumbled rocks, deep cracks and jagged rifts. It was dangerous ground and even the trees were stunted in the crumbling soil, as if they knew they had taken root on a fault line. Turkey was in a seismic hot zone and there were long stretches of the southern coast that stood on shifting, unstable land.

I came upon an intersection, made a left, accelerated round a curve and knew I had been in that uninhabited corner of the world before. Even as a psychologist I couldn't say whether it was an accident or if a subconscious hand had guided my decisions – all I knew was that, just down the road, I would see the ocean and, half a click beyond it, I'd find, figuratively speaking, the site of the shipwreck.

As anticipated, I reached the sea – a turbulent mess of currents dashing against the rocks – and drove along the clifftop. Ahead I saw the small bluff where, as a young agent, I had parked the car so long ago.

I stopped near an abandoned kiosk, got out and walked closer to the cliff edge. Safety – of a sort – was provided by a broken-down security fence. Signs were attached to it, displaying a message in four languages: DANGER OF DEATH.

Although nobody visited the place any more, it had once – long ago – been hugely popular with both sightseers and archaeologists. The constant earthquakes and landslides, however, had eventually become too much, the kiosk had fallen into disuse and the tourists had found plenty of other ruins equally as attractive and a damn sight safer. It was a pity, because it was a spectacular site.

I paused near the fence and looked along the cliffs. Stone steps and fragments of ancient houses descended eerily into the surging sea. Marble columns, parts of porticos and the remnants of a Roman road clung to the cliff side. Kelp and driftwood were scattered among the ruins and the wind-borne spray of centuries had crusted everything with salt, giving it a ghostly sheen.

Further out to sea, the outline of a large piazza was clearly visible under fathoms of water, a classic portico stood on a rocky outcrop with sunlight streaming through it – known as the Door to Nowhere – and the restless sea flooded back and forth across a wide marble platform, probably the floor of some grand public building.

It had been a major city of antiquity, a trading port long before the birth of Christ, but a huge earthquake had torn away the coast and lifted up the cliff. The sea poured in and drowned nearly everyone who had survived the initial jolt.

I walked along the fence, dirt spilling down and hitting the rocks two hundred feet below, until I turned the corner of the bluff. The wind was much stronger, the vegetation more stunted and the landscape even more unstable and I was forced to grab hold of a steel warning sign to steady myself. I looked down: jutting out into the water was an old wooden jetty, much diminished since I had last seen it.

It had been built decades ago by a group of enterprising fishermen who had realized that ferrying tourists and archaeologists into the ruins by boat was a far better way to earn a lira than hauling in nets and lobster pots. The main attraction back then hadn't been the shattered townscape or the Door to Nowhere but a long tunnel which had led to what was reputed to be the finest Roman amphitheatre outside the Colosseum. Renowned in the ancient world for the brutality of its gladiatorial contests, it was known as the Theatre of Death.

I had never seen it – nobody except for a few brave archaeologists had been in it for thirty years. The tunnel, the only way in and out, was barred and gated after a giant landslide had opened up huge cracks in its ceiling and even the tour operators were muted in their objections – nobody wanted to be caught inside that if the whole lot came down.

But it wasn't a Roman slaughterhouse or the other ruins that had taken me to the edge of the cliff. It was the old jetty that had brought back a flood of painful memories.

Chapter Thirty-three

ALL THOSE YEARS AGO, THE DIVISION HAD ARRIVED AT THE JETTY IN force. Just after sunset, eight operatives, casually dressed, a few with backpacks, had come down the coast on a decent little cruiser.

They looked like a group of youngish guys out for a good time. I wasn't among them: as the junior member of the team, my job had been to arrive separately, take charge of a specially purchased van, drive to the small bluff and park as close as possible to the abandoned kiosk. In the event that something went wrong, I was to evacuate whoever needed it to another boat waiting at a Bodrum marina. In the worst-case scenario, I was then to drive the wounded to a doctor who was on standby for just such an emergency.

I was inexperienced, and I remembered that I had a lot of fear on me that night: we had come to the furthest reaches of Turkey to kill a man.

His name was Finlay Robert Finlay – that wasn't his real name, his real name was Russian, but that was what we knew him by – an overweight guy in his late forties who had a big appetite for everything, including treachery. He had been a young consular official working in the Russians' Cairo Embassy when the CIA managed to turn him. Apart from paying him a handsome monthly retainer, the agency did nothing with him: he was a sleeper, and they let him go happily about his life and whoring, content to watch him climb the ladder. He was a bright man, so it was no surprise that, after a number of years, he became the KGB station chief in Tehran, working under deep diplomatic cover.

It was then that the agency decided it wanted a return on its investment. They were sensible and they only took from him the highest-quality intelligence and insisted that he didn't take any unreasonable risks. They had lavished too much of their love and gold on him to jeopardize it by being greedy. He quickly became one of the agency's prime assets, and they stayed by his side through half a dozen diplomatic posts, until he returned to Moscow and moved into the inner circle of Russian intelligence.

But a life like Finlay Finlay's leaves in its wake tiny clues that sooner or later come to the attention of counter-intelligence. Finlay understood that danger, and one afternoon in his summer dacha out-side Moscow he reviewed his career and came to the inescapable conclusion that, pretty soon, all those fragments would hit critical mass. Once they did, it would be *vyshaya mera* to him too.

He arranged to visit family just outside St Petersburg and went sailing in a little one-hander dinghy on a beautiful summer Sunday. Then he put a waterproof pack with his clothes in around his waist, slipped overboard and swam ashore in Finland. The distance wasn't far, but it was no small achievement given his size.

He made his way to the US Embassy, declared himself to the shocked duty officer and fell into the warm embrace of his CIA handlers. After being debriefed, he reviewed his bank accounts and realized that, between his retainer and the bonuses he had received for every piece of high-level intelligence he had delivered, he was an affluent man. The agency gave him a new identity, settled him in Arizona, kept watch on him and then, satisfied that he had adapted to his new life, let him slip from their consciousness.

The one thing that nobody could have anticipated, however, was that Russia would descend into the hands of outlaws masquerading as politicians. Fortunes were being made as the country's assets were sold off to those with the right connections, many of whom were former KGB operatives. Finlay watched it from his home in Scottsdale – nothing too elaborate, a nice three-bedder – and became increasingly frustrated. He liked the money, our friend Finlay.

He had been around the secret world long enough to have hidden away a safety-deposit box with several alternative identities and to know the value of what he still had in his head. He drove to Chula Vista, south of San Diego, one morning and walked through the turnstiles at the crossing into Mexico. According to the fake passport he was carrying, he was a Canadian with US residency. Travelling under the assumed name, he flew to Europe, made contact with his former buddies in Moscow and met them in a café at Zurich airport.

Finlay, or whatever name he was using at that stage, gave them a taste – a gourmet sampler, if you will – of everything he knew about the personnel and double agents employed by his former best friends in McLean, Virginia. It was so good that the Russians booked themselves in for the full dinner and another spy had come in from the cold.

Finlay was no fool – he held back the best of his material, dealing it out sparingly, all the time manoeuvring himself closer to those with the right connections. By the time he'd wound himself in tight, he was able to swap his best secrets for a gas-exploration licence here, an industrial complex at a knock-down price there.

When the CIA finally realized that one of its former assets was selling them out and called The Division in, Finlay was a wealthy man with a mansion behind twenty-foot walls in Barvikha, Moscow's most desirable suburb and, while he wasn't as rich as some of his neighbours, he was wealthy enough to have also purchased a luxury penthouse in Monaco.

He had changed his name half a dozen times and altered his appearance, thanks to an excellent plastic surgeon, but the rat-catchers at The Division tracked him down. We could have killed him in Moscow or Monaco – you could kill a man anywhere – but the real measure of a successful execution wasn't in the obituary but in the escape. Moscow presented the problem of getting in and out of the country, and the less than square mile which constituted the principality of Monaco – with over four thousand CCTV cameras – was the most closely monitored postage stamp on earth.

Finlay's penthouse, however, did offer us one advantage. Its picture windows and the French doors opening on to a terrace gave us the opportunity, by using a special microphone, to eavesdrop on what was said inside. The system wasn't perfect, it missed a lot, but one of the fragments it captured concerned a boat. We knew he didn't own one, so a quick scout around the marina, where all the luxury cruisers were moored, soon turned up the fact that Finlay and a small party were travelling to what was almost certainly the strangest party on earth.

Every year, for six hours before the tide changed, it was held in Bodrum.

Chapter Thirty-four

NOT LONG AFTER OUR EIGHT AGENTS HAD STEPPED ON TO THE JETTY, the revellers started to arrive in force. It was one party you didn't want to be late for.

The vast majority of them parked near the bluff and used specially installed ropes and ladders to climb down to the ruins. The chicks had their handbags and cells slung around their necks, skirts hoisted halfway up their asses, doing their best to maintain their grip and dignity. Of course, there was already a guy stationed below with a spotlight, picking out the most sensational underwear for the entertainment of those who had already arrived. Judging by the frequent bursts of wild cheering, a surprising number of women went out clubbing wearing no panties at all.

Every few minutes some young guy would dispense with the slow climb, grab a rope and launch himself into space. I figured that most of the amateur abseilers were smokehounds. In my experience, they were usually the ones too stoned to care much about personal safety. At least half a dozen times I saw them brush the cliff, land hard on the rocks, then high-five each other before firing up another blunt. And they say drugs don't cause brain damage.

The idea for the Rave at Bodrum – and the huge profits it generated – belonged to a German backpacker. He had washed up in Bodrum and, hearing about the ruins, had driven a scooter out at night to photograph the moon through the Door to Nowhere. Somewhere in his chaotic past, though, he had spent two years studying oceanography in America before dropping out, and he remembered enough to realize that a couple of times a year the ruins would be far less spectacular – a king high tide would submerge most of them.

But that meant there would also be a king low tide and far more of the old city would be revealed. For a start, the wide marble platform would be out of the water. He stared at it and thought: what a great dance floor that would make.

Two months later, after he had examined the tide charts and used a scuba set to dive and check his measurements, he and several buddies parked generator trucks on the bluff, ran cables for a light show down the cliff and moored barges with half-stacks of speakers just offshore. They cut holes through the fence, anchored ladders and ropes to concrete tripods so that the customers could get down and stationed a gorilla at every one to collect the door charge.

People were happy to pay. Where else in the world could you party in the middle of the ocean by starlight, get high surrounded by classic ruins and dance on the grave of twenty thousand people? Partygoers said it was the best dance party they had ever known.

The night I saw it, the annual Bodrum rave was huge and even more extraordinary. By then, there were ten barges with speakers anchored inside an arc of rocks, protected from the swell. On the largest of them, standing on a scaffold platform like the ringmaster at some futuristic circus, was a DJ known far and wide as Chemical Ali. Guys in the rocks used smoke machines to send what looked like a supernatural fog out across the water – the Door to Nowhere appeared to float on a cloud. Only then did they launch the banks of lasers and strobes.

In the middle of this maelstrom, a group of security guys grabbed a steel walkway and ran it out from the base of the cliff to the newly emerged marble platform with its four broken pillars. As the music grew in a crescendo, so loud you could almost touch it, the first of the partygoers, led by a dozen tall fashionistas, crossed the walkway and stepped on to an area nobody had walked on for two thousand years. Or at least not since the previous year's event.

With the driving music, the towers of lights and lasers, the gyrating silhouettes on the dance floor, the smoke casting a pallor on the ruins and the Door to Nowhere suspended, ethereal and mysterious, above the water, it made it easy to believe that, if the dead were going to rise from the grave, it would be on a night like that.

Well, one of the walking dead did show up – though he didn't realize it yet. He arrived on one of the scores of huge cruisers, nosing its way through the fog and mooring just outside the arc of barges.

As it bobbed among other mega-yachts, The Division's shooters, spotters and safety men were all at their posts. After alighting from their boat they had sent the decent little cruiser to wait in the darkness offshore, adjusted their earbud headphones and lapel mics and watched the crowd grow in size and confusion. Satisfied nobody had marked them, they melted into the masses, split apart and made their way to their predetermined positions.

The key man was a thirty-four-year-old black guy, one of the funniest and smartest people you could ever hope to meet. Like all of us when we joined the outfit, he had taken another name – in his case he had called himself McKinley Waters, in tribute to 'Muddy' Waters, the great Delta bluesman. Anyone who ever saw Mack, as we knew him, play slide guitar and sing 'Midnight Special' had to wonder why he was wasting his time in the intelligence business.

Mack was the primary shooter, stationed in a little hollow near the lip of the cliff, his rifle already assembled and hidden in the darkness next to him, swigging from a bottle of Jack that contained iced tea, looking for all the world like some dude getting loaded and waiting for the crowd to clear before he made his way down.

Further along the clifftop, in the shadows under a cluster of stunted trees, was the back-up shooter – a prick by the name of Greenburg, the sort of guy who made no secret he was gonna marry rich. He was hanging out with two others, looking like a group of white buddies trying to decide whether to pay the money and take the drop over the cliff or not. In reality, the other guys were spotters: apart from locating Finlay, their job was to warn the men, whose entire attention would be focused on shooting, if danger approached from somewhere outside their field of vision.

I was on the bluff next to the rented van. By accident, I had the best view and could see all the team at their stations. Hence, I saw the excitement ripple through them when Finlay turned up on time: in another few minutes he would be well and truly going through the Door to Nowhere.

His security team, all ex-KGB guys, emerged on to the recreation deck at the back of the boat and, binoculars raised, scanned the cliff side, the small beach and the dance platform.

Only when they gave the all-clear did anyone appear from inside: it was a group of young women, dressed to kill in Chanel and Gucci. They waited on deck while a speedboat was launched to deposit them directly on the dance floor.

I saw Mack put his bottle of Jack down and slide his hand into the darkness. I knew that he was expecting Finlay to emerge to kiss his four companions goodbye and he was going to be ready. The two spotters, worried about an advancing cloud of smoke, wandered away from Greenburg to make sure that they had a clear view. A safety guy came through the car park and headed towards the fence, ready to take everybody's back. I heard, through my earpiece, our three guys partying down by the water – a third shooter, another safety guy and a guy riding shotgun in case it got into a firefight with Finlay's goons – talking to Control. He was out on the boat that had delivered the team, getting an update from everybody except me. We all sensed that we were on the launch pad, ready to shoot.

The thing that none of us knew was that a group of men on another boat, its running lights out, were also taking a keen interest in everything that was happening on shore. Masked by the eddies of smoke and the looming bulk of the big cruisers, their modest boat was, to all practical purposes, invisible. And yet the men on board had a stunningly good view: they were all equipped with military-grade night-vision goggles.

The glasses had been supplied by Finlay's head of security, who didn't think the Bodrum trip was any way to run a railroad. To improve protection he had enlisted a group of hard men – free-lancers, but among the best in the business – to travel independently to Bodrum. They were briefed by phone, a container of equipment was waiting for them when they arrived and they cooled their heels for two days before being told to get on board a boat he had organized. It was that boat which was anchored just offshore.

In the darkness, the freelancers saw Finlay emerge from the bullet-proof glass of the sitting room and approach the young women. We saw him from the cliff side too. Mack let the target take two steps – just to make sure the goons next to him couldn't haul him back inside in time if a second bullet was needed. He had his finger on the trigger when the spotter nearest to him called a warning.

Another cloud of smoke was about to obscure his aim. Greenburg had seen it too and got to one knee, getting ready in case he had to take the shot. But Mack glanced at the cloud, figured he had time, aimed fast and fired. Nobody even marked the sharp *crack* of the discharge, thanks to the pounding music. The bullet hit Finlay but it was hurried and what had been intended to punch a large hole in his forehead and shatter his brain had hit him lower.

He fell to the deck with a chunk of his throat splattered over the Gucci dress behind him. He was still alive, writhing, but Mack's vision was obscured by the smoke and he couldn't take the second shot. One of the spotters spoke urgently into his mic, telling Greenburg to hit him again.

The security guys on board were in chaos but the men on the back-up boat had heard Finlay scream through their own earpieces as he went down and they were scanning the cliffs with their night-vision goggles. One of them saw Greenburg on his knee raising his weapon and yelled in Croatian . . .

A sniper next to him panned fast, locked on to Greenburg and pulled. Greenburg – his own finger about to squeeze – took the round in his chest and fell, thrashing. I was closest and, knowing he was still alive, I sprinted towards him.

It was breaking all the rules – the priority was the mission, not the safety of the team – and I was supposed to wait for Control to shout an order. But Greenburg was lying on exposed ground and would be shot again and dead in seconds if somebody didn't get him into cover.

Nobody knew where the hostiles were firing from, but Mack saw the danger instantly: if somebody at sea could target Greenburg, they could hit me. Screaming a warning, believing he was still obscured by the smoke, he crouched low and ran hard to intercept me and pull me to the ground. He liked me, we both worshipped in the house of blues and I think that played a part, but so did the fact that he was naturally a courageous man.

Halfway towards me the breeze ripped a hole in the smoke and the guys on the boat were very good – two bullets hit Mack just above the kidneys. But for the grace of God, it would have been me.

He dropped his rifle and went down screaming. I wheeled, got to him fast, threw my body over his and rolled with him – gunshots blasting the crumbling soil all around us – until we tumbled into the safety of a small depression. Partygoers were screaming – finally realizing that two men were shot and badly wounded – but they had no clue what was really happening, or where the shooters were located, and that made their panic even more acute.

Control had no such difficulty in pinpointing the source: he had been pacing the deck of the little cruiser when he caught sight of what he recognized as a muzzle flash through the smoke and shadows. When The Division had set out that morning, he'd had the good sense to throw on board a set of flashing blue-and-red lights, and he slammed them on the roof of the cabin and told the skipper to hit it.

The mercenaries on the back-up craft saw the fast-approaching boat with its flashing lights and immediately jumped to the logical, but incorrect, conclusion. In four different languages they yelled at the wheelman to plunge into the logjam of spectator craft, in the hope of losing themselves. They knew that, in a fair race, they wouldn't have a chance, and the last thing any of them needed was a shoot-out with the Turkish cops.

Their boat skimmed between other boats and passed so close to two of them that it shaved paint from their hulls. The screams from their occupants told Control that the unidentified boat had fled, so he ordered the skipper to turn and head for Finlay's mega-cruiser.

In the confusion, the flash bar allowed him to get so close to the back of the big boat he could see Finlay lying in a pool of blood. A couple of the women and a distraught crew member, believing that Control was a cop, screamed at him to get an ambulance or a Medevac chopper fast, but Control knew from the way Finlay was spasming and the big hole in his neck that they had done their job: he was in the last stages of bleeding out. He turned to his skipper and told him to get the hell out, and it was only as the supposed cop boat departed that the security chief realized he had just been face to face with the man who had ordered the hit. He didn't care by then – his meal ticket had just been cancelled and he was already working out how to cross the frontier before the Turks took him into a room and told him to grab his ankles because the party had only just started.

Control had been listening to the reports from everybody on shore and, as his boat roared across the water, satisfied that the mission had been accomplished, he ordered the men at the base of the cliff to head fast for the jetty, where he would pick them up in three minutes. He then ordered me to go to the back-up plan.

The two spotters had heard it all, and they grabbed Greenburg under the arms and dragged him to the van. He was already dead – the bullet to his chest had fragmented when it hit his ribs and the splinters took out so much of his heart and lungs he never really had a chance.

In the shallow hollow I had done what I could to stop Mack's bleeding. He was a well-built guy, but somehow I managed to throw him over my shoulder and get him into the passenger seat of the van. I laid the seat back, grabbed my jacket and bound it round his waist to try to further stem the loss of blood. He was still conscious and he saw the tag inside the jacket. 'Barneys?' he said. 'What sort of fucking bluesman shops at Barneys?'

We laughed, but we both knew he didn't have a chance if we didn't get him medical help soon. I swung behind the wheel and hit the gas, fishtailing through the parking lot, sending revellers scattering, while the spotter directly behind me was already on his cell, speaking to Control on what we all hoped was a sufficiently secure line.

As I turned hard on to the blacktop, the spotter hung up and told me I was to drop him and his buddy at the marina in Bodrum, as planned. They had to get out before everything went into lockdown: Turkey was a proud country and the Turks wouldn't react well to people being executed under their noses. The spotters would take Greenburg's body on board with them while I got Mack to the doctor who was on standby. Hopefully, he would stabilize the wounds and buy time for a stealth chopper from the US Mediterranean Fleet to come in low over the coast and extract us both. The chopper, with a doctor and two medical specialists on board, was already being scrambled and, once it had picked us up, it would head for the fleet's aircraft carrier, where there were operating theatres and a full surgical team.

Mack had a chance, and I drove even faster. It was a wild ride, and I don't think anyone in a mini-van shaped like a brick had ever covered the distance any quicker. We arrived at the marina and, in a stroke of good fortune, found it virtually deserted – it was Saturday night, and all the boats were either partying at the ruins or moored near Bodrum's scores of beach-front restaurants.

I backed along the dock, helped the spotters transfer Greenburg's body on board and then got back behind the wheel. We had a bad road in front of us and a world of trouble behind.

Chapter Thirty-five

WE SANG. MACK AND I SANG 'MIDNIGHT SPECIAL' AND ALL THE OLD Delta blues standards as we barrelled south through the deepening night, down roads I had only travelled once before in my life, terrified that I would miss a turn or take the wrong fork and finally cost him his life just as certainly as I had cast it into the balance up on the clifftop.

We sang to keep Mack's creeping unconsciousness at bay, we sang to thumb our nose at death, our unseen passenger, and we sang to say that we were alive and we loved life and that nobody in that vehicle was going to be taken easy or without a fight. It started to rain.

We had driven south, moving fast into an increasingly remote area with only the scattered lights of small farms to tell us where the land ended and the sea began. At last I saw the turn-off I was looking for, took it in a shower of gravel and started a long descent towards a secluded fishing village. We came round the tip of a headland, met the rain full on and saw lights huddled together at the water's edge. I reached the village and found a narrow street which looked familiar.

Mack had slipped into a kind of half-world, my jacket was soaked with his blood – and I drove one-handed, constantly trying to keep him awake and fighting.

Hoping to hell I hadn't made a mistake in my navigation, I turned a corner and saw a communal water fountain surrounded by dead flowers and with an old bucket tied to a rope and knew that I was close. I drew to a stop in the darkness, grabbed my flashlight from my key chain and shone it on the front gate – I didn't want to have a half-dead man over my shoulder and knock at the wrong door.

The beam of the flashlight picked out a brass plaque on the gate. Unpolished and faded, written in English, it gave the occupant's name and the details of his degrees – in medicine and surgery – from Sydney University. In light of the nature of the guy practising there, it probably wasn't the best advertisement for that august institution.

I opened the passenger door, lifted Mack on to my shoulder, kicked open the gate and headed towards the front door of the rundown cottage. It opened before I got there – the doctor had heard the car stop outside and had come to investigate. He stood on the threshold peering out – a face like an unmade bed, skinny legs in a pair of baggy shorts and a T-shirt so faded that the stripper bar it advertised had probably closed years ago. He was in his early forties but, given his love of the bottle, if he made fifty it would be a surprise. I didn't know what his real name was – thanks to the plaque on the gate, all the Turks in the area knew him simply as Dr Sydney – and that seemed to suit him fine.

I had met him a week earlier when, after Control had made the arrangements, I was sent to test the route. He had been told I was a tour guide escorting a group of Americans through the area who might need, in the unlikely event of an emergency, his assistance. I don't think he believed a word of it but, by all accounts, he didn't like the Turkish authorities very much and our substantial cash advance encouraged him not to ask any questions.

'Hello, Mr Jacobs,' he said. Jacobs was the name I was using in Turkey. He looked at Mack draped over my shoulder and saw the blood-soaked jacket tied around his waist. 'Quite a tour you must be running there – remind me not to take it.' In my experience, most Australians aren't easily rattled and I was deeply grateful for that.

Together we carried Mack into the kitchen and, though the doctor's breath reeked of booze, there was something in the way he straightened his back and cut away Mack's clothes and damaged tissue that told me he had once been a surgeon of discipline and skill.

I used whatever of my medical training I could remember to act as his theatre nurse and, with the hot water running, the kitchen bench swept clear to provide a table, the reading lamps from his study and bedroom pressed into service to illuminate the wound, we tried desperately to stabilize the shattered body and keep Mack alive until the chopper with its specialists and bags of plasma arrived.

Not once through that harrowing time did the doctor's hand shake or his commitment falter – he extemporized and cursed and dragged out from beneath the layers of booze and wasted years every idea and strategy he had ever learned.

It didn't work. Mack faded, and we fought harder, we got him back, then he faded again. With the chopper barely eighteen minutes away, the bluesman seemed to sigh. He lifted one hand up as if to touch our faces in silent thanks, and flew away. We fought even harder, but there was no calling him back that time, and we both fell still and quiet at last.

Dr Sydney hung his head, and it was impossible from where I was standing to see whether his body was trembling from fatigue or something far more human. After a moment he looked up at me and I saw in his eyes the despair – the anguish – it caused him to have someone die in his hands.

'I used to operate on injured children,' he said quietly, as if in explanation for the drink, the run-down cottage, the life in exile and the acres of pain he carried with him. I nodded, finding at least some understanding of what it must have been like to lose a young kid under the knife.

'He was a friend of yours?' he asked.

I nodded and, with a decency that no longer surprised me, he made an excuse and found something to do in another part of the house. I drew the sheet over Mack's face – I wanted him to have all the dignity I could give him – and said a few words. You couldn't call it praying but, out of respect, in the hope that his spirit was some-where close at hand, I said what I needed to about friendship, courage, and hopeless regret for breaking the rules up on the cliff-top.

The doctor returned and started to clean up, and I walked out into his living room. It was fourteen minutes until the chopper arrived, and a message on my cellphone told me they had identified a garbage dump behind town where they could land without being seen. Keeping the tremor out of my voice, I called and said they could stand the medics down: it wasn't a patient they would be evacuating, it was a body.

I got rid of the vehicle by giving it to Dr Sydney – it was small recompense for the effort he had made to save Mack – and my remaining concern was the Turkish cops. Trying to discover what

422

they were doing, I turned to the TV playing softly in the corner of the living room.

It was showing a Turkish news programme, but there was nothing about the killings at the rave or of a police operation heading my way. I used the remote to surf through the local channels – soap operas, Hollywood movies dubbed in Turkish and two more news programmes – but nothing to cause alarm.

Nor was there anything on the BBC, CNN, Bloomberg or MSNBC . . .

Chapter Thirty-six

I COULDN'T BREATHE FOR A MOMENT. I WAS STILL STANDING ON THE bluff above the ruins, remembering the past, but the thought of looking at the TV in the doctor's old cottage had stolen the air from my lungs.

If Dr Sydney could get the English-language news channels in a far more remote area, how come they weren't available in Bodrum?

I ran for the Fiat.

It was still early, there was little traffic and the drive into Bodrum was almost as fast as when I had had Mack lying in the seat beside me. I parked on the sidewalk outside the hotel, sprinted up the steps and saw the manager coming out of the dining room.

'Ahh,' he said, smiling. 'Was the trip of the mirrors with the largeness of glass a success?'

'I'm sorry,' I replied, 'I don't have time. I need to know about the TV service.'

He looked at me, confused – why the hell would I want to know about that?

'The bellboy said you can't get the English-speaking news channels in Bodrum. Is that right?'

'That is the truth very much,' he replied. 'The company of great thievery called DigiTurk which gives us the channels of crap has no such service.'

'There must be a way – I've seen the BBC, MSNBC and several others,' I said.

He thought for a moment, turned and made a phone call. He spoke in Turkish, listened to the response then cupped his hand over the mouthpiece as he reported to me. He said that his wife thought that some people bought digital boxes and accessed a European satellite which broadcast the news channels I was asking about.

'What's the name of the service – the satellite? Does she know?' I asked.

The manager put the question to her, then turned to me and gave the answer. 'Sky,' he said.

Sky was a British satellite broadcaster and I knew from living in London it was a pay service. That meant there were subscribers and, if people were buying decoder boxes, somebody in the organization would have a list of them.

I went up to my room fast and called the company in England. I got passed through eight or nine different phone extensions before I ended up with a helpful guy from the north country whose accent was so thick you could have served a Yorkshire pudding with it.

He was in charge of European subscriptions, and he told me that all the channels I was interested in were carried on Sky's premium Astra satellite.

'It's got a big footprint, that one – it was designed to cover Western Europe and reach as far as Greece.

'Then quite a few years ago, the satellite's software was upgraded, the signal got stronger and suddenly you could pick it up in Turkey with a three-foot dish. Of course, you still need the decoder box and an access card, but it means a lot more people have taken it up.'

'How many subscribers, Mr Howell?'

'In Turkey? We've got expats, of course – they take their boxes and cards with 'em when they move. Then there's the English-themed pubs and clubs – the tourists want their football. Finally, we have the locals who like the programming. All up, there's probably about ten thousand.'

'Can you break it down by area?'

'Of course.'

'How many people in the vicinity of Bodrum – say, a province called Muğla?' I asked, desperately trying not to let my hopes get too far ahead of me.

'Give me a second,' he said, and I could hear him tapping at a computer. 'It's a murder investigation, you said?' He was making conversation while he worked to get the data.

'Yeah, young American guy. He loved sports and TV,' I lied. 'I'm just trying to tie a few things up.'

'I got it,' he said. 'About eleven hundred subscribers.'

My spirits soared. It meant people in Bodrum could receive the television stations I needed. I looked out of the window and imagined the woman I was looking for sitting cross-legged in one of the white Cubist houses, watching a TV with a Sky box on top, grabbing soundbites from a host of different news programmes and working for hours to edit and code them. Eleven hundred boxes – it had narrowed the search for her dramatically – and I wasn't done yet.

'If you discount the expatriates and the bars, how many subscribers do you think there are?' I asked.

'Households? Most likely six or seven hundred,' he replied.

I was close! Six or seven hundred households was a lot of work, a lot of shoe leather to track down each one of them, but it meant the potential suspects were now ring-fenced. Somewhere among that group was the woman I was looking for.

'Is that a good number?' Howell asked.

'Very good,' I told him, unable to keep the smile out of my voice. 'Can you give me a list of the subscribers?'

'Sure, but I'd have to get authorization. No offence, but we'd need to know for certain it's the FBI who's asking.'

'I can get you an official letter in a couple of hours. After that, how long would it take?'

'It's just a download and printing it out. A few minutes.'

It was better than I could have imagined: very soon I would have a list of six hundred addresses, and the woman's would be one of them. We were on our way.

'Thanks,' I said. 'I can't tell you how helpful this is.'

'No problem. Of course, you're lucky it's only the authorized ones you want.'

It stopped me in mid-celebration. 'What do you mean?'

'Well, a lot of people tuning in these days—'

I started to feel sick.

'Use pirated boxes,' he continued. 'Chinese, mostly – if it's not Rolex watches and Louis Vuitton handbags, they're counterfeiting boxes and our access cards. They sell 'em through small electronic shops and internet cafés – places like that. It's big business. Once you've bought the box and card, the service is free. You there?'

'In somewhere like Muğla,' I said quietly, 'how many pirated boxes do you think there would be?'

426

'A place that size? Ten thousand – maybe more. There's no way of tracking who has 'em, it's totally underground. Next year, we think we'll have the technology to trace—'

I wasn't listening: next year we could all be dead. Ten thousand boxes and no subscriber list made it an impossible task. I thanked him for his help and hung up.

I stood motionless, the silence crowding in and the black dog of despair biting at my heels. To have had my hopes raised and then so comprehensively dashed was a hard break. For the first time since I had been press-ganged into the war, just for a few moments I thought I had a real way into the problem. Now that it had turned to dust, I was in the mood to be brutal with myself.

What did I really have? I asked. I had compiled a list of phone boxes; by a stroke of good fortune and the work of a team of Italian experts I had stayed in the game – and apart from that? Anyone who didn't need a white cane could see that I had very little.

I was angry too. I was angry at the fucking Chinese for not controlling the wholesale piracy of other people's ideas and products, I was angry at Bradley and Whisperer and all the rest who weren't there to help me, and I was angry at Arabs who thought that the bigger the body count, the greater the victory. But mostly I was angry at the woman, and the man in the Hindu Kush for staying ahead of me.

I walked to the window and tried to find a pocket of calm. The exercise with Sky hadn't been a complete bust: it had taught me that the woman almost certainly lived in the area, and that was real progress. I looked across the rooftops – she was out there somewhere. All I had to do was find her.

I tried to see in my mind which of the phone boxes she had been standing in, waiting for the phone to ring, but I had no data, and all I could draw was a blank. Yet I could hear the traffic going past and I listened to the muzak – the radio station, or whatever it damn well was – playing faintly in the background.

Come to that, I thought, where was the update on the music? What were Whisperer and those guys doing back home? Wasn't the NSA supposed to be trying to isolate, enhance and identify it?

I was in just the mood to vent my frustration so, even though it was late in New York, I didn't care. I picked up the phone.

Chapter Thirty-seven

BRADLEY ANSWERED AND TOLD ME HE WASN'T IN BED, BUT, FROM THE sound of his voice, he was clearly exhausted. Well, so was I. He started to ask about Dodge's death, just to maintain the cover, but I cut him short.

'Remember the music we spoke about?' I said. Of course he didn't, he had no idea what I was talking about. 'There was the sound of traffic, it was playing in the background—'

'Oh yeah, I remember,' he said, getting with the programme.

'What happened?' I asked. 'Somebody was supposed to be drilling down, trying to identify it.'

'I don't know, I haven't heard.'

'Get on to it, will you? Make some calls.'

'Sure,' Bradley replied, offended by my tone, immediately getting as irritable as I was. 'When do you need it by?'

'Now,' I replied. 'A few hours ago would have been better.'

Hungry as hell, I was on my third stale candy bar from the mini-bar, and sitting in the chair, staring out at the town and thinking about the woman, when the phone rang. It was Bradley, and he said that the music was pretty much a bust.

'They've filtered out the noise of the New York traffic,' he said. The reference to New York was meaningless packaging. 'And they've enhanced the music. It's Turkish, of course. It seems it's being played on a kaval—'

'A what?' I asked.

'A kaval. A wind instrument, like a flute apparently – seven holes on top and one underneath; they're the melody keys. It's a folk thing. The story is that shepherds would use it to lead their flock.'

'Great – we're looking for a shepherd driving his sheep through rush-hour traffic,' I said.

'Not exactly,' replied Bradley. 'It's pretty common – they say it's very popular with folk-music groups.'

'A kaval, huh? What was it playing on? A CD? Live? On the radio?'

'After they took out the background noise and enhanced it, they lost what they call the signatures – they can't tell.'

'Christ! They don't make it easy, do they?'

I looked across the rooftops and asked myself again: where had she been standing? Some place where you could hear traffic and music being played on a Turkish folk instrument called a kaval. *Where?*

'Here's another problem,' Bradley continued. 'They can't identify the tune either. The sample's not very big, but nobody seems to have heard it.'

'That's strange,' I said. 'You'd think if it was a folk tune, and with all their experts—'

'Yeah, I guess.'

We were silent for a moment and, when it became clear there was nothing more to discuss, I broached another subject. 'I'm sorry, Ben,' I said.

'For what?'

'Being a dick.'

'But you've always been a dick,' he said, deadpan as always. 'Anyway, I told our friends you were feeling the stress and starting to crack up.'

'Oh good, that should further my career,' I replied.

'Glad to help,' he said. He didn't laugh – it was Ben Bradley, after all – but I could tell from his voice that I had put things right with him, and I was thankful for that.

'One more thing,' I said.

'Sure.'

'Ask 'em to work out a way to send the recording, will you? Just the music, not the traffic.' I didn't know why but I wanted to hear it.

Chapter Thirty-eight

TWENTY MINUTES LATER, AFTER I HAD FINISHED SHOWERING, I WALKED out of the bathroom and found a new email on my laptop. It was from Apple, telling me that twenty-seven dollars had been charged to my credit card for music downloads.

I hadn't bought any music and my fear was that some jerk at the CIA had thought it might be useful to add to Brodie Wilson's already extensive collection of fucked-up music. I went to iTunes, saw a group of new tracks had arrived and realized that most of them were just packing – there was only one that mattered, and I knew it was from Whisperer.

On the night before I flew to Turkey – when we were working in his study – I saw on the wall an autographed copy of the Rolling Stones' *Exile on Main Street*, which, despite our fatigue, had led to a spirited discussion about whether it really was their greatest album. Who would have guessed that the country's Director of National Intelligence was a closet Stones expert? In scanning the new tracks, I saw that Bradley hadn't been joking when he said he had told our friend I was cracking up. Whisperer had sent me the Stones' '19th Nervous Breakdown'.

I put my cursor on it, hit play and listened for thirty seconds before it morphed. Planted in the middle, stripped of traffic noise and the woman's strange message, was the kaval music. Twice I played it through – it lasted for a little more than two minutes – then downloaded it on to my MP3 player. I thought it might give me inspiration as I headed out again to locate phone box after phone box.

It didn't; it gave me a headache.

By the time I had photographed the fourth one and decided to ask groups of neighbourhood women if they recalled seeing a woman waiting for a phone call and drawn nothing except confused looks or a wary shake of the head, I knew it was going to be a very long day. What was that Turkish expression? Digging a well with a needle?

Still, if you wanted to drink, sometimes that's what you had to do. I was walking down a narrow street, listening to the kaval and wondering again why none of the experts could identify it, when I stopped: something had just occurred to me. I was following the map on my phone, looking for the next phone box, and it meant I had to make a right. Instead I wheeled left and headed towards the centre of town.

Up ahead, I saw the purple fronds of the jacaranda tree I was look-ing for and, moments later, I caught sight of the guy from the record store, opening up the shutters that covered the glass windows. When he saw me, he smiled.

'I thought you'd probably come back,' he said, and indicated one of the classic guitars in the window. 'You look like a Stratocaster kind of guy to me.'

'I'd love to buy a Strat, but not today – I need some help.'

'Sure,' he replied. I helped him raise the rest of the shutters and then he led me through the front door and into the dark cavern of the music store. It was even better than I had thought: at the back there was a cabinet full of restored turntables for those who still believed in needles and valves, a better range of modern guitars than most stores in New York and enough vinyl pressings from the seven-ties to have made Whisperer weep.

I indicated his collection of Turkish folk instruments and told him I had a piece of music played on a kaval that I was hoping he could identify.

'A lot of other people have tried,' I said, 'but nobody seems to be able to nail it.'

'I wish my father was alive,' he said. 'He was an expert on the traditional stuff, but I'll give it a shot.'

I cued up the MP3 player and watched as he listened. He played it four, maybe five, times. Then he put the player into a docking station and played it through the store's sound system. Three tourists who had wandered in listened.

'Not exactly foot-tapping,' one of them, a New Zealander, said. He was right – the music was haunting, more like a cry on the wind.

The owner played it again, his dreamy eyes focused. Then he shook his head, and I wasn't surprised: it had always been a long shot. I started to thank him, but he interrupted.

'It's not a kaval,' he said.

'What?'

'That's why you're having difficulty identifying the tune – it wasn't written for a kaval. Almost anybody would have made the mistake, but I'm pretty sure it's a far older instrument. Listen . . .'

He played it again. 'A kaval has seven melody stops on top and one underneath. This is hard – you've really got to listen – but the instrument that's playing here has only got six stops on top and one below. There's no seventh stop.'

I listened one more time but, honestly, I couldn't tell – I had no idea how many stops it had. 'You're sure?' I asked.

'Yeah,' he replied.

'What is it then?'

'I can't tell you anything about the tune,' he said. 'But I think we're listening to a çigirtma. It's virtually forgotten – I only know about it because my father loved the old stuff. I heard the instrument once when I was a kid.'

'Why are they forgotten, though – they died out?'

'Not exactly – the birds did. For a kaval you need the wood of a plum tree, but a çigirtma is made from the wing bone of a mountain eagle. The birds have been endangered for years, so the instrument faded away – and so did the music written for it. That's why you can't find the tune.'

He removed the MP3 player from the docking station and handed it to me. 'You know the Hotel Ducasse?' he asked. 'You might get some help there.'

Chapter Thirty-nine

THE HOTEL DUCASSE WAS ONE OF THE PLACES I MENTIONED EARLIER – SO fashionable, people were drilling holes in the wall to get inside. It was on the waterfront, with a private beach, cabanas you could rent for the summer for a small fortune and a dozen flat-bottomed boats that ferried waiters, food and drinks out to moored cruisers. That was the low end of the establishment.

The exclusive section, up on the roof, was called the Skybar. I had come straight from the music store, and I passed through the hotel's art deco front doors, crossed several acres of Cuban mahogany flooring and skirted extravagant settings of Philippe Starck furniture before I found the Skybar's dedicated elevator. As I approached, I saw the guy operating it – dressed in designer black pyjamas – note my cheap FBI-style clothes and ready himself to say it was reservation only. But I have a pretty good death stare when I need it, so I set it to Defcon 1 and saw him decide that keeping me out wasn't worth dying for.

He zoomed me to the top and I stepped into a zoo. The Skybar's centrepiece was a pure white, vanishing-edge pool with a glass bottom and a huge view across the bay to the Crusader castle and – fittingly enough – the French House.

Facing the pool were a handful of ultra-luxurious cabanas which seemed to be occupied by several of Eastern Europe's leading kleptocrats and their families. Slightly elevated, they commanded the best view of the pool and its huge expanse of flesh and silicon: scantily clad women of all ages with bee-stung lips and bolt-on boobs, and young, hard-bodied guys in swimsuits so brief they were generally called banana hammocks.

At the opposite end to the cabanas was the bar and a small stage for a five-piece band. One of the guitarists was my objective, but getting there wasn't without its obstacles. The first of them was approaching me with a sympathetic smile and his hands spread wide in silent apology. It was the maître d' and, unlike his clientele, he was class all the way: French was my guess, Berluti handmade shoes, lightweight Brioni suit, gold-rimmed eyeglasses.

'I'm sorry, sir,' he said. 'Today, we are fully booked.'

I looked at the two dozen empty tables – it was early – and even more vacant stools at the bar. I smiled back just as pleasantly. 'Yes, I can see that.'

He already had his arm around my shoulder, guiding me back towards the elevator where the ninja was waiting to whisk me back down to the street where I belonged. I reached into my jacket pocket, and the maître d' assumed I was going for my wallet and a handful of bills to bribe him.

'Please, sir – don't embarrass us both,' he said, with genuine pain.

'I wasn't going to,' I replied, pulling out my gold shield.

He looked at it for a moment and put aside the shepherding shit while he considered what to do.

'Are you arresting someone, Mr Wilson?' he asked.

'Probably.'

He leaned closer – you could tell he was a terrible gossip – and dropped his voice. 'Can you tell me who?'

I leaned in equally close and dropped my voice to match his. 'Sorry, not allowed.'

'No – of course not. But you could probably say what the charge would be.'

'Sure,' I said, and indicated the pool area. 'Bad taste.'

He burst out laughing and shook my hand. 'Fuck, the place will be empty. You'll need a bus.'

He dismissed the ninja with a glance, raised his hand in a gesture to the distant barman and guided me back towards the acres of flesh. 'Be my guest, Mr Wilson – Anton at the bar will take care of your drinks.'

I thanked him, walked beside the pool and settled myself on a stool at the bar. I asked Anton for a coffee and turned my attention to the band. It was the bass player I was interested in – his name was Ahmut Pamuk, and he was in his fifties, neatly dressed, a guy who had obviously decided years ago just to play the groove and not look at the crowd. At the Skybar, that was probably wise. He was good, he knew his shit; the sort of man who had already given music the best years of his life and would probably be playing just one more gig until they laid him in the ground.

But the owner of the music store had warned me that he was one of the most unpleasant people you could meet and, watching him on stage, seeing him at his lifetime's work, I had some understanding why. For a real musician, a man who had been full of hopes and dreams, playing endless versions of 'Mamma Mia' and 'Yellow Submarine' would be enough to embitter anyone.

As Anton brought my coffee, Pamuk was in the middle of a set – the hits from *Titanic* – and I waited for him to finish. The owner had told me the guy had been collecting traditional and folk music for years. His father – a musician himself – had started it, worried that if it weren't collected and written down it would be lost for ever and, in later years, his son had picked up the baton. Apparently, Pamuk got by however he could – playing at the Skybar, pumping gas – all the time finding lost music, playing some of the instruments himself, noting it down like a lost language and sending it to the Turkish National Archives. According to the guy at the music store, if any local could identify the çigirtma tune, it would be him.

The set finished, the band left the stage to no applause, and I stood up. I gave Pamuk my name and told him that I had a piece of music I was hoping he could help me with. My idea had been to ask him to listen to the MP3 player, but I never got the chance: the store owner hadn't been mistaken about Pamuk's personality.

'It's the brunch crowd, and I've been on stage for an hour already – you heard the deafening applause, right?' he said. 'I'm gonna eat, I'm gonna have a coffee and then I'm gonna rest.' He turned to walk away.

'Mr Pamuk,' I replied, 'I'm not a musicologist or some foreign academic.' I flashed him the shield. He wasn't sure how to react but decided it might be wiser to at least pay lip service to cooperation.

'Okay, I'll give you a phone number. Call me tomorrow, we'll set a time,' he said.

'Tomorrow's not good enough. It'll have to be today,' I countered.

He glared at me, but he had never met the Defcon 1 before and buckled.

'From four o'clock I work at 176—' and he rattled off the name of a street that I had no hope of pronouncing, let alone finding, as I was sure he knew. Asshole.

'Write it down, please,' I told him, and motioned to Anton that I needed a pen. Grudgingly, Pamuk complied and, as I walked away, I slipped the address into my pocket.

I almost didn't bother: in light of his personality, I was certain the meeting was going to be a waste of time.

Chapter Forty

APART FROM HAVING TO STAB HIM THROUGH THE FLESHY PART OF HIS hand, my follow-up conversation with Ahmut Pamuk actually turned out to be quite pleasant.

After I left the Skybar I walked along the harbour, found a bench in the shade, slid the battery back into my phone and called Cumali at the station house. I hadn't spoken to her since Florence and I wanted to check any progress on the newly launched investigation into Dodge's murder.

As it turned out, very little had happened. Hayrunnisa picked up the call and told me Cumali had left just after 11 a.m. and wouldn't be back for the rest of the day.

'Where's she gone?' I asked.

'Just a few private things she had to attend to,' she replied.

I was about to press her when I realized it was Thursday and that Cumali's son had invited me to see the Grand Parade and the clowns. She had taken him to the State Circus.

I said I would call back in the morning and then spent another hour checking with people working near phone boxes – again to no avail – and realized that, with lunchtime approaching and most offices and stores closing, it was about to become a near-to-hopeless task.

With little choice but to take a break, I decided to turn my attention to the French House. My confidence had been badly shaken by the mistake that Whisperer and I had made: we had jeopardized our entire mission by assuming that the death of Dodge would be a case worth investigating. Such errors rarely went unpunished in the secret world and, on the plane back from Florence,

I had resolved never to let it happen again. Come what may, I was going to stay one step ahead of the cops. Knowledge is power, as they say.

The core question was simple: how did the killer manage to enter and leave the estate without being seen? Included in the files about Dodge's death that Cumali had given me was a reference to the company responsible for letting the mansion, and I figured that was the best place to start.

Prestige Realty was its name, and I had seen its flashy storefront a number of times during my walking tours. I glanced at my watch and saw that, if I hurried, I had a chance of getting there before it too closed for lunch.

I got within hailing distance just as a man was locking the front door. When he heard me calling to him in English he turned and switched on the smile that realtors reserve for someone they think might have just got off the boat. As soon as he saw me, he switched it off.

He was in his early forties with a full pompadour, an open-necked shirt and a rope of gold chains around his neck big enough to anchor a cruise liner. I liked him immediately. In a strange way, there was no guile to him – if you got ripped off by a man who looked like that, I figured you only had yourself to blame.

I introduced myself, told him I was with the FBI and that I wanted to discuss the French House. He shrugged and said that one of the local cops had visited him about a week ago and taken a photocopy of the lease. He was just the realtor and there was really nothing more he could add.

He was obviously in a hurry to leave and I apologized for taking his time – as a rule, I've always found it helps to be polite – and told him the local cop had called by when it had been an investigation into an accidental death.

'What is it now then?' he asked, surprised.

Obviously the word hadn't leaked out about the overnight developments in the case – although I guessed that what I was about to tell him would mean most of Bodrum would know by nightfall.

I looked at the glass front door and saw his name in gold letters. 'It's a murder investigation, Mr Kaya. The young American was pushed off the cliff.'

It shocked him – upset him, too. 'He was a nice man,' he said.

'Not like most of the assholes who rent mansions here. He talked, showed an interest – he said he was going to take me out on his boat. Shit – murdered?'

'You can understand why I need to talk to you.'

'I was just going to lunch—'

'Good, I'll join you.'

He laughed. 'You know that wasn't what I meant.'

'Yeah.' I smiled. 'But where are we eating?'

Chapter Forty-one

IT WAS A HIGH-END BARBECUE JOINT ON THE BEACH: A POLISHED DECK overhanging the sand, sails of white canvas filtering the sun, designer furniture and – not surprisingly, given my host – a front-line view of groups of tourist chicks sunbathing topless.

As soon as we sat down I asked him if he knew about the house's Nazi past and he looked at me as if I had forgotten to take my medication.

'You're kidding, right?' he said. He looked at my face and saw that I wasn't.

'Who owns it?' was my next question.

'I don't know, not exactly,' he replied, sort of shaken. 'I got a letter – this would be about seven years ago – from a lawyer in Liechtenstein saying he represented a charitable trust which owned the property. He said the trustees had decided they wanted it to produce an income.'

'Did you ask him who was behind the trust, who the real owner was?' I inquired.

'Sure. I even got my own lawyer to try to find out, but it led through a series of nominee companies into a dead end.'

I didn't say anything, but I knew most Liechtenstein trusts were designed to be impenetrable. That was the reason why the tiny principality – sixty square miles, sandwiched between Switzerland and Austria – was the first port of call for Europeans, primarily Germans, wanting to hide assets from their tax authorities.

'So the lawyer acting for the trustees said he wanted you to rent it out. This was after the renovations?'

'That's right – and it was good money for not much work. I

collected the rent, deducted the maintenance expenses and my commission and forwarded the balance to a bank in Liechtenstein. That was it.'

'Who had a key to the estate?' I asked. 'Apart from you?'

'Nobody has a key. Just codes. There are four gates, they're all on electronic keypads linked to a computer – you can't tamper with them.'

'Okay – so how does it work? A new tenant arrives for their stay, then what?'

'I meet their estate manager at the house – all these people have estate managers and personal assistants,' he said. 'I enter my six-digit code into the keypad and hit hash. The screen asks me if I want to change the code and I say yes. I then have to enter my code again, wait twenty seconds, and it tells me to put in the new code.

'I take a walk and the estate manager or the tenant enters their own six numbers – that way I have no idea what it is. We do the same thing at the other three gates.'

'Then they decide who to give the code to?' I asked.

'Exactly. They bring their staff with them – all security-checked, so it's not as if they give it out to strangers.'

'What about gardeners, the pool guy – people like that?'

'It's up to the tenant, but I've never heard of anyone giving the code to any locals. They make them ring the intercom on the trades-men's entrance, the security chief checks them out and opens the gates personally.'

'And at the end of the lease, it's the reverse, right? They enter their code and you replace it with yours?'

'You got it.'

I paused, thinking. 'And in winter, when there are no tenants?'

'There's no need for that level of security,' he replied.

'So – you give the gardeners and the pool guy your code?'

'Not exactly – there's a caretaker who stays on the property for part of the year. He lets them in and does some maintenance. He uses two rooms in the attic over the boathouse, but he has to move out when summer starts. Rich people don't like strangers on the property.'

'But he lives there eight months of the year?'

'Pretty much,' he replied.

'He'd know the house better than anyone?'

'I guess.'

'What's his name?'

'Gianfranco Luca.'

'Where can I find him?'

'He's got a summer job here on the beach – runs a little team that gives massages to tourists.'

The waiter was hovering nearby, and I signalled to him to bring the bill. Kaya offered to give me a ride back into the Old Town, but I said it was a beautiful day and I preferred to walk. He got to his feet, we shook hands and he gave me a business card – made to look like a gold ingot – and told me to call him if I needed any more information.

It wasn't until he had left, and I was waiting for my change, that I glanced down at the card and solved another one of life's mysteries. In the bottom right-hand corner was his office phone number.

The first seven digits were 9. 0. 2. 5. 2. 3. 4. – the numbers that someone had written down at the Eastside Inn and flushed down the toilet. I figured that whoever was living there had been making inquiries about renting an expensive mansion in the area. Something like the French House.

Chapter Forty-two

I DIDN'T HEAD BACK INTO TOWN – INSTEAD, I MADE MY WAY THROUGH the restaurant's car park, hit the beach and found a kiosk that rented out deckchairs and umbrellas.

I set up camp on the sand, put my shoes and jacket on the chair, rolled up my chinos and let the water surge across my feet as I walked along the beach.

At the far end, close to the base of a small bluff and half hidden among a scattering of boulders, I found Gianfranco's operation. Quite by accident, and moving through the shadow cast by the boulders, I approached it from behind.

Privacy was supposed to be provided by canvas screens with the name of his business on them, but they had been poorly arranged and I had the chance to observe him through a gap.

He was in his mid-twenties, olive-skinned, with two days' stubble and a shock of wavy hair. Yeah, he was good looking but probably not quite as handsome as he thought: his eyes were set too deep, and he was a little too muscle-bound.

Nevertheless, he must have seemed attractive to middle-aged German women who were on vacation and looking for fun and maybe something a little more physical in the hot Turkish sun. One of them was lying face down on the massage table, the top of her two-piece swimming costume unhooked and a towel covering her butt.

Gianfranco, in a white banana hammock and nothing else, was working one of his twenty oils – prepared from ancient recipes, according to the bullshit on his privacy screens – into the woman's back, lightly running his fingers over her side-boobs. She made no

443

objection and, having dipped his toe in the water, he leaned further over, slipping his massaging hands down under the towel covering her ass and bringing the white hammock within an inch of her face.

It was impossible to tell if his hands were inside her swimming costume or not, but it didn't matter – they would be soon. Remember the days when divorced middle-aged women went on vacation and the most adventurous thing they did was drink too much and buy some tacky souvenirs? No wonder the tourist shops in the Old Town were going broke.

As he kneaded her butt under the towel she complimented him on how strong his hands were. I guessed English was the only language they had in common.

'Yeah, I built 'em up as a kid,' he said. 'I worked in a car wash, I was an expert on the full wax and polish.'

'I bet you were,' she laughed, her voice growing throaty. 'Did you do interiors as well?'

'Oh, yeah,' he replied, 'they were my speciality.' He leaned closer. 'They still are, I just charge a little extra.'

'And how about a complete detailing? How much is that?'

He was close enough to whisper in her ear, and she must have thought it was okay. 'You take credit cards?' she asked.

'Of course,' he replied, laughing, his hands clearly inside her swimming costume by then. 'This is a full-service operation.'

'And I'm glad to hear it,' she said, her hand touching his muscular thigh and starting to move up towards the hammock.

It was a bit like watching an imminent train wreck – hard to drag your eyes away – but I feared she was about to let the banana loose, so I stepped between the screens.

'Gianfranco, is it?' I asked happily, making out that I hadn't noticed anything unusual.

The German woman instantly drew her hand away and made sure the towel was covering her butt. Gianfranco, on the other hand, was furious – abusing me for intruding and pointing at the privacy screens and telling me I would be lucky if he didn't break my ass.

I was content to let it blow through, but it seemed the more he thought about that unused credit card, the more he whipped himself into a frenzy, and he went to push me hard.

I caught his forearm in mid-air, so fast I don't think he realized what was happening, and pressed my thumb and index finger right into the bone. Krav Maga had taught me that there is a nerve there which, when put under stress, partially paralyses the hand.

Giancarlo felt his fingers go limp – it probably wasn't the only thing – and realized that his hand wasn't responding. He looked at me, and I smiled.

'I'm with the FBI,' I said cheerily.

The German woman had already got off the table, pulled her top up and was grabbing her few possessions off a chair.

'What do you want?' Gianfranco demanded.

I picked up his shorts from a table, tossed them to him and waited while he pulled them on one-handed. 'I'm investigating a murder at the French House,' I said.

'What's that got to do with me? I only work there in the winter.'

I noted the answer, noted it carefully, but I glided into the next question without any apparent pause. Just keep it normal, I told myself, no pressure.

'So I understand. A bit of maintenance, let the pool guy in, help the gardeners – is that right?'

'Yeah.' He was flexing his fingers, feeling the movement returning.

'How much do you get paid?'

'Nothing. Free board, that's all. I have to make enough on the beach in summer to keep me all year.' He glanced to where the German *Hausfrau* had disappeared. 'Thanks a lot, by the way. She was good for at least a hundred.'

I ignored it. 'You live above the boatshed, yeah? How do you get up to the house?'

'There's a set of steps behind, they go up the cliff.'

'Protected by a security gate and an electronic keypad. You use Mr Kaya's code?

'That's right – when he remembers to give it to me.'

'And if you don't use the steps, how do you get up there?'

'I don't understand.'

'Sure you do. There's another way on to the estate, isn't there?'

'You mean climbing up the cliff with ropes and pitons?'

'Don't be cute. How does someone bypass the gates and cameras and get up there?'

'I don't know what you're talking about,' he said.

I didn't respond, I just kept looking at him, and though he became increasingly uncomfortable, he didn't add anything to it.

I shrugged and let it go. I knew he was lying – he was so full of shit that if I gave him an enema I could have fitted him in a shoebox.

The reason I was certain was simple. When we had first started talking I had said I was investigating a murder. Everyone in Bodrum thought Dodge's death was an accident – even Kaya, the realtor, had found it hard to believe – and the thing that I had noted was that Gianfranco hadn't shown any surprise. None at all.

I couldn't tell what part he had played in the events at the house – my intuition was that it was probably very little – but he knew there was another way up and he knew what it was.

'Thank you for your help, Mr Luca,' I said. 'I'm sure we'll be talking again.'

He didn't appear overjoyed at that prospect and maybe I would have changed my mind and stayed to pursue things with him, but it was twenty to four: time to go.

Chapter Forty-three

I RETURNED TO MY DECKCHAIR, PUT MY SHOES ON AND WALKED FAST back into town. Using the map in my head, I made my way down half a dozen narrow streets, skirted the side of a plaza and, up ahead, saw heavy traffic passing down the road I was looking for.

I reached the intersection, looked in both directions to locate number 176 and realized I had been there before.

Suddenly, the world shifted on its axis.

In that one moment – that one crystalline dot of time – the balance of the hopeless investigation swung in my favour and I knew I had found the phone box I was looking for.

It was standing on the opposite side of the thoroughfare, ten yards from a BP gas station. I recognized it because it was one of the boxes which I had photographed on my first day. All around me was the sound of the traffic we had heard in the background of the Echelon recording. Number 176 was the gas station and – unlike the first time I had seen it – a man was sitting in a chair outside, ready to pump gas. It was Ahmut Pamuk and on a table in front of him were a clutch of leather- and woodworking tools he was using to repair a traditional Turkish string instrument.

Repairing an instrument today, I thought, playing one on a different occasion. A çigirtma, for instance.

I didn't move and, as I had done so many times before in my professional life, I excluded the confusion of the world and turned my mind inwards. I saw a woman approach: she either came on foot and walked close to the fuel pumps or arrived by car and left it on one side of the gas station – it was the only place to park in the vicinity.

She stepped up to the phone box, waited for the phone to ring and then held up her cellphone with its recorded message. There were no shops or houses nearby where somebody could have observed her – probably the reason it had been chosen – but her cellphone had been just far enough from the mouthpiece of the phone for Echelon to pick up the noise of the traffic and the faint sound of Ahmut Pamuk.

The musician would have been at his table, playing the strange wind instrument, probably writing down the notes of the folk song and preparing to send it to the archives.

I said nothing, did nothing, felt nothing. I ran it through my mind once more to ensure that my longing for information hadn't coloured my logic. Satisfied at last, determined not to surrender to any emotion, I turned and looked at every square inch of the gas station's office and roof. I was searching for pointers and only when I found them did I unchain my feelings and let my heart soar.

Against all the odds, working with nothing more than a couple of sounds captured by accident, I had found the phone box and – thanks to what I had just seen – I knew I had a chance of identifying the woman.

Chapter Forty-four

I CROSSED ONE HALF OF THE ROAD, CLIMBED OVER A RUSTY RAILING USED as a divider, dodged a swarm of oncoming vehicles and headed towards Pamuk. He saw me approach and didn't bother to hide his disgust. At least it allowed me to dispense with the pleasantries.

'You own or borrowed from someone a çigirtma?' I asked.

'A what?' he replied.

I was pretty sure my pronunciation wasn't that bad and he was just being a prick.

'A çigirtma,' I repeated.

He looked blank and shrugged. 'I don't know what you're talking about, American – maybe it's the accent.'

I managed to keep my temper and picked up a stitching awl – a long, pointed spike – he had been using to pierce leather for his repair work. I scratched the surface of his table with it . . .

'Hey – whaddaya doing?' he objected, but I ignored it.

'There it is,' I said, when I had finished scratching out the name of the instrument. 'Recognize it now?'

'Oh yeah,' he said, barely glancing at it. 'A çigirtma.' Strange, it sounded almost identical to my pronunciation.

'You were playing one here at the table, about a week ago – maybe a folk song for the archives?' I was only asking him to make absolutely certain I had found the right phone box: plenty of investigations have foundered on agents desperate for information leaping to the wrong conclusion.

'I don't know – I can't recall,' he said, with a surliness that was hard to believe.

I have to admit that I was amped – at last I was close to finding a tangible lead in the labyrinth – and maybe that was why I snapped. I was still holding the stitching awl – a nasty little bastard of a thing – and Pamuk's left hand was resting on the table. It was so fast I doubt he even saw it. I drove the end of the needle straight through the thin web of skin between his thumb and index finger, pinning his hand to the table. He screamed in pain, but he should have thanked me for being a good shot – half an inch either way and he would never have played bass again.

Immediately I grabbed his forearm to stop him moving – in such a situation, most people's impulse is to pull their hand away and, in doing so, he would have ripped the web of flesh apart and increased the damage dramatically. Immobilizing him meant that all he had was a puncture wound, which – painful as it was – would heal quickly.

It was funny, though, how a steel awl through the hand concentrated his mind. He looked at me, listening to every word I said, biting his lip with the pain.

'You're a good bass player,' I told him, 'maybe one of the best I've heard – and I know what I'm talking about – but it's not the world's fault it didn't work out for you.

'You don't like playing covers of other people's music? Then leave. Write stuff, put on concerts of folk music for tourists, do *something* – but drop the attitude.

'That's the advice, here's the warning. Lie to me now and I promise you won't be able to do any of those things, not even "Mamma Mia" for the ten thousandth time – you'll be lucky if you can strum a ukulele with your fucking teeth. Okay?'

He nodded, scared, probably thinking I was some sort of US government-sanctioned psycho. I thought of telling him that was the post office, not the FBI, but decided to let it ride. I ordered him to hold perfectly still, and I managed to extract the awl without causing any further damage. He gasped with the pain, but that was nothing compared with the yell he let out when I doused the wound with a liberal splash from the open bottle of raki standing on the table.

'Alcohol,' I explained, 'is a great antiseptic.' I grabbed a piece of white linen he had been intending to use to polish the folk instrument when he was finished and bound his hand. I did it expertly, just tight enough to ease the pain and restrict the bleeding.

'You were a doctor?' he asked.

'No,' I said, 'I just picked up a bit of knowledge along the way – dressing gunshot wounds, mostly.'

He stared at me and decided I wasn't joking, which was the attitude I needed.

'Were you playing the çigirtma – yes or no?' I asked again as soon as I had tied off the bandage.

'Yes,' he replied, thankful to have his hand back and flexing the fingers to make sure they still worked.

'How was my pronunciation this time – okay?'

'Not bad,' he said. 'It seems to have improved greatly, thanks to the needle.'

I couldn't help it – I laughed. I poured him a shot of the raki and took the edge off my voice.

'I want you to listen to a piece of music,' I said, pulling out the MP3 player. 'Is that you?'

He listened for a moment. 'Yeah . . . yeah, it is,' he replied, his voice full of surprise.

I knew then, without any doubt, that logic had not fallen victim to emotion.

'How did you record it?' Pamuk asked, indicating the MP3 player.

'Somebody came in to get gas,' I lied. 'A person in the car was on the phone and left a message on an answering machine in New York. The music was playing in the background. It's a murder investigation – I can't say any more than that.'

The last thing I wanted was to reveal the importance of the phone box – even allude to its existence – and I was pleased to see he was totally down with my explanation.

'New York?' he said, smiling. 'Wow – an international recording artist at last.'

I smiled and indicated what I had seen on the gas station's office and roof. 'You've got video cameras,' I said.

'Yeah, in case anyone drives off without paying. Armed robberies too, but there hasn't been one in years.'

'Listen, Mr Pamuk, this is important – what system is used to record the footage? Tape or disk?'

'It's old. Tape,' he replied. 'VHS.'

'Where is it – the system and the tapes?'

'They're both here – in the office.'

'Okay,' I said. 'How are the tapes catalogued, filed?'

He laughed. 'What filing? There's a box and the tapes are thrown in.'

'Then reused – recorded over?'

'That's right,' he said.

It was exactly what I had feared – that one of the cameras had captured the woman approaching the phone box – either on foot or by car – but that the tape had been reused and the footage wiped.

'Okay,' I said. 'Tell me how it works. Who changes the tapes?'

'We all do – whoever's working,' he explained. 'The first thing you do when you start your shift is make sure the right amount of money is in the cash register, and then you check the recording equipment.

'If the tape is close to running out,' he continued, 'you eject it, throw it in the box, select another one, rewind it and hit record.'

'So some tapes might not have been used for weeks or months, that right?' I asked.

'Sure – depends on which one somebody grabs. For all I know, ones at the bottom of the box might not have been used for a year.'

I took a moment to think: it was going to be a roll of the dice, that was for sure. 'What happens if somebody drives off without paying?' I queried.

'We go to the system, wind it back, take down the licence tag and call the cops.'

'Do you give them the tape? For a prosecution, anything like that?'

He looked at me and laughed in disbelief. 'This is Turkey, Mr Wilson. The cops trace the licence tag and go talk to the guy. Pretty soon he agrees to cough up twice the amount on the pump, which then goes to the gas station. He also has to pay a "fine" to the cops, which they pocket. Who needs a prosecution? Everybody's happy except the guy who did the runner, and nobody cares about him.'

The system had its advantages for me too – it meant that none of the tapes were at the Bodrum police station or drifting through the judicial system.

'And you look at the tapes on a TV in the office, right?'

'Sure,' he replied, then watched as I walked around the front of the gas station, looking at every camera, working out their fields of vision. It was going to be close, very close, whether they captured her – whether she came by foot or car, she would have had to walk to the phone box. If she had stayed very close to the kerb I didn't think any of the cameras would have picked her up. And that was even assuming I could find the right tape and it hadn't been recorded over.

'Are the tapes time-coded – you can see the date, hours and minutes running along the bottom?' I asked.

He nodded – yeah – and that gave me one advantage: thanks to Echelon, I knew the exact dates and times of both phone calls.

'All right,' I said. 'Take me into the office. I want to look at the tapes.'

Chapter Forty-five

AN HOUR LATER, ALONE, I WAS STILL SITTING IN FRONT OF THE ANCIENT black-and-white TV, its screen little bigger than my hand, and its definition about as good.

Beside me was a large stack of VHS tapes that I had already reviewed and a small collection of ones which I hadn't yet seen, the fast-diminishing repository of all my hopes. Maybe the Western world's too, but it was best not to think about that.

The office was cramped and, if it had been cleaned in the last decade, I would have been surprised. Despite the heat – air-conditioning hadn't yet reached BP in Bodrum – there was no chance of falling asleep. The chair I was sitting in was so wrecked and uncomfortable that I had to get up every few minutes to give my back and butt a chance of survival.

All the time, stopping only to throw another tape on the discard pile, the time code was flying by in front of me, threatening to send me cross-eyed before the day was over. Just in case I got myself confused, I had written down the date, hour and minute of each phone call and allowed a margin of fifteen minutes on either side just to make sure she hadn't arrived early or waited around afterwards.

Frequently checking the notation, I had come close a couple of times, watching the time code roar towards one of the appointed times, feeling my pulse race and the fatigue lift, only to see the tape stop abruptly and then find myself watching footage from a totally different week.

On one agonizing occasion I came within a hundred and forty seconds of the first phone call and I was certain the woman was about to walk into frame when the TV set suddenly went to a blizzard of static as the tape ran out completely and I was left staring in despair and disbelief. Ahmut Pamuk hadn't been kidding when he said the system was chaotic.

I was down to my last three tapes when he appeared at the door. 'Wanna coffee?' he asked.

I hesitated, looking sceptical, I guess.

He laughed. 'I know what you're thinking: Not more of that Turkish crap – so thick you don't know whether to drink it or chew it. I'm not offering that – I'm suggesting a cup of real American java, as thin as piss, so weak we Turks normally serve it in baby bottles.'

'Sounds perfect,' I said.

'One condition,' he replied. 'I'll go and buy 'em, I'll humiliate myself with the café owner on your behalf, but if anyone pulls in you have to pump the gas.'

'Okay,' I said. With just three tapes left, I knew the chances of seeing the woman were negligible, and I had pretty much given up – apart from a miracle, a coffee was just what I needed.

I had finished the next tape and was partway through the second-to-last one when Pamuk handed me the coffee. I took the top off, looked around to find a garbage can, discarded the lid and looked back at the screen. It had jumped nine days and, with a growing sense of wonder, I saw the code at the bottom counting down fast to the date and time of the second phone call.

I checked my notation just to make sure – confirmed it – and couldn't take my eyes off the screen. Behind me, Pamuk was standing in the doorway, enjoying his treacle-like coffee, and I knew that if I saw the woman I couldn't react – he thought I was looking for someone pulling in to pump gas and, if I proved myself a liar, that would open up a rat's nest of questions. Apart from that, there was a risk – however slight – that he would know the woman. Totally neutral, I told myself: keep it calm.

'Did you mean what you said before?' Pamuk asked, taking the opportunity to kick back and have a chat.

'About what?' I kept watching the footage, too frightened to try to skip forward in case I missed something.

'Me being one of the best you'd heard.'

'It's true,' I replied, watching the seconds fly by and click over into another minute. Keep going, I urged it silently: *Keep going*.

'Did you play yourself?' said Pamuk.

'When I was a kid – just good enough to know I'd never be great. I would have given anything to have had your talent.'

He said nothing. I wanted to look at his face to see his reaction, but I couldn't break my concentration. If I was going to catch sight of her, it would be very soon. I shot a glance to check the VHS player – there was plenty of tape left but, thanks to BP's security system, that was no guarantee. It could jump a day, a week or a month at any moment. I looked back at the screen, watching the seconds cascade past and feeling Pamuk's presence behind me.

He grew larger in my mind and a strange emotion settled on me – I suppose all my senses were supercharged – but I had the feeling, the certainty, that I had been put into his life for a reason. It reminded me of the priest I had met in Thailand long ago who said that perhaps our paths had crossed so that he could tell me something. It felt like it was my turn to pass it on.

My concentration didn't waver, my eyes didn't shift. 'You hate the work you do,' I said quietly, 'you hate the music you have to play, and that's enough to cripple a man's heart. Any man.'

On the screen there was no sign of a vehicle or a pedestrian – nothing. Maybe she was walking closer or parking her car and would stay so tight to the kerb that she would avoid the camera's field of vision altogether – and that was assuming the tape didn't run out or make one of its sudden jumps. I looked at the time code again, flying ever closer to the appointed minute for the call.

If I didn't see her soon, the tiny window would have closed for ever.

I kept my voice even, neutral, nothing to betray anxiety or excitement. 'I met a man once – this was many years ago,' I continued. 'He was a Buddhist monk and he told me something I've never forgotten. He said that if you want to be free, all you have to do is let go.'

Pamuk made no reply and, of course, I had no way of seeing his face. I watched the time code chew through the seconds – where was she?

Where was she?

'That's interesting,' Pamuk said at last, and repeated it: 'All you have to do is let go. Is that what you're telling me I should do – let go of the crap jobs?'

'I'm not telling you anything. But maybe it's what I'm really doing here – I've been put on the road to pass it on, so to speak. Take it as a gift, if you want.'

I saw a car on the screen. It swung through the frame as if it was going to park: a Fiat, I thought, dark-coloured, but it was hard to say on a black-and-white TV. I didn't sit forward in my seat, even though I wanted to. I just flexed my shoulders as if I were stretching.

I checked the time code – it was damn near perfect. Moments later, a woman appeared from where she must have parked. She was a Muslim with a headscarf on, the usual long dress, her head down as she hurried towards where I knew the phone box was located.

Halfway past the pumps, well away from the kerb, she reached into her handbag and pulled out a cellphone. Then she stopped, glanced around as if she were making sure that nobody was watching, and I saw her face for the first time.

I stared at it for what seemed like minutes but, according to the time code, amounted to slightly more than two seconds. She checked the time on her watch, moved towards the phone box and disappeared from sight.

I barely moved. I kept my attention on the screen even though my mind was racing, feigning what I hoped was just the right body language to convince Pamuk I had seen nothing that would interest me. A short time later – maybe a few minutes, but it was hard for me to judge – the tape ran out, and I never saw the woman emerge from the phone box.

I used the static as an excuse to turn and see if Pamuk had registered anything untoward. He wasn't there.

I had been so engrossed in what was happening on the screen that I hadn't heard a car pull in for gas or noticed that Pamuk had left to attend to it. I sat in solitude and silence for a long time, thinking about the woman I had seen. Finally, I got to my feet and walked out of the door. If nothing else, the fresh air would do me good.

Pamuk had just finished serving another customer and, as they drove off, he turned towards me. 'Find what you were looking for?' he asked.

'No,' I lied.

'Is that why you look so pale?'

'A few hours in your so-called office would do that to anyone,' I told him.

He smiled. 'I want to thank you for what you said – that thing about being free.'

'Don't mention it. Sorry about stabbing you with the needle.'

'I probably deserved it – about time somebody made me wake up.' He laughed.

We shook hands, and I walked away. We never saw each other again, but a few years later I was listening to National Public Radio and I heard him interviewed. I learned that by then he'd had a string of hits playing traditional instruments and had become a sort of Turkish Kenny G. His biggest-selling album was called *If You Want to be Free*.

Alone, deep in thought, I headed down the road and into the fading afternoon. I hadn't taken the VHS tape with me, the one thing that would have helped identify the woman, because I didn't need it. I had recognized her face when she had stopped to look around.

It was Leyla Cumali.

Chapter Forty-six

SHORTLY AFTER 9/11, WHEN THE US AIR FORCE STARTED BOMBING SITES in Afghanistan to try to kill the leadership of al-Qaeda, a woman living in a remote village became a legend in the mosques where Islamic fundamentalism flourishes.

The air force dropped several laser-guided bombs on a nondescript house but, unfortunately, the US intelligence community had got it wrong again. A man by the name of Ayman al-Zawahiri wasn't in the building – just his wife and a group of his children.

Out of nowhere, in the middle of a freezing night, the huge explosions levelled the house and killed most of the kids. Their mother, however – badly injured – survived. Almost immediately, men from the surrounding houses fell upon the ruins and, cursing the Americans and swearing eternal vengeance, tore at the masonry and rubble with their bare hands to get to the woman.

She was conscious, unable to move, but she knew that in the chaos of the attack she had not had the opportunity to put on her veil. She heard the rescuers digging closer and, once they got within earshot – frantic – she ordered them to stop. As the wife of an Islamic fundamentalist and a devout Muslim, she would not allow any man who was not a direct relation to see her unveiled face. She said she would rather die than be a party to it, and it was no idle threat. Despite the pleas of the rescuers and several of their womenfolk, she could not be persuaded otherwise and, several hours later, still unveiled, she succumbed to the effects of her wounds and died.

I had read about the incident shortly after it had happened, and I was thinking again about such a level of religious devotion or madness – choose the definition which suits you best – as I walked through the streets of Bodrum. In the back of my mind, it had been exactly that sort of woman I had expected to find using a pre-configured message on a cellphone to communicate with the world's most wanted terrorist. Instead I got Cumali – a modern working woman by most standards, driving up alone in her black Italian car, and I just couldn't square that circle.

Certainly the guy in the Hindu Kush was the first of a new breed of Islamic fanatic – intelligent, well educated, technologically accomplished – the sort of man who made the 9/11 hijackers look like the thugs and ruffians they were. At last the West had encountered an enemy worthy of our fear, and my private belief was that he was the face of the future – pretty soon, we would all be longing for the good old days of suicide bombers and hijackers. But however sophisticated he might have been, he was still a cast-iron disciple of Islam, and yet his only collaborator, as far as we knew, appeared to be anything but a fundamentalist. Yes, she dressed modestly in accordance with her religion, but Leyla Cumali didn't appear to be al-Zawahiri's wife by any stretch of the imagination.

I stopped outside a bar near the waterfront popular with Bodrum's large contingent of backpackers, and declined a raucous invitation from three young German women to join them. I glanced around and, further down the road, saw what I needed – a quiet bench deep in shadow – and sat down and called Bradley.

I interrupted him eating a sandwich at his desk and gave him a quick update concerning the history of the French House and told him about the real estate agent's phone number. I then broached the real purpose of the call. I said that the only other significant news was that the woman in charge of the investigation appeared to be very competent.

'Her name's Leyla Cumali,' I told him. 'Remember it, Ben – I think we'll be dealing with her a lot. She's in her mid-thirties, divorced, but apart from the fact she's only been here a few years, I don't know anything else about her.'

It sounded natural enough, but I hoped that I had hit just the right note to indicate to Bradley that he had to call our friend and get his people to find out as much about her as possible. Bradley didn't disappoint me.

'Cumali, you said? Wanna spell it for me?'

I gave him the spelling, but I made no attempt to inform

Whisperer that she was the woman in the phone box. As big a revelation as it was, I was worried. I didn't know enough about her yet, she didn't fit any profile I had imagined and I was scared that somebody in government – maybe even the president himself – would order that she be secretly picked up, undergo rendition to some Third World country and be subjected to whatever torture it took to discover the identity and location of the Saracen. In my view, that would almost certainly be a disaster.

From the beginning I had believed that the woman involved had a way of contacting him, and nothing had changed my mind that the most likely method was an innocuous message on an Internet forum – something like a dating site or buried within the personal ads of a myriad different electronic publications. Such a message, unremarkable to anyone else, would have meant volumes to the Saracen.

And yes, as smart as the system was, it had one other great advantage: it could be booby-trapped. One tiny alteration – changing the spelling of a word, for instance – would tell the Saracen that she was acting under duress and he had to vanish. Once he was warned that we were on his trail, I didn't believe we would ever catch him.

For that reason I wanted to warn Whisperer directly that rendition would probably be a catastrophe. I also wanted to be able to tell him more details about the relationship between a modern Turkish cop and a fervent Arab terrorist.

Once darkness fell, I knew I had a perfect opportunity to research Leyla Cumali's life in far greater depth.

Chapter Forty-seven

STILL SEATED ON THE BENCH, THE SHADOWS LENGTHENING ALL AROUND me, I dialled another number.

'Good afternoon, Mr Brodie David Wilson,' the manager said when he heard my voice. 'Perhaps you have more adventure for the help of me and the simple carpenter-folks?'

'Not today,' I replied. 'I want to know about the State Circus in Milas – what time does it start and finish?'

'You are a man of many great surprises – you wish to make a watching of the circus?'

'No, I was thinking of performing.'

He laughed. 'You are pushing my leg.'

'Yes,' I admitted. 'A colleague suggested going, and I was wondering how much time it would take.'

'I will go on to the line of the Internet,' he said, and I heard him hitting a keyboard in front of him. 'Yes, here it is – all in the language of Turkish-men. It is of great good fortune that you have the advantage of my orifices as a translator.'

'And excellent orifices they are too,' I said.

'The times are of the following – the Grand Parade starts at six of the night evening and the extravaganza of the final piece finishes at eleven thirty.'

I thanked him and clicked off. Darkness fell at around eight thirty so, under cover of night, I could be in Cumali's house by nine. By the time she drove back from Milas, it would be past midnight, giving me three hours to do the job.

It was an assumption, of course – an unquestioned belief that the circus would end on time. You would have thought I would

462

have learned how dangerous assumptions could be.

I glanced at a clock on a nearby building: it was 5 p.m. Four hours until my clandestine date at the old port, four hours to take a boat ride, four hours to find a secret pathway.

First, though, I had to find a store that sold building supplies.

Chapter Forty-eight

THE SMALL FISHING BOAT RAN PARALLEL TO THE GERMAN BEACH AND, AT the last minute, the weatherbeaten skipper threw its wheezing inboard into reverse, turned the wheel fast, and drew to a perfect stop next to the wooden jetty.

When I had first approached the old man sitting on Bodrum marina repairing one of the boat's winches and told him of the trip I had in mind, he had refused point blank.

'Nobody goes to that wharf,' he said. 'The French House is—' Unable to find the English word, he mimed a knife cutting his throat, and I got the meaning: it was forbidden.

'I'm sure that's true,' I replied, 'except for the police,' and got out my shield. He looked at it for a moment then took hold of it to examine it more closely. For a second I thought he was going to bite it to see if it was real.

Instead he handed it back, still looking sceptical. 'How much?' he asked.

I told him he would have to wait for me – all up, we'd be gone about three hours – and offered a rate I guessed was more than generous. He looked at me and smiled, displaying a handsome set of broken teeth.

'I thought you wanted to rent the boat, not buy it.' Still laughing at his enormous good fortune, he dropped the winch among his nets and motioned me aboard.

Once we drew alongside the jetty I clambered on to the boat's rail and, clutching a plastic bag from the building-supplies store, jumped ashore. The overhanging cliff towered above us, and I knew from experience that nobody in the mansion or on the lawns could see us.

Even so I was glad of the cover provided by the late-afternoon shadow and I couldn't really explain why: all I knew was that I didn't like the house, I didn't like the German Beach much either and I was pretty sure, if I was right, I wouldn't like what I found.

La Salle d'Attente – the Waiting Room – and I was already convinced, thanks to the location of the house, that the visitors all those years ago had come to wait for a boat. According to the half-forgotten stories, they would arrive in Bodrum without being seen, spend days in the sinister privacy of the estate and then be gone in circumstances which were equally as mysterious.

I figured that, back then, there was probably a cabin cruiser moored in the boathouse – a vessel in which the visitors could be hidden from view – while it headed out to keep a rendezvous with a passing freighter.

But to walk down the cliff by the path made no sense – it was totally exposed to the public. That was why I believed there was another way from the mansion into the boathouse.

I called to the skipper, said I was heading up the path, walked along the jetty and, as soon as I was out of sight, started to examine the boathouse. It butted up close to the towering cliff and in the shadows I quickly found what I was looking for – a door that gave access to the interior of the building. Although it was locked, the wood was old and it quickly gave way under the pressure of my shoulder.

I stepped out of the fading light and into the gloom. The place was huge and there, sitting on underwater rails, was an ancient cabin cruiser, perfectly maintained. I couldn't help wondering whose asses had sat on the plush seats in its darkened interior.

At one end was a pair of wide doors, worked by electric winches, which gave access to the water. At the opposite end were changing rooms, two showers, a toilet and a large workshop. Running up one wall was a set of steep stairs.

I opened the plastic bag, took out the device I had purchased and headed towards them.

Chapter Forty-nine

I STEPPED INTO TWO TINY ROOMS. DURING WINTER, IT WAS Gianfranco's apartment but now the furniture was shrouded in dust covers and everything else was packed away.

I turned on the handheld device and watched the needle on its voltmeter flicker to life. It was Swiss-engineered and expensive but, unlike most of the crap Chinese versions, I was confident it would work. The device was made for builders and renovators – it told you where to find power and light cables in walls and ceilings so that you didn't nail into them and electrocute yourself.

If there was a secret door or trapdoor in the boathouse, I figured it had to be either mechanically or electrically operated. The problem with mechanical was that it was complicated: you would need levers and pulleys, chains and counterweights. An electrical system, on the other hand, just required an electric motor, and I believed it was the more likely candidate.

I held the device up, placed its two prongs on the wall and started to search the length of it. I was trying to find a power cable that would lead to a hidden switch but, while the device found plenty of wiring, it all led to lights or power points. Once I had finished with the walls, I started on the ceiling and floor, but with no better results.

Moving downstairs, I realized that the wind had picked up and was rattling the sea doors – a storm was coming in – but I ignored it and stepped into the workshop. The room, full of power tools and shelves of paint, abutted the cliff and I thought it was the most likely location of a hidden door. I started at the back wall, working fast.

The needle of the voltmeter kept jumping – there was wiring everywhere in the walls – but each strand led to one of a host of power points and light switches, which turned out to be legitimate. The ceiling and cement floor – even under the workbenches – yielded nothing, and my spirits sagged.

Wondering if I had been too worried about the swastikas and had deluded myself, I moved into the changing rooms. Hope spiked when I found a switch under a wooden bench – only to crash when I found it worked the underfloor heating.

From there, I headed towards the showers but decided to sweep the toilet first. I was fast running out of possibilities.

The ceilings and floor were clear, as were three of the walls, but on the one which featured a handbasin and a mirrored cabinet above it, I got a signal.

There were no light switches or power points on that wall, but the flickering needle didn't excite me: I guessed there was a small light inside the cabinet. I opened the mirrored door and, apart from an old toothbrush, found nothing.

Using the meter, I traced the wiring along the plaster until I came to a right angle: the wall featuring the toilet and cistern stopped me. It was strange – an electrical cable ran straight along a side wall and disappeared into a corner. What was behind the toilet? I wondered. I tapped the wall – it was stone block or brick. Solid.

I went back to the cabinet and used the meter to search around it. The wire definitely terminated behind the cabinet. It was basically a wooden box, and I looked at it carefully: it was old, almost certainly fitted when the house was first built – but the mirror was new. I wondered if a maintenance guy – Gianfranco – had been asked to replace the mirror and, when he took the cabinet off the wall, had found something far more interesting behind it.

Using the flashlight on my key-ring and feeling with my fingers, I searched the edges of the box – if there was a switch behind it, there had to be a way to access it easily. It wasn't apparent; and I was starting to think of unscrewing the cupboard from the wall – or just getting a hammer from the workshop and ripping it off – when I found a small, ingenious lever hidden under the bottom edge.

I pulled it, the cabinet moved out from the wall and I could hinge it upwards: a perfect piece of German engineering.

Recessed into the wall behind was a brass button with a swastika etched into it. I pressed it.

Chapter Fifty

AN ELECTRIC MOTOR WHIRRED AND THE ENTIRE WALL HOLDING THE toilet and cistern pivoted open. It was masterly in the way it was built – the wall itself was made of stone blocks and must have weighed a ton, while all the water and sewage pipes were able to move without being torn apart.

Just inside the newly opened cavity was a large niche which housed the electric motor that operated the mechanism. A set of stone steps – broad and beautifully constructed – led down into gloom. I saw three brass switches on the wall and figured they were for lights, but I didn't flick them – I had no idea what might be ahead of me and, like any covert agent, I knew that, in darkness, lay safety. I considered finding the button which would close the wall behind me, but rejected the idea. It was safer to leave it open. If I had to run like hell back towards it, I didn't want to waste time fumbling for a switch and waiting for a door to open. It was a mistake.

I walked silently down the steps and entered a tunnel tall enough to stand upright in, well built and properly drained, with flagstones on the floor and a ventilation shaft built into the roof. The air was fresh and sweet.

The thin beam of my flashlight shone ahead and, before it was swallowed by the blackness, I could see that the tunnel was hewn out of solid rock. Somewhere ahead – through the cliff and far below the sweeping lawns – I was certain it would connect to the mansion.

I moved forward, and my weak finger of light caught a glint of bronze on the wall. As I got closer, I realized it was a plaque set into the rock. My German was rusty but it was good enough for the purpose. With sinking heart, I read: 'By the Grace of Almighty God, between the years 1946 and 1949, the following men – proud soldiers of the *Reich* – designed, engineered and built this house.'

It then listed their names, military rank and the job they had undertaken during the construction. I saw that most of them were members of the Waffen SS – the black-shirted, armed wing of the Nazi Party – and as I stood a million miles from safety the photo of the mother and her kids on their way to the gas chamber rose before me. It was a section of the SS that had operated the death camps.

At the bottom of the plaque was the name of the group that had funded and organized the construction of the house. It was called Stille Hilfe – Silent Help – and it confirmed what I had suspected ever since I had seen the swastikas on the wall of the library.

Stille Hilfe was an organization – ODESSA was reputedly another – that had helped fugitive Nazis, primarily senior members of the SS, to escape from Europe. It was one of the best clandestine networks ever established and you couldn't have worked as an intelligence agent in Berlin and not have heard of it. My memory was that they had provided money, fake passports and transport along secret routes that were known as 'ratlines'. I was certain the mansion had been built as the terminus to one of those lines, an embarkation point to take the fugitives and their families to Egypt, America, Australia and, mostly, South America.

I took a breath and thought how wrong I had been: despite the ventilation system, the air wasn't fresh and sweet at all. It was rank and foul, and I hurried forward, wanting to be done with the place and the terrible memory of the men who had once escaped down the tunnel.

Up ahead, the beam from the flashlight showed that I was approaching the end of the tunnel. I was expecting flights of steep stairs, so it took me a moment to realize I had underestimated the German soldiers' engineering skills: it was an elevator.

Chapter Fifty-one

THE SMALL ELEVATOR CAR ROSE UP THE SHAFT FAST AND SILENT. I WAS ON edge – I had no idea where inside the house it would stop and if anyone would be at home.

It jerked to a halt and I heard the sound of an electric motor. When the door finally opened I saw what it operated; the sheet-rock wall of a large linen closet concealing the elevator had slid aside. I stepped into the gloom, moved fast between shelves of neatly pressed sheets and quietly cracked open a door.

I looked out into a corridor. I was on the second floor, a part of the house I had never seen before. I could have left then – I had found the secret way into the mansion – but I heard a voice, muffled and unrecognizable because of the distance, and slipped into the long hallway.

The sound stopped, but I kept creeping forward until I found myself facing the grand staircase. On the far side, a door into the master bedroom suite was partly open.

From inside, I heard the voice again: it was Cameron, and it occurred to me that she might be talking quietly to herself, spending time in the bedroom with the memory of her husband. I remembered how she had said that if she laid on the bed she could smell him and imagine that he would still be there. Then I heard a second voice.

It was a woman's – a young American from the Midwest by the sound of it. She was saying something about a restaurant when she stopped abruptly.

'What's that?' she asked.

'I didn't hear anything,' Cameron replied.

'No, not a sound – there's a draught.'

She was right – the wind was coming along the tunnel, up the elevator shaft and seeping out of the linen closet.

'Did you leave the door in the boat shed open?' Cameron asked.

'Of course not,' the other woman said.

They both knew about the tunnel – so much for Cameron's Oscar-winning performance about loving her husband.

'Maybe the wind's blown open one of the doors downstairs,' Cameron said. 'There's a storm coming in.'

'I don't know, I'm just gonna have a look around.'

'I thought we were going to go to bed,' Cameron replied.

'We are – it'll only take a minute.'

I heard a drawer being opened then a metallic click. From long and unhappy experience, I knew the sound of a pistol being cocked when I heard it, and I turned and headed fast towards the linen closet.

The corridor was too long and I realized immediately that, when the unknown woman stepped out of the bedroom, she would see me. I pivoted left, opened a door and stepped inside a guest bedroom. I closed the door silently and, with my heart racing, stood in the unlit space, hoping that she would go down the grand staircase.

She didn't. I heard footsteps approaching, and I prepared myself to take her down and disarm her the moment the door opened. She passed by – heading for the back stairs, I figured – and I gave her a minute before I slid back into the corridor.

It was empty, and I moved fast to the linen closet, watched the secret wall slide shut behind me and waited for the elevator to descend towards the tunnel. Only then did I lean against the wall and concentrate, trying to imprint the exact sound and tone of the woman's voice on my memory.

In reality, I needn't have bothered – strangely, it was the smell of gardenias that turned out to be significant.

Chapter Fifty-two

I WALKED ALONG THE MARINA, SHOULDERS BENT INTO A FAST-RISING wind and my face hit by the spray being whipped off the ranks of advancing whitecaps. The summer storm – wild and unpredictable – was sweeping in, and already thunderheads were appearing overhead and flashes of lightning lit the horizon.

The ride back across the bay from the French House had been a battle against the wind and tide. When we reached the marina, even the skipper had looked green around the edges and had told me, laughing, that maybe I had got the better part of the bargain after all. I paid him and headed somewhat unsteadily towards the waterfront promenade.

At the end of the bay I found what I had seen a few days earlier: a ghetto of garages and down-at-heel shops which specialized in renting scooters and mopeds to the legions of tourists. I walked into the busiest of the outfits – a man was far less likely to be remembered among a crowd – identified the most common of the bikes, a Vespa step-through, gave an overworked attendant my licence and passport details and rode out into the encroaching storm.

I made one stop – at a shop selling mobile phones and other small electronic devices. I scanned the display counter, pointed out what I needed and bought two of them.

Around the corner, in a deserted alley, I halted at a rutted section of road and smeared the licence tags with mud to make them indecipherable. It was far safer than removing them – if a traffic cop were to stop me and complain that the tags were illegible, I would just shrug and say I had no idea. The purpose of the scooter was simple: to provide a fast escape in case things went wrong.

For that reason, it had to be parked at the back of Cumali's house, so, having made my way down to the old port, I circled behind the huge building housing Gul & Sons, Marina and Shipwrights and turned into a narrow road which led to the loading bays at the rear. Everything was closed for the evening and, by good luck, there were no other buildings overlooking the area. I parked the Vespa behind a row of garbage skips hard up against the brick wall that formed the rear perimeter of Cumali's property, and hidden by the night stood on the saddle.

As the first drops of rain splattered around me, the wind moaning through the steel roof of Gul's warehouse-style premises, I leapt up, grabbed the top of the wall, hauled myself up and moved fast along the top of it.

Twelve feet above the ground the wind was worse, and I had to use all my concentration to ignore the peals of thunder and keep my footing as I headed for Cumali's garage.

I clambered on to the roof, crouched low and crossed the rain-slicked tiles. From there, it was a jump across a small void to the back of the house and a grab on to an ornate iron grille that secured a second-floor window. I'm not as young as I used to be – or as fit – but I still had no difficulty in shimmying up a tangle of old pipes and getting on to the pitched roof of the home.

I knelt in the darkness, removed four terracotta tiles and dropped down into the attic space. It was unlined, unlived in, and I was pleased to see that Cumali used it as storage – that meant there would be an access panel, and it relieved me of the necessity of kicking my way through her ceiling.

Without replacing the tiles, I moved slowly through the attic and let my eyes become accustomed to the gloom. Against one wall I saw a folding ladder and knew I had located the access panel. Gingerly, I lifted it a fraction and stared down into the stairwell. I was looking for the telltale red blink of a sensor, but there was nothing and I knew there was no burglar alarm.

I opened the panel, dropped the ladder silently and slipped down into Cumali's dark and silent house.

I froze.

I wasn't alone. It was the merest hint of movement, a muffled sound – maybe a foot falling on a wooden floor – but I registered it as coming from inside the room at the front of the house. Cumali's bedroom, I figured.

Was it possible she hadn't gone to Milas at all? In that case, where was her son? Could somebody else be staying in the house – the nanny, for instance? I had no answers, but I had a stopgap solution – I pulled the Beretta out of my waistband and crept silently towards the door.

It was open a crack, but there was next to no light coming from inside. If it was Cumali I was sunk, but anybody else and I had a fighting chance – the likelihood of someone being able to describe me in the dark, taken by surprise and with their heart in their throat, was so low as to be negligible. I just had to remember not to speak – my accent would narrow the field of suspects to a fraction.

I hit the door hard, throwing it back on its hinges and bursting inside – just like they had taught me. The noise and suddenness of movement was designed to unnerve even the most seasoned professional. I swept the room with the muzzle of the Beretta and saw the eyes first – green – looking straight at me. Their owner was sitting on the bed.

Licking its paws.

It was the tabby cat that I had seen scratching itself inside the kitchen window. Dammit – I should have remembered she had a pet. Getting slack, I told myself.

Angry, I turned, went down the stairs and found myself in the living room. The curtains were drawn, the room made up of pools of shadow, but the first thing I saw was a TV in the corner and a Sky decoder box on top of it. I stared at it and thought of her sitting cross-legged on the floor, her son asleep upstairs, as she worked through the night composing and copying her messages.

To be so close to the heart of it galvanized me and I moved fast to the windows, made sure the curtains were closed tight, and turned on a lamp. The single worst thing to do when you have broken into a home is to use a flashlight – light leaks out, and nothing alerts a neighbour or passer-by faster than a beam of light sweeping around inside a house. The soft glow of a lamp, on the other hand, seems normal.

In a corner of the room was Cumali's chaotic desk, stacked with files and bills, only the computer monitor and its keyboard sitting in a clear space. I moved the mouse and the screen came alive – thankfully, like most people, she had left the computer on and I didn't have to worry about trying to unlock the password or removing the hard drive. I reached into my pocket and took out the two USB travel drives I had bought at the mobile-phone shop. I put one into the computer – the other was a spare, just in case – and I knew my way around Windows well enough to be able to ignore that it was in Turkish and get it to perform a full back-up.

With all her files and emails being copied on to the tiny drive, I set about searching her desk. I split it into four sections and did it methodically, examining everything and refusing to let myself be hurried. I used the camera on my cellphone to photograph anything of interest, but I knew in my heart I was just going through the motions – there was nothing that appeared to signify some sinister plot.

Among a pile of bills that were waiting to be paid was a file containing all Cumali's home and mobile-phone accounts, and I took several minutes to look through them. All the numbers she had called seemed straightforward – certainly there were none to Pakistan, Yemen, Afghanistan, Saudi Arabia or any of the other hot zones of Islamic fundamentalism. Nor did I see any billing codes that indicated they were relay numbers used to connect to a foreign phone number. They seemed to be Turkish calls – that was all – but I photographed them anyway.

Then the lamp went out.

I felt a spike of fear and, instinctively, I grabbed my gun. I listened closely but heard nothing, not even the tabby cat. I stood up from the desk and moved silently to the window, wanting to see what was happening outside. I pulled a corner of the curtain aside and looked into the street: the storm had become steadily worse and the whole area was in darkness. It was a power failure.

I should have asked myself, of course, if it was just Bodrum that was blacked out or if it extended further afield. Unfortunately, I didn't.

Chapter Fifty-three

FORCED TO RELY ON MY FLASHLIGHT, I RETURNED TO THE DESKTOP, finished with it and started on the drawers. They were even more barren.

On a scrap of paper – a half-completed crossword torn from a London newspaper – I found that someone had written the word 'clownfish' in the margin. Maybe they had been trying to work out a clue. Maybe not. It was scrawled, written quickly, and I couldn't tell if it was Cumali's handwriting or not, so I photographed it too.

A few minutes later, leafing through the pages of an old day-runner diary, I found a handwritten list of sea-life – all in English – which featured the same word. Again, it meant nothing to me – perhaps she had been trying to teach her son something – and I moved on.

Thanks to the power failure, I had far less hesitation in using the flashlight – everybody in Bodrum would be doing it – and I swept the room, searching the limestone walls and uneven floorboards, looking for a hidden safe. There was nothing, so I took the USB drive out of the computer – thankfully, it had finished copying the files before the power failed – went back up the stairs and made my way to the next most likely place to yield results: Cumali's bedroom.

I was about to start on the cop's bureau when the beam from the flashlight gave me a glimpse of a tall filing cabinet in her walk-in closet. I tried one of the drawers and – strange, I thought – found that the cabinet was locked.

I opened my wallet and took out a small set of picks and, though it had been years since I had learned the technique, the lock was so simple it took me less than a minute to throw the bolt. The first drawer was full of police case files – including several dealing with the death of Dodge – but behind them, in a gap at the back, I discovered the reason why Cumali kept it locked. She didn't want her son getting hold of the Walther P99 pistol I found there.

There was nothing remarkable about its presence – a lot of cops kept a stand-by side arm at home – but I located the serial number etched into its barrel and entered it into my cellphone for later checking. Who could tell? Sometime, somewhere, it might have been used or registered to somebody, and that could give me a vital clue.

The next drawer was almost empty – just bills that were stamped 'paid' and a file containing an itemized account from the regional hospital. Although most of it was in Turkish, the names of the drugs that had been ordered were in English, and I knew from my medical training what they were used for. I looked at the first page of the file, saw the name of the patient and the date and realized that, several weeks earlier, Cumali's son had been admitted with meningococcal meningitis.

It was an extremely dangerous infection – especially for kids – and notoriously difficult to diagnose fast enough. A lot of doctors, even those in emergency rooms, often misread it as the flu and, by the time the mistake was discovered, it was often too late. Cumali must have been fortunate enough to encounter an ER doctor who was sufficiently knowledgeable – and strong-minded enough – not to wait for the results of the pathology tests but had immediately put the boy on the massive doses of intravenous antibiotics, which had undoubtedly saved his life.

I kept going through the file, feeling good about what had happened – at last the little guy had caught a break. I got to the final page and glanced at Leyla Cumali's signature on the bill. I was about to put the file back when I paused. Perhaps it was because I had never really looked at her name written down before, but I realized something: I didn't know her surname at all. Not for certain.

The strict practice in Turkey was for a divorced woman to return to her pre-marriage name, but I remembered reading once that a court could grant dispensations. Say, against the odds, Cumali was her married name – it meant that there might be a clue in an earlier life, in a previous surname.

In everything I had searched I hadn't found a birth certificate, marriage licence, passport – anything at all – to show what name she had been born with. It was possible that the documents were kept in a secure location – a safe in her office at the station house, for example – but I couldn't be sure and worked faster, going through every drawer of the filing cabinet to see if I could find them.

The curtains behind me were closed tight and the wind was drowning out every other sound, so I had no idea that a car had come down the street and pulled into Cumali's driveway.

Chapter Fifty-four

IT WASN'T UNTIL LATER I DISCOVERED THAT THE BLACKOUT HAD extended far beyond Bodrum. To Milas, for example – which meant that the evening performance of the circus had been called off, the tickets transferred to the following week, and the audience had left hours early to make their way home.

I figure that the little guy fell asleep on the drive back, so Cumali stopped outside her garage, as close as possible to her back door. She picked him up, pushed the Fiat's door closed and carried him across an apron of concrete.

She slipped the key in the back door, opened it one-handed, and the blast of storm-driven wind entering through the missing four terracotta tiles on the roof would have told her instantly that something was wrong. If she had any doubts they would have been dispelled by the sound of my footsteps on the bare boards of the floor above.

She turned with her son in her arms, got back in the car and used her cellphone to call Emergency. I have no doubt that she gave the operator the confidential code – a feature of all police forces – which said that an officer was in trouble and needed urgent help. There was no other explanation for the speed and strength of the response.

Strangely enough, it was that urgency which gave me a chance – not much of a one, admittedly, but a chance all the same. In some situations you take what you're given and make no complaint.

The first squad car to arrive came down the road fast – no siren or bubble-lights flashing, in the hope of surprising the intruder – but drew up to the kerb a little too fast. The sound of gravel being thrown up, almost buried in the wind, was the first indication I had that something was badly wrong.

An agent without as many miles on the clock as I had might have gone to the window to look, but I froze and listened. I heard the metallic sound of a car door opening and, when the door didn't slam, it told me eloquently that the occupants didn't want to be heard and were coming for me.

Even though I was certain that the cops were outside I continued to sweep through the filing cabinet, unwilling to surrender the only opportunity I would ever get, continuing to look for a document – any document – that would tell me Cumali's birth name. I figured the visitors were waiting for back-up, which meant one thing was for sure: they wouldn't be entering the house in numbers small enough for me to handle. I decided to stay until I heard the next car arrive and then get the hell out.

I kept searching, attuned to every sound, cancelling out the howl of the wind. Less than a minute later I heard at least one more car pull to a stop. Perhaps two. Despite my earlier plan – call me stupid, if you want – I pressed on. In the bottom drawer, under a stack of old law-enforcement magazines, I found a large leather book, the type of thing which I had seen many times before – a wedding album.

It wasn't what I was hoping for but, under the circumstances, it was my best chance. I just hoped Turkish photographers were as business-minded as their counterparts in America. I opened the album at random, pulled out one of the photos and slammed the book back where I had found it, confident that one photo taken years ago wouldn't be missed.

I jammed the photograph inside my shirt, scattered some of the contents of the filing cabinet across the floor and upended two drawers from the bureau to make it look like an amateur burglary. I picked up the Walther P99 and cocked it – at least, in that regard, luck was being a lady. I had no hope of using my own gun, in case suspicion fell on me – any ballistic tests on the bullets could end up nailing me with certainty – but the Walther was completely un-connected to me. I headed for the bedroom door, ready to use the gun.

Lights in the house came on – the power to the area had been restored. Maybe luck wasn't such a lady after all. I wheeled right and headed for the stairs that led up into the attic – I had left them down and hadn't replaced the roof tiles, just in case I needed a fast retreat.

I heard footsteps – pairs of boots, actually – coming up the front steps, and I knew the cops were only moments away. Clambering up the stairs, I heard the key turn in the lock.

I made it into the attic just as the front door was thrown open, accompanied by a man's voice yelling in Turkish. I figured he was telling whoever was inside to throw down any weapons and show themselves with their hands up.

I hauled the ladder up, threw myself at the part of the attic where I had removed the tiles and crawled through on to the pitched roof. Sticking to the shadows, I elbowed my way forward and did a fast reconnoitre of the area. I noted Cumali's car in the driveway and clearly saw her sitting inside holding her son, while a group of her colleagues moved towards the garage and through the backyard. They had the place surrounded.

There was only one way out: a sprint over the tiles and a flying leap across the eighteen-foot-wide driveway to the roof of Gul's adjoining warehouse. No sweat – eighteen feet was no problem for me.

Sure. I hadn't jumped anything like eighteen feet through thin air since training and, even then, I was more wooden spoon than gold medal.

Chapter Fifty-five

I CONTINUED TO LIE IN THE SHADOWS, TRYING TO THINK OF A BETTER plan, when I heard a door thrown open below and, a second later, the shattering sound of a stun grenade exploding. Turkish cops didn't muck around. I figured they had made their way into Cumali's bedroom and any minute they would turn their attention to the attic space.

I needed no more incentive than that. I got up, crouched low and ran fast for the edge of the house. Between one heartbeat and the next my feet lost contact with the tiles and I was swimming in clean air, willing myself forward, stretching with my arms and chest, trying to reach out and grab the guttering on the side of the warehouse. I was falling and for a terrible moment I didn't think I had a chance, then my left hand touched the metal and slipped but my right hand caught and held. I swung like a bad trapeze artist and reached up and grabbed on with my failed left hand and hauled myself up on to the roof of the warehouse . . .

Unfortunately, the night wasn't dark enough.

I heard voices yelling, the sharp crack of a gunshot and I knew at least one of the cops near the garage had seen me. The bullet must have gone wide, and I was confident that nobody had any chance of recognizing me in the gloom. The problem was going to be escaping off the roof.

Already I could hear orders being yelled, the sound of mobile radios being activated, and I didn't need it to be translated to know that men were being told to seal off the warehouse. I had to find the maintenance stairs down from the roof, get into the building and run for the loading bays at the rear. Outside was the Vespa.

It was going to be a race and it got off to a bad start – one of the cops had called in a chopper.

The pilot had its searchlight on and I saw the bright finger of light approaching as I sprinted across the reinforced steel and climbed a ladder to an even higher section of the roof. I was heading for a pair of large cooling towers, figuring that Mr Gul and his Sons would make sure the water system got regular maintenance, and I wasn't disappointed. A locked doorway next to them probably gave access to a flight of stairs. I levelled the Walther at the lock and blew it apart.

I kicked the door open and half jumped, half ran down the first flight of steps. There was barely any light but I saw that I was in the boat-repair building – a cavernous, eerie place. Between towering walls lay a group of dry docks and several dozen luxury cruisers hanging from huge claws above. The motorized claws were attached to steel rails bolted to the rafters, allowing the large boats to be moved hydraulically from one work area to another without ever going near the ground. Some facility.

As the hanging boats creaked and groaned in the high wind, I headed down the next flight of stairs. Four overhead lights – the big vapour variety – exploded to life.

Allowing the cops to see my face would be as bad as being caught, so I dropped to one knee and took aim. Unlike the long jump, I had always been pretty good on the firing range. I hammered out four shots in rapid succession and took out each of the lights in an impressive blast of gas and falling glass.

In the gloom I heard Turkish voices cursing, more men arriving and the sound of large roller doors being raised. I knew that very soon they would have enough boots on the ground to search line abreast until they had me cornered. I ran back up the flight of stairs, climbed on to a steel gantry just below the grid of steel rails and sprinted for a control box. I could see cops spilling into the facility below and I just hoped that none of them would look into the rafters and see me silhouetted against the ceiling.

I reached the control box and thanked a God I wasn't even sure existed: six identical handheld devices were in chargers attached to the wall. I grabbed the first of them, switched it on and saw a numeric keypad and a display screen spring to life. I sprawled on the floor to conceal myself and, with no real idea what I was doing, working more by intuition than anything else, I aimed the device into the darkness and pushed its attached joystick.

The motorized claws holding a huge cruiser started to move, propelling the boat along the overhead grid. A group of four cops on the ground, all in uniforms with a lot of braid, looked up and saw the white and gold cruiser gather speed above them. The most senior of the cops, florid and overweight, his buttons straining against his belly – the Bodrum police chief, I figured – either took an educated guess or saw the glow of the handheld device and pointed at the gantry, yelling orders to his men.

Cops ran for access ladders on the walls and started climbing towards me. They were mostly young, hollering to each other, and I realized that a vacation atmosphere was creeping in – they knew a single man didn't have a chance against so many and they were sure going to make him pay for violating the property of one of their own. I had the feeling an accidental 'fall' wasn't out of the question.

Frantically, I experimented with the remote device. Each of the boats had a four-digit identification number hanging from its side and I realized that if I entered it on the keypad I could use the joystick to send each boat back or forward, left or right. As more cops arrived to help in the hunt, I lay out of sight, getting as many boats as possible in motion, hoping to create maximum confusion for when I made my run.

The only part of the device I wasn't sure about was a yellow button at the bottom – I had my suspicions, but I didn't want to fool with it. Instead, I ramped the white-and-gold cruiser up faster, turned it on to a track to converge with a forty-foot sloop and flattened myself.

One of the cops climbing the wall saw what was about to happen and screamed a warning. Everybody below ran fast – standing under two boats when they collided was no place to be.

The moment they hit, debris flew everywhere. The sloop parted from its claw, fell fifty feet to the floor below and exploded into kindling.

In the chaos and fear I scrambled to my feet. A forty-foot black Cigarette boat with twin gas turbines and a huge wing at the back – every drug smuggler's dream boat – was coming towards me. As it sped past, I leapt, grabbing a chrome stanchion on the boat's side, and hauled myself aboard.

Chapter Fifty-six

BEING HIDDEN ON BOARD A SPEEDING CIGARETTE BOAT MEANT THAT MY situation had improved – but it was also true that the starboard side of the *Titanic* initially held up a bit better than the port side. I was still stuck inside a warehouse with several dozen Turkish cops ready to rumble.

I rolled across the deck of the speedboat and for once managed to time things exactly – a beautifully restored Riva from the 1960s was gliding past in the other direction. I dived off the side of the Cigarette and landed on its teak stern. I sprawled across it, barely hanging on, and it carried me towards the loading docks at the rear.

Somewhere behind me there was a deafening crash – I guessed that another two big cruisers had collided – but I had no time to turn and look. A catamaran I had unleashed appeared at right angles out of the gloom, coming straight at me.

Its steel bow, reinforced for ocean-going journeys, would slice the Riva in half, but there was nothing I could do except hang on – if I abandoned ship I would end up as a pile of broken bones next to the kindling fifty feet below. I braced myself for the impact, but at the last moment the Riva pulled ahead and I watched as the big cat passed behind, stripping the paint off the hull right next to me.

Light split the darkness and I looked down and saw that the cops had wheeled in banks of work lights from the yard outside. My first inclination was to shoot them out but, on quick reflection, I decided it would almost certainly give away my position. Instead I had to watch as they tilted them up and started searching the grid and the rampaging boats for any sign of me.

Every second, the Riva carried me closer to the loading bays, but the cops on the lights were working methodically, lighting up sectors, and it was only a matter of moments before they would hit on the old boat and see me. I slid over the side, dangled for a moment and scanned the area beneath me for any cops. I registered it as clear but, in the confusion and urgency, I was wrong – a cop in a sharkskin suit was running in a cable for more work lights.

Hanging over the side of the Riva, clinging by my fingertips, I waited . . . waited . . . and let go. I fell twenty feet and almost ripped my arms out of my sockets as I grabbed hold of a horizontal pipe that fed water to the sprinkler system. I had no time to scream – hand over hand I moved along the pipe until I could drop down on to the roof of a storeroom. From there I reached the side wall and, while a dozen cops were climbing higher to find me, I scrambled from one handhold to another down the aluminium siding.

Still holding the remote device, I hit the ground while the cops on the work lights swept the rafters and boats above. I sprinted for the rear and rounded a corner – there was the loading dock, thirty feet ahead. Cops entering to search the joint had left one of the roller doors up and I knew that the scooter was only twenty yards away, hidden in the darkness behind the row of garbage skips.

Running fast, I caught a flash of movement to my left. I wheeled, the Walther rising fast to the firing position, but saw that it was only a street dog that had wandered in looking for food.

The dog wasn't the problem, though – it was the voice that suddenly barked a command from behind me. It was in Turkish, but in some situations all languages are the same.

'Drop the gun, raise your hands' was what he was saying – or a pretty fair approximation of it.

I guessed the guy was armed, and that meant he had me square in the back, from what seemed – according to the position of his voice – to be about ten yards away. Well done, Turkish cop – too far for me to jump you, too close for you to miss. I dropped the Walther but kept the remote.

The cop said something, and I guessed from the tone he was telling me to turn around. I wheeled slowly until I faced him. It was the cop in the sharkskin suit, kneeling down, still crouching to connect a cable to the work lights. He had a nasty little Glock pointed at my chest. But that wasn't the most surprising thing – that was reserved for his name. It was SpongeBob.

He looked at my face, more surprised than I was. '*Seni!*' he said, and then repeated it in English. 'You.'

As the full implication of the deep shit in which I found myself hit him, he curled his lip and smiled with pleasure. I said earlier I had made an enemy for life, and I wasn't wrong – for him this was payback with a lovely twist.

I saw that, behind him, the Cigarette had reached the end of the grid and was coming back fast towards us. SpongeBob, still triumphant, yelled over his shoulder into the cavernous space to come quick. Thankfully, I didn't hear my name mentioned, and I figured that he was keeping that as a big surprise. The Cigarette came closer, closer . . .

I heard boots running, approaching fast. The Cigarette loomed directly above SpongeBob and I only had a second to act before everything about the mission fell to ruins. I pressed the yellow button.

SpongeBob heard the rattle of chains and flashed a glance upwards. The claws holding the huge boat released. He was too alarmed even to scream – instead, he tried to run. He was no athlete, though, and the sharkskin suit was cut too tight to let him do much more than a strange sidestep.

The rear of the hull, housing the twin turbines and all the weight, fell first. It plunged down and took him on the skull, compressing his head into his chest, exploding his neck and killing him before he even hit the floor.

As his body found the concrete I was already diving behind a mobile crane. The Cigarette hit the floor and exploded into fragments of fibreglass and metal. While the steel of the crane protected me from most of the debris, I still felt a stinging pain in my left calf.

I ignored it, got to my feet and ran hard for the little I could see of the roller door through the clouds of dust and swirling debris. I heard the cops yelling, and I guessed they were telling each other to take cover in case more boats started raining down.

I saw the open roller door, made it through and burst out into the night. I sprinted for the garbage skips, saw the Vespa and was thankful I had exercised the foresight to leave the key in the ignition. My hands were shaking so much it probably would have taken me five minutes to fit it in.

The engine burst to life, I roared out from behind the garbage skip, hurtled between a stack of shipping containers and fishtailed down the road and into the night before the first of the cops had made their way out of the warehouse.

My only concern was the chopper, but I saw no sign of it and guessed that, once the police chief thought I was cornered, he had dismissed it. Whatever the reason, driving more soberly once I hit the busier streets, I reached the hotel without trouble and slid the scooter into the small garage reserved for the manager's old Mercedes.

I didn't even notice that I was wounded.

Chapter Fifty-seven

THE MANAGER DID. HE WAS ALONE IN THE FOYER, SITTING BEHIND A DESK on one side of the reception area, when he looked up and saw me enter. As usual – hand extended, his face alight with his signature smile – he came forward to greet me.

'Ah, Mr Brodie David Wilson – you have been on the relax with a dinner of the fine quality, I hope.'

Before I could answer, I saw his expression change: a shadow of concern and perplexity crossed his face.

'But you are wearing an injury of seriousness,' he said, pointing across his always impeccably clean tile floor to where smears of blood marked my path.

I looked down, saw a tear on the left calf of my chinos and figured that the piece of flying debris from the exploding Cigarette had done more damage than I had realized. The blood had flowed down on to the sole of my trainers and I had now traipsed it across the hotel foyer.

'Damn,' I said. 'I crossed the main road down near the BP gas station. There's a rusty railing they use as a road divider. I guess I didn't climb it as well as I thought.'

It wasn't a great explanation, but it was the best I could do at short notice and the manager seemed to accept it without question.

'Yes, I know this place,' he said. 'The traffic is of much madness. Here, let me be of helping.'

But I declined, insisting instead on making my way to my room, walking on the tip of my foot to prevent leaving any more bloody smears on his floor. Once inside, with my door locked, I took off my trousers and, utilizing a pair of travel tweezers, succeeded in pulling a jagged hunk of metal out of my calf. Once it was removed the wound started to bleed like a mother, but I had already torn a T-shirt into strips and I got it compressed and bandaged in a few seconds.

Only then did I open my shirt and turn my attention to the photo I had stolen from the wedding album. It showed Cumali and her then husband, smiling, arm in arm, leaving the reception for their honeymoon. He was a handsome guy, in his late twenties, but there was something about him – the cut of his linen pants, the aviator sunglasses dangling from his hand – that made me think he was a player. There was no way I could imagine him being a stalwart of the local mosque and, once again, looking at Cumali's beautiful face, I encountered the same damn circle I couldn't square.

I turned the photo over and saw that Turkish photographers were no different from their counterparts elsewhere: on the back was the name of the photographer, a serial code and a phone number in Istanbul to call for reprints.

It was too late to phone him so, with my calf throbbing hard, I opened my laptop to check for messages. I was surprised to see that there was no information from Bradley about Cumali's background, and I was in the middle of cursing Whisperer and the researchers at the CIA when I saw a text message from Apple telling me how much I had been charged for my latest music download.

I opened iTunes and saw I was the proud owner of *Turkey's Greatest Hits*, a compilation of the country's recent entries in the Eurovision Song Contest. Oh, Jesus.

I had to endure two tracks and part of a third before I found, embedded in it, a series of text documents. Although it didn't say so, it was clear that the researchers had hacked into the Turkish police database and found Cumali's human resources file.

Their report said that she had studied two years of law, dropped out, applied to the National Police Academy, and undertaken a four-year degree course. In the top tier of her graduating class, she had been streamed into criminal investigation and, after service in Ankara and Istanbul, her knowledge of English meant that she was posted to a tourist destination where it would be put to best use: Bodrum.

They found plenty of other stuff, commendations and promotions mainly – she was a good officer by the look of it – but it was all standard career stuff and it was clear that even from her time at the academy, the Turkish police had known her as Cumali and nothing else.

The researchers at Langley had also wondered if that was her real surname, and they tried to find an electronic back door to access marriage licences, birth certificates or passport applications, but they ran straight into a brick wall. Amazingly, Turkish public records couldn't be hacked. It wasn't because the government had adopted, like the Pentagon, some complex system of cybersecurity. The answer was much simpler – none of the archives had been digitized. The official records existed only on paper – probably bundled up, tied with ribbon and stored in endless warehouses. According to Langley, the only way to access anything more than five years old was by a written application – a process which could take over a month.

I stared at the report in frustration – as was so often the case with the agency's research, it was all tip, no iceberg. I figured that sooner or later they would resolve the question of her name but, as the lawyers say, time was of the essence. Pissed off with their work, I went to bed.

Thanks to Langley, the entire investigation now rested on a photographer in Istanbul I had never heard of and who might well have been retired or dead.

Chapter Fifty-eight

HE WAS NEITHER, ALTHOUGH BY THE SOUND OF HIS COUGH AND THE lighter firing up a constant stream of cigarettes, the dead part might have been closer than he wished.

I had woken before dawn, dragged my injured leg to the laptop, put the USB travel drive into a slot and started to work through Cumali's files. It would have been slow and grinding work, except that most of it was in Turkish and I had no choice but to discount the vast majority of them. Even so, you get a sense of things, and I couldn't claim that among the letters and work files I found anything that raised my suspicions: the mistake that most people make when they want to stop someone from seeing material is to encrypt it, which means that a person like me knows exactly where to look.

As I had suspected when I was in her living room, nothing was coded and, if she had been smart enough to hide any incriminating files in plain sight, I was damned if I could identify them. Nor was there anything in Arabic, even though we had good reason to suspect she knew the language.

Having drawn a blank with the files, I turned to her emails. Thankfully, many of them were in English, and I saw that she had a wide circle of friends and acquaintances, many of them other mothers with Down's syndrome children. Among the hundreds of messages I found only two that made me stop – they were both from a Palestinian charity associated with the Al-Aqsa Martyrs' Brigade, a group that frequently organized suicide bombings against Israelis. The emails acknowledged donations to an orphanage in the Gaza Strip, and my first reaction was to ask why – if Cumali really wanted to help kids – she didn't give to Unicef. On the other hand, charity was one of the Five Pillars of Islam and, if it was a crime to donate money to organizations associated with radical groups, we would end up indicting half the Muslim world. More, probably.

I marked the two emails with a red flag then put the USB drive into an envelope and addressed it to Bradley in New York. As soon as FedEx opened I would courier it to him to be on-passed to Whisperer for further analysis. I looked at the clock – it was 7 a.m. and, though it was early, I wanted to find out whether the photographer was dead or alive.

I called the number, waited for what seemed minutes, and was about to give up and try later when I heard an irritable voice give a greeting in Turkish. I apologized for speaking English, talking slowly in the hope that he could follow me.

'Can you speak a bit faster? I'm falling back asleep here,' he said, in an accent that indicated he had watched a few too many Westerns.

Pleased that we could at least communicate, I asked him if he was a photographer and when he confirmed it I said that I was planning a special gift for the wedding anniversary of two friends. I wanted to put together a photo collage of their big day and needed to buy a number of reprints.

'Have you got the code number?' he asked, more polite now that there was money to be made.

'Sure,' I replied, and read off the number on the back of the stolen glossy.

He asked me to wait while he checked his files and, a minute or two later, he returned and told me there was no difficulty, he had the file in front of him.

'Just to make sure there's no confusion,' I said, 'can you confirm the names of the bride and groom?'

'No problemo, pardner. The groom is Ali-Reza Cumali—' He went on to give an address, but I wasn't interested: the moment I heard it I knew for sure that the cop hadn't reverted to her previous surname.

'And the bride?' I asked, trying to keep the excitement out of my voice. 'Have you got a name for her?'

'Sure,' he replied. 'Leyla al-Nassouri. Is that the couple?'

'Yeah, that's them, Sheriff.' He laughed. 'I've never been quite sure how to spell her unmarried name,' I continued. 'Can you give it to me?'

493

He did, I thanked him for his help, told him that I would be in touch as soon as I had a full list of the photos I needed and hung up. The name al-Nassouri wasn't Turkish – it was straight out of Yemen or Saudi or the Gulf States. Wherever it was, it was Arabic. And so was the man in the Hindu Kush.

I grabbed my passport, headed out the door and almost ran to the elevator.

Chapter Fifty-nine

THE DOORS SLID OPEN AND, ALTHOUGH IT WAS ONLY SEVEN TWENTY IN the morning, I stepped out into what appeared to be some sort of celebration. The manager, the receptionist, the bellhop and other hotel staff were gathered at the front desk and had been joined by several of the carpenters and other friends of the manager who had helped me with the mirrors.

The conversation – all in Turkish – was highly animated, and coffee and pastries were being handed around. Despite the hour, somebody had produced a bottle of raki, and I wondered if they had won the lottery or something.

The manager approached me, smiling even more widely than normal, waving a copy of that morning's local newspaper. 'We have news of the greatest happiness,' he said. 'You recall the SpongeBob, the man of the biggest corruption, a curse on all citizens of goodness?'

'Yeah, I remember. Why?'

'He is dead.'

'Dead?' I said, faking surprise and taking the copy of the newspaper and looking at an exterior photograph of the marina warehouse with cops everywhere. 'It's hard to believe,' I said. 'How?'

'Squashed – flat like the cake of a pan,' he explained. 'Some man of idiot brain broke into a house belonging to a cop of the female.'

'Broke into a cop's house? Yeah – what an idiot brain.'

'Probably a Greek people,' he said, absolutely serious.

'When did this happen?' I asked, trying to act normal, just kicking it along. Everybody else was standing near the desk, and the manager and I were in our own private world.

'Last of the evening, while you were having your relax with the dinner of the fine quality. Just before you walk in with your bloody . . .'

He paused as a thought occurred to him and, though he tried to haul the sentence back, he couldn't.

'They say the killer ran from the boat place with a trail of the blood injury,' he said. He stopped and looked at me.

Our eyes met and held – there was no doubt he knew who the killer was. I could have denied it, but I didn't think it would have been convincing; or perhaps I could have issued some dark threat, but I was certain he wasn't easily intimidated. I didn't like it but I figured I had to trust my intuition and take a chance on him and his friendship.

'No, no,' I said finally. 'You're of the wrongness quite substantial. My relax of the fine food wasn't last night – that was the night before.'

He looked at me in confusion, about to argue, thinking I was genuinely mistaken, but I kept talking so that he didn't have a chance to blunder on.

'Last night you and I were here – in the lounge,' I said. 'You remember? It was quiet, there was nobody else around.'

Suddenly his eyes sparked as understanding dawned. 'Oh yes,' he said. 'Of course, that's right – the dinner was of the night previous.'

'Now you remember. Last night, you and I talked, you were explaining to me about the Greeks. It was a long conversation.'

'Oh yes, one of the longest. Those damn Greek peoples – nothing is simple with them.'

'True. You had a lot of things, a lot of history, you had to tell me. It was well past 10 p.m. when I went to bed.'

'Later, probably, 11 p.m. is more the time of my memory,' he said, with great enthusiasm.

'Yes, I think you're right,' I responded.

We looked at each other again and I knew my intuition about him had been right. The secret was safe.

He indicated the passport in my hand and dropped his voice. 'Are you leaving in the hurry not to return?' he asked.

'No, no,' I said. 'If anybody asks, I've gone to Bulgaria – I spoke about finding an important witness.'

I farewelled him and headed for the front door and my car. I opened the trunk, pulled out the rubber lining and found a way to access the right rear wheel arch. I removed the tracking transmitter held in place by strips of magnets and attached it low down on the pole of a parking sign.

With any luck, no pedestrian would see it and whoever was monitoring it at MIT would think my car was still parked at the kerb.

I got behind the wheel and drove for the border.

Chapter Sixty

ALL DAY I HAMMERED THE FIAT DOWN ENDLESS STRETCHES OF highway – stopping only for gas, passing the distant minarets of Istanbul in the afternoon and reaching the Bulgarian frontier in the early evening.

The hardscrabble corner of the world where Turkey, Greece and Bulgaria meet is one of the busiest road junctions in Europe and, once I had left Turkey and entered a sort of no man's land, I was surrounded by long-haul semis crawling towards Bulgarian immigration and customs.

After forty minutes and about a hundred yards' progress I called out to the driver of a Danish freighter stopped on the side of the road and asked him how long he figured it would take to clear the frontier.

'About eight hours from here,' he replied. 'Depends on how many illegal immigrants they find and have to process.'

Bulgaria had somehow managed to become part of the European Union and had quickly established itself as the organization's most vulnerable border, acting as a magnet for anyone who wanted to enter the Union illegally and travel on to other, richer, pastures like Germany and France. By the look of the trucks and people-movers, there was no shortage of chancers and people smugglers.

I thought about trying to get to the front and showing my shield, but rejected it: there was always a chance I'd meet some thickhead who was only too happy to show the FBI who was boss. Instead I undertook some brief preparations, pulled on to the shoulder and drove up the inside of the endless queue. I passed under two overhead structures with cameras and signs and figured that pretty soon the border patrol would come and find me.

Two minutes later, silhouetted against the twilight, I saw blue flashing lights as a car approached fast down the dirt shoulder towards me. It stopped about ten yards in front, blocking my path, and the guy riding shotgun – probably the more senior of the two – lumbered out and walked towards me. He was about my age, over-weight, and his uniform looked as if an even bigger man had been sleeping in it. You could tell he was ready to start yelling and order me back to the end of the queue.

I had about ten words of Bulgarian, gleaned from a visit years ago, and luckily they included 'I am sorry.' I got it out fast, before he could launch, and I saw that the phrase at least drew some of the venom from his snarling face. I couldn't tell from his eyes, because, despite the hour, he was wearing shades.

I kept talking, switching to English, throwing in the Bulgarian apology a few more times. I told him that I had been in his fine country before and had always been overwhelmed by the friendliness of the people. I was hoping that would be the case again now that I needed assistance. I was running late and was desperately trying to catch a flight out of Sofia, the Bulgarian capital.

He grunted and looked as if he was about to tell me he didn't give a shit – like I said, they were a friendly people – when he saw that I was handing him my passport. He looked at me quizzically; I met his gaze and he took the book. He opened it at the details page and found the five hundred Lev in banknotes – about three hundred US, a month's wages that far east – that I had put in there.

I had arrived at what was always the most dangerous part of any such transaction – paying off an official was a serious offence in any jurisdiction, and it was at that stage the guy in uniform could really shake you down if he wanted to. Five hundred to go to the front of the queue? Try twenty thousand – and your watch and camera, please – not to charge you with attempted bribery.

He asked for my driver's licence and, with that and the passport, he returned to his squad car. Vehicles that I had overtaken on the inside were now crawling past, hitting their horns in celebration of excellent Bulgarian justice and giving a thumbs-up to the two officers. I wasn't angry – in their position I probably would have felt the same.

The man returned and told me to open the driver's door. It looked like the real shakedown was on the way, and I was bracing myself, about to reach for my shield, when he climbed on to the door sill so that he was standing up next to me, holding the door half closed.

'Drive,' he said, 'and hit the horn.' I did as I was told, and he started signalling to several of the big semis to stop immediately, opening up a gap.

'Go between them,' he ordered and, to the accompaniment of huge air brakes hissing, I squeezed into a lane in the middle of the road which half a dozen languages said was for official use only.

'Faster,' the officer ordered. I needed no further encouragement, and floored it.

Followed by the squad car with its lights flashing and the officer still hanging on to the open door, we flew past the miles of semis and coaches until we reached a row of glass booths topped by various crests and a huge Bulgarian flag.

The guy clinging to the door took my passport, stepped into one of the booths, borrowed a seal from his colleague and stamped my passport. He returned, handed me the book and – I figured – was about to tell me his colleague also needed a contribution, but I was already hitting the gas and heading into the night before he opened his mouth.

I travelled fast, headlights stabbing into the darkness, revealing acres of forest and – as if life in the new EU wasn't surreal enough – clutches of women in micro-mini skirts and skyscraper heels standing on the roadside in the middle of nowhere. Major trucking routes in other countries had endless billboards; in Eastern Europe they featured prostitutes, and no country more so than Bulgaria.

I passed hundreds of them – Gypsy girls, mostly – waif-like figures in lingerie and fake fur, hard-eyed kids whose lives revolved around the cabin of a semi or the back seat of a car. If they were pregnant their services sold for a premium, and you didn't have to be a genius to work out that orphans were one of the country's only growth industries.

Porrajmos, I said to myself as I drove on, recalling the Romani word that Bill had told me so many years ago: I was looking at just another form of the Devouring.

At last, the young women gave way to gas stations and fast-food outlets and I entered the town of Svilengrad, an outpost of about twenty thousand people which had virtually nothing to recommend it except a pedestrianized main street and a wide range of shops that stayed open until well past midnight to cater to the endless stream of truckers.

I parked the car far away and found four of the stores I was looking for clustered together. I chose the most down at heel of them, the one that – as far as I could tell – had no video recording equipment or surveillance cameras. Inside, I bought the two items that had led me to drive seven hundred miles in twelve hours and had taken me from the edge of Asia into the old Soviet bloc: a piece-of-junk cellphone and a prepaid, anonymous SIM card.

I returned to my car and under a single street lamp in a dark corner of a Bulgarian town nobody had ever heard of, surrounded by farmland and young Gypsy hookers, I made a call to a number with an area code which didn't exist.

Chapter Sixty-one

USING AN UNTRACEABLE CELLPHONE ROUTED THROUGH THE BULGARIAN phone system, and fairly confident that MIT would not be listening, I waited to talk to Whisperer directly.

I had to tell him Leyla Cumali's real name, I had to report that she was an Arab and I had to reveal that she was the woman in the phone box. That was the first imperative of any agent who was still 'live' and far from home – to pass on what they had learned. It was the only insurance against apprehension or death, and they taught you from the earliest days that information didn't exist until it had been safely transmitted. But, more than that, I had to discuss with him the problem of rendition and torture.

The phone rang five times before I heard Whisperer's voice. 'Who is it?' he asked. It was early afternoon in Washington, and I was shocked at how weary he sounded.

'Dave, it's me,' I replied, deliberately using his little-known first name, just in case somebody was listening, keeping the tone light and unhurried despite my excitement and a thrumming anxiety concerning my surroundings.

Although he must have been surprised to hear my voice, he picked up the tenor of the conversation immediately. 'Hey, what's happening?' he said, just as casually, and I was reminded once again how good a case officer he really was.

'You know the woman we were talking about, Leyla Cumali?'

'The cop?'

'Yeah. Well, her real name is Leyla al-Nassouri.'

'Sounds Arabic.'

'You're right. It was her in the phone box.'

There was dead silence at the other end. Despite Whisperer's studied indifference, despite his years of experience and enormous talent, I had shocked the quiet voice out of him.

I didn't know it then, but the effect of my words was amplified by the rolling failure of all our other efforts. The hundred thousand agents working for a host of intelligence agencies, everyone supposedly looking for a man trying to build a dirty bomb, were delivering a lot of heat but absolutely no light. Deep down, Whisperer figured we were dealing with a cleanskin and that the chances of catching him in time were diminishing by the hour.

'Oh yeah – in the phone box, huh?' he said, recovering his voice and making it sound as if it didn't mean much at all. 'You sure about that?'

'No doubt. I met a guy who played an instrument – I won't try to pronounce it – made from the wing bone of an eagle. He showed me some footage.'

'Sounds weird,' Whisperer said, sounding as if it was all pretty amusing. 'How do you spell it? Al-Nassouri, not the eagle thing.'

I told him and, in normal circumstances, the next question would have been about where I was calling from, but I was certain he already knew. Given his job, all calls to Whisperer's cellphone were recorded, and I figured that he would have already scribbled a note to one of his assistants and had Echelon track the call.

While he was waiting for the answer, I kept talking. 'There's something I feel strongly about, Dave – very strongly indeed. You have to go softly; you should be careful who you talk to.'

'Why?' he replied. 'You figure some folks will come up with a bright idea? They might want to move in and start hurting people?'

'Exactly. We assume she can contact him but I'm pretty sure the system is booby-trapped.'

'A deliberate mistake under duress – something like that?'

'Yeah.'

He thought about it for a few seconds. 'I guess the guy would be foolish if it wasn't.'

'We could lose him totally.'

'I understand,' he said. There was another pause while he considered what to do. 'I'm gonna have to run this past at least one other person. You with me?'

He meant the president. 'Can you convince him to hold back?' I said.

'I should think so, he's an intelligent man, he'll get the problem. Can you nail this business down?' he asked.

'Find him? I've got a good chance,' I replied.

I heard a small sigh of relief – or maybe it was just his blood pressure heading back down to earth. 'Okay, we'll assume we're going with the confidential thing. I'll get the researchers back on to her,' he said.

'You saw their previous efforts?' I asked.

'Sure – not much good, was it?'

'Fucking hopeless. We've gotta colour outside the lines, use other people.'

'Who?'

Halfway across Turkey, following the white line for mile after mile until I was almost hypnotized, I had been thinking about the CIA's research and how the hell to compensate for it. Somewhere just south of Istanbul, I decided what we had to do. *Hai domo*, I said to myself.

'There's someone I know,' I said. 'I told him once that if I was in a corner and needed computer help, he'd be the guy I'd call. His name's Battleboi.'

'Repeat that,' Whisperer replied.

'Battleboi.'

'That's what I thought you said.'

'It's with an "i" at the end, not a "y".'

'Oh good, that makes a difference. Battleboi with an "i" – it's almost normal, isn't it?'

'His real name's Lorenzo – that's his first name. He's been busted for stealing the details of fifteen million credit cards.'

I heard Whisperer typing on a keyboard, obviously accessing an FBI database, and a moment later he was talking again.

'Yeah, well, you're right about that – Jesus, the guy must be in the hacker hall of fame. Anyway, two days ago he cut a plea deal with the Manhattan DA.'

'What did he get?'

'Fifteen years in Leavenworth.'

'Fifteen years?!' I responded. I started cursing the people responsible – fifteen years in the Big House, for credit cards? I wasn't sure he would survive it.

'What was that?' Whisperer asked, overhearing my muttering.

'I said they're assholes. He always claimed they'd bleed him for all the information he had, then double-cross him.'

'I don't know anything about that.'

'I guess not, but you've gotta keep him out – at least until we're finished. Tell him a friend of his – Jude Garrett – needs his help. I'll bet he'll outperform the other team, no matter what resources they've got.'

'Battleboi, for God's sake. Are you sure about this?'

'Of course I'm sure!'

'Okay . . . okay.' he said. 'How do you want him to get in touch with you?'

'I don't know – if he can steal fifteen million credit cards, I'm sure he'll find a way.'

We were finished with business, and suddenly I felt tired to the bone.

'Before you go . . .' Whisperer said and his voice trailed off. I wondered if he had lost his train of thought, but it turned out he was finding it hard to say, that was all.

'I told you once I envied you,' he continued, even quieter than usual. 'Remember that?'

'Sure, in the car,' I said.

'I don't any more – I'm just glad you're there, buddy. I don't think anyone else could have done it, it's been outstanding work. Congratulations.'

Coming from Dave McKinley, it meant more than from anybody else in the world. 'Thanks,' I said.

After we hung up I sat for a long time in thought. There was one thing I still couldn't fathom – Leyla al-Nassouri-Cumali didn't fit any profile that I could imagine.

Chapter Sixty-two

FOR THE TEENAGE BOY IN EL-MINA, THE RUN OF GOOD LUCK THAT HAD started with the unexpected gift of a cellphone continued unabated.

On a Wednesday afternoon, walking home from school, the phone rang and he spoke to the man who had given it to him. The Saracen said that he was calling from Germany, where he had been lucky enough to find both a mosque that conducted itself in accordance with his strict beliefs and a job that offered great promise for the future.

The boy started to ask questions, probably with the thought that he might one day be able to join the father-figure who had been so generous to him, but the Saracen cut him short by telling him that, unfortunately, he was heading to work, time was short and he had to listen carefully.

'Get a pen out – I'm going to give you an address.'

While the boy sat on a wall under the shade of a tree and rummaged through his backpack, the Saracen explained that he had already posted him a key that would open the garage at his old apartment. Inside were the boxes of medical supplies he had spoken to him about. Remember – the expired vaccines with their official dispatch dockets already attached? Once the boy had received the key, he was to open the garage and fill in the following address.

'Mark them to my attention,' the Saracen told him, 'at Chyron Chemicals in Karlsruhe, Germany. I'm going to spell it out, starting with the street address. Okay?'

Once he had finished, and had made the boy repeat it back to him, he said that he had already organized for the Beirut courier, with a refrigerated truck, to visit the garage on Saturday morning. Could the boy be there to meet him and unlock the door? Of course he could.

With that done, there remained only one more task. He told the boy to call the company in Beirut from which he had bought the industrial refrigerators and negotiate to sell them back.

'Whatever money you get, you can keep,' the Saracen said. 'That should guarantee you'll drive a hard bargain,' he added, laughing.

When the Saracen told him what he could expect to receive for the items, the boy could hardly believe it – it was almost six months' salary for his mother, who worked in a local laundry. He tried to thank him, but the doctor cut him short, telling him that he had to run to get to work on time. The Saracen hung up and, though the boy didn't know it, it was the last time they would ever speak.

The Saracen stepped out of a public phone box next to the Karlsruhe market square and sat for a moment on a wooden bench. It was close now: in a few days the garage would be empty and the ten thousand tiny bottles loaded on to a truck operated by a courier company which specialized in medical supplies.

The boxes that contained the precious vials would be displaying genuine dispatch dockets from a Lebanese hospital, their destination well established as one of the largest producers of vaccines in the world, and all of them addressed to a man who was an authentic employee of the company's warehouse department.

Chapter Sixty-three

THE BOXES ARRIVED FIVE DAYS LATER.

Their documentation showed that the courier had transported them to the port of Tripoli, where they had been loaded into a refrigerated container. A small Cedars-Line freighter had taken them across the Mediterranean and, several days later, they had encountered European customs in Naples, Italy.

How do I put this nicely? Italy, even at the best of times, isn't renowned for its thoroughness or bureaucratic efficiency. When the boxes arrived, it happened to be the worst of times. Continual budget cuts had taken a huge toll on the customs service, and its resources had been further depleted by a flood of containers carrying illegal immigrants risking the short journey from North Africa.

Even though the boxes secretly contained a Biosafety Level Four hot agent, none of them were opened for inspection, let alone analysis. The overworked officers believed what the documentation and transit history attested to: they were expired vaccines being returned to the manufacturer in Germany.

In Naples, the boxes were loaded on to a truck, driven north without any further inspection, crossed the unpatrolled border into Austria and from there headed into Germany.

They arrived at the Chyron Chemicals security gate – just another shipment among the hundreds that went in and out every day – at 11.06 p.m., according to the guards' computerized log. One of them saw the contact number on the documentation – a guy working in the warehouse – called him and said a delivery was on its way.

The boom gate lifted, the driver was waved through and three minutes later the Saracen took possession of his ten thousand vials of liquid Holocaust. The journey that had started so long ago with once-classified information haemorrhaging online was almost at an end.

The Saracen immediately stored the boxes in a rarely visited area of the warehouse reserved for discarded packaging and attached a sign in Turkish and German on the front of them: DO NOT MOVE. AWAITING FURTHER INSTRUCTION.

His original plan had been to sidetrack vials of a certain drug which was destined for the forty largest cities in the United States, empty them of their contents and replace with his own creation. It would have been a slow and dangerous process. On arrival at work on his first day, however, he had realized it wasn't necessary. The glass vials he had used in Lebanon were so close in appearance to those used by Chyron that even an expert eye would have been hard pressed to tell the difference. All he needed to do was put labels on them.

Immediately, he had started experimenting with solvents which would lift the labels off the legitimate drugs without damaging them. He needed the labels intact, and he found what he was looking for in a large art-supply store – a common solution which neutralized most commercial glues.

Ten half-gallon containers of it were already stored in his locker and the only job that remained for him was to lift the labels off the genuine drugs and re-glue them to the tiny bottles of smallpox virus. They would then be shipped to America in perfect disguise, distributed to the forty cities and, he was confident, the US health-care system would do the rest.

He was aware that changing the labels would be a long and laborious process but, fortunately, he worked alone on the graveyard shift and there was little real work to distract him. He had run it through in his head so many times – even spending one night timing himself – that he knew he would hit his deadline.

There were nine days to go.

Chapter Sixty-four

AFTER DRIVING THE SEVEN HUNDRED MILES BACK I ARRIVED IN BODRUM in the early afternoon, still trying to reconcile what I knew of Leyla Cumali's life with her role in the imminent conflagration.

I had stopped twice on the way for gas and coffee and, each time, I had checked my phone and laptop, hoping for news from Battleboi. But there was nothing, and the only email was two spam messages which had been filtered and gone straight to the junk folder. I was getting increasingly frustrated and worried – maybe the Samurai hacker wasn't going to be any better than the CIA – so when I saw the manager hurrying across the foyer towards me, I figured another disaster must have come down the pike.

It turned out I was so tired I had misread the cues: he was hurrying because he couldn't believe I was back. I quickly realized that he had thought my story about visiting Bulgaria was bullshit and that, having killed SpongeBob, I was gone for good.

'You are a person of the many great surprises,' he said, shaking my hand warmly. 'Perhaps all of the men of the FBI are just as you?'

'Handsome and intelligent?' I said. 'No, just me.'

He clapped me on the back and spoke quietly. 'There has been nobody of the visit for you. The newspaper say the man was of the robber type, probably for the drug using.'

Relieved at that break, I thanked him and went to my room. Immediately, I checked my laptop for emails, but there was still nothing from Battleboi and I figured that, despite my fatigue, sleep would be impossible – every few minutes I would be looking to see if there was a message.

Instead, I pulled out the files on Dodge's death that Cumali had

510

given me and sat down at the desk. While I was waiting, I would see if I could find a trace of an American woman, one with a Midwestern accent.

Chapter Sixty-five

I CAUGHT MY FIRST GLIMPSE OF HER AFTER FORTY MINUTES. IT WAS JUST a few words in a record of an interview, but it was enough.

Cumali and her team had asked Dodge and Cameron's friends to recount how they knew the wealthy couple and to list the times they had spent together in Bodrum. It was standard stuff, the cops trying to build a picture of their lives, and, thankfully, most of the transcripts were in English.

Among them was one with a young guy called Nathanial Clunies-Ross, the scion of a hugely wealthy British banking dynasty who had known Dodge for years.

He and his girlfriend had come down from St Tropez to spend a week with Dodge and his new wife. There was nothing remarkable in that – apart from him being twenty-six and having a hundred-million-dollar boat to cruise around on – and I ploughed through half a dozen pages as he catalogued the bankrupt lives of some seriously wealthy people.

On the last page he gave a brief account of a vodka-fuelled night at a popular dance club called Club Zulu just along the coast. He said that six of them had flown in by chopper and, near the end of the evening, Cameron had run into a young woman called Ingrid – part of a larger party – who was a casual acquaintance.

The two groups had ended up sitting together, and the most interesting thing, according to Clunies-Ross, was that one of the guys in Ingrid's party – he couldn't recall his name, but he was pretty sure he was Italian and probably her boyfriend – had described his adventures with middle-aged vacationers. 'He ran a massage service on the beach,' Clunies-Ross had explained.

I started reading fast, the fatigue vanishing and my concentration roaring back. I sped through the rest of his interview but could find no further mention of Gianfranco or, more importantly, of the woman called Ingrid.

I turned to the back of the file and found the documents supporting the interview, including screen-grabs from CCTV cameras at Club Zulu – grainy and distorted. The last of them showed a group of people, obviously pretty loaded, leaving the club. I saw Cameron and Dodge, a guy I figured was Clunies-Ross with his girlfriend – all cleavage and legs – and right at the back, almost obscured, Gianfranco.

He had his arm around an arresting woman – short-cropped hair, an even shorter skirt, tanned and lithe, one of those young women who seem totally at ease in their own skin. By a quirk of circumstance, she was staring at the camera – she had large eyes, set a little deeper than you might have expected, and it gave the impression that she was looking straight through you. All my intuition, distilled and sharpened through countless hard missions and a thousand sleepless nights, told me it was Ingrid.

I turned and rummaged through the other files: somewhere, there was a master list, an index of all the names that had arisen during the investigation. There were scores of them, but there was only one Ingrid.

Ingrid Kohl.

The index linked to the information the cops had assembled about her. I turned to Volume B, page 46, and saw that it was almost non-existent – she was such a no-account acquaintance, her interaction with Cameron and Dodge so minor, that the cops hadn't even bothered talking to her. They did, however, take a copy of her passport.

I looked at the photo in the book. It was the woman with the short-cropped hair at Club Zulu – Ingrid Kohl.

There was no interview, but some things were certain: she knew Cameron, she was a friend or something more intimate of Gianfranco's and she was American. The passport said she came from Chicago, the heart of the Midwest.

Chapter Sixty-six

I WORKED THROUGH OTHER FILES, HOPING TO FIND ANOTHER MENTION of her or more photos, but there was nothing – just the one reference by the visiting banker and a poor-quality image from the surveillance camera.

In the fading afternoon I kept returning to it and, even though I took a long march through the attic of my memory, I couldn't recall anybody as attractive as Ms Kohl. On a professional level, I kept trying to match a voice to the image and thinking about gardenias . . .

When the computer beeped, telling me that I had mail, I figured it had to be Battleboi and I turned fast to the laptop – only to be disappointed. It was more spam and it had also gone to the junk folder.

Where the hell was the Samurai? I asked myself in frustration, marking the crap messages for deletion. I saw they were for some prize-winning scam and hit the button to consign them to oblivion. Nothing happened – they were still there. I hit the button again, with the same result, and realized what a fool I had been. The messages, disguised as spam, were from Battleboi.

When I had first met him and we were sitting in Old Japan expunging Scott Murdoch's academic record, he had told me that he had recently designed a particularly nasty virus that looked identical to the countless spam messages circulating in cyberspace. It was so obvious that even the most primitive filter would recognize it and send it to the junk-mail folder. When the unsuspecting owner – thinking that the filter had done its job – tried to delete the message, he would inadvertently activate it. Immediately, it would download a virus, a spyware Trojan or any other program Battleboi deemed

514

necessary – for instance, a key-stroke logger to record credit-card information.

Having been busted by the Feds, he had never got the chance to deploy his new spam bomb, until now, and I knew that I had already downloaded the information he had discovered about Leyla al-Nassouri-Cumali. All I had to do was find it.

I opened the first of the spam messages and was delighted to read that I was the lucky winner of an online sweepstake. In order to claim my winnings of $24,796,321.81 it was only necessary for me to send an email and they would reply with an authorization code and a list of instructions. The other spam emails were reminders, urging me not to delay and risk missing out on my windfall.

I tried clicking on the payout button without the authorization, but nothing happened. I figured that what I was really looking for was an encryption code which would unlock a hidden file, and I was starting to wonder if Battleboi was going to send it in a separate mail when I realized I already had it.

I copied the numerals of my winnings, deleted the commas and dot, entered it as the authorization code and hit payout. It sure did.

A document opened and I saw a picture of Leyla Cumali, aged about sixteen, taken from a driver's licence. Underneath it was a list of everything Battleboi had found out up to that point and, glancing through it, I saw that he had – exactly as I had hoped – certainly coloured outside the lines.

He said that he figured – as Cumali was a cop – that she had to be educated and, as a result, he had decided to try to track her through her schooling. The strategy gave him one huge advantage: it greatly reduced the number of people he was investigating. Shocking as it was, over 45 per cent of Arab women couldn't read or write.

He took six Arab nations and started searching middle and high schools. He found only one Leyla al-Nassouri of the right age – in an online archive from a school in Bahrain where she had won an essay competition in English.

He lost her for a while but discovered that, in the Arabic language, Leyla means 'born at night', and he started trawling through blogs and social networking sites using several dozen variations of that. Under the name Midnight he unearthed a woman who had posted several items on a local blog about scuba diving in Bahrain.

He managed to access their database and learned that Midnight was the online handle of Leyla al-Nassouri, and it gave him an email address which she had been using back then. Figuring that she was over seventeen, and armed with her name and the email address, he tried to get into the Bahrain Department of Motor Vehicles in the hope that he could locate the details of a driver's licence. It took him over four hours of brute-force hacking, but he finally broke into their network and found her application. It provided the photo and also her date and place of birth.

She had been born in Saudi Arabia.

Battleboi said that she faded away and he could find nothing more on her, not until two years later, when he located a photo and a precis of her academic career at a law college in Istanbul.

'That's all I have at the moment,' he wrote.

I closed the pages and sat in quiet thought. I saw her again – approaching the phone box, speaking to a terrorist in the Hindu Kush, the most wanted man in the world – an Arab woman who got an education, went scuba diving, learned to drive and travelled far away to attend college.

Battleboi had done a great job, but things were no clearer. Leyla Cumali might have been born in Saudi, but it still didn't make any sense.

Chapter Sixty-seven

I WALKED. I HUNCHED MY SHOULDERS, BURIED MY HANDS IN MY pockets and grappled once again with the contradictions of Cumali's life.

I had left the hotel, wandered through a maze of small streets and, by the time I had tried a hundred different ways to square the damned circle, I found myself at the beach. It was late afternoon and still warm – the last flicker of summer before autumn really blew in.

I sat on a bench and looked across the foreign sea, turquoise and almost other-worldly in its brilliance. A father was splashing water with his three kids in the narrow zone where the water met the sand. Their laughter filled the air and, from there, it was only a small step for me to start musing about a little boy who had no father to splash water with and didn't even know what Down's syndrome was.

The kids' mother walked close to take a photograph of her children just as I was thinking about Cumali and the quiet heart-break she must have experienced when she saw the telltale single crease across the palm of her newborn baby's hand and realized that he was the one in seven hundred.

The whole world seemed to slow: the glittering water from the kids' buckets hung suspended in the air, the father's laughing face barely seemed to move, the mother's hand froze on the shutter. My mind had run aground on a strange thought.

Evidence is the name we give to what we have, but what about the things we haven't found? Sometimes the things that are missing are of far greater importance.

In all the time I had spent searching Cumali's apartment I hadn't seen one photo of her with the baby. There were none of her with

517

him as a newborn on her desk, not one of her playing with him as a toddler and no portraits on the wall. I hadn't found any in the drawers and I had seen none in frames beside her bed. Why would you keep an album of photographs of a failed marriage and have nothing of you as a family or of the little guy as a baby? Weren't they the things mothers always kept? Unless . . .

He wasn't her child.

Still the water hung in the air, the mother kept the camera to her face and the father was caught in the middle of laughing. I wondered why I hadn't considered it before: she had arrived with her son in Bodrum three years previously with her husband left far behind and no friends or acquaintances to contradict her. She could have told people whatever story she wanted.

And if he wasn't her child, whose was he?

The water fell to the ground, the mother took her photograph, the father threw a splash of water back at his kids and I started to run.

It was dinner time and I figured if I was fast enough I could get to Cumali's house before she did the washing-up.

Chapter Sixty-eight

CUMALI OPENED THE DOOR WEARING A CASUAL SHIRT, A PAIR OF JEANS and an oven mitt. As she wasn't expecting any visitors, she had dispensed with the scarf and tied her hair back in a ponytail – I have to say it suited her, accentuating her high cheekbones and large eyes, and I was struck again by how attractive she was.

She didn't appear embarrassed about being seen with her hair uncovered and a shirt open at the throat, merely pissed off at being disturbed at home.

'What do you want?' she asked.

'Your help,' I replied. 'May I come in?'

'No – I'm busy, I'm just about to serve dinner.'

I was ready to start arguing – to be as insistent as necessary – but I was saved the trouble. The little guy emerged from the kitchen, saw me and started to run. Calling happily in Turkish, he came to a halt, gathered himself together and gave a perfect bow.

'Very good,' I said, laughing.

'It ought to be – he's been practising every day,' Cumali said, her voice softening, pushing some wayward strands of the little guy's hair back into place.

'It'll only take a few minutes,' I said, and after a pause she stepped back, letting me in – more for her son, if that's what he was, than from any desire to help me.

I walked down the corridor ahead of them, making sure to look around, curious, as if I had never been in the house before. The little guy was right behind, chatting away in Turkish, demanding that his mom translate.

'He wants to take you on a picnic,' she said. 'He saw a programme on TV about an American boy. Apparently, that's what best friends do.'

I didn't joke – it meant everything to the child. 'A picnic? Of course,' I said, stopping to bend down to him. 'Any time you want – that's a promise.'

We stepped into the kitchen and, using her oven mitt, she went to the stove and pulled a tagine – a Moroccan casserole pot – off the heat, tasted its contents with a short wooden spoon and served herself and her son. She didn't offer me any – a real affront in the Muslim world, where, due to the prohibition on alcohol, most hospitality revolved around food – and it was clear she wanted to be rid of me as soon as possible.

'You said you wanted my help – what is it?' she asked, as soon as she sat down and started to eat.

'You remember a woman called Ingrid Kohl?' I said, thanking God for a cover story good enough to get me into her house.

She paused, having to think, while the little guy smiled at me and took a drink from his Mickey Mouse glass.

'Ingrid Kohl,' Cumali said. 'A backpacker . . . American . . . an acquaintance of Cameron, or something. Is that her?'

'Yeah. Have you got anything else on her?'

'She was peripheral; I don't think we even interviewed her. You came here at dinner time to ask about her? Why?'

'I think she and Cameron know each other. I think they've known each other for a long time. I suspect they're lovers.'

She stared at me, her fork halfway to her mouth. 'Do you have any evidence – or is this just wishful thinking?'

'You mean like the mirrors?' I said sharply. 'There's evidence – I just need to firm it up.'

'So you're telling me she knows how to get on to the estate, that she's a suspect?'

'That's exactly what I'm saying. But I have to hear her voice.'

'Her voice?'

'I'll take you through it when I know for sure,' I replied. I didn't want to get into a long discussion about Dodge's death, I just wanted to get her out of the damn kitchen and take the items I had already identified.

'Can you get the two women down to the precinct house in the morning?' I asked. 'I want to hear Ingrid's voice then put some questions to her and Cameron.'

Cumali was anything but enthusiastic. 'Cameron has already given an extensive interview. I'd have to know more—'

'I want to wrap it up quickly,' I interrupted. 'I want to get out of Turkey as soon as possible. With your help, I think I can do that.'

Maybe it was the hard insistence in my voice – more likely it was the thought of getting rid of me – but, for whatever reason, she gave in. 'All right, I'll call Hayrunnisa first thing tomorrow and get her to organize it.'

'Can you call her now, please?' I had already checked out the kitchen and couldn't see her handbag or cellphone. I was hoping it was in another room.

'Call her at home, you mean?'

'Yes.'

'No. Like I said, I'll phone her in the morning.'

'Then give me the number,' I replied. 'I'll do it.'

She looked at me, exasperated, then sighed, got to her feet and went towards the living room to get her phone.

I acted fast, meowing to the cat, which was watching me from the corner. It worked, making the little guy laugh and look in the opposite direction. I moved behind him and had the first item in my pocket before he saw it.

By the time he turned in my direction I was at the stove with my back towards him, and he couldn't see me reach for the second item. In order to divert him, I pulled my phone out as I turned to face him and started pulling silly faces and shooting photos of him.

It made him laugh again, and that's what he was doing when his mother walked back in, cellphone to her ear, talking in Turkish to Hayrunnisa. Cumali hung up and looked at me.

'She'll call them at eight in the morning and tell them to be in the office at ten. Satisfied?'

'Thank you.'

'Now, can my son and I have our dinner?'

'Of course,' I said. 'I'll let myself out.'

I bowed to the little guy, turned and went out the front door. I made a right, headed towards the nearest main road and started to run. I only stopped when I was lucky enough to find a vacant cab going back to town from the port.

I told the driver I wanted to go to some souvenir shops, and directed him towards the ones I had seen on my first day in Bodrum.

It was getting late, but I knew they stayed open all hours and that the largest of them was an agent for FedEx.

Inside, I bought half a dozen souvenirs and told the old guy behind the counter I wanted to express courier them to New York – all I needed was a box to pack them in. I addressed it to Ben Bradley at the precinct house and included a note so that if anybody in Turkey inspected the parcel they would think it was innocent enough – a cop on assignment was sending the guys at the office a few mementoes to make them envious.

I told Bradley to distribute the claret-coloured fezes among the other detectives, the plastic belly-dancer lamp was for his desk and the other two items were for our mutual friend. 'Don't worry, he'll get the joke,' I wrote.

Of course it was no joke – in another hour I would call Bradley and tell him exactly what I wanted done with the wooden tasting spoon and the Mickey Mouse cup.

Lift off the dried saliva and have it DNA-tested as fast as possible, I would say. Only then would I know the exact relationship between Cumali and the little guy.

Chapter Sixty-nine

THERE HAD BEEN A CHANGE OF PLAN. I ARRIVED AT THE STATION HOUSE a few minutes before ten the next morning to find that Ingrid Kohl had said she was fighting a cold and couldn't make it until later in the day. Maybe it was the truth – who would have known?

Cameron, on the other hand, hadn't even been spoken to – not personally. Hayrunnisa had called the boat, but the young woman's personal assistant had refused to wake her.

'My instructions are clear – she's not to be disturbed. When Madame gets up I'll ask her to call you.'

I told Hayrunnisa to phone me as soon as either of them arrived, but, as it turned out, I was sitting on the sidewalk of a nearby café two hours later – tracking the progress of the FedEx package on my cellphone, learning that it had made it overnight to New York and was about to be delivered – when I first saw Ingrid.

She was coming down the street towards me, a cheap bag over her shoulder, a pair of fake Tom Ford sunglasses pushed back on her head, a young dog – a total mutt – on a piece of rope. Current 'it' girls were all walking designer dogs that month, and Ingrid either didn't give a shit or was taking the piss out of them. I almost laughed.

Except for one thing: the grainy photo hadn't done her justice. She was taller than she had appeared and, in a pair of denim shorts and a thin white T-shirt, she revealed a sensuality which I hadn't anticipated. Her short hair had grown out a little, and it made her blue eyes seem even deeper set and gave the impression that she could look straight through you.

She was stunning, no doubt about it – five hip young guys staring from a nearby table proved that – but if she was even aware of it she seemed to give it no importance. Maybe that was why she could carry everything off – even the damned dog.

A long time back, I said that there were places I would remember all my life. People, too. And I knew then, sitting in a nondescript café under the hot Turkish sun, that the first sight of her would be one of those things that would stay with me for ever.

She stepped off the sidewalk and moved through the café's tables, heading towards the take-away section. As she passed the hip guys – Serbs, from the language they were speaking – one of them reached out and caught her by the wrist.

'What sort of dog is he?' the guy – designer stubble, his shirt unbuttoned, ink around one bicep – asked in accented English.

She looked at him with a stare withering enough to burn the stubble. 'Let go of my arm, please,' she said.

The guy didn't. 'It's just a question,' he replied, smiling.

'He's a German breed,' Ingrid said. 'A dickhound.'

'A what?' the guy said.

'A dickhound. I point a guy out to him and he brings their dick back in his mouth. Wanna see?'

The dog growled on cue and the smile vanished from the guy's face – his anger heightened by his four friends laughing at him. Ingrid pulled her hand away and continued towards the bar.

I sat and concentrated on the sound of her, but it wasn't as clear-cut as I had thought: she had been telling the truth about having a cold, and her voice was rasping and distorted by it. The acoustics in the mansion had also been totally different – the sheer scale of the place had added a sort of reverb – and I had only heard her at a distance. While my feeling was that it had been her in the bedroom, I couldn't be sure.

Full of doubt, I looked at her again, as she stood at the bar with the mutt, and I had to be honest. Maybe I didn't want her to be the killer.

Chapter Seventy

INGRID EMERGED FROM THE BACK OF THE STATION HOUSE, ACCOMPANIED by yet another kid-cop in dazzling boots. She tied the dickhound to the handrail of the steps and climbed towards Cumali's office.

I had left the café ahead of her so that I would be ready when she arrived and was sitting at a conference table in a corner of the office watching her out of the window. Cumali herself had begged off, saying she had to devote herself to a more pressing matter – the search for SpongeBob's killer.

'I was looking for Detective Cumali,' Ingrid said as she entered, not noticing me in the corner. It gave me another opportunity to hear her voice, but I was still too uncertain to call it.

'I'm afraid the detective isn't here,' Hayrunnisa replied. 'I think this gentleman can help you.'

Ingrid turned and saw me, and I watched her eyes drop to my dumb FBI-style shoes, run slowly up my shapeless pants then pause for a moment on the cheap shirt and unattractive tie. I felt like all I needed was a pocket protector.

Having seen her at the café, I had no need to return the appraisal and the cool indifference with which I stared at her gave me a small advantage.

Then she smiled and the advantage disappeared. 'And you are?' she asked. I had a sense she already knew.

'My name is B. D. Wilson,' I said. 'I'm with the FBI.'

Most people – even those without anything to hide – feel a frisson of fear when they hear those words. If Ingrid Kohl did, she showed no sign of it. 'Then I can't see how you can help me. I was told I was here to pick up my passport.'

She gave Hayrunnisa the withering look and I realized that the secretary had told Ms Kohl whatever had come to mind in order to make sure she showed up. It was probably standard operating procedure in Turkish police departments.

Rather than let Hayrunnisa twist in the wind, I answered for her. 'I'm sure we can do that. I just have a few questions first.'

Ingrid dropped her bag on the floor and sat down. 'Go ahead,' she said. She wasn't easily flustered.

I placed a small digital video camera on the desk, clicked a button, checked that it was recording both sound and vision and spoke into it, giving her full name from the passport copy I had in front of me, the time and the date.

I saw her looking closely at the device, but I paid it no attention. I should have. Instead, I turned to her and told her that I was a sworn law-enforcement officer and that I was investigating Dodge's death.

'It's now a murder case,' I said.

'So I heard.'

'Who from?'

'Everybody. It's the only thing American backpackers are talking about.'

'Where did you meet him and his wife?'

She told me they had seen each other at various clubs and bars but had never spoken. 'Then everything changed one night outside a club called The Suppository.'

'There's a club called The Suppository?' I asked. I mean, you'd have to question it, wouldn't you?

'Not really. Its name is The Texas Book Depository – you know, Kennedy and Oswald – run by a couple of hipsters from LA, but it's such a dump everyone calls it The Suppository.'

'Anyway, I'd just left with some friends when I saw a stray dog lying behind some trash. He'd been badly bashed and I was trying to work out how to get him on to my moped when Dodge and Cameron arrived.

'They called for a car and we got him to a vet. After that, if I saw 'em around, we'd talk – mostly about the dog.'

'So you knew Dodge well enough that if you walked into his house one night with alarming news he'd know who you were?'

She shrugged, appearing confused. 'I guess.'

'That's the dog, is it?' I asked, motioning towards the window.

'Yeah.'

I kept talking while I consulted my notes, just filling in the silence. 'What's the dog's name?'

'Gianfranco,' she said.

I didn't react. 'Italian, huh?'

'Yeah, he reminded me of a guy I knew – some dogs have just gotta hunt.'

I smiled and looked up. 'Have you got family, Ms Kohl?'

'Somewhere.'

'Chicago?'

'All over. Married, divorced, married again, separated. You know the deal.'

'Brothers, sisters?'

'Three stepbrothers; none that I care to know.'

'And you moved on from Chicago, is that right?'

'I went to New York, if that's what you mean – for about eight months – but I didn't like it, so I applied for a passport and headed over here. I'm sure you've got all that on some database.'

I ignored it and ploughed on. 'You came to Europe alone?'

'Yes.'

'Brave, wasn't it?'

She just shrugged, not bothering to answer. She was smart, but far more than that – she was self-contained, you got the feeling she didn't need anybody.

'How have you been living – money-wise, I mean?'

'How does anyone? I work. Cafés, bars, four weeks as a door bitch at a club in Berlin. I make enough to get by.'

'What about the future?'

'You know – marriage, a couple of kids, a house in the suburbs. The guy would have to dress sharp, though – somebody like you, Mr Wilson. You married?'

Yeah, I could go for her, I told myself. With an axe handle. 'I meant the more immediate future.'

'Summer's almost gone. Maybe I'll head to Perugia in Italy – there's a university for foreigners there that a lot of people talk about.'

I glanced up from my notes, checked the camera was working and looked at her. 'Are you gay or bisexual, Ms Kohl?'

She met the Defcon 1 full on. 'And tell me,' she replied, 'which side of the fence do you farm, Mr Wilson?'

'That's not relevant,' I replied evenly.

'Exactly how I feel about your question,' she responded.

'There's a big difference. It's been suggested that Cameron is bisexual.'

'So what? You need to get out more. A lot of modern chicks are – I think they got so sick of men they decided to try the other team.'

Before I could respond to the theory, I heard the sound of heels clicking on the linoleum in the hallway.

Cameron walked in.

Chapter Seventy-one

INGRID TURNED AND, THANKS TO A FORTUITOUS ARRANGEMENT OF THE chairs, I was looking at both of them at the precise moment they saw each other.

No flicker of affection, no secret sign of acknowledgement, passed between them. They looked at one another exactly as you would expect of casual acquaintances. If they were acting, they sure carried it off – then again, for a billion-two you'd expect a good perform-ance, wouldn't you?

'Hi,' Cameron said to Ingrid, extending her hand. 'I didn't expect to see you here. They said I could get my passport.'

'Me too,' Ingrid replied bitterly, and jerked a thumb accusingly in Hayrunnisa's direction. 'Mr Wilson here was just asking if you were bisexual.'

'Oh, yeah?' Cameron replied. 'And what did you tell him?' She pulled out a seat and sat down. She had no apparent anxiety either, and I had to admire their self-possession.

'I said you were – but only with black chicks. I figured as we were dealing with a male fantasy we might as well go the whole nine yards.'

Cameron laughed.

'Murder isn't a male fantasy,' I said.

I told Cameron it was now a homicide investigation, and I explained about the fireworks and taking the mirrors to Florence. All the time, however, I was trying to assess the two of them, to get some clue to their actual relationship – were they lovers or just two attractive women who had drifted into Bodrum and were nothing more than ships in the night? Was it Ingrid I had heard in the bedroom? Who was the woman who knew about the secret passage and – I was certain – had induced Dodge to go to the cliff and then tipped him over the edge?

'I have a photograph of Dodge and the killer in the library together. All I need is the face,' I said.

They both looked at me, shocked at the existence of the photo – that was gossip they hadn't heard.

'Was it your idea – developing the mirrors?' Ingrid asked, and I sensed a change in the atmosphere. She may not have thought much of my clothes, but she had a new-found respect for my abilities.

'Yeah,' I replied.

'Helluva thing to come up with,' she said thoughtfully.

I started to explain the difficulties facing somebody attempting to get on to the estate unseen. 'There has to be a secret pathway, a passage, so to speak.'

But I didn't get any further. Ingrid bent down and lifted her cheap bag on to the table. 'Sorry,' she said. 'I need something for my cold.'

While she was trying to find the throat lozenges, the bag slipped and spilled its contents on to the table and floor. Cameron and I bent and picked up lipsticks, change, a battered camera and a dozen other trivial things. As I stood up, I saw that Ingrid was gathering the remainder of her stuff off the table and putting it back in her bag. Still unclaimed was a glass tube with a picture of a flower etched into its side.

'Perfume?' I said, picking it up.

'Yeah,' she replied. 'I got it in the Grand Bazaar in Istanbul – some guy blends it by hand. It's a bit strong – can take out an elephant at fifty paces.'

I smiled, took the cap off and sprayed my hand. 'Gardenia,' I said.

She looked at my face, and she knew something was wrong. 'What are you – a fucking horticulturalist?' She tried to laugh, and took the perfume back, but it was too late.

All the doubts I had about her voice had been dispelled. I knew with certainty it had been her in Cameron's bedroom: when I stepped out of the guest room and headed for the secret elevator I had smelt the same unique scent hanging in the hallway after she had passed.

'No, not a horticulturalist,' I said. 'I'm a special agent with the FBI investigating several murders. Gianfranco, the guy you named your dog after – how long did you date him?'

She and Cameron heard the aggression in my voice and they knew that everything had changed.

'What's Gianfranco got to do with anything?' Ingrid asked.

'Answer the question, Ms Kohl.'

'I don't recall.'

'He showed you the tunnel into the house?'

'What house?'

'Cameron's.'

'There's no tunnel into my house,' Cameron offered.

I turned to her, surprised at my own anger – Dodge was her husband, and in all the interviews her friends had said that he adored her. 'Don't tell me there's no tunnel – I've walked along it.'

'So? Even if there is,' Ingrid interrupted, 'nobody ever showed it to me.'

'Gianfranco says that he did.' I was making it up, hoping to shake the hell out of her. It didn't work.

'Then he's a liar,' she shot back. Cameron had been badly thrown by both the information and my anger, but not Ingrid – she stepped up to the line and came right back at me.

'You believe him?' she said. 'Franco's your witness? A guy who feels up middle-aged women on the beach for ten and change. Any decent lawyer would tear him to shreds. Did you ask him about dealing weed, huh? Or find out that his name's not Gianfranco and he's not Italian – but what woman is gonna have a fantasy about getting head from a guy called Abdul? But you knew that, of course—'

She looked at my face as I was inwardly berating myself – I had sensed there was something in Gianfranco's English that was more Istanbul than Naples, but I hadn't taken the time to think it through.

'Oh, I see the nationality escaped you,' she said, smiling.

'It's not relevant. I don't care what his name or country is.'

'*I* care,' she responded. 'It goes to the question of credibility. Gianfranco's got none and so far you're batting on less.'

'You a lawyer, Ms Kohl?'

'No – but I read a lot.'

There was something in the way she delivered the line and turned her eyes on me that made me think of bare boards and a cold rehearsal room. I took a stab.

'Where was it – New York, LA?'

'Where was what?'

'You studied acting.'

Ingrid didn't react, but I saw Cameron glance at her and I knew I was right.

'You can theorize whatever you like,' she responded. 'If Abdul – I mean, Gianfranco – knows a secret way into the house, then I would say it's him in the photo. He probably killed Dodge.'

'That makes no sense,' I retorted. 'What's the motive?'

'What's mine?'

'I think you and Cameron are lovers. I think you both planned it and did it for the money.'

She laughed. 'Cameron and I are strangers. We've run into each other half a dozen times. The longest time we've spent together was in a vet's surgery. Some love affair.'

'That's all true for Ingrid Kohl,' I said. 'But I don't believe you are really Ingrid Kohl—'

'Then take a look at my passport,' she fired back. 'This is total bullshit. Jesus! Of course I'm Ingrid Kohl.'

'No,' I replied. 'I think you stole an identity. I think you're acting a part. I believe that, whatever your real name is, you and Cameron have known each other for a long time – maybe you even grew up together. You left Turkey Scratch, or wherever it was, and went to New York. Then both of you came to Bodrum for one reason – to kill Dodge. That's a capital crime and, even if you avoid the injection, you'll both spend the rest of your lives in jail.'

Ingrid smiled. 'Turkey Scratch? That's funny. You make that up – like you did the rest of it?'

'We'll see. I'm not done yet—'

'Well, I am.' She turned to Cameron. 'I don't know about you, but I want a lawyer.'

'Yeah, I need legal advice too,' Cameron replied, looking like a deer in the headlights. She grabbed her bag and started to stand.

'No,' I said. 'I've got a series of questions.'

'Are we being charged?' Ingrid demanded.

I didn't say anything – it was clear she wasn't easily bullied.

'I thought so,' she said into the silence. 'You can't hold us, can you? You don't have any jurisdiction here.' She smiled.

Cameron was already heading for the door. Ingrid picked up the throat lozenges and tossed them into her bag. As she slung it over her shoulder she turned and stood close to me. I couldn't help it, I felt like I was flying a kite in a thunderstorm.

'You think you're very smart, but you don't know about me or Cameron or anything. You don't know half of what's happening. Nowhere near. You're lost and you're grasping at straws, that's what this is all about. Sure, you figure you've got some evidence. Let me tell you something else I read – "evidence is a list of the material you've got. What about the things you haven't found? What do you call that?"'

It was my turn to smile. 'Good quote – a fine piece of writing,' I said. I knew then it was she who had killed the woman in New York and dumped her in a bath of acid.

'The quote comes from a book called *Principles of Modern Investigative Technique* by a man called Jude Garrett,' I continued. 'And I know where you got that book – you borrowed it from the New York Public Library on a fake Florida driver's licence. You took it back to Room 89 at the Eastside Inn, where you were living, and used it as a manual to kill someone. How's that for evidence?'

She looked at me expressionless – my God, it was a triumph of self-control on her part. But her silence told me it had rocked her world, ripped the canvas of her meticulous crime from top to bottom.

She pivoted and walked out. I figured that, within an hour, Cameron would be lawyering up, paying for a regiment of top-flight advisers, but it wouldn't help them much – I understood what they had done, everything from the day the Twin Towers fell to the real reason why there were lacerations on Dodge's hands.

I paid no attention, however, to what she had said about not understanding the half of it. I thought it was just boasting, cheap bar-talk, but that was underestimating her. I should have picked up every stitch, I should have listened and thought about every word.

I glanced up and caught Hayrunnisa's eye. She was staring at me, seriously impressed. 'Wow!' she said.

I smiled modestly. 'Thank you.'

'Not *you*,' she replied. 'Her. Wow!'

If I was honest, though, I agreed. Ingrid Kohl – or whatever her name was – had done a great job during the interview, better than I had ever expected. Even so, there was plenty of stuff on the camera that I knew would help convict her in court. I picked up the device and I couldn't help myself – I started laughing.

'What is it?' Hayrunnisa asked.

'You were right,' I said. 'Wow! It was no accident she spilled the stuff out of her bag – it was a diversion. She turned the fucking camera off.'

Chapter Seventy-two

I WAS WALKING ALONG THE MARINA, FOOTSORE AND HUNGRY, BUT TOO anxious to eat or to rest. It had been three hours since I had slipped the battery back into my phone and left Cumali's office and already I had covered the beach, the Old Town and now the waterfront.

Twice I had started to dial Bradley, desperate to hear the results of the DNA tests, but I stopped myself in time. I had stressed to him on the phone how urgent it was and I knew that he and Whisperer would have made arrangements to speed them through the lab. He would call the moment he had them, but it didn't make it any easier. Come on, I kept saying to myself. *Come on.*

I was halfway between a group of seafood stands and several rowdy nautical bars when the phone rang. I answered it without even looking at the caller ID. 'Ben?' I said.

'We got the results,' he replied. 'No details yet, just a phone summary, but I figured you'd want them as soon as possible.'

'Go ahead,' I replied, trying to keep my voice neutral.

'The little guy is definitely not the woman's son.'

My response was to exhale – I was so wired I hadn't even realized I was holding my breath. Why the hell was Cumali raising him as her own then? I asked myself.

'But the two individuals are closely related,' Bradley continued. 'There's a 99.8 per cent probability that she is the boy's aunt.'

'His aunt?' I said, and repeated it to myself. His *aunt*?

'What about the father? Can they tell us anything about that?' I asked.

'Yes – the father of the child is the woman's brother.'

So, I thought, Leyla Cumali was bringing up her brother's son. I

535

felt a rising tide of excitement – of sudden clarity – but I didn't say anything.

'That's all I can tell you at the moment,' Bradley said.

'Okay,' I said coolly, and hung up.

I stood still, blocking out the sound of the drinkers in the bars. Leyla Cumali's brother had a little boy and she was raising him – in complete secrecy – as her own child.

Again, I asked myself, why? Why lie about it? What was there to be ashamed of in taking care of your nephew?

I thought of the morning when I had met her at the corner park – of the anger that had greeted my intrusion and the furtive way in which she had gathered up the little guy. I recalled thinking then that I had walked into a secret. It wasn't normal; none of those things made any sense.

Unless, of course, the father was an outlaw – a soldier in a secret war, for instance. A man always on the move, a man wanted for *jihad* or terrorism or something worse . . .

Maybe such a person would have handed his son over to his sister to raise.

In those circumstances, Leyla Cumali-al-Nassouri would have reacted with alarm when an American, an investigator, showed up and discovered the boy's existence.

But what about the little guy's mother? Where was she? Dead, probably – bombed or shot in any one of the dozen countries where Muslim women are cut down on a daily basis.

I found a bench, sat down and stared at the ground. After a long time I looked up and, from that moment forward, with an overwhelming sense that I had reached a watershed, I no longer believed that Leyla al-Nassouri had been speaking on the phone to a terrorist. I believed she had been talking to her brother.

At last I had squared my circle – I understood the real connection between an Arab fanatic and a moderate Turkish cop. They hadn't been discussing the mechanics of a deadly plot or the kill-rate of smallpox. We had assumed they were and had gone charging through the door marked 'terrorism', but the truth was far more human: they were family.

Yes, she probably knew he was an outlaw, but I doubted she had any idea of the magnitude of the attack in which he was involved. There were countless Arab men who were Islamic fundamentalists and believed in *jihad* – twenty thousand on the US no-fly list alone – all of whom had some sort of price on their head and were trying to make sure that Echelon or its offspring couldn't find them. To her mind, he was probably one of them – a garden-variety fanatic. There was no evidence to show that she knew he was plotting murder on an industrial scale or that she was even aware he was in the Hindu Kush.

I started to walk fast, weaving through knots of vacationers, dodging traffic and heading towards the hotel. But what of the two phone calls? Why, at that critical time, had the Saracen risked everything to speak to her?

Like I said, I was finding clarity. In the filing cabinet in Cumali's bedroom I had found the bill from the regional hospital – the one that showed that the little guy had been admitted with meningococcal meningitis. I couldn't remember the exact date of his admission, but I didn't need to – I was certain it coincided with the two phone calls between Leyla Cumali and her brother.

Once she learned how gravely ill he was, she would have posted the coded note on the internet message board, telling the Saracen to phone her urgently. In her distress, she would have reasoned that a father had a right to know and, given her brother's religious devotion, he would have wanted to pray for his son.

Most sites that offer dating and personal ads automatically alert other users to posts that might interest them. The Saracen would have received a text message telling him that a fellow-devotee of an obscure poet – or something similar – had posted an item. Knowing it had to be bad news, he would have phoned her at the designated phone box and listened to her prerecorded coded message.

What a time that must have been for him. On a desolate mountaintop in Afghanistan, trying to test half a lifetime's work, three people dying of sledgehammer smallpox in a sealed hut, he aware that, if he was discovered, it would probably mean instant death, and then to be told that his son was critically – perhaps fatally – ill.

Desperate, he would have arranged to get an update from Cumali, and that was the second call he made. She would have told him that the drugs had worked, the crisis was past and his son was safe – that was why there were no more calls.

But there was one other thing I realized, and I couldn't avoid it – the Saracen must have loved the little guy with all his heart to have risked everything for a phone call. I didn't like it, I didn't like it at all – I knew from shooting the Rider of the Blue that if you're going to kill a man, far better it's a monster than a loving father.

I flew up the steps of the hotel, burst into my room, threw a change of clothes into a bag and grabbed my passport. I knew the Saracen's surname now, the same as his sister's – al-Nassouri – and I knew where the family came from.

I was going to Saudi Arabia.

Part Four

Chapter One

TURKISH AIRLINES FLIGHT 473 TOOK OFF FROM MILAS AIRPORT, BANKED hard through the setting sun and headed across a corner of the Mediterranean towards Beirut.

After leaving the hotel, I got in the Fiat, drove hard to the airport and took the first plane that was heading south – anything that would get me closer to Saudi Arabia.

My idea was to save as much time as possible. While I was in the air I would call ahead and organize for a US government jet to rendezvous with me halfway there – on the runway in Lebanon.

No sooner had the sparkling waters of the Mediterranean come into view and the FASTEN SEATBELT sign been turned off than I took my cellphone and headed for the bathroom. With the door locked and no time to worry about who might be eavesdropping, I called Battleboi in New York. First, I had to know where the hell in Saudi I was going.

Rachel-san picked up. 'It's me,' I said, without further identification. 'I need to talk to the big guy.'

'Listen,' I said, as soon as he had come to the phone. I didn't have time for small talk. 'You said you found the woman's application for a driver's licence—'

'That's right.'

'She was born in Saudi – where? What town?'

'Hold on,' he said, and I could hear him padding his way towards his office.

'The application's in front of me,' he said after a short break. ' "Jeddah", it says. A place called Jeddah.'

'Thanks,' I replied. 'Great work.' I was about to hang up, but he got in first.

'Did you hear what happened?' he asked.

'About Leavenworth?'

'Yeah. I told you they'd bleed me out then double-cross me. I hate this but . . . I have to ask . . . I need help.'

There was a catch in his voice, and he had to pause to master his emotions. 'I can do it – do the time, I mean – but I'll lose Rachel. She wants kids – I can't ask her to wait and give it up. Five years' reduction is all I'm asking. I don't know who you really are but—'

'That's enough,' I said, more harshly than I meant, but I couldn't allow him to go anywhere near the topic of my identity in case somebody was listening. 'I know people,' I said hurriedly. 'I promise – I'll do what I can.'

'Yeah, sure,' he said sarcastically and, while I understood that he had been used and screwed, I didn't appreciate it.

'I'm not like the people who nailed you,' I said, voice rising. 'If I give you my word, I mean it. I'll do *everything* possible. Okay?! Now, I've got a few problems of my own—'

'Sure, sure,' he said. I think he found my anger more reassuring than any words I could have said, and I hung up.

My next call was to Whisperer. Again, there was no need for introductions. 'I know his name,' I said quietly.

I don't think in the history of covert intelligence such a bombshell had ever been met by so much silence. After what seemed like an eternity, Whisperer responded: 'You mean the guy in Afghanistan?'

'Yeah. Name of al-Nassouri. He's the cop's brother.'

There it was – done. The organism had fulfilled its fate; it had relayed the information. If I had died then, it wouldn't have mattered – the mission would survive.

'What else?' Whisperer asked.

'Not much yet – born in Jeddah, Saudi Arabia,' I said.

'Saudi? Ask me why I'm not surprised,' Whisperer replied.

'Another few hours and I should have his full name and date of birth. I'm hoping to get a photo.'

'Where the hell are you?!' he asked suddenly. For only the second time in recorded history he had raised his voice. I figured that the automatic trace on my phone had just appeared on his computer screen and it was showing that I was in the middle of the Mediterranean. But it wasn't really about him being alarmed by my location – the emotion, the stress, the relief, had broken through for

Dave McKinley. We had a name, we had an identity, we had a man to hunt. Now it was just a matter of time.

'I'm on board TA473 en route to Beirut,' I said. 'I need assistance getting to Jeddah and a lot of help on the ground when I get there.'

'We'll talk about that in a minute. First, how long before you can give me an update with the rest of the details?'

I looked at my watch and did a fast calculation of flying time and document searches. 'Twelve hours – I should have what we need by then.'

'Sure?'

'Yeah.'

'I'm at the office now,' he said, 'but I won't be then. I'll be down the road – you know the place. We'll be waiting for your call.'

He meant the White House, and he'd be in the Oval Office with the president.

Chapter Two

I UNLOCKED THE BATHROOM DOOR AND CAME FACE TO FACE WITH HALF a dozen pissed-off passengers who had summoned a flight attendant. It was clear from the tilt of her jaw that she had justice on her mind.

'People have been knocking on the door,' she said icily.

'Yes, I heard 'em,' I replied. It was true, but what was I gonna do – hang up on the director of intelligence?

'You know it's an offence to use a cellphone in flight.'

I nodded. God, I was tired. 'Yeah,' I said. 'I know.'

'And you saw our video making that clear?'

'Sure, lady. But you know something – I don't *care.*'

The passengers glared at me, speaking in Turkish or Lebanese, as I went to my seat. Another ugly American, I guessed was what they were saying.

It was with some satisfaction then – after we had touched down in Beirut a short time later – that I realized we weren't heading to a gate. Instead we stopped out on the apron as a motorized cherry-picker, three police vehicles and half a dozen black SUVs headed out fast to meet us.

As the passengers and cabin crew looked out the windows, wondering what the hell was happening, getting scared, the icy flight attendant approached me.

'Mr Wilson?' she asked. 'Could you come with me, please.'

A British guy sitting in the next row stared at the squads of armed cops approaching. 'Jesus – all that for using your cellphone? The Lebanese don't screw around, do they?'

He was joking, and it made me smile as I grabbed my carry-on and followed the ice maiden down the aisle. Two of her colleagues were already turning a handle and releasing one of the cabin doors. As it slid open, the platform of the cherry-picker rose into place.

Standing on it was a middle-aged guy in a dark suit. He looked into the cabin and saw me. 'Brodie Wilson?' he said.

I nodded.

'Got your passport?'

I pulled it out and handed it to him. He checked the photograph, the physical description on the data page and entered the serial number into his cellphone. A moment later he got a Code Green and handed the book back.

'I'm Wesley Carter, Commercial Attaché at the Embassy,' he said. I had never seen him before, but I knew it wasn't true – without doubt, he was CIA station chief, Beirut. 'You wanna come this way?'

Watched by everybody on board, the ice maiden looking embarrassed, I stepped on to the platform and the cherry-picker lowered us to the ground. There were four more Americans in suits standing at strategic points around the SUVs, and I knew they were armed security. They watched as Carter shepherded me into the back of one of the vehicles and signalled to the Lebanese cops in the squad cars.

They hit their flashing lights and, travelling at high speed, we charged across the asphalt towards an adjoining runway.

'We've arranged a private jet for you,' he explained. 'It belongs to an Arab arms dealer, a sort of friend of ours. It was the only thing we could get at short notice. The pilots are ours, though – ex air force, so they're good.'

I looked through the armoured glass and saw a black G-4 corporate jet with an extended fuselage sitting in the distance with its engines running. I wondered how many rocket launchers you had to provide to the CIA's friends in the Middle East to afford one of those.

Carter spoke quietly. 'Whisperer told me you were way off the books, said you were looking for the nuclear trigger.'

I nodded. 'Isn't everybody?'

He laughed. 'You can double-down on that. Three thousand out of Beirut station alone – everybody in the region's helping. Nothing anywhere, though. What about you?'

I shook my head. 'Nothing yet.'

'I think he's flying solo.'

'Who?'

'Nuclear-boy.'

I turned to him. 'Why?'

'Human nature, I guess – if he wasn't, we would have heard something. People always talk; everybody gets sold out. Not far from here, there was a revolutionary guy – not a bomb-thrower but a fanatic, a lot of people said. He had a dozen followers who worshipped him, and they went through hell together. Even so, one of them sold him out. You know the story – Judas betrayed Jesus with a kiss.'

Now it was my turn to laugh.

'It was two thousand years ago,' Carter continued, 'and nothing's changed – not in this part of the world anyway.'

The SUV pulled to a halt at the steps of the G-4, and I grabbed my bag. 'Good story,' I said, and shook his hand.

I opened the door and ran for the steps. I heard Carter calling after me. 'Don't forget – those guys where you're going, they're garbage wrapped in skin. Good luck.'

I smiled – I didn't need luck. Even if the Saracen was flying solo, it didn't matter. In another few hours I would have his full name, date of birth, a history of his early life and probably a photo. That would be enough for Carter and a hundred other station chiefs like him to mobilize their men and those of other nations – the whole secret world, in fact – to find him.

Forty-eight hours was my estimate. In forty-eight hours we would have him: we were going to do it in time.

Chapter Three

ALL THE LABELS ON THE TINY GLASS BOTTLES WERE IN PLACE. AND THE Saracen had done it right on schedule.

He had worked tirelessly, but luck had also played a part – one of his colleagues had been in a car wreck and that had allowed him to pull a series of double shifts.

Right from the outset, he had organized the work like a production line, setting himself up in a section of the storage area hidden behind towers of flattened packaging. Undisturbed, he had a garden hose, a waste drain, a trash compactor, a commercial glue gun and various large plastic tubs at hand.

He filled the tubs with the chemical solvent, slit open the shrink-wrapped slabs of legitimate drugs and immersed the tiny glass vials in the solution for two point five minutes – the optimum length of time, he had found, for floating off the labels. He then laid the labels out in front of a space heater for two minutes to dry – the same time it took him to feed the unwanted bottles into the compactor, crush them to oblivion and hose the liquid drug they had contained down the waste drain.

The slowest part of the process was coating the back of the labels with the glue gun then reattaching them to his own glass vials. At first he had thought it was so slow that he would never make his deadline, but he soon found that not overthinking it, getting into a rhythm, treating himself like a robot with a glue gun, increased the throughput dramatically.

Fortunately for him, the warehouse had its own shrink-wrap machine to repair any packaging which had become damaged during the manufacturing and dispatch process. As a consequence, the Saracen had no difficulty in re-sealing his deadly bottles into the correct packaging.

By the end of his first evening's work he had one thousand tiny glass vials which were, for all practical purposes, identical to those used by Chyron. They were filled with a similar-looking clear fluid, fitted with the correct labels for a widely used drug, sealed in genuine plastic packs and plastered with legitimate bar codes, serial numbers and dispatch dockets. The only difference, impossible to detect by any other means than sophisticated chemical analysis, was that a potentially lifesaving agent had been replaced by the Saracen's home-made apocalypse.

Being a doctor, he knew the exact process that would occur once the vials hit America. A medical practitioner or a suitably qualified nurse would insert a syringe with a needle length of one inch or longer into the top of the bottle. The needle length was important, because the material they thought they were injecting had to be administered by what was called the intramuscular route. It would be injected into the deltoid muscle of the upper arm, and a needle of at least one inch was necessary to penetrate the muscle tissue of adults and older kids properly. In the case of infants and young children, a needle length of seven eighths of an inch was sufficient, but the injection would be given in the rear of the thigh.

No matter the age of the patient or the site of the injection, once the virus was in someone's body – and, with an intramuscular injection, there would be no misses – that person could not be saved. They could be described, totally accurately, as a zombie – one of the walking dead.

The Saracen also knew that one small group in any community – newborn babies – would be precluded from being given the so-called legitimate drug, but he didn't care. With ten thousand vectors unleashed and smallpox being an airborne pathogen, transmitted like the common cold, the only way for babies and anyone else to avoid infection would be to stop breathing.

With the one thousand glass vials completed, and confident he could go faster, he clocked off on that first night and made his way home brimming with hope and wild excitement. Dawn was just breaking but instead of falling into bed in his tiny rented apartment he started a ritual which he would follow for the next week.

He turned on the TV and watched the Weather Channel.

In the early hours of the morning, it carried a comprehensive update on the weather situation in the continental United States. To the Saracen's great joy, he saw that an unseasonal cold front was forming slowly in the north of Canada and was forecast to move across the United States. All the channel's experts were predicting that an unusually cold fall was coming early.

The seemingly innocuous development guaranteed that the impending attack would be, if it were at all possible, even more devastating. All airborne viruses – not just smallpox – were far more contagious in cold conditions, and most experts estimate that such conditions accelerate their transmission by at least 30 per cent. The reasons are straightforward – people cough and sneeze more, they take the bus instead of walking, they eat inside restaurants and not at sidewalk cafés. As the temperature drops, populations unwittingly wind themselves more closely together and provide a far better environment for the transfer of viral material.

Several days later, by the time he had finished processing the last of the ten thousand vials, the Saracen saw that the cold front was growing stronger and more widespread.

He moved the plastic-sealed packages into the warehouse proper, placed them in the right shipping bays for their intended destinations and checked one last time that all of their dispatch documents were in order.

In twenty-four hours, several trucks, part of the endless convoy which regularly passed through Chyron's European manufacturing plant, would pick up the packages and convey them the ninety miles through the town of Mannheim, past the huge US military base at Darmstadt and on to Frankfurt airport.

The flights to America would take about ten hours, the packages would then be transported to the company's regional freight centres and – about twelve hours later – be loaded on to trucks and delivered to doctors' offices throughout the United States.

Alone in the cavernous warehouse with only his thoughts and God for company, the Saracen was certain that in forty-eight hours the storm – both literally and figuratively – would hit the Republic.

Chapter Four

THE INTERIOR OF THE ARMS DEALER'S PRIVATE JET WAS SO UGLY IT HURT my feelings as well as my eyeballs. The walls were lined with a purple crushed velvet, the captain's chairs were upholstered in a deep-red brocade, complete with monograms, and all the fittings were in gold plate that was so highly polished it looked like brass.

But the plane was capable of flying very high – where the turbulence was less and the air thinner – which meant that, in the hands of the two US Air Force pilots, we would make it to Jeddah in record time. The craft also had one other advantage – at the back of the cabin was a door which led into a bedroom with a full-size bed, and a bathroom decorated in a combo of chrome, mirror and leopardskin.

I managed to ignore the decor and, after showering, I changed my clothes and lay down on the bed. I have no idea how long I slept but at some stage I woke up and lifted the blind and was surprised to see that night had fallen and we were flying beneath an endless field of stars.

I turned over and, in the solitude of flight, got to thinking about the huge effort I had made to escape the secret life, what it had been like in Paris for those few wonderful months when I was reaching for normal and how I wished that I had found somebody who loved me as much as I wanted to love them. I would have liked children too but given the circumstances – being swept back into the covert world, even now chasing shadows down dark alleys – the way things had worked out was probably for the best. Maybe later, when the mission was finally done, I thought dreamily . . .

It was with that thought in mind, somewhere between heaven and the desert, that I must have fallen back to sleep and, once more, seemingly out of nowhere, I saw the vision of myself on the old yacht, sailing across the endless sea, heading into the dying of the light.

In the midst of it I heard a distant voice I didn't recognize, but then I realized: it wasn't God, it was the pilot on the PA announcing that we were landing in fifteen minutes.

I swung my legs off the bed and sat in silence for a moment. The vision of death had troubled me even more than before. It was more vivid and more insistent, as if it were drawing closer.

Chapter Five

A HIGH-LEVEL DELEGATION WEARING IMMACULATE WHITE *THOBES* AND the characteristic red chequered headdress – two of which were braided in gold, indicating that the wearers were members of the Saudi royal family – met me on the asphalt at Jeddah.

They waited at the bottom of the steps – a dozen of them, whipped by the strong desert wind – with at least forty more guys with assault weapons standing near a fleet of black Cadillac Escalades.

The leader of the delegation – one of the men with the gold braid – stepped forward, shook my hand and introduced himself as the director of the Mabahith, the Saudi secret police. In his late thirties, with a weak handshake and hooded eyes, he had about as much charisma as the Angel of Death.

He indicated the rest of the group. 'These are all senior members of my organization. We flew up from Riyadh two hours ago,' he explained, pointing at an unmarked jumbo jet standing on the adjoining runway. I guessed they needed a plane that size to transport their fleet of armoured SUVs.

I smiled and lifted my hand in greeting to the team. I thought of asking why there were no women in the party, but I thought it might get us off on the wrong foot. Instead I thanked the director for his assistance. 'I spoke to Dave McKinley as I was leaving Turkey – I guess he called you immediately.'

The guy looked at me as if I had taken leave of my senses. 'I never spoke to Whisperer – President Grosvenor called His Majesty the King personally.' Little wonder we had a 747 and a small army on hand.

I had only been to Saudi once, and that was years ago, but I remembered it well enough to know that manners were of critical importance, so I turned to the delegation.

'It is a great honour for a member of US law enforcement to have the chance to work with the famous Mabahith,' I lied, yelling into the teeth of the wind. 'All of us in my organization – and indeed in our entire intelligence community – hold your force in the highest regard.' These were the same guys Carter had described as garbage wrapped in skin. 'As you probably know, we believe we are close to identifying the man who has been trying to buy a nuclear trigger. With the Mabahith's legendary skill, knowledge and intelligence, I am sure we can quickly bring this mission to a successful conclusion.'

They loved it. Everybody smiled and nodded, stepping forward to kiss me on the cheek and introduce themselves. With the formalities over, we headed for the Escalades and sped out of the airport towards a blaze of distant lights.

I had been to Jeddah on my previous trip, so I knew it well enough. There was only one thing to recommend it: say, you wanted to commit suicide and couldn't quite find the courage, two days in Jeddah would do the trick.

With no movie houses, music venues, bars, mixed-sex coffee shops or parties, there was little to do at night, and we drove down a high-way that was almost deserted. But that didn't stop the guys at the front using their flashing lights and, at a ton-up and with sirens screaming, we tore through the flat, featureless landscape.

We slowed only when we reached the Corniche and made a right. Through the window I saw the city's main mosque, with a huge parking lot in front of it – an area I had once heard was sometimes used for a far darker purpose – and then we swung past the Ministry of Foreign Affairs and headed down a side street. We stopped at a security checkpoint that was manned by armed men who looked like correction officers from a maximum-security jail. They probably were. The Mabahith was one of the only security forces in the world which ran its own prison system, and you didn't need a very big shovel to discover that the inmates were frequently tortured.

We approached a grim-looking building, pulled into an underground parking lot and travelled by elevator up to a huge conference room that was fitted out with work stations, overhead screens, video-conferencing facilities and glass-walled rooms full of hard drives and servers.

'Welcome to the war room,' the director said.

There were another hundred men – agents and analysts, by the look of them – at their desks, and they stood as we entered. Their boss spoke to them in Arabic, introducing me, then turned: 'Tell us what you need,' he said.

I told them that we were looking for a man, probably in his thirties, with the surname al-Nassouri. 'Apart from that, we know nothing about him,' I said. 'Except – he has a sister who was born here in Jeddah.'

I told them her name was Leyla, gave them her date of birth and said that we believed she had moved with her family to Bahrain. The director nodded, gave his agents a series of instructions in Arabic and took them off the leash.

He escorted me to a chair next to his own at the central console, and I had the opportunity to witness a unique event. I had read about it, of course, but I had never actually seen the machinery of a totalitarian state in full flight. For anyone who values privacy and freedom, it's a terrifying thing to behold.

The agents ordered up birth certificates, hospital admissions, passport and visa applications, archival lists of the membership of every mosque, school enrolments, academic records, confidential medical histories, Department of Motor Vehicles entries and, for all I knew, the records of every public toilet in the kingdom.

On and on it went – not just information about the target but about everybody of the same surname in order to vacuum up any family members. All of it was in Arabic, so I had no hope of monitoring their progress, but I watched in awe as the walls of hard drives spun and searched, men disappeared down into the bowels of the building and returned with old files of documents and a team of male typists seated behind the central console continually updated an executive summary to keep the director informed.

The team of analysts and agents ate at their desks, only pausing to grab a coffee or to yell requests across the cavernous space until, after three hours and with the room littered with print-outs and running sheets, one of the most senior investigators returned from the archives carrying a thin folio of official documents tied in red ribbon. He called to his boss politely in Arabic and, whatever it was that he said, caused everybody to stop and turn towards the director.

He took possession of the thin folio, looked at it from under his hooded eyes, demanded the latest version of his executive summary and turned to me.

'We now have everything we need, Mr Wilson,' he said. 'I have to admit I'm confused – I think there has been a serious mistake.'

'What sort of mistake?' I said, clamping down on the spike of fear, keeping myself calm.

'The name of the man you are looking for is Zakaria al-Nassouri,' he said, handing me a copy of an Arabic birth certificate.

I took it and looked at it for a moment. All I could think of was: what a long, long journey it had been to get to that piece of paper. All my life, in a way.

'The woman you mentioned,' he continued, 'Leyla al-Nassouri, had one sister and a brother. This brother – Zakaria – was born five years before her, also here in Jeddah.

'Their father was a zoologist at the Red Sea Marine Biology Department. Apparently, he specialized in the study of . . .' He had trouble with the Latin but took a stab at it anyway: '*Amphiprion ocellaris.*'

Dozens of other men in the room laughed – whatever the hell that was.

'Clownfish,' I said quietly, realization dawning. I slipped the birth certificate into a plastic sleeve and put it next to my cellphone. 'In English, they're called clownfish. I think the man I'm looking for took it as some sort of code name, probably to log on to an Internet forum.'

The director just nodded and continued. 'According to the archives, my predecessors in the Mabahith knew the father well. Twenty-five years ago, he was executed.'

It shocked me. 'Executed?' I said. 'For what?'

The director scanned a couple of documents and found the one he was looking for. 'The usual – corruption on earth.'

'I'm sorry but what exactly does "corruption on earth" mean?'

He laughed. 'Pretty much whatever we want.' Nearly all his team found it funny too. 'In this case,' he continued, 'it meant that he criticized the royal family and advocated its removal.' Suddenly, he wasn't laughing and nor were his agents – that was his family we were talking about.

'Executions are carried out in public, is that right?' I asked.

'Yes,' he replied. 'He was beheaded down the road, in the parking area outside the mosque.'

I hung my head – God, what a mess. A public beheading would be enough to radicalize anyone – no wonder the son grew up to be a terrorist. 'How old was Zakaria al-Nassouri?'

Again he consulted some files. 'Fourteen.'

I sighed. 'Is there any evidence he witnessed the execution?' The whole thing was such a train wreck, I figured anything was possible.

'Nobody was sure, but there was a photo taken in the square which several agents at the time believed was probably him. As a result, it was placed in the family's file.' He took an old photo out of a folder and passed it over.

It was in black and white, shot from a high angle by what was obviously a surveillance camera. It showed a teenager, tall and gangly, buffeted by a searing desert wind in the almost empty square.

All the body language – the total desolation in the way that the boy was standing – spoke so clearly of pain and loss that I had little doubt it was him. A cop was approaching, his bamboo cane raised, trying to drive him off, and it meant that the boy's back was half turned to the camera, his face averted. Even then, holding a photo of him, I couldn't see his face. I didn't realize it, but it was a bad omen.

I put the photo in the plastic sleeve, and the director moved on. 'Records from the immigration department show that, shortly after her husband was executed, the mother took the three children to live in Bahrain.

'I doubt that she had much choice – as a result of her husband's crime, she would have been an outcast among her family and friends. Good riddance,' he said, with a shrug.

'But, given their history, we continued to take an interest in them – at least for the first few years. Bahrain is a friendly neighbour and, on our behalf, it watched them.'

He reached across to another folder, causing the sleeve of his *thobe* to ride up and expose a gold and sapphire Rolex which probably cost more than most people earned in a lifetime, and took a number of sheets out of the folder. They were field reports from agents who were doing the watching, I guessed.

'She took a job,' the director said, scanning through them, 'and gave up wearing the veil. What does that tell you?' He looked at his men. 'Not much of a mother or a Muslim, eh?'

All the men murmured in agreement.

You never know, maybe her husband being decapitated had

556

something to do with her getting a job, I thought. Carter was right about them, but what was the alternative? Right now, we needed them.

'The boy joined a small mosque – very conservative and anti-Western – on the outskirts of Manama, the capital. Around the time of his sixteenth birthday, they helped pay for him to fly to Pakistan—'

I caught my breath. Sixteen was just a kid, but I did a quick calculation, working out which year we were talking about. 'He went into Afghanistan?' I asked. 'You're telling me he was a *muj*?'

'Yes,' he answered. 'Some people said he was a hero, that he brought down three Hind helicopter gunships.'

Suddenly I understood why he had travelled to the Hindu Kush to test his virus, where he had found the explosives to booby-trap the village, how he had managed to escape the Australians down long-forgotten trails. And I thought of another Saudi who had gone to Afghanistan to fight the Soviets – he was also a fundamentalist, a man who had hated the royal family with a passion and had ended up attacking America. Osama bin Laden.

'So he was in Afghanistan – what then?' I asked.

'We only have one more document,' he replied, picking up the thin folio fastened with the red ribbon. He opened it and took out an impressive-looking form written in Arabic and stamped with an official seal.

'We found this in the paper archives. It was sent to us about fourteen years ago by the Afghan government.' He handed it to me. 'It's a death certificate.

'As I said, there has been a mistake – he was killed two weeks before the war ended.'

I stared at him, not even looking at the document, robbed of speech.

'You see, you're chasing the wrong man,' he said. 'Zakaria al-Nassouri is dead.'

Chapter Six

I WATCHED A CRESCENT MOON RISE ABOVE THE RED SEA, I SAW THE minarets of the city mosque standing like silent guardians, I felt the desert crowding in and I imagined I could hear the pumps sucking out ten million barrels a day from beneath its sand.

With the death certificate still in my hand, I had risen to my feet and walked to a window in silence – I needed a minute to compose myself, to think. By an exercise of iron will I forced myself to work it through. Zakaria al-Nassouri wasn't dead – I was certain Leyla Cumali had been speaking to her brother on the phone. I had heard his voice on the recordings and I had met his son. DNA doesn't lie.

So what was its meaning, a death certificate from so long ago? It took only a moment to see the answer, and it was worse than anything I could have imagined. I felt my stomach knot and, I have to admit, for a few terrible heartbeats I felt like giving up.

But I knew that one of the hallmarks of every successful mission – perhaps of life itself – was a determination never to retreat, never to surrender. What was that verse of Whisperer's? 'To go to your God like a soldier.'

There were a hundred pairs of eyes focused on my back, and I turned to face them. 'He's not dead,' I said, with total conviction. 'It's impossible, he has a six-year-old son – we've seen the DNA.'

I saw the alarm spread through their ranks – was I claiming that Saudi intelligence had made a mistake or was incompetent? What a fool I was. In my distraction and despair, I had forgotten the importance of flattery and good manners. I grabbed the oars and rowed back fast.

'Of course, it takes an organization with the skill and experience of the Mabahith – to say nothing of its exalted leadership – to see things that we never could.' It was so saccharine it could have induced diabetes, but it did the trick: everybody relaxed, smiling and nodding.

I indicated the document. 'I believe that in the last weeks of the conflict Zakaria al-Nassouri bought his own death certificate – either in the backstreets of Kabul or by bribing an Afghan official to issue it.'

'Why?' the director asked.

'Because he had been a *muj*. He knew that people like us would always be dogging him. Maybe even then he was planning to fight a far bigger war.

'Once his old identity was dead, he took a new one. It wasn't hard. Afghanistan, Pakistan, Iran – the whole region was in chaos, corruption everywhere.'

I paused, face to face with my failure. 'I think somehow he acquired a new passport.'

The director stared. 'You understand?' he said. 'That means we don't know his name, his nationality, what flag he's travelling under—'

'You're right – nothing,' I said, trying to hide the devastation I was feeling.

'But somewhere,' I continued, 'somebody in the Arab world has heard about a man of the right age, an ex-*muj*, an exile, whose father was executed in Saudi. How many of them could there be? We have to find that thread.'

The director thought about it and I imagined the seconds ticking away on his million-dollar watch. 'If there's anything, it wouldn't be in the computerized files,' he said at last, thinking out loud. 'We would have already run across it. Maybe in the paper files . . . there could be something, a long time back.'

He spoke harshly in Arabic, issuing orders. By the flurry of urgent activity, I guessed that they were being told to call in reinforcements, to drag in more analysts and researchers, to summon men long since retired who might remember something. Dozens of the more senior agents scrambled to their feet, grabbed their laptops and cigarettes and headed for the elevators.

The director pointed at them. 'That's the main search party – they will start going through the paper files. I've got another two hundred men on the way, but I can promise it won't be fast. There's an apartment upstairs – why don't you get some rest?'

I thanked him, but I knew I couldn't. I looked at my watch: it was six hours until I had to make a call to the two men waiting in the Oval Office. I turned to the window and stared out at the star-strewn night. Somewhere out there was a desert so vast they called it the Sea of Emptiness and I thought again of the Saracen.

T. E. Lawrence – Lawrence of Arabia – knew something about that part of the world and the nature of men. He said that the dreamers of the day were dangerous people – they tried to live their dreams to make them come true. Zakaria al-Nassouri's daydream was to destroy us all. Mine was to catch him. I wondered which one of us would wake in the morning and find that their nightmare had begun.

Chapter Seven

THE CORRIDORS RAN FOR MILES. ON EITHER SIDE, TWENTY-FEET-HIGH motorized storage racks stood like monoliths – enter a reference number, a name or any other data on a control panel, and the racks moved silently to reveal the relevant archive boxes. It was like standing inside a computer hard drive.

There were eighteen identical floors, all filled with paper archives: the raw data of decade after decade of surveillance, betrayal and suspicion. Hidden far beneath the Mabahith's regional headquarters, linked together by a central atrium, the complex was overrun by men searching the storage racks and hauling out archive boxes. The director had been as good as his word and had pulled in every agent and analyst he could find.

I had made my way down from the conference room and taken a seat beside several of the senior agents at a command post suspended out over the atrium. I watched as teams of men on every floor unbundled yellowing paper files and searched through mountains of data looking for any reference – any mention at all – of a man whose father had been executed in Saudi Arabia all those years ago.

Three hours of watching them plough through files in Arabic, three hours in a windowless vault with guys who didn't touch alcohol but smoked thirty a day, three hours of counting every minute, and I was as close to desperate as I ever wanted to be. Naturally, when one of my neighbours said that the first squad was heading out to interview people who might be able to contribute something to the lost narrative, I grabbed my jacket to join them.

The three agents were hard guys, the youngest of them in his twenties, a man whose IQ was so low I figured they had to water him twice a day. We gathered up eight more of their colleagues on the way and rolled in a convoy of four black SUVs with so much *makhfee* on the windows it was like travelling in permanent midnight. I'm certain, though, it fulfilled its real purpose admirably: no ordinary civilian who saw them passing could have failed to be afraid.

For mile after mile we criss-crossed the sprawling city – four and a half million souls marooned in the middle of the desert, seemingly half of them employed by Aramco, the world's largest oil company – and interviewed people about a family which had long since vanished. We sat in the *majlis* – the formal sitting rooms – of poor houses way out in the suburbs and questioned men whose hands were trembling, we saw dark-eyed kids watching from shadowy doorways and glimpsed veiled women in floor-length *burqas* hurrying away at our approach. We visited an elderly man called Sa'id bin Abdullah bin Mabrouk al-Bishi – he was the state executioner who had beheaded al-Nassouri's father – in the hope that in his last moments the condemned man had said something about the career and future he had wanted for his son. After that we drove to a modest villa close enough to the water to smell the salt and, for some reason I couldn't quite explain, I took a photo of it on my cellphone. It was al-Nassouri's childhood home and we questioned the man who had moved in after the family had fled in case he had heard something in the following years.

Nobody knew anything.

Finally, we took a break, pulling into a roadside shack for coffee. We were sitting outside, listening to the idiot in his twenties go on about some chick he had met in Morocco, when a cellphone rang and I was asked to return immediately.

The team was gathered in an open-plan research area on one side of the atrium, the air filled with cigarette smoke. The director stood at a table, an archive box in front of him, plenty more of them piled on the floor. Spilling out of them were field reports, interviews with informers and records of hearsay and gossip.

The director said that they had accessed a box containing what had been thought to be worthless material concerning a number of conservative mosques in Bahrain.

'There was one slim file which proved to be of interest,' he said. 'It dealt with a small mosque on the outskirts of Manama, the capital.' He looked at me to make sure I realized the significance of what he had said.

'Zakaria al-Nassouri's mosque?' I asked, trying to keep my voice neutral, battling a surge of hope.

He nodded. 'The file contained the usual empty analysis and a few incomplete logs of membership, but buried among it was this . . .' He held up a three-page document in Arabic.

'About five years ago a low-level field agent interviewed a Saudi aid worker who had delivered food and medicine to the refugees in the Gaza Strip. While he was unloading trucks at a dilapidated hospital, he heard about a man who had been brought in earlier in the evening after an Israeli rocket attack.

'When his work was done he went up to see the wounded man to find out if there was anything he could do to help. The man, with shrapnel wounds near his spine, was going in and out of delirium, and the aid worker ended up sitting with him through the night.'

The director paused, looking at the document, checking his facts. 'It appeared the wounded man was a doctor and, at one stage, semi-delirious, he mentioned he used to be a member of the mosque in Manama. That was how the report ended up in this particular file.

'Everybody assumed he was a Bahraini. But he couldn't have been because, much later on, again in his delirium, he said his father had been publicly beheaded—'

I sat forward so quickly I was lucky not to fall off the chair. 'Bahrain doesn't do that,' I said.

'Exactly – only one country does.'

'Saudi,' I replied.

'Yes. It appears the man had been travelling in a car with his Palestinian wife and child when it was rocketed – whether the vehicle was targeted or if it was collateral damage, nobody knows.

'The woman died, but not immediately. In his rambling account, he said that he was holding her and she made him promise – promise before God – that he would protect their child. The little boy had survived with minor injuries—'

'Praise be unto Allah,' the whole room said in Arabic.

'But the mother knew,' the director continued, 'that for him the tragedy was doubly great. Not only had he lost her but he also suffered—'

'From Down's syndrome,' I said with sudden certainty.

'How did you know?'

'It's definitely him – al-Nassouri,' I said, getting to my feet, having to work off the flood of nervous energy. 'It's his son – I know the boy. Where did the hospital send the child – to an orphanage?'

'That's right.'

'Run by the Al-Aqsa Martyrs' Brigade – I've seen the receipts.' At last I understood why Leyla Cumali hadn't sent the money to Unicef.

'What else?' I asked, probably more harshly than manners dictated, but we were on a roll and nobody noticed.

'The dead woman's name was Amina Ebadi – at least that was one name she used: many of the Palestinian activists use aliases or *noms de guerre*. We've done a search on her, but can't find anything.'

'Yes, but what about him – what about the doctor?' I asked, my voice crackling with intensity. 'Did the aid worker get the name he was using?'

'That was a strange thing – the doctor was in terrible shape but, when the aid worker returned the following night, he'd discharged himself. Probably scared about what he might have said when he was rambling—'

'His name, Director? Did he get a name?'

'No.'

I stared at him. 'There's *nothing*?! Nothing more?'

He nodded. 'We've been through everything. The original report wasn't followed up. It didn't seem to have any significance—'

'Until now,' I said bitterly. I tilted my head back and tried to breathe. The news seemed to have sucked the air – and the energy – out of the room. The agents and the director kept watching me, but I tried to think.

I knew more about Zakaria al-Nassouri than any covert agent had a right to. I knew he was born and raised in Jeddah, that he had stood in anguish in the square where his father was beheaded and that his mother had taken him to live in exile in Bahrain. I knew the name of the mosque he had joined in Manama and that his fellow worshippers had arranged for him to go to Afghanistan and fight the Soviets. At the end of the war he had bought a death certificate, somehow acquired a new passport and vanished into the trackless Arab world. He had studied medicine, graduated as a doctor, met a woman who sometimes used the name Amina Ebadi and married her. Together they had worked on the undocumented and lawless

564

frontier – the refugee camps of Gaza: a hell on earth if ever there was one. I now knew that the married couple were travelling with their young child when they were hit by an Israeli rocket, killing the mother and injuring the doctor. The little boy was taken to an orphanage and the doctor must have asked his sister Leyla to reach out and save him. Full of hatred, without family responsibilities, using his knowledge as a doctor, enabled by the vast haemorrhaging of information on the Internet, he had set about synthesizing small-pox. He had returned to Afghanistan to test it, and we heard him on the phone, worried about his beloved child, the only link he had left to his dead wife.

And after that? After that, the music stopped and there was nothing. Who was he now? What name was he using? And – more importantly – where was he? 'A way in,' I said softly. 'Somehow you push forward and find a way back in.'

Nobody knew if I was talking to myself or offering a suggestion to everyone. I probably didn't know either.

'That's all we have on the man,' the director said, sweeping his hand across the floors of motorized files. 'There's no name, no identity and no trace. Not here, anyway.'

He was right, and the silence hung in space. Through the haze of smoke, I looked at the men. There was no way back in for any of us, hope was gone, and I knew . . .

We had lost him.

I forced myself not to show my despair and stood a little straighter. Bill had always told me there was no excuse for bad manners, and I owed the Saudi men something.

'You've done more than anybody could have asked,' I said. 'It was a thankless task, but you did it with talent and good grace and I thank you wholeheartedly.'

It was probably the first time they had heard genuine praise instead of empty flattery, and I could see on their faces the pride it brought them.

'*Jazak Allahu Khayran*,' I said finally, butchering the pronunci-ation but using one of the only Arabic phrases I recalled from my earlier visit. It was the traditional way of offering thanks: 'May God reward you with blessings.'

'*Waiyyaki*,' they all said, smiling kindly at my effort and offering the time-honoured response: 'And with you.'

It was the signal everybody needed, and they got to their feet and started packing everything up. I remained where I was, standing alone, desperately trying to find another way forward, a route, a path. A miracle.

I journeyed through the catalogue of my professional memory, I let my mind wander down every unconventional alley, but I came up empty.

I had identified the Saracen, but I didn't know him; I had located him, but I couldn't find him; he was somebody, and he was nobody. That was the truth, and nothing in the world was going to change it.

I looked at my watch.

Chapter Eight

IT WAS THE WORST PHONE CALL I HAVE EVER HAD TO MAKE. NOBODY WAS angry, nobody shouted or made accusations, but the sense of failure and fear was overwhelming.

After I had said goodbye to the director of the Mabahith, one of the black SUVs took me the short distance across town to the high-security compound that housed the US consulate. Carter from Beirut Station had called ahead and alerted them to my presence, so I had little delay in getting through the anti-suicide barriers and guardhouses.

Once I was inside, the young duty officer assumed I needed a bed for the night and started to show me towards a guest apartment, but I stopped him halfway to the elevator and told him I needed a telephone in the building's Tempest zone – an area specially engineered to prevent any electronic eavesdropping. The Mabahith and I might have ended on good terms, but that didn't mean I trusted them.

The duty officer hesitated, probably wondering who I was exactly, then started activating the electronic locks on blast-proof doors, leading me deep into the heart of the building. We passed through an internal security checkpoint, which told me we were entering the area occupied by the CIA, before arriving at a small room with only a desk and a telephone. The blandest place you have ever seen, distinguished only by its complete lack of sound.

I closed the door, activated the electronic lock, picked up the phone and asked the operator for the Oval Office.

The phone was answered immediately and I heard the president's voice. It was clear he was exhausted, but it was equally obvious that his spirits were buoyed by the expectation of good news. I had told them I would have the Saracen's full name, date of birth and

567

probably a photo. I had found them too, I just hadn't anticipated they would be useless.

Whisperer announced that he was on the line as well, and I think he guessed from my downbeat greeting that a disaster was heading down the pike. Like any good case officer he had learned to judge every nuance of a joe's behaviour. 'What is it?' he asked, his voice tightening.

I told it to them hard and cold and straight, like one of those accident reports you read in the daily news. I said that, despite all our efforts and the great promise of a few hours ago, we had nothing to work with. Nothing at all.

There was a terrible silence.

'One minute we were cock of the walk, next a feather duster,' Whisperer said finally. 'It's a bust—'

'Busted flat and out of time,' the president added, the exhaustion, stripped of its veneer of hope, coming through loud and clear.

'What about the others?' I asked. 'Everybody who's looking for the nuclear trigger. Anything from them?'

'A hundred thousand people and nothing,' Grosvenor replied.

'I figure we never had a chance. I think we ran into the perfect storm—' Whisperer started to say.

'A cleanskin flying solo,' I said.

'A cleanskin, yes. But not totally solo – no,' he replied.

'What do you mean?'

'In Afghanistan – he must have had help for at least a short period. A man flying solo can't grab three hostages.'

He was right, but it didn't seem important and, anyway, the president was already moving on.

'We'll pick up the woman – what's her name, Cumali? – as soon as possible. Is that the plan?' he asked Whisperer.

'Yeah. Pilgrim believes she's in the dark – am I right?'

'Pretty much,' I said. 'As Whisperer probably told you, Mr President, she has a way of contacting him, but I think it will be booby-trapped. She'll misplace a letter, use a different word – it'll warn him to run.'

'You may be right,' the president said. 'He bought a damn death certificate, he's smart enough – but we have to try.'

'I'll send a team in fast,' Whisperer said. 'We'll get her out of Turkey, rendition her to Bright Light.'

Bright Light was the code name for Khun Yuam, the CIA secret prison I had visited up on the Thai–Burma border. The story was that once somebody disappeared into Bright Light, they didn't emerge. It was strange – given the magnitude of the events which we were confronting – but I couldn't help thinking about the little guy and what would happen to him. Back to an orphanage in either Gaza or Turkey, I figured. Wherever it was, there wouldn't be much bowing and laughter.

'At dawn, or near enough, I'll issue an executive order,' Grosvenor continued, 'and close the borders. We'll isolate the country the best we can – airports, land crossings, ports of entry, everything we can think of.'

It was obvious they were still heading down the human-vector track and, even if they were right about the method of dispersal, over half a million illegal aliens entered the country every year – a good indication that any attempt to secure the borders would be of little use. Like the old virologist had said: sooner or later, we all sit down to a banquet of consequences.

Even though I didn't think their plan would work, I said nothing. I had no alternative, so it would have been churlish to tear it apart without having something better to offer. They were doing their best to keep the country afloat, that was all.

'We don't have to say it's smallpox,' Whisperer suggested. 'We could claim it's a highly virulent avian flu. As bad as it is, it's not freighted with the same terror. Once you say "smallpox" and add "sledgehammer", it's gonna be like Mount Everest – it'll make its own weather.'

'No,' Grosvenor replied – he had obviously thought of it too. 'What happens when the truth gets out? Our only hope is the co-operation of the public – given the chance, Americans always rise to the occasion. Betray them and you've lost 'em. One vector, one trace, that's all we need and we can track it backwards. I also plan to release the vaccine. I don't know if it will do any good, but we have to try everything and use what we've got.'

'Yes, Mr President,' Whisperer said. 'What about you, Pilgrim? Coming home?'

'I'll go to Gaza,' I said.

It was Whisperer who recovered first. 'An American alone in Gaza, without a legend? They'll be lining up with bomb belts and baseball bats – you'll be dead in a day.'

'I've spoken to the Saudis – they've got some people on the ground who can help.'

'That means the line will only be half as long.'

'Al-Nassouri was there – it's the only thread we've got.'

'You don't have to do it,' the president said. 'Not finding him is no reflection on you. On the contrary. When we first met, I asked Whisperer to stay behind – I told him you were the coolest sonofabitch I'd ever met. I didn't realize you were also the best. You've done an outstanding job.'

'Thank you,' I said simply.

'I won't send you a presidential letter of commendation,' he said, trying to lighten the tone. 'You've already got one of those.'

'And the golf balls,' I replied.

They laughed, and it gave me a chance. 'If I could ask one thing, Mr President?' I said.

'Go ahead,' he replied.

'There's a hacker we pulled out of Leavenworth who did some great work. Would it be possible not to send him back?'

'A pardon, you mean?'

'If it could be done,' I replied.

'What about it, Whisperer? You know this guy?'

'Yeah, excellent work – I'd support it.'

'Okay – I'll get his name from Whisperer and write the order.'

'Thank you, Mr President' was all I could say. I was thinking of Battleboi holding Rachel tight when he heard the news.

'Good luck, Pilgrim,' the president said, bringing the call to an end. 'I hope we'll see each other again in better circumstances.' He didn't sound very confident.

The line went dead, and I sat in the soundproofed silence, thinking that it would probably be the last moments of peace I would know for a long time. Maybe ever.

Gaza.

Whisperer was right – it was one of the deadliest places on earth. The only good thing about it was that there was nowhere to sail: at least there wouldn't be any old boats with patched sails waiting for me.

Elsewhere maybe, but not in Gaza.

Chapter Nine

IT WAS GERMANY, SO THE TRUCKS ARRIVED RIGHT ON TIME. IT WAS JUST after 6 a.m., with a light rain falling, when they drove through the security gates at Chyron.

Just as the drivers had done a thousand times before, they swung past the glass-fronted administration building, ran down factory row and stopped at the loading bays in the rear. The warehouse guy – the tall Muslim whose name none of the drivers could quite remember – was already at the wheel of a forklift, waiting to help load the boxes of pharma for shipment to America. He didn't say anything – he never talked much – but the drivers liked him: he worked fast and seemed a damn sight more intelligent than most of his colleagues.

The consignment was a large one – it included everything from pallets of vaccines to crates of antibiotics, millions of doses of different drugs – but even so, the Saracen had it loaded into the back of the trucks in under five minutes. He had all the documentation ready too, and the drivers knew that with him there was no need to check – it was always correct.

They grabbed the paperwork, ran through the rain, scrambled into their cabs and were heading back towards the A5 freeway in record time.

Had they glanced in their rear-view mirrors, which none of them did, they would have seen that the Saracen didn't move from the forklift: he sat in quiet contemplation and watched them until they were out of sight. He knew that the rain and the roadworks on the A5 – there were always roadworks on the '5 – would slow them down, that was why he had hurried, but not so much that they wouldn't make their designated flights.

At last he lowered his head, rested it on his forearms and floated in some place between prayer and exhaustion. It was over, it was out of his hands, and the relief was so overwhelming he felt tears sting the back of his eyes. The crushing responsibility of the last three years, the great burden of doing Allah's work, had been lifted. The weapon was flying free and the fate of the mission, the welfare of nations, the survival of whatever innocence remained in the world, rested on a system of border controls which the Saracen believed was so tenuous as to be virtually non-existent. But that was not within his control; he had done all he could: everything rested now in God's hands.

With a growing sense of freedom, he raised his head and stepped out of the driver's seat. He walked back inside the warehouse, went to his locker and cleaned it out. For the first and only time since he had started work at Chyron, he didn't wait for his shift to end: instead, he slung his backpack over his shoulder, passed unnoticed through the security gates and, heart soaring, walked down the empty road in the drizzling rain.

He returned to his tiny apartment – nothing more than a bed, and a table and a sink in a corner – threw out the food in the cupboards, packed his spare clothes in the backpack, put the keys on the table and slammed the door behind him. He made no attempt to pick up the wages that were owed to him, to get a refund on his rental deposit or farewell the men at the Wilhelmstrasse mosque who had been so generous to him. He left as mysteriously as he had arrived.

He headed fast through the waking town to the railway station, bought a ticket and, a few minutes later, the express train to Frankfurt came into view. There he would retrieve his luggage and medical kit from the long-term locker, go into a toilet stall and revert to the clothes and identity of a Lebanese doctor who had been visiting for a conference at the Messe.

For weeks, as his mission had moved closer to completion, he had increasingly thought about what he would do then. He had no desire to stay in Germany and no reason to return to Lebanon. Within days, he knew, a modern plague – the black pox was how he thought of it – would burst into the public consciousness. Its presence would start slow, like a match in straw, but it would rapidly become what scientists call a self-amplifying process – an explosion – and the whole barn would be on fire.

America – the great infidel – would be ground zero, the kill-rate astronomical. Deprived of its protector, Israel's belly would be exposed and at last it would be left to the mercy of its near enemies. As economic activity fell off a cliff, the price of oil would collapse and the ruling Saudi elite – unable to buy off its own people any longer or fall back on the support of the United States – would invoke a fearful repression and, in doing so, sow the seeds of its own destruction.

In the short term, the world would close down and travel be rendered impossible as nations sought safety in quarantine and isolation. Some would be more successful than others and, though a billion people had died from smallpox in the hundred years before its eradication, nothing like it had ever happened in the modern world – not even Aids – and nobody could predict where the rivers of infection would flood and where they would turn.

As the dying time – as he called it – came closer, he had felt a growing certainty that, whatever happened, he wanted to be with his son. If they lost their lives, then that was Allah's will and all he asked was to be with his child so that he could hold him and tell him that they had nothing to fear either in this world or the next. If it was God's plan that they lived, then, as soon as was practical, he would take him to Afghanistan. Together they would walk along shaded riverbanks, and perhaps he would show him the mountain slopes where he had brought down the fearsome Hind gunships. And as summer turned to autumn they would make their way through distant valleys to the fortress of Abdul Mohammad Khan. What better place to raise his son than among the devout and the brave? And when the time was right they would return to Saudi and laugh and grow old together in the land where the soul of his father was closest.

To be with his son? The thought had sustained him through everything in Karlsruhe. One night he had gone to an Internet café and searched the Web, and he had already found a rooming house suitable for a devout Muslim man in Milas.

Yes, he would re-emerge in Frankfurt as a doctor, take the train to the airport and board a plane. He was flying to Bodrum.

Chapter Ten

ON A PRIVATE JET AT FULL THROTTLE, IT TAKES ABOUT TWO HOURS TO FLY from Jeddah to the Gaza Strip, a slice of abject misery wedged between Israel and Egypt, home to one and a half million stateless Arabs and at least twenty groups identified by the State Department as terrorist organizations.

Beirut Station had arranged for the arms dealer's red and kitsch Gulfstream to be replaced by a CIA-owned Lear jet that was decorated in three shades of beige. At least it didn't give me a migraine. While that might have been an advantage, the downside was that there were no beds, something which turned out to be significant. I was forced to sit up and, with nothing more than end-less miles of oil derricks to look out on, my thoughts were my only company.

I have to say they were miserable companions. I don't think I'm a vain man but I do have a liberal dose of professional pride. Sitting in a plane at thirty thousand feet, there was no place to hide, especially not from the truth. I had met Zakaria al-Nassouri head-on, and he had defeated me.

Maybe I never really had a chance – he was too good, too smart, too far ahead ever to be caught. This was the person who had carried quicklime into the mountains of the Hindu Kush. Quicklime on the back of packhorses – for five hundred miles, through some of the most inhospitable land on earth! He had planned every step, every detail.

Certainly a man capable of that would have anticipated the day when somebody in my business would try to find him. Like a fugitive in fresh snow, he had swept the ground behind him. He bought a death certificate over fourteen years ago, and followed that up with a fake passport. As I said, maybe he was too far ahead to ever be caught.

And yet, as far as I could see, there was nothing we could have done differently. Of the ten people who knew the secret, the eight government officials had not only maintained their silence but acted with admirable speed. Without being boastful, the other two members of the group – Whisperer and myself – were among the best in the world, armed with all the resources and technology the most powerful country on earth could provide. We were apex predators and, like all apex predators, we were hard-wired to hunt . . .

I stopped to correct myself. Not every apex predator hunts. I could think of at least one that didn't. A shark hunts, but a crocodile lies silently in the reeds and waits for its prey to come to him.

At that moment, I realized what our mistake had been – we had been hunting him when we should have been trapping him. We never had a chance, not in a straight-line pursuit: his lead was far too great. But in a trap, a head start wouldn't have mattered.

Was there still time? Perhaps we had a card left to play, one more roll of the dice, a final round left in the chamber. Somehow we had to draw him out of the shadows and make him come to the waterhole.

I stared out of the window for what felt like a lifetime. I didn't see the clouds or the oil rigs, but I came to believe that we had a chance. I based it on one thing only, a lesson I had learned a long time ago in a banker's office in Geneva: love wasn't weak, *love was strong*.

I unbuckled my seatbelt and scrambled to my feet. I hadn't realized that clear-air turbulence was rocking the small jet, sending it pitching and yawing, but I had no time to worry about it. I headed towards the front of the cabin, nearly hit the roof as we took a sudden dive, grabbed hold of a seat back and half crawled, half rocketed, to where a CIA secure phone was located in a small closet.

I grabbed the handset and made a call.

Chapter Eleven

WHISPERER ANSWERED ALMOST IMMEDIATELY, BUT HIS VOICE, EVEN softer than usual, was so hoarse it sounded like acid running over gravel. There had been too much stress, too little sleep, too many disappointments for one man's plate.

I told him the mistake we had made in trying to run the Saracen down and explained what I wanted to try – not the detail of it, just the broad strokes. Thankfully, he was so experienced, he didn't need chalk on a board.

I said we had to delay the rendition of Cumali and convince the president to postpone his address to the nation. 'I need time for it to work, Dave,' I said.

He tried to laugh. 'You're asking me for the one thing we don't have,' he countered, and again I heard the years in his voice. 'We can't delay, I was speaking to him twenty minutes ago – it's impossible.'

I pleaded my case, I begged him and, finally, when that got me nowhere, I told him in anger that he had better listen to me because I was the best agent of my generation and, *fuck it*, I was telling him we had a chance. He said nothing for a moment, and I could tell that the raw vanity of it, so out of character for me, had shocked him. He told me to wait.

So I clung on, both literally and metaphorically, pitching and plunging through the turbulence while he called the president on another phone. A few minutes later I heard his footsteps return across the wooden floor of his study.

'I just spoke to Grosvenor,' he reported. 'He doesn't think it'll work, he doesn't believe in it—'

'Jesus!' I interjected. 'Did you explain our mistake?'

'Sure I did,' Whisperer replied tersely. 'I said we'd ridden out like a posse and we should have been desperadoes waiting for a train. How was that – clear enough?'

'And he still didn't get it?'

'You didn't let me finish. He said he doesn't believe in it – but he believes in you. You've got thirty-six hours.'

The relief flooded in. One more chance for salvation, one more chance for redemption. 'Thanks,' I said sheepishly.

'Phone us, good or bad. If it starts falling apart, he wants to know immediately. He's got the address to the nation written. He said no false hope, no letting wishing overwhelm logic. If it's a turd, don't try to polish it.'

'Okay,' I replied.

'You've got my number; here's another one in case there's a problem. It's Grosvenor's.'

As good as my memory was, I didn't want to trust it so I pulled out my cellphone and entered it on speed-dial under 911. I was still keying it in as Whisperer plunged on.

'Okay, so we've got thirty-six hours and we've got the outline of a plan. Now we work it. What's the first step?'

'A phone call,' I replied. 'We can't make it ourselves – it has to sound like the real deal. What's the highest-level asset we have inside Turkish intelligence?'

Given the country's strategic importance, I knew that the CIA – like every other major intelligence agency – would have spent years cultivating turncoats inside MIT.

Whisperer said nothing – I was asking him to discuss one of our nation's most closely held secrets.

'Dave?' I prompted him.

'There's somebody we could use,' he said reluctantly.

'Who?' I knew that I was pushing too hard, but I had to know if it would fly.

'For shit's sake – don't ask me that,' he replied.

'Who?'

'There are two deputy directors of MIT,' he said finally. 'One of 'em grew up Wal-Mart but prefers Gucci, okay?'

'Shit . . . a deputy director?' I said, taken aback. Despite my years in The Division, I could still be shocked at the scale of betrayal inside the secret world. 'He's not going to like doing this,' I said.

'He won't have a choice – he'll be scared I'll turn him into his government. Maybe they still hang traitors in Turkey. What are the details?' I heard the rustle of paper as he grabbed a pen to take notes.

When I had finished, he read the bullet points back to me, but he had done more than record them – he had improved and massaged them on the move and, once again, I thanked God for a great case officer.

'What now?' he asked. 'Call him and get him to do it?'

'Yeah, it's warp-speed if we're gonna have a chance.'

I rang off and, while Whisperer was dropping a bomb on a deputy director of MIT, I hammered on the cockpit door. I heard the voice of the ex-US Air Force pilot through the intercom.

'What is it?'

'Change of plan. Ditch Gaza, we're going to Bodrum.'

The door flew open. 'Where's Bodrum?'

I yelled the answer, but I was already turning back to the closet. I had another urgent call to make.

Chapter Twelve

WHEN HIS PHONE RANG, BRADLEY WAS IN A BAR ON THE LOWER EAST Side. It wasn't some hipster joint with tapas and a 'tasting menu' but a real place with nicotine ingrained in the walls and drinks strong enough to curl your toes. A last vestige of old New York – a cops' bar, in other words.

Ben was attending a farewell for some old warhorse and, thanks to the popularity of the retiree and the design of the speakeasy, the only place he could escape the crowd and noise was out in the street. As a result, he was holding a long-neck beer in drizzling rain when he got drafted into the front line of the secret world.

'Where are you?' he asked.

'In a CIA jet over Jordan,' I said. There was no point in masking it, I needed him shaken, to hear the clarion call.

'As soon as you hang up,' I continued, 'I want you to call the man you've been passing messages to. His name is David McKinley, he's the director of United States intelligence.'

I heard Bradley's intake of breath. 'Shit, I thought—'

'Forget whatever you thought. This is the real deal. Tell Dave I need a wingman fast. He'll organize a chopper to take you to an airport and get you on a government jet.'

'Where am I going?' he asked.

'Bodrum. McKinley will arrange the documentation – you're an NYPD detective investigating the murder of Ingrid Kohl.'

'Who's Ingrid Kohl?'

'It's the name of the dead woman you found at the Eastside Inn.'

'How do you—?'

'Later,' I said, as I thanked providence for Cameron and whoever

Ingrid really was: their crimes had got me into Turkey and had at least given us a chance.

'I'll pick you up at the airport,' I said. 'And Ben – make sure you bring your side arm.'

Six miles high, turning hard for Bodrum, the turbulence finally abating, I figured he wouldn't need it if everything went to plan. Then again, when had that ever happened?

Chapter Thirteen

DESPITE HIS VEHEMENT OBJECTIONS, THE DEPUTY DIRECTOR OF THE Turkish MIT made the phone call twenty minutes after I had spoken to Whisperer. It was to Leyla Cumali.

I never heard the conversation, of course, but some time later I read a transcript of it translated into English. Even from that document, devoid of all inflection and emotion, it was easy to tell that the MIT guy was a master of his craft. He had one of his assistants phone and schedule a time for Cumali to call him. She was given the number of MIT's switchboard and, by the time she had made it through various assistants, she would have been in no doubt that she was talking to a very powerful man.

Very politely, he said that he needed her help in a highly confidential matter concerning a foreign visitor. God, the relief she must have felt when she realized he wasn't investigating her.

'How well do you know Brodie David Wilson?' he asked.

The transcript records a pause – it would have been Cumali overcoming her surprise – but the spook encouraged her.

'Just your impressions, Detective – you're not giving evidence here,' he said, with a laugh. Damn, he was good.

He listened quietly to her account of me, interrupting now and again to make her think that he cared.

'Thank you, very good,' he said, when she had trailed to a stop. 'Have you felt at any time that perhaps he wasn't a member of the FBI?' he asked, starting to lay the pipe.

'No . . . no,' said Cumali, but then hesitated while she thought about it more deeply. 'There was one thing: he was clever – I mean, outstandingly clever – at what he did. I remember wondering if all FBI agents were that good.'

'Yes, that would make sense . . . him being very good,' the deputy director said obscurely. 'Tell me, did he ever make phone calls in your presence that led you to be suspicious or confused about their content?'

'No . . . He had a strange habit, though – I never noticed it, but my secretary did. Except when he was making a call, he always had the battery removed from his cellphone.'

Well, I thought, despite the make-up and the stilettos, Hayrunnisa was smarter than I had given her credit for.

'Why would he take the battery out?' the spook asked.

'I have no idea.'

'Then let me help. If somebody has a cellphone in their pocket, it can be turned on remotely without them knowing.

'Once it is powered up, the inbuilt microphone can be activated. Somebody who is tapping into the phone can then hear everything that is being said in a room. If the battery has been taken out, there is no risk.'

'I had no idea,' Cumali replied.

'So you're not aware that intelligence agents always do that?'

'Intelligence agents? Can you tell me what this is about?'

Working to Whisperer's instructions, that was exactly the question the deputy director wanted Cumali to ask. He played it like the expert he was.

'You are a sworn officer of the law – a highly regarded one, I might add. All this is highly confidential.'

'Of course.'

'We have cameras at the Bulgarian border which record all crossings. We also know the licence tag of Brodie Wilson's rent-a-car so, thanks to certain software we use, we learned that he entered Bulgaria. Do you know why?'

The licence-tag recognition system was bullshit – sure it existed, but Turkey wasn't even close to using it. Cumali, however, had no way of knowing that.

'No,' she said.

'Two of our men who operate over the border located him in a town called Svilengrad, where he bought a cheap cellphone, a SIM card and made one phone call. Have you ever heard him mention that town?'

'Never.'

'As a consequence of this, we became very interested in Agent Wilson. For reasons I can't discuss, we now believe that may not be his real identity. We think his name is Michael John Spitz. Do you have any response to that name, Detective?'

'None at all,' Cumali replied.

'Spitz is a member of an elite CIA group,' the deputy director continued. 'That would explain why you thought he was an outstanding investigator. Their job is to hunt terrorists.'

I could imagine the fear that must have struck Cumali's heart, sitting in her whitewashed house at the old port, suddenly jolted into thinking about the coded calls between her and the Hindu Kush.

Their job is to hunt terrorists.

In the name of Allah, she must have thought, who were the CIA after – her? Her brother? She knew that he was a wanted man, but what the hell had he dragged her into?

'We believe the homicide investigation is a cover,' the deputy director said. 'Something has brought him to Bodrum. Do you have any idea what he could be investigating?'

'No,' she lied. The transcript recorded that she said it 'forcefully'.

'Thank you, anyway, you've been very helpful,' the spook said. 'At the moment, we're not going to do anything. We'll listen to Spitz's phone calls and wait and see. But I'll give you a number, a direct line. If you hear anything, you are to call me immediately. Understood?' he said, before recounting the number and hanging up.

Whisperer and I had broken all the rules: we had arranged for the target to learn the truth of the mission. But in doing so we had baited a trap – Cumali was a detective and I was gambling everything that her instinct would be to investigate. She would want to know more – fear would make sure of that – and I believed there was only one place she could look: in my hotel room.

She wouldn't do it herself but, given her work, she would know plenty of criminals who could. It was now my job to make sure that everything was ready when they arrived.

Chapter Fourteen

FOR THE FIRST TIME IN MY PROFESSIONAL LIFE, I WAS OUT IN THE COLD – I was on a mission without a legend or cover.

The small jet had crossed Jordan and landed at Milas late in the morning. I passed through Turkish immigration without delay, grabbed my car and, instead of driving to Bodrum, headed fast into Milas. Just behind City Hall, I found a camera store and watched as a young woman took my phone and printed out a hard copy of the photo I had taken of Cumali's childhood home in Jeddah. The store also sold phone accessories and I bought another battery for the piece of junk I had purchased in Bulgaria.

I found a store catering to tradesmen nearby and picked up a hand drill, a small soldering iron, a bottle of all-purpose glue and half a dozen other items. I threw them in the car and drove hard to Bodrum. I arrived back at the hotel while it was still lunchtime, which meant the manager was out and I made it to my room without delay.

I pulled the battered Samsonite suitcase off the top of the wardrobe and carefully cut open the fabric lining that concealed the inside of the two locks. I drilled out the tiny keyhole of one of them then turned my attention to the Bulgarian phone. With the soldering iron I managed to connect the new battery in sequence – doubling the time the phone could operate – then opened up the menu. I spent a frustrating twenty minutes manipulating the software so that the camera would take a photo every two seconds.

I taped the jury-rigged phone inside the Samsonite so that its camera lens was hard against the drilled-out lock, giving it a clear view of the room. Before I went out, I only had to turn the phone on, glue the fabric back and return the suitcase to the top of the closet. I figured that the camera would be perfectly hidden, but the location had one other great advantage – people searching for something will look inside a box or suitcase but hardly ever examine the object itself.

I now had my own surveillance system, admittedly held together by wire and rope, but workable: I had to know for certain that the burglars had found what I was about to plant. Everything else depended on it.

I took the freshly printed photo of Cumali's old home and added a computer disk which included a copy of her Bahrain driver's licence, details of the scuba-diving blog and the precis of her college course in Istanbul. I put everything in a plastic file and placed it inside the in-room safe – a piece of crap with a battery-operated electronic keypad which any burglar worthy of the name would know how to power down, clear the code and open.

The photograph and documents were to convince Leyla Cumali that Michael Spitz was hunting her.

In addition, because they were genuine items, the so-called halo effect would wash over whatever else she found – I was counting on the scum-boys also to steal my laptop. Inside, Cumali would find two emails – totally fake – which I had drafted on the flight across Jordan. I was checking them, inserting them in my inbox at the appropriate dates, when the hotel phone rang.

A woman identified herself as being a secretary at the New York homicide bureau, but I figured it was bullshit – she was almost certainly one of Whisperer's back-office staff.

'The flight you are expecting is Turkish Airlines 349 from Rome, arriving at Milas International at 15.28,' she said.

I wasn't expecting any flight from Rome, but I guessed what had happened: Whisperer had figured a government jet would attract too many questions and had booked Bradley on a commercial flight.

I glanced at my watch: I had ten minutes if I was going to get to Milas in time. I finished checking the emails but didn't delete any computer files – the material which was genuinely confidential was protected by unbreakable 128-bit encryption, and its presence would lend credibility to the subterfuge. The computer itself was password-protected and there was some low-level code, but I was confident – as Whisperer had told me when he first gave it to me – that it could be busted quickly if somebody wanted to.

I put the laptop in the safe alongside the other material, turned the Bulgarian phone on, re-glued the fabric and went out the door fast.

The bellhop, the young guy behind the reception desk and the woman at the switchboard watched as I exited the elevator. I slid the room key along the desk and called to the phone operator, loud enough for them all to hear. 'I'm going to the airport. Any calls, I'll be back at five thirty.'

I knew that if Cumali was going to have my room turned over, the first thing she would do was try to discover my movements. Hopefully, I had just saved her and the scum-boys some trouble.

As I ran for my car I figured that, by the time I returned, they would have entered the loading dock at the rear, gone up the service elevator, picked the lock on my door and – to make it look like a plain vanilla hotel robbery – my room would be in chaos.

I couldn't have been more wrong.

Chapter Fifteen

I GOT TO THE AIRPORT JUST IN TIME: TWO MINUTES AFTER I ARRIVED, Bradley walked out of the customs zone.

I guided him past the men with massive urns on their backs selling apple tea, endless crowds of hustlers and beggars and an attractive Slavic couple who were almost certainly pickpockets and out towards the parking lot.

On the street, the wind was coming straight out of Asia, delivering a host of exotic scents, and loudspeakers were broadcasting a *muezzin*, telling Muslims that it was time for prayer. I saw Bradley looking at the chaotic traffic, the distant pine-clad hills, the minarets of a nearby mosque, and I knew it was setting him back on his heels.

'We're close to the borders of Iraq and Syria,' I said. 'A bit different from Paris, huh?'

He nodded.

'People in my line of work get used to alien places,' I continued, 'but you never get used to the loneliness. It's good to see you.'

'You too,' he replied. 'You gonna tell me why we're here?'

'No,' I said, 'but I'll tell you as much as necessary.'

We had arrived at the Fiat and, while I performed the usual deadly dance with the Turkish traffic, I asked Bradley to remove the batteries from both our cellphones. By the time I had explained why, we were on the freeway.

'We – that means the US government – are hunting a man,' I explained. 'We've been hunting him for weeks—'

'The guy everyone's talking about?' he asked. 'The one with the nuclear trigger?'

587

'There is no guy with a nuclear trigger,' I replied. 'That was a cover story.'

I saw the surprise on Bradley's face, and I knew what he was thinking – he had seen the president talking about it numerous times on TV. I didn't have time to explain the reason for that, and I kept going.

'A couple of days ago we thought we had him nailed, but we were wrong. We don't have a name, a nationality or his whereabouts. The only link we have is his sister—'

'Leyla Cumali,' he said, his eyes flashing in a moment of realization.

'Yes. In the last twelve hours she has been told that I am not here investigating a murder – that I am a CIA agent.'

'Are you?'

'No, I'm far beyond that. When we get to Bodrum, I believe we'll find she has organized to have my hotel room robbed. The thieves will have taken a number of items, including my laptop.

'It has several security features, but she will be able to access it without much trouble. Inside are two emails that she will find significant. The first will tell her that we intercepted coded phone calls between her and a man in the Hindu Kush—'

'The where?' Bradley asked.

'Afghanistan. She will read that we don't know the content of those calls – because they were in code – but given that she was born in Saudi Arabia, her father was publicly executed and her phone friend has been involved in the abduction of three missing foreigners, we think that she is part of a terrorist undertaking.'

'Is she?'

'I don't believe so, but the document gives details of her impending rendition to Bright Light.'

'What's Bright Light?'

'She'll search the Web and find a number of newspaper articles which claim that it's in Thailand, part of a system of CIA secret prisons.'

'Is it?'

'Yes.'

'What happens at Bright Light?'

'People are tortured.'

'Our country does that to women?'

'Our country does that to anybody.'

Ben had only been in-country for thirty minutes but already he was getting quite an education. I let him sit in sombre silence for a moment as I overtook a convoy of Turkish military heading to the Syrian border.

'Cumali is the sole carer for a six-year-old boy,' I went on, once the tank transporters were vanishing in my rear-view mirror. 'Obviously, the child can't be abandoned – so the document lays out the arrangements for his welfare.'

I pulled out my phone, replaced the battery, opened its photo file and gave it to Ben. On the screen was one of the shots of the little guy I had taken in Cumali's kitchen.

'He's Down's syndrome,' said Bradley, looking up at me.

'Yes,' I replied. 'The document says he will be picked up by our people and transported to an orphanage in Bulgaria, one of the poorest nations in Europe. Due to poverty and the fact that he is an alien, nothing will be done to cater for his special needs.'

Bradley didn't take his eyes off me; sickened, I think. 'The purpose of the document is to panic her,' I went on.

'I think you just might succeed,' he replied. 'Why?'

'We know she's able to contact our target. The problem has always been that, if we try to force her, she'll do it in a way that will warn him – he'll go to ground and we'll lose him completely.

'If, however, she thinks she's reading secret information and it panics her, she will contact the target voluntarily. No deliberate mistakes, and no clever warnings.

'He's the only person who can help her, the only person who can tell her what is going on. Even if he wanted to ignore her, he can't – he's an Arab, he's her brother and that makes him the head of the family.'

Bradley thought about it, then looked again at the photo he was still holding. The little guy was laughing – a child, just a pawn in the great game.

'You think this up all by yourself?' he asked. It wasn't admiration I heard in his voice.

'Pretty much,' I said.

'Is it always like this – your work?'

'No,' I replied, thinking about two little girls in Moscow. 'Sometimes it's worse.'

Bradley took a breath. 'Okay. So Cumali contacts her brother – what then?'

'She tells him about the second email.'

Chapter Sixteen

I DRIFTED OVER INTO THE SLOW LANE AND SCANNED THE TRAFFIC behind in the mirror. When I was satisfied that we hadn't picked up a tail, I walked Ben deeper into the shadow world.

'The second email claims to be from the deputy director of the CIA. It was dated two days ago and it reports that we have had a breakthrough concerning the abduction of the three foreigners in the Hindu Kush.'

'But you haven't, have you?' Ben asked.

'No. The man and the events are a mystery. He's a lone wolf, an organization of one. There hasn't been any gossip and no chance of betrayal. We've been looking for a ghost.'

I swung down an off-ramp, heading for Bodrum. 'But we have glimpsed him,' I continued. 'We know that he's been to Afghanistan twice. First as a teenage *mujahideen* to fight the Soviets and then a few months back to abduct the three foreigners—'

'Why were those people taken?'

'I can't tell you that.' Ben was offended, but I couldn't help it – there was no need for him to know, and that was the golden rule in the world he had entered.

'One aspect of the event, however, has been critical to our plan. Dave McKinley realized it – you can't abduct three people by yourself. Not in Afghanistan, not from different locations, not from fortified compounds. In that regard, our ghost must have had help. It has given us a way in.

'McKinley has done two tours in the 'Ghan and nobody in the Western world knows more about the country than him. He's certain it was old *muj* comrades, probably one of the warlords, who helped our man. Those ties run deep and would explain why, despite a thousand agents on the ground, we have heard nothing.

'The second email says that, in two days' time, one of those helpers – in return for a large cash reward and a new identity – will reveal the names of our ghost and all those who assisted him.'

We had reached the coast, and the setting sun was washing the azure sea with shades of pink. I doubted that Ben had seen anything as beautiful, but he barely registered it.

'If that were true about the cash reward, what would happen to the men he betrays?' he asked.

'They would be interrogated, then handed over to the Afghan government.'

'And executed.'

'Yes. The email doesn't reveal the traitor's name, but it makes it clear that I know it.'

'So, if your target – if the ghost – wants to save himself and his comrades, he has to find out from you the name of the turncoat and pass it on to the warlord fast.'

'That's right,' I replied. 'Our target has to come to the waterhole, he has to come to Bodrum and get me to talk. And he'll have less than a day to do it.'

'Then you grab him.'

'No.'

Bradley reacted. 'No?! What do you mean "no"? I thought—'

'Grabbing him won't help. The man has information we need. Let's say he has sent a package to America – or is about to – and we have no chance of finding it. We have to get him to tell us the shipping details.'

'Torture him.'

'No – same problem as with his sister. By the time we discover he has told us a raft of crap, it's too late. The package has already arrived. No, he has to tell us voluntarily.'

Bradley laughed. 'How are you going to get him to do that?'

'I'm not,' I replied. 'You are.'

Chapter Seventeen

'NO!' BEN WAS SHOUTING, STARING AT ME. I HAD NEVER SEEN HIM SO angry. I had just explained how we were going to force the Saracen to reveal the so-called delivery arrangements and, now that I had finished, he wasn't bothering to hide his disgust at even being in the same car as the idea.

'I won't do it. Nobody fucking would. What sort of person – what sort of mind – thinks up something like that?'

'Then give me a better idea,' I replied, trying to keep it calm. 'I don't like it any more than you do.'

'Oh, yeah? You're forgetting – you *chose* this life.'

'I didn't. If you recall, I was trying to leave it – this life *chose* me.'

I was pissed off – the last thing I needed was a lesson in morality. I hit the brake and swung into the parking lot of the café with the panoramic view of Bodrum and the sea.

'I'm not interested in a fucking view,' Bradley said.

'I pulled in so that you could have some privacy.'

'Privacy for what?'

'To talk to Marcie.'

Again, I stopped far away from the crowd on the terrace. I started to get out of the car so that he could be alone.

'What am I speaking to Marcie for?' he demanded.

'You told me once her parents had a beach house – in North Carolina or somewhere.'

'What's a beach house got to do with it?'

'Have they got one or not?!' I insisted.

'On the Outer Banks. Why?'

'Tell her to drive there – now, tonight.'

'Here's an idea – she might want to know the reason.'

I ignored it. 'Tell her to pick up as much food and bottled water as she can. Staples – rice, flour, gas bottles. She's got to remember gas bottles. As many as she can find.'

He stared, the anger gone. 'You're scaring me, Scott.'

'*Brodie*! The name is Brodie.'

'Sorry.'

'Don't be scared, you're safe up where you are – on the moral high ground. Can she shoot?'

'Sure. I taught her.'

'Get long arms – rifles, shotguns. I'll tell you the best make and model numbers in a minute. Once she's set up in the house I can walk her through how to convert 'em to full automatic. She'll need ammunition. Lots of ammunition.'

Bradley tried to interrupt.

'Shut up. Anybody approaches the house, at two hundred yards she tells them to back off. They keep coming, and she shoots to kill. No warning shots. Two hundred yards is important – at that distance there's no chance of her inhaling aerosoled particles and becoming infected.'

I saw the fear spark in his eyes. 'Infected with what?!'

'A virus. Highly contagious and resistant to any known vaccine. This version is being called evasive haemorrhagic, and it is believed to have a 100 per cent kill-rate. That is what is being sent into the homeland. Smallpox.'

Ben Bradley, a homicide cop from Manhattan, a hero of 9/11, someone taking only the second overseas trip of his life, an outsider drafted into the secret world less than twelve hours before, a guy sitting on an isolated lookout high above the Turkish coast, the bravest man I have ever met, was now the eleventh person to know.

Chapter Eighteen

WE WOUND OUR WAY DOWN INTO BODRUM IN SILENCE. BEN NEVER called Marcie – faced with a choice between two evils, and unable to come up with an alternative to my plan for finding out the truth from the Saracen, he chose the lesser of them.

'Take me through the arrangements again,' he had said, once he had overcome his shock – and fear – on hearing about the unfolding catastrophe.

When I had finished explaining the plan again and answered a host of questions – even down to the length of rope and how tight to make the noose – I put the car into gear, swept past the terrace and hit the road.

I concentrated on the driving, slowing only when we hit Bodrum and started to weave through the backstreets. Once I got close to the house I was looking for, I pulled to the kerb and parked a good fifty yards away. I pointed it out to Ben, made him name ten significant features and then repeat them. It was a standard way of imprinting a memory, and most studies showed that, even under extreme stress, a subject would remember six of them. Satisfied that, even in the pounding whirl of a live mission, Bradley would find the correct house, I pulled out and drove to the hotel.

While Ben went to the reception desk, I headed for my room, anxious to see how much damage Cumali's scum-boys had done. As I stepped into the elevator I saw the manager smile and take Ben's passport.

'Ahh, Mr Benjamin Michael Bradley,' he said. 'I will need of the credit cards three from you to put me on the side of the safe.'

'Say again?' said Ben.

Chapter Nineteen

THERE WAS NOTHING. I WAS STANDING JUST INSIDE MY HOTEL ROOM, and not a thing had been touched.

I closed the door behind me and moved to the closet, keyed in the code to the safe and opened it. The laptop and the plastic file were exactly where I had left them.

I swept my eyes around the room. Where the hell had I gone wrong? How had Cumali seen through it? Had the Turkish MIT guy tipped her off, either deliberately or inadvertently? I didn't think so – he had far too much at risk to blow it for one phone call to a lowly cop. So why hadn't she taken the bait? With my mind jumping from theory to theory, I walked around the room. I passed the unmade bed – I had put the DO NOT DISTURB sign on the door when I left so that the scum-boys wouldn't be disturbed – and stepped into the bathroom.

Everything was how I had left it. Unthinking, I bent to pick up a towel I had left on a stool and saw that the tube of toothpaste was sitting on the shelf where I had put it. Ever since I was a kid, I'd had a strange habit though– I had always laid my toothbrush along the top of the tube. Now it was sitting next to it. Somebody had moved them to open the bathroom cabinet.

I wheeled around, entered the bedroom and hauled the suitcase off the top of the closet. I was relieved to see that, even if an intruder had looked inside, they hadn't found the Bulgarian phone – it was still hidden inside the lining. I pulled it free of its tape, clicked on an icon, and opened the photos, which had been taken at two-second intervals.

I quickly saw that the scum-boys had come all right – they were just way better than I had anticipated.

The time code showed that two men had entered my room thirty-two minutes after I had departed. One photo showed them face on in perfect focus: a pair of hard-eyed hipsters in their early thirties wearing expensive leather jackets and carrying backpacks. Their quick, efficient movements and the minimum of conversation told me that they were professionals. I had turned the phone's microphone on, and that gave me a barely audible recording of their muffled voices. While I couldn't understand what they were saying, I recognized the language: they were Albanians. In retrospect, that should have set alarm bells ringing.

Their nationality also explained the ease with which they had entered the room. Standing in the background of one frame, I saw the bellhop – their countryman and fellow sleaze – being handed a wad of cash. I figured that, after they paid him, he returned to slouching in an alcove in the foyer, acting as their lookout in case I returned early.

There were thousands of photos – thank God the two batteries had held out – but by flicking through them and knowing exactly how professionals worked, I managed to build a picture of exactly what they had done.

The photos showed the leader – the one giving the orders – shrugging off his leather jacket and getting down to work. Underneath, he was wearing a skin-tight black T-shirt – chosen, I was sure, because it accentuated how ripped he was. A lot of steroids, I thought.

He pulled a digital camera out of one of the backpacks and, before they searched the clutter on the small desk, he photographed it so that they could replace everything in exactly the same position. I figured they followed the same procedure as they worked fast through everything else. No wonder, apart from the slightly misplaced toothbrush, I hadn't thought anyone had been inside.

They turned their attention to the safe and, though the photos weren't very clear, I could tell it offered no resistance. Muscleman would have turned its cheap circular keypad counter-clockwise and popped it out, revealing the power supply and circuitry. That allowed him to remove the batteries, clearing the code, and plug in his own keypad. A bracket of ten photos showed that he had the door open in under twenty seconds.

They took out the plastic folder and photographed the shot of

Cumali's childhood home before Muscleman produced his own laptop, slipped the disk into it and copied its contents. As soon as it was finished, they turned their attention to my computer. I didn't need to wade through all the surveillance photos to know what they did . . .

They used a tiny screwdriver to remove my hard drive and then inserted it into their own computer, bypassing most of my laptop's security features. With the help of code-generating software, they would have broken through the remainder of the defences and been able to access all my documents and emails within minutes.

From there, it was a simple matter to copy everything on to USB portable drives, return my hard drive to the laptop and put everything back in the safe. I flew through the rest of the covert photos and saw that the men had searched the other parts of the room, entered the bathroom and were out of the door, carrying everything they needed, twenty-six minutes after they had arrived.

I sat on the bed and looked at a photo of them leaving. My hand was trembling with relief: it had been successful; the first stage was over. Cumali had believed the phone call from our man at MIT and acted exactly as we had hoped.

There was no doubt that she would be able to read the stolen data, and that meant the next steps were now entirely in her hands. Would she believe what she saw in the emails? In my fatigue and anxiety, had I made some small but fatal error? Would she be sufficiently panicked – terrified of Bright Light for herself and a Bulgarian orphanage for the child – to code up a message and contact her brother?

Perhaps if I hadn't been so preoccupied with those questions, I would have paid more attention to the photo I was holding. I knew that there were seven major drug cartels operating in the area and that one of them, run by a lavender farmer out of Thessaloniki in Greece, had a heartfelt interest in the activities of American intelligence agents. Had I been more attentive, I would have thought about who was the most likely person Cumali would find to do her dirty work or maybe even recognized something about one of the men whose image I had captured. But I didn't, and there was a knock on the door.

I looked through the peephole and saw it was Bradley.

'Did the burglars come?' he asked.

'Yeah,' I replied.

He slumped down in a chair. 'What about that manager, huh?'

'The professor? What about him?'

He turned and looked. 'The professor! Professor of what?'

'English,' I said.

Bradley almost smiled – much to my relief. It meant he was overcoming the disgust he had felt at the role he had been given. In the event that everything went ahead, I needed him calm and totally committed: my life would depend on it.

Chapter Twenty

'WHAT HAPPENS NOW?' BRADLEY ASKED.

He had left my room, returned to his own, uupacked and showered. Looking less haggard and seemingly more relaxed, he was sitting with me in the hotel's dining area. It was 9 p.m. and we were picking at plates of meze, neither of us with much appetite, the anxiety bearing down. We were alone: the season was dying fast and the hotel's few other guests had already headed out to beachside bars and restaurants.

'The next step is that Cumali reads the fake emails. Then we hope she contacts her brother,' I replied.

'How will we know if she does?'

'Echelon,' I said.

'What's Echelon?'

'Something that doesn't exist. But, if it did, it would be listening to cellphones, fixed lines, emails, every communication in this part of Turkey. In particular, it would be monitoring one phone box four miles from here.'

'And if Cumali does contact him, when do you think she'll do it?'

The same question had been occupying my thoughts. 'She should have received the stolen information by now,' I replied. 'The way the Albanians took it means she won't have to spend time trying to unlock it – the passwords are already broken.

'Assuming she believes everything she reads, it'll scare her badly. She'll keep rereading it, trying to find other stuff on the hard drive, wasting time. Finally, the worst of the shock, maybe even a bout of nausea, will have passed.

'She'll sit at her computer in her old fisherman's house and post a message on an Internet forum or dating site.

'Almost immediately, the Saracen will receive a text message from the same site saying that someone who shares his interests has just posted an entry.

'He'll know what it means – he has to contact her urgently, probably at some prearranged time.

'Meanwhile, Cumali has to record grabs from English-language news programmes and code up a message. The anxiety will slow her down and then she's got to drive to the phone box and wait for him to call.

'I figure, by the time she's done everything, Echelon will hear something by no later than midnight. That's our drop-dead time. If it doesn't, I guess she will have seen through it, and we're finished.'

'And say Echelon does hear. McKinley will call you and tell you that the man is probably on his way?' asked Bradley.

'Yeah. McKinley's message will be short, he'll just say something like: Buddy, you're live.'

'Midnight,' Ben said quietly, and looked at a clock above the fireplace. 'Three hours to go.' He almost laughed. 'It's gonna be a long night.'

'Yeah,' I replied coolly. Over the years I'd had a lot of long nights and I had learned something about patience. 'Two choices – you wanna play cards or hear a story?'

'I don't know,' he responded. 'Is it a good story?'

'Judge for yourself,' I said. 'It's about a woman called Ingrid Kohl.'

Chapter Twenty-one

'NOT ALL DEATH WARRANTS ARE SIGNED BY JUDGES OR GOVERNORS,' I explained. 'This one was a pre-nup agreement.'

Ben and I had moved from the dining room into the lounge – a cosy place with an open fire, a lazy cat and a good view across the lobby to the front door – just in case Cumali or the Albanians had a different plan and came calling.

'The man and woman in question had known each other for six weeks when they decided to marry,' I continued. 'Her name was Cameron, his was Dodge and there was one point two billion at stake.'

'No wonder there was a pre-nup,' Ben said, lifting a beer.

If ever there was a night for a drink, I thought, this was the one, but I managed to push the idea aside. 'Cameron had been working as a glorified sales assistant, so she didn't have much bargaining power – or access to good advice.

'Needless to say, it was a tough agreement. If she divorced Dodge, especially in the first five years, she got next to nothing. On the other hand, as a widow, she got everything. So, if she fell out of love—'

'And wanted real money—' Ben added.

'Dodge hadn't signed a pre-nup—'

'He'd signed a death warrant,' the homicide detective said, raising his eyebrows, impressed.

'A couple of months later, Cameron decided she didn't want to be with Dodge any more,' I said.

'Another party involved?'

'There usually is. In this case, it was a woman.'

'Wow, this is the gift that keeps on giving,' Ben said.

'Now, you have to understand, there are a few things I don't know. I've had to guess at them, make some assumptions, rely on experience, but I know I'm right.'

He nodded. 'Sure. You're the one investigator I wouldn't argue with.'

'My intuition is that the two women had grown up together; I think they were lovers before Dodge entered the frame,' I went on. 'Anyway, let's call Cameron's friend Marilyn – I don't know her real name.

I stole a glance at my watch – only twenty minutes gone. I didn't know it, but apparently time passed slowly when you were waiting for the end of the world.

'They had left Turkey Scratch, or wherever they grew up, and moved to Manhattan, full of dreams, I suppose.

'Cameron got a job at Prada and Marilyn wanted to be an actress. In other words, she took a job in an office.'

'Then Cameron met the billionaire,' said Ben.

'Yeah, it was a whirlwind, but Cameron must have known it was her one chance at a fortune – lightning never strikes twice.

'Maybe she sat down and discussed it with Marilyn, perhaps it was all very civilized, but in my experience life's a lot messier than that – my guess is she dumped her lifelong friend. Whatever happened, she married him.

'One thing I'm certain of: Dodge never met Marilyn or even saw her – that was important for what happened later.'

'Okay,' Ben said. 'So Dodge and Cameron get married, but it doesn't work out.'

'It didn't take long. Even though I believe that Marilyn felt betrayed, Cameron re-established contact. She wanted to be rid of Dodge, but she had a problem—'

'The pre-nup.'

'Right. But the women saw a way round it – they could have each other *and* the money. Kill him.'

'What was their plan?' Ben asked.

'They didn't know. Then, one morning, a group of terrorists helped them out: 9/11.

'The office where Marilyn worked was located in one of the towers, but she was running late. She saw the planes hit and realized

603

that, as far as the world was aware, she was dead. For a would-be murderer, there was no better alibi.'

I looked up, and saw three fellow guests come through the front door and head for the elevator. As usual, the tradecraft was running in the back of my mind, and I knew that all the residents were now in for the night. In the next ten minutes the young duty manager would lock the front door, check that the loading bay and service elevator were secure and dim the house lights. I looked at a clock on the mantel – its hands were barely moving. Where was Cumali? Where in hell was Echelon?

'But Marilyn had to stay dead,' said Ben, dragging me back to New York and 9/11.

'That's right, so she walked through the smoke and body parts and found the perfect place to live off the grid. The Eastside Inn.

'She was an actress, and she used her craft to make sure nobody could recognize or describe her. Every day she played a different role.'

Ben nodded. 'Yeah – I never did get a photofit. She must have started planning right away. That took her to the New York library and your book.'

'Right. An appendix at the back deals with the clear-up rate of homicides in different countries. A few minutes' reading would have told her that there were a lot better places to kill someone than America.

'Turkey was perfect – there was little use of forensics, and investigators were overworked. Cameron would have had no trouble convincing Dodge to cruise the Aegean, but that created a big problem for Marilyn.'

'Dead people can't get passports,' Bradley said.

I nodded. The lights throughout the hotel started to dim, the cat stretched, Bradley and I looked at the clock on the mantel. A hundred and twenty-five minutes to go.

I took a break, walked over and poured myself a coffee. My hands were shaking.

Chapter Twenty-two

THEY WERE WATCHING THE CLOCK IN WASHINGTON, TOO. IT WAS MID-afternoon on the East Coast, and Whisperer had made his own estimate of when Echelon would hear a coded message from Cumali. It was even earlier than mine.

If it was going to happen, he calculated, it would be no later than 11 p.m. Bodrum time. He was either more of a pessimist – or a realist – than me.

When there was sixty minutes left by his count, he closed the door of his office, stopped all phone calls and gave strict orders that he wasn't to be disturbed. If the president needed him, there was a direct, secure line on his desk and, in the event of good news, the NSA would flash the details to him on a dedicated Internet channel.

In his heart, he didn't think it was likely. Experience had taught him that wishing didn't count for anything, and he had seen too much madness, too much fanaticism, to expect any terrorist plan ever to end well. On his first tour in Afghanistan, as a young analyst, he had been seriously wounded by a pregnant woman wearing a bomb belt and, as station chief years later, he had seen kids clutching grenades run towards GIs while asking for candy.

No, he was certain: very soon the president would order the closing of the borders, the panic would start, the queues for vaccine would stretch for miles, troops would be in the streets and the terrible search for suicide infectees would start. As soon as the president had finished addressing the nation, Whisperer would hand him the document which he was now starting to write. It was his resignation.

He wrote with his usual brutal honesty but with a sadness that weighed so heavily he thought it might crush him. A sadness for his country, for the citizens he had failed, for his kids who he barely knew, for a career that had started thirty years ago with such huge promise and was now ending in historic failure.

The clock on his desk ran down – the Internet channel was open, his screen alight – until it hit nothing. Time was up, there was no word from Echelon and, for once in his life, it brought him only misery to be proven right.

He opened his drawer and had the cuff around his arm to check his blood pressure when the secure phone flashed its bubble light. He picked it up.

'Nothing?' asked the president, not even trying to mask his anxiety.

'No,' replied Whisperer. 'Cumali obviously didn't swallow it – some small but critical mistake, I guess. Pilgrim calculates the drop-dead time differently – he says another fifty-seven minutes – but it won't change anything. What do you want to do – go to the people now?'

There was silence for a long moment as Grosvenor tried to bring order to his tumultuous thoughts. 'No,' he said finally. 'I gave him thirty-six hours. We play it out. He deserves that.'

Grosvenor hung up, devastated for the nation and its people, aware that the public and history would be merciless in their judgement.

An hour earlier, like Whisperer, he had also cleared his agenda and stopped his calls, so he now sat alone in the afternoon's swelling silence. He leaned his head into his hands and wished that Anne was still alive, he wished that they had had children, he wished that there was a family in whose arms he could find comfort and meaning.

But there was nothing, just a gale of fear blowing down the lonely corridors of his mind.

Chapter Twenty-three

BRADLEY AND I WERE IN A DIFFERENT CORRIDOR: WE WERE HEADING through the gloomy silence of the hotel towards my room.

With less than thirty minutes left before the deadline, I had wanted to walk off some of the crushing anxiety, and I had suggested to Bradley that I give him the Turkish police files concerning Dodge's death. Knowing that they would be crucial to a future prosecution, he agreed, and we said goodnight to the lazy cat and headed across the deserted foyer. We were about to step into the elevator when I stopped – I had a strong sense we were being watched.

There was nobody around, not even the duty manager, but there was a CCTV camera mounted on a wall, trained on the reception desk and its safe, and I wondered who might be in some office nearby observing us.

Quietly, I told Ben to take the elevator while I used the stairs – a group of assailants, Albanians for instance, would find it very difficult to deal with a target which suddenly split apart. The cop looked a question at me.

'I need the exercise,' I said.

He knew I was bullshitting, and I jagged left as he stepped into the elevator car. I took the stairs two at a time and met him without incident just as the steel doors opened. He stared at me and raised his eyebrows – I had the Beretta 9-mil out and cocked. 'Handweight?' he asked, deadpan.

I lowered it, and together we headed towards my room. I still had the feeling we were being observed, but the corridor wasn't equipped with cameras and, though I turned fast and looked behind us into the gloom, I saw nothing.

I unlocked the door and a thought occurred to me: the bellhop could still be in the building, ordered by whoever had recruited him to keep an eye on me. I closed the door behind us, bolted it and put the pistol on the coffee table, within easy reach.

'We were in Manhattan,' Bradley reminded me. 'Cameron and Marilyn had decided to kill Dodge in Turkey, but there was a problem.'

'Yeah, Marilyn needed a passport,' I said. 'So they started searching. They were looking for a woman in her twenties, a loner, new in town maybe, definitely somebody who wouldn't be missed.'

'Did they find her?'

'Sure.'

'Where?'

'A gay bar, Craig's List, Washington Square on a Sunday afternoon – I don't know, it doesn't matter. But Marilyn took her out on a date. Later in the evening she invited her back to the Eastside Inn with the promise of drugs and sex. Instead, she killed her.'

We looked at one another. 'She killed her for her identity, Ben,' I said.

Bradley said nothing, thinking about it, like any good cop trying to work out how to blow holes in it.

'You recall a woman at your seminar?' I continued. 'Turquoise shirt, very intelligent, sitting at the front?'

'Sure, I don't think she was intelligent, though. You told her women found you sexually attractive, and she agreed.'

I laughed. 'She said that the murder might have had something to do with identity theft, but I wasn't concentrating. Remember, those guys arrived and sat at the back? I should have listened, though – she got it right.'

'And you say the name of the dead woman was Ingrid Kohl?' Bradley said. 'That was the woman we found in the acid?'

'Yes,' I replied. 'Marilyn was dead. She had no identity, so she had to destroy Ingrid's face, her fingerprints and pull her teeth. She couldn't allow the body to be identified – she was going to steal her name and become her.

'Once the real Ingrid was dead, she had her wallet, her handbag and apartment keys. She cleaned out Room 89, sprayed it with industrial antiseptic, took one final pass, burnt anything else she found and headed out.'

'You think she moved into Ingrid's apartment?'

'I don't know. She chose a loner, so it was possible. Whatever happened, Marilyn would have immediately gone through Ingrid's possessions.

'In a few hours, she would have had a social security number and everything else she needed to get a birth certificate.'

'And with a birth certificate you can get a passport,' Bradley said.

'That's right,' I replied, and started to assemble the files relating to Dodge's murder.

I glanced at the digital clock on the night stand – fifteen minutes to go – and tried not to think of failure. There was still time – just one phone call and a short message was all we needed.

'So she's now Ingrid Kohl and has a legitimate passport with her own picture in it to prove it,' Bradley said.

'She flew to Europe,' I explained, 'established a history as a young backpacker and arrived in Turkey four months ahead of Cameron and Dodge.'

'What was the plan? How were she and Cameron going to kill him?'

'I'm not sure they knew, I think they were going to figure it out here – an accidental fall off the back of the boat one night, a hot shot of bad drugs, wait till he was loaded and drown him in the bath.

'But Ingrid got lucky – she met a hustler who used the name Gianfranco, a guy who knew more about the house where Dodge was staying than anyone.

'I think he had a scam going on – if there was nobody in residence he'd take young women through a secret tunnel and have sex with them in the locked mansion.'

'A secret way into the house?' Ben said. 'That must have been all Ingrid needed.'

'Yeah,' I replied, handing him the stack of files. Ten minutes left.

'Dodge and Cameron sailed into Bodrum on their boat and met Ingrid around the clubs – just casual, nothing special. Dodge had never seen Cameron's lover, so he had no reason to suspect Ingrid was anything more than she appeared.

'The two women waited till they knew he was alone on the estate – the night of a big fireworks display – and Ingrid made her way into the boathouse and along the tunnel. Dodge was in the library on a massive drug binge when a woman he had met burst into the room – of course, he assumed she had been let in by security.

'My theory is that – seemingly out of breath – she told him that a helicopter with Cameron on board had just gone down in the bay.'

'Shit,' said Ben, shocked at the ruthless ingenuity of it.

'Naturally, Dodge believed her,' I said. 'Not that he was in much of a state for rational thought – he was completely loaded, full of self-loathing and disgust too.'

'How do you know?'

'He had a series of cuts on the palms of his hands. The cops thought it was because he'd grabbed a bush on the cliff as he fell, but the wounds were too regular for that. He had been doing it to himself in the library. It's not uncommon among drug abusers – he was self-harming.'

Ben was silent. 'Poor guy,' he said finally. 'All the money in the world, and he's alone, sitting with a knife . . .' His voice was swallowed by the sadness of it.

'He grabbed a pair of binoculars, and Ingrid led him down the lawn,' I said. 'Desperate to see what had happened to Cameron, he stood on a railing. Ingrid probably offered to hold his waist.

'Everything turned out perfectly. Ingrid gave him a tiny push, he was flying through the air and a billion dollars was knocking on their door.'

I shrugged. That was it – finished. Ben looked at me.

'Ever seen one as good as this?' he asked. 'Even if the Turkish cops thought it was murder, there was nothing to connect Ingrid to Cameron.'

'Nothing at all,' I replied. 'How could she even be a suspect? There was no past relationship, no present involvement, no motive.'

Ben just shook his head. 'Brilliant.'

'Sure was,' I said. 'Both the murders – this one and the one in Manhattan.'

Ben had found a file he was interested in and opened it up: it showed the passport photo of Ingrid, and he stared at her beautiful face.

'If you're right about the rejection, I guess Ingrid must have really loved Cameron – to have been thrown aside in favour of some guy, to take her back and then to kill for her. Not once, but, as you say, twice.'

I had never thought about it like that. 'Yeah, I guess that's true,' I said. 'A strange sort of love, though.'

Of course, I should have remembered what Ingrid had said when I interviewed her – about not understanding the half of it. It was arrogance on my part, I suppose – I was so certain that I had unravelled the whole crime.

Bradley was too. 'How unlucky were they?' he said. 'They had committed what was near enough to the perfect murders, and they would have got away with it too – except the highest level of the United States intelligence community and one of its investigators became focused on this town.'

'Bad luck for them, maybe – not for us,' I said. 'Without Ingrid and Cameron I wouldn't have had the perfect cover – we would never have got as close as we have. God help them, but they were an important part of what could have been a great victory.'

'It's over?' he asked in surprise, looking at the clock. Four minutes to go. 'You don't think he's gonna call?'

I shook my head. 'I didn't tell you, but McKinley had his own estimate of when we could expect to hear. I was the outrider – he was an hour earlier.'

'What happens now?' he asked quietly.

'Get on the phone,' I said. 'Book the first plane home. If you leave at dawn, you can probably get back before they close the airports.

'Then do what I suggested – take Marcie and head straight for the beach house. Together, you'll have a chance.'

'Better with three,' he replied. 'Come with us.'

I smiled but shook my head. 'No, I'll go to Paris.'

'Paris?' he said, shocked. 'Cities are going to be the worst places.'

'Yeah, but I was happy there . . . I had a lot of dreams . . . If it gets really bad, I'd like to be close to that.'

He looked at me for a long moment, sad, I think, but it was hard to tell. Then he started to ask me how long it would take for the virus to burn out and other—

I held my hand up, signalling him to be quiet. I thought I had heard something outside in the hall. We both stood frozen, listening. Then we heard it together – footsteps.

I grabbed the Beretta off the night stand and glided silently to the peephole. Ben drew his pistol and trained it on the point where the door would open.

I looked through the spyhole and saw the shadow of a man on the wall. He was coming closer.

Chapter Twenty-four

THE MAN STEPPED INTO VIEW – IT WAS THE BELLHOP. UNAWARE HE WAS being watched, he pushed an envelope under the door.

I waited until he had left before I put the pistol down and picked it up. Watched by Ben – heart racing, my thoughts veering between hope and ruthless restraint – I opened the flap and pulled out a single sheet of paper.

I read it, felt the wall of anxiety collapse, and shook my head in wonder.

'What is it?' said Ben.

'I'm a fool,' I replied. 'There was never going to be any message that Echelon could hear. Cumali didn't need to go to the phone box – the man is already here.'

'In Bodrum? How do you know?'

I indicated the letter. 'She wants to pick me up at eleven in the morning – she's invited me to go on a picnic with her supposed son.'

'No, you're wrong,' Ben responded. 'What can happen if the boy's there?'

I laughed. 'He won't be,' I said. 'She'll make an excuse. Why else would she suddenly invite me to a picnic? She can't stand me. No, her brother's here, Ben. Tomorrow, I'm going to meet him.'

Bradley's doubts died under the weight of my certainty, and I saw the look on his face – I could tell he was dreading the role he would now have to play. To be honest, I wasn't looking forward to mine either.

I unbolted the door for him. 'Call Whisperer fast. Just tell him: Buddy, we're live.'

Chapter Twenty-five

I HAD COME TO TURKEY AS A PATHFINDER AND ENDED UP AS A LURE. Consequently, I had made no effort to put my affairs in order before I left and now I found I had to do it fast.

As soon as Bradley had left to call Whisperer, I sat down at the small desk, pulled out a piece of paper and, late as it was, started to write my will. In normal circumstances – with just a government pension, the annuity from Grace and a small collection of paintings – I wouldn't have bothered.

But things had become more complicated. When Ben and Marcie had blown my cover and forced me to leave Paris, one of the few things I had thrown into my bag were the two letters from the New York lawyer about the deaths of both Bill and Grace.

The elderly lawyer's name was Finbar Hanrahan, the son of penniless Irish immigrants, a man of such integrity that he threatened single-handedly to give lawyers a good name. He had been Bill's lawyer since before he had married Grace, and I had met him many times over the years.

With the two letters in hand and back in New York, I had made an appointment to see him. So it was, late one afternoon, that he rose from behind the desk in his spectacular office and greeted me warmly. He led me to a sofa in the corner from which there was a view all the way up Central Park and introduced me to the other two men in attendance, one of whom I recognized as a former secretary of commerce. Finbar said that they were lawyers but neither of them was associated with his firm.

'They have read certain documents and I have asked them to be here as impartial observers. Their job is to ensure that everything I do is by the book and cannot be misconstrued or questioned later. I want to be scrupulous about this.'

It seemed strange, but I let it ride – I figured Finbar knew what he was doing. 'You said in your letter there was a small matter of Bill's estate that had to be finalized,' I said. 'Is that what we're dealing with?'

'Yes,' he said, 'but there's an important issue we have to resolve first.' He looked at the two wise men, and they nodded. Let's do it, they seemed to be saying.

'You may not know this,' Finbar said, 'but Bill cared about you very much. More than that, he believed that in some way you were special – he thought you were destined to do something very important.'

I grinned. 'Yeah, one of Grace's friends told me that. Obviously, he'd become unhinged.'

Finbar smiled. 'Not unhinged, no – although he did become increasingly concerned about you. Especially after you left Harvard and went to live in Europe. Frankly, he didn't believe you were involved in the art business at all.'

The news didn't surprise me – Bill had been not only intelligent but also highly intuitive. I didn't reply – I just looked at the elderly lawyer, poker-faced.

'Bill had no idea how you earned money,' he continued, 'and was worried that you had become involved in a business that was either illegal or, at least, immoral.'

He waited for a reply, but I nodded and made no comment.

'He said that on several occasions when he tried to talk to you about it, you were not what he called "forthcoming".'

Again, I just nodded.

'So, this is my question, Scott: what exactly do you do?'

'Nothing right now,' I replied. 'I'm back in New York to see if I can find something that might grab my interest.' I didn't think it was a good idea to tell him I was looking for cover, running from my past.

'Yes, but before that?'

'I worked for the government,' I said after a pause.

'Well, it seems like half the country does that – although I use the term "work" loosely.' He had a pretty wry sense of humour, old Finbar. 'What exactly did you do for the government?'

'I'm sorry,' I said. 'I've been told not to talk about it.' I saw the two wise men exchange a glance – they obviously didn't believe it.

'Told by whom?' Finbar said, ignoring them. I felt sorry for him – it was clear he really wanted it to work out.

'By executive order,' I replied quietly.

The former secretary of commerce raised his eyes – it was getting too much for him. 'You worked in Europe, but the White House won't allow you to discuss it, is that right?'

'That's correct, Mr Secretary.'

'There's got to be somebody – a superior or someone – we can talk to about it, even in general terms,' Finbar said.

'I don't think that's possible,' I replied. 'I've probably gone too far already.' And anyway, The Division – which had never officially existed – had already been buried.

Finbar sighed. 'Bill was very clear, Scott – we can't go forward unless I'm satisfied about your integrity and honesty. You'll have to help us—'

'I can't – I've given my word not to speak about any of it. I signed undertakings.' I think they were surprised at the harshness and finality of my tone.

'Then I'm afraid . . .' Sadly, the lawyer looked at the other two men for confirmation, and they nodded. 'I'm afraid we have to terminate this meeting.'

I stood up, and the others did the same. I was disappointed that I would never know what Bill had intended, but I didn't know what else to do. The former secretary of commerce was putting out his hand in farewell when a thought occurred to me.

'I have a letter of commendation which might help. It concerns an event I was involved in some years ago.'

'An event? What sort of event? A charity run or something?' the former secretary asked.

'Not exactly,' I replied. 'Some parts of the letter would have to be blacked out, but I think you could see it.'

'Who's it from?' Finbar asked eagerly.

'From the president. It's handwritten on White House stationery.'

The three men didn't say anything. Finbar looked as if he'd have to bend down and pick his jaw up off the floor. The former secretary was the first to recover, still sceptical.

'Which president?' he asked.

'Your old boss,' I said coldly. I didn't like the guy much.

'Anyway, call him,' I continued. 'I'm sure you have a number. Ask him for permission to read the letter. Tell him it concerns a young man and a terrible event in Red Square – I'm sure he'll remember.'

The former secretary had no response, and Finbar filled the silence. 'We should stop here,' he said. 'I think we've stumbled into an area concerning national security—'

'You sure have,' I replied.

Finbar looked at the other two lawyers, addressing the former secretary. 'Jim, if you wouldn't mind – could you make that phone call later, just as a formality?'

He nodded.

'In the meantime, we're in agreement then?' Finbar continued. 'We're satisfied – we can move forward?'

The two men nodded, but I could tell from the way the former secretary was looking at me that he had been in the Cabinet meeting when the death of the Rider of the Blue had been discussed. He had probably never thought he would come face to face with the man who killed him.

Chapter Twenty-six

FINBAR TOOK A FILE OUT OF A WALL SAFE, THE OTHER TWO LAWYERS shrugged off their jackets and from our eyrie I looked out at rain squalls sweeping down the park towards us, still with no idea what was going on.

'As you know, when Bill died his very substantial wealth was held in a series of trusts which then passed – in their entirety – to Grace,' Finbar explained, opening the file.

'There was, however, one small but special part of his life that was quarantined in a separate corporate structure. What it contained had been built up over years and, quite honestly, Grace had never shown any interest in it.

'Before he died, Bill made arrangements, with my help, for this to pass into your hands. I think he was worried that if Grace outlived him she would make no provision for you.' He smiled. 'Bill was obviously an intelligent man – we know how that turned out, don't we?'

I grinned back. 'She did give me eighty grand a year.'

'Only at my insistence,' he shot back. 'I told her that if she didn't make some gesture you would probably contest the will and might well end up with a fortune.'

'That must have turned her stomach.'

'Damned right it did. Bill wanted these arrangements kept secret until after Grace's death – I think he was worried that she might challenge it and crush you with legal fees.

'With her gone and, satisfied of your integrity, everything is now in place.' He reached into the file and took out a bundle of documents. 'The first part of Bill's arrangement relates to a property in SoHo. Have you ever seen it?'

'I've never even heard of it,' I replied.

'It is an old tea warehouse with a cast-iron facade and a huge space inside. Several people have said it would make a magnificent home. Why they would say that, I have no idea.'

Finbar – a widower with no kids – lived in a fourteen-room pre-war co-op in Park Avenue's most elite white-glove building, so I wasn't surprised that he thought a converted warehouse was one step above a garbage skip.

'Bill had it made airtight and put in sophisticated humidity, fire and air-conditioning systems. This building and all its contents are what he wanted you to have.'

He gave the bundle and a sheaf of other documents to the two wise men, and they started signing and witnessing them.

'What contents?' I asked.

Finbar smiled. 'Bill was very orderly, a completely rational man, but in one segment of his life he never disposed of anything—'

'The art!' I interrupted, caught between shock and wonder.

'That's right,' Finbar replied. 'As you may know, there was hardly an unknown artist he didn't support by buying their work – sometimes whole exhibitions.'

'He told me once,' I said, 'that most people's idea of charity was to give money to the United Way – he supported starving artists.'

'And that's exactly what he did – year after year, cheque after cheque. But he had the eye, Scott – that was the remarkable thing – and he kept everything he bought.'

'In the tea warehouse?'

'That was why he converted it – he stacked it inside like lumber. Warhol, Roy Lichtenstein, Hockney, Jasper Johns, Rauschenberg – the list is endless. This is an inventory.'

He pushed a print-out across to me and I leafed through it – every page was littered with what had become household names.

'What about Grace? After Bill died, she never asked about any of it?'

'As I said, she had no interest. I think at some stage he must have told her that he'd sold whatever he still owned and the proceeds had gone into one of the trusts.'

He slid another thick document across the desk. 'Naturally, I had to keep the canvases insured and that meant regular valuations. This is the most recent information.'

I took the list and saw that next to each canvas was its estimated value. On the last page it had been totalled. I stared at the figure and saw that I was a very wealthy man – maybe not as rich as Cameron, but over halfway there.

The three men watched as I got to my feet and walked to the window. The rain was starting to hit, and I couldn't tell whether it was that or the tears in my eyes that was clouding my view. Even at the end of his life, when he was doubting my character, Bill had tried to take care of me. What more could I have asked? He was a wonderful man and, once again, I realized I should have treated him better.

I turned and looked at Finbar, and he handed me all the documents – signed, sealed and delivered.

'Congratulations,' he said. 'You're now the owner of one of the finest collections of contemporary art in the world.'

Chapter Twenty-seven

ALONE, SITTING IN A BUDGET HOTEL IN A BACKSTREET OF BODRUM, writing my last will and testament, I had to decide what would happen to a treasure trove of canvases which most museum curators would die for.

The collection was completely intact. Although I had spent a lot of time in the silence of the tea warehouse – wandering among the towering racks of paintings, pulling out masterly works that nobody had seen in decades – I had never sold any of them. They were too much a part of Bill, and my feelings about them – as well as the wealth they represented – were still far too raw for me to deal with.

Strangely, though, the disposition of them in the event of my death presented no problem to me. I figured the answer must have been bubbling away on the back burner of my mind for hours, if not longer.

I wrote that I wanted the Museum of Modern Art to be given one hundred canvases of their choice, on condition that they put them on permanent display. I directed that they should also be granted the folio of Rauschenberg drawings that was the reason Bill and I had visited Strasbourg so long ago. I then described the photograph of the peasant woman and her children walking to the gas chamber that I had seen at the Natzweiler death camp – the photo that had haunted so many of my dreams – and requested that the museum acquire a copy of it.

I said that the rest of the canvases, including the warehouse in which they were stored, were to be sold and the proceeds used to endow a William J. Murdoch Home for Orphaned Roma or Gypsy Children.

I then came to the most difficult part of the exercise. In conclusion, I said, I wanted the Museum of Modern Art to mount a small display at the entrance to whatever gallery featured the one hundred works. The display should consist of the Rauschenberg drawings, the copy of the photo from the death camp and the following dedication: 'Bequeathed to the people of New York in memory of Bill . . .'

I sat very still for a long time and then laid my pen down. I was unsure what to say next, incapable of finding the words that would do proper honour to Bill's memory. I thought of us driving up through the pine forest of the Vosges mountains, I remembered the crouching evil of the gas chamber, I felt again the strength of him as I slipped my hand unbidden into his, I saw the instant happiness in his eyes as he looked down at me, and suddenly I knew the words that would mean everything to my foster father: 'Bequeathed to the people of New York in memory of Bill Murdoch – by his loving son, Scott.'

I finished by appointing Finbar Hanrahan, counsel-at-law of Park Avenue, and James Balthazar Grosvenor, President of the United States, as executors. I figured if I was going to die for my country it was the least he could do.

I called down to the front desk, heard the young duty manager's sleep-addled voice and asked him to come to my room. Without letting him see the content of the document, I had him witness my signature and I then sealed it in an envelope and addressed it to Finbar.

I put that envelope inside another, scrawled Ben's name on it and a note: 'In the event of my death, please deliver the enclosed letter by hand when you return to New York.'

I slipped it under the door of Ben's darkened room and went back to my own. I locked the door, kicked off my shoes and lay fully clothed on the bed. In the stillness of the night, two lines from an old poem whose name or author I couldn't remember drifted into my head:

> *I slept, and dreamed that life was beauty;*
> *I woke, and found that life was duty.*

Life was duty. Like any soldier going into battle, I thought of the conflict that lay ahead. To be honest, I didn't hope for success or glory. I just hoped that I would acquit myself with honour and courage.

Chapter Twenty-eight

ELEVEN O'CLOCK IN THE MORNING, BARELY A CLOUD IN THE SKY, unseasonably warm for that time of year, and Cumali arrived right on time.

I was waiting on the sidewalk in front of the hotel, dressed in trainers, a pair of chinos and a summery shirt flapping loose – a perfect look for a picnic, I thought. The Beretta was tucked into the back of my trousers, but it was there purely for decoration, part of the legend of an unwitting covert agent: I knew it couldn't save me and that I would lose it the moment I got jumped. The chinos had deep pockets, and that was why I had chosen them – the real weapon was in one of them and, by slouching forward, acting relaxed, hands buried in my pockets, I could keep my hand on it.

The black Fiat pulled to a stop and I saw that Cumali was alone. If I needed any confirmation about what was really happening, she had just given it to me. Smiling warmly, I went to open the front passenger's door. It was locked, and she indicated the rear seat. Apparently it was okay for a Muslim woman to lead a man to his death but not to share the front seat with him.

I opened the rear door and climbed in. 'Where's the little guy?' I asked.

'It's a field trip for kids from the school,' she replied, 'and he's been allowed to go along. We'll be joining them for the picnic – he wants to show off his American friend.'

As an actress, she was a good cop – she had thought too much about the lines and they came out stilted.

'What sort of field trip?' I asked, carrying on like everything was fine.

'Archaeology – "dumb ruins", as the kids say.' She laughed, and it seemed to ease her anxiety. 'An interesting place – I think you'll enjoy it.'

Somehow I doubted that. 'Is it far?'

'A fair distance by car,' she said, 'but I've got a share in a half-cabin cruiser. If you don't mind being deckhand, it's quicker and a more spectacular sight. Then we can bring my son back the same way – he loves the boat.'

Somebody knew what they were doing. It was easy to tail a car, but a boat was almost impossible – the field of vision was too expansive and there was no traffic to hide amidst. They were making certain I didn't have help following me.

'Sounds cool,' I said.

I wasn't feeling it. Despite my years of training, despite the plans I had laid, I felt the tendrils of fear unfurl and tighten around my throat: it isn't an easy thing to do, to walk knowingly into harm's way.

Cumali turned the wheel and headed down into a hidden cove with an old jetty and a few dozen small boats at anchor. Because I was sitting in the back, I hadn't been able to see whether she had brought with her the one piece of equipment that was crucial to my plan. If she hadn't, I was going to have to abort. 'Have you got your phone?' I asked.

'Why?' she replied, alert, looking into the rear-view mirror, scanning my face.

I shrugged. 'We don't want to be on a sinking boat waving for help, do we?'

She smiled as the anxiety receded. 'Of course.' She fumbled at the waistband of her jeans and held it up.

The mission was on: there was no turning back now.

She pulled into a parking spot and I unbuckled my seatbelt. 'Anything to unload?'

'There's a picnic basket in the trunk. I don't drink alcohol, but I brought some beer and there's plenty of food – help yourself.'

The condemned man ate a hearty meal, I thought, and almost laughed. I realized the stress and fear were starting to get the better of me and made myself lock it down. I pulled the picnic basket out of the trunk and turned to follow Cumali on to the jetty. She was crouching to cast off the mooring line from a little half-cabin launch, old and wooden-hulled but well-maintained. I wondered how much it had cost them to rent it for the day.

She stood up and, unaware that she was being observed, paused to stare at the small cove. It was beautiful in the morning light – the turquoise water, the deserted beach, the whitewashed houses – and in a moment of epiphany I realized that she was imprinting it on her memory, saying goodbye. I had wondered earlier if I had panicked her enough, and I saw now that the threat of Bright Light and a Bulgarian orphanage had terrified her. I figured that she and the little guy would be leaving very soon with her brother, probably driving hard for the border with Iraq or Syria. Thinking about it more, I understood that, if I went missing, she would be the prime suspect, and that left her little alternative. For all of us, our time in Bodrum was coming to an end.

She broke free of her thoughts and stepped down into the launch's cabin. By the time I got on board and stowed the hamper she had started the engine, powered up a small VHS radio next to the wheel and was talking in Turkish into the mic. She put it back on the cradle and turned.

'Just letting the harbour master know where we're going, what our route is,' she said.

It was a nice touch, but she wasn't talking to the harbour master, she was speaking to her brother and whoever was with him, letting them know that we were on our way. I had already worked out our destination, of course.

Chapter Twenty-nine

THE RUINS OF THE DROWNED CITY CLUNG TO THE CLIFF, THE OLD STEPS followed their eternal path into the sea and the Door to Nowhere was a silhouette under the harsh noonday sun.

Cumali had slowed down as we approached, allowing me to view the ruins in all their glory, and I had reacted with appropriate wonder, as if I had never seen them before.

The cliff face and the parking area on top were as deserted as ever, and the only sound as we passed the sunken dance platform was the wailing of a few circling gulls. Their mournful cry seemed a fitting accompaniment as Cumali steered the little cruiser up to the rotting jetty.

I grabbed the mooring line, swung off the deck and made the boat secure. On the beach, host to clots of tar and the bodies of two dead gulls, hordes of crabs ran for cover like roaches in a tenement kitchen. I hated the place.

Cumali came to my side, carrying the picnic basket, and I took it from her, indicating our surroundings. 'It doesn't look like much of a spot for a picnic.'

She laughed, more relaxed now that she had got me to the designated place and her part in the plan was almost over.

'We're not picnicking here. There's a tunnel that leads into a Roman amphitheatre – the experts say it's the best example in the world after the Colosseum.'

I did my best impression of being pleased. 'Sounds great. Where are the kids?'

She had obviously thought of it – or her brother had. 'Already here,' she said easily. 'They came by bus; there's a path that comes down into it from the road.'

I knew it wasn't true – the area had been reconnoitred when the hit on Finlay Finlay was being planned, and Control had warned us that, if things went wrong, not to shoot open the gate on the tunnel and try to find refuge in the ruin. It was a dead end; there was absolutely no way out.

'I'm looking forward to seeing the little guy,' I said as we picked our way across kelp-strewn rocks.

'He's so excited,' she said. 'I could barely get him to eat his breakfast.'

We found a rough path that led towards a dark opening located in the side of the cliff just above the beach.

'It's the start of the tunnel,' she said. 'The dignitaries and generals used to arrive by barge. Accompanied by fanfares, they walked down it and into the amphitheatre.'

'I would have thought the place would be better known, there'd be more tourists,' I suggested.

'Years ago, it was packed, but they did so much damage it's just for archaeologists and school groups now.' The lies were coming more easily to her.

'What's the amphitheatre called?' I asked.

She said something in Turkish, which, of course, I didn't understand.

'In English?'

'I don't think there's a direct translation for it, I'm not sure what it means.'

I guessed she didn't think it was a good idea to tell me I was about to enter a place called the Theatre of Death.

We stopped at the mouth of the tunnel and I saw, half hidden in the gloom, a gate made of heavy, rusted bars. If it had ever been chained and padlocked, it wasn't now. 'They don't keep it locked?' I said.

'The only access is by boat, and hardly anyone knows about it. It hasn't been locked for years,' she said.

That was their first mistake. I could just make out marks in the rust where a chain had been pulled free, probably cut through a few hours ago. It didn't help me, but I found it reassuring – it meant they were hurrying and overlooking details. Experience told me that would be an advantage.

Cumali pushed the gate open and was about to step inside when I stopped her. 'Here, let me go first,' I said, acting like a perfect gentleman.

I think good manners are very important when you are being led to your death. It also meant that, if everything went to hell, I would have a clear field of fire in front of me.

I walked through the gate, headed into the darkness and felt the sweat start to pool around the Beretta nestled in the small of my back. I knew that at the other end of the tunnel the Saracen was waiting.

Chapter Thirty

BRADLEY HADN'T ENCOUNTERED ANY DIFFICULTY IN FINDING THE RIGHT house. As planned, he had left the hotel five minutes after I was picked up by Cumali and, using a detailed map I had drawn for him, walked straight to Bodrum's best-stocked store for boating supplies.

Three minutes later he left the store carrying a plastic shopping bag holding the one item he had purchased and, once again following my map, headed south-west. After eleven minutes he turned into the street he was looking for and saw, halfway along it, the Coca-Cola distribution warehouse. He approached it, crossed the street and stopped in front of a small dwelling.

After checking its appearance and recalling six items about it, he was certain he had located the correct property. He opened the gate, passed the garden gnomes and knocked at the door. The time was 11.25: he was right on schedule. A few seconds later he heard a woman's voice from inside calling in Turkish and, though he didn't understand the language, he was sure that she was asking: 'Who is it?'

He said nothing in reply, just letting the silence boil and, as most people do in such a situation, the woman, the little guy's nanny, opened the door. Bradley's plan had been to push hard once the door was off the lock, step inside, slam it behind him and confront the woman in the privacy of the house.

It didn't work. In discussing it with Bradley, I had failed to take into account the fact that the woman was severely obese. When Bradley pushed hard on the door it hit the stationary bulk of her and stopped. It gave the surprised young woman just enough time to push back hard and start yelling. It looked for a moment as if Bradley was going to be locked out and the whole plan would founder. Reacting fast – thank God – the cop pulled out his pistol, rammed it through the gap straight at the terrified nanny's teeth and yelled at her to step back.

She didn't recognize all the words, but she got the message. She retreated a step, Bradley scrambled inside and, still pointing the gun at her, slammed the door behind him. The woman was too scared to scream and that gave Bradley the chance to pull a curtain aside and look out of a narrow window. To his relief, nothing was moving outside, and he realized that three Coke trucks manoeuvring into the warehouse, engines roaring, had swallowed her cries.

He turned back, saw that fear had really taken hold and she was shaking hard. Before he could say anything, a face appeared out of the doorway at the back of the house and looked down the hallway at them. It was the little guy.

Bradley's gun was obscured by the bulk of the woman, and he lowered it so that it was out of sight and smiled at the child. That was all the boy needed. He walked forward, grinning back, talking away in Turkish.

The nanny moved to take hold of him, protective, and that – combined with Bradley's grin – seemed to calm her, and the shaking turned into a tremor rather than a full-on quake.

'What is he saying?' Bradley asked, indicating the little guy, making his voice sound as friendly as possible.

The nanny swallowed, trying to moisten her throat, and forced her mind to summon up the limited English she had acquired working for different families over the years.

'He say – you American?' she managed to get out.

Bradley smiled at the little guy. 'Yeah – New York.'

The nanny translated for the boy, still holding him tight. 'He ask – you friend of bowing man?' she said.

Bradley looked confused – bowing man? What the hell was that? But the nanny came to the rescue. 'He mean FBI man.'

'Ah,' Bradley responded. 'Brodie Wilson. Yeah, he's my friend.'

The little guy said something, and the nanny translated for him: 'Where is the bowing man?'

'He's with your mom,' Bradley replied.

'Where they go?' the nanny translated for the little guy.

Bradley didn't want to alarm the child and had what he thought was a good idea. 'They went on a picnic,' he said.

As soon as it was translated, the boy dissolved into tears, seemingly inconsolable. Bradley had no way of knowing that it was the boy's dearest dream – to go on a picnic with his American friend – and now they had left him behind.

Bradley stared, confused. Through the child's tears and grief, the nanny managed to understand what the problem was and explained it for Bradley's benefit.

The cop bent down, kept the gun out of sight and told the boy that everything was okay, his mom would be coming to get him soon, but first they had to play a little game.

As soon as the nanny had translated it, the boy smiled at Bradley, reassured, and gave the cop one of his best bows.

Ben and Marcie had never had any kids, so Ben considered children pretty much an alien race, but he couldn't help being deeply affected by the child's desperate longing for something as simple as a picnic. He felt the revulsion well up, sickened by the prospect of what he had to do, but he also knew he had no choice. One kid's suffering was nothing compared with the carnage of smallpox, and he motioned for the nanny to lead the way down the hall.

In the kitchen he immediately drew the blinds and locked the back door. Only then did he turn his attention to its architecture. It was a traditional Bodrum house, and the kitchen, like most of its kind, had a very high, steeply raked roof to help dissipate the heat. In the middle, high above, a light hung from a beam. It was supported by a heavy brass bolt and Bradley knew it would be perfect.

He turned to the nanny, demanded her cellphone and attached it to the charger lying on the kitchen counter. It was good thinking – if the phone ran out of juice at a critical moment, everything would fail.

Speaking slowly and clearly, he told the nanny it was his absolute intention that both she and the boy would get out alive. 'It won't happen, though,' he said, 'if you try to escape, answer the door or touch the phone. You will do everything I say, understand?'

She nodded and, with that, Bradley sat down with his gun within instant reach, opened up the plastic shopping bag and took out a large coil of thick rope.

The little guy – intrigued – came and sat beside him. Together, they started to make the noose.

Chapter Thirty-one

I LED CUMALI DEEPER INTO THE TUNNEL, THE WALLS DECORATED WITH fragments of ancient mosaics, huge cracks bisecting the vaulted roof from centuries of quakes, the silence pressing down on us.

On either side were the ruins of what were called the *hypogeum*, the underground vaults and cells which housed slaves and animals used in wild-beast hunts, and I felt the deep melancholy of the place surrounding me. It was as if misery had taken root in the stone.

Cumali pointed at the barred pens, talking a little too fast, a little too nervously. 'The cells would only hold a few hundred people,' she explained. 'The huge spectacles and naval battles, which would often kill thousands of prisoners or slaves, were almost exclusive to the Colosseum.

'Here in the provinces, without the wealth of a Caesar, it was mostly gladiators and the re-creation of famous myths. Of course, those stories were wildly popular too – lots of violence and killing, but not much plot.'

'Sounds like a Hollywood movie,' I said, through my parched lips, trying to act normal. Cumali didn't seem to hear.

We turned a dog-leg, came out of the tunnel, and I saw the amphitheatre for the first time. Cumali had been telling the truth about it – the symmetry, the stacked decks of almost intact marble colonnades and the sheer size of it were remarkable. So was the stillness. In the harsh midday sun, the Theatre of Death felt like it was hushed and waiting, ready for a new performance to begin.

'Where is everybody?' I asked.

'Above us,' she said. 'There's a platform with a great view of the arena. If we follow the colonnade, we'll find a set of steps and they'll take us up to it.'

She turned to lead the way, and I glimpsed the first of them. He was standing deep in a ruined passage, unaware that, to a trained eye, darkness is often a relative thing – he was dressed in black, a pool of greater gloom in the shadow. I guessed that his job was to move behind me and cut off any chance of escape down the tunnel.

I swept my eyes around the arena, acting like any interested tourist: the Saracen and his hired help would have me triangulated and, from the single data point of the hidden man, I had a good idea where the others would be.

Cumali, walking a little faster, pointed to the middle of the site. 'Two thousand years ago, the sand on the arena floor would have been dyed a deep red,' she said.

'To disguise the blood?' I asked.

'That's right.'

I located another member of the team, a thickset bull of a man, standing in a honeycomb of crumbling arches just above us. I was surprised – he was in his sixties, far too old for this rodeo, I would have thought – and there was something about him that pinged my memory, but I had no time to dwell on it. Cumali had led me into a towering, crumbling passage – a dead end, I was sure – talking all the time to allay her nerves.

'Of course, the bodies had to be removed before the next event could start. Two men dressed as mythological figures would enter the arena to supervise it.

'The first was supposedly Pluto, the god of the dead. He would hit the corpses with a hammer, showing that the man, woman or child now belonged to him.

'The second was Mercury, who, according to myth, carried a wand and escorted souls to the underworld. In this case, the wand was a hot iron and he would touch the bodies to see if the person was really dead.'

'So even faking it was no escape.'

'None at all,' she said.

We walked deeper into the gloom. Up ahead, sunlight was spilling through the shattered roof, and I guessed that was where I would meet Zakaria al-Nassouri face to face. My journey was almost over.

I had to time everything perfectly now. I couldn't make a mistake – my life and everything else depended on it.

I slipped my hands deeper into my pockets, nice and relaxed, and I was certain that the men watching me from the darkness had already registered the small bump in the waistband at the back of my trousers. They would be smiling, I thought, knowing that I wouldn't have time to get my right hand out, reach behind, draw the pistol and start shooting.

Dumb American.

I had been taught how amateurs worked – they would be concentrating on the pistol, thinking that was where the danger lay, not worrying about my left hand, which was wrapped around the only weapon I cared about: my cellphone. It was powered on, ready to go, every button on the keypad set to speed-dial the same number – Ben Bradley's phone, in his pocket, back at the nanny's house.

In the seconds before the men jumped me, all I had to do was hit a button on the keypad. Any button.

Bradley wouldn't answer: he would recognize the number and it would start a countdown. Exactly four minutes later he would pick up the nanny's cellphone, take it off the charger and dial Cumali. She would look at the caller ID, see that it was the nanny and, worried there was a serious problem with the little guy, would answer. She would then learn something that would change everything.

The four-minute gap was crucial. It was the period I had estimated would elapse between first being grabbed by the muscle and the Saracen emerging from the shadows. If his sister's cellphone rang too soon, the Saracen might realize that something was wrong and turn and vanish into the ruins. How could I coerce a man who had already run?

If Cumali's phone rang too late, I was going to be in a world of trouble. The Saracen was desperate for information about the supposed traitor, and he didn't have much time. He wouldn't waste it on a polite conversation and I figured he would have something like a twelve-volt truck battery and alligator clips close at hand. As every torturer knew, that instrument was highly portable, easy to acquire and, if you didn't mind how much damage you caused to the victim, extremely fast. I wasn't sure I would be able to hang on for very long.

Four minutes – don't screw it up, Ben.

We passed a mound of rubble and trash – shards of broken glass, empty beer bottles, the polished steel lid of a freezer box. Groups of kids had obviously broken in over the years and partied hard.

Next to the mound was a long marble trough. Once used by the dignitaries to wash their feet, it was fed water from a stone gorgon's face. One end of the trough was broken, and I should have paid it more attention – it had been blocked with rocks and the trough was full. But my mind was in another place: I was waiting to be attacked, waiting to hit the magic button before they had my arms pinned to my back.

We stepped into the sunlight filtering through the shattered roof and I saw that the path ahead disappeared into a huge fall of masonry.

I had reached the dead end, I was trapped in a box canyon, and the index finger of my left hand was the only thing between me and disaster.

Chapter Thirty-two

'WRONG TURN?' I SAID, INDICATING THE WALL OF RUBBLE AND TURNING back towards Cumali.

She was no longer alone.

The first of the hired help had stepped out of a side passage, blocking any escape route, not trying to hide himself, looking straight at me. It was Muscleman who had broken into my hotel room, still in his leather jacket and an equally tight T-shirt. Maybe it was because my senses were highly charged, perhaps it was seeing him in the flesh, but I realized then that I had seen a photo of him long ago – laughing on the deck of Christos Nikolaides' converted ice-breaker as it rode at anchor in Santorini.

I suddenly knew which of the drug cartels Cumali had asked for help and why. When an old man up in Thessaloniki had heard it concerned an American intelligence agent, he would have been only too happy to agree.

'Looking around too?' I said to the man. 'I guess you're with the school group, huh?'

I couldn't let them think that I suspected anything; they had to believe that their element of surprise was complete, otherwise the Saracen might realize it was a trap.

I heard a footstep on gravel – Muscleman was the diversion, the attack was coming from behind. No time to think, just make a decision. Yes or no? Launch or not?

I pressed a button on the phone, firm and short.

It was the right decision. My finger had barely left it when they hit me – two of them, very fast, very hard, halfway to being professional. I was going down to my knees, but before I fell completely

635

I got one of them in the larynx with the point of my elbow and sent him reeling and gasping in a flood of pain. The other one had me round the neck, driving his fist into my face, and I felt my cheekbone go. I could have retaliated, but I was putting up a show. There was no point in having the crap beaten out of me, I would need all my strength for what was coming.

I clutched my cheek and sprawled into the dirt. Already I was counting. Four minutes: two hundred and forty seconds.

Two hundred and thirty-two. Two hundred and . . .

The man with the bruised and swollen larynx had stumbled back to join the other attacker, and I glimpsed his face. It was the bull of a man – squat, with closely cropped hair and a cruelty in his eyes that you rarely saw in men outside of prison. I'd seen him before, his expression too – on a mugshot provided by the Greek police – and I recalled that he had a very thick jacket indeed. It was Patros Nikolaides, the father of Christos: the old godfather himself had left his walled compound.

He and his Helper ripped the pistol out of my belt, shredded my shirt, grabbed my crotch and tore off my shoes to see if I had any concealed weapons. They cut open my pockets and removed my wallet, keys and phone before Nikolaides called to Cumali.

'You got 'em?'

She tossed him a pair of police-issue steel handcuffs and he and the Helper wrenched my arms behind my back and cuffed my wrists so tight I knew that, in twenty minutes, the tissue would be dying from lack of blood and I might lose the use of my hands for ever. Satisfied that I was immobilized, they got to their feet, picked up their weapons, smashed my cellphone, dropped it next to my discarded Beretta and puffed themselves up. They spoke in a mix of Greek and Albanian, but it wasn't hard to work out what they were saying – these American agents weren't half as good as they thought they were, especially when they ran up against genuine hard-asses from the Balkans.

With that, the old bull stepped forward, a decent Glock pistol in his hand, and looked down at me – hands cuffed, lying with my face in the dirt – and kicked me hard in the ribs with the toe of a steel-capped workman's boot.

'That's for my throat,' he rasped, then motioned to Muscleman and the Helper – both armed with Skorpion machine pistols – to drag me to my feet.

I forced back a wave of nausea from the blow to the ribs, stood unsteadily and looked at Cumali.

'What's happening?' I asked through clenched teeth. I was gasping, trying to deal with the wild shards of pain in my chest and face. For once, I wasn't faking anything. This was no walk in the park.

One hundred and seventy-eight seconds.

'You shouldn't have crossed the Bulgarian border in your rent-a-car,' Cumali said. 'That was stupid – it's monitored by cameras equipped with licence-tag recognition.'

She didn't try to keep the note of triumph out of her voice. It was clear: she had outwitted the elite American agent.

'Bulgaria?' I replied. 'I've never been to fucking Bulgaria.'

She shook her head, sneering. 'And you've never been to Svilengrad and you don't know about Bright Light and an orphanage for a little boy. Your name is Michael John Spitz and you are an intelligence agent, a member of a special CIA group.'

I paused just enough to make it appear as if I had been startled but was trying to cover it.

'I don't know what you're talking about,' I said. 'You know I am an FBI agent, here to investigate a—'

Wham! The steel-capped boot caught me just under the kneecap and I dragged in a lungful of air to try to combat the exploding pain. I would have crumpled if Muscleman and the Helper hadn't been holding me.

'Don't fucking lie,' Patros Nikolaides said with a smile. It was nice to meet a man who enjoyed his work.

One hundred and thirty-two seconds.

Then I saw him.

The most wanted man in the world stepped out of the side passage, leaving the shadows behind and moving into a wedge of light.

He was tall and muscular, just as I had expected a former *muj* warrior would be, and not even the cheap western suit he was wearing could conceal the coiled tension in him. 'Dangerous' was the word that instantly came into my pain-racked mind. I looked straight at his dark eyes, and it was impossible not to see the sharp intelligence in them. Be careful, I told myself, be very careful.

His beard was neatly trimmed, the jaw set, the lips drawn in a determined line – he had an authority, a sense of command about him. 'I believe you have been looking for me, Mr Spitz,' he said quietly.

'My name isn't Spitz and I have no idea who you—'

I saw the bull's boot go back and I braced myself for the detonation, but the Saracen raised his hand, stopping him.

'Please,' he said to me, as if the lies were hurting him. 'My sister, praise be unto God, has contacts in Turkish intelligence. She discovered who you really are—'

'Your sister?' I said.

He ignored it. 'She knows nothing of my work and little about me, especially in recent years, but she is aware of what happens to Muslim men hunted by agents like you. The whole Arab world knows.'

'I am an FBI agent,' I repeated through a red mist of pain. 'My name is Brodie Wilson, I am investigating a murder.'

'I don't have much time. I am going to ask you some questions and you are going to tell me exactly what I need to know. Yes?'

'How can I tell you? I'm not Spitz! I don't know what we're talking about.'

Ninety-eight seconds. That was all – and Bradley's call couldn't come soon enough. My knee was ballooning up and bringing with it increasing waves of nausea, my chest was a field of pain and I was finding it increasingly difficult to speak because of my cheek.

'Don't put yourself through it,' the Saracen said. 'You are an American, Mr Spitz – a man without God. When you stand at the abyss, when you are being broken on the wheel, who will you be able to turn to for help?

'You have made tiny mistakes, left enough evidence in your wake, to end up here. No, you're really not that good.

'Why do you think those mistakes were made? Whose hand was protecting me? Who do you think delivered you to this place? It wasn't Leyla al-Nassouri. It was God.'

I said nothing, slumping a little, as if defeated. Muscleman and the Helper loosened their grip a fraction as they tried to support me, and I launched myself forward, using my head as the only weapon I had, hitting Nikolaides' face with the top of my skull, splitting his bottom lip, feeling it spurt with warm blood, sending him flying backwards and making him spit two lower teeth.

Another few seconds wasted. *Come on, Ben – not long now. Cheat a little.*

The bull, bellowing with pain, hurled himself towards me and was only stopped by the Saracen's shoulder as he stepped between us.

'We're wasting time,' he said, and looked at Muscleman and the Helper. 'Get started.'

I would have liked to have kept chatting, I would have liked to have chatted for another sixty-three seconds, but they didn't seem interested. The two Albanian thugs dragged me back down the passage, and I was confused – I thought they would have had the truck battery or whatever equipment they needed right at hand.

The confusion vanished when I saw the overflowing marble trough and realized what it meant. Mentally, desperately, I tried to shift gears – I had prepared myself for pain, not terror. I had figured I could withstand the alligator clips or pliers ripping out my fingernails for a brief amount of time, but now I dragged my feet, trying to run the clock down – every second was going to count. If I started to talk, everything would be lost.

Forty-two seconds. The drug courier at Khun Yuam, the tough guy with the machete scars across his chest, had lasted twenty-nine.

The Saracen stopped at the marble trough and spoke to his sister in Arabic. I couldn't understand the words, but his hand motion was eloquent enough – he was telling her to take a walk. What was about to happen was not suitable for a woman to witness.

Thirty-eight seconds. Don't let me down, Ben.

Chapter Thirty-three

BRADLEY WAS TIMING IT TOO, BUT HE WAS USING A WATCH SO HIS COUNT was different – and more accurate than mine. He figured forty-six seconds.

The obese nanny was drenched in sweat and her legs looked as if they were going to buckle at any moment. Worse still, she was standing in a pool of urine – she had peed herself the moment she realized what Bradley had in mind. At gunpoint, working to my instructions, he had ordered her and the little guy into the centre of the room, directly under the sturdy roof beam. Now, seven minutes later, the woman continued to whimper and beg for help in Turkish and, though the boy had overcome his first fit of fear and yelling, he was still crying and asking for his mother.

The whole event was tearing Bradley's nerves to shreds and, when he wasn't checking his watch, he stared at the floor looking as if he was going to vomit. Despite her distress, the nanny noticed it and couldn't work it out: maybe he wasn't such a bad man after all. It encouraged her again to muster her limited English and implore him to release them.

'Quiet!' Bradley yelled, repeating it even louder and raising the gun at her when she still wouldn't stop.

She shook again with tears, the little guy's sobs grew more pitiful, and all Bradley wanted to do was to get it over with. It was ahead of time, but he took the nanny's phone off the charger and – despite my insistence that he had to stick absolutely to the schedule – he rationalized it by telling himself it would take time to dial Cumali's cellphone and there would be a delay while she answered.

It rang four times – *come on, come on*!

It answered – thank God, he thought – and he heard a woman's voice speaking in Turkish. He only caught a few words before he talked loudly over her, asking if it was Leyla Cumali and telling her to listen carefully . . .

The woman kept speaking, her tone unaffected. It was if she was a . . . Bradley realized – it was an automated voice.

The nanny – tottering on her feet, all three hundred pounds of her bearing down on her weak knees, saw through her tears that something was badly wrong: Bradley was close to panic. He was breathing hard, not saying a word – the voice was speaking in a language he didn't understand, he had no way of deciphering it and he didn't know what to do. This wasn't in the manual – where the hell was the Turkish cop?!

He looked at his watch – thirty-two seconds until the four minutes was up. He was about to hang up and try again when the voice, out of courtesy to the phone company's customers, repeated the message in English: 'The subscriber you are calling is either out of cellular range or has their mobile phone switched off.'

Bradley lowered the phone and stared into space. Oh, Jesus.

Chapter Thirty-four

CUMALI HAD WALKED DOWN A FLIGHT OF BROKEN MARBLE STEPS AND entered an area which, more than any other, had attracted legions of archaeologists and historians to the ruins.

Deep underground, in a vaulted space still decorated with fragments of mosaics and frescoes, she stood beside a reflecting pool, its surface as still as death. It was the centrepiece of what had once been a temple, a place where the highest officials made offerings to their gods in thanks for a safe journey. Cumali had first seen it years before, and had returned to its mysterious beauty in the belief that being so far underground would make it impossible to hear Spitz's screams and desperate pleas. She didn't realize it, but the sub-terranean space was equally good at deadening cellphone reception.

She stared at her face in the mirror-like water, telling herself that whatever her brother was doing to the American was little different from what had been visited upon Muslim men at Abu Ghraib and Guantanamo Bay. Bright Light, too.

Comforted by the thought, she walked on, passed the end of the reflecting pool and headed deeper into the temple's catacomb-like passages.

No sound or signal would ever find her there.

Chapter Thirty-five

MUSCLEMAN AND THE HELPER HAD RETRIEVED A SHORT WOODEN PLANK that had been hidden among the mound of rubble and trash. I fought and struggled, trying to chew up time, but my injured knee and the pain in my chest meant they had little trouble binding me to the wood with heavy leather straps.

I was face up, trussed so tight I couldn't move, when the Saracen's face appeared above me – impassive, his hand reaching down and taking my wrist. He was a doctor, and he was checking my pulse. He gave a grunt of satisfaction – he knew from my heart rate I was scared.

He pointed at Nikolaides. 'When I'm finished,' he told me, 'the man with the dental problem will question you about a murder your intelligence agencies committed in Santorini.

'He wants to know who ordered the attack and the names of those who did the killing. You understand?'

'Santorini? I don't know anything about Santorini.'

They didn't look convinced. Nikolaides threw a bucket to Muscleman and picked up a length of dirty towel from the rubble. They were about to start.

The Saracen kept looking at me. 'You can avoid this,' he told me. I said nothing, and he shrugged.

'When I was in the Hindu Kush, some people helped me. As you know, one of them has decided to betray us. Obviously, I can't allow that to happen. I want you to tell me the name of the traitor.'

'Even if I knew it,' I replied, 'once I told you, you'd just kill me.'

He nodded. 'I'm going to kill you anyway.'

'I figured – otherwise, you'd be trying to hide your faces.'

My best guess was that I would end up in a waterproof shroud, probably already hidden in a locker on the half-cabin cruiser, and it would likely be years before a fisherman finally hauled it aboard. If Ben didn't come through, I just hoped I was dead before they put me inside.

'If you know you're going to die, what's the point of suffering first? The name, Mr Spitz.'

'I am an FBI agent. I came to Bodrum to—'

'I've seen an email!' he snapped, his face coming close to mine. 'From the deputy director of the CIA.'

I did my best to look shocked. He registered it, and smiled. 'Now – the name of the traitor.'

'I'm an FBI agent—'

Exasperated, he signalled to Nikolaides. The Greek wrapped the dirty towel over my face, covering my eyes and nose, jamming my mouth open. Nikolaides took both ends of the rag behind the plank and tied it tight. I was in darkness, already finding it difficult to breathe, my head bound so firmly to the plank I couldn't move.

I felt them lift me and, in my private blackness and terror, I knew they had me suspended over the water.

Twenty-nine seconds by my count – the same amount of time the drug courier had endured. Despite my own weaknesses, even though I had always doubted my courage, I only had to withstand it for as long as he did.

They started to lower me down, and I dragged in a breath. The towel stank of sweat and engine oil. The last thing I heard was the Saracen: 'You're shaking, Mr Spitz.'

Then the water hit me.

Chapter Thirty-six

IT WASHED OVER MY TORSO AS THE PLANK SANK INTO THE TROUGH, chilling my genitals and aggravating the open wound on my chest. I dropped lower, helpless, and felt the tide hit the back of my strapped skull and cover my ears.

Then they tilted the plank backwards.

Water flooded across my face. Trying not to panic, unable to use my arms or twist my body, I took another huge gulp of oil-stained air and only succeeded in sucking the moisture faster through the towel. Water ran down my throat, and I started to cough.

A wall of water hit my face and I wasn't coughing any more, I was choking. In darkness, my head tilted back, I had no idea whether the water had come from a bucket or if they had plunged me deeper into the bath. The sensation of drowning – of a terrifying need to drag air through the sodden towel – was overwhelming.

Instead, fluid was flooding into my nostrils and mouth and running down my steeply inclined throat. The gag reflex kicked in, trying to save me, and became a rolling thunder of spasms and choking.

More and more water was hitting me, and I was becoming disoriented. I had only one thought, one belief, one truth to cling to: eighteen seconds and Bradley would call. Seventeen seconds and salvation would be at hand. Sixteen . . .

I was bound so tight I couldn't thrash and kick despite the cascading terror. More water entered my nose and mouth, seemingly drowning me, and the constant gagging and spasms were turning my throat raw. I would have screamed, but the filthy towel and surging water prevented even that release. With no way to express itself, my terror turned inward and reverberated through the hollow chambers of my heart.

My legs and back jerked instinctively, trying to make me flee, using up precious energy, and I felt myself being tilted further backwards. Water swamped me. Another surge of gagging hit. Where was Bradley? He had to call.

A fragment of my whirling mind told me I had lost count of time. How many seconds? There was nothing but blackness and the desperate urge to breathe. To endure, to survive, not to falter was all that was left.

I spun through darkness and overwhelming fear. My head was tilted even further back and I was plunging down. Maybe it was just another huge bucketful of water, but I felt as if I was deep under the surface, choking, gasping and retching in a watery grave, desperate for air, desperate for life.

I knew I could endure no more, but suddenly I was rocketing up, the water draining off my face, and I could drag air through the towel. It was tiny and insignificant, but it was a breath, it was life and they were standing me upright. Bradley had called – he must have!

I tried to suck more air into my throat – I had to be ready to play my part – but I kept gasping and retching. Then the towel was gone and I was pulling in breaths as my chest kept heaving, with my windpipe shuddering and spasming.

I knew that I had to control it, I had to be in command – by God, it was the Saracen's turn now to sit down to a banquet of consequences.

A hand slid inside my shredded shirt. I blinked the water from my eyes and saw that it was him, checking the rhythm and strength of my heartbeat. I caught sight of the old bull standing behind him, laughing at me through his stained teeth, enjoying my distress and fear.

A surge of wild panic tore through me: nobody was acting as if the tables had been turned. I knew then that there had been no phone call. Where the hell was Ben?

I slumped – I was alone in the Theatre of Death and, this time, I really was dying to the world. I would have fallen to the ground, but Muscleman and the Helper were holding the board, and kept me upright.

'The name of the traitor?' the Saracen asked.

I tried to speak, but my throat was ripped raw and my mind, awash with adrenaline and cortisol, was struggling. Instead, staring down at the ground, I just shook my head – no, I wouldn't be telling him any name.

'That was thirty-seven seconds,' he replied. 'It was longer than average and you should be proud. You've done as much as anyone could expect. But it can go on for minutes if we like. Everybody breaks; nobody can win. What is the name?'

My hands were shaking, and I didn't seem able to stop them. I looked up and tried to speak again. The first syllable was so soft it was inaudible, and the Saracen leaned in close so that he could hear.

'Put the towel back on,' I whispered.

He backhanded me hard across the face, splitting my lip. But he couldn't scare me any more. In a corner of my mind, I had found a small reservoir of courage – I was thinking about Ben Bradley and those sixty-seven floors.

Muscleman and the Helper upended the plank and carried me back to the trough. The Saracen was about to reattach the towel when Nikolaides called out, telling him to step aside. I saw that he had picked up a stonemason's hand hammer – a heavy, brutal thing – from among the equipment they had hidden next to the rubble.

When I was flat on the board, my shoeless feet directly in front of him, he pulled his powerful shoulders back and swung as hard as he could.

The hammer hit me full force on the sole of my left foot, bursting the flesh and crushing the matrix of tiny bones and joints. A searing, vomit-laden flash of pain – like a massive electric spear – went through my shin, up my leg and into my groin. He might as well have been crushing my testicles. I would have passed out but, somehow, my howling scream tethered me to consciousness.

Nikolaides laughed. 'See – his voice is stronger already,' he said to the Saracen. 'Sometimes, the old ways are still the best ways.'

He hit me again. It was closer to my toes, I heard more bones crunch and I screamed even louder. I was going over the waterfall into unconsciousness, but the Helper – standing next to my head and cheering the old bull on – slapped me hard across the face to keep me in the present.

He called to the bull: 'Another one.'

'No,' ordered the Saracen. 'This has taken too long already. If he passes out we'll be here all day.'

He turned to me. 'Tell me the name now.'

'I am Brodie David Wilson. I am an FBI—'

They put the towel back in place and lowered me towards the water.

Chapter Thirty-seven

CUMALI HAD WALKED THROUGH THE REAR OF THE TEMPLE, PASSED between the remains of thick masonry walls and entered an underground space called the *spoliarium* – the area where dead gladiators were stripped of their weapons and the bodies disposed of.

She wondered what was happening above – surely it couldn't be long before she heard her brother calling out to tell her that it was over and they could leave.

What a waste, she thought – Spitz was a brilliant investigator, certainly the best she had ever known. The idea about the mirrors in the French House alone was evidence of that. He would have got away with the whole subterfuge of his identity too, except for driving across the border in a rent-a-car that could be traced to him. Didn't they have cameras with licence-tag recognition in America? They probably invented them. Strange that such a clever man would make a mistake like that.

Of course, she would never have known who he really was except for the call from the man at MIT. And what about those guys? One phone call and then nothing – no follow-up questions, no approaches to check on Spitz's movements or details. By using her drug-world contacts, she had found out more about him with one break-in than Turkish intelligence had achieved with all their resources. In fact, it didn't seem as if they were very interested in Spitz at all.

A terrible thought struck her – what if the American hadn't made a mistake by driving across the border? Say the deputy director of MIT was in their employ, or somebody had re-routed her call and she hadn't been speaking to him at all? What if all the clues she had

649

followed had been planted? Imagine if it was a sting. It would mean that she had been supposed to show the information to her brother and get him to emerge from the shadows.

'In the name of God—' she said, and started to run.

She passed the vaults where the gladiators' weapons and armour had once been stored and raced up a long ramp towards the Porta Libitinensis – the Gate of Death – through which the bodies of the dead entertainers were removed.

She had almost reached its ruined arch, the whole arena spread out in front of her, when her cellphone – no longer in the dead-spot – started to ring. She pulled it out and saw that she had at least a dozen missed calls. All, like the current one, were from her nanny.

She answered, desperately frightened, speaking in Turkish. 'What is it?'

But it wasn't her nanny's voice that replied. It was an American man speaking English.

'Leyla Cumali?' he said.

Terrified, she yelled, 'Who are you?'

But he didn't answer, using instead the exact words the two of us had planned in my hotel room: 'I have sent you a video file. Look at it.'

In her confusion and fear, she didn't seem to hear, demanding again to know who he was.

'If you want to save your nephew, look at the video,' Ben demanded. 'It is shot in real time, it's happening now.'

Her nephew? Cumali thought. They know everything.

Hand shaking, almost in tears, she found the video file and opened it. She watched it and almost collapsed, screaming into the phone, 'No . . . please . . . oh, no.'

Chapter Thirty-eight

I WAS DROWNING AGAIN – THIS TIME IN PAIN AS WELL AS IN WATER. I WAS fighting for my life, fluid cascading over my face and my shattered foot, generating surge after surge of agony. It was fast becoming the only consciousness I knew.

My head was tilted back, my throat open, water flowing down and triggering endless spasms of gagging. My chest was heaving, my lungs screaming and my body collapsing. Terror had chased out every rational thought and had me cornered. I had tried counting again, but had lost it at fifty-seven seconds. That seemed like a lifetime ago.

Behind the blindfold, I had travelled beyond the last star. I had seen the void at the end of the universe, a darkness without form or shape or end. I knew that they had damaged me in a place far beyond pain, scarred me in my soul.

A wisp of memory found me in my corner. Whisperer had said something. He had said, if it ever got too much for me, I should finish it. Roll to my rifle and go to my God like a soldier. But that was the final cruelty of it – because the torturers controlled the amount of water, I couldn't even open my throat, flood my lungs and drown myself quickly. Even the last dignity, the one of taking my own life, was unattainable. I was forced to go on, to suffer, to stand at the Door to Nowhere but never be able to step through it.

The Saracen checked his watch – the American had already endured for one hundred and twenty-five seconds – longer than any man he had known, far longer than he had expected, approaching the mark set by Khalid Sheikh Mohammed, a great warrior, a follower of the One True God and a courageous student of the Holy

Qur'an. Surely he must be ready to talk now? He motioned to the two Albanians.

I felt water stream from my hair and the filthy towel rip free of my face as they pulled me out. I was shaking, my body completely out of control and my mind not far behind. The terror was physical, every fear in my life made manifest. I couldn't speak but as I returned from the abyss the pain in my foot came back with a wild ferocity and I felt myself plunging into a welcome unconsciousness. The Saracen hit me hard on my broken cheek and the surge of adrenaline stopped me.

He forced open my eyelids and looked into my pupils, seeing how much life was present, while his other hand probed my neck until he found an artery, checking to see if my heartbeat was irregular and threatening to fail. He stepped back and looked at me – gasping for air, trying to control my tremors, forcing aside the pain in my foot.

'Who are you?' he said so softly I was probably the only one who could hear it.

I saw the concern and confusion on his face, and it gave me strength. In our epic battle of wills, I was dying but I was winning.

'The name?' he said.

I shook my head weakly.

'Give him to me,' Nikolaides said, exploding with impatience.

'No,' responded the Saracen, 'you'll end up killing him and we'll know nothing. We've got hours if we need them.'

'Until somebody sails past to look at the ruins and gets curious,' Nikolaides said.

'Go and move the boat then,' the Saracen replied. 'Put it behind the rocks so nobody can see.'

Nikolaides hesitated, not accustomed to being ordered around.

'Go,' the Saracen said. 'We're just wasting more time.'

The bull glared and gave in, turning to the two Albanians, ordering them to help him. The men vanished down the main passageway, and the Saracen looked down at me slumped against the trough, still bound to the board, my wrists swollen and twisted out of shape, the steel cuffs cutting into the flesh and my fingers as white as the marble from the lack of blood. He poked my shattered foot with the toe of his shoe and watched me wince. He did it again – harder – and, despite myself, I cried out.

'It's only going to get worse,' he promised quietly.

He lifted back his shoe to kick the raw flesh, but he never got the chance. From out of the darkness of the side passage, we heard a voice.

She was yelling in Arabic, frantically.

Chapter Thirty-nine

FROM WHERE I WAS LYING, I HAD AN UNOBSTRUCTED VIEW AS CUMALI ran into the light, fear written all over her face, the cellphone clutched tight, her brother racing to meet her.

For a moment I wondered what had happened: in my mind, the plan was shattered and I was finding it difficult to process even the most rudimentary information. I couldn't conceive that Bradley was alive; I didn't remember that one phone call could still save both myself and the mission.

I watched in confusion, trying not to surrender to the pain in my foot and wrists, as Cumali reached her brother and thrust the phone at him. He spoke in Arabic, but it was clear that he was demanding to know what was wrong. Gasping for breath, Cumali just pointed at the phone. The Saracen looked at the screen . . .

His beloved son stared back, innocent and uncomprehending. Tears streaked the little guy's face but, because he was being filmed, he was trying his best to smile. He had a hangman's noose around his neck.

The Saracen stared at the still frame, his entire universe trembling, everything he thought he knew and understood shaken to its foundations. He looked at me, murderous and volatile. Somebody was threatening his child! He would—

He flew towards me, his eyes incandescent with anger, and in my wounded mind a gear finally meshed. It was the phone call I had tried so hard to count down to, the one which I had desperately wanted to hear. It was the only explanation for the woman's distress and the Saracen's anger . . .

Bradley had come through!

I tried to sit a little straighter, but I was still strapped to the board. Despite a wave of pain, I managed to remember what I had rehearsed in my hotel room when my mind and body were whole and terror was something which only other men knew. I had guessed that the moment of greatest danger would be when the Saracen realized it was a sting and that his child's life was in the balance: he might lash out in fury and kill whoever was close at hand. I dug down and recalled what I had to say.

'Be sensible and you can save your son,' I said, half faltering.

'How do you know it's my son?!' he yelled.

'You can save him if you want,' I repeated, not bothering to explain.

His sister had recovered enough to start screaming at her brother – half in Arabic, half in English, all in anguish – telling him not to waste time, to ask me what he had to do to save the child. The Saracen kept staring at me, unsure whether to surrender to logic or anger.

'Look at the picture!' Cumali yelled. 'Look at your son!'

She pushed the phone closer to his face and he looked again at the child's image. He turned to me . . .

'What is happening? Tell me!' he demanded.

'Speak to the man on the phone,' I replied.

The Saracen put the phone to his mouth and spoke in English, venomous. 'Who are you?!' he said, trying to assert control.

I knew Bradley would ignore it – just as we had planned, he would tell the Saracen to watch a video clip he was about to send. The first shot would be of a clock or watch to prove that it wasn't faked, that we hadn't staged it, that it was happening as we spoke.

The Saracen played the clip. He saw the clock and then he seemed to stagger. His sister, watching too, clung to him, crying out in a mix of Arabic and Turkish. The clip showed one end of the rope attached to the brass bolt that had once supported the kitchen light. The other end was the noose around the little guy's neck. He was standing on the shoulders of the obese and sweat-drenched nanny. When her weak knees gave out, she would fall and the boy would hang.

It was a horrific scene, and it was no wonder that Bradley had objected so vehemently to it, but I needed something so shocking that the Saracen would have no time to act or plan. In truth, I couldn't take all the credit – if that was the word – for devising it.

I had read about it years ago – during the Second World War, Japanese troops had made captured European fathers support their kids in exactly the same fashion. They had then forced the children's mothers to watch until their husbands stumbled and fell. Of course, to the Japanese, it was sport.

The Saracen lowered the phone and looked at me in hatred. While he stood rooted to the ground, Cumali flew at me, about to rip and tear at my injured face.

Her brother hauled her back – he was trying to think, his eyes darting around the walls of the ruins. It was a better indication of the prison in which he found himself than the bars of any cage. My mind was starting to function and I knew I had to keep the pressure on, to deny him any chance of disrupting the script I had written.

'I and my people won't tolerate any delay,' I said. 'Listen to the phone again.'

Robotic, in shock, the Saracen lifted the phone and heard a woman at the other end sobbing, hysterical, speaking to him in Turkish. It disoriented him – it was a language he didn't understand – and he handed it to his sister.

She started to translate into Arabic, but I stopped her. 'In English,' I demanded.

She told her brother it was the nanny. 'She's pleading,' she said. 'She can barely stand! She says, if we can't save her, at least save the child.'

She grabbed the Saracen's shirt, losing control. 'What in God's name have you done? What have you led us into?!'

He threw her hand off and she stumbled backwards, breathing hard, staring at him in fury.

'We estimated that the nanny would probably be able to stand for another six minutes,' I said. 'Of course, we could be wrong. It might be less.'

I was making it up but, in the desperate circumstances, nobody challenged it. The Saracen looked at the image on the phone and then at me. I knew that he was reeling, uncertain what to do.

'You're his father,' I said quietly. 'Your son is your responsibility – save him.'

I had learned long ago in Geneva that love wasn't weak, love was strong. Now I had gambled everything on the power of it. The Saracen said nothing, immobilized – unable to think or decide –

caught between his grand plan for the future and his son's life.

I had to force him, and I reached down into my fragmented mind and remembered what I had to say. 'What value is a promise,' I said, 'especially one to a dying wife? But go ahead if you want to – break a promise made before Allah.'

He stared at me, breathing in shallow gulps, scared. 'How do you know that? Who told you about Gaza?!'

I made no reply, and he turned away from the two of us. He was lost in darkness, trying to find a way out of the prison, thinking – I was certain – about holding his dying wife, how his son was his last tangible link to her and the sacred promise he had made to her and to God to protect him.

I saw his shoulders slump, and then his voice broke with sudden anguish. 'What do you want?' he said, turning towards me. 'Tell me what to do.'

Cumali, sobbing in relief, threw her arms around him.

'I have to let the man on the phone know that I'm alive and safe,' I said. 'Untie me.'

The Saracen hesitated – once he released me he knew that there was no going back – but he didn't get any more time to think about it. Cumali stepped forward, released the leather straps that bound me to the board, took a key out of her pocket and unlocked the cuffs.

They fell to the ground and I almost passed out from the flood of pain as the circulation started to return to my swollen hands. I managed to grab the side of the trough and haul myself upright. As soon as I touched my battered foot to the ground, the explosion of crushed nerves almost sent me back into the mud, but somehow I stayed on my feet and put my hand out for the phone.

The Saracen gave it to me, but I didn't raise it to my face – instead I reached my hand out to the two of them.

'Weapons,' I said.

They both handed over a pistol – the cop's was a standard Beretta 9-mil, but the Saracen's, probably provided by Nikolaides, was a SIG 1911 Stainless, made in Switzerland, as good a weapon as you could ever buy over the counter.

I shoved the Beretta in my pocket and kept the SIG held loosely in my swollen fingers. Given the state of my hands, I wasn't sure I could even fire it. I shifted the weight on my damaged foot, fought back a wave of nausea and raised the phone to my mouth.

'Ben?' I said, my voice rasping and broken, probably barely recognizable to him.

'Is that you?' he asked.

The sound of the cop's voice, something I thought I would never hear again, almost overwhelmed me. I slumped for a moment and realized how they had nearly destroyed me.

'Sort of,' I said, after a moment. 'I'm gonna open the mic, Ben,' I continued, trying to remember the details I had so meticulously planned. 'You'll hear whatever is going on. If something happens to me, shoot the nanny – okay?'

I saw the information register with the Saracen and Cumali, and I lowered the phone. Despite the freshly dug craters in my mind, I knew I had to move fast. I turned to the woman.

'Go down the tunnel, stay hidden and watch the beach. When you see the others, head back fast and warn me. Remember – get smart and sign them up to attack me and the man in Bodrum will hear. You know what he'll do.'

She nodded and ran, desperate to make it work, desperate to save the boy. In her anxiety and fear, I doubted she even realized she had become my closest ally.

I turned and looked at the Saracen. I knew that, no matter how much agony I had gone through, the really difficult part lay ahead: I had to get him to tell me the truth and not defeat me with lies and disinformation.

'My name is Scott Murdoch,' I said, through the pain of my injuries. 'I am an American intelligence agent. I am going to ask you some questions.'

Chapter Forty

I HAD LAIN AWAKE IN MY HOTEL FOR HOURS THE PREVIOUS NIGHT thinking about how I would interrogate Zakaria al-Nassouri if I ever got the chance.

I decided my only hope was to ask a relentless wave of questions, never giving him the opportunity to guess which ones I knew the answer to and which ones I didn't. I had to mix knowledge and ignorance so effectively that he would be loath to risk any lie at all, and I had to do it so fast that he wouldn't have time to think and weave.

I knew it would have been difficult a few hours ago but, wounded in body and mind, I had no idea if I could manage it now. One mistake, one successful deception, and it would have all been for nothing.

'If you lie, give me one incorrect answer,' I told him, 'I will shoot you and turn the phone off. As you know, the man in Bodrum has his instructions concerning your son. Clear?'

I didn't wait for an answer. 'Who recruited Patros Nikolaides?' I said, worried that my damaged throat would fail me.

Straight off, the question wrongfooted him. Nobody had mentioned the old bull's name, and I could see the Saracen was wondering how the hell I knew it. Already he was on the defensive.

'My sister,' he replied, trying to show he wasn't shaken.

'When she was twelve she won an essay competition – what for?'

'English . . . English comprehension.' Who the hell did they speak to, he must have been thinking, who would know details like that? His mother—?

'What hospital treated the shrapnel in your spine?'

659

'Gaza Infirmary.'

I was flying all over the world, leaping across decades—

'Did your sister ever go scuba diving?'

'My father taught her – when she was young.' It was probably correct – their father had worked at the Red Sea Marine Biology Department.

'How many Hind helicopter gunships did you bring down?'

I checked the phone's microphone, desperately hoping Bradley was taking notes – in my state, I wasn't sure I could remember the answers.

The Saracen was shocked – now we were in Afghanistan. 'Three, some say four,' he replied. I could see it in his face: *who is this man?*

'After the war with the Soviets, where did you buy your death certificate?'

'In Quetta – Pakistan.'

'Who from?'

'How do I know?! It was in the bazaar.'

'Who provided you with a new identity?' I looked straight at him.

'Abdul Mohammad Khan.' His reply was one micron softer than the others, and I figured it was a betrayal. Good.

'Keep your voice up,' I said. 'The address of your childhood home in Jeddah?'

'You know – you've seen a photo of it.'

'I've been there, I took that photo,' I replied. 'Where were you stationed when you fought in Afghanistan?'

'The Hindu Kush, a village called—'

I talked over him, letting him think I already knew the answer, keeping the pace relentless. 'What nationality was your new identity?'

'Lebanese.'

I had got my first one: I had a nationality and, with that, I knew we could start to trace him if we had to. The walls were closing in.

In the house in Bodrum, Bradley was holding the phone tight to his ear – trying to hear everything, paper scattered on the bench in front of him, scrawling notes furiously because of the speed I was going.

He said later that he was almost certain – to judge by my voice – that I was dying on my feet.

Chapter Forty-one

I FELT LIKE IT TOO. I SCOOPED A HANDFUL OF WATER OUT OF THE TROUGH and threw it on my face – anything to keep going, anything to lessen the pain and cool what I feared was a blossoming fever. 'Who is Sa'id bin Abdullah bin Mabrouk al-Bishi?' I demanded.

'State executioner,' the Saracen replied.

'Country?'

'Saudi Arabia.'

'How do you know him?'

He paused, and I realized that the wound was still raw even after so many years. 'He killed my father.'

'Faster,' I warned him. 'What was your date of birth?'

He had barely begun before I hit him with the next one. 'What blood group are you?'

He only got half the answer out when I swerved again. I had to keep him reeling—

'What is the common name for *Amphiprion ocellaris*?'

'Clownfish.'

'Where did you receive your medical degree?'

'Beirut University.'

'Who paid?'

'Scholarship – the US State Department.'

I didn't react, but yeah – it figured.

'What mosque did you attend as a youth in Bahrain?'

I couldn't recall the name, but the Saracen's answer sounded right.

'With which radical group was it affiliated?'

'The Muslim Brotherhood.'

'Name the last hospital you worked at.'

'El-Mina District.'

That was the second one: hospitals had employment records and they would show the name he had been using since he had first acquired the Lebanese passport.

'Who was the medical director? . . . What year did you start? . . . Which month?'

The Saracen had no choice but to answer – the speed was unsparing, but it was costing me dearly. My small reserves of energy were rapidly depleting, and I was certain now that an ache at the back of my head was a symptom of fever – I figured an infection from the open wounds was starting to pour through my body. *Go faster*, I told myself. *Faster—*

'The name of the boy's mother?'

'Amina.'

'Ebadi?'

'Yes,' he replied, staggered at my knowledge.

'How many other names did she use?'

'Four.'

'Tell me the relationship between Al-Aqsa Martyrs' Brigade and your son's orphanage.'

'They funded it.'

'How was your wife killed?'

'A Zionist rocket.' God, the bitterness in his voice.

'What was the name of Nikolaides' son who died in Santorini?'

'What?' he countered, confused and desperate. 'We're back at the Greeks?!'

He had no idea where we were going next, and it gave me strength. I realized every detail of my epic journey counted – I was using every thread; for once I was picking up every stitch. Nothing had been wasted. *Nothing*.

'The name of the son?' I demanded.

He tried to recall, maybe not even sure he had ever been told it. 'I don't . . . I can't . . .' He was panicking. 'Christopher,' he said, but he wasn't sure. 'No, no—'

'Christos,' I said, and gave him a pass.

'Where were you the day before you came to Bodrum?'

'Germany.'

I figured it was true – it had to be somewhere close.

'How long were you there?'

'Two months.'

'The name of the street of the mosque you attended?'

'Wilhelmstrasse.'

'Which town?'

'Karlsruhe.'

'Name the three foreigners you killed in the Hindu Kush.'

'I don't . . . I don't remember—'

'First names! What did they call each other?'

'Jannika—'

I didn't wait. I couldn't recall them either. 'Did you use a Web message board to communicate with your sister?'

'Yes.'

'Who was Clownfish?'

'My nickname.'

'What illness did your son have when you were in the Hindu Kush?'

He stared at me – how the hell did I know his son had been ill?

'Influ—'

In desperation, he was trying a lie, testing me, but I looked straight at him and he thought better of it.

'Meningococcal meningitis.'

'Too slow. And don't try that again. What is the name of the largest hotel in Karlsruhe?'

I hadn't heard of the town, and I needed another fact to make sure we didn't focus on the wrong place. I felt the fever getting worse.

'Deutsche König,' he said.

'Did you work there?'

'At the hotel?'

'In Karlsruhe!'

'Yes.'

'Where?'

'Chyron.'

It meant nothing to me, and I wasn't even sure I had heard it correctly. 'Full name.'

'It's American, that is its—'

'Full name!'

The Saracen was sweating, probably trying to imagine the sign at the front of the building, but he blanked. I raised the phone to speak to Ben – as if I were threatening the boy. He got it—

'Chyron Pharma-Fabrik GmbH.'

'Name of the mosque you attended as a child.'

I didn't care – I saw the Saracen relax, just a tiny easing of the muscles around his jaw, and I knew that Karlsruhe and its chemical factory was the hottest of the hot zones.

'Your address when you were working in El-Mina?'

The Saracen could barely keep up, but he gave a street name and a number. He hadn't finished before I hit him again – 'Name three people I can verify it with.'

He gave them, but I didn't care about El-Mina either, even though I guessed that was where he had synthesized the virus.

'What job did you have at Chyron?' I was back where I wanted to be – in the hot zone. I could tell from his face he didn't share my enthusiasm.

'Shipping clerk.'

'Name of supervisor?'

'Serdar—'

'What shift?'

'Graveyard.'

'What is Chyron's primary business?'

'Pharma – drugs.'

'What sort of drugs?'

'Vaccines.'

I gambled. Probably the biggest gamble of my life, but a doctor didn't get a job on the night shift in a drug company's shipping department for nothing.

'When did the virus leave Karlsruhe?'

He paused fractionally, and I put the phone to my mouth, ready to pull the pin. He stared at me for a moment longer.

'Yesterday,' he said quietly.

I felt granite towers of mystery collapse and a blitz of relief so intense that for a moment I forgot the pain. I knew it now: in the last twenty-four hours a vaccine contaminated with the smallpox virus had left a company in Germany called Chyron Chemicals.

It was already in America, or close enough, and my urgent thought was: how big? What was the scale of the attack?

'How many doses?' I said.

'One hundred.'

It was the tiny inflection, the dropping away of the sound at the end, as if he were trying to shrug it off, that warned me. I still had the phone at my mouth. The SIG was in my other hand and I pointed the barrel straight at his face—

'I'll only do this once. I'm going to ask you again. How many?'

He seemed to slump. 'Ten thousand,' he said.

It took acres of self-control not to react. Ten thousand?! The number had to be true, it was too extraordinary to be a lie, and in that moment I put the last piece of the puzzle together. Given the scale of the attack and the time of year, the virus could only have been hidden in one place. I was certain I knew where it was and what he had planned. For the first time in what seemed like half a lifetime, I had no more questions.

I leaned against the trough – I was in pain, beyond exhaustion and, with the fever steadily colonizing my body, sweat was starting to run down my cheeks.

I looked up and saw al-Nassouri staring at me. He knew why the interrogation had stopped – I had found everything I needed, and all of his years of work, the very thing which had given his life weight and meaning, was in ruins. He was about to say something, probably to curse me in the name of his god, but he didn't get the chance. We saw Cumali running hard towards us.

'They're coming,' she called, stumbling to a stop.

'Together?' I asked, rapidly shaking off the exhaustion. 'Anyone straggling?'

'No, together.'

It gave me a chance – if they were strung out, the man at the back would be warned by the gunfire, and I didn't like my odds against some jerk with a machine pistol. Surprise – and hitting them in a group – was the best weapon.

I heard Bradley yelling on the phone, worried that something had happened, wondering why the hell the questioning had stopped. I lifted it fast.

'Problem,' I said. 'Hold tight, three minutes—'

I stuffed the phone into my pocket and started flexing my swollen fingers, trying to see if I could fire the SIG. One thing was certain – because of my damaged foot, I wouldn't be able to stand or even crouch. What I needed was help.

Chapter Forty-two

THE BERETTA FLEW THROUGH THE AIR. I HAD TAKEN IT OUT OF MY pocket and tossed it quickly to Cumali. She caught it and looked at me, surprised.

'Anything happens to me,' I said, 'the man in Bodrum won't accept any excuses, he'll shoot the nanny. So you'd better make sure I live. Got it?'

She was about to nod, but her brother interrupted. 'This is no work for her, she's a woman – give me the gun.'

I stared at him with incredulity, but then I checked myself – given his background and beliefs, I should have anticipated it. 'No,' I said.

'You know that I was a *muj*,' he continued, arguing. 'I've killed before, and I'm a better shot. Give it to me.'

'No,' I said emphatically. 'I don't trust you – and, anyway, you're the decoy.'

He reacted – the decoy? I had no time to explain, and I turned back to Cumali. 'Ever killed anyone?'

'Never.' She didn't look as if she liked the idea much.

'Just remember then – you're not shooting a man, you're saving your nephew.'

I told her to move fast to an area of fallen stone that would give her cover and a clear view of the three men. 'Your target is the old guy,' I said. 'He'll be slower, and he's only got a handgun. I'll try and nail the two with the machine pistols.

'I'll be sitting. The decoy will be standing, acting like he's interrogating me. The moment you see me roll on to my shoulder – open fire.

666

'Aim at Nikolaides' chest – when he goes down, keep shooting, okay? Noise always helps.'

I grabbed the polished steel lid of the old freezer box and positioned it against a fallen column. I lowered myself to the ground and leaned against the water trough, my back half turned to the approaching enemy.

When they saw me, slumped and facing away from them, they wouldn't suspect anything was wrong. Nor would they see the SIG in my lap. The polished steel of the freezer lid wasn't much of a mirror, but it would work: it would give me a clear view of the battlefield and the exact position of the three hostiles as they approached.

I heard Cumali whisper: 'They're coming!'

I slid the safety off the SIG, hoped that in her anxiety the cop had remembered to do the same, and waited with the Saracen standing over me. I was breathing hard, a broken man whose eyes happened to be focused unwaveringly on the polished steel lid of the freezer.

I saw the reflection of Nikolaides and the other two as they entered, and I forced myself to wait for the moment snipers called 'maximum kill'. Four seconds . . . three . . .

The sun shifted slightly on its axis and a shaft of direct light pierced the shattered roof. It hit the cool-box top and the sharp glint called the three men's attention straight to it.

Nikolaides was no fool – he realized that the steel lid had been moved. He squinted hard and saw me watching them. He screamed a warning to the Albanians, hurled himself aside and drew his pistol.

I dropped to my shoulder and started rolling into a firing position. Cumali opened up with the Beretta, but wasn't good enough to hit anything, let alone the sprinting bull.

I rolled over and over through the mud and dirt, crying out as the pain from my battered foot and injured chest shot through me, drawing aim on Muscleman. He was wheeling with his machine pistol, about to blast the crap out of the water trough and anything nearby, including me.

The Saracen, unarmed, was in mid-air, attempting to scramble to safety behind the rubble.

Upside down, on my back, I had my finger on the trigger, but it was swollen so badly I could barely feel a thing. In desperation, I fired a burst of three at Muscleman, working hard to spread them.

Normally, my first shot would have at least hit the target, but this was anything but normal and the first two missed completely.

The third got him in the groin, nowhere near deadly, but the range was so close it hurled him backwards. He dropped the Skorpion and clutched at what was left of his genitals.

Cumali, spraying bullets as she tracked with the fast-moving Nikolaides, didn't have a clue about what else was happening on the field. She missed the old bull by a mile but shot the Helper through the throat. He collapsed immediately.

She kept firing, chasing Nikolaides even though he was fast approaching the water trough. Bullets splattered in the mud all around me.

Jesus! I would have yelled a warning, but nobody would have heard it over the screams of Muscleman trying to stem the blood pouring from his crotch. I tried to roll to safety but got slammed backwards. A rush of pain erupted in the soft flesh of my shoulder and I knew one of her wild shots had hit me.

I managed to get to one knee, aiming the SIG fast at the blurred shape of the unwounded Nikolaides. I cursed my damn finger which could barely pull the trigger and saw that my left hand, supporting the barrel, was shaking like a mother.

I squeezed off four, very fast, but all I could do was hit the old bull in the legs, knocking him to the ground, sending his pistol flying. I wheeled fast, knowing I had to finish it quickly or I wouldn't have the strength. I saw the dickless Muscleman lunging for his machine pistol.

I shot on the turn – for the first time actually rising to the occasion – putting two in his chest, which was nothing fancy but good enough to kill him.

Nikolaides – bleeding, unarmed – saw Muscleman crumple. Sprawled in the dirt, he looked up at me, hatred and confusion in his eyes. I guess he had thought it was going to be simple, an easy morning's work, but somehow I had survived waterboarding, turned my captors against him and still shot well enough to put two of them down.

'Who the fuck are you?' he snarled.

I saw his eyes register his pistol lying almost within reach. I couldn't help remembering how he had smiled when he smashed my knee with his steel-toed boot, and the force of the hammer blows on my foot.

668

'They used to call me the Rider of the Blue,' I said. 'I was the person who ordered the killing of Christos in Santorini.'

Nikolaides' face twisted – he was this close to revenge only to fail? He howled, and a massive burst of energy coursed through him like a death rattle. He hurled himself at the pistol. I fired twice and, at that range, his head pretty much exploded.

I turned away – there wasn't any pleasure in taking a life, even that of a man like him. The day I felt there was I knew it would be time to leave the battle for ever. I levelled the SIG at Cumali – she was drenched in sweat, the adrenaline pumping so hard I don't think she really comprehended what had happened – and told her to remove the clip from the Beretta.

'Now keep hold of the gun, point it at the ground and fire three times,' I said, making sure there wasn't a round still left in the chamber.

'Now drop the weapon,' I said and, once it was in the dirt, I told her to follow the same procedure with the two machine pistols and Nikolaides' pistol.

'Now bring all the clips to me.'

She picked them up, handed them over and I put them in my pocket. With all the weapons separated from their ammunition, I pointed at the handcuffs, which were lying on the ground where she had dropped them, the key still in the lock.

'Cuff him,' I said, indicating the Saracen.

He had dragged himself out of the rubble and was supporting himself by leaning against the water trough, deep in the canyons of despair, wondering why his god would have forsaken him at the final hour.

'Hands behind his back,' I told her.

As she fitted the cuffs I saw that hordes of flies were already settling on the corpses, and I knew it was nothing compared with the feeding frenzy when the intelligence services of half a dozen countries descended on him.

He raised his lowered head and looked at me. I had the SIG in one hand, still trained on him, and with the other I was starting to rip strips off my shirt to combat-bandage my shoulder and stop the bleeding. Our eyes met, and we both knew that whatever was left of his life, he would never get another chance to complete his volume of dark history.

'I love him,' he said simply. He meant his son.

'I know that,' I replied. 'It was the only weapon I had.'

Cumali handed me the key to the cuffs and I put it in my pocket with the ammunition. I pulled the bandage tight with my teeth, tied it off and, with the pumping blood slowed to a trickle, I took Cumali's phone out of my pocket: the three minutes were almost up.

'Still there?' I rasped.

'Christ,' he replied. 'How many dead?' He had heard the gunfire through the mic.

'Three. It's over – you can let them go.'

A moment later he told me that the nanny was collapsing to her knees and he had cut the little guy down. I turned and looked at the Saracen and his sister and let them read it on my face – the woman and the child were safe.

The Saracen, sitting in the dirt next to the trough, hands cuffed tight behind his back, bowed his head, and I knew he was praying. Cumali shuddered, surrendered herself to a tidal wave of relief and started to cry.

I was about to hang up – I knew I had to make another, critical phone call – but the fever was coming on hard and my head was spinning. In the whirling confusion, there was something I had to know.

'Would you have shot the nanny?' I asked Ben. He didn't reply, and I knew that was answer enough.

'Would you?' he countered after a moment.

'That's the difference between us, Ben,' I said softly. 'It's why I was made for this business and you weren't. Of course I would have.'

Shaking, and not just from fever, I hung up and motioned Cumali over. I couldn't walk – God, I was so drained and hurt I could barely stand – and I needed her to lean on. She supported me under one arm, letting me take the weight off my mangled foot, and I turned to look at the Saracen.

'Try to come after me,' I said, 'and I'll shoot you both.'

He nodded, and we looked at each other one last time, both our lives changed for ever. I remembered what a group of British soldiers had said after the Argentine war: it was only their enemies who knew what it was really like on the front line.

I said nothing to him – what was there to say? – and I motioned Cumali to start moving out, leaving him handcuffed in the dirt. The only key was in my pocket, the weapons rendered useless, and I knew for certain that there was only one way out of the ruins – by boat – and I was taking the only one of those with me. Confident he was trapped, I knew that, probably less than twenty minutes after I made the next call, scores of men from dozens of different agencies would arrive. Not that they would have much to do other than arrest him – there was no plot to unravel, no network to roll up, no co-conspirators to track down. The soft kill of America was almost over.

Hurrying now, I started to dial the second call, my fingers swollen and shaking, trying to remember the number I had been given but which was stored on my smashed cellphone.

Dragging one foot, helped by Cumali, I headed back down the crumbling passage, deeper into the gloom. There was one thing, however, that I had overlooked, and for the rest of my life I would wonder about the mistake I made.

Chapter Forty-three

CUMALI LED ME THROUGH THE BARRED GATE AND, AS I STEPPED AMONG the rocks, the dazzling sunlight hit me hard.

The short distance from the water trough had been the most painful journey of my life, every step like one more blow. The waterboarding, the loss of blood and the escalating fever were turning into a flood and taking a critical toll on whatever strength I had left. I felt the past and the present melding into one.

I leaned against a boulder and ordered Cumali to get the cruiser from its hiding place and bring it up to the old jetty. As she headed off to a tiny cove behind a jumble of rocks, I hit the last digit of the number and heard the phone beep as it made the international connection. It was answered immediately.

My voice was barely audible. 'Mr President?' I said, as best I could.

'Who is this?' a man replied, too young to be Grosvenor.

'I need . . . I need to speak—'

'I can barely hear you. Identify yourself, please.' He sounded like a marine.

I was weaker than I had ever thought possible, damaged beyond measure, but I knew what had happened. I was using Cumali's phone, and the White House communications system had identified the call as originating from a completely unknown source. Sure, I was phoning the president's direct line, but they weren't going to let a call like that go through until they knew who it was. Hence I had been diverted to a high-security communications centre buried deep in the Colorado mountains and I was speaking to one of the eighteen hundred marines and technicians who manned it.

'Identify yourself,' the marine signalman repeated.

'My name is Sco—' but I knew that was the wrong thing to say; a name would mean nothing. Standing in the pounding sun, my eyes aching, I felt myself drift from my body. As if from on high, I looked down on myself.

'I can only just hear,' the signalman said. 'Repeat, please.'

I barely registered it. I was watching the old bull wield the stone-mason's hammer and I heard someone screaming in my head. I realized it was my own voice – but the only sound on the beach was the engine of the approaching boat and the scattered gulls circling overhead.

'Pilgrim—' I managed to say. At least I thought I said it, but I couldn't be sure – maybe it was just in my mind.

'I couldn't catch that. Repeat.'

Silence. I was watching a little boy with Down's syndrome run along the sand and jump into his father's arms.

'Are you there? Say again, please.' The signalman's voice dragged me back.

'I . . . am . . . Pilgrim,' I said.

The signalman heard it. At the start of every shift for the past month, one order had been drummed into the heads of every marine more than any other. If they heard a word, a certain code name, it had to be given priority over every other communication. The signal-man was hearing it now.

'Are you there?! Please hold, sir. Please hold, Pilgrim!'

He entered a series of rapid commands on his keyboard, calling up a list of officials who had to be told immediately – *Pilgrim is live; Pilgrim is in contact; Pilgrim has come in from the cold.*

The first person on the list was the National Security duty officer, seated at his desk in a small office in the White House. It was very late – just after 4 a.m. on the East Coast – when he picked up his phone and heard an anonymous voice: 'For the President. Pilgrim.'

Even though the duty officer was certain the commander-in-chief would be asleep, his instructions were clear, and he immediately rang the phone in the president's bedroom.

Grosvenor was a long way from sleep, though: more than twelve hours earlier Whisperer had called and told him about the hopeful message from Bradley. He was sitting in an armchair looking out at the lights of Washington, not seeing any of them, when the phone rang. He grabbed it, shocking the duty officer, who had expected a delay. Grosvenor listened as the man stumbled over the message.

'What was that?' the president barked, anxiety getting the better of him.

'It's Pilgrim,' the duty officer said at last. He heard Grosvenor murmur something that sounded like 'Dear God', but he couldn't be sure. Why would the president be praying?

'Are you there, Pilgrim?' I heard Grosvenor's unmistakable voice even though the line sounded hollow and alien. Somewhere in my fractured mind I understood that they were encrypting it in Colorado.

'Ten thousand doses,' I whispered.

'Ten thousand?!' the president repeated in disbelief.

'Already there,' I said. 'He's using our own doctors – probably starts in a few hours.'

At some stage, after leaving the water trough, my training must have kicked in and, without realizing it, I had rehearsed what I needed to say. My throat was burning up and I desperately wanted a drink, but the moment I thought of it I forced the idea aside, frightened that the gag reflex would kick in. I tried to stay focused.

'From Chyron,' I said, my voice fading.

'Repeat that,' the president said.

'It's a drug company . . . Karlsruhe . . . in Germany.'

Another voice came on the line. It was Whisperer, and I knew they must have patched him in and he had been listening. 'Can you spell it?' he said.

I tried several times, but I couldn't get past the first few letters; my mind was struggling.

'Karlsruhe?' Dave said, trying to confirm it.

I had never heard his voice so gentle, and I wondered why. I hoped he was okay.

'There's a hotel there. The Deutsche König,' I managed to say, before my voice trailed off again.

'Great, that's great,' Whisperer said.

The president probably wondered if I was dying, but, despite the stakes and urgency, he didn't try to force me on – I think he knew that somehow I was getting there.

'Keep going,' was all he said. 'You're a damned hero. Keep going.'

'I should have asked for batch numbers,' I rambled, weaker than

ever. 'I forgot things . . . The Saracen hurt me, you see . . . There was
a child—'

'Yes, we know,' Whisperer said.

'We shouldn't have done that . . . It was . . . I just didn't know any
other way—'

'Of course you didn't,' Whisperer replied. 'It's over now.'

From somewhere I found a burst of energy, and it helped bring
some clarity. 'It's a vaccine,' I said. 'It's in vaccine bottles.'

'What vaccine?' Whisperer asked, still in that strange, gentle voice.

'Flu shots,' I said. 'He put it in flu shots. The season is here,
immunization starts tomorrow.'

There was silence at the other end – I think they realized that I had
done it. Two phone calls from the Hindu Kush had somehow led to
doctors' offices throughout America. Then Whisperer confirmed it,
telling the president they had it all: the day, the manufacturer and the
method. I thought they were about to hang up – there must have
been a million things to organize – but instead Grosvenor spoke to
me.

'Where are you?' he asked.

I didn't reply. It was done. And I was squinting at the sun, thinking about the long journey that lay ahead of me.

'He's on the coast,' Whisperer said. 'Nineteen miles north of
Bodrum. Is that right?'

I still said nothing. I was gathering my strength, marshalling whatever resources I had left – I was going to have to crab my way across
the sand to the old jetty.

'Can you hold on, Scott?' Grosvenor asked, increasingly alarmed.
'I'm sending choppers from the Mediterranean Fleet for you now.
Can you hold on?'

'We'll have to tell the Turkish government,' Whisperer interrupted.

'Fuck the Turkish government,' Grosvenor told him.

'No, don't! Don't send anybody,' I said. 'I won't be here.'

Grosvenor started to contradict me, wanting to know what I
meant, but Whisperer stopped him.

'It's okay, Scott – I understand. It's okay.'

'Damned if I do,' Grosvenor said. 'I'm telling you, the choppers
are coming.'

'He's injured, Mr President . . . They hurt him—'

It was time to go, and I suddenly started worrying that I had

675

forgotten something. 'Did you hear?' I told them. 'Ten thousand doses . . . Chyron . . . flu shots.'

'Yes, we heard,' the president replied gently. 'I want to say on behalf of the—'

I hung up. It was done. All of it was done. To endure – wasn't that what I had said I had to do? To endure.

Chapter Forty-four

THE TIDE HAD BEEN SURGING HIGHER AND, ENTIRELY BY ACCIDENT, IT helped me. I limped and staggered across the sun-baked sand, heading for the wooden jetty, and had no choice but to pass through the encroaching water.

When I was ankle deep, the sudden coldness of it calmed the pain in both my foot and mind. I stood for a long minute, allowing it to cool the fever and letting the salt sting and cleanse the open wounds.

With a clearer mind, I reached the jetty, grabbed a handrail and made my way to where Cumali was waiting. She had brought the little cruiser in stern first and had the motor idling. I hadn't told her – we hadn't talked about anything – but her journey was at an end. I was heading off alone, and I knew that what lay ahead of me was hard enough, especially in my condition, and I was anxious to start.

That was when we heard the gunshot.

We turned, looked at the Theatre of Death and I realized what I had overlooked, the mistake that I would wonder about for the rest of my life. Did I do it deliberately?

Certainly when I left the ruins I was exhausted, I could barely walk and I had to make the urgent call to Washington. Of course I had taken every precaution by unloading the weapons and keeping the clips. But that was all in my conscious mind. In a far deeper place, did I know that there was another weapon? One that was fully loaded – my own Beretta, the gun which the Albanians had taken from me at the fall of masonry and discarded next to my smashed cellphone? Did I leave it there for the Saracen to use on himself – and, if so, why?

Obviously, he had remembered it, and the moment I heard the

gunshot I knew what he had done: with his hands cuffed behind his back, he had stumbled or crawled deeper into the passage and sat down next to the weapon. He had worked his hands down over his buttocks, picked up the pistol, manoeuvred it between his thighs, lowered his face so that the barrel was almost in his mouth and pulled the trigger. He probably knew the old song too:

> *When you're wounded and left on Afghanistan's plains,*
> *And the women come out to cut up what remains,*
> *Just roll to your rifle and blow out your brains*
> *And go to your god like a soldier.*

Cumali realized as soon as I did what the gunshot meant, and she started to run for the ruins. I grabbed her, but I was so weak she shrugged it off. It was only the urgency of my voice that made her stop.

'Listen!' I yelled. 'When they come, tell them that you knew nothing. Say that in the end you saved my life, tell them about the man you shot. Say that you set me free, that you betrayed your brother. Tell them anything! I'm the only one who knows – and I won't be here.'

She looked at me, confused. 'Why are you doing it?' she demanded. 'Why would you do this for a Muslim woman?'

'I'm not doing it for you!' I replied. 'I'm doing it for the boy – he deserves a mother.'

I grabbed the roof of the boat's cabin and started to haul myself aboard. Cumali ran for the tunnel, but I knew it was a forlorn mission. Her brother was a *muj*, he had brought down three Soviet Hind gunships: he wouldn't have missed.

Chapter Forty-five

CLUTCHING THE CAPTAIN'S CHAIR, FIGHTING THE FEVER AND PAIN, I edged the small craft away from the jetty and headed into open water. I swung south, hugging the shore, and ran with the throttle wide open, travelling fast.

The wind had veered round, blowing hard against the tide, and the bow ploughed through the steep swell, sending up sheets of spray and making the old engine howl. The journey might have finished me, but I forced myself to close the pain out and used my one good shoulder to keep the wheel on a course that was straight and true. Finally, I came round a headland, entered a long stretch of water sheltered from the wind and felt confident enough to lash the wheel off and let the boat take care of itself.

I went below and started to search. In a for'ard closet I found an old backpack and used it to hold the SIG and the ammunition still in my pockets. Next to it, wrapped in a sailbag, I found a heavy water-proof shroud already fitted with lead weights. There was no logic to it, but I was in a distressed state and I didn't feel like travelling with my own burial sheet. I opened the window, threw it out and watched it bob and sink in the foaming wake.

Under a rear bench seat, I found what I was looking for: the vessel's first-aid kit. It was probably twenty years old, but it had never been opened and it was surprisingly well equipped.

I took it back to the wheelhouse and used swabs to clean my smashed foot and a pair of scissors to remove the burnt flesh from where the bullet had entered my shoulder. I opened a bottle of anti-septic, eighteen years past its use-by date, and poured it on the wounds. It still worked – shit, did it work – I howled in pain and remained just conscious enough to be thankful that nobody could hear me.

So it was, with my wounds bound with yellowing bandages, reeking of antiseptic and equipped with a crutch adapted from an oar, that I finally saw the section of coast I was looking for. On the last breath of day, a long way south and a storm rolling in, I turned the wheel and passed between the clashing rocks that sheltered a secluded fishing village. The first squalls of rain meant that the jetty was deserted, and I drew up next to it unobserved.

I brought the small craft in by her stern, kept the motor running and tied her off tight to a bollard. I jammed the other oar through the spokes of the wheel to lock it in position and threw the backpack and makeshift crutch on to the jetty. With the engine straining to take the boat back to sea, the mooring line was pulled tight, and I used it for support as I crawled up next to the crutch. Armed with a knife I had found on board, I slashed the mooring line and watched the boat launch itself towards the darkness of the clashing rocks. Even if it managed to make it through the channel, the surrounding coast was so rugged I knew it would be thrown ashore and smashed to pieces before dawn.

I slung the backpack over my shoulder and settled myself on to my crutch. Looking like a soldier returning from some distant war, I made my way past two shuttered cafés and into the backstreets of a tiny town I barely remembered.

Chapter Forty-six

THE CURTAINS WERE DRAWN IN THE MEAN HOUSES AND THE STREET lights were few and far between. In the gathering darkness, I made my way down a narrow street and – just when I was worrying that I had made a wrong turn – I saw a communal water fountain.

The old bucket was still tied to the rope and the flowers surrounding it were as dead as they had always been. With my body almost spent, I limped past it and reached the old cottage, the lettering on its brass plaque almost illegible now. I knocked hard on the door and, after what seemed an age, it opened and I saw Dr Sydney standing on the threshold – unshaven, his baggy shorts swapped for a pair of frayed chinos and teamed with an old Oktoberfest '92 T-shirt – but otherwise little changed in the intervening years.

While the booze had probably continued to play havoc with every other organ, his mind – and his memory – were holding up remarkably well. There was something in my face that he recognized, and I watched him dredging through the past to find a name. 'Jacob, isn't it?' he said.

'Near enough,' I replied.

I saw him take in my bandaged shoulder and foot, the ragged clothes and my haggard expression. 'You're looking well, Jacob,' he said, deadpan.

I nodded. 'You too, Doctor. Nicely turned out, as always.'

He roared with laughter. 'Come in. We can keep lying to each other while I see if we can save that foot.'

He led me inside and I realized what a strange thing memory was – the rooms seemed much smaller, the distances far shorter, than the night we had carried Mack along the same route. In the kitchen, the

681

Australian got three lamps into position, laid me on the kitchen bench, stripped off the bandages, took one look at my foot and hit me with a massive dose of IV antibiotics and an even larger amount of painkillers. Thankfully, when it came to medicine, subtlety wasn't his strong suit.

He decided that, despite the swelling and purple bruises, neither my ribs nor my kneecap were broken. Fractured, maybe, but there was no way of telling without an X-ray.

'Feel like a drive to the hospital in Milas?' he asked.

He saw the look on my face and smiled – 'I didn't think that was an option' – and told me he would splint and bandage them as best he could.

After that, he injected a local anaesthetic, cleaned and sutured the gunshot wound and told me I was a lucky man.

'I don't feel like it,' I replied.

'Half an inch difference and it wouldn't have been a hospital for you, even a makeshift one. It would have been the morgue.'

With the rest of the wounds taken care of, he turned his attention to the havoc wrought by the hammer blows. He had been a pediatric surgeon, highly experienced with victims of car wrecks, so I believed him when he told me that the bruising and swelling would eventually take care of themselves.

'There's little I can do about the small bones that have been broken without scans, X-rays and an operating theatre,' he said, smiling. 'A steady hand would help too.'

He decided to manipulate the bones individually into the best position then set and bandage it, hopefully holding everything in place.

'You're going to have to do intensive exercise to keep the ankle mobile and prevent the muscles of your lower leg from atrophying. Maybe it'll work.'

I nodded, and he adjusted the lamps in order to start. 'This is going to hurt.'

He got that part right. Sometime after midnight, the work was done and he called a halt – I was slipping in and out of consciousness, and I think he doubted whether I could take much more. Holding me under the arms, he got me off the bench and we crossed the kitchen, entered the living room and headed for a stairway leading to a disused bedroom.

Halfway there, I heard voices coming from a corner of the room and saw the old TV again, tuned to CNN. It was the evening news and the network's Washington correspondent was reporting on the frantic efforts since early in the morning to locate and seize ten thousand doses of flu vaccine that had been accidentally contaminated with potentially lethal traces of engine oil.

I didn't want the doctor to know I had any interest in the event, so I told him that I needed to rest a moment. Holding on to the back of a chair, I looked at the screen.

'The alarm was first announced by the president in a 6 a.m. press conference,' the correspondent reported.

'Simultaneously, the FBI and local police agencies across the country started locating and securing all flu vaccines manufactured at a plant in Karlsruhe, Germany, operated by Chyron Chemicals.

'The president delivered high praise to the staff of the Food and Drug Administration who uncovered the problem and alerted the White House in a 4 a.m. phone call—'

'Ready?' The doctor asked, and I nodded, letting him help me up the stairs. I wasn't surprised by the story Washington was relating. What was it somebody once said? In war, the first casualty is truth.

I reached the bed and lowered myself down. My head hit the pillow, the doctor turned out the light and I drifted into a strange unconsciousness.

Chapter Forty-seven

THE FEVER ROCKETED DURING THE CONFUSION OF DAYS AND NIGHTS that followed and the doctor barely had a chance to leave the small room. He told me later that he had sat at my side, sipping on a bottomless glass of Jack and listening to me roam across a remarkable dreamscape.

He heard tell of a man tied to a plank drowning in an endless ocean, a father beheaded in the blistering sun, a city littered with people bleeding out from an incurable virus, a child with Down's syndrome hanged by the neck. He said, smiling, that the mind was a strange thing – how, under the onslaught of a fever and high doses of medication, it could invent such terrible fantasies.

If only he had known.

Worried that the horrors were growing worse, and convinced that it was a bad reaction to the drugs, he decided to wind them right back. Maybe it was the adjustment to the medication, or perhaps nature just ran its course, but the fever peaked and the nightmare memories diminished. When I finally managed to take some solid food he decided to venture into the village to pick up some groceries and other supplies. I figured he had probably run out of Jack.

He returned a troubled man. He told me that a man and woman had arrived, claiming to be tourists on a road trip, and had made supposedly casual inquiries at both village cafés about whether any Americans had passed through recently.

I always knew that Whisperer and his legions would find me – people talk, Echelon listens, somebody would have gone into the archives and found the account of Mack's death all those years ago. I didn't fear the strangers, though, I knew they had been sent to help me in case I needed it – and yet I had no intention of talking to them. I was a ruin of a man, but I had done my duty, nobody could ask any more than that, and how I stumbled my way through the wreckage that remained was entirely my business.

I told the doctor nothing about the interlopers, but I noticed as the day wore on that he was becoming increasingly worried about what had turned up on his doorstep. That night, for the first time, I made my way slowly down to the kitchen and discovered that he was quite a cook. As he seasoned what he called his signature dish – lamb marinated in thyme and garlic – he asked me if I still sang the 'Midnight Special'.

'Do I think about Mack, you mean?' I replied. 'More times than I ever imagined.'

'Me too,' he said. 'A terrible night. Just after you left I heard a chopper come in. They picked up his body, huh?'

'Yeah.'

'Where was he buried?' He tried to make it sound casual, but it was a strange question and I knew where he was heading.

'Arlington,' I replied.

'He was in the military?'

'Sure – he just happened to be a fighter in a war that had never been declared.'

The doctor put his herbs down and turned – he had arrived at his point. 'You too, Jacob? Is that what you do?'

'Worried, Doctor?'

'Of course I'm fucking worried! I've been worried since the night you arrived. As soon as you went to sleep I opened your backpack. There was a SIG covered in gunshot residue and enough ammunition to arm a small African country. Now two people turn up and I'm wondering when the shooting is going to start.'

He was a good man, he had done the right thing by me, and he deserved an honest answer. 'Yeah, I'm a soldier too.'

'Enlisted or mercenary?'

I smiled. 'Drafted on this occasion.'

'CIA, or something worse?'

'I like to think better, but your mileage may vary.'

'And the people in town?'

'They're ours. They're here to check that I'm okay.'

'You're sure?'

'They're not killers, Doc. If they were, we'd already be dead. There's nothing to worry about – I give you my word.'

I could see it reassured him, and I was glad I had done it. A few days later, just after dusk, there was a knock at the door. There was something about it – the loudness, the fact that the front gate hadn't creaked on its hinge, the time of day – that worried me.

I nodded to the doctor to answer it and limped as fast as I could to the old bedroom, where a narrow window offered a decent view of the front door. A guy in his thirties was standing there – dressed like a tourist, but so hard-wired, so full of tension, that the clothes would have fooled only the most casual observer.

The doctor opened the door and the tourist told him that he wanted to speak to the man who had arrived at the house a few weeks previously. The doctor told him the only other occupant had been his brother, on a family visit, who had returned to Australia a couple of days earlier.

The agent just nodded. I figured he had been told to play it cool. 'Well, if your brother comes back,' he said, 'and you happen to discover that he's an American with a bullet wound in his shoulder, give him this, will you?'

He handed over a sealed package and left. Standing in the kitchen a few minutes later, the doctor watched me break the seal and spill out a clutch of letters. His eyes widened as he saw that the first envelope was embossed with the seal of the President of the United States.

He was even more surprised when I ignored it and looked at the others. I recognized the handwriting on one – it was from Whisperer – and I put it next to the president's.

Two letters remained. One was in an NYPD envelope with Bradley's details on the back and the other – written in a strange scrawl – was addressed to the Oval Office with a note to 'Please pass it on to the man who sometimes uses the name Jude Garrett.' I knew who it was from.

I picked those two up, limped across the kitchen and went up to my room.

Chapter Forty-eight

I READ BRADLEY'S FIRST. HE SAID THAT AS SOON AS HE HAD LEFT THE nanny's house she had phoned the local cops and told them what had happened.

Because she worked for Cumali, she had no difficulty convincing them that the story was true, despite its extraordinary nature. A black American wasn't exactly hard to locate and, alerted by an all-points bulletin, a prowl car picked him up before he had even reached the hotel. They slammed him over the hood, disarmed him and took him down to the precinct house. He was fearing the worst – some Turkish form of enhanced interrogation – but by then all hell was breaking loose at the Theatre of Death.

American choppers from the Mediterranean Fleet had already been dispatched at the president's order – not to pick me up but to secure the Saracen and collect evidence. Grosvenor phoned the president of Turkey, alerted him to their approach and told him that they had located the man attempting to buy the nuclear trigger. As a result, MIT operatives and the Turkish military all converged on the ruins. With two Turkish Navy destroyers standing offshore, half a dozen US helicopters on the beach and two hundred military personnel and intelligence agents in the ruins, the order went out to put Bradley on ice until the situation became clearer.

After five days in a cell – and following a direct request from Grosvenor to his Turkish counterpart – Bradley was released and had his passport returned. He went back to the hotel and had a tearful telephone reunion with Marcie, who, once she had recovered, asked him when he would be home.

'A few days,' he said.

'What?!' she cried.

A cop to the very end, he wasn't leaving without organizing the extradition of Cameron and Ingrid for the murder of Dodge and the woman at the Eastside Inn. The next morning, less than twelve hours after his release, he returned to the precinct house and went to Cumali's office. Hayrunnisa told him in hushed tones that her boss was still being 'debriefed' – and sticking steadfastly to the story that I had recommended to her, it seemed – so he asked to see whoever was in charge of the murder investigation. After a flurry of phone calls, the kid in the shiny boots escorted him to the luxurious office of the Bodrum police chief.

I recalled the man – I had seen him when half of his force were pursuing me through the boat-repair facility, the night that I pancaked SpongeBob. The chief was in his fifties, big and florid with pampered skin and a neat moustache, the gold buttons of his impressive uniform threatening to burst at any moment. Despite the eau de Cologne he was wearing, he had a smell about him, and I couldn't say I was surprised by what Ben reported.

He wrote that the chief said he had received extensive legal submissions from lawyers acting on behalf of both Cameron and Ingrid: as I had anticipated, the moment the two women had left their interview with me they had immediately gone and lawyered up. The chief said that the submissions led him personally to review all the evidence.

'Naturally, I had to discount everything supposedly discovered by the man calling himself Brodie David Wilson. He wasn't even a member of the FBI and had entered the country under false pretences. As we know, he had his own agenda in complicating and prolonging the case.

'My own review showed that the work of the Turkish detectives was outstanding, as usual. It was clear that their initial finding was correct – Mr Dodge had died by misadventure. His fall was a tragic accident.'

Ben stared at him in disbelief, but the big Turk didn't seem to notice. He smiled, lit another cigarette and spread his hands wide.

'Of course, I didn't want to make that judgement on my own, so I presented the evidence and the legal submissions to one of our most esteemed local judges. He too could see no reason for holding the two women and the other material witnesses in Bodrum any longer.

'He suggested – and I agreed – that we return the passports and release them on bond, pending any further inquiries.'

'Release them?!' Ben asked, taking it hard, again acting as the champion of the dead. 'How much was the bond?'

The Turkish cop tried to blow him off. 'There were ten of them . . . I'm not sure . . . There's a file, I'd have to—'

'How much?' Ben insisted, not bothering to hide his anger.

The chief dropped all pretence of civility. 'Two hundred thousand dollars each,' he snarled.

Ten people – two million dollars! It was a fortune – but not to Cameron. Ben didn't need to ask what she had done – of course, she would have paid the bribe and bought their way out.

'When did they leave?' he asked in despair.

'Three days ago. They got on board the huge cruiser and an hour later were sailing out.'

'What if your "further inquiries" turn up something?' Ben asked bitterly. 'What do you do then?'

'We write and ask them to come back. But, as I told you, I'm sure that won't be necessary.' Ben said the guy was almost smiling.

As I mentioned, I wasn't surprised. With the FBI out of the picture, armed with all of the work which I had done, the Bodrum police chief and a corrupt judge had seen that they had Cameron cornered and did what generations of their Ottoman predecessors had done. They put their hand out.

Ben wrote that there was little he could do – the two perps had left Bodrum, and Cameron's payment had guaranteed that all the material witnesses had scattered too. He thought perhaps he could pick the case up in New York, but he was realistic enough to know that, with limited resources, and one killer officially listed among the dead at the World Trade Center, unless the two women returned to America, he had little hope. With that much money, they certainly didn't need to go back – they could travel the world for the rest of their lives.

I sat in silence for a few minutes, thinking about the two women and their crimes, but even then I didn't recall it. No, the comment Ingrid had made to me about not understanding the half of it never even entered my head.

Chapter Forty-nine

THE SECOND LETTER, THE ONE ADDRESSED TO JUDE GARRETT VIA THE Oval Office, was from Battleboi.

It was better written than I could have imagined and, knowing the big guy, I was certain that he must have sweated over it for hours.

'I was in handcuffs and shackles,' he said, 'one of ten prisoners inside a bus with barred windows. We were heading across the runway at La Guardia to take a Con Air flight to the Big House down in Kansas when two black SUVs with their sirens going made us stop.

'I figured that whoever the guys inside were, they must have had a really high security clearance to drive across an airport but, apart from that, I wasn't interested.

'That morning, I had written to Rachel telling her not to wait for me and I was trying to work out how I would deal with fifteen years in Leavenworth.'

He told me that the two US marshals on board the bus – guys who hadn't stopped sneering at him because of his size and eccentricity – got out and met the men in suits who were scrambling out of the SUVs.

The most senior of the suits – who turned out to be a high-ranking executive in the Department of Justice – showed his ID and started barking orders. As the convicts watched through the barred windows, the two marshals immediately got back on board and made their way through the prisoners.

'They stopped next to me, unlocked the chain securing me to the seat and led me towards the door. I asked them what the hell was happening, but they didn't answer. They probably didn't know themselves.

'On the runway, the executive officer handed me a letter. I ripped open the envelope and saw that it was from the Oval Office, but I didn't know what it meant – for once in my life, I couldn't compute.

'By the time I finished reading it I was pretty close to crying. It was a presidential pardon. "For services in defence of your country," it said.

'God knows who you are, but you said you would do everything possible to help me, and you did.'

He wrote that, after the formalities were completed, he made his way back to Old Japan, ran through the apartment without even taking off his shoes and found Rachel in a corner of their bedroom, distraught. She looked up, saw him and thought for a moment it was a dream. Then the dream smiled, reached out his arms to her and, being the son of devout Catholic parents, told her in wonder, 'It's the Gospel of St Mark, babe – chapter sixteen, verse six.'

She had no idea what he was talking about and didn't care – she let him fold her into his huge embrace, kissed him and, after they had stood for a long time in silent gratitude, he sat down and wrote the letter to me.

'You gave me a second chance – a chance for life, a chance for love, a chance for kids. How do you thank somebody for that?' he said.

'I suspect that we'll never see each other again, but always remember, on this date every year we will set a place at our dinner table for you and wait for your knock on the door.

'Travel safe and may God, by whatever name you know Him, protect you.'

Chapter Fifty

THE FOLLOWING DAY, AFTER MY NORMAL ROUTINE OF EXERCISE AND physiotherapy, I took stock of my health. While it was clear my foot was healing, I had to admit that if I ever wanted to regain the complete use of it I had to increase dramatically the amount of work I was doing.

I discussed it with the doctor and, that night – after dinner, with the village in darkness – I ventured out for the first time. Slowly, forsaking my makeshift crutch for a walking stick, I made my way down the narrow streets and along the waterfront, dragging my foot in a strange limp as I became increasingly tired, but forcing it to function.

It was slow and excruciating and, after two hours, I finally made it back through the front gate and collapsed in the living room. The doctor was already in bed, and after I recovered I took the opportunity to search through his groaning bookshelves. At the back, covered in dust, I found a copy of the Bible, presented to him on graduating in medicine by his father.

I looked up the Gospel of St Mark, chapter sixteen, verse six. It was the King James's version and, even if you are not a believer, the words are still very beautiful. I sat for a long time, thinking about Battleboi and Rachel, and, though I can't say that I prayed, I was thankful that at least one good thing had come out of the whole terrible enterprise.

The following night, despite the pain and fatigue, I walked the unforgiving streets again. And the night after that, and the night after that. I never saw anybody, I never spoke to anyone – I was a shadow in the darkness, but a shadow growing stronger.

A month later, having ventured further and further afield, I felt confident enough to put my foot to an extreme test – a ten-mile walk along a coastal path and down into a rarely visited fishing village which the doctor said was one of the most beautiful on the coast.

'Make sure you visit the boatyard,' he said. 'They still use the old crafts; it's the last one working in wood.'

Setting off early on a cold and sharp-edged morning, I hiked through the empty hills of southern Turkey, the smell of pine and the restless sea my only companions and, to my surprise, I did it relatively easily. I was still limping, and I had to rest from time to time – but there was no more of the vicious, debilitating pain, and I knew that my time at the doctor's was coming to an end.

The coastal path eventually wound down into the village – untouched by tourism, an authentic jumble of cottages and boat-sheds, home to men and women whose lives had changed little in hundreds of years.

After a lunch of fresh seafood in a sleepy café, I made my way to the boatyard at one end of the small cove and found that the doctor was right – it was a lovely thing to see the old kilns aglow, smoke hanging in the air and the artisans bending and shaping lengths of timber as they repaired the squat fishing boats for the next season. Nobody paid me any attention, and I wandered past the stacks of drying wood, thinking about how many great skills the world had lost, how many things of value had passed without any of us even noticing. The old men with their chisels and hand saws were once the most highly paid members of their community, and what had we put in their place? Financial engineers and young currency traders.

I turned a corner – and stopped. At the back of the yard, under a sagging canvas roof, perched high on wooden chocks, was a timber-hulled ketch. She was about seventy feet long, probably half a century old, and even though she was unpainted and her masts hadn't been stepped, it was clear that she would once have been a thing of beauty.

Whoever owned her had used the almost lost skills of the yard to start restoring her but, by the look of the dust on her transom, they appeared to have run out either of cash or interest. I walked closer and dragged aside part of the canvas roof so that the light fell more evenly on her. I had always thought that there was nothing quite so sad as an abandoned boat, but the work that had been done on the ketch was outstanding, and it gave her a dignity that belied her distressed circumstances.

Thanks to Bill's lessons on Long Island Sound, I had learned a lot about boats and I knew just by looking at her that she was a craft that could weather almost anything.

'She's for sale,' a man's voice said from behind, his English excellent for such a sleepy part of the world.

I turned and guessed it was the owner of the yard. He was in his thirties, with a ready smile, a man probably trying to make something out of the business and keep his village alive.

'A wealthy Russian found her and brought her here,' he said. 'In her time she won the Fastnet, the Transpac, the Sydney to Hobart and most of the other blue-water classics.

'When we got her she'd been rotting at a mooring in the Greek islands for years, so we started from the keel up.'

'Then what happened?' I asked.

'The Russian stopped calling; more importantly, the bills weren't paid – I guess he either went broke or another oligarch had him killed.'

Probably the latter, I thought: that was the way most business disputes were settled in Russia. The owner of the yard indicated an old ladder leaning against the side of the ketch. 'Please,' he said, and I climbed up and on to the broad teak deck.

I saw that the cabin was set well back, slung good and low, while the wheel sat high to give a commanding view of the sea. It was easy to see why the Russian had rescued her.

I wandered into the wheelhouse, went below and walked quietly through her galley and bedrooms. During the years when I was sailing, I had heard men say that, once in a lifetime, a boat would talk to a sailor, and I knew – for better or worse – that the ketch was meant to be mine.

The owner had followed me on board, and I emerged from a for'ard hatch and found him near a set of winches. 'How long to paint her?' I asked.

'A week,' he replied.

'Getting a suit of sails would be a problem—'

'We've still got the originals – they're patched, but they're okay. Come to the office and I can show you her records.'

Twenty minutes later, I had negotiated a price and added an extra twenty grand to update the navigation equipment and have her stocked with food, fuel and water. I borrowed the owner's cellphone, went outside and called Finbar Hanrahan in New York to arrange to have the money transferred into the owner's account.

The old attorney didn't ask what it was for – on hearing that I was in Turkey, he probably assumed I was on government business and didn't press me. Before hanging up, I asked him to also send thirty thousand to Dr Sydney to compensate him for everything he had done. I had already decided I wouldn't be going back, I would sleep on the boat to supervise the work that needed to be done. I had my backpack and, inside, were the SIG and the letters – there was nothing else I needed. Anyway, I never liked goodbyes.

I returned to the office and remembered one thing I hadn't inquired about. 'What's her name?' I asked.

'Nomad,' said the owner.

I nodded. If I had had any doubt that the ketch was meant to be mine, the name dispelled it. I think I mentioned – in a very old use of the word, 'Saracen' means a wanderer, a nomad.

Chapter Fifty-one

I PUSHED OUT EARLY ON A MONDAY MORNING AND, WHILE THE BOAT WAS really too big for one person, the skills I had learned from Bill came flooding back and I discovered that, as long as I wasn't too ambitious I could handle her well enough.

She must have cut a strange sight, though, with her freshly painted hull, faded sails and a patched spinnaker, but it wasn't worth worrying about: it was so late in the year and winter was coming on so strong that the only other craft I saw were always well off on the horizon.

As I grew in confidence and my seamanship returned, I found that Nomad still had a stunning turn of speed, and after three weeks I was beating fast towards the boot of Italy with the idea of heading up the Adriatic Sea towards Split in Croatia.

I pulled into a tiny outpost on the western shore of Greece – no more than a general store and a decrepit jetty – to top up my fuel and buy supplies. The elderly owner fuelled the boat's diesel, put the fruit and milk I had purchased into cartons and threw in a pile of *International Herald Tribunes* that had gone unsold over the previous months.

'You might as well have them; I'm just going to burn 'em.'

Two days later, sipping coffee in the late-afternoon sun, making my way along a deserted coast, I was down to the last few papers when I encountered an item at the back of one of them, almost lost next to the finance pages. It was nothing much, the sort of thing you might read all the time, simply a report that Greek police had found no suspicious circumstances concerning the death of a young American woman who fell from her luxury cruiser off the coast of the party island of Mykonos.

'The woman, the former wife of wealthy auto heir, Dodge—'

I sat forward and scanned the paragraphs fast until I found the name: Cameron was dead. According to the police, she fell from the back of her cruiser while intoxicated – the story said that the local medical examiner had found a cocktail of recreational drugs and alcohol in her system.

In the middle of the text was a photo of Cameron and Ingrid arm in arm, posing with Ingrid's stray mutt outside an impressive baroque building. With an increasing sense of dread, I flew through the story to find out what it meant.

A few paragraphs down, I got the answer. It said Cameron had only just remarried, tying the knot with Ingrid Kohl, a woman she had recently met in the town of Bodrum, Turkey.

'The two women were among the first to take advantage of new German legislation allowing same-sex marriages,' the report said.

'They had flown to Berlin and were wed at the City Hall four hours after the law came into effect, a ceremony witnessed by two strangers whom they had recruited off the street and their dog, Giancarlo.

'The couple then began their honeymoon by returning to their boat moored near—'

I got to my feet and walked to the starboard rail, trying to breathe. The sun was melting into the sea, but I barely saw it. Ingrid had been right: I didn't understand the half of it. But I was certain that I did now.

All my experience – all my intuition – told me that the moment they had left Berlin as a married couple, Cameron's life was effectively over. Though I couldn't prove it, I was convinced that the masterful plan Ingrid had developed in the maelstrom of 9/11 had one secret codicil which Cameron had known nothing about – Ingrid was going to make sure that she was the one who inherited Dodge's fortune. But didn't Ingrid love Cameron? I asked myself, always the investigator. But I already knew the answer – she had been betrayed and abandoned by her long-time lover. She didn't love Cameron, she *hated* Cameron.

Of course, working to my belief, she would have had no difficulty in concealing her true feelings: she was an actress, and she would have played the part right up to the end. Once they were married, she knew that she didn't even have to get Cameron to write a will –

as the legal spouse, she would inherit everything, even if Cameron died without making one.

The rest must have been easy – a long night of partying, a walk to the stern, a last kiss in the moonlight, a slender hand that tipped Cameron over the rail as the big cruiser powered on.

In the dying light I hung my head, angry with myself that I hadn't foreseen it, even though – God knows – I had been warned. I left the railing and went back to look at the date on the newspaper.

It was months old, too much time had passed – the boat would have been sold and the rest of the money transferred through a maze of untraceable offshore companies until it finally ended up in a bank like Richeloud's.

Somebody as smart as Ingrid Kohl – or whatever her name was – would have had a new identity and a new life waiting, and I knew that she would have disappeared already into the anonymity of the world, protected by her boundless intelligence and ingenuity.

She was the best I had ever encountered and yet . . . and yet . . . I had a strong feeling that somewhere . . . on some strange shore . . . in a street of some foreign city . . . in Tallinn or Riga . . . in Dubrovnik or Krakow . . . I would see a face in the crowd . . .

Chapter Fifty-two

I SAT ON THE DECK UNTIL LONG AFTER NIGHT HAD FALLEN, THINKING about the two women and the events which had drawn us into each other's lives.

As a covert agent, darkness had always been my friend but, since my visit to the Theatre of Death, I had a fear of it which I suspected would outlast everything else in my life. I got up to switch on the running lights and check my course. Halfway along the deck, I stopped.

It seemed that my course was already set. I stared at the arrangement of the stars, the position of the moon and the pitch of the sea. When I listened, I heard a silence so loud it screamed.

I had been there before.

It was the vision of the future that I had seen the night I looked out of the window of the Oval Office. Just as I had glimpsed back then, I was alone on an old yacht, the sails patched and faded, the wind driving me into darkness, the boat and I growing ever smaller on a limitless sea.

Now this was the night and this was the moment, and I waited alone, barely willing to breathe, as the sea rolled towards me. *Nomad* heeled over and white water foamed at her bow as the wind backed a little and rapidly grew stronger. We were travelling faster and I stepped to the railing to work the winch. The rigging started to sing under the strain and, though there was not a soul on the dark-painted ocean, I was no longer alone.

Bill Murdoch was on the other winch, his wide shoulders pumping, yelling and laughing at me once again to get her damned head up into the wind.

Up for'ard, a woman scrambled to set the running lights. Because my mother had died when I was so young I remembered very little of her and it was a source of secret pain to me that with each passing year I could picture less and less of her face. Tonight, lit by the navigation lamps, I saw her clearly, every detail.

Voices, speaking in Polish, came from behind me. The woman whose photo I had seen as she held her children tight and walked them towards the gas chamber was on board with me now. She was sitting in the cockpit, grown old and happy, with her adult kids and grandchildren all around her.

Yes, things were dying, and it had certainly been a vision of death that I had seen, but it wasn't mine – it was another kind of death. I was bidding all the ghosts of my past goodbye. Just like the Buddhist priest had told me on the road to Khun Yuam all those years ago: if you want to be free, all you have to do is let go.

And under that vaulting sky, sailing on the wine-dark sea, I realized that I was born to the secret world, I was meant to be an agent. I didn't choose it, I had never really wanted it, but that was what had been dealt to me. I had started on the journey thinking it was a burden, and that night I saw that it was a gift.

And I knew that not this year, but maybe next, I would return to New York. On a certain day, at an appointed hour, I would go to a building near Canal Street, ring the buzzer and walk up the stairs to Old Japan.

The apartment door would open and, inside, I would see a table set for three, because I knew that the man who lived there would always keep his word.

As Rachel watched, Battleboi would laugh and reach out his huge arms towards me. After a moment we would look at each other and he would ask me why I had come.

I would smile and say nothing, but in my heart I would know the answer, I would know exactly what I had put behind me: it was what was written in the Gospel of St Mark, chapter sixteen, verse six.

That was the part of the epic story about coming back from the dead, being restored to life. 'He is risen,' it says.

He is risen.

Acknowledgements

I think it was John Irving, the winner of both the National Book Award for a novel and the Oscar for a screenplay, who said that writing a movie is like swimming in a bath and writing a novel is like swimming in the ocean.

I had read that comment long before I embarked on *Pilgrim* but even then I wasn't prepared for just how big the ocean was and how much effort it would take to cross it. I could never have done it without a host of people on the support boats calling out encouragement and occasionally yelling 'Shark!' if it looked like I was flagging. It would indeed be churlish of me not to acknowledge them and give them my heartfelt thanks.

First to Doug Mitchell, a truly great film producer and an even better friend for more years than I care to remember. He not only gave me wise counsel, but supported and believed in me when those things were sorely needed. To George Miller – a film director and an Academy Award winner himself – who once walked into an office where I was working and asked if I would be interested in working with him on a screenplay. That started a journey, an inquiry, into storytelling that has never stopped and will probably continue until – as we said in *Road Warrior/Mad Max2* – 'my life fades and the vision dims'.

I must thank the entire team at Secoma Group in Europe, especially Tony Field, Louise Knapp and Carolina Scavini – all highly accomplished in the business world – for their friendship, unstinting loyalty and great practical help. They have looked after so many things, and helped in so many unheralded ways, I know that I will never be able to adequately express it. I am aware that for a writer that is not a good thing to admit, but that is the truth of it.

To François Micheloud and Clément Bucher, friends of longstanding and business associates, who have guided me through the intricacies of life in Switzerland and have made our lives far more enjoyable and interesting for it. It was their suggestion that I accompany them on a visit to the concentration camp at Natzweiler-Struthof – a grim and terrible place where I stood alone for a long time looking at a photo of a woman with her children on their way to the gas chamber and the germ of an idea was born.

Bill Scott-Kerr is the publisher of Transworld, of which Bantam Press is an imprint. His unbridled enthusiasm, intelligent notes, incisive editing, brilliant marketing, unflinching support and profound knowledge of the arcane workings of the publishing world – a topic worthy of a Dan Brown novel, in my view – have surpassed anything I ever expected. Or probably deserved. I just hope that I get the opportunity to keep travelling down the road with him and the rest of the outstanding team at both Transworld and Random House.

The same sentiment applies to Steven Maat, my publisher in the Netherlands, who was the first person to buy the manuscript – at that stage, only one-third finished and from a debut novelist into the bargain. I have always thought that the Dutch were a courageous and intelligent people and now I know for sure! Thank you, Steven.

Jay Mandel in New York and Cathryn Summerhayes in London have represented the book – and fielded countless crazed emails from me – always in a gracious, very smart and suitably ruthless way. They are both literary agents at WME and they have done a truly outstanding job. Long may they prosper.

I must also thank Danny Greenberg in Los Angeles, who has been a friend as well as my motion-picture agent for more years than either of us would probably like to contemplate. The fate of the film rights for the novel rest with him and I know they couldn't be in better or more accomplished hands.

Don Steele is in grave danger of giving lawyers a good name. An entertainment attorney at Hansen, Jacobson in Los Angeles, he is one of the truly good guys – and a fine lawyer to boot – in a town that has far too few of either. It is not surprising that he works at the firm where he does – Tom Hansen has great taste and intelligence and gathers like-minded people around him. Thanks to both of them.

I must offer a special mention to Brian and Sandra Maki for all the support and faith they have shown – both to me and to the project – over so many years. Brian, a voracious reader, waded through every draft of the novel and always came back with a host of useful suggestions and a wealth of grammatical corrections. We may not always agree on correct English usage but that doesn't diminish for one moment his enormous contribution! Great thanks to both of them.

Jennifer Winchester helped in ways which only my family and I will ever fully appreciate. Patient and unflappable, she was always there and never lost her temper or got irritable – even when I seemed to be permanently doing both. Thank you to her and also, especially, to Marinka Bjelosovic, who has worked so hard on our behalf for the last eight years. I am sure, to her, it must seem like an awful lot longer.

To my children – Alexandra, Stephanie-Marie, Connor and Dylan – thank you so much for the boundless support and unquestioning belief. You make it all worthwhile. I have to make special mention of Dylan. Every morning he would come into my office, look at the pages I had done overnight and nod his head. 'You're doing well, Dad,' he would say each time. He was four years old, couldn't yet read – and I have no doubt it will remain the most heart-warming review I ever receive.

Finally, to Kristen, my wife – my best friend, my sounding-board, my companion on every step of this journey – thank you. She listened to countless bad ideas, knew how to bury them gently, and always recognized the good ones when I was fortunate enough to have them. The mistakes in the book are all mine but whatever is good in it is due in enormous measure to her. I could never have done it without Kris's unstinting help, counsel and encouragement. *I Am Pilgrim* is dedicated, with love, to her.